MOTHER
LONDON

MICHAEL MOORCOCK

MOTHER
LONDON

A NOVEL

HARMONY BOOKS/NEW YORK

Copyright © 1988 by Michael Moorcock

Published in 1989 in the United States of America by Harmony Books, a division of Crown Publishers, Inc., 225 Park Avenue South, New York, New York 10003

Originally published in 1988 in Great Britain by Martin Secker & Warburg Limited

HARMONY and colophon are trademarks of Crown Publishers, Inc.

Manufactured in the United States of America

Library of Congress Catalog Card Number: 88-034766

ISBN 0-517-57183-8
10 9 8 7 6 5 4 3 2 1

First American Edition

This book is dedicated to the memory of my
friend Pete Taylor and is also for Brian
Alford wherever he may be

ACKNOWLEDGEMENTS

Thanks to Clare Peake for permission to quote "London, 1941" by Mervyn Peake.

Quotations from Wheldrake's *Penultimate Poems 1897* are published by permission of the copyright holder.

Several broadsheets and popular songs quoted are from *Curiosities of Street Literature* collected by Charles Hindley, 1873, reprinted 1966 by John Foreman the Broadsheet King, and *The Minstrelsy of England* ed. Edmonstoune Duncan, 1905.

Love's Calendar is published by permission of Lorcenius Music Co. Ltd. 1887.

Madcap Mary and Gentleman Joe is from *The London Rakehell; or, Harlequin Upon the Town* by M. C. O'Crook, 1798.

Thanks are particularly due to my wife Linda Steele for her research and editorial work on this book.

CONTENTS

LONDON, 1941

Half masonry, half pain; her head
From which the plaster breaks away
Like flesh from the rough bone, is turned
Upon a neck of stones; her eyes
Arid lid-less windows of smashed glass,
Each star-shaped pupil
Giving upon a vault so vast
How can the head contain it?

The raw smoke
Is inter-wreathing through the jaggedness
Of her sky-broken panes, and mirror'd
Fires dance like madmen on the splinters.

All else is stillness save the dancing splinters
And the slow inter-wreathing of the smoke.

Her breasts are crumbling brick where the black ivy
Had clung like a fantastic child for succour
And now hangs draggled with long peels of paper,
Fire-crisp, fire-faded awnings of limp paper
Repeating still their ghosted leaf and lily.

Grass for her cold skin's hair, the grass of cities
Wilted and swaying on her plaster brow
From winds that stream along the street of cities:

Across a world of sudden fear and firelight
She towers erect, the great stones at her throat,
Her rusted ribs like railings round her heart;
A figure of dry wounds—of winter wounds—
O mother of wounds; half masonry, half pain.

Mervyn Peake, *Shapes & Sounds 1941*

PART ONE
ENTRANCE TO THE CITY

I do not know how many tons of high explosives have been tipped out upon the gigantic target of London since the Battle of London began on August 24th, 1940. The result is a grim city, a shabby city, except round and about Guildhall, where several famous streets have been burned to the ground.

The people of London, having developed a technique of living in the face of repeated danger, now accept the preposterous, and what was until so recently the incredible, as the normal background of existence. I often think that the ability to reduce the preposterous and the incredible to the level of commonplace is a singularly English gift.

H. V. Morton's *London*, February 1941

The Patients

"BY MEANS of certain myths which cannot easily be damaged or debased the majority of us survive. All old great cities possess their special myths. Amongst London's in recent years is the story of the Blitz, of our endurance."

Setting aside his antique fountain pen David Mummery pauses to stick a newspaper picture of the Temple beside the article he is preparing which will again be favourable to the City's freemasons and must surely guarantee his entrance into their brotherhood; then London's subterranean secrets will at last be his. Mummery wets his lips with a blue flannel. Lately his mouth has been dry all the time.

Calling himself an urban anthropologist, and with an impressive record of mental illness, Mummery lives by writing memorials to legendary London. Peeling dried glue from his swollen fingers, he glances up at the brassbound mahogany clock with a mercury pendulum which blends into a wall of miscellaneous but chiefly patriotic images and, lifting the lid of his 19th-century clerical desk, replaces the notebook beside an old ear-trumpet which holds his pens. As he gets up he begins to sing what is for him almost a lullaby. Blake, in the main, has a calming effect.

"Bring me my bow of burning gold . . ."

A crowded museum of ephemera, of late Victorian advertisements, Edwardian crested ware, 20s and 30s magazines, wartime memorabilia, posters from the Festival of Britain, toy guardsmen, Dinky delivery vans, lead aeroplanes, his room's surfaces are covered by confused and varied strata, uncatalogued and frequently unremembered. Mummery can explain how these are his sources of information, his revelatory icons, his inspiration.

At the centre of this great collage is a framed newspaper photograph of a V2 rocket flying over London. This V2 is Mummery's private *memento mori*. He believes it might even be one of the bombs which almost killed him as a child. He glances past stacks of books and ancient boardgames on his window sills to the thinning mist outside. Almost invisible, the low December sun is dimly reflected by the cold slate of terraced roofs. After reaching his hands towards the embers of the small fire he lit at dawn in the black cast-iron grate he opens the doors of an old Heal's wardrobe and begins methodically to dress in four or five layers of clothing; lastly adding a large black bearskin hat to expose only a hint of pink flesh and his unusually bright eyes when he lets himself out onto the dowdy landing and runs downstairs to leave his lodgings where Maida Vale borders on Kilburn and catch his Wednesday bus. Lately he has been feeling painfully cold.

The V2 moves with steady grace before the blustering East wind as it crosses the channel and reaches Brighton, passing low enough over the town for people in the Pavilion Gardens to see it rush by, the yellow fire from its tail glaring against the broken cloud; it will reach Croydon in minutes then in a further minute South London when, its fuel gone, it will fall on the suburb where David Mummery, almost five years old, plays with his toy soldiers. Forty-seven feet long and carrying two thousand pounds of explosive, this sophisticated machine, the combined genius and labour of amoral scientists, serf technicians and slave workers, is about to bring a miracle into my life.

David Mummery is also writing his memoirs. Some of these have yet to be made coherent; some are still in his mind. Some he has considered inventing.

Small and bundled, Mummery presents a shapeless profile as he walks rapidly beneath dark leafless planes to his stop, congratulating himself that as usual he is a few minutes ahead of the main rush-hour crowd which must soon begin its progress up a High Street already roaring with traffic from the suburbs. It gives him familiar satisfaction to be only third in the queue when the throbbing scarlet double-decker draws in for its passengers to mount. Finding himself a downstairs seat two rows back from the

6

driver's cabin he rubs a neat circular spot on the fogged window, peering out with quirky pleasure as the bus approaches grey unthreatening Paddington.

Frequently Mummery imagines the city streets to be dry riverbeds ready to be filled from subterranean sources. From behind the glass he watches his Londoners. *This fabulous flotsam.* They come from Undergrounds and subways (*their ditches and their burrows*) flowing over pavements to where myriad transports wait to divert them to a thousand nearby destinations. The mist has dissipated. A cold sun now brightens this eruption of souls. Through streets enlivened by their noise small crowds flow: through alleys and lanes and narrow boulevards. At this distance Mummery loves them: his impulse is to remove his woollen gloves, reach through his overcoat, his muffler, his jacket, his cardigan, find his notepad and record how the sunshine glitters off worn stone, new concrete and dirty red brick, off frozen flesh; but he makes his hands remain at rest in his lap: presently he has no need of scenery: he must devote himself to the Masons. Having delivered his latest manuscript (*Five Famous Whitehall Phantoms*) to his publisher on the previous Monday he is free from any immediate financial considerations and now desires almost painfully to be back near his canal and his old women, with his personal nostalgia. As the bus passes a curved metal railway bridge and runs under a white flyover he thinks of the millions of predestined individuals driving or being driven in a million directions, their breath, their smoke, their exhausts softening the sharpness of the morning air.

Momentarily Mummery feels as if London's population has been transformed into music, so sublime is his vision; the city's inhabitants create an exquisitely complex geometry, a geography passing beyond the natural to become metaphysical, only describable in terms of music or abstract physics: nothing else makes sense of relationships between roads, rails, waterways, subways, sewers, tunnels, bridges, viaducts, aqueducts, cables, between every possible kind of intersection. Mummery hums a tune of his own improvising and up they come still, his Londoners, like premature daisies, sometimes singing, or growling, or whistling, chattering; each adding a further harmony or motif to this miraculous spontaneity, up into the real world. *Oh, they are wonderful like this, today.*

7

". . . but she's only a beautiful picture, in a beautiful golden frame!" An old song as ever on his delicious lips, Josef Kiss mounts the footboard of the bus, much as a pirate might swing himself into his victim's rigging. Eccentric clothes swirl about his massive person. Advancing into the body of the vehicle he appears to expand to fill up the available space. He plucks off his leather gloves, unbuttons his Crombie, loosens his long scarf. Watching him partly in reflection, partly from the corner of his eye, Mummery half expects Josef Kiss to hand the garments to his conductor, together with a generous tip. Mr Kiss places himself across the left front seat and sighs. As a matter of principle he makes everything he does a pleasure.

At Mr Kiss's back an orange-haired woman with chapped skin and a nose rubbed red by coarse tissues reassures herself, speaking to her friend: "I thought I'd better see the priest. It couldn't do any harm. Well, I saw him. He said it was all nonsense and I wasn't to bother myself about it and to have nothing to do with Mrs Craddock. That suited me down to the ground."

Really lovely eyes and hair but she'll kill herself at this rate.

"All aboard, please. There you are, love. Mind that bag, sir, if you please. Thank you, thank you very, very much. Thank you, sir. Thank you, madam. Thank you, thank you, thank you very much." With insane patience, his face hanging in regular folds under his grey hair so he resembles a natty bloodhound, the conductor scurries about his aisles and stairs. "Cheer up, love, it'll all be over by Christmas. There's going to be a whip-round for my retirement. Keep talking, that's the secret, Mr Kiss. You know that as well as I do." He speaks in a quiet moment between Westbourne Grove and Notting Hill. Grey, massive houses, monuments to the optimism of the late Victorian bourgeoisie, once multiple-occupied, the background to a scandal which destroyed lives and careers and rocked a government, slowly being reclaimed from the exploited immigrant by the upwardly mobile whites, go slowly by on both sides, behind trees. "But this is nothing. The tourist routes in the summer are murder. They never know where they're going. You can't blame them for it, can you? Imagine what we'd be like in New York. Or Baghdad. And how's your sisters?"

"Hale as ever, Tom. Oh, very well."

"I thought that was where you were coming from. Give them

my best when you see them. Tell them I miss them. Tell them I'm retiring. I'll be in Putney, though. Not too far." Tom winks as he steadies himself on the vertical chromium rail before the bus takes a lumbering turn, putting the renamed cinema and the Bhelpuri House at its back. Both will be gone in a year, making way for some empty title, a new development.

"They say they can't afford London Transport any more, Tom." Josef Kiss regards their surroundings with the greed of someone who has regretted too many disappearances and losses. His gentle smile suggests resignation.

The conductor shifts his money-bag in order to sit down on the seat across from Josef Kiss. His response is to chuckle. His chuckling helps him maintain his equilibrium. "They could buy and sell the Duke of Westminster."

Mr Kiss's smile indicates a broad consent. He glances casually back and does not recognise Mummery.

There is no dishonour in flight. There is no blame in failing to enter the fire. I did nothing to harm her. But he could not know he was my rival. In some distress, Mummery rises, disembarks and runs, an awkwardly animated stuffed beast, for the Tube at Notting Hill, taking the steps two at a time, careering through the barrier, waving his weekly pass, flying down the escalator in time to force himself through the doors of a Circle Line train for High Street Kensington where he changes to a Wimbledon-bound District Line and sits alone as the carriage sighs and rumbles as far as Putney Bridge where he jumps out, dashes through the exit into Ranelagh Gardens, momentarily claustrophobic amongst the oddly arranged terra-cotta houses, to the trees and steeples and undecorated slabs, the hullabaloo of the bridge where traffic jostles to cross the Thames, and there before him is a Number 30 bus heading South. He leaps to the platform just as the bus moves forward again and the river is revealed, beyond it The Star and Garter and all the other rosy English Domestic brick behind tall bare trees on the further shore. For a moment the light turns the water to quicksilver. Gulls rise and fall around the bridge. Mary Gasalee is aboard, seated on the bench behind him, next to Doreen Templeton. They are patients at the same Clinic. Neither woman acknowledges Mummery. Perhaps his big hat disguises him. Mummery lapses into the comfort of despair. He imagines himself falling before their

9

eyes into the water, describing an exceptionally beautiful curve, his expression beatific; he begins to radiate forgiveness, a profoundly elaborate form of self–pity.

"Mary Gasalee, that boy's in pain."

There's no pain in the fire, she thinks, but she turns her head. The boy stands on the platform waiting to get off. The water seems reflected in his grey pallor. He holds the handrail with all his strength. His face is thin; those might be spots of fever below his dulled eyes. Dumbly he challenges her glance. *He's not mine,* she thinks and looks out at the passing shops, at Macdonalds, Mothercare, at W.H. Smith and Our Price. As the bus continues up Putney High Street, the boy jumps free. His mustard–coloured duffel coat flaps like useless wings. *He's not my yellow doll.*

Doreen Templeton gets up first. They have reached their stop. Mary follows her. They step down to the pavement. "Couldn't you *feel* his pain, Mary?" Again and again Doreen Templeton wraps herself in her coat. They walk slowly up the hill towards the open Heath, a few bushes, some scruffy trees. "I could. But I'm very oversensitive, as you know. Maybe I imagined it."

Mrs Gasalee is no longer responsive. She believes Doreen Templeton's apparent concern for others is merely another way of getting attention. Doreen's sensitivity is at best mere imposition, a sentimental exercise, for she never does anything about her "intuitions". While Doreen is not stupid (she sometimes admits her self-deceptions) she is completely selfish. Mrs Gasalee has now disliked her for five months. Doreen has yet to notice; she continues condescendingly to describe her own highly tuned mental condition and its effect on the less blessed, like her family and her former husband. Mrs Gasalee's replies to Doreen are from old habit ritualistic, only apparently engaged. Content to have mere confirmation, Doreen never questions them.

They reach the green gate of the converted vicarage, the NHSS Special Clinic. Mrs Gasalee begins to tremble out of many causes. Doreen sighs. "Well, love, here we go again."

From the debris flies the Black Captain, his hands stretched towards the infant Mummery immovable amongst brick and plaster, one of the V2's few survivors.

Behind them, hesitating until he sees them pass through the gate, David Mummery looks back down the hill to where Josef Kiss turns the corner; today his has been the slower route. Mr Kiss always comes by the same bus but Mummery usually varies his own journey since it is one of his few ways of relieving the tedium of overly secure habits which, even when they torture him, are preferable to uncertainty. Mummery craves the familiar as an alcoholic craves drink but dignifies these cravings as an example of his own nobility, of his enduring love. Thus he still nurtures his passion for Mrs Gasalee, preferring to yearn for her rather than risk a new romance; holding on to familiar and simple childhood verities and letting the past remain golden, tarnished only by the unthinkable shadow of others' needs and ambitions. He longs for the emotional intimacy he knew with Mary Gasalee and is determined, though she will not return to him again, never to experience the same intimacy with another woman: his enduring love, his self-congratulation, is a deception presenting itself as a definition.

"Mr Kiss." Mummery lifts his hat. "Can you eat fire?"

Josef Kiss throws back his head and roars.

"My dear boy!"

With his usual mixture of trepidation and pleasure David Mummery waits for his rival's generous arm to enfold him so that side by side they may enter the doors of the Clinic. His misery subsides, as he knows it must, for he is recognised at last.

Upon the dark green and cream walls, a post-war hangover, are pictures of Cornwall by R. Wintz, chiefly pastels and gouaches of St Ives before the Formica signs engulfed it. Some of the brown steel-framed armchairs contain other regular patients. They call themselves The Group and are unusual only by virtue of certain individuals.

From his corner seat Mr Faysha's benign smile greets Mummery and Mr Kiss. The tiny muscular African is about sixty, his beard and hair both grey, his skin so youthful he resembles a schoolboy preparing for a role in a nativity play. Hardly able to glance up, as if frozen in mid-dive, Ally Bayley is poised on the edge of the next chair. She is the youngest of them, hiding under a weight of curly brown hair, her clenched fingers revealing fresh scabs. Reading with gloomy arrogance from a fairly recent number of *Country Life* Petros Papadokis, a Cypriot, ignores her. He attends the Clinic only, he insists, under pressure from the Islamic Mafia who run his local medical centre. Beside him an older man with red curly hair and the slightly bloated good looks of a 1950s English film star, an empty pipe gripped in his mouth, sports the corduroy suit, woollen scarf and Fairisle pullover of a vanished Bohemian Soho. Admitting it is not his real name, the older man calls himself "Hargreaves" because he fears a publisher will discover his attendance at the Clinic and stop commissioning his paperback covers. "Hargreaves" is particularly wary of Mummery, whom he has run into once or twice in editor's offices. "Morning, old boy." His reluctant courtesy amounts to a snub.

Doctor Samit, in his usual grey pinstripe three-piece, throws open his office door and grins out at them revealing strangely even teeth which are probably cosmetically treated. "Hello again! We'll be ready in a minute. I saw Miss Harmon coming up the road. Is everybody here? What terrible cold weather, eh?"

"That new chappy, the pie-shop chappy, hasn't turned up yet." Doreen Templeton believes he lowered the tone last week. "And we're waiting for Old Nonny as usual."

"But where's our Mr Mummery?" Doctor Samit is surprised. "He's always on time. Oh, do forgive me. I didn't recognise you, David."

Apologetically, with a trembling hand, Mummery removes his hat. "I'm a bit paranoid about keeping warm this year. I don't want another dose of flu."

"And Mrs Weaver's probably off sick again." Doreen Templeton reports the remaining absentee. "She was looking seedy last week, you'll remember. Her bronchitis gets to her around Christmas. I can't recall a Christmas it didn't." She enjoys reminding them that she has been "In Group" longer than anyone apart from Mrs Weaver herself who nowadays only comes for the company when she feels like it.

Cold air blows in as the outside doors are opened and they can smell the powerful scent of lavender before they see Old Nonny, whose clothes in spite of the weather remain bright blue, lilac or violet, even her hat, even her eye-shadow. She has wound several chiffon scarves around her neck and wrists wherever her skin shows outside her blouse and cardigan. "Stay!" With almost theatrical command she addresses her invisible Lulu. As optimistic and as ebullient as her mistress, the pomeranian will wait in the drive.

"Good morning, everybody." She has the strangest of accents, ancient London English on which are layered a thousand other influences and aspirations. "Good morning, Doctor Samit, darling. And how's our dusky quack?"

The doctor straightens his perfect cuffs and offers her his habitually sardonic bow. "The better for seeing you, Mrs Colman, thank you." Nonny claims to have wedded Ronald Colman in 1941 just before the church and all its records were bombed. "How," he asks laboriously, "are you, is more to the point."

"Fighting fit as always. Strong as a horse. I'm not here, doctor darling, because of my health. I'm here because like most of us it's the only way I can stay out of the bin. There's nobody sick here, as you well know, unless it's poor Mrs T. Good morning, dear." And laughing in the face of her declared enemy she turns her back. "What ho, Mr Kiss!" She winks. "Had any good parts lately?" She was, she said, on the stage herself before the War, as Eleanor Hope. She met Ronald Colman through Alexander Korda when she auditioned for *Hearts of Oak*. "He should have got the OBE, at least, for what he did." She turns to a startled Mr Papadokis. "The sisters wrote to the king, you know, but never heard back. Did they Mr K?"

Embarrassed, Doctor Samit utters a professional chuckle. "Well, well, well."

Old Nonny waves her chiffon in eccentric patterns. "Stuffy in here, isn't it?"

Doreen Templeton's thin features become whiter and narrower, her lips tighten and her eyes are furious slits. Even Ally enjoys her dramatic discomfort, for Old Nonny never loses in these exchanges, which is why Doreen chooses to address her next remark to the ceiling. "She really should get rid of her pans. I blame those home helps." Several times Doreen has offered the theory from *Reader's Digest* that Old Nonny having contracted Alzheimer's Disease from ingesting too much aluminium therefore has no business at the Clinic.

guts nobody bitch all blood me no salt doss ist eine ferbissener

Mary Gasalee frowns and becomes startled, grateful when Josef Kiss, noticing her reaction, rises in stately fashion to be beside her. "I suppose it's time to get my prescription again," she says. "Are you okay?"

He presses the hand she lifts into his. "Oh, dear. Oh, dear, Mary."

Glancing across at them Mummery pretends to notice nothing. Long ago, when he was a teenager and she in her thirties, she gave him up for Josef Kiss whose tolerance, security, and variety of experience Mummery at any age was incapable of providing. Even now, considering himself no longer a child because he has endured the discomforts of treatment and therapy, Mummery's insights are merely conventional and his attempted sympathy lacks understanding. He means well but his fear makes him ungenerous. He can say only what he feels will please her since she is his main chance of returning to the golden past where he briefly enjoyed being the object of her romantic idealism: her twin soul. Her enthusiasm had made him feel of value in the world. At one point it had seemed she might go back to him, but no doubt she had only been getting her bearings. Yet he lived in hope. For him hope had always been preferable to reality. Mary Gasalee had realised what it would mean to be the perpetual source of Mummery's self-esteem and had refused that burden. Only dimly aware of her reasons, Mummery enjoys the sensation of sadness rather than jealousy while continuing secretly to envy her intimacy with Josef Kiss, who at different times had commended the Clinic to them both. Mummery wonders why Mr Kiss is shaking his head.

pork all leave Jerusalem pork all go into Babylon

The retiring actor visits Mrs Gasalee once a week, on Saturdays, when he likes to help her with her week's shopping. On Sundays she sees her friend Judith. Wednesday is Mary Gasalee's only other constant. Mr Kiss's physical life, however, is one of strict routine which he refuses to change. His routine and his own particular medicine are his protection against a chaos he is willing to risk perhaps three or four times a year and then usually only in the controlled environment of the Abbey, his costly asylum. Each year he saves for his few weeks' sabbatical. He is divorced.

Dobrze! Czego Pan chcesz? Lord Suma fought the Cockney Bulldog that night, beyond Waterloo, but fell like a collapsed barrage balloon. The Bulldog had him stuffed, they say, and used him as a couch in his Blackheath mansion. It was raining. I was so miserable I almost went back to the tattoo parlour. There's some comfort in those needles. But it's a habit, too. I've seen people just like Lord Suma. Not an inch of skin left. He was a

Londoner, it turned out, from Uxbridge. Could have fooled me. She's got that scent back. Is it natural or does she put it on?

"Come along everyone." Miss Harmon throws wide the double doors to the Meeting Room. "Let's get stuck in, shall we?"

Obedient they rise, merge and in single file enter a room with dark blue carpet and grey velvet curtains. On the eggshell walls hang more pastels of the seaside, the Cotswolds, an alp. A coffee table, some floral easy chairs, three straight chairs and a sofa are at facing angles on the carpet. Taking their usual places, with the exception of Ally Bayley, they appear to relax.

I should have looked up that healer he recommended. This is doing me no good I don't know about him but it's right across London there isn't even a tube stop for Temple Fortune is there it's all mock Tudor it gives me the shivers they say he's very good, though. The electric shocks did nothing but make my hair fall out.

Mummery positions himself to look through the tall window onto the chilly heath with its miscellany of ugly trees, road signs and ruined grass. By comparison the interior is pleasant.

One V-Bomb landed on the common. Nobody realised it would be followed so closely by another. By mine.

Placing his pencil and notebook on his chair's arm and acknowledging Miss Harmon, Doctor Samit opens the session. "So what have we been doing with ourselves since we last came together? Who wants to begin?"

Gently Miss Harmon leans forward. "How about you, Ally? What happened to your hand?"

At once Ally begins to sob. "He just left me," she says. "Broken milk bottles over the step and I couldn't stop bleeding. The people from the pub came out with flannels. I was so ashamed."

Ally's stories make them all uncomfortable. She cannot find it in herself to leave her husband.

"He's subhuman, Ally." Old Nonny's eyes glitter with outrage. "He's a beast. He's worse than most. He should be put away. Can't you get into one of them shelters?"

"He came after me." Ally returns to her private tears, rocking herself silently in her chair. They are unable to disturb her. Mr Faysha's own eyes are filling. He puts a tiny hand near her on the next chair, in case she should find it useful.

"And what about the rest of us?" Miss Harmon's hair hangs in

15

dark, lank slabs at the back and sides of her long head. Her prominent nose and chin help her cultivate a crudely Pre-Raphaelitic appearance. She wears a dress of William Morris material normally used to cover furniture. Occasionally, when half-dreaming, Mummery will start awake, convinced that one of the armchairs has come to life. "How have we all been?"

Under Miss Harmon's and Doctor Samit's conduction, some eagerly, some reluctantly, some resentfully, some gladly, the others recite accounts of their week or tell stories of adventures which have the ring of truth or else are clearly invented. Mr Kiss enjoys these sessions. His tales are anecdotal and frequently sensational, even humorous. He cannot easily stop himself from entertaining whereas Mrs Gasalee recounts as a rule something she has heard from an acquaintance, sad stories concerning small injustices and frustrations, how she feels the help she gave or offered was inadequate. Sometimes she will admit having over-heard people telepathically, but she knows this tends to make a few patients, and certainly Doctor Samit, embarrassed. Old Nonny tells of famous friends, unlikely events, incredible gatherings, chance meetings with household names, not a few of whom are long dead, and requires no response save the occasional nod or exclamation. Doreen Templeton listens through all this with disbelieving resignation and then discusses how badly people behave towards her even when she tries to help them. Mr Papadokis, in a low murmur which makes them strain to hear, if they make the effort at all, with eyes on the ground, speaks chiefly of troubles with his wife and mother, with his three children, his brother, his sister-in-law. "She says such filth. She asks about my girl-friend's knickers. She can't be clean. She's not Greek. You know." Only occasionally does his voice rise, taking on a note of rhetorical protest. "What is it? How can I be responsible for that? Am I Superman? I said."

With a shrug Mr Faysha accepts his turn. "Oh, it's just the usual old stuff." The movements of his hands and shoulders are apologetic. His smile is perpetually gentle. "But what am I to do?" For forty years he has been married to an Englishwoman. They still live in Brixton but are thinking of moving. For years they suffered the prejudice of their white neighbours; now it is the young West Indians who give them most trouble. Mr Faysha is inclined to dismiss his personal problems and drift into a general philosophical argument. "What can you do about it?" he asks The Group. "We're definitely victims of history I'd say, wouldn't you?" He was sent here from the mental hospital after he bit a taxi driver who refused to take him home one night from the West End. He was surprised to discover Mummery, but it has become a comfort.

Mr "Hargreaves" announces that he remains full of disgust for what he still terms The Establishment. Once again he lost his temper with his students at the art college where he teaches twice a week. The college will sack him if he does it again. He struck a youth. "Hardly touched him. I'm only violent where art's concerned. The little fool said something silly about Pollock. The usual sort of half-witted philistine pun. Well anyone will tell you I've never been a fan of the abstract expressionists but this know-nothing attitude you get from kids these days just makes me blow my top. I didn't mean to hurt him. I didn't hurt him, really. Fifty years ago it would have been twelve of the best taken as a matter of course. Not any more. Anyway, the crux of it is, I suppose, that I'm born out of my time. Even in the way I paint. I always wanted to be a Pre-Raphaelite."

Miss Harmon's smile is one of quiet yet profound sympathy.

They sit patiently through his familiar discourse. All Mr "Hargreaves" ever expects is a chance to express his anger once a week. Meanwhile Arthur Partridge comes in, to be introduced again. "You all met Arthur last week," Miss Harmon reminds them. Arthur shuffles on the spot, grinning about him.

This is a kindergarten they turn us into children and then tell us we must learn to fend for ourselves they diminish us and accuse us of lacking self-esteem they steal our dignity while offering admonitions of our failure to confront reality.

Arthur is a baker and even now his hands appear white with flour. They lie at his sides as if waiting for the oven. "You'll get the hang of it." Doctor Samit points with his pencil. "Sit over there, Arthur, next to David, please."

Mary Gasalee opens her eyes, wondering who spoke last.

They said the first bomb was a lucky escape. The second was a miracle. But Mr Kiss knows all about bombs and miracles and so does Mary G.

Mummery remembers Arthur Partridge's peculiar, unfinished tale of a threat from the sewers. He is interested in the story since his next book will be about London's underground waterways. He first went down several years ago in search of legendary subterraneans. The Fleet's pig herd was rumoured to be moving back to its old pastures, inhabiting the river just below Holborn Viaduct, having gone wild since the early 19th century. Mummery hopes Partridge will provide him with some authentic folklore or simply some small additional anecdotes, for he continues to justify his attendance at the Clinic as research, feeling no further medical need of it though he admits the pills still help. He is a stickler for taking them, refusing to run the risks Josef Kiss runs of deliberately releasing himself from the course. "Those pills are our anchor, young Mummery, but sometimes it's as well to cut the cable and let our ship drift into more interesting waters. That's why I maintain my habits, It's between destinations that fresh adventures occur!"

Mummery once accompanied Mr Kiss on several such adventures but the thought of fresh ones now disturbs him. Of late he has been increasing his own dosages, since the medicine has less and less effect. Tremors now seize him from time to time, making him fear that his problem has more to do with cerebral palsy or some related disease than with his psychological constitution.

This grows more hideous. Have they no idea what damage they cause us? They're without sympathy, it's true. But worse, they're without intelligence.

Oh, God, there's no pain in the fire.

Those ladies. They would be a comfort more to him than to me. I wish they were transferable.

Arthur Partridge sits on the edge of the sofa between Mummery and Mary Gasalee and describes a creature he knows cannot exist but which he is sure swallowed the dough he was preparing for a special order of wholemeal rolls. Mummery knows better than to get out his own notebook. All he can do as usual is try to memorise interesting details. Not that there is much to Partridge's account. It lacks, Mummery, decides, real imagination. It even lacks a sense of reality. The poor baker's tale has the deeply banal quality frequently distinguishing the truly mad from those who, like so many in The Group, are touched by a sort of divinity, who are, as Miss Harmon sometimes condescends to tell them, "special". Mary Gasalee for instance with the unnerving knack she shares with Josef Kiss is almost always able to guess what people are thinking. Mr Kiss

18

frequently reveals powers bordering on the supernatural. Mummery himself has a firm faith in the miraculous; he believes he can predict the future. For this reason he gave up his Tarot party tricks. Not that he is otherwise disturbed; believing that some people are simply better at reading the coded signs of language, gesture, choice of clothing and so on around them, he takes these gifts for granted. He and his friends share this sensitivity, he believes, with many artists, though they lack genuine creative talent, which is why Josef Kiss when he gave up his original trade could never become a great stage performer, why Mummery's attempts at fiction always fail. When the authorities actually tested them at the National Physical Laboratory, with picture cards and other well-used devices, the results proved disappointing to researchers anxious to believe only in certain forms of extra-sensory perception.

These Bills of Mortality. Our friendship was never the same. And so we cross the generations, the genes. The genre as we know it. Yes, cried Robert Du Baissy, we must bring havoc. It's their only salvation. In a magazine read by his father he recalled a picture, a demon drinking tonic wine. "Merry on Earth! Miserable in Hades!" But he remembered most the demon's green wrist against the red flame and a gun coin nutridot he said checking off his list say a fivepenny piece sixpence would be better a meal the size of a sixpence sounds good ah, well, tenpence a lunch? That won't get us very far he was a lad Simon his name was or we called him that anyway heading off up the Northern Line Bartholomew Fair then he went back to Morden it must have been on Oak Apple Day

The time has arrived for further responses, for analysis, for self-examination, for Doctor Samit to suggest what they should think about until next week. Each person responds differently; some are merely dutiful, some spiteful, others careless, one or two pathetic. Mr Partridge says very little. Mr Papadokis is lugubrious, enigmatic and boring. Ally cries for a while and says she feels much better. Mr "Hargreaves" raves ritualistically, his true anger already expended.

When it is over Josef Kiss reaches magnificently for his Crombie. "Well, young David, you'll be wanting to get to your canal. Are you satisfied with the new one?"

"My canal." Mummery knows an instant's happiness. "And my

bloody memoirs. I'm talking about the Blitz, our bombs. Oh, yes, I think so."

Mrs Gasalee looks back at him in sudden amusement.

David Mummery

MUMMERY HAD WRITTEN: I was born in Mitcham, famous for its lavender, between the aerodromes of Croydon and Biggin Hill, about nine months before the beginning of the Blitz. My first clear memory is of a rainy dawn sky with searchlights like fingers waving in final paralysis against the grey of barrage balloons while a few Spitfires and Messerschmitts wheeled and dived almost languorously in the penultimate manoeuvres of an air battle, their distant guns like the barking of tired dogs.

My childhood was happiest during the War years. By day with friends I hunted for shrapnel and the wreckage of combat planes; we explored ruined houses and burnt-out factories, leapt between blackened joists and swaying walls above chasms three or four storeys high. At night I slept with my black-haired mother, the local beauty whose royal-blue eyes saw little and whose nervous heart sensed everything in the security of our Morrison shelter, sheets of steel and wire mesh surrounding the dining room table.

We have never had a soldier in our family. My father, Vic Mummery, the speedway rider, was trained as an electrical engineer and did essential war work. He was good-looking, glamorous enough to have his pick of the ladies, especially those who recalled his prewar fame. He waited until the end of the War before leaving my mother who refused to tell me he had gone. Later she explained that since everyone's father was away she had assumed I wouldn't notice his departure. It seems not to have occurred to her that I might wonder why my father had left when everyone else's was coming home.

I was delivered in a small house in a nondescript street called Lobelia Gardens by a doctor named Gower, a Welsh incompetent whom my mother adored to the day of his justly premature death. He lived in the house across from ours and his wife loathed my mother, whose womb was affected as a result of his unhygienic laziness. Built in the early thirties, with a touch or two of mock-Tudor, a hint of Hollywood pebble-dash stucco, the road had even then failed to fulfil its early promise but I remember the house with great affection. It contained panelling known to my parents as Jacobean, a great deal of oak, including built-in cupboards glazed with coloured panes, a dining-room suite and two or three solid bedsteads. I have been fond of oak ever since. The front door had a large stained-glass representation of a galleon in full sail.

In the summer there was the endless and verdant Mitcham Common, with her ponds on which oildrum rafts and army inflatables were sailed, especially after the destruction of the Luftwaffe in the Battle of Britain, a soft green golf-course, copses, unthreatening marshes, stands of poplars, cedars and, of course, her elms. She had pedestrian bridges of wood and iron spanning a railway, sandy bunkers and depressions where all day long I sprawled and read and ate unseen. I do not remember ever learning the limits of Mitcham Common. Save for two small woods, which I discovered later, it was what remained of the countryside between London and Croydon. With the growth of a middle class determinedly taking advantage of the railways, thousands of small, similar streets had flowed around the Common, forming links of concrete, brick and hard asphalt with Croydon, Sutton, Thornton Heath, Morden, Bromley and Lewisham, no longer townships but suburbs bordered by the cultivated flowers and trees of Surrey and Kent, the Green Belt.

School might have been a better distraction if I had not already learned to read. The lessons were boring and the food disgusting. Within a fortnight I found it necessary to vomit over the head-mistress's desk when I was taken to her office by my teacher because I refused my lunch. Mrs Fallowell sat on her side of the desk and I was situated on the other, my plate of cold, grey, congealing mince, pale cabbage and watery mashed potato in front of us amongst her forms and test papers. I can smell it now. It still makes me gag. Disapprovingly Mrs Fallowell had discussed, as people did, the starving children of Russia. Those who remembered when it was plentiful were puritanical about food. I knew only rationing and what were called shortages; consequently I was part of Britain's healthiest generation. I missed nothing. I could never understand why adults grew so enthusiastic over a rabbit leg, a fatty chop or even a chocolate. Throughout the War my grandmother lived on pigeons which her massive cat Nero caught for her in the street. Another early memory is of pink bird feet sticking up through piecrust. One weekend in 1945 a lucky V2 rocket destroyed the school, freeing me to return to my ruins and my adventures.

My mother, also born in Mitcham, had known its broad Common, its vast commercial lavender fields, its Fair and gypsies, before her family moved back a mile or two to South London, where they had looked down on Brixton from a respectable part of Tooting. Their house of hard grey-yellow brick was a cut above most others, she told me, because it had steps leading up to the front door, showing it possessed a basement which suggested at least one live-in servant. In fact my grandmother did most of the work and gave birth to thirteen children. Eight survived infancy. Five survived the Blitz. Three are still living.

Our ancestors, including Sephardic Jews, Irish tinkers, French refugees and Anglo-Saxons, were shadows, vague legends, probably because there was more than one illegitimate birth in our fairly recent history, which could also be why I look back on a line predominantly maternal. People said we seemed Irish. Together with her raven hair and striking eyes my mother had a soft rose complexion, while her sisters were all high-coloured redheads and in their photographs the three youngest look stunning.

By the thirties my grandfather, refusing to give up drink, had been thrown out by my grandmother and lived in one room in Herne Hill. They expected him to die of the whisky. A master baker, he had written for the trade journals. "That's who you get your talent from." My mother had been his favourite. My grandfather's only triumph was to die of emphysema from smoking. A great dandy, he gambled away, family folklore had it, several fortunes. In keeping with the majority of our neighbours our status depended less on our present situation than on a mythical past.

"That's your ancestor." I remember my Uncle Jim standing with stern pleasure on the staircase of 10 Downing Street, where he lived. He wore a black coat and pinstripe trousers: his hair was thin, a reddish brown. He had a soft, ruddy face; his tobacco-stained hand on my shoulder was gentle. The portrait we contemplated was one of dozens, all former Prime Ministers, which crowded the walls. It was of Disraeli. I felt there was a family resemblance. I was ten. Without my mother's knowledge I had been visiting my uncle regularly in the school holidays, taking the bus to Westminster in the hope of a tip, perhaps half-a-crown. I was rarely turned away. My friends and I spent a good deal of our holidays contacting relatives who might be good for a couple of shillings. Others I could count on were my father's parents in Streatham, my Aunt Kitty in Pollard's Hill, my Aunt Charlotte in Thornton Heath. Until her own daughter was born I was my Aunt Charlotte's favourite.

Reaching Number Ten I would try to use the knocker and would always be stopped by a policeman who either recognised me or would send inside for my uncle. Usually he would arrive personally at the door to greet me, dispatching one of the messengers or policemen to buy buns: "With icing on them. You've got kids, Bill. Whatever boys like best." Then I would take the old lift to his quarters where his wife Iris, crippled by rheumatism and absorbed in her *Watchtower*, would greet me with the honeyed whine which, childless herself, she considered appropriate. She used much the same tone with animals, and I knew she hated them. She made a crude stab or two at kindness, but her own incurable pain was her dominating interest. When I planned to become a writer her most generous act was to give me her old Pitman Shorthand primer (she had been my uncle's secretary in the Treasury). Most Christmases she remembered to send me a subscription to *The Warcry*. She followed both the Salvationists and the Jehovah's Witnesses and later my Uncle Jim died prematurely as a result of her conversion to Christian Science. I never blamed her for taking to these desperate faiths but I could not forgive her for imposing them upon him and for putting his cat down the day before his funeral. My uncle was honest, amiable and generous. What disappointments had made her so opposite?

For some years I kept a collection of Winston Churchill's cigar butts taken by me from his ashtrays. Most were at least six inches long. When I was sixteen and determined to overcome the nausea I felt whenever I caught a whiff of burning tobacco I smoked them all. My uncle had predicted a great career for me, first in journalism and then in politics, but my act of smoking those miserably old cigars was probably a strong indication that I would never be a Member of Parliament, let alone a Cabinet Minister; I lacked the appropriate foresight.

Since my father's flight and my grandmother's death in 1948 my Uncle Jim had provided moral support to my mother, cold-shouldered by many members of her own and my father's family who also treated me with singular caution. Sometimes I felt my relations regarded me as a sort of unexploded bomb; in my presence they frequently affected heartiness, would pause in mid-sentence, changed the subject or began to mumble. This weight of mystery made me deeply curious about their supposed secrets. Later, with painful disappointment, I learned they had restrained themselves merely from mentioning my father's infamy or my mother's disgrace. It was generally agreed that my mother was somehow to blame for driving my father off. It was a common notion in those days that a wife who could not keep a husband had failed one of life's major tests.

I remember opening a local newspaper, still full of troop movements and little maps, looking for the cartoons and finding instead a neat square hole mysteriously cut from the centre pages. Years later I came to realise the censored section was a report of the court case when my parents were legally separated. They were not actually divorced until she was 71 and he was 77, an event which caused my mother some trauma and in which I participated as a go-between since they were still terrified of confrontation.

After VE Day, when he packed his bags, I saw my father once or twice a year, at Easter when he would deliver an egg, and in December for the presentation of birthday and Christmas gifts. Clinging to his strong impersonal back I would sometimes ride on his motorbike pillion. I never missed him, though I enjoyed the occasional intrusion of his masculinity into a world predominantly filled by women and children. While I welcomed his bounty it never seemed superior to my mother's. I was to discover that his visits were primarily at the urging of Sheila, his common-law wife, whom my mother persistently refused to call by name and still continues to characterise as a heartless hussy. While by no means a bad man Vic Mummery was, I think, emotionally lazy.

My father was also born in Mitcham, in a detached rather than a terraced house and was therefore a cut or two above his wife. His mother was Kentish. She had died shortly after giving birth to him, of poisoned blood, and his father had married another country-woman who doted on Vic even more than on his half-brother, her own son Reggie. I visited my remaining grandparents almost as frequently as my Uncle Jim. In a Victorian maisonette where Streatham bordered Mitcham, not far from the great South London Crematorium, they no longer lived in the splendour of detachment. Theirs was a street of miniature redbrick Gothic terraces, like ancient almshouses, full of rich stained glass and ecclesiastical porches endlessly reproduced, row upon row, at the end of which ran the main road where stately trams, all crimson paint and dented brass, moved with the purpose of ships of the line. I could rely on my grandma for sweets from her part-time job at the nearby chocolate factory, and on my grandad for money. Less prone to mythologising their family's past, they were a more trustworthy source of information for me in my attempts to distinguish fiction and folklore from reality. My own mother tended to believe her stories even as she created them, and her sisters never felt it their duty to set me straight, so I learned to watch their expressions when I retold certain tales and learned when my mother's memory of events did not marry with theirs.

Though not neutral, my surviving grandparents had fewer loyalties to my mother's accounts but best of all were the stories I heard when I was sent to the West Country, to stay with my grandma's family, ancient Lovelucks, with Somerset and Devon Lovelucks, servants at great houses, tenants of mighty farms, chauffeurs to the nobility, claiming kinship with Norman baronets. From these Lovelucks came ordinary unembroidered accounts of my father and his half-brother as boys and of my grandmother's girlhood. Most of the Lovelucks were my grandma's peers, without children or with children abroad or at the War. As the only grandchild I received considerable attention but when others were born I slowly lost my prestige. Invitations took on a formal reluctance and then ceased altogether so that as War was succeeded by an austere Peace the dunes of Westward Ho, the wheatfields, woods and moorlands of Polperro and points south became no longer accessible and soon, aged seven, I was discovering the miserable monotony of boarding-school's full-time rural life, developing a horror of the Home Counties and of health food I have yet to conquer.

London is my mother, source of most of my ambivalences and most of my loyalties. In 1948 we moved to London proper, to Norbury SW16, to Semley Road and a brand new semi-detached built on the levelled rubble of a house which had received a direct V1 hit in 1944. The 109 went from the bottom of Semley Road up London Road via Streatham, Brixton and Kennington, to Westminster where I could visit my Uncle Jim in Downing Street. North of us was Brixton. Nobody my mother knew lived in Brixton any more, and all her relatives had moved from Tooting since it had ceased to be the "old Tooting". Her family had occupied one of the finest houses off Garrett Lane. Of her seven siblings the women had all married, Oliver had joined the Navy, Jim had become a Civil Servant, from Treasury to Foreign Office to his job with Churchill, and Albert, the oldest, had trained boxers in his gym somewhere on the borders of Kent. He had also bred greyhounds, I think, near Beckenham. Like most Southwest Londoners I knew very little about Southeast London. Albert's son had become a diplomat and his daughters had "gone into medicine". One was married to an editor on *The Times* and my mother regularly insisted I contact her to further my own journalistic career. Unusually I had relatives of the same generation who were working-class, middle-class and upper-class. We even had French aristocrats through my father's Aunt Sophie who married a Baron and died a very grand lady in Paris. They mixed fairly comfortably on special occasions and only two of my ferociously rising aunts were snobs. I had many confusing role models as a child; for a time I wished desperately to know my place and was even uncertain what to call myself or my trade. My education was sketchy. I received a minimum of erudition at Cooper's Hall, an obscure and experimental public school which soon expelled me. I was even unsure of my mother's status. My Uncle Oliver believed she was being "kept" by a rich businessman who supplied my school fees. She eventually told me that my Uncle Jim, secretly so my Aunt Iris should not know, had paid for me. All that school ever did was threaten my friendship with Ben French, a marvellously enjoyable companion until the day he lost his life to a casually popped Largactyl and half a can of Special Brew.

Back at home I was enrolled in an appalling private school, run by two tyrannical women who liked to wear their WVS uniforms to class, where I was bullied by two brothers, the Newby boys; they were held up to us by our parents as examples of perfect respectability though we knew them to be sadists. I remember our triumph when Chris, the younger Newby, was hanged for his part in the murder of a policeman: he was just old enough to receive the death sentence. When the case came into the newspapers it at last gave meaning to my own misery at the little thug's hands. When his older brother, Derek, was sentenced to life in Copenhagen for the manslaughter of his girlfriend all of us who had suffered at their hands knew deep satisfaction. Our parents were duly shocked but almost immediately forgot how they had insisted we emulate the brothers. I remember my mother in the front room of our house in Semley Road watching with approval Chris Newby lifting his neat little school cap to the vicar. I could not mention that the reason I no longer had a similar cap was because Chris had stolen it and urinated over it.

Josef Kiss and I stand by the gate of the Semley Road house where I grew up. Behind us is a small enchained patch of sunlit green and a brick church. "And you were happy, were you, in this?" With his stick he sketches the outline of the pleasant, nondescript suburban villa which still keeps its original trees and shrubs, its various rosebushes, its wooden fence, its vines, its air of tranquil security.

"I was happy," I tell him, "most of my life. Until the business you know about, which led to our meeting."

"Well, Mummery, are you happy again?"

"I'm determined to be," I say.

Mary Gasalee

MRS GASALEE came out of the flames. Trembling, she sat on a bench beside Brook Green, Hammersmith, watching the pupils swaggering through the gates of St Paul's Girls School. She had a burn scar on her back, the exact imprint of a hobnail boot, perhaps where she was stepped on by a would-be rescuer during the Blitz. Hearing, as she believed, the thoughts of the children, she smiled carefully, with no wish to disturb anyone. These girls helped her recreate the events and feelings of her own past. Her girlhood had been a happy one before sex came too soon to confuse and subjugate her so she no longer knew her own soul. She focused her green-gold eyes on the towers of Phoenix Lodge Mansions at the corner of Shepherd's Bush Road where she had lived for several years, occasionally alone. Her daughter now maintained that flat as a pied-à-terre which was still not too noisy on her particular floor though the traffic between Hammersmith and the motorway was constant.

The boy is in pain. Rejecting this she again allowed herself to be absorbed in a multitude of unformed desires and cloudy notions, of a world unspoiled. Soon she must go to Goldhawk Road to get the prescription which for a while would block out those children's voices, happy, sad, despairing or impossibly gay. As usual she knew a sense of regret at her potential loss.

I don't believe you can be called Utterfuck and not know it's funny if I find out it was Shelagh I'll kill her mummy's been in touch with that I could still do with chocolate fourteen eighty-seven was the defeat of who the hell I hope we get Groggy for assembly that smell's more roses than violets and it's really really good but it couldn't have been one of the really big bombs roll on roll on roll on . . . Most had few words in their heads, just states of mind in the main agreeable, while some poor self-conscious soul occasionally emitted a burst of sickening agony all the worse because it had no source in any reality save the victim's cruelly washed brain; or so it seemed to Mrs Gasalee who had learned not to respond. The burden of others' pain had brought her to her present pass where she must now rise reluctantly and move on to the pseudo-hygiene of cracked Formica and smudged emulsion, the day-patient's surgery, a begrudged and temporary sanctuary beyond Shepherd's Bush Green on the bleak road from the White City.

didn't ask him for a penny then farted the minute she was finished

She was no longer proud nor particularly frightened of what she had learned to call her overactive imagination, which invented voices, even whole identities for people. In the end she had been glad enough to accept the prescription. Little more than a century ago people like her had been burned, tortured or driven from their villages. David Mummery's theory was that their mutual condition was a product of what he called urban evolution: as a Brazilian native of the rain forest was able instinctively to use all his senses to build up a complex picture of his particular world, so could a city dweller read his own relevant signs, just as unconsciously, to form an equally sophisticated picture. Mummery found nothing alarming or mysterious about their condition, believing that most people chose to ignore the available information while certain cynics turned it to their advantage and became confidence tricksters, modern witch-doctors, publicists, predators of myriad varieties. Unable easily to block the wealth of information provided by a great city, he, she and Josef Kiss were like powerful wireless receivers who must learn how to adjust their fine tuning to keep a required station. She was not sure she accepted this.

punks me growup me pants me smell all that pork

She wondered what Patrick Gasalee would have made of her if he had survived the fire. Her husband had always joked about her living in another world and had seemed to love her for it, but in time he would probably have been frightened by her dreaminess and perhaps even ashamed of her. She only remembered him sporadically. She had married at sixteen because he had been about to go to War and she had become pregnant almost at once. They had been alone for a while, a couple, when they spent a happy few weeks together after Patrick's parents evacuated to his Aunt Rose in Lincolnshire. Taking a job as an usherette just up the road from the flat, Mary enjoyed all the latest pictures for nothing, three times a day, six days a week; on Sundays they had a different show, usually older films. When Patrick went off to fight she had already made plenty of local friends who were pleased to help her through and when the baby was born almost the whole of De Quincey Road turned out to help. When Patrick returned to Wood Green on leave from Africa his baby was two days old. The leave was due to him but they had made it compassionate and flown him home. Brown and cheerful, healthier than he had ever been in London, he was delighted by the baby and she felt more in love with him than ever. He made them both sleep in the Morrison shelter in the parlour while he used the upstairs bed. When the bomb hit it blew the whole house apart. Patrick had been killed outright. There had been nothing left of him. His body had burned in the fire.

Just before she went into her coma Mary was in shock, unable to remember her own name or the baby's. In hospital they decided she had a form of amnesia familiar amongst the War's casualties, akin to senility, but they could make no more tests until she woke up from her long sleep. Now she had clear memories of her girlhood, of her dreams and few of the Blitz. She was still not entirely certain what had happened when the bomb hit and could not quite recall what Patrick had looked like since all his photographs had been destroyed when his mother and father were killed after their return to London. Unrecognised by her comatose mother, her daughter Helen, last of the Gasalees, had grown up in Earl's Court with Mary's cousin's children.

Mary's gratitude and love for her cousin Gordon Meldrum was profound. Good-hearted and conscientious, he had ensured Helen's security as well as her education. Having spent many holidays with the Meldrum relatives in Aberdeen, Helen had developed a profound attachment to Scotland, the background to her first novel, *The Forgotten Queen*, which was accepted by Mills and Boon who published her next five historical romances in the two years before she was offered a large advance from Collins for her seventh novel *Laird in Waiting*, and she was twenty-four when she completed it. It became a best-seller. Eventually Helen moved to a slender Gothic house, built for one of Scott's imitators, a mile or two from the centre of Edinburgh; she shared it with her close friend, her secretary-companion Delia Thickett, a relationship which comforted Mary Gasalee who had only a few pleasant experiences of male lovers.

Once or twice a year Mary enjoyed visiting Durward Hall where the two young women were at once solicitous of her comfort and considerate of her privacy; a more relaxing version of the retreat she had once stayed in, but that had been run by nuns with whom she had little in common. She belonged at Helen's; she knew the security of familial love.

With few anxieties about her, Mary was proud of Helen and watched for book reviews, eagerly telling neighbours when "Maeve MacBride" was giving a television or radio interview. Helen was a great Woman's Hour favourite, especially on the subject of Highland folklore and history. Her books were serialised in *Woman* or *Woman's Own*, in the *Daily Mail*. She was described as "the voice of Scotland's heart" and remained amused by the fact that she hadn't a drop of Scottish blood – though sometimes she thought her mother, with her weird second sight, might have more than a touch of Celtic feyness.

Born Mary Felgate in Seven Sisters Road not a mile from Holloway Women's Prison, Mary had been raised with fierce concern by her Grandma Felgate who swore Mary would not meet her mother's bad end. Mary's clothes had been so thoroughly mended and washed that people thought she must be a paroled charity case and at school had nicknamed her "Workhouse".

When Mary was eight Grandma Felgate, already wizened into a tightly determined and economical four foot eleven, moved them to Clerkenwell, to a Peabody block of wholesome flats erected in 1900 for the deserving poor at Bowling Green Lane, just off Farringdon Road where the focus, the chief landmark of Mary's new territory, became Smithfield Meat Market in which, with the other children, she learned to play and to earn an occasional penny. She had loved Clerkenwell. Grandma Felgate had died when Mary was fifteen and had already worked for a year in Gamage's Department Store, Holborn, where she had been chosen for special training. By the time Patrick Gasalee from Electrical Goods caused something in her to twitch, her only surviving close relative was Grandpa Felgate who, though he had doted on her as a little girl, had lately shown her the same neutral interest he reserved for everything save himself, and had been happy to see her married and gone as soon as she was sixteen.

Now Helen's birth was impossibly confused in Mary's mind with the sensation of falling, the baby held tightly in her arms, head over heels into flames. She had in fact not been badly burned and the Auxiliary Firemen had said it was a miracle, but sometimes, when asked to state her own or her daughter's birthday she would automatically give the date of the night her husband was killed, when she emerged from the incendiary's debris, Monday 30 December 1940.

In her own mind Mary Gasalee had actually been born again in 1955 at the age of almost 31. That summer enough of her memory had returned for her doctors to believe a relapse into coma would be unlikely and eventually they let her go into a baffling world building itself great white towers, laying all that was prewar with pale plastic and polished board, where the new words she heard were "smooth", and "clean", and "creamy". These postwar Young Turks identified cornices, railings, old leaded picture glass, finials, corbels, ornament of every kind with the sub-Wagnerian posturing of Nazism, the corrupted romanticism of the Right, so they smashed the pretty tiles of Victorian villas, boxed over the fancy fireplaces, ripped the picture rails and ceiling roses from their plaster; but Mary, who remained a prewar child, saw only a continuation of the Blitz and grew afraid of their fierce practicality and their puritanism. Helen was completing her first GCE exam at the Godolphin and Latymer School in Hammersmith where she had won a scholarship and it was agreed she should be left undisturbed until the holidays, especially since earlier that year Gordon's wife Rachel had died of cancer. To her own relief, Mary was put by Gordon Meldrum on a train to visit his sister in Aberdeen, a city she found far less shocking than the new, off-white London, where Helen eventually joined her for several weeks.

Her daughter's generosity, openness and frank concern impressed Mary. In the awkward surroundings of the hospital she had only a hint of her daughter's character. In Scotland Helen took her for long walks through the countryside and beside the ocean, helping her explore Aberdeen and nearby towns. With wonderment Mary regarded the great grey northern sea. She had never been out of London.

For her Scotland still remained a magic land and she would feel almost guilty when the train from Kings Cross to Edinburgh crossed the border. It thrilled her to imagine she broke with all London's realities, and Helen and Delia were pleased to encourage this fantasy. They drove her to fairy castles and picnicked in secluded glens or on peaks overlooking wild valleys. During the past five years she had found in the Highlands every confirmation of what she read in her daughter's romances, yet when the train took her back into London with its noisy dirt Mary Gasalee found quite a different reassurance and felt this was probably in the long run better for her.

She had felt shy with her daughter at first, for she lacked the education, the middle-class accent, the confident way of controlling the world which thanks to the Meldrums Helen had acquired, but in Scotland where they both spoke "Southern" and were more or less outsiders, these barriers had swiftly melted and never appeared again.

called it his curiosity made a fortune short-changing those bitches from South Ken I never could stand that child's smell sort of stale god you get sick of illness after a while never ate a vegetable in his life and spent half his time complaining of constipation the other half sitting on the loo flushing himself out with laxatives that can't be good for you my mother got cancer of the colon is it and they said it was that rana ib sab'n afak my guest my guest oh no

Freshly seeded with three months' supply of the calming drug, Mary buttoned her cardigan while staring with calm curiosity at the instruments arranged in a stainless-steel tray next to the couch.

"And what about headaches?" Dr Bridget finished washing her hands at the little sink behind her desk and rolled down her sleeves. Once the house from which her surgery was converted had been grand for this part of the world. The embossed wallpaper displayed vaguely oriental representations of Sky, Land and Water, with ornamental ceilings from which, Mary guessed, had once hung gas chandeliers to fill a comfortable home with warming light, *Fire*. "Any problems there, Mary?"

Mrs Gasalee resented this particular use of her Christian name, an increasingly common means of exerting authority. Since her release, hospitals had started it but the police had now also adopted the technique. She had been brought up to address other people with more respect. But she could think of no graceful means of objecting. "I've been very well, just lately, thank you, Dr Bridget."

"Everything ticking along nicely at the Clinic?" Dr Bridget sat down and sighed. "The memory improving is it, Mary? Do take that chair, dear. You always look like the boy in that painting. When Did You Last See Your Father?"

"He was a soldier, I gather." Mary's gaze wandered to the window, and the little strip of green where two West Indian girls in school uniform wrestled. Their mothers chatted nearby, enjoying some minor respite, poised beside the zebra crossing. "Possibly Canadian."

"Yes," said Dr Bridget. She did something to a lock of her mousy hair, holding the heel of her hand hard against her cheekbone for a moment, her brown eyes imitating patience. "Yes, dear, you've mentioned it. I was joking. So all we need is our other prescription topped up, to help us sleep and so on."

"I don't know about you," Mrs Gasalee made a crude stab at retaliation, "but I could do with some more tablets myself."

Frowning Dr Bridget packed more hair into place. "It's usually fifty isn't it, Mary dear?"

"Usually fifty, yes." Careless in defeat. "Dear."

Dr Bridget scribbled with her ballpoint. "No more constipation problems? No bad depression?" This was her own ritual. Though Mrs Gasalee did not respond her silence went unnoticed so she said: "I suppose I could do with a few tension tablets. The ones for the migraines." She noticed a black smudge on her left thumb, like soot. It emphasised the remains of a fingerprint.

Dr Bridget pursed unpainted lips and swung again in her seat to look at her file cards. "It's been nearly a year since your last prescription. That's very good. Things are looking up for you are they, Mary?"

Mrs Gasalee watched the thin red pen make an addition to her prescription form. From the doctor's drawer came a sudden scent of rose essence. Dr Bridget tore the paper off the block and offered it between two long fingers. She uttered a smile which told Mary

35

Gasalee that only affirmation would bring approval. "Otherwise all's well, eh?"

Mrs Gasalee nodded slowly.

"And how's that famous daughter of yours?" Dr Bridget's dark desperate eyes seemed to note that Mary's pastel Fairisle and heather-mixture skirt, her tan boots, were only of medium quality.

"Writing away up in Scotland." Mary would not let Helen support her. If anyone deserved help in his old age it was Gordon, now in Devon. This was absolutely no business of Dr Bridget's.

"Got a best-seller going according to *She*, eh? But I suppose that's all exaggerated. Like pop stars." Dr Bridget's stare became reflective. Her nose wrinkled. Slowly she began to push her pad away from her. "I expect she's muddling along like the rest of us."

"Oh, I expect so." Mary welcomed a flush of angry pride. "In her castle up there on her island. But she keeps Irish wolfhounds, of course, and you'd never believe how much Chum they get through in a day."

Irritated by this consultation's failure to follow a predictable course, perhaps blaming herself, Dr Bridget said, "Well, I must get one out of the library some day."

"Every little helps." Mary drew a breath. "They get paid for the borrowings now."

As Dr Bridget rose, her eyes wandered to the side of her own face as if searching for further rogue locks. "No more nightmares, I take it."

Mrs Gasalee, half-way to her feet, grew wary and, straightening her skirt, walked quickly to the brown-and-white door. She folded her hand over the knob. At the corner of her vision she detected a lick of fire. Knowing it to be nonsense she feared she might one day will a flame to life. Her grandmother, a firm believer in the reality of spontaneous combustion, had known of at least five accredited cases, including her own uncle who had died drunk aboard his barge on the canal, boiling and bubbling and giving off yellow fumes until he was nothing but a mess of fat and sulphur on the planking, with a nasty hole in the carpet, too. It was a year before they got rid of the smell. It had sometimes occurred to Mary that she, rather than the Luftwaffe, had set off the explosion which had killed Pat. All the doctors had explained how common it was to feel guilt for the death of those you survived, but Mary remained unconvinced by their arguments. Her strong dislike for Dr Bridget bothered her. She grew anxious to leave lest merely by pointing one of her neat, stubby fingers she made the obnoxious woman flare like a chip pan.

"Nothing like that." Opening the door Mary slipped through and closed it tight behind her while Dr Bridget's receptionist gave off a pert, meaningless smile. Diana was combed and frizzed to resemble a tropical plant, predominantly red and yellow. Mrs Gasalee liked people to look colourful.

"All right then, Mrs G?" Diana's smile took on warmth.

"Right as rain. Bye, bye, Di."

My life, my real life, began in fire. Mary Gasalee passed the old Shepherd's Bush market where she had once gone to spend time with the budgies and the tame mice. Beside the bland formica of the BBC Theatre she crossed the street to set foot on the Green's mud. The heavy traffic surrounding her on all sides gave her a secure feeling as if the wagon train had completed its circle. Overhead she saw a kestrel, one of a pair nesting in the roof of the old dancehall, hovering as if to stoop upon the two shabby drunkards, their broken veins tracked over their faces like ketchup, who moaned indistinctly at her from their bench. One had a half-healed mess on his forehead. She knew he was grateful for the wound which saved him the effort of climbing to his feet to beg. As usual she paused to give each a fivepenny piece in the same way she always made a contribution to the altar fund when leaving a church. Knowing they could sometimes be aggressive she walked quickly across the Green until she reached the underpass taking her back to the road for Hammersmith and ultimately Queen's Club Gardens where she had a small basement flat. She was one of the few who still rented in a square growing daily more gentrified. Helen had tried to persuade her to buy the flat outright, with her help. "You can't go wrong these days, mum. It could be in your name, or both our names." But Mary Gasalee had always rented her flat, since she moved from Phoenix Lodge and before that Bayswater, and it would no longer seem hers if Helen bought it.

to Holborn on up towards Seven Sisters und dein des Menschen Antlitz dein des Menchen Glieder und sein Atem Einziehend durch die Pforte der Geburt

By the time she reached Olympia the sun was out again, giving a

37

little unexpected warmth to the stark branches of the few trees growing near the railway. It brought a sense of respite, and she drew a clear breath of the winter air before crossing Hammersmith Road for North End Road.

Gradually the little shops which served the wealthier residents of West Kensington gave way to the kebab bars, cluttered grocery stores, cheap electrical retailers, dowdy drapers and hardware shops run by recent immigrants and she turned at length where some of the shop fronts began to appeal to the young middle-classes slowly taking over the bijou terraces around Star Road which for almost a hundred years housed a clientele poorer than the one the original developers had envisioned. Indeed, only now were the brick villas achieving that dreamed-of respectability.

Before she went home Mary made her customary stop at St Andrew's Church where Star Road became Greyhound Road. The church had taken her fancy because its 19th-century builders had consciously tried to make it look rural, succeeding in creating something more impressive than what they had hoped to emulate. St Andrew's had a wonderful carved porch, a beautiful spire, an air of tranquil dignity.

Within the dappled semi-darkness of oak and coloured glass Mary knelt in prayer. *Please God, do not let me be wicked. Do not let me release or be consumed by any power you have chosen to invest in me. Do not let me fail to understand your intentions when the time comes. I pray for the soul of Patrick Ambrose Gasalee, my late husband, and for other poor sufferers who have perished and continue to perish in terrible wars, Lord. And please help Josef Kiss to help himself because I am sure you agree it's about time he was married again. He is wasted as he is. Thank you and amen.* She had no formal knowledge of the Church and most of her attempts at appropriate language were taken from what she saw on television. She had a horror of attending any kind of regular service and went to great lengths to avoid the vicar or other worshippers.

Humming to herself now, Mrs Gasalee left the chill of St Andrew's and crossed Greyhound Road to enter the unnatural calm of the Gardens, an unspoiled enclave of great red mansion blocks surrounding a rather unkempt tennis court, some flower beds and a number of rich evergreens. She let herself into the shabby door of Palgrave Mansions. The entrance hall was as gloomy as the church but offered neither the same security nor hope. She said good afternoon to Mrs Zimmermann, a white-headed hen with a mottled brown beak who always came to stare as she went by, held her breath against the ghosts of a thousand overcooked vegetables, descended to the deepest haven of her basement and let herself in to her own black front door. As usual through the remains of the late afternoon light her two chocolate-point Siamese cats came running according to habit from the back of the flat, voicing loud familiar sounds, half-complaint, half-greeting, and purring as soon as they reached her legs. Picking one up in each arm she held them like babies, bellies upward. They lolled, little lordlings, squinting with pleasure into her delighted face.

"Hello, my lovely boys. You're angry with me aren't you? You never do know when it's Thursday." Rocking the ecstatic animals in her arms she entered the comfort of her kitchen. Unusually this flat had never been modernised in the fifties. It still had its massive black Victorian range against which the cats loved to sleep and on which her kettle was already gently boiling while over it on pulleys hung a wood and cast-iron drying rack holding her day's washing, a few underclothes, a blue jumper, a couple of shirts. With a black rod she knocked the lever at the back of the chimney to widen the flu, then opened the fire door to peer into a familiar and hellish landscape. The range needed no more coke for the moment. It suited her to base a good deal of her domestic routine around the stove's demands. She hardly ever used her gas cooker. Removing her coat she hung it in the tall wooden cupboard behind her, then from her little refrigerator at the end of the scrubbed pine counter furthest from the stove she took a tin of Meaty Chunks. Her Siamese grew alert, standing on hind legs to paw her thighs. Humming cheerfully, she filled two identical plastic bowls, one of which she had marked Gabby and the other Charlie in honour of Rossetti and Swinburne who she had fallen in love with when she saw them played on television. She mashed the food carefully, breaking up the lumps.

Opening the baking compartment of the stove, she again checked the temperature before returning to the fridge and removing the pie she had made that morning. Protecting her hands with a cloth she positioned her pie on the upper rack. "And that's my supper sorted out." She bent her stocky body to offer the cats their bowls. While they ate she unwound her scarf and took off her cardigan. With her gloves and her handbag she balanced these on an old hallstand just outside the kitchen. The stand was festooned with so much miscellaneous clothing she could only just see her face in a fragment of the mirror. She was still surprised to be over sixty. She looked less than forty, as if all those years in the coma had not counted, as if she had begun to age only after leaving hospital when she had looked hardly older than Helen. *Nuns look like this, but not doing what I've done.* Faintly disturbed she wondered if she were paying a price in a bargain she couldn't remember making. Or had she yet to pay?

For a second she saw David Mummery's nervous features beside her own. She recalled his pale body, the fragility of his bones, his delicate flesh. He seemed to have taken on weight and colour recently, but not health. She knew a moment's sadness for him, then returned her attention to herself. Nothing could depress her now the surgery was behind her and she was safe in her home again. It was silly to be upset by good fortune. *It's the pure life you lead, Mary.* She moved an old fur jacket in order to address a little more of her face. *Think what you'd look like if you'd kept on going with the insatiable Mr Kiss!*

She began to smile. She was always amused by those particular memories.

"Bless him."

Josef Kiss

"MR KISS, have you ever eaten fire?" The admiring lad chanced his luck.

Josef Kiss was tight today and shook with something like laughter. Standing with straight glass lifted beside the shining wood and faded tapestry of the settle, he was huge enough to dwarf even the mighty furniture around him. At his age, with his subtle makeup, he was magnificent rather than grotesque. He had been boasting how with a minimum of talent he had earned his living in almost every aspect of the theatrical profession and so gave serious thought to young Bashall's question.

"Unless you count the time my cooker exploded as I bent over a pan of baked beans I can answer truthfully: Only in pretence, Sebastian. I admire those who can." He drew sluggishly at his pint. "I had a cameo role as a circus personality in *Writs*. My old friend Montcrieff, also. You take what you're offered." A further consultation of his memory. "For a very short while I was a sharpshooter's assistant. His name was Vittorio something. He was interned on the Isle of Man during the War and I lost touch. An unjust fate, the Isle of Man, for anyone save an unrepentant Nazi. Were you ever there?" He became more animated. "Shrouded in fog, Sebastian, summer and winter. Not merely Britain's answer to Siberia, I assure you, but a refinement. I played a season in Douglas in 1950. The people are grim, the beer is dreadful and the architecture owes much to modern Ireland in its unremitting ugliness. The pubs are open all day. Their urinals are full of inebriated Dubliners leaning on their arms over filthy porcelain, groaning and vomiting 'Oh, Jesus. Oh, dear Jesus!' while in the public bars their wives, coarsened by Man and God, stare listlessly over halves of Guinness through murky windows at children bloated with crisps and lemonade, endlessly tugging the levers of one-armed bandits. It is not worth the same time it takes you to travel to France just to see a horse-drawn tram or sit on the hard benches of a miniature railway for the privilege of glimpsing, should the mist divide at all, a cove or two almost as pretty as Devon's. It is called a tax haven, I believe. My own theory is that captured tax evaders are exiled there. Her Danish settlers were either convicts or those Vikings who failed to qualify for Valhalla. No one in their right mind would volunteer to live there. As for their tailless cats, I'm sure that any Manxman would find a cat's tail a delicacy compared to his normal diet." Mr Kiss leaned his back against carved mahogany in what had once been the snug of The Sun and Roman before its conversion to a single vast horseshoe bar.

With his third pint of Director's Sebastian Bashall's attention had wandered. His small gnomish face grew vague. "You ate fire on the Isle of Man?"

"Presumably many do. Merely to keep warm. No. That was where the unfortunate sharpshooter was sent. My mind-reading was never very successful in the provinces so I, to my shame, was a sort of pierrot. I forget the name of the theatre. One of those summer shows people went to out of desperation before landladies installed Television Lounges in their boarding houses. Oh, how I longed for Blackpool that year. I'm not one to mourn the passing of Summer Concert Parties. Television is a kinder employer and a more reliable paymaster and, better still, one rarely has to leave London. It was the TV Commercial saved both my life and my dignity. Why Sebastian were you asking about fire?"

The young estate agent turned so that for an instant his own glass was brought to red-gold life in a shaft of winter sunlight. All this so transfixed him that he replied almost distantly: "I was wondering how it was done, that's all."

"The trick is not to keep the fire in your mouth too long. You can try it for yourself. Look." Mr Kiss took a box of Swan Vestas from beneath his cape. Removing a match he struck it. Then he opened his red lips to engulf the flame. "There. The palate is fairly sturdy

42

and the lack of oxygen in one's mouth soon stifles the conflagration. You must be the fourth young man to ask me that question this week."

"A fire-eater on the news burned his face off."

Josef Kiss picked up his own glass, briefly defeated by the sight of so much remaining beer. "Once more the mysteries of London's coincidences are solved and clarified. The ordinary explanation is always a welcome antidote to ambiguity." He replaced the glass on the damp mat, drew a breath, then took his drink back to his face for a single, manful swallow.

"My round, Mr Kiss." Sebastian exposed his watch. He was due back at the office in fifteen minutes. Through the crowd of laughing cigar-smokers, the local business gentry in their glossy suits and crisp shirtings, he hurried across dark carpet to the bar and waved a couple of pound coins at the sturdy, tattooed publican, Peter Edrich, whose greying red hair curled with sweat from supervising his massive Victorian erection of brass, mirrors, bottles and polished wood, tending and wiping his levers, his toggles as he had tended a ship's engines, long ago in the Age of Steam. "A pint and a half of best please squire." Sebastian glanced beyond the clouded glass, across a busy stretch of the Mile End Road, to his own office. Behind the display boards of the front window he saw familiar figures at their desks. Gerry Pettit had left half-an-hour before him and was still not back. Sebastian relaxed. Thursday was never a heavy day for estate agents round here. Usually he only took likely purchasers to The Sun and Roman, his own preference for lunch being the smaller, cheaper pubs of the sidestreets, but he enjoyed Mr Kiss's regular Thursday visits and could even justify their meetings as work for Mr Kiss brought intelligence of most other London districts and always knew what an average family house was selling for anywhere from Ealing to Epping, from Barnet to Bromley.

Mr Kiss seemed in particularly good form today, so Sebastian decided to risk a further question, something which had been on his mind for a while. "Sorry if I seem overcurious, Mr K," he proffered the pint, "but where do you actually live yourself? I mean you seem to be familiar with so many bits of London. I know you don't come from round here."

Josef Kiss touched his mouth to the straight glass, exhibiting as much relish for this, his fifth, as he had for his first. "In confidence, Sebastian, I divide my time between Town – that is the West End, Kensington, Chelsea and so forth – the City, which is to say the City of London and the East End – the Western Suburbs, chiefly Chiswick, Acton and Hammersmith – the Northern Suburbs from Camden to Finchley – the Southern Suburbs, Battersea, Brixton, Norwood et cetera – and the Eastern Suburbs, as far, say, as Dagenham or Upminster. I have homes commanding all four points of the compass."

"I was under the impression you lived . . . where?" Sebastian Bashall again considered his watch. He had seven minutes remaining. "White City?"

As if a chord was struck in his brain Josef Kiss blinked. "White City or Black, dear lad," he said absently, "there are no greys, at least, in the world of Josef Kiss." He lifted the glass to swallow half its contents. "I have a pied-à-terre in Acton – rich and concentrated, though its exterior would never betray it – another in Brixton, that perpetual nerve-centre of London working-class life and as traditional a home for unsuccessful theatricals as Brighton is for the successful. I have seen racetrack gangs come and go. I have witnessed the rise and fall of the Brixton Chain Gang, so called because the heavy bicycle chain was their favoured weapon, as well as other coteries of violent young men. You will not recall the epic Teddy-Boy clash on Tooting Common between the Chain Gang and the Balham Blackshirts, which resulted in several deaths and many serious woundings. Though the area now attracts a better class of resident it remains interesting to me. I also maintain a little home in Hampstead, looking on to one of the Heath's least attractive views. My main residence, however, is near Fleet Street. I like to think it keeps me at the heart of things. One of the few private seventeenth century houses remaining in those expensive alleys."

"Near Doctor Johnson's, then? The Cheshire Cheese?"

"I'd never have called him that, dear lad, whatever his short-comings. I see you've finished your half. Would you care for another? Swiftly?"

"I'll be getting back, Mr Kiss. I suppose you could make a packet if you sold your Fleet Street place, eh?"

"Sadly it's held, as it were, in trust."

Left with a further puzzle Sebastian Bashall buttoned up his jacket, tucked his short plaid scarf down inside it, drew on his corduroy overcoat, called "See you next week then!" and pushed through the doors towards his office.

Josef Kiss rounded with a smile upon orange-cheeked Audrey who in her white overall gathered plates containing the remains of jumbo sausages, beans, chips, puddings and military pickle. "A delicious Shepherd's Pie today, my dear."

"Well," a movement of her shoulders told him she was too busy to chat, "I'm glad you liked it, love."

Draining his glass on his way to the pegs by the cigarette machine, Mr Kiss stood it carefully on a table and took down his wide-brimmed hat, his long muffler, his umbrella. He was a stickler for every convention associated with the English eccentric, conventions which afforded him considerable privacy and discomfited no one; they stated exactly how far he wished to remain distanced from his fellows.

With sudden alacrity, and a general flourish in the direction of the publican and various acquaintances, he left the warmth and press of The Sun and Roman, taking enormous, ponderous strides East towards Bow and The St Clement's Arms where in a few minutes he was due to meet his old friend Dandy Banaji whose "London Byways" column was one of the few enduring features of *The Bombay Daily Mail*. Their relationship was to some extent professional. Appearing weekly as "information and general expenses" on Banaji's pay sheets Mr Kiss supplied basic intelligence for the column and had achieved the status of a regular character, being frequently referred to as "The Ancient Resident" or "Our London Friend".

As the sun came through again, making even the frozen heaps of dirt-crested snow look relatively fresh, Mr Kiss's heart began to sing. The listless movement of the traffic was at odds with the general mood of the day and he checked an impulse to shout to the cars and lorries, to urge them to pull themselves together, and look more cheerful.

"You're an old fraud, Kiss." He followed this with a satisfied yawn. "But at least you no longer do much harm to anyone." Because of his habit of colouring and embellishing his conversation and so keeping people at a remove he had led the estate agent to believe he owned at least four London houses while in fact his four rooms were all bedsitters which he had accumulated almost by accident. He frowned, thinking the traffic had increased, but then he realised he was hearing human voices.

Twenty minutes of relative security and tranquillity on the South Suburban Line. I didn't start buying a paper till I got interested in my stars and then of course later it was the telly programmes. I must admit this led to me taking an interest in the news. Some of it really shocked me. That's why I came to get into politics. After I got into local government I hardly looked at a national paper and when I eventually became an MP I stopped reading papers altogether. Nowadays I don't even read books. My wife. What are those golden builders doing near wonderful ever weeping Paddington? The meat of Smithfield used to stink by eleven in the morning. That's why we come here my wife and I. It was during the war originally. We were refugees from Copenhagen. We thought the light was so beautiful. She returned to Denmark but I remained. Theobald's Road. The clockmaker's.

Mile End Road was a consort of disgruntled noises. The bad weather got everyone down. This was the worst winter since 1947, that hideous year when he was convinced he would die. Doing pantomime at the Streatham Grand, his consolation was being chosen at the last minute to be the Goose. The costume was usually hated for its stuffiness, but he played his part with grateful vigour. According to local notices he had been the star of the season, but the freezing journey home at night to Endymion Road, when he had to walk not much more than a mile, had been one of his worst ordeals. At the end of the performance he would simply remove the goose mask, drag his topcoat over the rest of the suit, wrap his scarf about his off-white throat, set his hat on his head and, gripping his umbrella, waddle on great yellow feet back to Brixton, careless of all curiosity. Twice he was stopped by policemen who, listening to his story sympathetically, would agree at last that no law stopped a man from walking the streets of London dressed as a goose. One mild summer evening some ten years later he had strolled the same route up Streatham Hill only to have his jacket slashed from neck to waist by a Teddy Boy's razor, but soon afterwards, as he was fond of saying, the economy took a rise, allowing the youth of South London to trade their razors for reefers and dress much more attractively. For a while there was real peace in Brixton.

He knew he was drunker than usual. "Life goes up, old boy. And life goes down again. Surely there are some areas of progress." The few people still at large on the Mile End Road began to distance themselves from him. He saw their white breath as blank speech balloons, as if a cartoonist experienced a sudden failure of creativity. *He's one of the leaders of the National Front. He took over the White City, Shepherd's Bush, Harlesden. But he's diabetic, see, and slowly going blind. He won't be treated in hospital. Thomas his name is – a great friend of Dylan Thomas actually. They were related. I know for a fact a baby was born in St Mary's that had two faces. One on the front of its head like normal the other on the side. It's these pakis and jewboys from Golders Green buying up all the land. That yard's full of vermin. Mrs Taylor's had no electricity. There's no inside toilet, no gas. The house is as filthy as they are. What's happened to us? I can remember everything. I can remember everything. I knew I'd find you here you Telling fortunes in the laundry while it rains Jack's got a hammer. I thought I'd better tell you.* Mr Kiss smiled as usual, wondering how much of all this he imagined or embellished, then he sighed, pushing with an air of finality through the narrow door of The St Clement's Arms and its density of regulars to wave his brolly at the small figure of Dandy Banaji hunched on a stool in the corner of the bar under the television, wearing a gabardine trenchcoat over his tweed jacket, check shirt and flannels. Mr Banaji lifted a shy hand. "What's it to be, Kiss, old boy?"

"The usual, thanks, old boy. How's life?"

"Oh, you know. I saw Beryl on Monday. I interviewed her for the paper. She asked to be remembered." When Mr Kiss offered no response Mr Banaji added: "She's doing well, it seems, in an unpopular job."

"A perfect promotion for a sleazy antiques dealer. The middle-class black economy was a boon for her."

"Kiss, what a rotten cynic you are!" D.M. Banaji held up his fingers to attract the jet-haired barmaid's eye then pointed at Mr Kiss and himself. Molly's raspberry-coloured arms rippled as she pulled a pint of Flowers then a pint of Eagle, her smile tender: "You're looking healthy, Mr K. This cold weather must agree with you." Resting for a moment against the bar she adjusted something within her green satin blouse. "Her career has been a perfectly honourable one," Mr Banaji said.

"Not my sister!" Josef Kiss accepted his Flowers with a wink. "Even when she ran her junk shop the totters would go anywhere

47

else before they'd do business with her. When she got to Bond Street that all changed, of course. The wealthy may be less generous than the poor, but they're considerably more foolish. How does she turn a profit on the side, I wonder, as Minister of Arts?"

"She sent you her love. She said to give her a ring if you and I wanted to have dinner with her and Robert."

"You're a good soul, Dandy." Mr Kiss raised his glass as if it were the first of the day. "By God, you need this, don't you? Dreadful winter. Cheers."

Studying Josef Kiss with kindly concern, Dandy said nothing. Most people suffering from his friend's condition found alcohol reacting badly with their drugs but Mr Kiss improved if he drank only beer. They had been meeting since 1940 when the government had offered amnesty to Indians who would come to England from exile in America. A member of the Indian National Congress Mr Banaji had begun working for Intelligence even before Japan entered the War. One night he went to the Windmill Theatre where Josef Kiss had resumed his famous act, his original turn. Singled out of the audience to go up on stage Dandy was deeply impressed when the mind-reader revealed details of his life and circumstances still either classified secret or known only to himself. After the show he sent his journalist's card to Mr Kiss's dressing room, thinking he might convince his department to employ this obvious psychic against the enemy, but Mr Kiss had dismissed his singular talent as trickery and luck, a certain instinct for people, and was thoroughly amused by Mr Banaji's astonished admiration. The Indian had been unprepared for Mr Kiss's skilful blocking of questions, his apparently amiable insistence that he possessed nothing more than a knack for good guesswork, but he agreed to be Mr Banaji's guest for lunch the next day. And so they had become friends.

Gradually Dandy Banaji learned to understand that Mr Kiss was so terrified of his own talent that it was possible to have only the most superficial conversations about it. After a year of courtship, when Dandy always bought the drinks, the meals, the tickets to the cinema, he concluded that Mr Kiss possessed a profoundly complex and sophisticated psychological shielding. One night, as they sat together in Aldgate East Underground Station sheltering from an air-raid, he felt able to offer his opinion. "Your spiritual protection,

Josef Kiss, is appallingly thorough. You are like one of those invulnerably armoured beetles. I feel in the presence of a specialised species at once more highly evolved than my own yet almost certainly doomed to early extinction."

This amused Mr Kiss. "You've improved my ego no end, old man." He then became serious. "But I'd advise you to be very careful what you say to me for there's nothing more dangerous to my type of madman than admiring hyperbole. If you really are my friend you'll ensure I keep my feet on the ground and you will *never* out of some puritanical zealotry of your own attempt to pierce my armour!" Pointedly he changed the subject, recounting an anecdote of Whitechapel before the Blitz.

Within a few days Mr Kiss was arrested. After a brief stay in West End Central Police Station, he was sent to a mental hospital in Tooting. When they at last gave visiting permission Mr Banaji was confronted with a doped wretch unable to control spittle oozing from slack lips. A doctor told him Mr Kiss had found a prop broadsword and a Scottish costume at the theatre and claiming to be both a direct descendant of Brian Borhu and Charles Edward Stuart, recruited a dozen drunken Argyll and Sutherland High-landers from a pub near Kings Cross and led them on an assault of Buckingham Palace. The royal family were not at all popular in the Blitz's early months and were somewhat sensitive to such demonstrations since Mr Churchill had yet to improve their public image. Hating to see Mr Kiss so pathetically contrite, Mr Banaji eventually secured his friend's release on condition he continued taking his barbiturates. Thereafter Dandy Banaji privately swore never again to risk encouraging Mr Kiss's self-destructive mania.

On his release Josef Kiss went to see his agent, intending to change his act, but the man had already decided to stop representing him. Similar incidents in the past had demanded too many embarrassing explanations to various theatre managers. "And now you've upset the bloody king. Which could mean curtains for my knighthood. All that charity work wasted."

In turning his back for the last time on telepathy Josef Kiss discovered a new agent who, by encouraging his minor ability for acting, allowed him to earn a fair living from small parts in films, television cameos and eventually, most profitably, commercials whose royalties were enough to sustain the habits which kept him sane and gave him all the public recognition he required. Because his knowledge of London was so thorough ("a walker never gets as miserable as a sitter, dear boy") Dandy Banaji was only too pleased to pay for the privilege of accompanying Mr Kiss on his expeditions and to write about them for the paper. Their relationship had become both intimate and equable and also mutually profitable, a perfect marriage. And nowadays Mr Kiss's periods of incarceration were always voluntary.

When first visiting Josef Kiss in the Abbey Dandy Banaji was concerned about the older man, but Mr Kiss had been utterly normal and full of reassurance. "The only problem in this place is the thieving. I'm not always sure who it is, an inmate or a nurse. It's commonplace here. Rife, dear lad." He had introduced a permanent resident, his soulmate, he said, Mr Moonboy, who resembled a saintly spaniel.

Dandy Banaji had been sad to learn from a neighbour, a porter at the Abbey, that Moonboy had died three months earlier. He had sought Mr Kiss out in the pub where at Friday lunchtime he always held court, The Old King Lud at Ludgate Circus, for the Welsh Rarebit he said and a decent pint of Guinness.

"I'm thinking of finding a fresh retreat," Mr Kiss informed him. "Moonboy was the spirit of the Abbey. He was saner than any of us." He had lifted browned cheese dripping Worcester Sauce towards his scarlet, salivating mouth. "A good deal saner than you, Banaji, with your odd trade. Saner than me, too. No doubt his relatives got him in there simply on the strength of his name. Nobody else in the family was called Moonboy. But every loony should be a Moonboy, don't you think? There's no point in grieving. He was happy enough. We're none of us free, Banaji, as you're fond of complaining." Reaching out a hand to which grease clung like pearls he almost let it fall upon his friend's shoulder, then thoughtfully took a paper napkin and wiped his fingers. "The people at the Abbey, the regulars, all loved him, even some of the guards. And you know as well as I do what character it takes to get a kind word from those roughs. Still, I believe they've lost my custom. There's a place in Roehampton I'm thinking about. Or possibly an actual monastery. It might be interesting to be possessed."

Now Mr Kiss finishes his pint of Eagle and sighs.

"Well, old boy," Mr Banaji raises his voice as closing time is called by Molly from the far end of the bar, "and where are we off to today? Weather permitting."

"This afternoon I think we'll stroll around Battersea to observe the migrated young of Chelsea who have crossed the river; the interloping tribe which has now claimed the entire border country, a wave of conquest familiar in history. And they are still spreading. I have even seen a pocket or two in my native Brixton." He begins to resume his outer clothes. "I also have some doggerel for you, should it prove intelligible to the good folk of Bombay. You can explain it by some reference to the Moghuls or if you like, the British. Poor souls. All the British have left to dominate these days are their weaker countrymen." And embracing Dandy Banaji about the shoulders Josef Kiss leads them from The St Clement's Arms towards Mile End Tube Station, declaiming:

> "Where once the naked naphtha glared
> Why darling now glare I.
> While the cot that sheltered costers
> Has become a listed lie.
> It's as swish as you could wish for,
> Twelve wine bars to the mile,
> And in place of your deserving poor,
> You'll soon observe, I'm sure,
> Three stockbrokers, two banking men
> And a high-up in the Law.

"We shall take the early curry at our Star of the Raj. What do you say, Dandy."

"You must let me write that down," Mr Banaji is tactful, "as soon as we're on the train."

"I have a copy with me. They probably can't use it."

"Oh I'm sure the editor will pretend to be very knowledgeable and not admit his bafflement." Mr Banaji allows his features to relax into a happy grin, for he is in Mr Kiss's hands now. His steps lighten as they pass through the gateway of the station and head for the down escalators. "But they'll pay for it, and that's something, isn't it?"

"The very foundation of our partnership, dear boy."

Riding upwards on the long incline towards the surface David

Mummery recognises them as they descend towards him and hastily he removes his fur hat. He has developed a morbid anxiety of not being recognised. The sight of the two so cheers him he waves with increased enthusiasm as he rises above them. "Mr Kiss! Dandy!"

"Mummery! Mummery! What on earth are you doing with that dead cat in your hand? You need help, lad! You must come with us. We're off to look at the Battersea gentry!" Extravagantly and with genuine emotion Josef Kiss beckons him to follow. But Mummery is set on his own specific release.

"It's the good old canal for me, finally, while there's still a bit of light. Enjoy yourselves!"

From the depths out of sight in a tunnel comes the sweet music of a violin, a classical busker.

"What beautiful harmony." Josef Kiss cocks his head as a train enters the station. They reach the deepest level. He leads them forward. "Quickly, Dandy. Several changes must be accomplished. Mummery reminded me how very soon it gets dark now. We must cross the river before sunset." They enter the tunnel glowing with tile and posters. On its curve a young woman in long black draperies begins to play a new piece. Mr Kiss tosses a coin towards her open fiddle-case. Dandy smiles his hurried appreciation as with closed eyes she throws herself into a sonata's first movement.

"Oh, London! London!" And Dandy, riding high on all these combined sensations, shakes his head, allowing the city to absorb him.

PART TWO
HIGH DAYS

LONDON! There is a resonant sound and roll in the very name of the world's greatest city. It affects us like the boom and reverberation of thunder. There is a note of majesty in it, accompanied by a throb as of doom. It is the fullness of life which impresses us most in London – the pathos, the passion and the power of restless, striving multitudes. This it is which thrills and fills us, as sea-captains are thrilled and filled by the vastness, might and mystery of the sea. While there are many aspects in which London may be viewed, we are chiefly impressed by it as comprehending the whole of human life in all its varieties, moods and conditions. Comedy and tragedy; the ripple of laughter and the rain of tears; love and hate; luxury and squalor; strenuous labour and debasing idleness; dainty civilisation and disgusting barbarism; a splendid Christianity piercing the dusk of the city with the cross on the summit of St. Paul's, and a squalid heathenism rotting in filthy dens and filthy alleys on the other side of the Thames; in short, all the elements which go to make up our conception of that bewildering mystery which we call life are here congregated and exemplified in a vastness and intensity without a parallel among the cities of the world.

– R. P. Downes, *Cities Which Fascinate*, Kelly, 1914

Queen Boadicea 1957

JOSEF KISS came back to the city, to Liverpool Street Station in a cloud of steam, to find a Spring mist lying on the wasteground where London Wall joined Wormwood Street. He shrugged his caped shoulders as if to rid the Worsted of locomotive grime, of foreign dust, of all Amsterdam, and made his way, cracked Gladstone in one hand, ivory-handled gamp in the other, towards the ornate red mass of a Victorian public house standing alone amongst rubble and hoardings and fresh-dug pits which had survived every form of German bombardment but was soon to be brought low by concrete banks for here the city was redeveloping on land where the rubble of War was only recently cleared. Already the great pub's brick and stucco was threatened from across the street by grey crowcatcher's walls, by clean, unfeatured glass. Josef Kiss, still relatively young, yet assuming age as part of a disguise, passed into the empty warmth of the private bar, the day's first customer, noisily expelling the hard-boiled-egg smell of trains from his nostrils and holding up his hand for his usual pint quickly dispensed by the host Mick O'Dowd in shirtsleeves, whose skin was always copper, whose eyes were dull pewter. O'Dowd remarked that Mr Kiss's thirst seemed unusually urgent.

"Dutchman's fizz doesn't much agree with me, Mick." Drawing off his cape Josef Kiss hung it on the hatstand's blackened mahogany. "Although Mrs Kiss, who now lives there, thinks I'm merely narrow-minded. I've heard about the European beers of strength and character, especially in Germany and Belgium, but I

57

can't adapt to them, any more than you could face bland cheese and sliced ham for breakfast. Now there's a memory I'd exorcise. Have you a hot pie and perhaps some mash?"

"Two eggs and three rashers me, with tomatoes, fried bread and potatoes on Sundays, rain or shine, with the exception of the War, of course. Give it five minutes, Mr Kiss." O'Dowd paused behind his bar. "So you've come from Harwich?" His khaki cardigan was reflected in the dusty engraved mirrors behind him, framed by smiling girls in shorts and sweaters, by happy tars in uniform, advertising Players and Senior Service cigarettes. They stood on dark red and blue carpet, greasy mock-Persian.

"All night at sea from the Hook, sitting up in a hard chair with black waves too high to be anything but nerve-racking and thirty of my South African cousins, drunk as only Boers can get, singing offensive songs in English and what I'd guess were even more offensive songs in Afrikaans, trying to co-opt me into their festivities and telling me not to be 'zo bleddy mizribil'. They have enjoyed, I gather, some rugger victory."

Sligo women on the council vandalism at the Mozart and Beethoven estates and only up five minutes still that's Bow for you and nothing much else as much of a dynamiter as this he dropped a jumping jack or two into a pillar box and calls himself a mollyflogger too

"They know how to celebrate all right, those blokes." O'Dowd was admiring. "But you're glad to be home, eh?"

Josef Kiss absorbed his draft Guinness and spread himself with a sigh across a bench's scarlet padding. Due in Soho for lunch with his agent in an hour, he did not trust the man to keep their appointment. Another pint and a pie would sustain him on the final leg across town and be some sort of insurance against lunch's cancellation. "I see from your board outside that tonight won't be restful, Mick, for your regulars."

"Oh they don't mind the bit of skiffle once a week. It brings in the youngsters. You'd be surprised how much beer they get through. And the pretty little girls. All students you see from the Poly most of them. There's no harm in them and it's good for trade."

Mr Kiss held his peace, having disdain for English folk-music, let alone anything more exotic. The washboard and the tea-chest had removed the last vestige of art from musical entertainment, he thought, taking melancholy pleasure from the pub's heavy curtains, its brass rails, dusty wood and vaulted ceiling decorated with grimy cupids and smutty naïads: this noble gin-palace had once given audience to hopeful young Music Hall performers. Now its upper floors were tramped by noisy bearded lads in check shirts who sang about cities never seen, cottonfields they could barely imagine, railway companies whose names they confused with rivers. *He's gone where the Southern cross the Yellow Dog.* "Frankly I view them much as Christ viewed the moneylenders in the Temple."

"Now, now, Mr Kiss." O'Dowd gave out an embarrassed grin, pulled the second pint, left it to settle and hastened through an archway connecting him to the broader reaches of the public bar where five of his regulars, in dirty grey suits, whose cropped heads made their ears seem huge and prominent, were going on with a game of poker O'Dowd believed they had started in 1946 when the side of the pub had been rebuilt and regular trade restored. For the past twelve years these Irish men had worked as casual labourers hired on a daily basis for a multitude of contractors in the Liverpool Street area and could see another twelve years of decent pay ahead. Every morning they took the Number Eight bus from Kilburn and took it home every weekday night. On Saturdays they knocked off at noon; on Sundays they went to Church and their local pubs.

I bought my first suit it was a three-piece and spent a fortnight looking for Lime Street Station I thought I was still in Liverpool

Left alone, Josef Kiss took stock of his visit. His wife, contentedly settled in Amsterdam with an ex-detective whose thrillers were a local success, remained sullen and unforgiving of his madness and what she regarded as his folly in relinquishing his profitable mind-reading act; yet she refused to divorce him because she said this would disinherit their two sons and their daughter. He had frequently argued that the premise was false in law and that anyway he had nothing worth inheriting, but she had held her ground. This time he had given up early after the ex-policeman had taken himself disapprovingly out of the picture. Mr Kiss felt Laurens itching to arrest him: they were natural enemies. Moreover the children displayed guilty embarrassment whenever his presence gave them pleasure; he would eventually have to cut himself away from them until they were older. He feared they must soon come to resemble the Dutchman. It was inevitable. Smelling his food, he turned his head to look beyond the little red velvet curtains on their blackened brass rail, out into the crowded street. The mist still refused to lift. It married with the Portland facings of the steel-framed sixteen-decked blocks and here and there appeared to take concrete shape, to form a giant beside other giants: *Tombstones to a vanished future, our single chance at Grace*, thought Josef Kiss. *Gone.* O'Dowd with a plate, knife, fork and napkin in one hand, lifted the wooden flap dividing them and bent to place an aromatic pie on the table.

"I'll fetch over the pepper and salt. And will you be having your other pint?"

"As soon as you like, Mick."

Looking forward to the end of the War, Josef Kiss had not imagined the Angry Young Man, an iconoclasm which swept the city after Labour's failure to bring off the New Millennium, the rapid disintegration of the Empire, the folly of foreign adventures. Everyone had anticipated a better future after the enemy's defeat but what they had really hoped for was an improved past which the socialists had failed to deliver. Mr Kiss did not blame Labour for this, but was presently content to assume the posture of High Tory since radicalism was so universally approved of in London.

Wearied by beer, by his encounters and by his own company, he moved his elegantly elephantine body upwards, pausing as he engulfed himself for the outside to proffer a dignified bellow in the direction of an invisible O'Dowd. "Next week. Next week, as usual." Unless, he privately determined, the pub allowed still more jazz and skiffle, in which case he would bow to the triumph of the tone-deaf and find a fresh base for his Monday evenings. Since the Central Line would get him swiftly into Soho he decided to take the tube from Liverpool Street to Tottenham Court Road. By arriving early in his agent's Greek Street office he would allow Bernard Bickerton no excuse for forgetting to take him to Romano Santi's a few doors away. This was currently Mr Kiss's favourite restaurant, but he could only afford to treat himself to it once a week. His agent had hinted at lucrative television work advertising, if he had not misheard, a new line called Frozen Cod Pieces. Mr Kiss could only guess delightedly at the nature of the commercial. Perhaps they wanted him to dress up as an Eskimo Henry the Eighth.

As he came up from the tube a brilliant sun struck deep into the crevasse of Oxford Street, which he regarded as a spiritual base, and his growing good humour seemed reflected in the faces of shoppers filling up the lunch-hour pavements. *Mr Bulhary had better pay up today am I unusually sensitive that notices different qualities in engine smoke and car fumes that likes to watch sunsets crawling through Battersea fogs but she's a character skulls can't show that can they Edinburgh will be a relief he thinks.* Whistling he turned left towards Soho Square with its battered statue of Charles the First, its tiny mock-Tudor gardener's hut like an Elizabethan Wendy House. Here the birds offered in full throat substantial counterpoint to his own "One of the ruins the Cromwell knocked about it!"; borders are full of daffodils and early tulips and above his head fresh leaves shone pale upon the trees. He was ready for all disappointment as he advanced down Greek Street towards Bernard's green and brass door, the cleanest of Georgian restorations, rang a glittering bell and was admitted by little Mrs Hobday whom he called The Human Canary; she was all of a flutter in her yellow hair, her familiar suit, trilling at him gaily as any wild songster. "We weren't, weren't, we weren't expecting you, you, for another twenty, twenty, twenty minutes, Mr, Mr Kiss. Will you be all right down here for a bit? Mr Bickerton has people in his, his office just now. Just now. So –" She flapped a bright blue arm towards the ill-lit rear where padded chairs and a coffee-table were arranged beneath walls sporting posters of Bernard's better-known clients.

"If you'd be kind enough to take charge of this." Placing his bag on the floor he laid his brolly across it. "Look after them until I return?"

"Of course, of course. In my cubby, cubby, my cubby hole." Coyly nodding she pushed open the door next to the glass window marked RECEPTION behind which she typed on a massive Imperial and answered a telephone. "Yes?"

"Much obliged to you, Mrs H. Is Mr Hobday better?"

This courtesy added to her confusion. She uttered a kind of joyous gasp and blushed as if he'd flattered her. "Oh, so k– so kind, yes, yes, yes, indeed. Fit as a flea. He's indestructible, indestructible, is Mr Hobday. He'll live to a hundred."

"And Tiddles?"

"Oh, the cat. The cat. We had to get rid of, get rid of him." A descent into mourning silence.

Mr Kiss displayed concern. Then the phone began to ring and with an apologetic wave she gathered up his things, rushed into her little cubicle and closed the door. Smiling enthusiastically at him she spoke rapidly into the instrument then, head on one side, listened with her whole attention to the caller.

Josef Kiss, unburdened, yawned and padded towards the waiting-room, relieved he was expected. He had no further cares. Uncritically he read through an issue of *Country Life*.

Down the stairs over his head enthusiastic voices gave out assurances, grateful protestations, as Bickerton saw visitors from his office on their way. Two pretty young women, in full skirts supported by several petticoats, in bolero jackets and pink blouses, in small hats which they had pinned to their platinum hairdos, in Chanel Number Four, in nylons and highheels, stepped carefully to street level where Mr Kiss, a kindly patriarch, smiled over his magazine observing them not by gender but by type, for they were almost identical twins, their similarities enhanced by make-up. "Oh, ladies, tell me what you *do*!" He was eager.

They were surprised to find him there. The plumper sister giggled. "Juggle," said the other. "And acrobatics. Don't we, Eunice? I think we've got '*Sunday Night at the Palladium*'."

"You'll find it wonderful. And an evening there guarantees you a year everywhere else."

"Yes." Looking at him with friendly curiosity, Eunice allowed her hand to stray towards her perm. "We sing and dance, too. All the *Boyfriend* numbers. And *Rock Around the Clock*. All the Bill Haley numbers." She glanced at her sister. "Don't we, Pearl?"

"Well, juggling and acrobatics is steadier." He smiled to show encouragement for their ambitions. "Fashions change so in music. Do you skiffle?"

"Oh, no!"

"Josef! Josef!" With firm good humour Bernard Bickerton shouted down. "Leave my girls alone and come up here. They're on their way to the top, those two."

Josef Kiss arose and bowed. "A pleasure, ladies."

"And you." Eunice expressed kind condescension. "Are you an actor, then?"

Mildly encouraged by her wish to detain him longer he expanded: "A theatrical, I think you'd say. A bit of a has been," on impulse tenderly he took her hand and lowered his lips to it, "I fear, in your world. You're going to the top."

"Oh, I love old-fashioned men."

"I was always a novelty. My name is Josef Kiss. I wish you success."

As if to encourage him further Eunice paused, but Mr Kiss had taken from the encounter as much as he desired. His wife, his horrible time in Amsterdam (where new shoes had rubbed blisters on both heels) were satisfactorily diminished. A further bow, to the not unamused Pearl, and he set foot upon Bernard's thick, green stair.

All their girls were flowers and all their boys were animals. Rose, Leo, May

His agent, distinguished in greying hair and well-cut brown pinstripes, consciously cultivating a remarkable likeness to the film-star Stewart Granger, spoke with dry mockery. "Those little popsies aren't interested in an old lecher like you, Jo."

"We should all lunch together some time." Mr Kiss merely wished to unnerve his agent. "At your expense. Could they learn mind-reading, do you think?"

"Be careful, Jo. They're strong as horses, the pair of them. They could have you for breakfast." His warning over, Bernard suddenly adopted an apologetic stance. "Look, Josef, I know I promised Romano's but believe it or not they're booked solid today."

"*Booked!*" Mr Kiss flared his substantial nostrils.

"Absolutely solid. A coach party of local government officers from up north. Doubtless on the razzle at public expense. But there it is. We'll go to Madam Mahrer's over the road. Okay?"

Josef Kiss replied with amiable ferocity. "Bernard, Madam Mahrer's is Tuesday evenings and, if Jimmy's is too crowded, Saturdays. Never today. Oh, Bernard!"

"You like the grub there." Bickerton became touchy. "I know you do. You recommended it when I first moved here."

Two walls of his office were lined with shelves containing every sort of filing device and a score of scrapbooks; its windows looked onto a miserable courtyard containing several strata of litter from surrounding offices and restaurants and a pregnant tabby washing herself beside a rotted tea-chest from which spilled damp scripts.

Bernard's other wall, pale green and cream, was decorated with framed newspaper cuttings praising stars of stage, screen and radio. Josef Kiss, seating himself in the only armchair, watched his agent pour two whiskies.

"What's wrong, then?" Bernard handed over the glass. "German food too much like Dutch? How was your wife and that rozzer, by the way?"

"Blooming like spring bulbs. The children too. Red cheeks and heads growing rounder by the hour. They're turning into Edam cheeses and are content. No, I'm fond of Madam Mahrer's food. I'd happily eat it daily. But she is Tuesday evenings, not Thursday lunchtimes. Thank you." He pretended to sip the whisky to which he had an aversion.

"What's the bloody difference, Josef? Not everyone gets a free lunch out of me. I could have taken Yvonne and Collette."

"Is that Pearl and Eunice?"

"Can it matter much where we have lunch? What's wrong with today? What's right, come to that, about Tuesday?"

"Don't think me whimsical, Bernard. Tuesday's when her awful dog goes to the vet for his treatment. Surely you've seen the beast? She dotes on it. Unchecked, it wags what remains of a tail amongst the tables. Day and night it's allowed to run free. If you complain, if you raise your voice even slightly to it, she refuses to serve you. You're not allowed back, either. She always keeps reserved signs on every table. You've realised, haven't you Bernard, that the dog's disintegrating in front of your eyes? It's mangey. Bits fall off it as it moves. Because we fear his mistress and love her food it believes itself popular. In any just society it would have been stoned to death. It wheezes. More than once it's made me gag. It sits down beside my chair as I lift a fork of rotkraut to my lips. It has forced me to leave the lion's share of an excellent pork chop, which no doubt it finished later. She's cheap, she's wholesome, she's generous with her portions, she's been known to give credit. She's a wonderful cook, Bernard, but her dog is disgusting. So I limit my visits to Tuesdays, when she has it oiled or grafted or whatever they do to it, and Saturdays, when she discourages it from the public rooms, perhaps because she's afraid drunks will attack it. That dog is the rotten apple of her eye. It's the fly in an otherwise delicious ointment. The serpent in Eden. What time do you propose we go there?"

"About now. One?"

"Why not the Quo Vadis?"

"Too expensive. The bill would absorb my whole commission."

"I thought this advertisement film was going to be lucrative."

"There's still an audition, though they're close to being committed. They say you've the right shape for it. All the other portly actors have been snapped up by Bird's Eye. I've got you an 'Armchair Detective'."

"Whose victim am I to be this time? And what's my trade? Deaf and dumb beggar? Forger? Renegade publican? Jeweller? Pawn-broker? Burglar? Petty blackmailer? Small-time gang boss? Do I die in the first five minutes or am I saved until the second act?"

"You're a milkman who sees too much. It will help you get into your Fish Finger role."

"You mentioned Cod Pieces."

"I know you liked that. But they saw the snag in time. Now they want you to sell Sailorman's Fish Balls."

Josef Kiss knew quiet contentment. "Almost as good. Well, let's get over to the Widow Mahrer and hope her foul dog's already attached itself to some other nauseated diner."

In the restaurant's murk through which the old owner, white lacetrimmed pinafore over long grey flannel frock, could be seen at work in her back kitchen beyond the glass pastry cabinet which as usual contained only a single plate of strudel, where Teutonic gilt and chrome mingled with the last decadent flourish of Belgianate Art Nouveau, Bernard Bickerton gestured with a bread roll, advising how best potential employers were impressed, and Josef Kiss listened respectfully for he trusted Bernard considerably.

Mr Kiss ordered the venison and mixed vegetables, a favourite he could rarely afford, while Bernard, revealing a bottle of red Graves, insisted it was the finest claret produced since the War and the dog, having exposed its horrible hindquarters only briefly, disappeared for the duration of the meal, making the lunch near-perfect. Later in a contented daze the large actor accepted three envelopes from Bernard. Two held the details of his appointments, one contained payment for residual rights from the BBC play shown in Australia, enabling Mr Kiss to pay easily for that afternoon's pre-arranged pleasure. In the warmth of the Greek Street sunshine, as they stood together outside Madam Mahrer's heavily crocheted window, Mr

Kiss with dignity thanked Bernard for the lunch, for the work, for the money. Holland had become less than a memory. The future grew brighter and hazier. "I've left my bag at your office. You won't mind if I pick it up just before five? I shan't disturb you."

Having so thoroughly earned his client's approval Bernard became expansive. "Whatever you like. You'll be at your Holborn number? Behind St Alban's Church?"

"Until June. Then I take the room overlooking the Heath. I'll miss Leather Lane and the delightful secrecy of Brooke's Market but for another five bob a week I get the whole of Hampstead in exchange. The landlord's a bohemian and a gentleman. Neither can be said of the present oaf with his sinister speculations."

"Now you're off to the Mandrake Club?"

"For a brief glass, perhaps. I don't know. It's a perfect day."

"I suppose it is." Bernard drew on some gloves.

They parted.

Wally couldn't've been more impressed, mum. The cheapjack it's typical a penny a pound aint bad North or South we were a family but not what you'd call united they're all Poles in South Ken now. Oh, my heart it can't last much longer it'll just explode one day and they'll find me dead on a barrow in Berwick Street it's the Chinese fish and chips and I ought to know enough to stop then he says I'll give you a monkey to stand in for him nobody'll even know it's you he'll know I said

With slow relish Mr Kiss strode through Soho's side streets and alleys lifting his hat to any lady of the town he recognised. A few were out early, trawling for the remains of lunchtime businessmen. Arriving at St Anne's Court, a narrow 18th-century passage in pungent condition, the tottering upper rooms sheltering prostitutes, the lower housing seedy restaurants and magazine shops, he rang the bell for Number Eight's top flat, a complicated Morse, and was at last electrically admitted. Deliberately he climbed the creaking stairs relishing the anticipation of joy, smelling coffee and gin, pasta and strong disinfectant, and reached the overfurnished two-room flat where Fanny, whom he visited almost always at this hour on this day when he was not working, awaited him, ready in her professional silks and furs. A red-headed motherly thirty, Fanny gave specialised comfort to what she called nice gents. She already had the kettle boiling as Mr Kiss removed his cape to immerse himself in plump arms, sweet scent, her smooth ambience. Elaborately if conventionally making use of rouge, eye-shadow, vermilion lipstick and long black artificial lashes, Fanny pecked him on the mouth, stroked his magnificent hands and asked how life was.

"It couldn't be better." When he had folded his cloak over the back of the armchair he removed a small brown-paper parcel from an interior pocket. "I didn't forget you, dear, in Amsterdam."

With spontaneous delight she unwrapped the gift, letting out a sound like a pleasantly startled chicken. "It's really lovely, Jojo!"

She displayed the decorative blue and white china clog on her pink palm. "I love Dutch pottery. I love pottery really. And everything. I'll put it with my Doulton pig, shall I?" And she crossed to the Welsh dresser where all her plates and souvenirs, her china cockerels, cats, castles, potties and aeroplanes, mementos of a hundred English seasides, were ranked, shining in the shaft from her dusty attic skylight.

"Now darling, let's get our old trousies off, shall we?"

Trembling. Oh, help. Here she comes. She's looking at my legs. Phew. Sonnie Hale and probably Jack Hulbert. Those were the days couldn't get more than a small one into the valley of death rode the six hundred but the war was on and that had its good and bad sides caught her in bed with an ARP chap after that there was no looking back

Taking the short cut between Wardour Street and Dean Street David Mummery carried a banjo on his self-important tartan shoulder, heading for the tube unaware of retracing Josef Kiss's progress almost exactly. His short buddy, the belligerent Patsy Meakin, was sermonising on the heroic career of Woody Guthrie who, through folk-singing refugees from McCarthyism, was now more celebrated in England than his homeland. "I got this letter from him. The poor bastard can hardly write any more. On a scrap of paper bag. He wished me luck. He asked me to say thanks to everyone who'd written to him. What a great bloke, eh, Davey? All his problems but he's still got time to think of me!"

David preferred Jack Elliott's versions. Guthrie's disciple with his partner Derrol Adams, with Peggy Seeger, Dale Parker, Dominic Behan or A.L. Lloyd could be found almost any night of the week at various skiffle pubs, coffee bars and folk-cellars. David had no interest in records or legendary musical heroes. He preferred Long John Baldry's Leadbelly imitations at The Skiffle Cellar or at

Bunjy's hearing Dixieland jazz from Ken Colyer. He would agree the originals were better but he had no abstract interest in the music and his chances of seeing a resurrected Bunk Johnson or an octogenarian Memphian bluesman were poor; but he kept his tastes to himself because what he did for fun his friends embraced as a religion.

After the bombers stopped went back to growing peas and stuff in his allotment an intimate friend of H.G. Wells my uncle Rex said he'd founded the Church of St John the Rapist well they soon sorted him out up there He was a twin his sister went to Australia then to India. She's in South Africa now they said there was a Gypsy Tomb on Tooting Common not that long ago

David and Patsy descended the stairs to Tottenham Court Road station's neon concourse. By the ticket machines, leaning against sooty tiling, Mark Butler in clean jeans and fresh blue flannel, home from Eton for the Spring vacation, lifted his gorgeous eyes from his tea-chest and awkwardly saluted, a good-looking boy embarrassed to admit in what he called "the real world" that he belonged to Pop. Eager to be accepted by David's friends who enjoyed his mixture of flattery, unworldliness, enthusiasm and learning, who called him their class enemy, he fascinated them and was treated as a wonderful exotic bird bewilderingly anxious to learn to be a sparrow while his black skin, the fact that he was the son of a Jamaican baronet, compounded their confusion. David had met Mark at one of his cousin Lewis's poker games. Lewis Griffin had left Eton the year before, deciding mysteriously to do PPE at Imperial College and meanwhile renting a house near Fulham Palace to hold a seemingly endless party where gamblers, debs, American remittance men, artists, journalists, pop singers, beat-niks and criminals came and went at random. As a result of his weekend visits to Fulham, David had met almost everyone he knew in London. Lewis was the only son of David's Aunt Mary and Uncle Robert. A banker, Robert Griffin lived at Hayward's Heath. He had, he told David's mother, written Lewis off.

Slowly the three young men walked to the corner of the poorly lit corridor leading to the Northern Line platforms.

"Where's Mandy?" Mark's voice echoed slightly, emphasising his hesitation. "I thought she was coming to bottle for us."

Jealous of his girlfriend's interest in Mark, Patsy was offhand.

"Mandy's coming on after her class. With Emily and Joss." Patsy wanted Mark to be interested in Emily, who played washboard. Her brother Joss made noises with a mouth-organ but was better on the kazoo he currently disdained. With the air of a buffalo hunter unscabbarding his rifle, Patsy took his steelstrung Spanish guitar from its bag while David swung his banjo onto his stomach. Having upended his tea chest Mark was retying string to its broomhandle. When he had it right he could make the thing sound like a real bass. Mark's other instrument was the cello. Their missing friends were all learning to paint at St Martin's School of Art round the corner.

David tuned his banjo to Patsy's guitar. Patsy had musical talent. He smiled and bowed comically to people who passed, most of whom recognised a skiffle group. Some smiled back. Others glared. Many pretended not to look. A small boy made bleating noises at David's straggly beard. "Look, mum, Lonnie Donegan." His giggle caused David to blush. He considered Lonnie Donegan a commercial hack.

My sainted aunt Mr and Mrs Morgenthal said they'd saved it up Like a flood sweeping such a lot away. Statues and everything Oh my heavens what next? You're crazy you've no idea what profound respect come I love you you're like what I mean what I feel like an idea come to life there can't be anybody else but you sweetest person ever knew proposing can't call that sleazy can you if it's love it won't do him any harm what he doesn't know can't just inevitable twin souls look we were meant for each this is no good unless what harm

Patsy struck the first chord. Clumsily David followed. The only one with a reasonable voice he had been able to insist on his playing an instrument too. "Let's do 'Talking Little Rock Blues'." He glared after the disappearing child. "Not on your life!" Patsy's mouth grew firm. They were here to earn their fares to Liverpool Street. David bowed to commercial wisdom. "It takes a worried man to sing a worried song." Disdained by purists because it was borrowed from Burl Ives, the number got pennies into the canvas cap Patsy had bought from a war surplus shop because it looked so much like Guthrie's railroad hat. "I'm worried now but I won't be worried long. . . ."

She should have been here by now I suppose this means I was expecting if her mother wasn't so bloody stupid there was this murder and the woman

was going to hang that's it the Lyon's Corner House they must be as old as
the hills my dad played in the gypsy orchestra they had bass fiddle not that
row I won't listen to the news I won't listen to the news I won't listen to the
news I won't listen to the news I won't listen to the news I won't listen to

A thickset young man with a boxer's damaged face and sporting a three-piece black suit stopped to listen until the song ended. "You're not bad mate." Not looking at David directly, he shot his cuffs to reveal sharp linen, diamond links. His attempt at a friendly overture, his display of power, could not disguise an habitually threatening note to his voice. "Play here often?"

"We do this for peanuts." Patsy's learned Glasgow accent thickened in equally aggressive response. "We've been on the wireless and we do proper gigs."

"Made any records?"

"Not yet." Mark was the only one not nervous. He smiled. "Just an amateur disc in a booth really."

At this the young boxer displayed disapproving surprise. "Bit posh, ain't you, for a shwartze?"

"Can't be helped, I'm afraid." Mark remained amiable. "Maybe you're a bit common for a weisse?" His retort assumed equality but was received with a deep frown, a silent pursing of lips, then the boxer said pointedly to David; "I run this club up East. You ever there?"

"We're doing a gig at the Queen Bee later, actually." By now David was too nervous to be discreet.

"What, the old Liverpool Street Boadicea?" The boxer's smile was openly contemptuous. "That's not the East End, chum. That's where all the commies go, don't they! Upstairs. Planning the fucking revolution."

"Not on Thursdays. We're Thursdays. Us and a couple of other groups." Puzzled by the man's refusal to listen to him Mark made a vague gesture.

"We've got jazz bands in our place. Well-known boys. And we're thinking of branching into skiffle." From a waistcoat pocket he removed his black and gold visiting card. "I'm Mr Fox. Reeny's brother. You know Reeny? She goes to all your student parties. Reeny from the Angel? With Horace her old man? Come up the club early next week. Ask for me. I'll give you some work. And tell Sambo he's all right so long as he brings along the old smokerola okay?" Mr Fox made a dignified turn and trotted out of the station.

Mrs B can't have no more dinners for sinners you've got to laugh a good job in Morocco what in the Foreign Legion I said but really it's a cook

"I take it I'm Sambo." Mark was laughing. "But what on earth's smogorola?"

"Tea." Patsy considered the card. "Reefers, old chap."

David was uncertain. "He's that friend of Kieron's. Harry used to work for him and his brother. You know, with the dud money and the morphine."

"Harry's dead, Davey. They found him in the river. Poppo had to identify him, remember? He was murdered."

"That's right. And John Fox killed him."

"Blimey," said Mark, impressed at last.

Thomas à Becket 1963

TOWER HILL, suddenly green after a long winter, her fortress ethereal in dawn light, was empty of people when Mary Gasalee came down from the Leman Street publishers where she was a receptionist on Mondays and Tuesdays and where she had just spent a hectic night with David Mummery for what they had called old time's sake. It had been their first meeting since 1959 when she had decided to return to Josef Kiss. Her left calf beginning to cramp, she seated herself carefully on a bench facing the White Tower, the Thames like cooling steel beyond it, and took out some bread she had meant yesterday to feed the ravens. She felt their upkeep as a personal responsibility, for if the birds ever left the Tower of London then England would fall, which was probably why their wings were clipped; this morning only one of the huge knowing birds was on the lawn, hopping cautiously her way, his head tilted to one side as if in recognition, opening his red carrion throat to caw.

"Grif likes rye I know." And she fished in her bag for the appropriate slice. Curls from her auburn hair irritated her face. Her underclothes had become uncomfortable. Her tweed suit felt awkwardly askew. She longed for a bath. Gladly she had left Mummery asleep in two chairs and hoped he would wake before anyone came in. He was, after all, only a freelance. *Nobody knew the true Nell Gwynn and London can keep a secret better than any city. She has unacknowledged catacombs, uncharted rivers, a wealth of subterranean mysteries deeper even than the bones of her dinosaurs.* A magnificent dawn disc, pale as Honesty, now climbed the sky above the Royal Mint's stone splendour and its rays fell upon her raven's blue-black quills. In the silence, all she could hear was the bird's beak at work, like a distant axe.

She had slept with Mummery chiefly from curiosity, for he seemed to be growing up. He was plumper, more self-assured, less opinionated, yet keeping that enthusiasm bordering on obsession which was his great attraction. He had spent much of last night describing how the Queen Victoria Street excavations revealed the existence of a Romano-Christian soldier's cult some two hundred years before Constantine and how there were traces of an earlier temple to Andrasta, a Celtic war-goddess, bronzed shields, silver torques, possibly a clue to the lost tomb of Boadicea. Speaking in such detail, so rapidly, he had confused her. She had enjoyed his intensity of expression but had thought to warn him he might be getting a little high. He had been in St Jude's twice for relatively short stays since she had last seen him. He had reassured her but eventually, as always, he had exhausted her. His brain was as crowded as *London's Hidden Burial Grounds*, the manuscript he had written for Cradle Press which required radical editing because he had tried to get too much into one small book. Her boss Mr Frewer wanted David to turn it into two separate volumes but would not double the advance. In the pub the previous evening David wondered if she thought he should get an agent. He had been paid between a hundred and two hundred pounds each for his seventeen books with Cradle and was not very good at negotiating terms for himself. Mary could only refer him to Josef Kiss. Were theatrical and literary agents the same?

Her answer had disappointed him. "The Scaramanga sisters say Josef's been cheated out of thousands by his agent. Wouldn't it be like substituting one crook for another? Adding another crook to the payroll, actually."

"I suppose it depends how much more money he gets for you." To change the subject she had kissed him.

He belonged to what he called a "liberationist group" which met Wednesday evenings in a Moscow Road pub near where he now lived. He had lost faith in political parties and described his fabulous vision of the coming age, assuring her the Millennium really was just around the corner. His idealism had momentarily inspired her agreement to go to tonight's meeting if her friend Judith would come with her since she did not want him to think her willingness to go out with him showed an intention to resume their affair. She was contented with Gilbert Dolman, whom she saw chiefly at weekends and who was undemanding, gratefully surprised by the length of time she was prepared to spend with him. He had a quiet sense of humour, looked older than she, though he was 36 to her 40, wore bow ties, natty sports jackets and flannels, had sandy hair, spectacles and played guitar in a semi-professional dance band. Managing a jazz record shop in High Holborn, he had no wish to control her life, while his only important ambition was to visit New Orleans before he died. He was also the cleanest, tidiest man she had ever known and at present she found these characteristics especially comforting.

Completing his meal Grif croaked at her as if offering her something in exchange for the bread. She bent forward.

"What is it, birdie?"

Croaking again Grif hopped a foot or two closer. Could she communicate with his tiny, oddly benign brain? But all that came were black and white shadows, a smell of rye, a minor sense of frustration. "I don't understand."

Marching past on his way to work a uniformed messenger in navy and cream, a peaked cap, a medal ribbon, a silver lanyard looped from the left shoulder, heard her speak and he responded: "Yes, indeed. A lovely morning, isn't it? Yes, indeed!" The old soldier's gloved hand saluted with automatic cheer.

She became terrified someone might again decide she was mad and she fell silent. As if disgusted by its failure to communicate, the raven spread its wonderful wings and ran towards the Tower and the moat. She began to wonder about Josef Kiss, who had now been at The Abbey for half his usual time and whom she would visit this afternoon. She was alarmed to find herself thinking that Grif had tried to warn her of something amiss with her old friend.

To take her mind off so much superstition she determinedly planned the rest of her day, hoping Judith would agree to come to The Archery with her, especially since she needed to speak to David again and had forgotten to ask for his phone number when last night he had promised to help her track down her past. She already knew that the street where she was born had been obliterated and replaced by ranks of stained concrete tower blocks; that her grandmother's house in Clerkenwell had also been blitzed, with the church where she had married and the hospital where they had taken her after she and her baby had been bombed. She bore her mother's surname before marrying Patrick so she was probably illegitimate but had been too nervous of contacting any Feldgates in the phone book so Mummery had offered to ring them one by one on her account. "I do research stuff all the time," he had said. "I like the research best. Half my life's spent in Westminster Reference Library."

It seemed to her he had remained fundamentally solitary since their parting. Maybe it was a condition common to people with their problems. During those intervening years his relationships had been brief, unsatisfactory, frequently culminating in a resumption of his treatment and he had given up telling fortunes after a friend's parents both died within a fortnight of each other, as he had predicted in the Tarot. He would only use his gift in his writing now. "Intuitive connections can open up whole new areas, Mary." After a while he had asked about her own health and she laughed and told him how she had learned to ignore the voices more easily. "I'm not exactly Joan of Arc. Though if I am inventing them maybe I could be a writer too. You'd be surprised what I hear, just sitting on the bus." He became serious again, trying to persuade her to suffer the experiments of his friend Dr Bill Christmas, one of the leading lights at the National Physical Laboratory in Richmond. Calmly she had reminded him how the whole idea made her nervous. "Besides, I'm probably just barmy. I won't go back inside any kind of institution again. I've lost too much time as it is."

David apologised. "Bill calls me his talent scout." He asked what tablets she was taking these days.

Mary got up from the bench. She was worn out. Her legs ached dreadfully. She had enjoyed her night with Mummery chiefly for its novelty but now she wondered if she had been right to give in to impulse and what the impulse had really been. Did she miss him? More likely she associated him with Josef, whom she did miss, though Josef's paternalism which had protected her in the early years of her discharge was presently too constraining. While Gilbert Dolman did not offer everything she wanted, neither did he threaten. Attracted to madmen but mad herself, she must be

75

consoled only by the conventionally imaginative. Occasionally she did long to be normal with a character better adapted to the world's expectations; then she reminded herself she had the satisfaction of her friendship with Judith, who was intelligent, beautiful, sane and who valued her for her oddness. These days Mary had come to be cautious in her relationships with men.

Because it felt easier and the day was bright, she turned from Tower Hill Station in preference for the Monument, wanting to go straight home on the District Line to Hammersmith, run herself a deep bath, feed the canary and relax until after lunch. In the relative tranquillity of near-deserted streets the cool sunshine made her light-hearted and she felt slightly wicked, just a little more adventurous than usual, even though the whole thing, begun in a pub, consummated on her boss's dusty carpet, had a somewhat sordid aspect. She wondered if she would tell Judith about it and what Judith might say. Her grin widened and she felt like whistling then as she crossed St Dunstan's Hill when the only car waiting at the signal began to hoot loudly, making her pause until she saw the light was in her favour. The bright red brand-new sports car continued its furious noise. Frowning she regarded it with curiosity as a window slid down and a hand waved. "Mary! Mary! Mrs G!"

Slowly she approached the crimson car, peering through the glass at the driver until she recognised at last the smooth, handsome, pink and white features of Kieron Meakin, as charming as always, beckoning for her to get in. She hesitated while with smiles and gestures he insisted; then she stooped, trying to fold her already ruined skirt under her as she almost fell into the low seat. "This is a bit of a nifty job, isn't it?" He smelled of expensive tobacco.

"You still in Brook Green, Mrs G? I haven't seen you for yonks. Where've you been hiding yourself?" His working-class accent was almost gone, replaced by something faintly Old Harrovian, presumptuous and slightly brutal. He made authoritative movements with his gearstick and advanced the car rapidly towards London Bridge. "You don't look any older than eighteen, as usual. Shall we go South for this? Can anyone tell you apart from your daughter? What's her name?"

"We're very alike," she said. "You haven't changed, yourself. Have you got a portrait in your attic, Kieron?" She felt as if she were in a dream, with one adventure following another.

76

He guffawed in recognition of their mutual good fortune. "It must be the blameless lives we lead."

"How's that brother of yours?"

"Patsy's over in Ireland until Tuesday. He's doing fine."

"Settled down a bit?" Wanting to ask Kieron to drop her off at the nearest tube, Mary found she was eager to hear his news. "Where are we going by the way?"

"Brook Green, of course. For a cup of tea and a chat?"

"I don't believe you. But it's very kind."

"Which bit don't you believe?" He wore an expensive tweed jacket and strong perfume which she took to be After-Shave. His fair hair was, if a bit long, elegantly cut, and his complexion was flawless. Only his light blue eyes looked a little bloodshot. "About the lift?"

"The chat and the cup of tea."

He looked at his large gold wristwatch. "Well, I've been driving since last night. All the way from York. What I could really do with is a quick drink. We can have that chat, then I'll drop you off home."

"I never could resist you, Kieron."

"Few can, Mrs G." Putting an arm around her shoulders he leaned to kiss her cheek. "I'm more than glad to see you."

"You're doing well for yourself at any rate." She paused. "Where would you get a drink at this time in the morning?"

"Over the bridge." They approached the grey stone arch across a glittering Thames. On the other side Southwark with her towers was like a magic city. "And give me two minutes to park." They went by the defiantly nondescript portals of London Bridge Station, already beginning to discharge city workers. "Here they come, the poor buggers." He turned into a sidestreet, took an alley, with ancient warehouses on one side, an elaborately moulded marble and brick façade on the other. Careless of traffic which might need to pass through the alley Kieron stopped the car, got out and came round to open the door for her. He bowed. He reached past her, blew his horn, then escorted her to what she thought at first must be a church. It had a high Gothic arch and was of blackened oak, fastened by enormous iron hinges. She noticed the terra-cotta mouldings, depicting monks of olden days picking hops and brewing beer, and knew it must actually be a pub.

77

In response to Kieron's hearty knocking the door was opened by a yawning middle-aged woman with streaked blonde hair, wearing a crimson satin dressing-gown. "Oh, hello, Kieron. Might have guessed who it was. We're not up yet."

"Don't worry, Sonia, all we want's a quick double, then we'll be on our way. This is Mary, by the way. I love her more than I love my own mother."

"Hello, dear." Resigned, Sonia stepped back to let them in. "You can't stay parked there forever. We've got a delivery at nine-thirty."

"We'll be well gone by then." Kieron straightened his shoulders, his tie, his cuffs, winking at Mary. "Come on. We've got the place to ourselves."

As Sonia disappeared upstairs they entered a magnificent hall with massive oak beams, perhaps the most impressive she had ever seen. Everywhere the theme of monastic life was continued, in paintings, friezes and reliefs. The fixtures were 19th-century Gothic, with more than a touch of art nouveau. The beer-engines might have been designed by William Morris. It was a wonderful dream of Olde England. She had always liked this style, though it was unfashionable. What surprised her was that nothing had been modernised. There was copper and pewter and dark marble, oak tables and benches; even the old gas-lamps were sinuous brass. "It's lovely." She watched Kieron behind the bar making the drinks. "Like a fairytale."

"I knew you'd like it. All my best friends do. I'm having a whisky. What'll it be, Mrs G?"

"A gin and tonic, Kieron, if you don't mind. I'm not a great drinker, but I've been up all night, too." She was delighted to see she had surprised him. He thought her an innocent, perhaps a little puritanical. He enjoyed both protecting her and shocking her. "G and T it is." He reached for the bottle. "You been out on the razzle, Mrs G?"

"You might say that. Just a little fling."

He brought the drinks to the carved table. "Sorry there's no ice. Now you've got me all curious."

"Then you'll have to stay that way."

"Well, well, well." He sipped his whisky. "So don't you work round there, somewhere?"

"I do." She saluted him with her glass.

"You and the boss, eh?"

"Whatever you like to think." She was thoroughly pleased with her secret. "You're doing well for yourself. Are you still in business with your brother?"

"Patsy and I remain the perfect partnership."

"You've given up the house-breaking, I heard." She pursed her lips, though actually she found it hard to think ill of him. "And the smuggling? What are you now, a publican?"

"I've only a small interest in the Thomas à Becket. And that's for sentimental reasons. I've liked the place since I was a lad. I was brought up down the road, you know, in Peckham. Where the rest of my family still is. All my no-good aunts and uncles and my rotten dad. Then I moved to Kent. How's young Davey? I haven't seen him for years, since I sold him a very nice little Olympia portable."

Involuntarily she laughed, "It's good to see you, Kieron. I don't often meet David. I remember the typewriter. When it broke down he was too scared to take it in for repair. He thought you'd stolen it."

Kieron rounded his charming eyes in mock surprise. "Why should he possibly think that, Mrs G?"

"Because you sold it to him in three minutes for thirty shillings and it was brand new in its case. He said you seemed in a hurry at the time."

Lowering his head Kieron offered her the expression which had conquered a hundred hearts and saved him from jail at least a dozen times. "All that's behind me now."

"You've gone straight!" She was cheerfully disbelieving.

He shrugged. "Virtually. Good wages, and the coppers aren't a lot of trouble. It's almost a social service. There's a lot of people approve of us now."

"Where would that be?"

"Hampstead, mainly. Dick Turpin's old patch. You still see his ghost riding Black Bess and all that. You could say me and Patsy was following in his footsteps. Jolly highwaymen, we are. Twentieth-century knights of the road." He winked. She was his confessor. He felt safe with her. She was not sure she wanted his confidences.

"You're holding up cars as they come round by Spaniard's Inn!" She shook her head to show she required no more information.

"Nothing so dangerous. Anyway, Mrs G, it's you I want to hear about."

Pressed into serving this devil I decided to bide my time. Eventually, however, I swore I would be avenged. Cool as a cucumber and blood all over his face. Micky told me to call the police. I just stood there.

"I lead a very dull life now." She wondered if she were blushing. Kieron had helped arrange her abortion.

"It can't be duller than being with Davey. No offence, but he's not the liveliest little bugger in the world, is he? I've read those books he does, though. Not bad. You wouldn't believe it was him."

"Well, I would." Mary was firm.

"I'm not knocking him." He was anxious to keep her good will. "But you know what I mean. Anyway, how is he? I meant to look him up."

"He's moved to Bayswater. I might see him tonight. There's a pub where he meets some friends." She forced herself to swallow the gin which she had only accepted because Kieron thought she would refuse. "The Archery?"

"A nice pub."

"You must know every pub in London."

He considered this seriously before shaking his head. "Not over there. Alien territory for me, Notting Hill and Bayswater. Full of whores and shwartzes. Not a place for a nice young man. And Greeks!"

She was sly. "I thought they were mostly Irish, still, in Notting Hill."

"I wouldn't know, Mrs G. My dad might be bloody Irish but I'm a Cockney boy. The best thing ever happened to the Gate was the West Indians. They livened it up a bit. It's a bloody sight classier now. You don't remember what a miserable dump it was, do you? In spite of the riots."

"David said that was just some Teds chasing a few black lads they thought got all the girls. It was the papers made it a riot."

"Don't they always." Unselfconsciously bored by the conversation, Kieron swallowed his whisky. "Come on, I'd better keep my promise and get you home."

The drink seemed to have increased her tiredness. When she looked around the Thomas à Becket the monks moved, turning their heads to smile at her. Under their feet the carved slogans shimmered. BRING THEE TO ME MY GOODLY WASSAIL BOWL became BORING THE TOMMY GOLLY WALSALL BOW. A bad sign. She should get to bed and sleep as soon as possible. Meanwhile she regained control of her senses. "That would be nice."

Kieron's words were fuzzy, obscured by a sound like ocean on shingle, so she could only nod and pretend to understand him as she strained to hear. Alarmed in case the voices would come into her head she was glad the city was still relatively deserted when they returned to the Porsche and drove through South London's sidestreets. Kieron was proud of his expert familiarity and it was not very long before they had passed Clapham Common and crossed the pink and grey stone, the late-Victorian grandeur of Hammersmith Bridge.

There was a moment on Haverstock Hill when it occurred to me she might be a murderess. Only without a saint she had managed to keep it all away from the house itself. Couldn't you manage a minute or two on Saturday?

"You really are tired, aren't you?"

His voice woke her. She had fallen asleep just before they reached Phoenix Lodge. Its motor still running, the car had stopped in the forecourt of the block. "I can't remember which one's yours."

She felt a moment's panic, fearing she had left her handbag behind, but it was at her feet. She searched in it for her keys. "I'd love to make you a cup of tea."

He kissed her cheek. "You're totally buggered. I hadn't realised. I think the gin was the last straw. Let me have your phone number."

The few moments' sleep had, as so often happened, brought her a respite. She felt ill, but the madness had gone away. She found her notebook and wrote the number. Neatly she folded and tore the page out, handing it to him.

"I might look Davey up. Is he at The Archery most nights?"

"Wednesdays is all I know. Everyone's welcome, he says. Want that cuppa?"

"A couple of spaniels in Orpington are wondering what's happened to me." He arranged his cuffs.

"You really did come out of your way, didn't you?" She was touched. "It'll take ages to get home."

"Not in this. Half-an-hour. It was good seeing you again, Mrs G." He put the number in his pocket. "I'll give you a ring. Maybe you, me and young Davey will have dinner some night, yes?"

"That would be lovely. I'm glad you're doing so well." She knew she would not meet him again unless it was another accident. He was impulsive, childlike, generous of his time and money and forgot all about you as soon as you were gone, a catlike quality at once bewildering and attractive to her. "I'll tell David you asked after him."

She waved as Kieron drove back into Shepherd's Bush Road, the way he had come. Somehow he managed to flourish the car, the dash he cut actually giving him the air of an old-time highwayman. Stewart Granger in something romantic. She hoped he would not get himself into serious trouble in Hampstead. Perhaps he was doing nothing more exciting than selling expensive motorcars. Wasn't that what a modern knight of the road would do? *More likely stealing them.* The voice was distinct and unfamiliar.

She drew a deep breath and with her keys extended aimed herself at the outer door. The redbrick turrets and gables of Phoenix Lodge Mansions were still sleeping. Even the milkman had not yet delivered. She managed to reach the shadowy inner hall where it seemed giants stood on guard.

That red-gold burnish covered his whole face so that as I watched him on my body his entire appearance was of heated metal. Never a god, sadly, he was far too ugly to be a god. Sie betraten das dunkle Haus.

She disciplined herself, taking slow, even breaths. It was demeaning to panic. The rapid beating of her heart, the flood of adrenalin, only brought on hallucinations which had ordinary physical origins. She paused, straightening her shoulders while the stairs ahead began to writhe in monstrous, snakelike movements. She had brought no tablets out with her because she hated to rely on them. Expecting to be home last night by seven she thought she would not need them. There were some in the bathroom.

Pissing in his mouth she said I never thought it was any way for a wife of mine to make a living . . .

She glared at the stairs until they stopped twisting, steadied herself once more, then took the next flight to arrive at last on her own swaying landing. *Bugger you make you squeal make you sing for your fucking breakfast you bitch who the hell do you think wants to hear you . . . Come where I like . . . fuck who I like . . . you want the same again do you then shut your fucking mouth Christ what a slag and meanwhile the rain over the Easterly part of Scotland will continue through the morning . . .* The peeled white paint of her front door was unthreatening. There were no more voices from behind her or, which would have been worse, from within. She got her key into the lock. She was grinning with relief by the time she closed the door behind her.

"Oh, Mary Gasalee, you certainly are no bloody Joan of Arc!"

Then, as she went from room to room opening all the curtains, letting in the magnificent spring sunlight, a sweet, joyful effusion of birdsong filled the flat. Her canary woke to greet her.

83

Captain Jack Cade 1968

AS PATSY MEAKIN raised his head above the level of a worn tombstone one of the season's new ferns brushed his cheek and made him jump. He sniffed hard, afraid of losing the amphetamine sulphate he had just inhaled under cover of these obscure monuments, trying to focus his 16mm camera through the trees' dappled light, across the bright glaze of the canal beyond. He could not understand why his client should want pictures of an ordinary house but it was his first paid cinematography job since he had left the London School of Film Technique two years before. He guessed it was some sort of spying operation and was almost as excited as if he were taking part in an episode of *The Avengers* or *The Man from UNCLE*. In Carnaby Street he had bought himself a special jacket for the occasion: it was Regency cut burgundy velvet. His nightly activities on the Heath kept him in funds.

The smell of bracken and fresh-mown grass was enough to take Patsy back into the fantasies of his childhood. Crawling closer to the railings above the canal he got the thatched roof of the little cottage in frame. Amongst all the municipal building, the half-abandoned industrial sites, it was incongruous. The great Kilburn gas-holders dominated the cottage and a canal as filthy as it had always been, though one or two optimists still fished along its banks. Further south, the concrete columns of the new motorway were being raised. Perhaps his client's interest lay in a connected property deal. Everyone was speculating on the Westway.

The cottage he was trying to film was almost invisible from any

84

angle. By climbing a tree he had seen it was a mixture of stone, clapboard and brick which might have been there since the beginning of civilisation. A variety of outhouses were apparently of similar age but the high yew hedge made it hard to get any decent shots, especially of the inhabitants. From time to time came peculiar animal noises, or a high voice would call a name, but although Patsy's imagination made much of the idea of unnatural orgies his zoom failed to find the source in spite of his shooting from every possible angle; gradually he grew more fascinated by his subject than by his fantasy. Belonging to an earlier century yet evidently inhabited, the cottage frightened him a little, reminding him of a ghost story he had read. It even had its own mooring steps to a narrow basin off the main waterway: Patsy thought he saw a small wooden rowing boat tied there. Zooming in again he moved his left hand through a clump of stingling nettles and his yell was taken up with apparent mockery by a large green bird perched in the oak immediately overhead. The bird, possibly an escaped parrot, flew erratically away over the canal towards the cottage. Deciding he had done enough espionage Patsy pulled himself from the nettles. The vast cemetery was beginning to freak him. When he delivered the film to his client's agent, Reeny Fox, and collected his fifty pounds that would be the end of it.

Patsy had still to work out what Reeny's (or rather, he was convinced, her brother John's) business was with the thatched cottage. The place was a curiosity, but the Foxes were interested neither in history nor in aesthetics. Burglary was not their style either, though kidnapping could be. Patsy did his best to hold this notion at bay. Seven years ago he had let John and Reeny involve him in a bungled attempt to kidnap and rob an American businessman with whom he regularly played poker. The man proved to have less than ten pounds on him and with him still in the stolen Granada they had quarrelled about what to do with him. Then John's unstable brother Bobby had smashed the American in the face and Patsy had pushed them both out of the car before things went any further. John had even thanked him for that. Specialising in procuring and drug importing, Reeny was good at moving people and goods illegally from country to country while John's talent was for running clubs and certain kinds of protection racket. He also had a small booking agency for rhythm–and–blues bands

playing the pub circuit and used the moronic punch-drunk Bobby
for frightening people. Patsy frequently advised them to stick to
what they knew and avoid the ambition which was getting the
Krays in trouble. Other fiascos had included an attempt to raid a
sweetshop in Dalston, which had put Bobby in hospital for two
months and jail for another year when the old woman shopkeeper
had set on him with a coal shovel. Patsy's association with the Foxes
had begun when he had been busking on the Continent and they
had employed him as a courier. At last understanding the volume of
heroin he was carrying in his haversack, he had rejected Reeny's
further offers and drifted back into business with his brother
Kieron.

Reeny had gone out of her way to assure Patsy that the filming
job was "absolutely on the up and up, dear. Okay, it was a bit
naughty of me, the last one. Perhaps I should have mentioned there
were PPK thirty-eights in the case, though they were in parts and
wouldn't have gone off or anything. In fact I sent the ammo by
post. Still, no harm done really, was there? And it was good money
and a nice holiday in Abyssinia, was it? Or was that you?" She had a
figure, Patsy often said, like a sack of potatoes. Even when, as she
frequently did, she removed her shapeless frock at parties she
looked exactly the same. She was even shorter than Patsy, about
five feet one, and almost the same width. She had told him the film
was being made "for a business colleague who's extending his
interests." It was possible John was getting into property speculation, in common with a lot of the East End villains, but perhaps he
simply planned to buy the cottage for himself, as a hideout. A place
sandwiched between the canal, the motorway construction, the
cemetery and the gas-works was not the ideal site for a block of
bijou residences and the picturesque hangover from an earlier
century's rural landscape could scarcely be worth a lot. The secrecy
must involve John's wanting the place as somewhere he could go to
ground if necessary.

Swinging his camera in its case, Patsy lit a cigarette, strolled back
towards the main gate, paused occasionally to read the inscription
on some particularly elaborate tomb, and decided he too wanted a
carved black marble angel weeping over him when he was dead. If
he ever got to make real films it would be worth saving up for. His
diploma had not yet got him a job and he was still forced to work

with Kieron. Two years earlier he had expected to be on location in Africa by now, or possibly working with some top Hollywood director, knowing he had much to contribute to the poetry of violence, yet ironically it seemed it would have been easier to bullshit his way into the business without trying for qualifications now he realised how much talk and how little action there was in the film business.

The speed gave Patsy a floaty lift and he sang to himself as he wandered between the graves. "So long, it's been good to know you. So long, it's been good to know you . . ." He paused to shrug off sudden tears, recalling Woody Guthrie's death about a year ago. He had not realised how swiftly his hero had declined into Huntingdon's disease. He regretted leaving music, particularly since people much less talented had risen from the same coffee bar and pub circuits he had played with the Greenhorns, but he had been too proud to commercialise his art. Only Joss and Mandy had done well, with Joss remaining bass player and lead singer in Iron Butterfly through all their line-up changes and becoming a tanned megastar living near San Francisco, while Mandy fronted her own blues band getting favourable or unfavourable notices as fashions came and went. She lived modestly in North Finchley now with a Chinese boyfriend and her two little girls.

Coming through the stone gates of the cemetery into Harrow Road's heavy goods roar Patsy looked at his watch. He had three-quarters of an hour to get to Cannon Street and The Captain Jack Cade where he had agreed to meet Reeny for lunch. He had hoped to develop and print the film but would give it to her in its bag, telling her to have it done professionally. Later he would have time to visit Battersea Park where the Pearly Kings and Queens were holding a charity Spring Parade. He had always wanted to film them in their full finery, with their ponies and carts. Maybe David Mummery would like to write a set of documentaries with him about London for American TV. With all the current England swinging and bobbies on bicycles crap it must be the best time to break into, for instance, CBS. It would earn him cash and get him good credits, maybe give him his ticket to Hollywood. Mummery's little tourist guides had just the right tone and if Davey still lived in Notting Hill he would phone him with the proposition. They could both take a share of the easy money now around.

Whistling like a finch in full throat Patsy jumped the first bus he saw going East, knowing it was to be his lucky day. As his snakeskin boot struck the platform the wind caught his long red hair, blowing it behind him, filling out his velvet jacket, making his beads rattle and glint so for an instant he resembled a huge bird, fabulous and Celtic.

"Someone like you shouldn't be allowed to live," he heard a woman say as he climbed the stairs to the top deck. She was speaking to the man next to her on the seat but he felt a pang, a memory, for those had been Ginny's words to him when he had last phoned her, trying for a further reconciliation, though even this did not affect his mood for long. He sat smoking a Capstan Full Strength in the front seat, noticing how the sunshine enlivened the grey buildings, the dirty orange walls, the filthy streets as they approached Edgware Road. "I kissed my girl by the gasworks wall." There were plenty more like Ginny. He found it impossible to believe he had let himself get so obsessed with her. She could rot as far as he cared. Stuck-up little cunt. Let daddy find her a nice harmless stockbroker.

Patsy winked at a shy young woman with long chestnut hair and wearing an Afghan dress who seated herself across from him. "Lovely day, darling."

She coloured.

"And where might you be off to this fine Friday morning?" Patsy offered her the remains of a boyish grin but he lacked his brother's charm. When she looked out of the window she aroused in Patsy a mild, predatory lust. "Come on now, lassie, if people like us can't communicate what hope is there for the rest of the world?"

She turned her pretty, oval face but did not meet his eyes. Patsy experienced quiet satisfaction; the appeal to comradeship usually did the trick. "I'm going to the demo," she said. "You know, at the Old Bailey. You know, for *Frendz*."

Displaying his camera case by the strap and thickening his entirely spurious Scottish accent Patsy grasped his chance. "Really? I'm covering it for the alternative press ma'self. I do a lot of work for *International Times, Oz*. All of that." If that didn't get her in the romantic kidneys, nothing would.

Still wary, she allowed herself to relax a little. "Yeah?"

"I'm Captain Klix, darling. I do all the big demos. All the stars' parties. All the rock and roll gigs."

Her colour still very high she made a regular nodding motion by way of acknowledgement. Her large brown eyes were emphasised by heavy mascara and her only other make-up was a pale lipstick. "This is the first real demo I've been to. I promised I'd go."

"Promised who, darling?"

"The guys from the *Frendz* office, you know. I was in the Portobello doing some street-selling last Saturday. I was in the office. You know Jon Trux? John May?"

"We're old buddies." Captain Klix made a shape with his fingers. "I'm going along myself when I've delivered some movie material. Why don't you come with me? Have a quick drink, then we can go together."

"I said I'd be there by one."

"Please yourself, darling. Well, maybe I'll see you. In case we get split up for any reason, give me your phone number. I need a chick for some pictures I'm doing. Nothing too sexy, you know. You'd be the perfect model."

"We're not on the phone. But I'm often in *Frendz*." When she turned for relief towards the window Patsy began to whistle and was surprised as she rose from her seat.

"Getting off already?"

"Changing. Aren't you?"

"I'll stay on for a bit." He saw that they had reached Marble Arch. If he went with her he would not only lose face, he would be late for his appointment with Reeny, and he needed her money. "Is your boyfriend at the demo?"

She grinned and waved sardonic fingers.

He watched her as she walked towards Oxford Street into the lunchtime shoppers, a fairy-tale princess in all her bright brocades. "Little prick-teaser." Patsy addressed the world in general. "They're the ones get themselves into trouble." He would drop in on the demo for a while, though he knew very few of the people there. It would be worth filming the event in case something happened and the TV news people weren't around. He might also score some dope and pull the hippy chick.

The counter-culture had taken Patsy by surprise and only received his interest because of the pretty girls it attracted. All his previous bohemian dalliances, with beatniks, socialists, the jazz and folk scenes, had been disappointing since the few girls around had usually been plump, short-sighted and more interested in talking about sex than doing it. Patsy knew he was a few years too old for his long hair and beads to be completely convincing but he offset this by presenting himself as an investigatory photo-journalist and an artist. If it promised the joys of teenage dolly-birds, good drugs and the chance of an orgy or two, he was willing to look a bit of a twit and the fact that he was older than most of them made even his stalest lines seem fresh. They had got him Ginny, after all. The amount of general bullshit they accepted meant he had no conscience about his lies. He laughed aloud. "Captain fucking Klix! I should bloody cocoa!"

When he left the bus at Farringdon Street he still had fifteen minutes to walk to Cannon Street. Exotic in his double disguise he made his way through crowds of released office workers contemptuous of the attention he attracted from them. A little out of breath, he went up Ludgate Hill and got his second wind by the time he passed St Paul's near the new office blocks, their massive glass slabs glaring in the sun, arrogant and alien conquerors. He deliberately avoided the Old Bailey. Here and there he spotted little pockets of brightly-dressed young people making for the Court. It looked to be a fair-sized demonstration.

Turning the corner into Cannon Street Patsy reached what was for him the true City of London where some years earlier at The Captain Jack Cade, a medieval façade just across from the railway station, he had last performed for the New Socialist Folk Club. The pub was built on the original site of London Stone which Jack, one of the last working-class heroes to lead a rebel army into London, had struck with his sword, declaring the people masters of the City. The Jack Cade symbolised the high hopes and failed ideals of Patsy's contemporaries and perhaps for that reason he had chosen to meet Reeny here rather than in Soho, which she preferred, or the East End, where her brother and his friends held power. Besides, in Soho there was always the chance of running into some old, unwelcome face to remind him of a favour or some money owed. Pressing back the doors of the oak-panelled saloon bar, fancying himself an outlaw in a Western, Patsy elbowed his way through city gents, ignoring jokes and nervous remarks about his clothing, knowing that this confident heartland of City conservatism now courted his kind since the Beatles had become honoured millionaires, for the merchant bankers, continuing to hold the real power, could no longer be certain who represented actual rebellion and who represented fresh capital, another factor which made Patsy cynical of hippy Revolution.

Seated at the table near the back of the pub Reeny was reading a copy of *Penthouse*, drinking her usual port and lemon, her hair shining with fresh henna; the blues, oranges and crimson of her face rivalling her sensational halo. Typically she was dressed in a shapeless purple frock, several turquoise, jade and malachite necklaces covering her bosoms, and Patsy already smelled her perfume mingling with the smoke from the Gitane between her pudgy, beringed fingers. Looking up as he emerged from the press of pinstripe and worsted she coughed by way of greeting and moved to let him sit beside her on the padded bench. "Dead on time, Pat. What's yours?"

"A pint of Guinness?"

Reaching for her handbag she began to rise until Patsy said, "I'll get it, love. Another for you?"

"Might as well." She put a pound note in his hand. "Save me feet."

Returning with the drinks Patsy asked after her self-effacing mate. Rumoured to know in detail every illicit shipping operation from Dover to Macao, Horace hardly ever left their house.

"He's been a bit poorly, actually." Reeny was touched by Patsy's question. Few realised the affection she felt for her husband. "Sat up in bed when I left, with a cup of hot orange, two wholemeal bickies and the new *Times Maritime Atlas* I bought him for his birthday. Just a sore throat and sniffles." She scratched under her purple arms and ran carmine fingers through orange hair. Their corner of the pub was so gaudy it seemed like the transformation scene from *The Wizard of Oz*. "Did you make the film all right?"

He handed her the bag. "Don't take it out. It's got to be developed and printed."

"He's got someone set up to do that." Opening her wallet she removed five ten-pound notes stapled together. "Here you go, Pat. And if there's a snag you'll do it again within the week."

"As agreed." Sighing, Patsy sank a relaxing glass.

Shits at the Ministry. Speculation runs rife. I'm afraid principle was never my strong point. Knockers? Hardly the description, old boy. Still got the Rover? How's the wife? Ha, ha, ha. Ha, ha, ha. Ha, ha, ha.

Over near the window Judith Park, dressed in her severe best, wiped a paper napkin across her mouth smiling at Geoffrey Worrell to demonstrate how much she had relished her Shepherd's Pie.

"I really hadn't expected it to be so crowded." He sucked in his lower lip. "Next time we'll go to a restaurant."

This reference to the future was encouraging since he liked her designs and wished to publish ten of them as Greetings Cards, promising, if the first ten went well, to commission more. Pleased by the amount he offered, Judith was disappointed that it should be a flat fee, for Mary Gasalee had advised her to demand a royalty and she wondered if she would ever find the moment to ask Geoffrey about this, given that his black hair, uneven teeth, blue eyes, soft brown skin and strong hands made her knees weak and his every gesture displayed his fascination with her. To her own somewhat disapproving surprise she found she did not care if he was married or single. Of late she had become tired of compromise, of talking herself into mediocre affairs, of finding the best in boring men, and for the last ten months had chosen celibacy, even refusing her ex-husband their accusatory evenings. Today, however, she was ready for anything and her pulse quickened as she experienced the kind of half-terrified glee she had known when young and determined to sleep with a boy. Nonetheless her enthusiastic responses to Geoffrey, the inane eagerness with which she answered his simplest question, took her aback. Afraid he must think her a fool, she tried to restrain herself but he was merely flattered and grew increasingly eloquent about the problems of modern colour-processes.

She determined to get him on his own. "Perhaps we could continue this meeting outside. I mean, if you want to. It's so warm and lovely now. We could just walk a bit."

He uttered his hearty approval. "I hate town pubs anyway. But don't you love a good old country ale-house?" He told her about his local a few miles from Oxford and its wonderful beer, waved a familiar hand at the barman while opening the door for her. Reaching for her portfolio, "Let's take that, shall we?" A comforting smile, the faint, sweet smell of some rich tobacco.

"Oh, really, it's not heavy." She relinquished it, permitting herself a single broad grin as they headed for Queen Victoria Street and the river. This commission being important, Judith had prepared herself carefully, knowing her Mary Quant haircut made her look years younger; neither did it matter that she had chosen black court shoes for Geoffrey was a good three inches taller. During her ten months of celibacy she had grown determined only to make a fool of herself over someone completely desirable and Geoffrey, in his Harris Tweed jacket, sturdy Cavalry Twill trousers, well-polished brogues, was the perfect stereotype. As they wandered through the traffic under a dreamy sky Geoffrey continued his discourse on the problems of colour printing while she made little responsive noises and came as close as she had ever done to fluttering her lashes, sublimely tolerant of herself now in this marvellous spring weather. It was too early in the day to dare anything much but when the time came she knew she could even come up with a smouldering look.

Every so often Geoffrey would pause, suggesting, unconvinced, that he might be boring her, and with unbridled hypocrisy she would deny this. It seemed everything she said contributed to his pleasure. They reached the embankment where gulls climbed and dived in the spring currents: mallards squabbled like clowns on the bright water. He began to tell her how he would love to show her the Oxfordshire countryside at this time and without a blush she announced that Oxfordshire and the Cotswolds were her favourite parts of England. She was committed to becoming the best twin soul Geoffrey Worrell had ever shown a good time.

They paused beside some historic old battleships moored to concrete, *President, Chrysanthemum, Wellington*, and he knew a little about each. It was wonderfully relaxing, she said, to stroll like this with someone with whom you really felt at ease. She said it was as if she had known him for years; he reminded her of her favourite brother. On the subject of relatives he asked if she were married and she mentioned the divorce. How very courageous she was, he said, to start life over again. His own wife was a marvellous woman but only the children kept them together. "I think my job is a bit of a rival. Nothing she's interested in, you see." Determinedly sympathetic in spite of a sudden and unexpected twinge of conscience, Judith had mentally already burned her bridges. The future was now almost entirely a question of nerve.

"She has her own areas." As they came alongside the leafy lawns of the Inner Temple Garden, Judith wished she could sit down for a moment but all the benches were occupied. She stared coldly at an old derelict feeding sparrows from his palm. "But publishing isn't 'her thing', as they say. She's a tremendous mother, of course. The kids are very lucky."

While Judith was happy to continue this ritual she had no experience of what to do next, for it was at this point, if not earlier, she usually stopped. Then inspiration struck. "I think they probably have a pretty tremendous father, too." And she brushed her hand against his manly tweed.

At that moment as she looked towards the green shade of the Garden she saw a massive outline emerge from the trees. Josef Kiss was, by no means unusually, in mid-monologue. Judith knew a frisson of superstition, for Mr Kiss's companion was her ex-husband Dandy Banaji. While not particularly alarmed, she could not possibly continue to perform her elaborate and uncharacteristic courtship of Geoffrey Worrell before an audience which would be openly astonished, so winningly she seized the great brown-green arm. "I'm terribly sorry, Geoffrey. I've just seen someone I'd rather not talk to. Could we go back for a little bit?"

With patriarchal chumminess his hand fell upon her own. Making polite small-talk, he affected to notice their surroundings and with the lightest of pressure kept her arm in his. "It's really not a big mystery." She was apologetic. He grew gallant. "Look, if you don't think I'm being a beast or anything, I'm on my own in town this evening. I suppose you wouldn't be free for dinner?"

"I'm not sure." She pretended to think. "I had planned – Oh, but I've enjoyed this so much. Yes, I'd love to."

"I could pick you up. You're in Chelsea, aren't you?"

"Fulham, really. Holmead Road's just past World's End. Off King's Road. Not very salubrious. Do you know it?"

He smiled benignly down. "I can find it easily. Your phone number and address is on the backs of your cards."

"Of course." For years she had never known a mood as exhilarating. She wanted to laugh aloud. She was actually salivating. "You wouldn't mind if I got a taxi now? I've one or two things to do."

With courtly authority he stepped before a passing cab to flag it down. "Seven-thirty?"

"I'll look forward to it."

Calling her address to the driver she fell back in the seat, delighted and horrified by her behaviour. For a second she glimpsed Dandy's frowning eyes following her as she sped by.

"There are only three other churches like it in England," Josef Kiss pronounced. "One in Cambridge, one in Northampton and the other in Little Maplestead, Essex. What's wrong, Dandy, old lad? Not interested in the Knights Templar?"

"That was Judith, my ex-wife. All dressed up. With him." Dandy pointed at Geoffrey Worrell already hailing a second taxi.

"Looks like an off-duty solicitor to me." Mr Kiss was teasing. "Maybe she's going to try for alimony."

"She had her portfolio with her. He must be a publisher. None of my business, really, only I could have sworn she saw me. It's not like Judith."

"Maybe he's her new beau, old lad. Is he really Judith's type, though? A bit of a Hooray Henry."

"Don't be too certain." Dandy returned his attention to Mr Kiss. "She's always had a secret crush on your agent."

"My God! Judith's a woman of discernment. For all his reasonable taste in suits Bickerton is one of nature's lounge-lizards!"

Dandy Banaji changed the subject. "It probably wasn't Judith at all. What were you saying about the Temple? Something to do with Jerusalem?"

But Josef Kiss was now watching the mallards showing off their gaudy charms in the water below Blackfriars Bridge. "It seems a lot of trouble to go to for one little duck."

Nell Gwynn 1972

IN PALE denim, washed out yet irredeemably clean, David Mummery left the Freedom Bookshop in Red Lion Street, crossing High Holborn to cut through Lincoln's Inn Fields and smell something of the spring before arriving at his cousin's air-conditioned office in Chancery Lane. To present a more attractive contemporary image to his girlfriend and the people he wrote for, he had recently let his beard and hair grow, but remained resentful of the enormous pressure the world of fashion was able to bear upon him. Even the patients in his last mental hospital had been amused by his ignorance of current slang, his refusal to use what little he did know. Since there was no police charge he had got an early release, but he remembered the chief nurse's parting sneer, "Who's a cool cat, then?", as he walked out to the driveway and entered the taxi his mother had brought.

Time is a mad spider. Oh, the slush on those pavements. No movement this man go. Banacheck no bredrin bruk I heart extra hurry come-up no way I be ignorant. Paupers the lot of them stink not just clothes I'll be on my way okay just give me the chance. There isn't any bloody number forty six!

The sunshine and the apparently improved disposition of most Londoners in recent years was a consolation, of course. The world had grown considerably easier for him and he no longer felt the subject of everyone's attention. London was uncharacteristically at one with herself and though Mummery put the beginning of his change at the release of the Beatles' first single, most of his friends saw it entirely as a manifestation of Labour's 1964 victory.

96

The atmosphere was also invigorated by recent American immigrants who had discovered in London some kind of creative promise, a vitality and sense of aspiration which they believed was presently stifled in their own culture: an almost-concrete Utopia that was a direct extension of the American Dream, though Lois, his Virginian lady friend, was already beginning to express mild disappointment in London's failure to realise the potential she had seen in the city. Mummery argued that the English had always been filthy, foul-mouthed, lazy, small-minded and rapacious. "Like Japan," he had told her, "ours is a nation which survived through most of its history by piracy, mainland raiding and, when all else failed, colonial adventure. It was the Victorians, with their inspired hypocrisy, who refused this truth. The poor buggers who actually swallowed that idealism are the ones who are still suffering. John Osborne, for example. You'd do better to treat us as the xeno-phobic barbarians we are."

Lois had said, "You sound perfectly complacent about it."

"We're a nation in decline, Lois. A genuinely decadent civilis-ation. That's its real attraction, as a golden twilight which can't possibly last. No point trying to improve us. We know we're going down the drain. And we don't care."

He should, she believed, try to think more positively. She loved him. It was important he improve his life. Flattered by her concern, he knew she must eventually write him off as one of her failures. She was not, after all, fighting his congenital madness, his weak character: she was trying to deal with an entire cultural inheritance. She was at odds with History.

You wouldn't believe how little we did man but they tortured us anyway, then we all went to England. Bloody him love fucking what. How many redskins got lung cancer?

Passing into the glass elegance, the exotic shrubbery, the hi-tech smoky plastic of his cousin's offices Mummery gave his name to a grey-haired desk-sergeant who, impressed that he had an appoint-ment with the boss, asked him to take a seat, picked up the phone and murmured briefly into it. Mummery was pleased by his cousin's surprising success. In a heavily publicised romance Lewis had married the daughter of a titled Press Tycoon and risen rapidly. Two years ago he had founded *London Town*, designed to be a rival to *Vogue* and *Queen*. His recipe had succeeded. There was now an

American edition and five foreign-language editions. As the magazine's principal shareholder Lewis was worth more than his own father, who still refused to deal with him.

Mummery was not kept waiting. A message came down and he was directed to a burnished copper and slate lift which took him smoothly to the top. Passing more foliage and tasteful interior design Mummery reached a desk where a soft young woman stood in a smart, short sage-green dress and perfect pale blonde hair smiling at him through subtle make-up to say she was Mr Griffin's assistant and ask him to fall in behind her, then led him to a studio overlooking Fleet Street, various Inns of Court and, beyond, the brilliant Thames. Smoothly she suggested he seat himself but before he could oblige in came Lewis Griffin, grinning all over his face, scarely changed since his gambling days, a cigarette in his left hand, his extended right hand glowing with the kind of patina usually associated with a well-kept antique. "David! This is marvellous. At last!"

For the past few weeks Mummery had written a column called "London Pride". When the first piece had appeared last Thursday he received an invitation to call on his cousin who was delighted to discover he was working for the magazine. Pleased that nepotism had not played any part in the acceptance of his work, Mummery was equally glad Griffin should still feel friendship towards him. They had grown apart since Griffin gave up his Fulham house.

Griffin led Mummery into the depths of potted shrubbery, a vast office with a peach-coloured carpet, some pastel easy chairs, large, delicate-looking desk and an even wider view across London. "Not bad, eh? Haven't I come up in the world? I thought the bloody thing would last a fortnight. Can't complain, eh? It's better than winning the Irish Sweepstakes."

Not expecting this frankness from his cousin, Mummery was at a loss. With his black hair and eyebrows, his cosmetic teeth, his slightly puffy good looks, his three-piece Cardin suit and his striped Jaeger shirt, Griffin resembled a younger partner in the family bank and should therefore be radiating smug, ill-mannered confidence.

"We'll have lunch at the Wig and Pen, if that suits you." Seating himself in one of his easy chairs Lewis swivelled to take in his view. "Didn't you and I get stoned there a few years ago?"

Mummery began to smile.

"Stuffy, mediocre food, but full of the most incredible characters, the people who're running this country, controlling its opinions, deciding its justice! You'll be amazed. They're all sozzled or senile or both. Well worth a visit. I told Tommy Mee to join us. Do you mind? Tommy's keen to see you again."

Mummery was disappointed. Married to Lewis's sister, Mee had recently won the Kensington East by-election as a Tory. He had freelanced for Mee at London Transport Publicity where Mee, learning of his mental problems, had since adopted a condescending, bullying manner towards him.

"I'm not that fond of Tommy, as a matter of fact."

"Damn. I'm really sorry, Davey. I can't get out of it now. He gave me the impression you were buddies. We'll dump him as soon as we've had lunch. Then we'll drop into El Vino's for a drink."

Resigning himself to an unpleasant hour or two, Mummery accepted the offer of a Campari Soda, drank it quickly, then accompanied his cousin from the calm of the penthouse down to the confusion of Fleet Street's refurbished alleys and the Law Courts where they crossed the road to enter the Wig and Pen Club, which was somewhat smaller than Mummery remembered, with a bar, a small dining-room, some narrow staircases, wooden panelling and faded, uninteresting 19th-century carpets and paintings; in appearance and clientele little different to most of the local pubs and just as full of smoke and hearty, masculine laughter of the kind that bound comrades together. Almost everyone but Mummery was wearing dark clothing.

As soon as they were seated in a corner near a leaded window overlooking what Mummery thought might be a courtyard and had picked up the menus, Tommy Mee charged in, waving as if to an electorate. He was slender, sandy-haired, with projecting teeth, blue-green eyes, a swarthy drinker's face and a style of suit which, ten years earlier, had been considered gentlemanly amongst rising advertising people. He shook hands violently with Mummery saying he was glad to see him still on the right side of the wall, then, adopting a respectful tone and attitude, grasped Griffin's arm before releasing his grip on Griffin's hand. Lewis, it emerged, was thinking of buying some property, chiefly for new offices and shops. Mee was in a position to advise him.

While Tommy Mee expanded on the centrification of industrial

99

sites, the redevelopment of prime locations, Mummery steadily ate steak, kidney and mushroom pie, chips and cauliflower cheese, and drank a pint of thin pale ale.

"London's going to get an enormous facelift in the next ten years," Mee said. "And what's more, for the first time ever, the population will start to fall. That's a huge advantage to anyone who knows what's going on."

"What part of the population?" Mummery's interest was genuine.

Surprised by the interruption Mee blinked. "The part which can't afford to live here any more!" He straightened the bottom edge of his Regency waistcoat. "They'll all go out to the fresh air. To Milton Keynes and Harlow and places. That way everyone's better off. It's what the New Towns are for. Money's an abstraction, David. Even your lefty friends understand that. Nobody's more successful at building castles in the air and then asking for a grant to maintain them. Eh, ha, ha, ha. Prices don't rise according to production costs but according to what people are willing to pay. Clothes, food. Drugs. You name it."

"But property isn't abstract. People have to have shelter. It's a necessity, surely."

"Oh, indeed!" And Tommy Mee chuckled in his face.

Box upon box of used matches. Went off to be a drummer boy. Found playing their harpsichord at three in the morning. All strut and puff almost fell in the pond. Told me he wished to do the honourable thing by me. Ys xeber ka ek, ek herf sec hey. In mourning for eleven years. Made him wear a black condom, my wife said.

Now Griffin proved as good as his word. With an excuse about deadlines he hurried them through the meal, told Mee he would telephone him at the House of Commons, then drew Mummery down to Fleet Street, turning right into the complacent gloom of El Vino's which still had a quarter of an hour before closing time. "Tommy's a creep. I should have known better. He's useful to me and I don't want any family trouble. My wife thinks he's a scream. Are you married yet, Davey?" They both drank large brandies, leaning against the noisy bar.

"I live with a very brainy American girl."

"I envy you." Griffin nodded to an acquaintance. He lit a Sullivan's. "New blood. Do you get over there much? New York's wonderful, isn't it?"

"I haven't been yet." He felt obscurely ashamed. "Maybe this year."

"Don't believe a word they say. And Los Angeles is marvellous too." Griffin upended his glass. "Look, Davey, I'm really sorry about Tommy. Have another?" He signed to the barman. "Would you and your lady friend come to see us? Please. I know Catherine's planning a small dinner. Just some nice people. Perfectly casual. Nobody like Tommy, I promise."

Mummery was further heartened by this evidence of friendship. "That'd be smashing, Lewis. Thanks."

"Seven-thirty next Wednesday?" As he paid for the second round Griffin allowed himself to glance at his watch. "Fuck! I've got this TV thing in half-an-hour. Okay? I think your pieces are tremendous. Nostalgic without being sloppy. And funny. Very good. You know where we are in Chelsea? Thirty-two Paradise Passage."

Mummery had not been invited to a dinner party for some time. Most of his friends entertained only in cheap restaurants so it would make a change to see some of the richer members of his family again, and Lois would be impressed by Griffin's casually wealthy style. It was a side of English she had not yet encountered.

Cheerfully tipsy, he parted from Griffin outside the bar and set his face towards the narrows of Drury Lane where members of various counter-culture journals were holding a kind of war-conference above the printing shop which served most of them. These papers did not always pay, he had few opinions in common with the other contributors, but Lois approved of his nod towards radicalism and the editors showed real enthusiasm for his more inspired ideas.

They were old enough now, so old they were almost all noses now but a cheap cut don't make much difference. Come across the scattered bones of a shotdown German pilot. Someone had already cut the parachute off. A lot of the uniform was gone, too, by then. And of course the watch and stuff. Keep your house cold, I say, and you'll never be short of company. Children will want to cuddle you. Cats will sit in your lap. Dogs will remain loyal. Kerner ho gia! Shabash! Tum humara bat janter hi? Pop it in like a good boy, then.

Climbing at last the cracked, uncarpeted stairs to a top landing, he was greeted warmly by a fair-haired young woman in a white suede Indian Maiden outfit. "Hi, Dave!" He did not remember her name or the paper she worked for. She leant unsteadily against the wall near the door trying to do something with a portable tape-recorder. Mummery entered a large room filled by a circular table, miscellaneous chairs, R. Crumb, Grateful Dead and Black Panther posters, its surfaces covered in dusty newsprint, corners stacked with old magazines and browning file copies. Most of the young men round the table consciously resembled characters from Italian Westerns with long hair, wide-brimmed hats, cowboy boots, big belts, massive buckles, fringed buckskins, denim shirts. The smell of hash was pungent and enticing. Seating himself in a vacant chair Mummery listened in silence to an argument about distribution strategy and the possibility of several papers combining. Circulations were down. Even the police paid little attention to them; people who had originally brought style and talent to the radical press were selling the same material to better-paying markets, including the music papers. There was no longer a widespread demand for the evangelical prophesying popular in the late sixties. Dick Barron, darkly aggressive, a little too fat for his black leathers, said they had been stoned so long they hadn't noticed times changing. "We've made all the impact we were ever going to make. We should either pack it in or find new targets. Otherwise it's just a wank."

Fooling around in the back brain said it was a process of regeneration it certainly had me shaking all over the bloody floor I might have died for all they cared . . .

Mummery accepted the joint as it came by, unable to share their disapproval of Barron's cynicism. "We've got to keep the faith, man." Pete Baldock, in a stained beige jacket and a green velvet shirt, raised his bloodshot eye. "Let those other bastards get jobs on *Sounds* and *The Village Voice*. What's wrong with peace and love?"

"This could be our hour, you know . . ." The young man next to him, clean-shaven, with round, grey eyes and dirty blond hair, was new to Mummery. "You know. Our hour."

Mummery smoked the joint down as far as he could and waited for another to come his way. He began to relax. He realised how nervous he had been in his cousin's company. Hash worked better than any tranquilliser, so he was content to remain at the meeting until there was no more. "It's historical." He felt he should contribute. "Dick's right."

"We can't give up our revolutionary strategy now!" Jim Enevoldson, the American editor of *Frendz* since the fourth staff uprising that year, looking like a lumberjack in his heavy black beard and plaid shirt, had been in Amsterdam until a month ago. "I can't believe this is happening!"

The long convoluted argument became increasingly abstract as everyone grew more stoned. In this familiar situation, where no action was called for, Mummery felt comfortable. He was convinced he had lived through a Golden Age which had lasted up to the making of "Let It Be". Older than most of the others, he had known the true awfulness of 1950s austerity; he enjoyed a better life than anything he had ever expected; National Service had been abolished before his call-up, the economic revival had arrived in time for him to enjoy it, and he was not going to complain, just because the best of times were passing.

At five-thirty Dick Barron rose from the table. "I'm going up The Nell Gwynn."

Feeling companionable, Mummery went with him. They stumbled cheerfully down the stairs, out into the crowded street, the warm rush hour of Drury Lane, to Holborn Viaduct and their favourite local, with its brightly coloured terra-cotta fruits and flowers, its Elizabethan interior, cast-iron roses and plaster brambles in reds, greens and yellows, and its huge oak-framed mirrors. Upstairs, years earlier, Mummery had been a regular at the Folk Club. Now there was only poetry. "If you're going to sell out, Dick, then sell out gracefully and do it for a lot." Mummery ordered them both double whiskies. "I'm a regular with *London Town* now."

"I'm writing fiction, myself. At least you get royalties. And songs, of course." Elbows on the massive bar, they watched the others drift in. Barron leaned close to Mummery. "See that bloke in the corner?" He indicated a narrow-faced, white-haired solitary man of about fifty at a small table near the open door. "He's the copper arrested me two years ago. He comes in here every day hoping to nick somebody else. He doesn't even recognise me. Pathetic, isn't it?"

"You'd think he'd know who you were."

103

"They can't tell us apart."

The policeman turned his head revealing the set, wary expression of a neurotic terrier. Dick Barron lifted his glass and winked. "Evening officer."

Mummery, with his persistent fear of arrest, looked away in alarm to show he was not part of Barron's challenge. "You know what today is? It was in my first column. It's Oak Apple Day, when the Chelsea Pensioners wear an oak-leaf to remember Charles the Second's restoration."

What a bloody tragedy those poor little babies. Is Mrs Saleem still alive? I have no wish to continue their tradition but I have little hope. People aren't so bad I was looked after very kindly. To fuck the little bitch then she'd know who I was all right. Yüzmeden yüzmeye fark var. I saw it all before in Wicklow.

"The past's flapping about me like a tarpaulin in the wind, threatening to smother me again. But it's like it's stuck to my body." Theatrically, "Hargreaves" stubbed out his Gauloise. He was loose in baggy corduroys, like an understuffed toy, his coarse skin flushed, his hair unruly. "Don't go, Heather. Stay for one more. You've plenty of time."

"I'm catching a train. I told my mother I'd be home for supper. I do understand, Joe." Carefully, so that she did not get her heavy velvet sleeve soaked by the beer spreading across his table, she reached across to pat him. Her Pre-Raphaelite hair swayed against his face. Her Pre-Raphaelite jaw dropped in a display of sympathy. His pain was almost as uncomfortable as her own. "I'll see you tomorrow, you know. At school."

"It's tonight I'm worried about. I don't want to sound melo-dramatic or anything . . . "

She got up before he could threaten suicide again. She took her purple cape from the coat-stand. It was getting boisterous in the Nell Gwynn. The *International Times* people had gathered around a small, white-haired man and were shouting at him, apparently nervous about another police raid on their offices. "I'll give you a ring, if I can," she said. "Later."

"How many others are there? At this moment? Today? Tonight? Are they all like me? I sought him out. I searched for him across an entire city. Sweetheart! Oh, sweetheart! Love me again."

104

At this point, before her teacher could resume his grizzling, embarrassment came to Heather Churchill's rescue, providing her with the will to leave. "Try to stop drinking and go home, Joe. Or stay at your friend's in Notting Hill. Leon's always glad to see you."

For the moment he had dismissed her. With his head in his hands he whispered to himself. It was almost a year since Donald had left London, returning to Bury after his release from hospital. Donald had been beaten up and robbed on Hampstead Heath by someone be believed to be a casual pick-up and by the man's accomplice who had been waiting in hiding. Donald had screamed for help but Joe thought he was playing an emotional game and had gone home to Chalk Farm. By the next day when Joe found out the truth Donald, badly knocked about, had refused to speak to him.

Stopped at the door by a mumbling boy trying to tell her about a tunnel leading from the pub into a secret world of perpetual summer, ruled, as far as she understood him, by a benign and immortal Good King Charles, Heather called back to Joe. "Go home. Paint a picture. You need to paint a picture."

She pushed past the messenger from the Summer Kingdom and entered the street. The station lay on the other side of Holborn Viaduct's red, gold and green Victorian Gothic ironwork. Below the viaduct as she crossed, in Farringdon Street, a man pushed a huge cart loaded with every kind of spring flower. As high above him as she was, the delicious scents of freesias, narcissi, hyacinths, lilies and roses were powerful. Hands on the rail, she wondered if she had time to get down the steps to stop the man and buy a bunch for her mother. Looking at her watch she all at once knew panic. She had three minutes. Searching for her ticket in her handbag she ran for the station entrance, then, as she crossed the concourse, confused by the shouting tannoy, a starling flew low over her head, making her cry out. She snapped her bag shut and with long strides headed towards her platform, knowing with intense relief that she would catch the train.

Staggering in pursuit, Joe Haughton saw her duck away from the bird and sprint with her red hair flowing, giving him the first idea for a picture he had had in ages. Suddenly, from habitual despair, he grew enormously cheerful. Heather meanwhile disappeared behind the barrier, but he was determined to ask her tomorrow to model for him. Tonight, before the image deserted him, he would do the initial sketches. Straightening his shoulders he searched for the exit closest to the Central Line which would take him to Notting Hill. Overhead, through glass and elaborate cast iron, he saw more birds massing in the blue evening sky, their voice a single ululation. In his mind Heather ran with her hair tangling starlings which struggled to rejoin a flock forming a wide, dark cloud disappearing like smoke into the distance where a train crossed cornfields. Arms outstretched she ran towards the river. There was a possibility that in her panic she might drown.

He had an impulse to warn her, but her train had already left the platform. He scratched his head, amused to note how the excitement had returned and with it his confidence. She was his subject now; her fate anything he might imagine. Reaching St Paul's underground station he ran whistling into the depths to buy his ticket. He would prove to everyone that all he needed was his work. He had a canvas stretched and by tomorrow could have the whole initial preparation done. Heather would sit for a couple of hours, to get her colours right. There was even time to submit the picture to the RA. People would be astonished. It would be his best.

The train came squealing in and he stumbled aboard, almost falling into an empty seat. Drawing on the flyleaf of his paperback, he determined his picture's proportions. Once he nodded off and almost went past his stop, but by the time he ascended into the Notting Hill air and walked down Kensington Park Road, with its cherry blossoms and its thousands of birds in evening chorus, he was again wide awake and enthusiastic. The effects of so many self-pitying pints dropped away, making him feel ten years younger. He would walk straight home to Adela Street to clear the decks for tomorrow. Turning into Ladbroke Grove, seeing the tall grey walls of The Elgin, familiar and comforting, he decided to look in, just to let Leon know what he was planning, and pushed open the doors of the saloon bar, passing through the murk to the back room where Leon usually played pool. Standing near the jukebox under the electric light, Leon rested on his cue like a Greek warrior upon his spear, a handsome Trinidadian whose air of refined, private humour Joe found attractive. Leon greeted him with a friendly nod. "Your game next, man."

Unwilling to check his excitement, Joe shook his head. "Can't make it tonight, man. I've got an idea for a painting. I need to get home."

"Nice one, man. I'll see you, then." Lifting his cue in salute Leon returned to his table while Joe shoved through the newly arrived crowd of gypsies who, because of the recent murder there, had been banned from the Kensington Palace Hotel across the street. Stopping only to buy haddock and chips from the shop below the railway bridge, Joe moved with happy stride towards his little studio flat with its view of the canal.

For the first time since the height of his affair with Donald he whistled his favourite Noël Coward songs.

Pikki-pikki porker no company a me. Let him go up his own batty for all me care. Bloodclot cut no style round here. Sucked it dry feel like it's going to drop off all shrivelled. Get the stake and there's no way I can't double it by the morning. Horny horse all over white make him lucky if you got virgin. Be silver hair, be gold stick out, be ruby eyes, be tail made of copper. Down all the way from Queensland and kept on going but she never knew enough to stop him until they found the van in Redcliffe Gardens three years later. Same bloody air on a G-string. Flew out, big clear all got crosses on us. All got crosses now. Horny horse make water white, make sky all red, make trees go gold. Horny horse bring silver spray. Make me happy. Happy, happy, happy day. No more pork in Babylon. Pork all flee Jerusalem.

Sherlock Holmes 1981

CROSSING HUNGERFORD Footbridge between the Royal Festival Hall and Charing Cross Embankment Josef Kiss paused to watch a train roll by on his left then contemplated the monumental buildings downriver, the gulls fighting against the wind, the agitated water, the tourist boats lit by fitful, untrustworthy shafts of sunlight, coming to moor alongside their piers. For a moment he saw this landscape still populated by monsters, by mud and giant ferns, when prehistoric summers, humid as any in Mississippi, lasted for centuries, and he longed to witness some translation, at least some improvement in the climate, for it seemed the previous winter had lasted forever. Elsewhere, as the rattle died and the two forty-six began its familiar passage to Lewisham, a clarinet sounded, a jazz tune made mournful as it was snatched up on the wind. "Italy," said Josef Kiss, by way of a challenge to his own city. "Rome, next year, my love, if this goes on."

Dismounting from the bridge's last step he slipped a careful coin into the busker's corduroy cap then headed determinedly for the great stone terraces of Northumberland Street. His lunch at County Hall with his sister had upset him. She wanted him to act as a man in the street for her party's new advertising film. The idea was so absurd it had momentarily cheered him, confirming that his sister would not know a man in the street if her Daimler ran over one on a pedestrian crossing. Telling her that as an anarchist he was morally against the whole electoral system had alarmed and disgusted her, as he had hoped, so that she had released him almost at once. She planned to stand again for the Tories in the next election. She made a perfect Member, he said, and must surely soon be selected for high office. She had agreed.

The red race has come to the end of its time. Going round and round, round and round, searching every station, seeking out my nation, don't find me destination. Me got to live me. The new generation. It isn't just a fashion. Not just a rhythm or a simple pattern. More the education of a poetic imagination. Shout and then run like buggery. Italian news from Mr Parrott.

Northumberland Street, its high, regular Victorian Arcadian houses blackened by a thousand bygone fogs and looking as if they had only ever been designed for official business, public residences, had one welcoming feature: set back from the road, beside Craven Passage, which ran into the echoing gloom of Charing Cross arches, stood a public house Josef Kiss still called The Northumberland though it had been rechristened for almost twenty years. Having discovered a reference to The Northumberland Arms Hotel in The Hound of the Baskervilles its owners had justified a profitable change by installing in an upper room a Sherlock Holmes exhibition bought from the Festival of Britain. Now a regular's evening at The Sherlock Holmes would frequently be interrupted by the sudden arrival of fifty studious Americans led by a guide who would take the party upstairs for five minutes, bring them all down again, order fifty half-pints of bitter, which most of them were too polite to describe as undrinkable, and leave within quarter of an hour. Josef Kiss had come to enjoy this spectacle, though it was as well to arrive early to get a place at the new Edwardianate bar. Today he just had time to refresh himself before the pub closed at three.

He entered a sea of plaid sport jackets and deerstalkers, all of them below eye-level, and realised at once he had come upon a party of Japanese. He smiled pleasantly at them, as an uncle to favourite nephews, wishing them "Good afternoon", raising his broad-brimmed hat, since the Japanese were amongst the few nations these days who appreciated old-fashioned courtesy. He felt no resentment of these earnest strangers who filled what he still sometimes termed, with his usual sardonic theatricality, "one of my regular watering-holes", for in his opinion tourism had brought variety to London, had kept alive many institutions, had helped maintain public services which would otherwise have foundered and, best of all, now provided him with constantly fresh audiences when it came upon him expansively to hold forth. He saw his relationship to London's tourist millions as essentially symbiotic. Without them, he had decided, he should have shrivelled up, and the city with him.

Bowing and lifting, beaming and nodding, Mr Kiss reached the bar in time to order himself a pint of stout in a straight glass. "Your interest in our famous detective is flattering," he told a mild-looking American couple who had arrived without a guide, "but have you heard of Doctor Nikola, a villain both more intelligent and more attractive than Moriarty? It was in the very passage which runs beside this tavern, on a foggy November evening in 1894, that Nikola was responsible for the demise of three Metropolitan policemen, two knights of the realm, a High Court judge and a military gentleman of rank. All corrupt, incidentally. You will find this, and much more, recorded in the tales of Guy Boothby, whom I heartily recommend. Kipling and Conan Doyle also were his fans. Sadly, these days, you have to look for them in secondhand editions."

The husband produced a notebook to record the information.

"You ought to be doing this lark, Mr Kiss." The lanky landlord of The Sherlock Holmes gestured towards a young woman in blazer and flannel skirt who at that moment was ushering her group upstairs to observe the Baker Street study. "Was there really a Doctor Thingy?"

"As real to the readers of *Pearson's*, Arnold, as Holmes to the readers of *The Strand*. A sinister creature to be sure, but more popular even than the Man Bat of The Charing Cross Hotel, who lived for three years undetected amongst roofs and attics above the station, surviving chiefly on human blood and parts of corpses stolen from the hospital morgue. That would have been around the turn of the century."

Arnold shuddered. "I mean it, Mr Kiss. You should do it for a living."

"And lose my amateur status?"

"I'll never understand why you gave up the halls."

"Sanity, Arnold. Television is my bread and butter and tourism's my private pleasure. I'm content. London endures. Her stories endure. People's demand for Romance endures. And I retain confidence in human nature. I'm no cynic, Arnold."

"Well," Arnold wiped a glass, "it makes a change from the bloody Sleuth of Two Twenty-One bloody B, and I can't complain about that. I don't even like detective stories."

Josef Kiss had reached his afternoon's limit. Tipping his hat once more to the Japanese party, he re-entered the blustery sunlight, moving resolutely towards the clearing of Trafalgar Square and the National Gallery where he intended to spend half-an-hour with a Whistler. At four he was due in St James's Park, near Duck Island, for what the director described as a couple of quick retakes, a soft-focus piece on the enduring Victorian values of someone's Beef Tea. He was, in the eyes of advertisers, directors and viewers alike, the epitome of Antique Virtue and was grateful for the work. The role of genial Admiral Filet had lasted him almost nine years, bought him the freehold on two of his flats, the remaining twenty years lease on a third, and enabled him to make a good offer for the long lease of the fourth. Investing his income in tiny properties gave him security, anonymity and, if necessary, the opportunity to assume a fresh identity. His building-society accounts were in widely separated areas and at least ten pseudonyms. He had spent the rest on travel and his sanctuaries, where he enjoyed the relaxation of un-medicated madness for a few weeks, at little danger to himself and none at all to others. He had taken endowment policies for his children, who occasionally visited him in London and were as good as Dutch by now. He hoped when he died to be revealed as something more than the sum of his apartments.

Here she come no other feeling like her Christ it hurt it hurt it hurt so goddam bad. The West is dead. Babylon go under. Pork all gone from Jerusalem. When will you pay me say the bells of Old Bailey. That's where I saw her in the crypt of St Martin's, after we came out of the Wagner wasn't it? Twelve years gone and not a penny to show for it. Jeg spurgte om de havde hørt nyt fra Angkor . . . Se debe pagar la entrada? Hal arga bokral? Mist put there no more. Is it?

Leon Applefield, feeding pigeons in the company of his niece Bianca, glanced after Mr Kiss's billowing cloak as it passed Nelson's Column and was reminded of an old TV serial he had watched as a child in Trinidad before his parents came here. "There goes Zorro!" He grinned at a mystified Bianca.

"Can we buy some more seed, Uncle Leon?" She had ketchup and orange juice staining her white lace front. Her mother would kill him.

"Sure, honey." Elegant in his long leather coat, his butcherboy cap, he strolled, her hand in his, towards the old man with a tray of birdseed round his neck. Because his sister needed to visit her husband in hospital Leon, with free time since C & A had accepted his nightwear designs, had offered to take Bianca. His own daughter had returned to Scotland with her mother, but Bianca was not really much of a substitute. Tessa was livelier, perhaps brighter, certainly wittier. They enjoyed joking together while Bianca responded with eager seriousness or blank puzzlement. She was, he supposed, "Well-trained".

The pigeons fed for a third time, Leon suggested they walk down to St James's Park and look at the pelicans. When he had described a pelican she agreed. By five o'clock Leon could return the child, but his sister Amber had arranged for them all to eat out at a smart hamburger place with her middle-class North London friends whom Leon loathed. He had to mix with people like that during working hours and thought it unfair of Amber to expect him to waste his evening with a bunch of trendies at Camden Lock, but he could not in conscience refuse his sister. Her husband Victor had after all broken his leg helping Leon decorate his new flat. His deadlines met, Leon was mildly depressed and preferred his old Notting Hill haunts, shooting pool with his mates, listening to gossip in the Mangrove, smoking ganja at All Saints Road; harmless pursuits which Amber found threatening. She clung firmly to her middle-class origins while for his part he felt burdened and threatened by them. Acceptance by his poorer black con-temporaries meant a great deal more than the chance of talking about mortgage rates with white leftwingers owning huge houses in Islington. He planned to split as soon as he could and cross the street to the Music Machine where he knew for certain he could pick up a girl for the evening. He might pose as a drug dealer or something equally romantic. Nobody knew better than Leon Applefield how to appeal to their strangely repressed Home Counties imaginations. He was almost like one of them.

The park was crowded, layered with a hundred shades of green, its water smooth. Bianca ran up to it. "Careful honey," Leon said. He sighed for his grandma. "Noisy river never killed nobody."

"Is that a pelican, Uncle Leon?" She had returned to tug at his coat.

"No, honey, that's a swan." He marvelled at the child's inexperience. Did Amber take her anywhere or show her anything?

As they walked beside the artificial lake the wind dropped and he began to recite the names of the exotic fowl which filled the royal waters. His walks with Tessa had taught him to recognise almost every duck, goose and coot which came to them for nuts, but Bianca was chiefly interested in the black swans and the gulls, which Leon hated. He tried to redirect her attention to a beige and brown tufted duck more timid than the rest, his own favourite, but Bianca became unreasonably nervous of it. He looked back through trees and shrubs heavy with spring blossom, towards the white palaces and government offices which Tessa had once believed to be the property of fairy princesses. "Only Mrs Thatcher," he had said. "And she's not much of a princess for anyone." From beyond the banks of trees even Horse Guards Parade might have been magical, but Bianca refused to engage her interest until they came upon the little mock-Tudor miniature manor-house of Duck Island where a movie camera had been set up and a team of self-important technicians redirected the public around them. A single policeman did his best to display his boredom. Leon let Bianca lead him towards this crew.

The object of her attention was a large, fat man, his face covered in make-up, brown flannel trousers rolled above his bare feet and calves. In a grey shirt, a pair of wide braces, and with a knotted handkerchief on his head he held a primitive fishing-rod in one hand, a sandwich in the other and listened with dignified concentration to a middle-aged man in a leather jacket with thinning hair and an unmusical voice, half-placatory, half-arrogant, who offered instructions. At length, obediently, the old man sat down on a small canvas stool and cast his line into the dirty waters of the pond. A woman in jeans ran from a mobile canteen with a steaming cup of liquid and placed it carefully beside the fisherman. "Get ready everybody!" The director raised pinched, pink features to the sky. "Okay, Fred! Action!"

Bianca had grown animated. "I know that man, Uncle Leon!" She was impressed.

"What is he, honey? A friend of your mum's?"

For the first time since they had left the house she laughed. "Don't you remember him?" She sang a snatch whose words were obscure but whose tune was familiar.

Leon shook his head. "Sorry, honey. What's he in? *Blue Peter? Playschool?*"

Her giggles mocked his ignorance until she was all but helpless. "You know! It's Admiral Filet!"

At last Leon recognised the commercial. "So it is. Well, maybe he's been marooned and is having to catch his own fish for a change."

Give her one tonight if we get off early enough no doubt she wants it playing hard to get not likely once I get hold of her there's no way you could drown in that depth is there you'd have to go over to Charing Cross or somewhere don't they break their necks or something first smell that wonderful lilac it makes you want to live forever wouldn't you do it if you could always be here in the springtime Michael Denison and Dulcie Grey wasn't it oh it's all gone now this violence has taken over everything though you've got to remember what violence was going on everywhere else is it like a habit does it have to be satisfied somehow no matter what couldn't we ever get off it shit in my pants if I don't find one soon this fat old fart thinks he's Laurence bloody Olivier only another three hours to bumtime Mavis.

Bianca grew deeply puzzled. "He's not wearing his uniform. He always wears his uniform."

"Maybe he lost it in a shipwreck." The crowd around the temporary barrier was now big enough to make Leon uneasy. "We'll just have to wait until he's on television to find out. Come on, Bee-Bee, it's time to meet mummy."

She let him lead her from the park, across Horse Guards Parade, past the Admiralty, the surrounded soldiers, into Whitehall where he looked towards Westminster and paused. "I should have got his autograph, Uncle Leon. He's my mum's favourite star."

To Leon's relief a vacant taxi stopped at his signal. "Camden Lock, please." He opened the door for Bianca to precede him. Before starting off the driver turned. "You know the market's only open Saturdays and Sundays, do you, sir?"

"It's okay. I'm meeting someone." Leon felt obscurely resentful, as if he had been foolish to reply. He watched the clouds move rapidly through the blue sky wondering how he could avoid his next ordeal. He saw it as a set piece: The Middle Class Family's Hamburger Evening. A subject for Bosch or Bacon. His failure to engage with these rituals was the chief cause of his split with Maggie. Life at Elgin Crescent had been an endless series of chaotic dinner parties crowned each week by an even noisier and more crowded Sunday lunch where the men got into egocentric arguments about politics and money and the women shrieked intermittently at their ill-behaved children. When a husband was alerted by a familiar voice his sole recognition of his family was, "Oh, just relax, for God's sake. Let 'em run about and enjoy themselves." As the only black man at these bouts Leon grew furiously bored by requests for his opinion on Africa, American Civil Rights or Immigration.

For a pleasant moment he considered taking Bianca off to The Elgin and introducing her to the diversions of pool, but he lacked the nerve. Moreover, she was too short to see more than an inch above the table so there was every chance she would damage the baize. He consoled himself that, when he and Tessa were in Los Angeles, they would play as much pool as they wanted at Barney's Beanery.

He wondered why these people embraced family life with such relish.

Perhaps their peculiar tribal habits, their vague liberalism, their inactive agreement about what angered or disgusted them, were means of maintaining a *status quo* to which they were as committed as any of their more frankly rapacious contemporaries. He had grown impatient with their discussions about H-Bombs, vivisection, dying fish, Women's Rights and clubbed seals while they ate and drank as much in an afternoon as people living a few hundred yards away could buy in a fortnight. He started to tell them this. Their hypocritical posturing was a true sign of a culture in decline. When he informed his wife he was voting Conservative in last year's election she had decided they were incompatible and made him leave. He had not wanted to go. He attempted to compromise but finally his anger was greater than his need to stay with her. In the second month of Margaret Thatcher's rule he had moved to Powys Square where a friend illegally sublet him a

Housing Trust flat. Under the name of Nigel Simonson he settled in to find, almost immediately, his luck changing. He now had customers for everything he designed. Meanwhile he played down his success to avoid the disapproval of his friends and in case Maggie demanded alimony as well as their house and Tessa's support. When she put the house up for sale and returned to Glasgow he thought briefly of buying it from her but he had no real wish to go back to what he had escaped. He was more at ease in Powys Square and so were his girlfriends. All he missed of family life was Tessa.

Fuckemcunt, fuckemarse, fuckemouth, fuckemtit no fucking bitch scares Micky Phelps got a Dirty Harry manstopper, got a Marine knife, got a Commando kit, fuckem killem, fuckem killem all the Soho bitches, go down Villiers Street see all the stuckup bitches wonder if I could get a new one in the Spring Sale but they never have my size what's that funny smell?

As the Number 15 bus turned into the Strand Mary Gasalee thought how lovely Charing Cross Station could look when the sun was on it. She was reminded of Oxford's colleges. She returned her attention to the notebook resting in her lap. Recently she had decided to write down her random thoughts, every notion, every flash of memory. Then, when she had time, she pursued what she could. Today she was on her way to Aldgate to look for the Chop House where Ron Heinz had taken her soon after she left the hospital. Ron had been born nearby. They had met at the half-way hostel. He had killed himself two years later.

"Are you sure, Mary, that this won't be too traumatic?" Judith looked carefully into her face again. "What with all the bombed houses, all the ruins, you don't want to discover another that's been bulldozed down."

"Oh, it won't matter." But Mary acknowledged with a grateful motion of her hand her friend's concern. "I'm glad you're with me. It was nice of you to come."

"Thank Geoffrey's umpteenth business trip." After several years of uncertainty Judith had married her publisher. "I've nothing much to do, anyway. I hate it when he goes away. I'm sure he's faithful but I can't get it out of mind that he might not be."

"Geoffrey's all right, surely."

"Well, I got him off his wife, so it would be easy enough for someone else to do the same. He'll fall for any old line." And Judith laughed loudly for they were alone on the top deck of the bus. "I never actually meant to marry him, you know, but I made a stand on principle. And that's how I became a homebreaker. Disgusting, isn't it?"

Privately Mary agreed. While remaining fond of Judith she disapproved of her behaviour, particularly since Geoffrey was no great catch and her friend had virtually given up her painting since her marriage. "Well, did you get what you wanted?"

Judith detected irony in Mary's voice. "Yes. Are you sure this bus goes all the way to Aldgate?"

Mary tried to lighten her tone. "It's about the only thing I'm sure of!"

"We don't have to eat any actual eels there?"

"Judith, it's not an Eel and Pie Shop. It's a Chop Shop. Lamb chops, pork chops, steaks, sausages, bacon, grilled or fried, mash, chips, peas, onions, bread and butter, tea. Delicious. Marble tables, mahogany booths, cast iron. You've never felt safer sitting down to a meal. And all for one-and-six or so in 1956. It was Ron's favourite. He used to get tremendously enthusiastic. He remembered lots of other bits of the old East End from his childhood. There was a joke shop – jokes and toys, really – he liked to go into, just to look. Tall doorway and dark emporium beyond, crowded to the ceiling with old, exotic stock. Cardboard boxes full of ancient tricks. And a couple of general stores. And a pub. All torn down, I suppose. But the Chop Shop was a bit further up so there's a chance it's still there. He was such a happy-go-lucky sort of chap."

"But he must have suffered from depression, too."

Mary looked out of the window as they moved gradually along Fleet Street. "I suppose so."

"It's as if someone's determined to wipe out every bit of your past." Judith was joking. "Doesn't it sometimes seem like that? Don't you ever feel funny?"

Est-ce de l'eau potable? Full of the joys of Spring put the lot on the same bloody horse god knows what milk-float it used to pull that rhubarb will be lovely when it comes up she really likes a nice bit of brass . . .

"Yes. But I've Helen, you know. And she's tangible enough. We're not strangers. She's got another book out this week." Mary suddenly wished she were making the trip alone. Her mind, not

117

exactly wandering, was filling with all kinds of words and pictures. These often brought flashes of clarity, distinct memories, fresh as if she were living them, and she could hear many voices, some evidently nearby, from the bus and the street; others from her past. Within her mind time was no longer linear. *Walk towards me.*

Ladies this heat can't last though all your lips are pressing to hold it I will never leave you if you say you'll be true mother, mother what are we going to do with you if you won't look after yourself the whole bloody vehicle swallowed up by the street as if it had never been and the whole thing filled in on top that was happening everywhere around here . . .

Judith Worrell thought Mary might be becoming too morbid again. "Did you ever find out why Ron killed himself?"

"His cat died. He had a Siamese cat, very much like my biggest one. It got leukaemia." Mary was sorry to be disturbing Judith.

"I didn't mean to hit a sore spot." Judith cleared her throat.

"You're not, dear. It isn't you. It isn't you." Mary turned widening eyes on her friend.

Looking for a bit of fun I'll give it to them you never know your luck. Find the old kind if you can they're so much handier. My Harold's feet are all we talk about . . .

"Mary! You're crying. What's wrong?" Judith dropped her voice. Two men were sitting down at the back of the bus. One of them looked at her as if in recognition then dropped his gaze.

"I'm not unhappy." She clasped Judith's hand. "A bit barmy, perhaps. But I'm very happy. I can smell all those beautiful roses. In the park. A bower. You know, a tunnel of roses. It was wonderful. Nothing but roses. I used to walk round and round in it. And there's the greenhouse. Don't worry about the blokes. You have to put up with that. It's hateful but I'm used to it. It's actually better when they're foreign and there are no pictures. The roses! Oh, Judith!"

Keeping hold of Mary's hand Judith attempted to control her nervousness. The two men were now speaking intensely in a guttural, unfamiliar language.

Bir seyi söylemesi baska, yapmasi baskadir. Could be worse but I don't know what I'll tell him if he asks me straight. Get off here and take the tube or should I just phone up?

"An arbour, is it?" Mary could no longer resist the memory. "And outside, in the centre, was a lawn. And on the lawn was a dovecot. With white doves coming and going. The roses and the sound of these doves! I can't tell you where it is. It's as clear as if I was there now. How long ago was it? I might be a kid. There wasn't much of that in Clerkenwell. It couldn't be Josef's could it? Josef's memory?" Mary's eyes were still open. She was smiling. Judith in turn began to cry.

I'm not ashamed of my sexuality or how I exercise it. I can't say I do good or harm in the end. But I do admittedly cause confusion. There are pigeons down there. Look. They want to build a wall round Greater London but where will the government go? Guildford? Dogs, cats and real foxes. Common foxes. Hear that thunder? Can't you understand that awful pain? Can't you? Stewing in her own juice. That made me laugh. Lazy liggers trying one on, tying one on Northern lights late in the day, soppy old dears, playing my banjo in a one-man band, a disenfranchised city, it's not going to get any better, especially for women . . .

"Did we go on holiday? Somewhere in Kent? Just a day out on the train. Was that Hever? Like a Tudor rose-arbour. It wasn't Canterbury. There's other kinds of flowers in the centre, around a fountain, and all the doves in their little houses."

Mary lifted her head up as if inhaling perfume. "I'm not at all sad, dear. I'm happy. But I'd love to know where I am."

Princess Diana 1985

"YOU PROBABLY think it's all down to the Knowledge. The Knowledge is the start, true, ma'am, but it's not really what the job's about. You've got to have instincts for roads and a good sense of the past. And people. I try to tell them that. They'll never know what's actually in my head. I like to drive at night. That's when the city's bones show. It helps you." The taxi-driver drew up outside the great Doric gates and removed his pipe from his mouth. "All Greek Revival here, see. Portland Stone." His curly grey hair, horn-rimmed glasses and soft, tanned square face emphasised a broken nose. "This is Kensal Green Cemetery. Is it the one you thought?"

Four-in-hand cutting a dash monkey never gobbled no bad bananas, sold up to do it I'll never know why . . .

"It looks huge." Mary craned to look inside. "Are there any other entrances?"

"This is the main one. Shall I drive you down to the chapel?"

Encouraged by the sight of Josef Kiss crossing the road ahead of them she opened her wallet and paid the driver. "That's very kind of you." She gave him a pound tip. "No."

"And thank you, madam!"

"Josef!" Mary stood on the pavement. She waved. He came about like a clipper under full sail, smiling with pleasure as she entered his field of vision. He wore a pale panama hat, in acknowledgement of the sunshine, a cream three-piece suit, a black armband. His cane was on his crooked left sleeve, in his left hand he carried his gloves. His age was hinted at by his careful movements rather than by his features. "I had hoped you would come, my dear. But you didn't know him awfully well, did you?"

"He was a friend of David's really."

"Then we're both here for Mummery. Well, anyway, it will make a good turnout. There are few in this world who ever achieve the funeral attendances they deserve." He removed his stick to offer her his arm. "My only reservation was that I would not wear black. Black is for one's nearest and dearest. Your navy, if I may say, is an excellent choice."

"I didn't really have much in the way of black." She stretched to kiss his cheek. "People don't, do they, these days? Unless they're under twenty-five."

"In which case they have nothing but. I suppose it's a sign of our miserable times. Mummery said it was an accident. A drug and a can of lager. What awful luck."

"Largactyl," he added.

With that hesitant, unnatural way of walking common at funerals, they moved between the gates and down the gravel avenue towards the chapel. "There's a family, apparently. The inquest said it was accidental death. What was he? Thirty-something?"

"Forty-four. Everyone said he'd be killed in a car accident, he drank so much. He seemed strong as an ox, yet he died in his sleep. David said he'd been working very hard."

No black shadow gonna get this boy's arse. Take it easy, take it careful. That sky was like a giant knife got me in the head. The trees are no protection.

Behind them several small groups kept themselves to themselves. Mary and Josef climbed steps into the cool columns of the chapel where David Mummery, one of the ushers, greeted them. He kissed Mary and shook Josef's hand. "The family's on the left." Like an automaton he indicated the pews on the right. "Sit wherever you like over there."

Mary recognised Mr Faysha from the clinic and one or two others she remembered from parties. She hoped her smiles were not inappropriate as she slipped into a row near the back, unbuttoned her coat, picked up two copies of the Order of Service and handed one to Josef beside her. The chapel was discreetly undecorated, rather cold, she thought, in its classicism. There was some geometric mosaic, some urns of flowers, a kind of altar on which the large polished pine coffin was already resting. The place reminded her of an air-raid shelter. There was something to be said, she decided, for a full Church funeral. She thought she heard a whisper at her back but it was nothing.

A somewhat feeble-looking pale creature appeared apologetically before them all. He wore Anglican robes, the vicar, and his executive drone made reference to "our dear relative and friend Benjamin".

I don't feel safe on the tube the way I used to. During the War it was the best place to be. Freemasons, they said he'd joined but there was nothing in his room. What a horrible way to die. And he didn't mean to. He couldn't have meant to. There was no note. They couldn't have thrown it away. The Astoria was his favourite. It was the nicest of them all. Always promised he'd take me deer-hunting in Richmond Park. He was no Errol Flynn, though not at all bad-looking. A real shame. A real waste. Still he's probably happy. Do they have a heaven for homos?

To Mary's relief the first hymn was a long version of Jerusalem, sufficiently rousing to rid her of some tension. Elsewhere people had begun to weep and she felt obscurely guilty for not joining in; but she could at least share the singing. "And now the time returns again; our souls exult, and London's towers receive the Lamb of God to dwell in England's green and pleasant bowers!" As she sang she could see with Blake that vision of a perfect London, where slums and misery were abolished and God's perfection touched every building, every grassy park and spinney. It was how others visualised Heaven; it was what many had hoped to see after the bombing. Then, above the somewhat uneven rendering, she heard the vicar's well-bred tones, scarcely altered even as they were raised in song, giving unnatural respectability, a deadly middle-class acceptance to those fierce, demanding words. Was it the function of the modern Church to moderate ambition, to dampen enthusiasm, to frown upon aspiration either spiritual or temporal? And could it cheat even at this moment these mourners of a wholehearted expression of their grief? Mary Gasalee, finding here at least a challenge to which she could respond, sang out with all her heart, uncaring save for the dead and the bereaved.

David Mummery, immediately behind her and to one side, was

astonished to hear her. Of late he had become used to her hesitancy, considering her somewhat caged and timid, but here she was like a wild lark revelling in her pure, unselfconscious voice, so beautiful he could not help but join in. Josef Kiss was equally inspired together with many others on their side of the chapel, until the words rang as they were meant to ring and a whole trained choir might have been celebrating the rising of Ben French's soul to Paradise. Careless of the perturbed, perhaps even disapproving, looks from Ben's family filling the two front pews across from the aisle, Mummery knew most of them thought Ben's death to be his own fault, an inconvenience, a final reflection on his friends and lifestyle. For his part Mummery, angered as usual by sudden bereavement, had developed a hatred for the three people who had been with Ben the night he died and had been afraid to call an ambulance in case Ben blamed them when he woke up in hospital. Both men were bearded, off-colour, in shabby jackets and flannels, seated near the front, while the coarse-featured woman who now claimed to be Ben's true love stood close to the coffin and wept, clutching at the hand of Hector Brown, red-eyed and dazed, Ben's companion of almost twenty years. Hector was tiny and dapper, unusually gentle, and had been left by Ben to run their small-holding in Yorkshire so Ben could come to London and finish his new book. As usual Ben had picked up a casual companion, this time a woman. Then he had died.

"The fields from Islington to Marylebone, to Primrose Hill and Saint John's Wood, were builded over with pillars of gold; and there Jerusalem's pillars stood."

Hector had prepared this version of "Jerusalem" especially for the service. It had been Ben's favourite hymn.

Originally Mummery had felt sympathy for Ben's relatives, but it was soon obvious that few of them cared much for him. The father, pinched and vaguely crazed, plainly did not wish to be there at all. Ben's will had named only Hector. The mother, with dark, soft features, her lips curved at their corners so that in her sadness she seemed to offer a ghastly grin, was equally distressed by her son's death and nervous of her husband's disposition. The family wore dark, cheap clothes. Only the brother, whom Mummery had mistaken for one of the undertakers, seemed prosperous. Alone among her family the sister, considerably younger than Ben, with

123

permed golden hair and a slightly dusty rabbitskin coat, responded with wholehearted grief, trembling so much she could hardly hold the typed hymn sheet, the Kleenex in her gloved hand sodden with tears and mascara. Ben had told Mummery she had occasionally attempted to intercede with their father, only to be threatened physically for her pains, the issue being not Ben's homosexuality but his decision to divorce the wife he had married when he was eighteen. Ben's father had been of the opinion that certain face-saving compromises should have been made. What hideous bargains had Mr French and his own wife struck over the years? Mummery remembered the dark, ill-smelling house from his childhood. Ben had spent as much time as possible, sometimes weeks at a stretch, at his friend's.

As the chapel service ended the heavy coffin was lifted on the shoulders of Ben's brothers and cousins who carried it towards the doors. The family followed, with Ben's friends coming up from behind, a good many of them typically homosexual men and women, while others were bizarre in old Afghans, in Chinese silks and fringed buckskins, the bohemian survivors of a bygone age, like veterans of some long-lost civil war. Mummery was almost amused. In the midst of these he and his colleagues from the clinic seemed reasonably conservative. Even Josef Kiss, while affecting the costume of an earlier and more exotic period, had the air of a retired imperial dignitary.

Get the heat out of my groin they're going to see the hardon any minute what the fuck is it about death does this to me every time? It can't be natural. It's fear. It really is fear. It's always bloody fear. That's terrible.

The procession moved along gravel pathways, between oaks, chestnuts, elms, past heavy memorials, past marble and stone and ornamental concrete, a host of sword-bearing angels, of weeping or smiling angels, of angels whose joyous hands pointed from grave to heaven. All the great shrubs were in leaf, but wild brambles and ferns grew everywhere as if Kew's botanical aristocracy had been overrun by Wimbledon's commons. Alerted by a small discrepancy in the rituals, Mummery looked back and saw, distanced from the other mourners by a matter of feet, "Hargreaves" in loose dark suiting, his face glittering with tears. Drawing in to Mummery, Hector said with a hint of unusual sarcasm, "Now who on earth's that one?"

"I know him." Mummery became aware of the rich flowers on a recently sealed sarcophagus. "But I didn't know he knew Ben."

"Some one-nighter, I suppose." Hector had learned to live with Ben's promiscuity but continued to hate it. "He could charm them, couldn't he, the bastard." His face displayed immediate disapproval of his own words. Hector loathed bitchiness. He had insisted on behaving pleasantly to Lizzie, who claimed to be Ben's chief confidante, his muse, though Mummery had told Hector that Ben had been trying to drop her for weeks. On the night of his death she had gone to his Queens Park flat, trying for what she called reconciliation. Ben had treated his casual affairs with women or men equally callously and had been about to return to Hector. In fact he had died avoiding Lizzie, for Mummery was convinced it was on her account he had swallowed the pill, seeking escape in sleep.

The coffin tilted slightly as the relatives rounded the corner near the canal railings, taking the last few yards towards the freshly dug grave, and at this point Mummery lost control of himself, shuddering as he wept, grateful for Hector's sudden, comforting grip on his arm. He stumbled, blinded, while on his right Mary Gasalee held his elbow and behind him Josef Kiss murmured, "Bear up, old chap. Bear up, bear up, bear up."

As they reached the overturned clay, the family again took up one position, the friends another, divided by the pit, while the vicar began those intonations intended to comfort but which succeeded in causing Mummery among others to stare away for fear their disgust would be displayed. As the undertakers lowered the coffin by its tapes, Mummery moved his attention from across the canal with its unfamiliar view of Bank Cottage's high hedges and saw through the elms almost a silhouette: "Hargreaves", still holding back, possibly afraid to reveal his own homosexuality by close proximity to the dead man. Mummery wished he could offer Joe Houghton some gesture of inclusion.

No longer filtered by thin clouds, the sun emerged in full. The birds who had made Kensal Rise their permanent home, laying generation upon generation of eggs in its old trees, uttered excited songs in the fresh noon air. Mummery, able to see his watch, noted it was almost lunchtime and supposed they must find a pub in Harrow Road afterwards, to complete the day's miserable rites, but he did not look forward to the sentimental recounting of Ben's supposed virtues and talents which would be Lizzie's chief contribution to any memorial drink.

Unexpectedly "Hargreaves" appeared on the far side of the grave, facing the vicar. He had two sheets of paper in his right hand. As the vicar flung the last symbolic sod upon the settled coffin Joe Houghton raised his voice, defying interruption:

> "Is this the great star-dreamer,
>   who sailed in coldest space,
> With a sun-wind in his topsail,
>   and a hard moon on his face?"

The vicar swung in questioning terror towards the family who in turn glared accusations at Ben's equally baffled friends. But "Hargreaves" was alone, spontaneous; for days he had rehearsed this moment: Ben would not go under without at least one sincere and personal declaration.

Mummery could imagine Ben giggling delightedly at everyone's embarrassment. Now determined to hear "Hargreaves" out like a Christian, the vicar folded his hands beneath his robes and stared with pursed lips patiently into the grave.

> "Call him Hermes-Aphrodite,
>   who loved in spite of sex,
> Who sailed beyond all Systems,
>   call him Regina, call him Rex!"

It dawned upon the vicar that these verses had evangelical as well as sentimental content and he began to try to gather courage from a supernatural, or at least moral, source to intervene.

> "He was the laughing rider,
>   he was the gadfly hero,
> Honour him, you lesser ones,
>   for he sails where you can't follow!"

Then "Hargreaves" bent, kissed the paper, and threw his fluttering valediction onto the coffin.

"Well . . ." Two tiny spots of red had appeared beneath the vicar's eyes. "I do wish . . ."

Houghton turned his back. He walked slowly towards the distant gates, the picture of renewed self-esteem.

In history these will never be more than a few filing cards lost in whatever tea chest in whatever attic they live until they're destroyed or bequeathed to some obscure archive. Mabel's got the crabs I'll swear it's her who else could it be that girl get fum-fum a me wis ki bat per mat jao voh Islam laya hyckian le rehi thi . . . He's lost his chance of ever being buried in a Jewish cemetery . . .

"It's always best to arrange things ahead of time. If there's to be an unconventional element." The vicar made feeble placatory motions. "I am so sorry, Mrs French." Ben's mother, perhaps seizing her only chance, was releasing tears at last.

"I thought it was lovely," she said.

"He's an insensitive lunatic!" The veins in Mr French's cheeks pulsed and darkened. Mummery remembered how this had fascinated him as a child. "I bet they knew exactly what he was going to do!"

Mummery, having paid all possible respects to his old friend, decided to take advantage of the confusion and moved swiftly away from the excitement, followed by Mary Gasalee, Josef Kiss, Mombazhi and Alice Faysha, her tolerant features set in an expression of mild surprise. "We can probably all get into my car," said the African ex-sailor when they were clear. "I take it you don't want nobody else along. Where to, David?"

"Can you get to Fenchurch Street?" Mummery opened a rear door in the Fayshas' little Escort which was parked near the chapel. "Ben used to read poetry in a pub down there." He climbed in.

"The Princess of Wales." Josef Kiss followed. "A fine Queen Anne exterior somewhat spoiled by its orange and blue New Elizabethan inside."

Mummery shifted to accommodate Mr Kiss's bulk. "It's The Princess Diana now and they've redecorated to Hollywood Cockney. Ben loved it."

Settled on the other side of Mummery, Mary Gasalee stared through the car's window. "What's that boy doing? I've seen him before."

Thin, grey-faced, the boy glanced back at her. In his navy anorak and jeans he waited on the kerb beside the traffic lights until on the green signal he started across Harrow Road, heading into a maze of dusty, decrepit streets, the unrisen parts of West Kilburn.

"He looks innocent enough to me." Mr Kiss carefully studied her face.

"Is he the boy who stole your handbag?" Mummery tried to catch another glimpse. "Was he at the funeral?"

Mombazhi Faysha put his Escort into gear, reversing clear of the other cars outside the chapel. In her new hairdo Mrs Faysha turned to smile at Mary Gasalee. "I know who you are. But we weren't actually introduced, were we? I'm Alice." Twisting in her seat, she offered her hand.

"I've heard about you." Mary smiled, glad that Alice seemed all that Mr Faysha had said she was. "We've heard about one another, I expect."

"He likes you lot. You always cheer him up, he says."

By the time they headed east everyone had shaken hands. Leaning forward, Mary explained to Alice Faysha how "Hargreaves" was a member of their group. Everyone knew his real name but pretended not to. "But we weren't aware he was a friend of Ben's."

David Mummery took one last, long look at the tall trees of Kensal Rise. Above the oaks, close to the canal, there hovered what he knew must be a kestrel. Like the foxes and badgers they had discovered the city to be congenial, with easy pickings for a bold beast. He admired their instincts for survival. "Oh, damn!" he grasped Mombazhi Faysha's shoulder. "We've forgotten Hector. We can't leave him there. It wouldn't be fair."

"Do you want me to go back?" Mr Faysha was reluctant. "I'm not sure we can take anyone else."

Alice tapped the steering wheel. "Oh, he'll squeeze in with me. Come on, Momb, we'll fetch him. He's no bigger than you!"

They're coming in from Middlesex, from Surrey, Kent and Essex, from Hertfordshire and Berks. They're swanning in from the Shires. To steal the benefits of our life and all our work. From Bucks or Beds. We're surrounded by them. Bloodsucking sods. They've got the Law on their side. The fucking Government on their side. They've got economic history on their side. And they're not scared of anything any more. Most of the people who could have frightened them off are in exile, lost in the townships outside Beaconsfield, Wycombe and Chelmsford.

Waiting out of sight in the bus shelter, Joe Houghton saw them turn round for Hector. He had anticipated pursuit, not from angry relatives but from concerned acquaintances like Mummery and for the time being he wanted to avoid such company. He had fulfilled his obligation to Ben and now was exhausted. He had meant to go home and work on his portrait of Ben who had for the past two months been sitting for him but he realised he could not yet face the picture. He did not care that he had made a fool of himself at the graveside. In the time he had known Ben he had never found the courage to declare his love and the funeral had been his last chance.

Where Harrow Road met Ladbroke Grove Joe Houghton turned roughly south and when he had reached the grey iron canal bridge he knew he was still too distressed to go home at once so instead he descended the steps to the towpath where the Council had placed a new green bench beside the water. Once horses had dragged brightly decorated, evil-smelling barges all the way from the Midlands to the heart of London, their drivers as proud of their calling as they were of the foulness of their language; nobody could offer more disgusting or hideous insults than the great bargees. The flat boats had brought coal for the power stations, for the electricity, for the gas. By this route it was still possible to get to Oxford, perhaps even to Leeds or Lancaster. Behind him a neat grass bank dotted with early daisies and late daffodils sloped down from the new brick of the council flats, a fragment of that postwar dream he himself had once shared, of a landscaped urban paradise, of airy vistas and good housing, alive with light, where people lived in security and dignity. That dream's singular failure still astonished him. Was its failure simply the result of the positive relish with which the British embraced almost any compromise, no matter how unsuitable? He was reminded of the singing he had heard as he stood outside the chapel. Again there were tears on his face as he made up his mind to apologise to David Mummery for rushing away. He had not meant to offend or hurt. He glared along the canal at the peculiar mixture of unkempt industrial brick, of modern housing, of rotting terraces, of grass and concrete, of moss, rubbish and delicate saplings. "And did the Countenance Divine shine forth upon our clouded hills? And was Jerusalem builded here among these dark Satanic mills?"

That could be his final homage. He would give Ben French back to Blake. The finished painting, of which Ben was the central image, began to take shape in his mind. He promised he would not destroy this particular canvas. It would hang somewhere, even if he had to donate it to an institution. Perhaps, too, he would incorporate some of the words of his homage, in the style of Blake.

"Bring me my bow of burning gold! Bring me my arrows of desire! Bring me my spear! O clouds, unfold! Bring me my chariot of fire!"

He was on his feet again, enthusiastically striding towards Willesden. The painting would celebrate everything he loved or had hoped to achieve. It would offer to the world what the world had always refused him. It would be his act of redeeming generosity, of release. The painting would be the best he had ever done and completing it would free him once and for all of the petty, self-destructive creature he had become. He looked up into massing, brilliant cloud glowing with the sun's warmth. The poem he had written for Ben was bad; he knew he had no talent for poetry. But he did not care: for the first time in his life he had overcome his selfishness, his fear of disapproval, and as a result he understood, late as it was, what his work had lacked. From now on he would be vulgar as Blake had been vulgar. He would be brash. He would risk banality. That was what he owed to Ben; the only thing he owed to himself!

Kensal Rise Cemetery came again into view, this time on the far side of the canal, looking like a magical forest. On his left the great gasholders towered, a vast abandoned fortress, and in their shadow was a high yew hedge hiding what he supposed must be some municipal construction, perhaps a relay station. He strode over an elaborately baroque cast-iron footbridge above a narrow basin in which was moored a single old-fashioned wooden rowing-boat, heavily varnished. Having crossed the bridge he stopped to salute from his side of the water a love that never was, the departed vessel which had carried all his dreams.

Till we have built Jerusalem in England's green and pleasant land!

On the other side of the dense old hedge, Elizabeth Scaramanga, doubled by her arthritis, heard the man's voice dying away. Clearly he was a little unsure of the words and she was tempted to help him out, to join in the hymn, but prudent habit restrained her impulse and a little sadly she remained silent, having no desire to risk the modern world's attention.

Her lips formed a kiss as she made small juicy sounds, pushing her fingers deep into a basket of rich-smelling chicken-meal,

130

drawing out a fourth and final handful which she scattered expertly about her feet. For over forty years and at this time virtually every day she had made it a firm habit to feed her fancies.

PART THREE
THE UNHEARD VOICE

Roast and boiled beef have kept their ascendancy wherever English speaking people form communities, and it is significant of this fact that Keen's Mustard is as truly appreciated among our Australasian brethren as it is in England and in London City itself. It is, in fact, the natural piquant accompaniment to roast and boiled pork, beef, ham, and other meats, salads, and made dishes, to poultry and to some kinds of fish, and among gourmets, to *mutton*.

Let the depreciator of cold mutton try a slice or two with the piquant addition of some fine mustard deftly commingled with a dash of walnut or mushroom catsup, and he will no longer despise the cold roast shoulder or the succulent boiled neck, eaten with a discreetly chosen salad . . .

It is really affecting to stand here at the Wellington Statue in front of the Royal Exchange, to look across to the Mansion House at lunch-time, and listen to the suggestive chiming of that old tune in praise of the national dish. The changes that have taken place in the surrounding neighbourhood are vastly significant of the progress of a beef-eating people . . .

Gossip About London City, Keen, Robinson & Co, 1892

Waiting Rooms 1956

THE BRIGHT hospital frock's thin flowery folds clung like a half-shed chrysalis to Mary Gasalee's skin as she looked beyond the conservatory glass at the distant willows, cypresses and poplars, fancying them the heads of giants pushing up through the placid surfaces of lawns and ornamental waters. Within, the deep jungle warmth smelled almost salty; it was rich. It was primaeval. A single crow against the unclouded sky might have been a pterosaur planing towards some nest of amniotic mud. Things decayed swiftly here. Mary spread her fingers in the yellow rays. *These are the hands of Mary Gasalee.* Many nurses affected to admire her remaining treasure, her wedding-ring: silver wound with gold, the moon imprisoned by the sun. It had an ancient air attached to it. Mary Gasalee whistled but the words evaded her and very soon the tune too disappeared, back to wherever her other memories found sanctuary.

She sat in the peaceful company of four women, two of them amiably senile, one whose lobes had been cauterised in a factory accident and the fourth, like herself, an amnesiac, though Joyce's memory loss was considerably harder to explain and took a different form. Sometimes Joyce could recall at least eight completely different versions of her past, not one of which, according to her relatives, remotely resembled her real history. Determinedly schizophrenic, every time a personality was exorcised by Doctor Male and his team Joyce could assume a fresh one and again escape the doctors without having to leave her bed, let alone Bethlehem Mental.

Like Mary, they sat in old-fashioned wooden garden chairs arranged to provide a view past all the summer flowers of the green geometric gardens and pools, the strolling patients and their visitors. *Nobby blimey nobby blimey nobby blimey snot the gripes.* Currently Joyce's features were at rest; only when a personality was threatened did they twist and pinch and grow ugly. She had delicate pale skin, silvery hair, narrow bones, gaunt features, huge grey eyes. Normally she was happy, for normally there was a pleasant story running in her head. *Annabel blushed at Sir Rupert's forwardness, but she could not control the sensation of pleasure which suffused her entire being.* It astonished Mary Gasalee how, at that subtle moment between third person and first, these banal creatures could assume three dimensions.

Concentrated by the glass above, the sun grew hotter. Mary thought she might catch fire. She got up to shift her chair. Movement for movement, Rachel, the surgery case, imitated her, while Mrs Parsons and Mrs Tree, grey and venerable as spectres, chuckled out at a private world of their own desire. Mrs Parsons saw geese and pigs in a farmyard; Mrs Tree observed an aerodrome from which all kinds of planes, chiefly piloted by Edwardian celebrities, came and went. *Lillie Langtry climbs into the cockpit of her Gloster Gladiator. It's not difficult to guess where she's off to! And who's this in the Avro 642 taxiing up behind her? Oh, I should have guessed. It's Queen Alexandra, handsome as ever. Good afternoon, listeners, and welcome to Croydon. Those of you who have just joined us might like to know that Mr Max Beerbohm intends to try out his new Junkers J84 in about half-an-hour. He's wearing a rather elegant tan-coloured suit . . .* Rachel waited for Mary to reseat herself. Mary fanned her face with her hand. Rachel too began to fan.

"How hot it is. I think I'll take a turn around the grounds." When Rachel did what she was doing now it made Mary uncomfortable. Not wanting to hurt Rachel's feelings, but because the woman was never allowed unaccompanied out of the building, it was as graceful an escape as Mary could make. She left Rachel uncertainly standing and entered the cool gloom of the recreation room. "All right if I go?"

Sitting in the shadows reading *The Daily Graphic*, Nurse Coggs nodded without looking so Mary opened the side door into the garden. "Oi, no you don't, lovie," Nurse Coggs called to Rachel.

All the patients were treated as if they were pets, though some like
Mary, better trained than others, were allowed an extra degree of
freedom. The heat of the garden, almost as muggy and confining as
the room, made Mary gasp. But it was dry heat which really
disturbed her. The roses were beautiful in all their variety of scent
and colour; she felt drunk. Her sandalled feet touching gravel she
walked carefully out across the lawn, pausing beside a thoroughly
trimmed fir tree to wipe her handkerchief across her forehead. She
had never known a summer like it. Queen Mary, Joseph Lowe, Mrs
Cocker, Arthur B. Goodwin, Muriel Adamson, Madame Hardy,
William Lobb, Great Maiden's Blush . . . Pink and crimson and
yellow and white; old, sweet roses.

"Our friends the hybrid teas."

"How do I know them so well?" She saw over her shoulder the slow
bulk of a gentleman making its way towards her. "Have we met?"

"I am Josef Kiss." He extended a cupped hand. She stretched out
her own and it was lightly kissed. They were at once playful and
ironic. She might have sighed. He was handsome, a radiant
Buddah. "Mr Kiss? I'm Mary Gasalee."

"You rival these in beauty, Miss Gasalee."

"I am Mrs." Flattered, she gave the roses her best attention.

"A child bride? Dear me. I hope –"

"A child widow, Mr Kiss." Smiling she stooped to sniff at the
Captain F.S. Harvey-Cant, at its rich, pink heart. "I was brought
here long before I woke up. To the Special Wing."

"What? You were asleep?" His fair hair was soft, his skin dark
cream. His eyes were enormously blue.

"Yes, since 1941. I was seventeen. Now, of course, I'm over
thirty. But I don't feel thirty."

"You look fifteen." He spoke rapidly, almost to dismiss this
observation, then quickly recovered himself. "Half your age, I
suppose. Mummery's age. Well, indeed! So you're The Sleeping
Beauty. You've become a legend here. How were you revived?
And why aren't you free?"

"I simply woke up. I can go when all the tests are complete.
When they're satisfied."

"Can they be?"

"When they're sure I'll look after myself properly. I have to
prove it."

"Ah, yes."

"You?"

"I must prove I will not try to disrupt public meetings, make a fuss in restaurants, upset small applecarts, inconvenience a stock-broker or embarrass my sister. I am not mad, merely unduly irascible. Well." He paused, drawing his loud paisley dressing-gown about him. "Well, I have friends in high places, you know."

"In the government, you mean?"

"Soon." He was thoughtful. "Pretty soon, I'm sure. But not exactly friends. Meanwhile Doctor Male is my brother-in-law. I could put in a word."

"Oh, there isn't a rush. Not after fourteen years. What do we know, after all?"

"I apologise." He bowed. "This is my weakness. You must remind me of it. You must forgive me."

"It's not weakness, Mr Kiss, to be kind."

"They tell me it is. And I believe that it is."

She thought him close to tears. He turned to sniff with a kind of voluptuous savagery some scarlet fuchsias. He was the first man she had met who possessed a power equal to her own. She did not want to startle him into leaving. "I think I would appreciate your advice."

"Mary Gasalee, you have had only the most specific and intense experience. Perhaps there's no harm in that. But it is not what they call 'worldly'. Make no mistake, here we meet in Paradise. Here evil is easily defined and contained. We are protected."

"But not free."

"You recall freedom, do you? What? Before the Blitz?"

"I married young."

"When the world hadn't changed. It would be hard to see you damaged."

"I have been hurt, Mr Kiss. They tell me I had a baby I have not seen, nor had any part in its raising, nor – " she motioned helplessly. "I was bombed. By fire. It all fell in. We were down in it. My husband – it's last week for me – was killed. And passion. I know that. I had a baby."

"You must think me horribly presumptuous. I did not say you were a stranger to experience. I suggested you were not worldly." He straightened his huge solid body. "Do you know a boy here, by the name of Mummery? I was seeking him out. He's borrowing my *Magnets* and *Gems*."

"Oh, I know. Billy Bunter and Co!"

"They, too, were the War's victims. He's reading my old copies. From my own childhood. I let him have one of each a week. It takes his mind off cowboys. He follows the serials of twenty years ago with the same freshness and relish as I followed them. It provides us with something in common. But I am due a *Magnet* back."

"He's a child. In this place?"

"Fifteen and highly strung. They're observing him. Tests. Like your own, I suppose. For the holidays. He leaves school this year and then they have even less control. They've told his mother they're trying to save him. Is that kind?"

"I don't know."

"You have no sarcasm. I'm sorry. You're new-born after all, eh? Into this wonderful summer. The best since 1939."

"That was very lovely. I borrowed a bike. We went to Hever. Not all the way by bike. We took the train, too. Yes, you're right. That was a good summer. I have depths, Mr Kiss, and my own peculiar intervening memories."

"You think me condescending? Perhaps I am." He advanced and she fell in beside him. They rounded a hedge. There on the lawn near a fountain whose copper mermaids drooled thin streams of brownish water into a lily-filled pond, eating an apple and lying on his stomach, his bare legs waving, the laces of his plimsolls untied, his shorts khaki, his shirt pale blue with rolled-up sleeves, his hair mousy, clipped back and sides, his skin pink and growing pinker in the sun, was a boy, reading, absorbed, apparently more than content. "Vernon Smythe was at The Green Man, gambling and smoking," Josef Kiss told her, "and now I believe he's being blackmailed."

"I always liked him."

"I think we were meant to. He had more of the author's character than most of the boys. Mummery! Here's someone else who knows the difference between Tom Merry and Harry Wharton."

The boy moved his head reluctantly, revealing hazel eyes, glazed by his imagination, browner skin on his face, a long nose, cupid's lips. Mary Gasalee wondered what was happening to her. Perhaps it had nothing to do with the men. But she had not experienced such sensations since long before Helen was born, with Pat, and then nothing as intense. *Oh, God, it's delicious, but it's so weakening. It can't be right.*

"Enjoy it?"

The feeling that they must be parts of a single personality joining together for the first time had nothing to do with her previous sense of loss: fifteen years, her husband, her child, much of her youth. This was a feeling of resolution; it offered her satisfaction. It made her happy.

"Only half a page to go. But yes, it's good. The best so far."

"I think so. It was one of my very favourites. Do you know Mary Gasalee? She's here, too, with us."

The boy was trained to politeness. She could see he wanted to finish his story but felt obliged to rise. She patted in his direction and towards the ground. "No, no, no. Read on. Don't spoil it. We'll still be here in an hour, I think."

They were close to a wall, red and pitted, veined by vines, rising to terra-cotta tiles at the top and then the tall wire. There was traffic on the other side. This had been a country mansion. Now it was surrounded by major roads and was closer to London's centre than to any real field, for the Angel had expanded about it a hundred years ago and Islington lay on every side. From the top of the house, a fairy-tale tower, circular and roofed by fancy slate, rising to a point on which stood a vane's remains, there came the sound of rehearsing violins and cellos for next week's concert. Meanwhile, below this, six or seven elderly men played a querulous game of cricket, waddling back and forth, striking at invisible balls, banging on the wicket.

"This simplifies." Josef Kiss led her on. "It's not so different, Mary. 'Mary's' all right, is it?"

"As rain." She recalled she had been a quick-tongued girl, rarely at a loss. "No objection. But you're Mr Kiss to me. At least for now. You don't mind?"

"Of course not."

She felt more comfortable, though the pleasant hunger of desire was still within her. She paused to breathe in the speedwell, the candytuft, the Swan River daisies, for they had arrived at the borders of an Old English Garden.

"There's a garden very much like this, but smaller, in Kensington. A roof-garden." Mr Kiss was clearly taking equal pleasure in her sensations. His hand was warm beside her arm. "You know it?"

"I was never over that way." More scents, so strong.

"When we're both at large we'll go there."

"I'd love to see Kensington. We meant to get to the museums, you know. But when we had the chance, we wanted the country. Castles, too. Arundel's nice. Leeds, was it?"

"Your people are from Kent are they?"

"No, not at all. I never knew this before, not in any detail, but one of the psychologists tried to get me to remember by doing a sort of family tree. Do you believe in blood, Mr Kiss?"

"What? Loyalties?"

"Sort of inherited personalities."

"I'm not sure. Why? Do your ancestors worry you?"

"I only have one set. My father's a mystery, perhaps American or Irish. And Gasalee, of course, is a false trail. It was my husband's name. His people were from Suffolk. I looked the name up. There's a Gazely in Suffolk and some people called Gayslee were slavers, pirates and smugglers out of the East Anglian ports. Very well-to-do in the end. Pat said his grandad had owned ships. Some went into industry and moved to Peterborough. Well, that goes no-where, of course. We were all Felgates, much more common. It just means field-gate, doesn't it. A road leading into a field! A gate into a field!" She laughed. "What's that? Nothing. Now Kiss on the other hand is really unusual." It was as if she had never relaxed before, never really talked before. She wondered why in his presence she felt so valuable. "It's exotic," she said slowly, with relish.

"People think it's Polish or Jewish, but it's as old an English name as any. Kissers were cordwainers, they worked leather. And Kiss comes from that. All the way back to Domesday, as unremarkably ancient as your own."

"Oh. I'd hoped."

"They were gypsies on my mother's side."

"They said my father was a tinker."

"There you are, then. We have our second sight from the travelling people." He touched her lightly on the shoulder to show he spoke in play. They had reached another wall. The grounds had seemed huge at first but now contracted with every extra day she spent here. They still heard the violins, the cricketers, but a bee buzzing on its way to a clump of iris seemed much louder. They sat down carefully on the lawn. The sweet smell of the cut grass was delicious. Overhead the sun continued to throb and the steel-blue sky shimmered. She stretched her neck backward, as if to be kissed.

"I shall be sorry when my time's due," he said, speaking to break a mood which she now knew they shared. "But I'll leave my address and so forth. You'll look me up? It would be good to have a friend from here. Normally, there are none. This time, there are two, with luck."

"You come regularly to Bethlehem?"

"Yes. Yes." He was so amused he began to shake. "Isn't it Josef's destiny? And Mary's?"

At this blasphemy she shot up. "Oh, no. You shouldn't. Oh, please."

"I'm sorry. I had no idea. So few English people . . . "

She frowned. "It's religion, isn't it? It's not in there. The memory, I mean. But Patrick took it seriously, I'd guess." She found her mouth was dry. "I'm so sorry. I know it was only meant as a joke. You haven't offended me." She became anxious again in case he should go. She tried to be funny. "But where's the holy baby?"

"No, no, no." He raised both hands. "There's no need. I'm extremely sorry."

"It might have done some good. We never went to church much. My granny. God-fearing, but not religious." Mary forced her body back against the lawn. She cleared her throat. "Afraid of God, I mean. A very primitive religion. But I read a lot, you see, when I was growing up. And I found an interest in Christianity. It seemed worthwhile. The idea." Slowly she put her head at an unusual angle.

"You're a reader, of course. What have you read lately?" he showed real interest. "What did you read before?"

"I began to read a lot of non-fiction when I first came awake. And magazines. Things to bring me up to date. It's funny you know being like Rip Van Winkle. But that wore off. Not a lot had changed, really, since the War started. Not for ordinary people. The names in the newspapers were a bit different. But it was all just as patriotic and I can't easily get on with that. My background. That's funny, isn't it? I'm not worried about missing the coronation and so on, though I was sorry poor King George died before he was sixty. I think he meant well. My grandma was interested in all that. My grandpa when he was alive was a solid republican. He hated them. Well, I'd read fiction mostly, before I mean. Silly stuff like Baroness Orczy and *Sexton Blake* and P.G. Wodehouse. I hated children's books, but I liked the serial stories. I suppose I had no taste. I went back to them but I got bored. These days I like Jane Austen. She's clever and she cheers me up. The Brontës seem to be forever gasping and shouting and shoving at you. And people get punished too much." She turned her open face towards him, smiling again, forgetful of her shock. "I've read dozens of the Macmillan Illustrated Classics in the library here. Have you ever read *Jacob Faithful*? Captain Marryat's really enjoyable. So's Mrs Gaskell. Fenimore Cooper. Thomas Love Peacock. It's the most wonderful mixture. And all with lovely pictures. George Eliot, Maria Edgeworth, George Borrow. I suppose you think it's a retreat?"

"From what, dear?"

"This."

"What is there to confront? Surely Mrs Craik must always be superior to Nurse Coggs."

"You know Nurse Coggs?"

"She ruled the men before she was transferred to Women."

"She's nice enough. The doctors treat us with a sort of cautious jocularity, and that's far more demoralising than her Head Girl manner."

"I think we're here to be demoralised." Josef Kiss blew out his cheeks. "I've never been entirely clear why they like to demean us so. You'd probably have to be one of them to understand. Something to do with power. What I want is also to do with power. Do you desire power, Mary?"

"If it preserves my privacy, Mr Kiss. I'm not sure I can follow you. Power? Sometimes I think I can read minds. But that's a common delusion in here."

"Very common. Is yours a delusion?"

"Oh, probably. Perhaps you could tell me."

He ran the palm of his hand over the shorn tips of grass. "Unfortunately *they* tell us. Maybe the language is the problem. They try to change us simply by altering the descriptions but I don't believe they know what they're describing. Do you know, Mary?"

"I'm not very analytical. You evidently like to get to the bottom of things." Warm beneath her flesh, the earth seemed to move sinuously but did not threaten her. She loved it. She would keep talking, displaying whatever interest was necessary to make him stay with her. Then came a picture of herself as a silly adult behaving like a child. She looked hard at him. His expression was mild, dreamy almost. Her embarrassment diminished when she realised he was merely considering her statement. He was listening to her and this alone was unfamiliar, almost frightening.

"Not altogether." He rolled onto his belly at eye level with some marigolds which blazed as if burnished. "My wife, who is now in Amsterdam, thought me incapable of getting to a problem's roots. Perhaps because I was successful in her case she believes I impose a kind of alternative reality on the world. Perhaps my reality was stronger than hers. Anyway, I am accused of that, among many other crimes."

"A criminal?" A speckled butterfly, perhaps a Silverwash, approached the daisies.

"I think she'd have it so. I don't know."

"Did she leave you?" Mary's tone was neutral.

"Went with our children. For a Dutch bobby."

"How awful." She widened her eyes.

"So you can see I might ask myself, 'Was she right?'"

"You've a strong personality, but it's gentle, too. And you don't attack."

He shook his head. "I don't attack you, Mary. But I am not everyone's friend."

"So what's your line?" The show on television had fascinated her. Every Sunday she prayed nobody would make a disturbance while it was on. Although some doctors thought TV bad for patients, the nurses were its champions. She enjoyed quoting slogans from it. It made her feel a little more up-to-date and part of society at large.

"Actually, I once did read minds for a living until it proved too dangerous. I've worked the halls in most capacities and fairs, circuses, private functions. For a while I was a professional toastmaster and after-dinner speaker. I'm an all-round theatrical, you see. Objecting to the touring and my lack of any real success,

146

my wife wanted me to return to my original trade, the mind-reading, because I had been so good at it. But that was how I first joined the lunatic ranks, Mary. I was raving. I was frothing. I have never been so bad since. But once you're defined in this world it is usually for good, so it's easy for me to take a break in the bin from time to time. Within reason I can even choose which bin!" He spoke lightly but without irony. "I'm an old hand. I have been in asylums since 1940. Since the beginning of the War. So we have that in common, you could say. Not a real comparison, I'll grant."

"I love . . ." Mary sat up straight, brushing loose cuttings from her back. It stuck everywhere. She was like a creature made of grass. It was all over her legs and arms. Yet it stopped the sun from burning her. "Well, Mr Kiss. If I'm to remain on Nurse Coggs's good side . . ."

"You will have to keep a rein on yourself out there." He gestured towards the wall, supporting his bulk on his other hand as he also righted himself. "But in here, not so much. Are you planning to practise for later?"

"I know what you mean," she said carefully. "And I suppose I am practising. You think I should not?"

"Ah, well. My own motives are in doubt."

"I'll meet you this evening – no, I'll meet you at the same time, same place, tomorrow. Yes?"

He was up, shadowing her whole body with his own. He held out his massive, sensitive hand, his eyes a deeper colour, his smile hardly visible. "Yes, Mary. It will give shape to my next twenty-four hours."

"Now I must run." It was not a phrase she usually employed. It was from the wireless. But that was true of much of her language that was not from books. He did not seem to mind. Or perhaps he was used to people who talked like her. Until now, in the real world at least, she had known only working-class people. Her other chief experience had come from films. She had liked Charles Boyer. She thought David Mummery looked like a young Charles Boyer. She supposed most of the stars had changed. The television mentioned names completely new to her. As if to demonstrate her truthfulness she began to run back towards the house.

Josef Kiss was less disturbed by but equally attracted to Mary Gasalee. *Remarkable girl, entirely self-educated, and the strangest accent,*

147

impossible to define. I suppose she learned how to talk again. Was she like a baby? Male will tell me. She's no child now. Her own must be fifteen or so. Around Mummery's age, I suppose. Male was fascinated. I should have listened better. Her skin is . . . It vibrates. It warms you. She glows. Oh, I don't know. I don't know. What else separates us but years? Too much, perhaps. The stimulus is extraordinary! But would it be fair? There was a tiny pain in the middle of his forehead. He scratched the spot. He brought his feet about to point again towards the distant wall. David Mummery must surely have finished the serial and want to discuss it.

Miss Pauline Gower, who has carried over 20,000 passengers since 1930, when she first received her 'B' Licence, flies in partnership with her friend Miss Dorothy Spicer, niece of the well-known socialite, Mrs Tree. Tonight they are bringing the distinguished Russian general, Alexei Nicolaevitch Kouropatkin, Commander-in-Chief of the Northern Armies, from Paris to Croydon, flying the new Dewoitine D-332 Air Liner presently on loan from Air France . . .

Mary Gasalee saw that the darkened recreation room was deserted. Through a gap in one blind a shaft of sunlight fell on the smooth, grey surface of the ping-pong table and silence suggested recent activity, perhaps some patient "throwing a fit", as Nurse Coggs usually put it. The atmosphere was often like this after a patient had been sedated and taken away, as if the others shrank back into themselves, afraid of attracting the same treatment.

Glad not to be observed, she sought the semi-darkness and settled in a cane chair facing the glare of the conservatory. The four silhouetted figures remained where she had left them. Rachel was gently rocking herself, as she usually did when she had nobody to imitate, and one of the senile patients was clearly sleeping. Sensing Mary's presence Joyce turned her head but could not see into the shadows. *My thighs were first blistered then calloused and scarred by that saddle, yet I came to love the country and the simple Winnahoo people, believing myself part of them just as they found it impossible to distinguish between their land and their own personalities. This is a common feature amongst the Indians of both North and South America.* Surreptitiously Mary pulled pieces of grass from her legs and arms, thinking of Josef Kiss and trembling, thinking of David Mummery and becoming delighted by her own wickedness. Was it right to seduce a boy? He was lovely. She shook her head, feeling she might be demonically possessed yet she experienced only lust for David and Mr Kiss. Meeting them on the same day was a coincidence. Nonetheless she was not entirely convinced she was sane. She recalled the nurses talking about "shipboard romances" and their stories of daring expeditions into other wards, secret meetings, elopements. Perhaps it was an inevitable fixation unless you were like Rachel, or were senile. She had overheard Doctor Male talking about the symptoms of Huntingdon's Disease, one of which was enormously increased sexual energy coupled, he had said, with an equivalent reduction in the super-ego. In other words, she assumed from her own reading, a man or woman might be turned into a kind of De Sadean Beast from the Libido. Amused and unconvinced by these reservations she was sure that what she experienced was nothing more nor less than wholesome lust and she knew it was shared by Mr Kiss at least. The problem was not why she desired both man and boy but how she should fulfil that desire. She felt increasingly that she had been cheated of almost fourteen years of real life for which she had to make up, and this meant that at times she was inclined to follow every impulse and risk any emotional danger to anyone to discover what might have been taken from her, but her common sense let her know this was fantasy, unfounded in any reasonable logic, and she must accept merely as bad luck being knocked senseless in the air-raid and as good luck her survival. There must be many like her and many more killed outright. She drew a deep, trembling breath.

"What's the matter with us?" As Nurse Coggs opened the wired-glass double doors from the main hall behind her rose the small routine metallic sounds of a psychiatric hospital, the smell of disinfectant, medicines and urine, the little cries and muffled shouts, the queer laughter. "Sitting in the dark. The sun too much for us? We don't want to get heatstroke, Mary. You and I are the only ones here who aren't barmy, and I'm not so sure about me." Such observations were standard from the nurses, some of whom believed mental instability to be catching like a virus from overexposure to the patients. "What is it? Just wanting some peace and quiet?" She sat down in her chair, pushing her black nylon legs out in front of her, picking up her newspaper, sighing. She scratched absently and generally about her bulky person. She bore the smell of a recent cigarette.

"Did something happen while I was out?" Mary spoke casually, not wanting to be disturbed, knowing if she was careful Nurse Coggs would give her no trouble.

Nurse Coggs grunted. "It's funny how you can always guess what's been going on, Mary. We had a visit from Eleanor. She'd just woken up and decided Napoleon had landed at Dover. Maybe it was a Zeppelin attack on Westminster Abbey. The usual stuff. We got her back to bed. She'll be all right. But you can never tell with Old Nonny. One day she'll be cracking jokes, putting you in stitches, just as normal as anyone, and next day it'll be like this. I don't know. All the same old boring rubbish you hear from half the boring people in here. Oh, dear!" To express exasperation Nurse Coggs shifted noisily in the wicker chair. "Was it nice in the garden?"

"Still very hot."

"I'll be glad of my weekend. I'm going down to the coast with my husband. His brother lives near Brighton, at Seaford. I love the pier. Did you like the seaside, Mary?"

"I've never been. Just to the country, to Kent and places. Some kids went to the sea but we couldn't afford it at the time. When the money got better I had a bike. We went to Arundel once, on the train. That's only a mile or two from the sea, isn't it? If someone asked if I lived on an island I wouldn't be able to tell them. Not from my direct experience." And she smiled.

"Oh." Nurse Coggs was back in *The Daily Graphic*.

"I think I'll go to the library." Mary got up. She was asking permission.

"You don't half get through a lot of books." Nurse Coggs raised frowning eyes in consent. "Do you really read them all?"

"It doesn't take long with time on your hands."

Entering the cool hall she crossed unlit marble, for the shades were drawn at the front windows and the great dark door was bolted. She greeted with a wave Noreen Smith from the office and another nurse whose name she did not know and reached the hall, climbing wide stone steps to the next floor. Everything here was stone and hardwoods. Incongruous modern floral pictures ranged the walls while both plaster and timbers were nicked, chipped and poorly repaired. In one of her less original roles Joyce had recreated herself as a Southern Belle inhabiting the shell of some vandalised antebellum mansion; this staircase was perfect for a hooped skirt. Turning the carved oak door's handle, Mary went into the library to be greeted by Margaret Hezeltine, lengthy and angular, a professional librarian who was a sort of trusty in spite of her inclination to tear up books of which she disapproved. "Ah, Mary! My favourite customer!" She treated her as she had once treated favourite girls at the school where she had worked until, mysteriously, she had been dismissed, then imprisoned, then eventually sent to Bethlehem Central. "What's it to be today? Jane Austen? But you must have read every one. And you didn't like Ann Radcliffe. I can't say I disagree. So . . . ."

"I'll just have a search through the Macmillan set again." Mary felt obscurely self-conscious.

"Scott?"

"Not Scott. But I might have another crack at Disraeli." In Margaret's company she found herself lapsing into the language of *Girls' Crystal*. "He defeated me with *Sybil*." She wondered at her own potential for mimicry. She could imitate almost anyone now, even Doctor Male, and although this ability made life in some ways easier it also frightened her. Someone less certain of themselves might have had identity problems.

The rows of books, arranged so that all aisles could be observed from the central desk, so that nothing could be done under cover, stretched towards the windows, surrounding the walls. The sun was excluded by green, unpleasant blinds. There was a smell of polish and dust and old paper. Margaret not only arranged her charges with detailed precision, she also cleaned them regularly. Spines were rubbed up, jackets were wiped free of any stain. Sometimes Mary came across tiny repairs to pages and careful straightening of dog-eared corners.

A third inhabitant of the room, the little old man they called Ernest the Policeman because of his country accent and claims to be a Chief Inspector with the CID, read only detective stories or what he called "True Life Crime" books. His small, gnomish features, his shifty, morbid eye, stared suddenly at her with baleful accusation. When he had first been sent to Bethlehem Central he had tried to arrest everyone, including the Head Doctor; now he contented himself with solving cases he heard on the wireless. He returned, with a small, secretive motion of his shoulders, to the

Agatha Christies, all of which he had read a dozen times, then he pulled out a book at random and shuffled to the desk where his mystery was stamped in unapproving silence by Miss Hezeltine who watched him disgustedly until he left, then returned to some busy, invisible activity below the level of the counter.

The rows of Macmillan Classics had been donated by Mrs H.E. Standlake, and Mary liked them largely because they did not attract many other readers. They were ranked in their own shelves at the end of the Fiction section; at least half had never been read until she found them. Pages were uncut, smelling of the day they were printed. She enjoyed the apparent anonymity they shared, each with a dull red spine stamped in faded gold, subtly embossed with a simple floral motif, frequently illustrated by the same person. She knew the names and styles of the illustrators as well as she knew the authors. Fred C. Pegram, H.R. Millar, C.R. Brock, H.M. Brock, Chris. Hammond, Hugh Thompson, F.H. Townsend, J. Ayton Symington and more. She recognised several of them from her girlhood, from the *Windsor Magazine* and other old bound volumes which often had been her only available reading, given to her by dealers in Farringdon Road because they were unsaleable. Farringdon Road was round the corner from where she had grown up. On certain days the long row of bookstalls had seemed to stretch all the way to Ludgate Circus, where she was forbidden to venture, past Barts and Smithfield, the old London names known to everyone, and under the Viaduct. On summer afternoons, during the school holidays, she went frequently to the book market and was soon known to the stall-holders, most of whom enthusiastically recommended their own favourite authors, who refused to sell but gave her the cheap editions, the battered old volumes, the paper-covered, double columned classics she attempted to buy. And above on the Viaduct the ladies in their stone robes, representing all the Victorian virtues of commerce and learning, seemed to regard her with benign approval. Even after she had left school and got her job in Holborn at Gamage's, less than two minutes from the Viaduct, she continued to visit Farringdon Road in her lunch break. Her grandmother, fascinated by her love of reading, had made only a token complaint or two. Her grandfather, growing so abstracted, had told her that education would be the salvation of the working class and begged her to give up novels in favour of more improving works like *The Martyrdom of Man* and *The Outline of History*.

From one of the shelves close to the top she plucked down *Sybil*. Even Fred Pegram's illustrations had not been at their most inspired. She pretended to be looking at the pictures but was simply enjoying the privacy and silence of her sanctuary. Eventually she took the novel up to Margaret Hezeltine. "If at first you don't succeed!" she said brightly.

"That's the spirit. Good girl." Miss Hezeltine put a neat imprint on the label. "See you tomorrow, perhaps."

"Or the day after." Mary hefted the book.

As she walked out to the landing a hearty shout greeted her from above. "There you are!" Doctor Male, swarthy, weedy, with untidy black hair and dark eyes, wearing his pinstripe suit, his tie badly knotted, a dissolute marmoset, came down the stairs. "Mary! Mary! Mary! We've been looking everywhere for you. We should have known you'd be in the library."

She grew mildly alarmed, wondering if they had noticed something strange in her behaviour. Was she going to be isolated? Did they intend to thwart her seduction plans even before they were properly formed?

"Oh, there's nothing wrong." He arrived beside her, scarcely any taller than she. "They want you up in the interview room. They've put you forward. You're going to be reviewed." He produced a testy grin. "Would you mind going up? Up." He pointed. "I'll be there. It's all right."

There was still time she decided to make love to both, though Josef Kiss must be the first. *Awakened by a Kiss. Yet the boy would be safest for me, but not safest otherwise. Too young. Even Patrick had to find out things from my grandad.* She pressed *Sybil* against her stomach as she climbed a further flight. The door of the anteroom was open, revealing some tidy polished oak, chairs and tables. On this side of the house there was no direct sun. She stood looking into the antiseptic emptiness of the room. *I was always a bit plump but he said he liked me better like that so there never seemed any point in changing or trying to change. It was lovely, then. We were all pretty happy – very happy, looking back. That was before the War and the Fire. I used to cook him a bit of smoked haddock for his Friday tea. And we always went to the pictures of a Saturday.* She knew the role that would satisfy them but they had given her no time to rehearse.

Josef Kiss strode naked through her mind. She began to tremble, leaning against the door frame.

"Go! Go! Go! There's nothing to worry about, Mary! Go! Look, you silly girl, you've dropped your book. Go! You've got the best chance of any of us of getting out of here! Go in! Go. Just be yourself, Mary." Doctor Male came up, jocular and urgent, wanting to get home. He stooped. He handed her the fallen *Sybil*. "You're okay, aren't you?"

"Okay," she said. And pulling at hair sticking to her face she made her way in, inhaling the beeswax smell, seeing no dust at all on any surface, staring at the doors which must open and through which she must soon progress, to be reviewed. *I suppose it must have been the shock of Pat's getting killed like that made me lose my memory. The queer thing is, I don't seem to have any ill-effects. I feel perfectly able to take up where I left off, though of course the baby's grown and everything. I can get a job easily. Your belly glows like brass what a gentle beast you are and your cock is soft gold never hurting. I have dreamed this. I have dreamed of you both.*

"Go, Mary, Go!"

With a perfectly ordinary smile, she did as he commanded.

Gypsy Gardens 1954

I'M HAVING trouble with this, wrote David Mummery in his report when he still wanted to trust Doctor Male. The most crucial year of my life? I suppose it was 1954, when I realised my mother was mad and I became anxious about our family history. There is nothing wrong with me, as I'm sure I mentioned at the time. My first memory is of bombs, of searchlights, silhouetted planes, monstrous explosions. My Uncle Reg recalls coming into the bedroom of our house in Mitcham and seeing my mother holding me up to the window. Together we watched the Blitz.

My Uncle Reg knew more family history than anyone else was prepared to reveal. Reg Mummery was my father's brother. He raced and worked on bikes with him in the early days. He had lived next door to us at the time. My mother kept in touch with his wife. I saw him more frequently than I ever saw my father.

My father was Vic Mummery, the Speedway King. He worked for a munitions firm I think, over in Croydon. Even before he left I hardly ever saw him. My mother alone sometimes took me on trips to the country and the seaside; a kind of semi-evacuation, I suppose. My mother was highly-strung, changeable to some degree, but she appears to have attempted consistency while I was growing up. True, she had a dramatic way of displaying her unhappiness. I remember her standing at the top of the stairs shortly after my father had gone, swaying there, then falling and sliding face-forward towards me. Had I called her? Perhaps. Was it my fault, her fall? She did not seem badly hurt.

Another time, when we had moved to a different house, she did exactly the same thing. Then, because I was older, I went to find some *sal volatile*. I pulled out the stopper and bent over her to put the smelling-salts bottle under her nose. The ammonia dripped out, ran down her upper lip and into her mouth. She was up immediately, swearing at me, accusing me of deliberately trying to poison her.

By now, of course, I suspected that her fainting spells were engineered, but my mother's considerable melodramatic talent never disgusted me. I admired her for it. When she could no longer move me emotionally I came to be impressed by her manipulative skill, by her shades and tones. It would be hard for anyone to try to blackmail me through guilt or shame. I learned resistance at the feet of a great mistress. I came to regard her "turns" as legitimate contests between us. I would never desert her, or indeed, feel anything but continuing sympathy, but I would not allow her to succeed in her object, whatever it was, by these means. It might only be a wish for me to accompany her on holiday or simply to go out to the pictures. When she asked me anything directly she received a fair and considered answer. In other words I attempted to teach my mother to behave more reasonably, but I was never very successful. By the age of fourteen it had dawned on me that my mother did not want me as a son or indeed a husband. She wanted me to fill the role vacated by my grandfather! As soon as I realised this, I began to understand not only how I should deal with her but what she was asking of me. In refusing her, I no longer resisted blindly. I held back specific kinds of attention which I did not think a young boy should be expected to give his mother.

None of this explains my insanity, my ability since childhood to hear and see what was inaudible and invisible to others, my periodic bouts of dementia, my paranoia. My relations with women are, I am told, fairly normal. My relationships have been about as long as those of most of my friends. I am only difficult to live with when I don't keep a check on my brain but this is not a sign of deep psychological wounding. My mother and I were close. We had survived the War together.

I must admit I have a fondness for ruins. I loved the bombsites the way most kids did, because they offered freedom and adventure. We liked nothing better than a bombed house, particularly if it was still roughly intact. We learned to walk from beam to beam, from joist to joist, avoiding the treacherous boards and plaster; we learned to test walls; we learned what to push to destruction, to make the rest of a house more or less safe. We could tell which roofs were likely to fall on us, which would hold, as we ascended swaying staircases into airy space, heading for attics no adult dared attain and discovering storehouses of weatherbeaten treasures. We once pushed a piano from a top storey all the way to the bottom of the brick-strewn garden, crushing hollyhocks and roses and raising a huge cloud of dust which gave us away so that we had to climb carefully back to the ground and run for it.

Cellars sometimes frightened us. We expected to find bodies there amongst the stinking mattresses and rotting wood of makeshift shelters. Usually there was water in them and they would reek of ancient excrement, urine and stagnation. We put matches to pipes to discover if they contained gas; we drank from dripping taps whose water had never been turned off. We dragged bath-tubs across the Common and launched them on ponds, trying to reach the islands and always sinking before we had gone more than a few yards. Our days of childhood were golden; our parents were still relieved that the bombing was over and had not learned the nervousness of the secure and well-to-do.

Nobody worried about the Bomb, for we had escaped the bombing. As children we thought nothing of making guns from steel tubing and packing them with gunpowder to attack our favourite targets. Those guns could put a ball-bearing through a corrugated-iron fence as a matter of course. We had rocket launchers, grenades made from pieces of pipe packed with gunpowder and lit with Jetex fuses from our model aeroplanes. We made Molotov cocktails from our parents' precious paraffin. And we made flamethrowers with bicycle pumps filled with petrol and lit at the moment you pushed the handle in, producing a fiery stream which burned for a few seconds before it went out. You could dip your hands in it and light them, impressing anyone who didn't know the trick: it was the fumes which burned, not the skin. I learned to eat fire by this means, but the only time I tried to chew razorblades I cut my mouth and tongue severely. I'm still not sure if it was possible to do or whether the man who displayed the knack was actually deceiving me. We knew it was bad to eat glass, for people died of that.

We shot at one another with Sten guns whose breeches had been blocked but which were otherwise identical to those used by the British Army. We played with abandon amongst those ruins, under the summer skies, and I believe we played with more pleasure than any child knows these days, for all their video games and elaborate toys. We wandered an enormous territory, widening it as we grew older by means of the battered second-hand cycles given us by relatives.

School was for me a prison in which people who had not earned the right exercised their authority over me. By the age of ten I had been tortured at two council schools, a public school and a private school. Only the nature of the pain altered. I was always bullied. I had taught myself to read by the time I was four. I read all the textbooks and became bored within a week of any new term. The principal of the public school told my mother he didn't think we were compatible, though there had been aspects of the place I had actually enjoyed: the surrounding woods, the farm with its pigsties, the old Tudor house itself, which was full of secret passages easily discovered. We used the passages to raid the larders at night, to get into the grounds without being seen. I wriggled through them three times, attempting to abscond, became lost soon after escaping and was caught by local people. I was very fond of the uniform and I continued to wear the green corduroy knickerbockers and brown jerseys long after I left.

Before I was returned to my mother most of my fellow students were convinced I had been raised by wolves in the Indian jungle. Kipling was not, at that point in Coopers Hall's political history, considered progressive so my plagiarism went undetected, though some had grown sceptical when I climbed a big oak near the art rooms and had to be helped down by my housemaster, while the catcalls of my enemies, led by Tommy Mee, demanded that I demonstrate my forest skills. Soon afterwards I caught mumps and in the infirmary experienced my first vision of Christ, a conventional head and shoulders, with a blue robe, blond hair, a fair beard, pale skin and blue eyes. He smiled at me, his fingers held in an attitude of benediction. By the time I reached home I had also seen Sir Francis Drake, King George the Sixth, not yet dead, Sir Henry Morgan the pirate, and a whole miscellany of less distinguished ghosts. After my initial excitement and knowing the school had punished me before for what it called my imagination I decided not to let anyone there know about these visitations. Eventually I entrusted my friend Ben French with my secret. Ben came from the council estate a few streets away. His mother worked as a cleaner at a nearby school; his father, they said, had been a well-bred American who had served with the RAF even before the War began.

When I recovered from the mumps the summer holidays had not yet started. While mother was at work and Ben was at school I cycled down to Mitcham Common, past the rebuilt parade of shops, the Circulating Library, the Funeral Parlour and the Dairy, to an area known as the Rocky, to the stables, to visit my gypsy friends. Ma Lee and her stocky daughters Marie and Phebe were welcoming as usual, but the boys had come to regard me as a bit of an interloper, now too posh and too effete. We had been inseparable in the early days of peacetime but now they prowled about the yards shouting at the horses, throwing stones at walls, kicking at tufts of grass in obvious resentment while I sat in the parlour drinking tea and telling the ladies what school had been like and what the ghosts had seemed to be saying. All three wore big gold earrings and Ma Lee had gold teeth. Their heavy jaws overshot their mouths; their olive skins were coarse under dark curly hair and boys and girls looked pretty much alike in old jumpers, moleskin trousers, wellington boots. My first girlfriend was a gypsy. Marie and I slept together, though she was two or three years older than me, and in the morning she got out of bed and fainted. Nothing had taken place between us as far as I knew. She had been minding me when my mother had gone on one of her business trips.

Ma Lee would read my fortune in the tea leaves. I don't know why she taught me women's secrets. Marie showed me how to read cards, not the fancy Tarot the hippies use, but old-fashioned playing cards. Phebe could see your future in your palm. Old Man Lee accepted his wife's valuation of me and taught me to ride the little ponies bareback. I can smell those stables, those ponies, the sweat and the wet sacking, the oats, the droppings – and it's mingled with Marie's *Eau de Violet* which she wore from the age of seven. Old Man Lee let me help muck out the stables and feed the ponies and harness them up to their fancy carts using brasses shaped like the sun and the moon and the stars: there were no other brasses on gypsy ponies. At my pleading, Marie taught me a little of her language, though now I suspect she knew very little herself. *Rom* was Man and *Mort* was Woman; *Chur* was Thief, *Distarabin* was Prison. *Tamo* was what she sometimes called me and that meant Little. Their word for horse was *Prad*. Soon I had a fair idea what the people around me, especially the boys who liked to keep me in the dark, were talking about. A lot of the gypsy language and canting slang survived into the patois they use in the theatre and from there the homosexual world.

Ma Lee had me in mind I think as a bridegroom. She often told the girls how she wanted them to better themselves; she thought it was unambitious to sell clothes-pegs from door to door, to whine at commuters to buy lucky white heather, to tell the fortunes of drunken fools in fairgrounds. Every so often the whole family would depart, harnessing their ponies to old, carefully maintained vans, then head into the countryside, to attend the various fairs where they would buy and sell horses. The reason so many gypsies had originally settled in Mitcham was because of the fairs, though some time before the War horse-trading had stopped. They still had "true-Romany" relatives who travelled and lived as tinkers but now they even referred to themselves as didicoys. Only the youths were ashamed of their parents' soft lives. Ma Lee said it had been miserable on the road; she always longed for a little house like the one she had. "But my mum and dad never saw the inside of a house. Never saw anything but an old wooden van, like what we now use for show, to tell the fortunes in."

One Easter I became separated from Marie and my friends at the big annual funfair and some gypsy boys jumped me in the dark behind the generators and beat me up. I still smell machine oil and think of blood. After that my mother made me stay away from the gypsy camps. I would still go when I dared. Marie was offended by what had happened to me yet could not heal the breach. Gradually, after my mother and I moved to Semley Road in Norbury, we stopped meeting. I miss her. She married a local greengrocer and, as her mother had feared, spent most of her days outside serving on the stall.

I began to see much more of Ben French who, like me, had little in common with the other local boys. Until he was called up for the RAF we did almost everything together. People thought we were brothers. We built tree-houses in the woods. We made canoes. We went adventuring together on our bikes. His sister was run over by a delivery van outside the baker's in Norbury High Street in 1954. I think that must have contributed.

The summer I was sent home from Cooper's Hall I stayed a week with my Uncle Jim at Downing Street. Except when I could confuse the tourists by moving the curtains of the windows so that they would look up hoping for a glimpse of Mr Attlee, the Prime Minister, I did not have much to do. My uncle took me once to the Festival of Britain, so it must have been 1951. My Aunt Iris didn't come. She said we would enjoy it more without her. We wandered through the crowds, reluctant to join the queues for the Dome of Discovery, stared at the Skylon and wondered what it was for, had an icecream or two and returned to Downing Street. The exhibition was supposed to celebrate Britain's wonderful future. I remember being disappointed.

Sometimes, when there was a large crowd outside the front door of Number Ten, my Uncle Jim would take me through an empty building and into the house through a side door. There was a fair-sized back garden surrounded by a high wall and planted with old-fashioned flowers, with hollyhocks and marigolds and daisies, but I wasn't allowed to play there. I could go and sit on a bench and read if I wanted, but Mr Attlee, said my Uncle Jim, didn't much care to be bothered by children.

The house, which I explored as much as I could, having little else to do, seemed of infinite size inside, while from the outside it seemed relatively small. I believe it was actually two houses joined by a corridor, which is why I remember views of Horse Guards Parade, but then I had no clear idea of its geography. My first memory of Winston Churchill was seeing him in some kind of blue silk pyjamas and a tin hat, yelling for my uncle while outside we heard the whistle of a V-Bomb, the crump as it went down somewhere near the river. My uncle seemed to be constantly at his beck and call. He actually took more interest in me than his successor, Attlee. He seemed convinced I was my Uncle Jim's son. "Your boy's growing, Griffin. Where's he at school?" The smell of cigar smoke and brandy was almost overwhelming. "Don't go into politics," Churchill told me. "It's a mug's game. Be sensible, follow your dad into the Civil Service."

While I stayed at Downing Street that summer I read my way through most of Dickens and a good part of *Encyclopaedia Britannica*. On Sundays I walked up almost deserted Whitehall. It was hot and there was dust on the road. At weekends there were scarcely any cars in London. My Uncle Jim took me to the National Gallery and then to the Leicester Square Odeon to see *Pinocchio*. "Your Aunt Iris would love this," he used to say, but I knew she hated going out. He had a ponderous dignity, like a stage butler; his hands were very soft and gentle. "I'll hold the fort, don't worry," my Aunt Iris said. "You two enjoy yourselves." Her face was lined and grim. I learned that she was in constant pain.

At Downing Street I was also introduced to Hopalong Cassidy. My Uncle Jim loved Westerns and read at least a dozen a week. Most of them were repetitious and boring, but the Clarence E. Mulford paperbacks with yellow and black spines and paintings of cowboys and outlaws from the 1920s were wonderful. They had an authenticity for me which made the Bill Boyd films I saw later seem disrespectful and watered down, sanitised versions of what for me was an enduring myth. Similarly I was disappointed in the Tarzan films. I continue to associate Number Ten with the Bar-20 Ranch and Tex Ewalt remains a more memorable resident than Mr Churchill, who struck me as a rather pathetic man, perhaps because by the time I met him his time was passing. He had, for instance, none of the bitter, mocking irony of Tex Ewalt, who hid his feelings behind his own legend, rather like Alan Ladd in most of his films, especially *Shane*.

I remember many of the famous politicians I have met for their smell more than anything. Only Sir Alec Douglas-Home seemed to have no scent whatsoever. He shook hands with me the first time we met, at a BBC reception, and asked how I had been. "Good to see you again." He looked like an amiable skeleton, his mouth a little less mobile than a ventriloquist dummy's. He was short, scarcely any taller than Prince Philip, who had in those days a rather dated manner, perhaps from keeping too many public engagements. When these people did find out who I was they would enthuse with delighted relief about my Uncle Jim. My Uncle Jim was a much-loved servant of the great. Anthony Eden, whom my uncle also worked for, smelled of old linen, of winding-sheets and dry-cleaning fluid. Macmillan, whom my uncle admired most of the Prime Ministers, was like country leather, turf and musty paper. I never had the chance to sniff a Socialist premier, though Nye Bevan, of whom I was in awe, smelled strongly of canned vegetable soup.

Of course, after 1954, I was *persona non grata* at 10 Downing Street.

I climb the stairs at my Uncle Jim's. I pause before the cold pictures crowding the walls; some are ancestors and some are old family enemies. "Don't listen to Winston," says my Uncle Jim. "You go into politics. It's the time to do it. There'll be changes. You must see they're changes for the better. Just promise me you'll do it straight. No messing about with the Liberal Party first." He makes me sit in the Cabinet Room, my cap on a minister's peg, staring at a black blotter marked mysteriously "1st Lord". I wonder how many lords there are. Is there a 20th Lord? I am not sure I'm up to the responsibility, not at eleven. Yet I love my Uncle Jim as much as I love my mother and I feel obliged to do my best to please him.

There are shadows in the walled garden and the strong smell of lavender. I long to be back with Marie. I run in my pyjamas through the house to see the sun setting upon the trees of St James's Park, far away. A flock of birds rises over the tall neo–classical silhouettes. Herons flap their wings and disappear; they are like something out of heraldry. I can hear distant cries from the water. I can see soldiers in red wool and gold metal riding horses across the parade-ground. I feel vulnerable in my night-clothes, my bare feet touching marble, polished wood, oriental carpet. I hear voices below. I smell baked meat and boiled vegetables, wine and tobacco, and the voices are raised importantly, knowing and aggressive. I'm not at all sure I can do anything but disappoint my Uncle Jim. Perhaps Mr Churchill had a better measure of me. All I can promise him at this moment is that I shall not stand as a Liberal candidate. My heart begins a heavy, frightened pounding. I am frightened by what might happen to me if I'm caught alone on the marble stairs below the famous portraits. I experience a thrill of helplessness which is almost sexual, perhaps because I am close to so much power. I run softly back through the empty passages and apartments, up the dark green carpeted steps to my room.

My Uncle Jim and my Aunt Iris sit on either side of a leather couch, listening to the news on the radio. Now whenever I hear the football results read out I see them sitting stiffly and in silence, as if already dead. As I move on they look up, alert, perhaps to give the housemaid orders.

My great-grandmother on the Mummery side was a housemaid at Hever Castle in Kent. She saw the Astors build their model village beyond the moat and make the place wonderfully comfortable: an idealisation of the Middle Ages. She was a woman famous for her long Venetian red hair and soft pale skin. "It looked as if her head were on fire." William Mummery, my grandfather, was born at the castle. "She used to tell us what lovely people the Astors were, even Nancy. When I met them I was too young to get any clear impression of them. She was a personal maid, not a skivvy. Hever was the best job in the country in those days. Every modern convenience. Better than Cliveden. Her aunt, you know, died a Countess in Paris. Sophia, her name was. I've got the death certificate somewhere. It was posted to my mother. I think she was Sophia's next of kin by that time, but I don't think there was much money." He had been fifteen and already at work when he learned of his mother's death by drowning in the River Eden, near Ann of Cleves' Bower, at the point where the new watercourse was laid. Apparently she had forgotten the river had been redirected and had fallen in at night.

My grandfather managed an import and export office in the City. He spoke a lot about Bills of Lading and the comings and goings of cargo ships. In 1954 I looked for his office. I knew it was near Fenchurch Street. I thought I would find it on the far side of a field full of wild grasses and purple flowers, of parts of brick walls and concrete slabs, the rusty wires sticking out of them like blasted trees, victims of some specific plague, but I never discovered his particular firm. There were model ships in every window and I had thought only his office would display a steamer.

The furthest I ever cycled, with my friend Ben French, was to Hever, near Orpington, because of my grandfather's stories. The castle grounds were closed to the public so we put our bikes against the flint wall of the churchyard and went to look for my buried relatives. Most monuments in Hever are of local sandstone and the weather had washed away all but this century's inscriptions. I found no Mummerys. It was a hot day and my bottom was sore. Ben had a three-speed BSA but mine was a heavy butcher's delivery Raleigh which I kept in his shed because my mother refused to let me have a bike until I was eleven. The Raleigh had one advantage: the big metal basket over the undersized front wheel could carry my black-and-tan terrier Brandy whose loyalty to me and dislike of almost everyone else was legendary. Brandy would run beside me until he grew tired, then he would sit down suddenly in the road and bark, waiting for me to notice him and turn the bike back so he could jump into the basket, sitting in front of me, panting and grinning, growling occasionally at a cat or another dog.

I had a childhood I am inclined to find idyllic. There were undercurrents, of course, and dramatically violent arguments with my mother which generally ended in mutual tears and apologies. I became used to intensity, believing it the norm. Other children seemed to have rather lacklustre existences, living so evenly they might never have been born. Yet this intensity was based firmly on ordinary human experience, with nothing morbid or exaggerated about it, and I never hungered as so many of my contemporaries did for bizarre or exotic sensation. I have seen half my generation dead or ruined; lost in an increasingly alien world of Low Tories and imperial ghosts; of shameful and wasteful military adventures, of grocery-shop philosophies, the same that made the last Empire of the French the wretched sham, the miserable, cruel, self-serving society it was. And those Little Englanders are so supremely self-satisfied, smug as bishops, they're unaware of the quicksand slowly engulfing them. But make no mistake, they'll be standing on our shoulders when they eventually succumb. Today's world belongs to Tommy Mee.

I was loved as a child; I was secure. I trusted many and was rarely betrayed. The few who occasionally betrayed me were seen to be fallible but I continued to trust them. No parent remembers every promise given to a child. I remained happy, confident and independent. I failed exams but nobody made me feel guilty. I succeeded in everything that interested me. Though doubtful of what exactly I planned to do, my mother gave me general encouragement. When I sold my first article to a local paper at thirteen she was delighted. The neighbours congratulated me; my teachers took pride in me, though continuing to warn me I should pay better attention to certain lessons. I was punished for my frequent truancies, my failure to produce homework and my larking in class, all perfectly normal. My only evident abnormalities, for my age, were an enthusiasm for atonal music, particularly Charles Ives, and my enjoyment of books regarded as difficult by my contemporaries.

Some people chose to see me as a lonely child, but I actually preferred my own company much of the time. I had friends to call on when I required them, especially Ben French. We were like brothers. Sometimes he had to go to the Midlands to stay with relatives and later, because he was a couple of years my senior, he would be at work during the day or doing his National Service. He found that joining the Air Training Corps got him exactly what he hoped for, a job in Whitehall he could attend daily like an ordinary position and live at home, with weekends off. Because of his success I was encouraged to join the ATC. Ben had sensitive, rather refined features, and his favourite reading, like mine when we first met, was Richmal Crompton's William books. We were both interested in chemical experiments. Much of our time was devoted to mixing gunpowder. This was a hit-or-miss business, involving many unplanned explosions, for the stuff had to be tested batch by batch. I spent half my boyhood with most of my eyebrows missing and much of my hair singed off. The ceiling of my room was blackened like the windows and frequently the curtains caught fire. My mother seemed to accept this fairly equably, perhaps because she could imagine worse. Although erratic, our production of gunpowder was sufficient for our various needs.

We were both interested, too, in toy soldiers, which we collected fairly methodically, visiting a tiny shop in Streatham, near the Common, for most of our Britains' models. We were only really interested in Britains'. We sent away for their catalogue and it was the size of a large phonebook, full of regiments and the armies of all nations, of model farms and zoos and railway figures. We used it as our bible. We discussed what to save up for, what odd jobs would bring us a naval landing party or some additional Camel Corps figures. These lead soldiers, available in such variety into the middle fifties, had all but disappeared by 1960. It alarmed me when plastic figures without any real specific uniforms and only broadly categorised by nation took their place. Now I can't afford to buy the lead figures; they have become the preserve of lunatic collectors. My first series of articles, to a boy's magazine, was on the subject of toy soldiers.

If I wasn't lonely, neither was I disturbed. I had wholesome interests, ordinary hobbies, normal activities. I looked outward, rarely deliberately inward. You encourage me to write because you think it will reveal some clue to my condition. My childhood will not provide it. The answer is in my genes, my biological chemistry, my inheritance. Who knows, I might actually be psychic!

My Other Uncle Jim, married to my mother's sister Daisy, took an interest in my toy-soldier collection. He was headmaster of a minor public school near Richmond and had served in South-East Asia during the War. He had a superb collection of blowpipes, shrunken heads, carved idols, ivory, peculiar head-dresses and necklaces which he had picked up while waiting for rescue in the jungle through most of the War. He had parachuted from a burning plane in 1942 and landed amongst friendly tribesmen, so deep in the interior that neither Japanese, Dutch nor British knew of their existence, though the tribesmen had a fair idea of what was going on. Eventually he learned of the American and British landings after the Japanese deserted the area, and his friends took him downriver in a canoe. I was never sure if he had really wanted to return to the West. Two weeks later, however, he and his considerable baggage were back in London. He had given away some souvenirs but the majority remained in their house, which was attached to the school. He occasionally used them to frighten his pupils into good behaviour, since rumour was he had shrunk the heads himself and was a dab hand with a poisoned dart.

My Other Uncle Jim was from Cork and had a clever, sardonic way of telling stories. I think I learned from him. Eventually he confided he had wanted to remain in the jungle village, where he had a local wife, since life with my Aunt Daisy had never been pleasant for him, but had been afraid she would discover his whereabouts and come to find him. Rather than live with this terror, he had given himself up. I think he was joking. I found his view of my Aunt hard to understand, since she doted on me. For some reason she never treated me with the contempt she reserved for her husband and her two sons, who were firmly under her thumb, even after the accident. When I stayed with them she sided with me in quarrels, cooked me special delicacies, encouraged me to acts of independence which would merely in conception have terrified her own sons. My Other Uncle Jim kept his head down, agreeing with everything and ignoring as much as he could. His power was all outside the home. Most evenings he sat in his study leafing through maps of distant Asian countries. My Aunt Daisy also greatly admired my father, whom she described as having guts. I never enjoyed my visits, partly because of the tension, partly because I found my cousins feeble and unimaginative. They're permanently institutionalised now, maimed in the accident which blinded my Other Uncle Jim and scarred my Aunt Daisy; some sort of domestic explosion.

I have very little to do with them, though I return regularly to Mitcham to visit my mother. I meet my father perhaps twice a year, usually in public houses of his choice. He drinks cautious half-pints and yearns for the Isle of Man before the War. The old gypsy yards have gone, replaced by graph-paper buildings, square-built of square blocks. Even parts of the Common have disappeared. The fairs these days are miserable things and there isn't a trace of lavender.

After my Uncle Jim died my Aunt Iris stayed in their large ugly house in Hove for another ten years. Eventually becoming senile she was taken to a Home. I never visited her, either. Perhaps it wasn't fair of me to judge her as harshly as I did: her disease had twisted her personality as much as it had her body.

At least my Uncle Jim was spared Margaret Thatcher. Tommy Mee is one of her junior ministers now. My Uncle Jim thought Edward Heath was a mistake. My uncle was at heart a Tory radical with a haughty dislike of socialism and a high respect for the men of principle who filled the postwar Labour Party. He spoke well of them and after some heart-searching agreed to serve Attlee, though he didn't care much for Gaitskell. "As for the Liberals, their principles are meaningless these days. They can't apply them." Once he took me with him to a large house near the Mall. In it I was forced to experience the company of some obnoxiously accented and ill-mannered children who I learned later were members of the Royal Family and their friends. My uncle was to apologise to me. "I had forgotten how out of touch they are allowed to be." I have nothing against the little Prince of Wales except that as he grows more and more popular on the current wave of nostalgic illusion, he has begun to take himself seriously. Once he was appropriately apologetic but nowadays actually believes himself to be both intelligent and humane. He speaks proudly of helping the tenants work the land and how important it is by this means to experience the life of the commons. Daily he grows more pompous. Some have blamed his wife for this. I blame public will (and perhaps his own secret depression): the public has a habit of turning icons into fools. My Uncle Jim was a great royalist but always insisted it was the duty of parliament to keep the monarchy in its place. The moment politicians came to believe in the divinity of kings, however disguised, the country would, he said, be in serious trouble. "Sooner or later we shall go the way of France." It was the worst fate he could imagine.

My Uncle Jim, while investing his faith in a democratic parliament, disliked the daily business of parliamentary politics. His initial attraction had been to the Foreign Office and later the Treasury but his loyalty to Churchill, both in the issue of anti-appeasement and most other positions of the thirties, meant he followed his hero into Downing Street and by some alchemy remained there, serving a succession of Prime Ministers and acting as an unofficial go-between with the Civil Service. He was a permanent secretary but no one was ever wholly clear about his function. Even the official reasons for his knighthood were rather vague. This state of affairs had come about during the War and had proven so useful he had remained in his flat under a variety of titles after Churchill left, looking down on the sightseers, watching the famous inhabitants come and go, a kind of vizier with little superficial power which was, he said, exactly how he wanted it. Apparently Wilson tried to make his role official and my uncle objected, won his case, considered his situation and, in 1965, retired. He told me Wilson's brand of politics was distasteful to him. It was lacking in depth. While he regarded Eden and Home as somewhat simple-mindedly honest, if poor organisers, he could exist in their atmosphere. "Wilson's air is unbreathable to me." Yet he saw nothing better in the up-and-coming Tories.

My Uncle Jim told me none of this until he returned from Rhodesia. The habits of discretion which had made him a sort of Jeeves to a variety of Wodehousian characters remained with him, but in his last years, before the Christian Science and the cancer, he opened up, at least to me. Because my uncle had loved Churchill I never voiced my real opinion of him, though it seemed to me even that old man was preferable to what we have now. When this country's political leaders lack vision and idealism, no matter how disparate, said my Uncle Jim, we fall back on our kings, queens, princes and princesses; always a bad sign, for we come to rely on dreams rather than policies. What made me curious about the House of Windsor was how from a family of impoverished Germans it accumulated so much wealth within a relatively short space of time. It would be ironic if the next King Charles were to succumb to the follies of the first. We shall see.

My Uncle Jim saw a lot of himself in me, and I still regret I could do nothing to fulfil his ambitions. Honestly, I think the time impossible for following in his footsteps. He belonged to a less disillusioned, more realistic age. Besides, I am now a certified madman and I believe that certification is of crucial significance if one desires a career in politics.

In my mid-teens, when I became fascinated with my own mental processes, I began actively to encourage my voices and visitations. This led to what happened in 1954. My mother was by now a director of a local company making office furniture for an international market and was away sometimes for a week at a time. I lost sleep and got "high", babbling to anyone who would listen about what I saw and heard, telling them what they were thinking, what they most desired from life, and I also suffered from minor delusions which was partly why I was put into Bethlehem Mental for those first few weeks, when I was fifteen, to be studied. By you. But nobody seemed on the right track. I was drugged, as you know, but in those days your drugs were not sophisticated and only partially stopped the voices getting through. I did find a wonderful escape, however, in the stories of Tom Merry and Co. of St Jim's, of Billy Bunter and Harry Wharton, which were loaned to me by another inmate who has since become a close friend. It was a peculiar feeling at first to go from the world of George Bernard Shaw to the juvenile never-never land of Frank Richards and *The Magnet* and *Gem* weeklies published years before my birth, but it was superior therapy. I calmed down immediately. My friend, a regular patient at the hospital, was cleverer, if you don't mind me saying, than any doctor, helping not only me but many others. I won't reveal his name. I know how jealous you doctors can get. I sometimes think of him as a kind of latter-day apostle, risking everything to go into the leper colony and bring comfort, hope, sometimes healing to abandoned souls.

These ideas are useless to you, if you are trying to analyse me with a view to affecting some kind of cure. My life is not untypical of many, save for its details; only my madness is divine. My delusions, as you see them, are easy for you to categorise. I share them with thousands of others. Yet still it never occurs to you to think seriously for a moment that because there are thousands of us we might possibly be right. You cling to your theories as others cling to desert mirages or their lunatic faiths, your only certainties. The difference might merely be in the intensity with which I and the others live our lives. Fear no more the heat of the sun nor the furious winter's rages, for we have analgesic gum and pills to purge and strong steel cages. You tell us that we grow irritable quickly. Who would not grow irritable with such inane and condescending questions? I live in this world of colour, of sound, of touch and sexuality so much more vivid than your own that sometimes it seems my body can hardly contain it all; and when I am overwhelmed, when I fail to remember how to behave in order to remain at large in your society, then I am caught again, trussed up, put away. Then you proceed to tell me how I am not myself, that I am raving, that I suffer from delusions of grandeur, because I refuse to pretend you are my masters. Was this what happened to Joan of Arc? Why do you want me to lie to you? Why is it so important? Why do you pretend all the time? What do you fear? The realisation of how unjustly you maintain your power?

The Common is sweet. I lie in the grass reading *Love Among The Chickens* and eating a Cox's Orange Pippin, occasionally drinking from a Tizer bottle, while not far away my dog Brandy runs in and out of the bushes. I have an Edgar Rice Burroughs and a Baroness Orczy with me and all the hours in the day to read them. I can smell the paper. The sun in the blue sky seems unmoving. This is a timeless place, far from traffic and any interruption, a summer afternoon amongst so many perfect summer afternoons in my ideal childhood. White hunters, warrior women, comic manservants, heroic dandies, gentlemen swordsmen and philosophical cowpokes crowd within. The world with all its hateful thinkers, its greedy, malicious and violent respectable suburban citizens, is too far away to affect me here. Perhaps I have the second sight, as Ma Lee suggested. Could it be that simple, do you think? I told you what you were thinking, Doctor Male, and you praised me for my cunning, for my clever guess. Are my periods of dementia merely the result of a lack of success in controlling my gift? Is it this you resent? This talent? Shouldn't you be investigating the world I can see? The world you're blind to? Oh, I don't really care. I'm not dead. The worst you can inflict is brief discomfort. What good can this do you? It probably does more good for me.

With my friends I am strong. There are the three of us. We are united. The father, the son and the holy virgin. We hold steady and we help the rest as best we can. My body shakes as if all the power you have repressed in me threatens to burst out of every pore, every sinew and vein.

The ruins are comforting. On certain occasions they rise up to protect me. In the warmth the weeds are growing and butterflies, bees, wasps, move erratically through the air. I lie behind a wall with Doreen Templeton: my trousers are down, her skirt is up. We shiver and grin as we investigate our differences. The bombs brought me security, sexuality, escape and adventure. We children of the Blitz are not to be pitied. We are to be envied. We are to be congratulated because we survived; so if you must pity someone then pity the relations of the dead and the parents of my dead contemporaries, my friends; but we are happier than any generation before or since. We were allowed to play in a wider world.

Today I know what you're thinking. Tomorrow I shan't know because you will have given me another injection. Will that make you safe enough? Or will you only feel secure when you have drugged me into death?

I'm wondering, just at present, what I can see from my window. There are bars and it's high overhead. The room's comfortable enough, with a good bed and nice sheets and pillows. I've plenty of books and a tape-player with a selection of music. But I'm puzzled by the movement outside. Perhaps it's nothing more than a tree come suddenly into leaf. I'm tired and I suppose my mind's hazing. I'll go back to Mahler. Currently I find his *Kindertotenlieder* inspiring; it leads me back into my free mind where intellectual thought ceases and I am again only myself.

Lost Stations 1951

JOSEF KISS sits in one of his tiny flats watching warm evening sunshine be absorbed by the English revived redbrick square shaded by high plane trees, in which a coster's barrow from Leather Lane and an old lady in a greasy coat with a rabbit-fur collar sit at rest. Brooke's Market, which has not known trade for two hundred years and is a haven sought by only a few, is a matter of yards from the Prudential's Gothic grandeur, from bustling High Holborn which boasts in parts a frontage far older, Staple Inn's leaning Tudor terraces where Josef Kiss buys his tobacco and his wine-gums, across from Gamages Department Store where he buys toys and clothing, from Hatton Garden and the world's diamonds. His wife knows nothing of this room; it is where he comes to rehearse, to be himself, to think about the world. Sometimes he pretends to be in Bradford or Dundee; at other times he tells her he works late-night clubs. The landlord knows him as Professor Donnol, one of his pre-War stage names. The square has only a little bomb damage, to the Butterfield church opposite, a masterpiece of Eastlake-inspired domestic 19th-century architecture, the epitome of everything Mr Kiss finds comforting and aesthetically pleasing. Whenever Harrow's mock-Tudor grows too much for him he retires here. The tiny square's tranquillity increases as the office workers leave and the faint sweet smell of tobacco from the Old Holborn factory fills the air; a clang or two comes from a late-working warehouse in Brooke Street, where Chatterton died, from a trolley-bus or a tram.

Mr Kiss returns to his Shelley and the Elgar Violin Concerto from his mahogany radiogram, a Third Programme broadcast, hardly a crackle. The wireless set stands on eagle claws between bookshelves neatly crowded with poetry and light novels: A. E., Rossetti, Yeats, MacNeice, Peake, Thomas; Dornford Yates, P. G. Wodehouse and John Buchan in pictorial dustwrappers; a dozen duller spines by W. Pett Ridge, some mint Gerald Kersh. Against rich Victorian wallpaper framed posters feature himself, his aliases: Signor Dante, Doctor Donlon, Tarot the Telepathist, Mandala the Mind Reader and Igor Rasputin, chosen for him by a succession of managers. If anyone were to see these he would be embarrassed; similarly he would not wish to be judged by his reading-matter, for even the poets have Drinkwater, Betjeman, Chesterton and Flecker in predominance. Here Mr Kiss can quote Alfred Austin, Wheldrake, and the obscurer late works of Swinburne, for this room does not aspire to profundity but to reassurance; Mr Kiss thinks of it as his priest-hole, just a step across Southampton Row from Bloomsbury, a short walk to Fleet Street and a pleasant stroll, in this sort of weather, to The Black Friar which is of a period and a style with Brooke's Market and remains his favourite pub. This, he says, is the finest part, the true centre of old and new London, neither City nor West End, neither slum nor residential district. Both of them drapers' assistants his paternal grandparents were married less than a mile away in St Jude's, Gray's Inn Road, and lived in Argyll Street, though neither church nor house still exist; Argyll Street is a wasteland soon to be flats, St Jude's hall is a nurse's hostel, the spire and chapel blown apart in the Blitz. Mr Kiss's mother was born above a shop in Theobald's Road, five minutes from his flat, his father in nearby Verulam Street, and came by the Brooke's Market premises because for a while his father had a part-interest in the building. He thinks of it as the peaceful eye of the London hurricane, a cone of silence: to reveal this secret place would be to risk too much for he happens to believe in a tangible evil which actively intends to seek out good and Brooke's Market is so far virtually untouched by Chaos, thanks perhaps to the influence of St Alban the Martyr, a church of discreet novelty, built to please and console a local population. Even Hitler's bombs failed to damage the square's integrity, though they wiped out so many of the surrounding streets.

Sitting naked in the warm light, his attention neither on Shelley nor Elgar, Mr Kiss thinks about his supper. In the cubby-hole near a door on which is arranged a variety of outer clothing is a porcelain sink, a miniature gas-stove, a small selection of canned and packet goods, some fresh vegetables, a half-bottle of claret, a teapot, a nest of blue enamel saucepans, a few spices. Crossing to his narrow bed, his huge graceful body like the kind decorating some 17th-century voluptuary's ceiling, he stretches out, thoughtfully fingering his supine privates and considering his choices; he is a marvellous ape, content in its captivity, caged because it chooses to be caged, a creation conceived by Blake, mortal godling and divine beast combined. In his mind Wheldrake's lines from "Ode to the Capital" replace the genius of Shelley's.

> LONDON! Mother to Half the Sphere;
>   Mother to Commerce: Mother to Ease;
> Parent to Truth; Mistress to Lies;
>   Mother to Innocents; Dam to the Wise;
> Matriarch to Empire's Rule of Peace:
>   Mother to Legend: Let Fools despise!

How desperate poor Wheldrake must have been, he thinks, to receive the Laureate's wreath. And it did him no good. His great rival Alfred Austin received the honour. After that Ode, in 1895, he returned to his more cheerfully decadent mode. But he had written it in Holborn, before he moved to Dorking to be closer to Meredith.

During the War Josef Kiss came here whenever he had the chance, to shelter. While having nothing against the specially built bunkers, the underground stations and cellars, in Brooke's Market he felt invulnerable. Here he conceived his eldest boy, though Gloria never knew where she was. He had not turned on the light. She had thought it was the flat of a friend. Lust that time drove out caution. He remains subject to impulsive decisions and his immediate emotions.

If I had not met her would I still be here? he wonders. *She was too young for me. But what else could she have done? I matched her needs of the time. And now there are those children whom I love. Did she flower too early? Am I to blame? Was there too little life in her and did I drain most of*

175

it before I realised what was wrong? I do my best now in the direction of duty and consideration, yet sometimes it seems she merely wanted the fling, followed by the babies, followed by a life of slow self-destruction; or is my own reading wrong? I love to fly and now she hates to fly. I love to sing and she blocks her ears whenever I open my mouth. She's as good as handed me an ultimatum: If I go mad again she'll not visit me. Those soft shades of lilac and magnolia, that water how it glows no warmer silver existed it could be gold but I still love you, matron that you are, and wish to walk with you again, amongst those trees, into the hothouses. Like at Kew, where you wrapped your legs around my thighs and gasped into my face, careless of them all. What is it I have done? Change? I can't.

Amongst those monstrous cabbage plants, with great pods dropping and cracking everywhere that tiny jungle where we planned larger expeditions until the War came to stop us. "What a summer, eh, Gloria, and you still wanted to become an actress. They said you looked like Gloria Stuart, but I thought you lovelier than that.

"Oh, you are still more beautiful than any star I've seen, but you plumped for Harrow. Perhaps just to bide your time. Perhaps to wait me out. Perhaps to put up a notice one evening when I return home proclaiming I'm no longer welcome. I have my bolt holes. There is nothing I need in Harrow save you and the children.

"We kept them coming, all through the War, like fools. There were souls to spare, Gloria, Gloria, Gloria. You say I've grown stranger, but I haven't. I don't change. I merely hold myself in check. It's the best I can do, Gloria, for you and me and the kids. There's too much that hurts and frightens you now that the War's done.

"Taking you to Brighton was a mistake, you said. You hadn't realised there was no sand. What am I hurting in you? The sun's bad for me, you say. It sort of expands me. But you enjoyed my expansions in the Tropical Plant House. How can I be cautious and at the same time be in love? One must wither."

"Soup," says Josef Kiss. "Here's a tin of Royal Game." Kept for a celebration, something to do with the Festival of Britain which is almost over now. He enjoyed it as much as the kids, if not more. Gloria thought highly of the joke railway and the showboat at Battersea and the boys took a sober pleasure in the Dome of Discovery, while little May stayed on the Galloping Horses until she was nearly sick. This feels like a real family outing, Gloria had said. *But I couldn't identify what was wrong with me at other times.* I think you talk too much, she said. *And I can't understand you. Or couldn't. These days I hardly listen. Then you get hurt when I don't remember what you said.* "I have to listen out for the kids, see, that's what's on my mind." *But when I kept quiet she said she couldn't stand it: I was moody. I am too simple for her, or too complex.*

"Or too wrong. Love, dear heart, is clearly not enough. And neither's money. What can help except that I stay away, become an enjoyed rarity. Yet already it looks as if I'm merely an interruption now, an irritation, an unwelcome stranger, Gloria. And I'll add a dash or two of wine. It'll taste like the best you get at Rules. But I could do with jugged hare. Josef Kiss. What do you say, Josef Kiss? Jugged hare? I don't mind if I do. With the theatrical fraternity? Rather! That's the stuff to give the troops."

And he again remembers a uniform, an RAF uniform, soon after they had agreed to have no more children, at least until the War was properly over. Even then it was rare to see an RAF uniform running hell-for-leather along a back alley in Harrow. "Gloria was my own creation and that's what she resents. Who can blame her for dropping off the odd pilot?" The soup must take its own time to cook. Another can is unlikely to turn up for a while. This is Victory. Yet it feels as if the War is still waiting to re-start.

Something has to be done to make people feel it is really over. Even if it means bringing Churchill back. Which is an irony in itself. He has his *Magnets* and *Gems* here, carefully put away in box-files, marked in years and issues; some of them listed in series titles. He looks at them with hope, but nothing stirs tonight. He returns his eyes to the Royal Game; he sniffs. Oh, it's strong. He hums to himself, taking his wooden spoon to the pan, to stir and sample, careful not to splash his flesh. "A change of flesh, indeed, indeed. But better still a change of mind, a change of head. Here's control for you. Here's the goal, a tasty tin of soup. It's not enough, Mr Kiss." He groans at the memory of happiness. "That's the worst of hells!" cries Signor Dante, the Man to Whom No Mind is a Secret. The pale green in the sky, the sweating palms of Kew, the stink, so sweet and grand, of a rain-forest's undergrowth. *Oh, God, the dirt of that glassy temple, its pods and blooms, her thighs hard around my hip, her lips glowing, the silvery glass and the water beyond.* "What ducks, Mr Kiss. What geese, what larks!" *And there's Jenny Wren a-*

177

nesting. Gloria! How many nests has Jenny Wren to build? And how many will last the summer and the hatching of the eggs? Will the fledgelings fall, Jenny? Will Jenny's nests begin to unravel? Too many nests for Jenny Kiss, the wren who thinks he's a cuckoo. The soup. Don't let it bubble. Don't let it even murmur once or the flavour's spoiled. Smell the game! Smell the wine. Smell the slivers of pheasant and venison, of the King's Royal Deer. *Smell Gloria, hard against me under the high glass.*

Now we taste it. Turn off the gas. Take down the brown rye Soho bakery bread; cut two slices. No butter until tomorrow. Lay out the big plate, put the bread and the bowl on the plate, pour the soup, half of it, out into the enamel bowl, white with a blue rim. Pom, pom, pom, to the Elgar cello, drawing its way through *allegro, ma non troppo,* almost at the conclusion. Take the soup and the bread to the window, lay it down between two small vines, return for half a glass of claret, good enough for its price, a treat, a memory of last year in Paris when Gloria came, nervously and bereft of habitual responsibilities which, he believed, she retained in place of happiness. Leave the kids with Mrs D, he said, and come on to Italy with me. To Rome. I'll show you the Mediterranean and the blue Aegean, you won't believe it. But they had been two days in Paris before the boat train left for London with them on board, enjoying the luxury of sleep, at least for him: not a wink, she said, for her, the very thought of sinking in that metal coffin, already below the waterline, lying in the carriage and unable to open a door, down like a stone, without a chance; didn't it occur to him? Not so it loses me any sleep, he had said. He tried to crawl into her bunk to comfort her but there wasn't room. "You're squashing me," she said, "I feel bad enough already." What is it, Gloria, claustrophobia? "You should know," she said, "you're always in and out of those bins." Claustrophobia, he said. "That's it. Honestly, Jo, I appreciate that you mean well but I'll never do this again. And the rocking!" Could you fly? he asked. "Me? Never!"

The Elgar ended, Josef Kiss turns the dial for Big Bill Campbell's Rocky Mountain Boys. "I'm an old cowhand from the Rio Grande." He sips his soup, he dips his bread, peering amiably into the silent enclosure. He loves cowboy and hillbilly songs and here, surrounded only by warehouses and offices, he can sing for all he's worth. "And my legs ain't bowed and my cheeks ain't tanned."

The other half of the soup is poured. "Last night as I lay on my saddle and looked up at the stars in the sky I wondered if ever a cowboy could drift up to that sweet by-and-by . . ."

Josef Kiss has known straitjackets and padded cells, bars and turnkeys, horrible doctors and psychoanalysts. He has known pills and injections and electric shocks: everything but surgery. He has also enjoyed more than his share of cleaning receipts, tram tickets and the contents of wallets, once part of his trade. – Tell me, sir, am I right, does your name begin with G? Thank you, sir. Thank you George. Now, you're married sir, I believe? Yes? And your wife's name, sir, begins with M – your wife's name, sir, if I'm not mistaken, is Marjorie. Thank you. Thank you very much. You're from Edmonton. You've just bought a new suit. You're having a squalid, half-hearted affair with a girl from the next door shop and you wouldn't have been in the theatre tonight if she hadn't thought better of the proposed trip to Southend, so now you're stuck for something to do, having already made your excuses. Oh, I'm not condemning you, I suppose, but it would be wonderful to read better minds. Minds which did not make you think you were divining the thoughts of perverse rodents.

"I didn't begin in business as a cynic. I was an idealist. I knew I had a gift. But all I could do was sell it for a few grubby bob a night in the halls. And by and large you don't get many George Bernard Shaw's and H. G. Wellses and Professor Huxleys in the ninepenny seats of the Empire Theatre, Kilburn, on a wet Thursday night. The violence. The frustration. The dreadful, quaking misery of people."

– You have a pet dog I believe, madam, and his name is Pat. He's a sheepdog? And your husband loves it more than he loves you and you'd cheerfully poison the beast if you could? Am I right, madam? Am I right, sir?

"Okay, Kiss, on your bike. Back to the bin where you belong. How many people are going to book you again if you go on like this? How many managers want to be told exactly how much they're on the take, how they're worried what their wives are up to, how they imagine in lurid detail the cruel things they would like to do to the magician's young assistant? Go on, Kiss. Off you go."

There is a tangible evil at work in the world. Mr Kiss has learned the hard way to control his sense of urgency, to make no full scale announcements, to let them think he has given up. He has learned it's illegal to warn the world of the Devil's army camped about the city, slowly but surely winning all the souls it needs.

"And you, sir, you believe Herr Hitler has some valid points, do you not? Round up the Jews in this country, too, and kick them all out. Stop worrying on behalf of the bloody Poles. What have they ever done for us? Am I right, sir? Thank you very much. No, sir, I am not calling you a quisling nor a traitor. I am not suggesting you lust to thrust your penis into the tiny cunts of nine-year-old girls. Of course not, sir. Forgive me, sir. My mistake. Yes, sir, I will gladly leave the stage, but I will not hang myself by piano wire from a meathook. Goodnight ladies, goodnight gentlemen. Music, maestro, please!"

Why do you have to say such nasty things about people? Gloria asked. It's no wonder they get angry. I'd get angry.

Oh, Gloria, I'm too scared to read your thoughts. Once I refused from nobility of sentiment. Now it's merely terror keeps me away. Would God the power the gift to give me no more to see myself as others see me.

– You are what we call a Sensitive, Mr Kiss, here at the Steiner Institute. We would gladly help you train those powers. Presently you are like a wireless set without a proper tuner. We can teach you to get the BBC, Radio Luxembourg, Radio Paris, Australia, you name it. At will.

"It was too much for me, that notion. I wanted it gone, not trained. Not stronger. What was their game? I asked them for help. Everyone I saw was the same. I could use my gifts for the good of mankind. Yet when the War came and I volunteered for Intelligence work I was turned away. Dandy asked too late. Gloria said I was being stupid, that I had every excuse for making the most of the War. The halls were crying out for acts.

"No! Stay back! I want no women here tonight!"

The last of the soup wiped clean by a morsel of wholesome bread, Josef Kiss sips his final inch of wine. He's tempted to save the label, not of the wine but the soup. "It will be a long time before I see another tin of Baxter's. Maybe if some more location work comes up in Edinburgh I'll meet that woman again."

Mary MacCloud had been connected through marriage to the soup family. He had sold his body for two tins of Scotch Broth and one of Royal Game. He was not ashamed. It had always seemed a more than fair exchange. War, after all, was War.

"And Austerity is something worse. Da-da-da-da! Deep in the heart of Texas!"

He washes his dish, his pan and his spoon. He replaces his Shelley. He ponders his Buchans and Guy Boothbys, he fingers a Cutliffe Hyne. But nothing moves him. A cry from outside draws him to the window to watch three small children wheeling an old pram across the courtyard. They could be his own, reduced to poverty, come to haunt him, to call him back to Harrow. He takes a step away from the window wondering if he will ever bring Ronald, his eldest, here one day; but it's probably too late. What would they make of it if he were to die and someone revealed his dens, these sinless nests?

A small breeze rustles leaves and the plane trees sway as if wearily in the still warm light. It's time for evensong. The children move off towards Bleeding Heart Yard. He is always mystified by the Market's being so frequently empty when so many families live in the old blocks all around, as if special territories have already been apportioned and Brooke's Market left out of every calculation. Some evenings he can sit on any one of several benches and not see a soul; read a novel, eat a picnic meal, even sing to himself without disturbance. It feels as safe as the bailey of a mediaeval fortress. But his safety would disappear if anyone else knew he lived here.

At last he takes down an old copy of *The London Magazine* for February 1909 and reads without much interest an article by Wilbur Wright about flying from London to Manchester. *With motors a little better than we possess today and with operators of somewhat greater experience and skill, men will make such journeys as that between London and Manchester without extraordinary danger. The danger to the future winner of the prize will be due to the fact that, in order to accomplish the feat before others, he will be compelled to attempt it a little before conditions are ripe.* This is followed by a long article concerning Valeska, the Woman Detective; Mrs Frederic Harrison's *No Votes For Women* – she was a famous beauty and there is an engraving of her; a further set of pictures of beauties, none of whom Mr Kiss finds attractive, some tricks one can do with matches and a part of *Don Q's Love Story*, the serial by K. and Hesketh Prichard. Josef Kiss reads it, knowing there is little chance of his ever discovering how it will end.

At exactly seven o'clock he goes to his jacket hanging on the door, feels in his pocket for one of the mild barbiturates the hospital makes him take which he keeps loose, since it's easy to mislay a bottle and he hates to be seen taking pills in public. He believes the barbiturate will increase his sense of boredom, yet still he lacks the will tonight to go out. He had looked forward to this evening at home. Gloria believes him to be auditioning for the job of ringmaster at a circus based in Birmingham, but now he would rather be with her and the children. He could put his clothes back on, take the tube to Harrow and be home for eight-thirty with the excuse the appointment was cancelled but he has a fear of interrupting her. He cannot forget the rapidly disappearing suit of RAF blue.

If his mood refuses to lift he will head for the Embankment in time for the sunset. In Essex Street he could meet his sirens, but surely it won't come to that? Something here must give up its potential for pleasure and escape. Big Bill says "Adios" for another week and Josef Kiss, turning off his wireless, puts on a record: Duke Ellington's "Caravan" is guaranteed to improve his mood. The bakelite arm of the gramophone reflects the black disc's 78 revolutions per minute. "Dooo-doo-dada-dada-doo-da-da." Lean back on the bed's many cushions, smoke a Winterman's cigarillo, look at the mementoes to an ignoble past and wonder if a season at Bexhill might save his bacon this summer. Money's tight and Gloria might be forced to return to the British Home Stores part-time, which would inevitably break any pax. Tomorrow morning he will drop in on his manager. He could do with another Ealing character part. *Whisky Galore* and *Passport to Pimlico* had kept them going nicely. All they'd given him was a line or two, but they seemed to think he was right for their specifically imagined backgrounds and had promised him something else as soon as it was available. Gloria had cheered up considerably at the chance of coming with him to the set and getting Stanley Holloway's and Alec Guinness's autographs for the children. She had expected it to be the start of something bigger. "Now you've got your foot in the door they'll give you more work. You'll become well-known. You'll be a star, Jo!" She had resented his pointing out the drawback to this vision, which was his lack of acting ability. He came over well visually, every director agreed on that, but give him a long speech and he at once lost conviction. Three or four lines, preferably well spaced out through a scene or, if possible, an entire picture, were within his true limits, disappointing nobody. "You do so well in your act."

"A crowd is a crowd. I'm addressing human beings, not a camera. And they're my own words."

"You don't want the work."

"Perhaps."

But he is himself on stage. Or rather he becomes the self he developed for public appearances, whether in a restaurant, on the boards of the Victoria Palace or at the tavern. His familiar barriers could be automatically raised, but give him an acting part where he must play someone else, perhaps someone like the creature he occasionally imagines himself to be, and he becomes anxious, for he has only one suit of armour; it serves him for every occasion. To make alterations to that armour might create weaknesses in the carapace, exposing his mind to all the other minds in the world. He has tried to explain this to Gloria but she is convinced he is over-dignifying his neuroses. There is always the chance she is right but he can't risk too much of his sanity to put her notions to the test; particularly when she will only perceive his risks as matters of pride or ego or something even less significant. He knows he risks his freedom and, worse, his dignity, for that's the first thing they attack when you are admitted to an enlightened post-war Mental Hospital where they boast of their high success rate, curing homosexuals by means of electricity. Personally, Mr Kiss has an affection for the electric shocks which increase his sense of well-being, though he says it is sometimes as if you have been mechanically masturbated in a government-run brothel. Gloria refuses any knowledge of these processes and long since relinquished responsibility to Beryl Male. *You are an animal to them, if a complex one; they would reduce the complexities, those doctors, if they could. Many still prefer the scalpel's cure for mental problems and would take my lobes off now if it were not for Beryl's preferring to have a lunatic rather than a vegetable in the family, though both must threaten her political career.* Beryl was now on Westminster Council, still dealing in old furniture, hounding widows for their paintings and china. On how many levels could she pose as a benefactress? What if she should one day lose patience and let the knife slice behind his eyes? He has his memoirs, she thinks. He has his hideouts. She would never risk *The Daily Mirror's*

183

pad-toters and camera-flashers in greasy brims and nasty mackin-toshes always with an eye out for a rising Tory. His blackmail, such as it is, remains entirely a figment of her suspicious mind. He has no intention of shopping her. He has never taken enough interest in the details of her ambition. Like studying the feeding habits of vultures, he says, it's best left to the experts.

As Beryl Male inhabits her brother's nightmares so he inhabits hers. He fears her rise to power. She fears his determination to resist the acquisition of power. She's had more than one word with Gloria, whom she has described as common. Their parents, though in debt and despair, kept their own shop, a drapers and haber-dashers in Theobald's Road. Gloria's parents were working-class. Her father had actually been a flusher in the sewers, an expert, proud of his trade; he had also done the cab-driver's Knowledge and possessed a green card, but he enjoyed solitude. People tended, he would say, to leave a sewerman alone. It didn't stink much down there in those echoing passages, glistening with damp, shining with phosphorus, which were warm. It was sweet. Once, soon after Mr Kiss and Gloria were married, he had taken his son-in-law down into the great arched vault rising twelve feet high over the River Fleet, little more than a stone's throw from Brooke's Market. He had been proprietorial in his love for this particular stretch. Mr Kiss had felt that any moment Gloria's dad would clap his hand on his shoulder and confide that one day he wanted all this to be Josef's. Mr Lightstone had been killed during the Blitz, trying to save people trapped in a bus which had driven into a fresh crater at night near Southampton Row tram depot. Mr Kiss had come to love him almost as he loved Gloria. Mr Lightstone had been a man of considerable comic intelligence. Before he died he had passed on much of his lore.

Mr Kiss's own parents were killed when their train received a direct hit from a V-2. They had been leaving at long last to stay with Mr Kiss's aunt in a village outside Oxford, in the Cotswold foothills. Mr Kiss had been under sedation in Friern Barnet hospital. Beryl had come to see him, relieving, she said, Gloria, and had broken the news. Beryl had seemed almost happy, perhaps glad to lose a link with their lowly past. Josef had wept and tried to sign himself out; they had given him more injections, straight chloral hydrate he could have sworn, judging by the headaches. When he came out, released by Beryl, who had not yet married Doctor Male, she had asked him to go to their parents' ramshackle three-storey flat over the shop. She was selling up to pay off debts, she said, and needed him to go through the personal stuff, keep what he wanted and get rid of the rest. Anything of value had been put aside. It had been almost too much for him. In the end he had taken some photographs, lockets, a few letters, an embroidered handkerchief his father had given his mother in 1914, the year he was born.

The handkerchief has his mother's initials on it, AK, a pink embroidered heart and blue letters. "With Love", trimmed with white lace. Framed with the photographs, it hangs between his posters. His mother was a tall woman, almost five foot ten with black ringlets, a heavy jaw, green eyes and the look of a gypsy. She claimed the Petulengros as relatives. Her father, whom she did not remember, had been born outside a van in Epping forest. The gypsies were born outside and they died outside. It was part of their religion. She had a little crystal ball, all that was left of his effects, for his van and its contents had been burned with his body. That was a ritual left over from Indian times, she said. Romany was closely related to Sanskrit. Hundreds of years ago her ancestors had come from beyond the Indus, bringing their mystic knowledge with them. Her family name had been Hatchin, an old term, she said, for settled gypsies. She had been an indifferent if hard-working seamstress but she and his father had both preferred leisure to money, so though they were not lazy they were never rich. Sometimes she laughingly suggested they take to the roads again, leave London and pick up what work they could in the towns and villages they passed through, but there were enough itinerants about in the early thirties and Daniel Kiss saw no joy in competing with people forced out of their homes. London, he said, was still wealthier and safer than almost anywhere else in the world if you knew what you were doing, and he was London born and bred as all his people had been since the walls first went up. "Feet first is how I'll leave this city." Alice Kiss said she should never have married a gorgio. But she loved him. Josef can't think whom Beryl takes after. He still wishes his father had been able to fulfil his simple intention of dying in his own city.

His penis has expanded slightly under his unconscious hand. This brings a memory. *Oh, ecstasy, ecstasy. Don't run against it, don't confront it. Oh, god – that was what it was like finally in the heat. Ecstasy. Can't, won't fight it. Don't fight the heat. Oh, god, this is more than heaven. It must be what hell offers and then takes away. I can smell the saturated mud, the fleshy leaves, the mighty blossoms, swaying there, the sun poured through silver to make such light, brilliant gold. Are you all right, sir, says the keeper, finding me alone with my trousers at an angle.* "Just a spot too much heat." *Too much heat, Gloria, in 1939, with all your eager offerings, your magnificent love. What happened to it? Did it die when our world ceased to have continuity, lost so much of its past? You became unenthusiastic after they had me put away. Yet you remained loyal for at least a year or two after that. Perhaps you felt betrayed by me. I'd made no secret of my gift, though it's true I had made light of it. You thought it merely my charm. You didn't believe me. How can that be betrayal?* He closes his eyes. "Ah." Duke Ellington is automatically switched off at the end of the record. "Gloria! Was it War or my passion that finally made me mad?"

– You realise, Josef, that you're merely imposing your own ideas onto reality. You will come to understand this.

"I wish you wouldn't use my first name in that familiar way."

– Let's not avoid the issue, Josef, shall we?

"The issue, Doctor Male, concerns my self-respect and your rudeness. I understand your drift, doctor. But you're wrong, and I'm right. I want help. I have always wanted help. You're so chained to your theories you are no better able to analyse than a worm under a stone, a creature fixed in its habits as you, Doctor Male. I impose nothing. You on the other hand impose on me. What are you trying to discover, doctor? Whether I'll bend to your will, come round to your point of view? You should, I think, consider this. But when my insistence on my own sanity becomes proof of my madness there scarcely seems room for discussion. I hope you won't think me rude if I suggest that your approach is at very least tactless?"

The medication dries Mr Kiss's mouth and deters further speech. The barbiturate makes him doze off, forgetful of his sensuality, his happy memories of passion, his cruel recollections of a dozen hospitals. *It's coming through, sir. It's a bit hazy. Ah, yes, the truth. The truth is, sir, I have made my living from the age of fourteen out of a party trick first demonstrated before I can remember. My mother was proud of it, my father uneasily tolerant. Beryl feared it because hers was a mind which drew its strength from secrets, from spying, from gathering to herself the details of other people's private lives. I always knew what she was up to, though I hardly ever betrayed her. But she was two years older than I. I found it hard to imagine she could own any kind of fear of me when I was so frequently at her mercy.*

Rising again, hugely yawning, his skin glowing like gold, the colour of pale roses, Josef Kiss walks once more to his window, paces again to his bookshelves, his radiogram, his sink and his stove, delicately puts out his little cigar, switches on his wireless, finds the concluding strains of a Mozart symphony, its coda an intensified memory, a poem distilled and redistilled from a poem. What he would give for a little artistic talent, something to divert all this stuff, to channel it and confer positive value on it! The sun has not yet set. It seems to be refusing to set. Brooke's Market outside grows mellow but somehow continues to hold the light. He has noticed this phenomenon before, how light remains here when outside the skies grow dark blue above high roofs, above Prudential spires, revealing stars, when it might still be early evening in the square. He opens a window to receive the sweet scents of curing tobacco and blossoms, of the little window-boxes the people keep, of Leather Lane's stalls, the fumes of Gray's Inn Road, the trees hidden everywhere in London, the grassy lawns which are there because Edward the Second was determined to give the country good lawyers and founded the Inns of Court, of the wild flowers on nearby bomb sites, of poppies and bindweed and coltsfoot. Unlike certain other great capitals London has always been prepared to reach accommodation with Nature, never caring to suppress her, nor to tame her much, where she can maintain a presence; but it has always been up to Nature to make her own way. There are badgers and foxes, they say, in the old forgotten catacombs, the lost vaults and abandoned subways.

The breathing in of London's air improves his spirits, lifts his heart; he holds his face out to the trapped sunlight and he smiles. It is the smile of a new-born demigod. From behind him a murmuring voice ceases and Grieg begins. He fills his lungs. Leaving his window open he turns, padding on his great square feet across a perfectly clean yard or two of Kashmir, and finds at once the collected poems of Hardy which he sets beside his single easy chair, near his gas-fire. At his sink he fills his kettle and begins to prepare a pot of tea. The bad spell, whatever it was, is broken. He's making the most of his seclusion.

Pleasure is so much easier to recall than pain, and that perhaps is why we continue with our strivings and our hopes. He licks red lips, smooths with the heel of his hand his gypsy eyebrows. But to recall such profound pleasure is a curse. "A curse, Signor Dante!" He looks at his posted likeness, in pointed beard and Mephistophelean cap, red as blood, which frowns out at him. "A curse you know very well. Yet here we are, restored again, ready again, cheerful again, cheerful enough, at any rate, Signor Dante. What more can we hope for just now?"

The kettle begins its faint, uncertain whistling, a hesitant call for him to come and make his tea. He heats the pot, he takes down his caddy and puts in three spoons of Assam. The water, poured from on high, rushes down to strike the tea, and steam for a second engulfs his face.

Josef Kiss sighs and sets the lid in place.

Lavender Walls 1949

MRS GASALEE lies as she has lain for almost seven years, dreaming in her guarded bed. The room is tiled in green and blue; at intervals there are mosaic scenes from the lives of saints, stylised neo-Byzantine, laid when nuns still ran Bethlehem Central and Mother Superior interviewed relatives of would-be patients here, but now this wing no longer has its own name, is merely 'Special'; only the tiles and the smell of carbolic remain of a time, almost exactly a hundred years ago, when Protestant charity raised this sanctuary for the mad. And Mary lies at its farthest end, a nurse to watch for signs of waking or of dying. Certain nurses would refuse this duty but others volunteer. Mrs Gasalee in repose might be a saint herself, her lovely face unlined by the world, her red curls on the pillow growing as she sleeps, cut and washed by Sister herself; clad in white, her skin sometimes seems translucent when the sun's rays strike her.

Her present attendant is Norman Fisher, a bored young trainee nurse from Main Wing who has hitherto dealt only with what his colleagues call Ravers and Droolers. This job is his alternative to the Army which he hoped to escape as a Conscientious Objector but the old wartime sobriety remains so they gave him the choice of becoming a miner or working in a mental hospital. He thought this would be easier. It is harder but more interesting and he thinks he will make a career as a male nurse since there are worse jobs offering far less power and there is a certain amount of fun to be had with at least some loonies.

Mrs Gasalee's breathing increases a fraction as it sometimes does when a man is beside her. "She's frightened of them," says Sister Katy Dodd, her real protectress, "but no one will listen to me."

Norman Fisher has brought along his treasured Yank comics, the coloured ones you can get from people who work at American bases, not the lousy black-and-white kind which cost threepence at Woolworth's and don't even have all the stories. He notices no change in Mrs Gasalee's breathing because his copy of *Master Comics* is open and with a feeling of intense pleasure he begins to read *The Sheriffs' Convention*, starring William Boyd as Hopalong Cassidy. – *Somewhere in the Twin River Hills – We shore made a slick git-away after our last job, Bronco – Yup! But I'm achin' tuh git back intuh action, Chip!*

Outside the window of this little wing is a walled yard where dustbins are stored in a large pine box coated with pungent creosote, its lid covered by tarcloth; the wall is brick but the yard was once a garden for the Mother Superior's contemplations, so shrubs are trained against it and in the summer all you can see is buddleia, lavender, clematis; old plants, gnarled and uncared for, but rich and entrenched forever. The window, raised a few inches, has a little mesh screen to keep insects from getting in. Unconscious of the scents, but made a little drowsy by them, Norman Fisher reads on, his lips barely moving. – *I should've known better than to turn my back on a desert rat like you! But I know just the type of treatment you need! WHAM! I've never seen these varmints around here before and nobody's going to see them around for a long time – except for Mesquite at the County Jail!*

Norman reads slower, savouring the story's conclusion as another might savour a remaining drop of wine. – *Er-er-er, thar's one favor yuh kin do fer us, Hopalong. If the folks back home ever heard whut happened tuh us, we'd never be able tuh live it down! – Don't worry! I won't breathe a word of it! We sheriffs have got to stick together! – That proves yo're jest as fine a man as everybody says! (For more two-fisted action, following the adventures of the famous sheriff in his own magazine . . . Hopalong Cassidy Every month! Only 10c).* Norman turns and reads an advertisement for *Mechanix Illustrated* and another for the 100 Famous Michigan Rainbow Mix Gladiolus (100 bulbs $1.69) before going on to his next favourite story, featuring Nyoka the Jungle Girl in *The Mad Leopard. Trader Tom* and *Colonel Corn* and

Korny Kobb will follow, then some more advertisements, then *Lumber Jack* and *Freshman Freddy*, then what Norman calls 'the written story', two pages of text: "Bloobstutter's Initiation" by Rod Reed. Only then will be begin *Bulletman, the Flying Detective*, and then *Bear Scare*. Finally *Captain Marvel Junior*, his favourite story character, and the main feature this month will cap his pleasure. Norman is a Captain Marvel fan, unlike most of his friends who claim Superman as their preferred hero. Norman also favours Lash LaRue over Hopalong Cassidy, but Lash's adventures are much harder to come by.

Norman's inner world is populated with flying champions and two-fisted cowboys, with people of magical strength and agility whose enemies possess faces permanently twisted in expressions of greed and hate. His pantheon includes Spy Smasher, Mary Marvel, Commando Yank, Golden Arrow, Ibis the Invincible, Phantom Eagle, Wonderwoman, Rocky Lane and Monte Hale. He yearns to go one day to America where their adventures are portrayed limitlessly. He has two more magazines when he finishes this one.

While Norman imagines himself a mighty boy Mrs Gasalee lies dreaming in her white unruffled bed, the smell of lavender coming unadulterated through the window and filling her. She dreams of the sun and the people who live there, gentle wraiths able to visit Earth only briefly because it is too cold for them even at the core but they would love her to join them: they beckon to her. They smile. Unable to move, she shakes her head. Merle Oberon, wearing a dress of black velvet, with black curls falling to her white shoulders, a double string of pearls at her throat, pearls and gold dropping from her ears, tries to lead Mrs Gasalee to the sun people but fails. It's impossible at present.

Merle has never been a sweeter friend, but even she cannot help. Mrs Gasalee is frozen. There is a world beyond the sun, a kind of park, apparently without boundaries, and it is full of flowers. Although she can see children in it their faces are hard to make out. Hearing some laughter, she is fairly sure they're happy, but the park is too ordinary to be heaven. Merle touches Mrs Gasalee's arm. This is not where she must go, where she sat amongst the armoured women who talked so easily and were so relaxed. One of them was Joan of Arc herself while another bore a strong resemblance to the Marquise de Pompadour, though without her shepherdess's costume and long cane it was not entirely possible to be sure it was her. They had given up their skirts for steel, all of them, and were carrying the War to the enemy. They had been kind to Mrs Gasalee. They had been so kind they made her weep. They made her helpless. When she enters these lands Merle Oberon is only one of her guides. Sometimes Katharine Hepburn or Louise Rainer come, sometimes Elisabeth Bergner or Janet Gaynor, but only Merle knows the sun people. She is their go-between. There is a forest of huge lilies, all colours, where Louise Rainer takes her; a tranquil lake with yellow sands is Janet Gaynor's favourite spot. Here Mrs Gasalee meets their friends. Janet Gaynor entertains the women of Hollywood, the elite. Men rarely enter Mrs Gasalee's dreams. She has no intention of waking and at present no one is trying to force her back, though she is aware of their presence today.

All the records went up in the War. I can smell that mysterious smoke. There's no smell like it. I can't see the source . . . Is it a building? Yes. It's coming off a roof. A flat roof. Not a chimney. Just the roof. That's funny. The smell's so strong. Oh, God. I can't continue. What's going up? The records?

Singing a little song from another age, Merle Oberon leads Mrs Gasalee through white streets away from the ugly smell. *Old Jenny, creeping Jenny. Ah, Jenny, weeping Jenny. Sweet old Jenny girl.* And now everything is calm again.

– What were you trying to do, then?

– I was trying to free the starling from the tar. The dump was burning and all the tyres had melted. There was this stinking film on my skin like when the oven caught fire and grandma's joint burned. The bird died. It was a summer afternoon over near King's Cross somewhere, the school holidays. But that's why the birds burst so frequently now, only of course in my imagination. Is that a river, Merle?

– Flowing fast towards Ludgate Circus? I suppose it must be. What do you want me to talk about?

– Nothing in particular.

They stand hand in hand on Holborn Viaduct looking down.

– Isn't the water clear as a bell? I used to come here to buy my books. The changes are all for the better.

– *Since you ask I will set before you my incredible history! You know my name. It is MR ATOM! Listen closely, for my story concerns YOU! My fate is bound up with yours in a way that Dr Charles Langley never could have guessed when, on the morning of a certain summer's day, he brought me to life . . .*

This is the city of sweat, of mists and succulents. Mrs Duxbury's lodger is a black man, you know, but I mind my own business. Her Bob was in the ARP.

Norman Fisher takes his time with his next comic. This is the cream. It is all Captain Marvel stories. – *Einstein said matter IS energy! Now, by the use of energy, I shall create living matter . . . I shall give my robot a brain, flood his metal veins with the very stuff of life! Even now the atomic energy ray is gradually transforming him into . . . Z Z Z Z z z z Z Z Z Z z z z z Z Z Z Z z z z z Z Z Z Z BOOM -- Out of the wreckage I was born. But Langley was wrong. Life did not come to me slowly, by a gradual transformation . . .*

Norman pauses, reining back from his pleasure to glance at Mrs Gasalee who looks dead until he peers carefully to see the faintest movement: a mirror would reveal a slight mist, as if she hibernates like the badger on the cigarette card he carries in his wallet; the card is all that is left of those he gambled away as a child. – *It came to me with an explosion, and all the power of the atom itself surged into me! I was no mere metal robot, with only enough life to stagger about on mechanical legs . . .*

– Well, dear, are you feeling better? Merle fingers her necklace pearl by pearl making it clear she hopes to leave.

– I'm okay, says Mrs Gasalee, I really don't want to keep you. I'll be seeing you soon, I'm sure.

– Of course. Here's the boat.

Merle runs down the steps of Holborn Viaduct and waits on the concrete jetty as the gaily painted barge is guided in; it is as if Queen Elizabeth takes the state barge to Kent or Mary Queen of Scots prepares for execution. In the days before she began to dream Mrs Gasalee saw all Merle's films: *The Scarlet Pimpernel, The Private Life of Henry VIII, The Private Life of Don Juan, Folies Bergère, The Dark Angel* and *The Children's Hour*. While Patrick was away she went to the pictures all the time. She starts, thinking the barge is melting, but it is only disappearing into a mist coming up fast from the Thames, rolling up like smoke, threatening to clog her lungs; yet turning she sees the other side of the Viaduct bright with clear sunshine as she remembers it from the last time she was here with rubble, broken furniture, helmeted men in dark uniforms off in the distance picking through the wreckage. She must be on her way.

Up Holborn from St Paul's comes a procession to rival the Lord Mayor's. Women in silver and gold armour ride white horses, ride chestnuts and palominos, raise banners, their metal warhats held in the crooks of their arms, their hair bobbed, like Joan of Arc's. Their flowing surcoats decorated by scarlet thread, by royal blue and bright yellow, by quartered arms, they ride with relentless dignity as if this is not a sleeping Arthur returned to life but a sleeping Guinevere leading an army drawing strength from the deeds of Boadicea and her daughters: *The Women of England Shall Save Our Country*. She recalls the poster's promise.

The yellow doll lies on the opposite pavement near the balustrade and Mrs Gasalee wonders if she has time to run across and pick it up but the procession is almost upon her so instead she waves. A few women smile at her as they go by but most fix their eyes on their important goals, the saving of their nation, their war against all oppressors. Riding in one brass chariot Gladys Peach is so pregnant she should not be out, but she has a spear and a helmet like the rest. Mrs Gasalee wonders should she volunteer and if so where? She looks away, over the little bright rivers which run like mercury below, towards St Paul's – If God could save St Paul's why couldn't he have saved my Patrick and my . . . There are loud trumpets sounding; loud enough to deafen her, to force her hands to her ears.

– Somebody may be pinned under the wreckage! . . . *SHAZAM! When Billy Batson speaks the magic name, Shazam, there is a crash of thunder and lightning that calls down CAPTAIN MARVEL, the world's mightiest mortal! – Billy's right! I'm glad he called me!* The procession passes and Mrs Gasalee crosses the empty street and looks for the yellow doll but it seems someone else has found it so she stands against the painted iron balustrade seeing miles of sparsely populated wooded hills where the city thins to north and west and becomes a golden land of little villages: a vision of rural paradise, the steeples of churches glittering in the afternoon sun. The mist now forms a silencing wall on the Ludgate Hill side of the Viaduct as she walks up Holborn in the procession's wake towards Gamages and the Prudential's red towers, noticing as usual that it must be Sunday since nobody else is on the street and every shop is shut, wishing she had asked Merle to stay with her, when,

rounding the Hatton Garden corner, comes Katharine Hepburn, all practical beauty.

– Not feeling sorry for yourself, I hope, Mary.

– No, of course not. They embrace. She and Katharine both have the same kind of hair, the same loose blouses and divided skirts, both wear tall boots, as if they have just returned from riding. The sun is warm. Mrs Gasalee is not afraid of it because she knows its gentle inhabitants can do no harm to her.

Arm-in-arm she and Katharine walk towards the white marble of Oxford Street, a wide boulevard. – We'll have some coffee in Bond Street.

– *CAPTAIN MARVEL! Dr Langley's somewhere under the wreckage! There's just a chance he's still alive– – I'll do what I can!*

Mrs Gasalee thinks about the yellow doll, for Katharine has a profound knowledge of the world and, while being more down-to-earth than Merle, is just as kind. Mrs Gasalee looks up in surprise at the streaked sky, for it is already evening. The men on the roofs seem to be some sort of officiates. They wear loose white and gold robes, like priests, and their movements are ceremonial, their hands full of metal, and she means to ask Katharine if they are druids preparing some ancient sunset ritual performed since before the Romans came here, but Katharine has noticed nothing odd and hurries past Oxford Circus and the silent department stores, towards what, from its size and proportions, spanning the whole of Oxford Street, must be Marble Arch. The marble glistens as if with water. She has never seen anything as massive. Not quite sure if she has been here before or, indeed, if she should be here now, Mrs Gasalee is mildly disquieted, but this feeling disappears with the tune Katharine begins to hum.

– *"Jerusalem fell from Lambeth's Vale, down thro' Poplar & Old Bow, Thro' Malden & across the Sea, in War & Howling, death and woe . . .* London's changed a good deal since I was first here, says Katharine.

– It's changed a good deal since I was first here, says Mary Gasalee. – It's changed in a way at least. Some of it's the same. Some of it's as I always imagined it. I wasn't allowed to go very far out of Clerkenwell, you know. My grandma took me shopping and that, later, but we didn't have much call to go West. We couldn't afford it. Or East, for that matter, where we knew nobody. We were about in the middle, weren't we? Not the middle of the old City, but in the middle of London as it is now. Very handy for you, people said. So it was, if you had anywhere you wanted to go. It was good for the pictures. But I moved to Tottenham, you see, when I was married. That's miles from anywhere.

– Don't cry now, says Katharine kindly. – There's a lot of nice things about Tottenham. Weren't you ever in the Garden of Rest? And the recreation ground? You thought you'd be safer. Patrick did. You weren't to know. You didn't make the decision.

– I wasn't given much to decisions. It never really came up. I mean, I didn't think I could. Or wanted to. I still don't want to, Katharine. I just don't want things to have happened.

Looking up from his comic, Norman Fisher wonders if the faint noise came from the patient. Her mouth isn't moving, her eyelids are still. Then he hears the sound again, like a distant fly, could swear it comes from her, from her depths. Norman is conscientious in spite of himself. He is growing to like the lady and understands why people enjoy sitting with her, for at least she's no real trouble. Being with her is a kind of rest; it cheers you up. Sometimes the row and the way patients paw at you gets you down in Main Wing. Going to the window he thinks after all a bee or a fly might have been trapped on the mesh but finds no sign of the insect. He leans to bring his lips close to her face. "Hello, love. Okay are we?" Conscience satisfied, he sits back with his comic. – *What a tragedy! Dr Langley is one of the world's leading scientists! One of his experiments must have gone wrong! Langley's still breathing! But he's terribly hurt! He needs medical attention right away!*

– You should pull yourself together Mary, says Katharine. Start looking to the future. You could make a lot of yourself. Mrs Gasalee remembers the confused fear and despair of other women in her position: Joan Crawford, for instance, in *Paid*. Joan often found the price of ambition too high, would lose the love of children, friends, husbands and wind up embittered, unhappy, alone. Was any worldly power worth that? And was such power always needed to achieve what Katharine so frequently urged her to do?

On little chrome chairs Mary Gasalee and Katharine Hepburn take coffee at a pavement café, observing a bustling Bond Street. They themselves are unnoticed, for everyone else is intent on shopping, dashing in one door and hurrying out another.

Proprietors bow and scrape. Mary recognises the clientele. Only the carriage trade comes to Bond Street. She longs for the Eel and Pie shop in Clerkenwell Road where her grandfather always took her on her favourite outing and where you could have as much mash as you liked. She would stick her sausages in the mash to make them look the way they were supposed to look in her comics, in *Chips* and *Rainbow* where someone's reward for virtue usually took the form of food, but the sausages never stuck up exactly as they should, just as wedges of cake could never be bitten to make a perfect half-circle. Mrs Gasalee spent much of her girlhood trying to get nature to imitate art. In the Eel and Pie shop most people knew her grandfather and would often seek his advice. "What do you fancy for the three-thirty, Alf? Who d'you reckon, Arsenal or Villa? You putting any money on Joe Louis?" Her grandfather would always give grave consideration to these questions and offer a measured answer. On a Saturday he would be surrounded by a dozen or more novitiates. Pressed into the corner of the booth, given a glass of Tizer whenever she ran dry, she was perfectly content to enjoy the mysterious company of those men. Sometimes her grandfather produced a folded pink newspaper and with a stub of pencil would flick ticks against columns, just as fast as he added up figures. "He's got a gift, has Alf," said one man to another. "Your grandad's got a real gift," she was told. "He never goes bust!"

"I never go bust because I hardly ever put any of my own money on." Her grandfather was a tall, thin man, with pure white hair, a white shirt, black waistcoat and trousers. He rarely wore a jacket. In the winter he would put on his overcoat before taking her to the Eel and Pie Shop where he always enjoyed a plate of jellied eels. They kept him healthy he said. They kept him fit. "That way, Mary, you never lose. If you're going to gamble, girl, always do it with someone else's money. Anyway, the knack would go away if I tried to rely on it. I've seen too many chaps come unstuck. I wouldn't try to make a living off the horses. It's like a woman who thinks she can do well by going with a lot of different blokes. There are always more losers than winners, girl. That's life." He hardly ever joined the other men in the public houses, though he would often enjoy indoors a bottle of Guinness shared with Mary's grandmother, usually at dinnertime, sometimes afterwards. "He's

197

better than most," said Mary's grandmother. Usually she wasn't much given to praise, especially to anyone's face. Her little house had a red velvet cloth on the oak drawleaf table in the parlour. There was a kitchen, a pantry and an outside lavatory. Upstairs were three rooms: one for her grandparents, the little front one for herself and one for the lodger, Mr Marrable, who had lived in Wales. They had wallpaper with large dark roses on it, a good quality staircarpet and there was always a strong smell of beeswax, for Mary's grand-mother kept a proud house. Some people in the street said she was stuck-up.

– You're miles away, says Katharine. Is there anything wrong with the coffee? Don't you like it here?

– I feel a bit awkward, says Mrs Gasalee. It's too posh for me, really, though it is very nice of you to bring me, but I think I'd be happier in Holborn, in Cawardine's where the coffee's the best in London. You get all sorts of people come specially from miles away.

– But you shouldn't feel awkward, Mary. You have great poise. How old are you now?

– Seventeen I think. Or maybe eighteen. You know what it's like.

– You should be growing up. You've the makings of a lady. A woman of substance.

– That's what my grandma said. She wanted me to better myself. It's not easy in my circumstances.

– Then change them.

Katherine hails a taxi and they drive through Regent's Park where herds of zebra and gnu look up from their grazing and Mrs Gasalee thinks she sees a lion stalking behind a clump of rhodo-dendrons. Huge birds flap overhead. They might be prehistoric, they are so large. As a little girl, whenever her grandfather wanted to give her a special treat she was taken to the Zoo and she rode on Jumbo. Sometimes she also went on the camel. They had special saddles to carry six children at once. But there had been more cages and a greater variety of animals in those days. Perhaps the predators had eaten the smaller animals? She remembers her grandfather predicting they would. When the wireless mentioned an open zoo he had dismissed the notion as foolish. Overhead something roars. She looks up but the sun dazzles her.

– I'll take him to the nearest hospital. – Good work, Captain Marvel! We'd never have reached him in time! MEANWHILE . . . – EEEOOWW! I'm seeing things. That thing can't be real!

Norman feels sleepy and would like to take a nap but is afraid Mrs Gasalee will come to life or choke herself and he will get the blame. It would be the end of this job and the only alternative is the pit.

Putting down his comic Norman again crosses to the window, hoping for a breeze to revive him, but the air is heavy and grows hotter. The door ajar, he goes outside to the cubicle and pours cold water into the sink, spashing his face until he hears another small sound and returns. Mrs Gasalee might have moved her head a fraction and her lips have certainly opened. Norman stares and listens but her breathing is unaltered. His gaze shifts to his comic lying on the bed. The comic's bold blues, reds and yellows seem to emphasise the fragility of her perfect left hand with its gold and silver ring. It is as if she has just been born fully formed, as yet unspoiled by the world, and for a second he thinks she might be some kind of miracle, but the idea is too fanciful. Norman knows exactly what the differences are between reality and the kind of ideas found in comics. He also knows what sanity is, and recognises insanity. This ability makes him particularly useful to the hospital and he has every chance of promotion. Unlike so many of the nurses, he is rarely infected by the lunacy around him. They say everybody goes mad in the end except the few like Norman who are immune. He returns to the window to look at the blossoms on the walls and smell the lavender at last. He yawns and scratches at his face before digging in his nostrils with his little finger. The cold water has done nothing to wake him up. Back in his seat he picks up his comic. *– NEAR A RAILROAD CROSSING . . . TOOT! TOOT! – I am strong, yes! But what shall I do with my strength? THAT IS THE QUESTION!*

They have reached King's Cross Station's grey and orange spires. – This is where I leave you, I'm afraid, dear. Katharine leans forward to kiss her. I'm going to the country for the weekend. With Spencer. But I'll see you when I get back. What are your plans?

– Oh, I'll probably . . . Then Mrs Gasalee begins to cry. Katharine takes Mary's face to her shoulder, briefly patting the back of her head. – There, there, Mary. Chin up, my girl. You'll be fine. You've just got to decide on a plan, that's all.

Mary cannot stop weeping.

– My train's going, says Katharine. I really must leave. It's the only one for Boston today.

Calming herself, Mrs Gasalee disengages to stand on the concrete watching as Katharine walks rapidly under narrow arches into darkness. Mrs Gasalee turns to discover more arches leading out towards Gray's Inn Road and approaches the middle one, hearing a distant cheering. The arch becomes a colonnade passing through an old churchyard before she can reach the street. There are worn, grimy gravestones; it is evening, faintly misty, peacefully warm, the time she enjoys most, particularly when the graveyard is grown about with thick shrubs and gnarled trees, its great marble angels announcing an unshaken confidence in the afterlife. Looking through some twisted elms surrounding a particularly elaborate tomb, she glimpses yellow and realises she has found the trail of the doll again, but the little paths between the graves form a surprisingly complex maze and it is some time before she is on the other side of the tomb. By the time she stands amongst the elms she has lost her sense of direction. The yellow doll has disappeared, but she is much closer to the tall cemetery gates topped by lacelike metal spires. Passing through them she finds herself in Gray's Inn Road, walking towards St Jude's Church, presumably on her way home.

– *You say nothing was found in the wreckage? – Nothing that could be identified! We put a security guard around the place when we found out it was Dr Langley's laboratory just in case any valuable secrets might be uncovered. But that explosion did a thorough job of demolishing the place! It's a miracle Langley survived.*

Norman is surprised. The story seems over before it has begun, with Captain Marvel in the last frames of the page flying back to Station WHIZ in order to change into Billy Batson and read the news. He gives attention to his charge, wondering if she smiles, then shrugs at his own folly and returns to Captain Marvel, pleased to discover that there is more to come. Meanwhile, outside the window, an orderly wheeling two large cans on a squeaking trolley lifts the lid of the dustbin box and starts to transfer the contents. In an exaggerated gesture of distaste Norman puts his fingers to his nose. "Phew!"

– *Hear me, representatives of the world! I am mightier by far than all your armies and navies! I can destroy you all . . .*

Glad to be in completely familiar territory, Mrs Gasalee takes the short cut through the backstreets off Theobald's Road where every day has an independent identity: Saturday is for the secondhand book stalls and going with her grandfather to the Eel and Pie Shop. Sunday is for reading or the Zoo, or some other special outing. Mondays grandma does the washing and serves cold meat for supper, with big, floury boiled potatoes. On Tuesdays she helps Mrs Kitchen sort magazines and newspapers to be collected by the hospital lorry. On Wednesday she takes care of Mr and Mrs Layborn's youngest while they go to the pictures. They always give her at least twopence, sometimes sixpence when they're a bit late. Thursdays her big homework has to be ready for turning in by Friday morning so Mr Maincastle can mark it over the weekend. On Friday they go to the King's Cross Cinema then have fish and chips from William Roy Hamer's Fried Fish Shop in Leather Lane, the best in London. Mrs Gasalee wishes she knew exactly what day it is. It feels as if it's the summer holidays, the obvious explanation for her own freedom. When she turns into Hatton Garden she realises she has been walking in the wrong direction altogether and begins to retrace her steps to Clerkenwell Road, cutting over into Warner Street where she can see the outlines of the Post Office behind Phoenix Place and, with some relief, knows she will be in Calthorpe Street in a matter of minutes, yet still wonders what it is she's forgotten. – *I have told you what I can do! Now I will show you my power –* THUS! *– AGGGHHH!*

Norman, gripped by the horror of the event, can't be sure if Mrs Gasalee moaned or if he imagined it. – *I saw that! You murderer! – Another challenger! I will deal with you, too! – HOLY MOLEY! You must be Dr Langley's robot! – I am – MR ATOM!*

Norman pauses before he turns another page.

Mrs Gasalee looks back. Above the familiar grey and red rooftops of Clerkenwell and Holborn she sees the risen mist. It has not advanced but grown higher, diluting the sun. Pausing to catch her breath, she decides it would be foolish to go into the mist when all here is clarity and certainty, yet she feels she should not head for Calthorpe Street and will win approval, though she is not sure from whom, if she returns to the Viaduct. Perhaps the army of women in their samite and polished steel wait for her to join them beyond the mist? She closes her eyes, feeling lonely. She needs one of her friends, but her friends never visit Calthorpe Street and grandpa isn't there any more. Has grandma gone too? As she shivers with horror tears return to her eyes, so she sucks in her lower lip, puts her tongue firmly against the roof of her mouth, contracts her throat and rocks so nobody will know she's crying. While no more tears escape she can deceive any passerby, but she is filled with enormous grief. When the mist rises higher she suspects it is not mist at all, but white smoke from some enormous, purifying fire which she must find the courage to enter and be cleansed to make the pain and the tears go and enable her to distress no one, not even herself.

In the empty street without even a face at a window, in the empty street of her girlhood Mrs Gasalee rocks and refuses to weep, turning feet shod in such fine riding-boots, the twin to Katharine Hepburn's, and forcing them to take step upon step upon step; step by step she goes back towards the smoke, her nostrils filling with the not unpleasant smell of it, like burning leaves and twigs on an autumn fire. Step by step Mrs Gasalee goes back to Clerkenwell Road, back to Hatton Garden, down towards the junction where the Viaduct begins and as she goes she is mourning something she cannot remember, grieving for ghosts who refuse to haunt her; step by step, and now the tears can't be held. They pour from her. She shudders with so much terrible grief. She lets the tears run down her cheeks and onto her breasts knowing she must surely ruin her beautiful silk blouse. Gasping, she is hardly able to move. She is exhausted and yet must still try to reach the Viaduct and the smoke hiding all of Old London, rising round St Paul's and the Old Bailey and the Monument and the Mansion House like a wall. Is that what is burning? The City? Is that why she's weeping?

She feels faint as the smoke sucks oxygen from the air and she coughs, her throat as sore as when the hospital took her tonsils out, and she wishes she wore sensible shoes now because the boots make it harder for her to keep her balance.

– *Very well, then! You now have a further demonstration of my power! Death and destruction shall be your lot if you choose to defy me! Choose wisely, mortals!*

– I never wanted to choose, says Mrs Gasalee, but everyone told me I must and I suppose I was happy to do what they thought best. I moved to Tottenham for the baby's sake.

Shaking with enormous sobs she turns back from the smoke and runs, no longer unsteady, until she enters sunlight again, Soho Square. Sitting on a bench, she takes bread from a bag beside her and begins to feed the little birds, shooing the pigeons who always take too much. She sat with Patrick once in Soho Square after they had seen *Gone with the Wind* at the New Empire. The picture had been magical and for a joke she called him Rhett and herself Scarlett. By coincidence Merle Oberon comes through the square's Greek Street entrance and waves. There is warm concern in her voice. – I wondered where you'd got to. Are you feeling all right?

– I had a bit of a spell. I can hardly remember what it was. But I'm fine now. Maybe it's my time of the month.

– I know what you mean. Merle has changed her black velvet for something more ordinary, a pink cotton dress with padded shoulders, a little summer hat with a veil and white court shoes. Sitting beside Mrs Gasalee she takes off her white gloves and dips her fingers into the paper bag to take out a stale crust and break it up in her lap, throwing crumbs to the little blue-tits and bullfinches.

– And what did you do today?

– Since I saw you earlier? Wasn't that today?

– No, dear. We last met on Sunday.

– I remember now. I think I went to the Zoo with Katharine. We saw some wildebeeste and probably a lion. Have you been working?

Merle is clearly reluctant to talk about her own day. She sighs, relishing the square's tranquillity. Traffic noises are far away in Oxford Street and Charing Cross Road, but here they could be in a previous century. – I love that little statue of Charles the Second, don't you? I wonder if he was really that size? Are all monarchs short? I met Edward the Eighth, you know. The Duke of Windsor, I mean. He was extremely handsome but scarcely taller·than me and I'm almost a midget. His brother is the same. They look so tall in the magazines, too. Do you think they use trick photography, the same as in the films?

– I'm sure I don't know. Mrs Gasalee is embarrassed, for while she is used to anger directed at the Royal Family she has never experienced this casual, almost contemptuous gossip. – My grandad thinks they should all swing.

– Oh, that would be terrible! What would future generations do for history plays? Imagine if we *all* got dictators! I can't see it, can you, Mary? *Edward the Eighth* sounds fine, just like *Henry the Fifth*, but I wouldn't fancy a job in *The Tragedy of Mr Chamberlain.*

– My grandad says they have half the money in the country and if they gave up their wealth we'd have no hungry people. He says they should stop visiting miners and feed miners' families instead.

This conversation is not to Merle's taste, so Mrs Gasalee changes the subject. – Do you think this lovely summer will last forever? I wouldn't complain!

It would be awful, thinks Mrs Gasalee, to lose Merle's friendship.

Merle smiles, flinging bread to a sparrow.

A golden haze is rising out of the surrounding Soho streets. Mrs Gasalee can smell coffee and perfume. – The sun people are here! She is disturbed. – Why are they in Soho?

– I think they came on the bus. Merle is a little distant.

Mrs Gasalee is anxious to make up for any offence she may have given. – To do their shopping, I suppose.

– I suppose so. Half turning Merle looks directly into Mrs Gasalee's face, revealing her tears, and Mrs Gasalee realises she has completely misinterpreted her friend's mood. They embrace, mutually comforting. – What's wrong? What's wrong? Again Mrs Gasalee feels her own tears rising. – What's wrong, Merle? Oh, my dear!

– My baby died. Merle takes a deep breath. – My baby died just as she was born. I'd wanted you to look after her. But now she's dead.

Chilled, Mrs Gasalee can think of nothing to say. – Merle!

– *Captain Marvel was clever! He foresaw the difficulty! Already he had built this thick-walled lead prison where I am now caged! Even MY strength cannot help me escape from this place! After this broadcast, I will be allowed to speak no more! This is my last message to the world. You, who have made me your prisoner, BEWARE lest I return to destroy my keepers! . . . BEWARE!*

Norman experiences his deepest satisfaction as he begins the story's last frame. He is sure there is even better to come.

Mrs Gasalee and Merle Oberon walk hand in hand through the narrow streets of Soho where the sun people are buying wine and groceries, ordering meals and drinks in the cafés and calmly going about their business. Apart from their faces, which are dignified and sweet, they are hazy in outline. Some of them recognise Mrs Gasalee and greet her with pleasure but she and Merle do not stop;

they cross Shaftesbury Avenue to be caught in the rush hour, a street full of traffic. Everyone is going home. After Gerard Place the two women pass through Leicester Square, Charing Cross Road and from William IV Street cross the Strand to walk down Villiers Street until they can enter the gardens beside the tube station. Here on a bandstand a little silver band plays *Land of Hope and Glory*, a favourite tune. The pressure of Merle's hand on Mrs Gasalee's is becoming painful. They do not pause in the gardens but cross the grey road to the Thames embankment and stand beneath an obelisk, Cleopatra's Needle which Nelson carried out of Egypt, to stare into pearly water.

— *There you are folks! A final message from Mr Atom, in his underground lead prison! I hope you all take his warning to your hearts! For Mr Atom is a menace the world cannot safely ignore!*

Norman moves on to the Wheaties advertisement.

The river begins to flow faster than usual and has become multicoloured, like seashells. From under Waterloo Bridge a bright flotilla emerges. Old, shining banners in red, gold, blue and white flutter on masts. Merle squeezes Mrs Gasalee's hand still tighter. — I shall have to leave you soon, my dear.

— I'm not lost, says Mary Gasalee.

Changing Posts 1944

"THERE'S NOTHING like a record of mental illness," Josef Kiss put the kettle on the gas, "for saving one's face as well as one's skin."

In the only easy chair Dandy Banaji watched his friend carefully cut a small Hovis, preparing their tomato sandwiches.

"Much better than being a conchie," Mr Kiss drew a tomato from its brown paper bag, "or having flat feet or being a bugger or enjoying the reputation, as in your case, of a Red Republican. Who wants a loony in the army? As a private, anyway."

Amused as usual, Dandy moved his fingers on the chair's floral arm. "You see, old boy, I'd always had you down for a noble pacifist. You shouldn't have told me the truth!"

"You're a pacifist, are you, Dandy?"

"Oh, well, pretty much, you know. Gandhi and all that." This efficient little room with its foldaway bed, its spartan selection of highbrow books and gramophone records, its limited creature comforts, was not what he had expected and was so strange to find behind the pale window nets of suburban Brixton whose every house was a warren of bed-sitters, whose streets were inhabited, if inhabited at all, by embittered and run-down theatricals, by seedy journalists, by isolated drunkards and ancient women exercising ancient dogs. As always he found Brixton more depressing than alarming; this traditional territory of racetrack gangs, whose lethal coalhammers were carried in special pockets, whose other weapons were razors and cycle chains, had most of its hoodlums in the forces or grown too old to cause much trouble. Even with the bombing,

Josef Kiss had told him, Brixton was much quieter than it had been.

Mr Kiss reached towards his urgent kettle. "They're keeping you busy, I hope, in your Top Secret job?"

"Off and on, you know, Josef. With the Japs on the run I don't think anyone will have much further use for me. I might be sent to India."

Mr Kiss had on his red velvet smoking jacket. He paused to feel in a pocket. "Going home? Permanently?"

"The Labour Party has committed itself to Independence. So I'll probably return as something of a hero. Not to be sneezed at, a chance like that."

"Certainly not." Having poured boiling water on the tea Mr Kiss opened, in Dandy Banaji's honour, his can of condensed milk. "And well-deserved. Where will you be going?"

"If I went it would be home to Bombay."

"No sailing date, as yet?"

"None at all." Smiling Dandy accepted his tea. "You know the Civil Service. Oh, marvellous stuff. Hot and sweet, just how I like it."

Mr Kiss prepared the sandwiches. From habit he cut the tomatoes thinly and with his serrated knife laid them carefully on the sparsely buttered bread, sprinkling them heavily with salt and pepper. When he had five sandwiches from three tomatoes he cut them crossways from left to right, then from right to left, to make twenty little triangles. "I wish they could have been cucumber. I know they're your favourites at this time of year. I was late in the queue as usual. I'm working until two. In that little West End Club." He placed the sandwiches beside the earthenware teapot and cups on the tiny table between them. "Assisting a clairvoyant."

Mr Kiss lowered himself into his ladder-backed chair. "He's not a true clairvoyant, of course. People are reassured by his fakery though. I receive the articles from the audience and hold them to my head – ration books, identity cards and so on. Then I give him clues by code. It's easy enough to learn. So many 'No-nos'. So many 'Um-yeses', – you know how these things are done, do you? He's pleased with me, but he's planning a season at Southend soon and I'll only go with him if he increases my money." Mr Kiss sighed. He glanced towards the window.

"So we might not be seeing you for a bit?"

This brought his attention round. "I'll try to stay in London. Southend's only an hour or so on the train from Liverpool Street. Though it might eat into any increase."

For a while they chewed in silence.

"To tell you the truth," Dandy Banaji slowed down on his last two little sandwiches. "I'm rather looking forward to some good international cricket again. When the War's over."

Josef Kiss wiped seraphic lips. "Not my game, I'm afraid. I used to watch a bit of Ice Hockey at Streatham or go to White City for the dog racing. I have the odd flutter on the National or the Derby. My mother was the one for that. Always picked the winners. Without fail. Year after year. I belonged to an archery club when I was a lad, believe it or not. An order of toxophilites which had an ancient Charter to set up targets every weekend in Gray's Inn Fields. Many of us joined because Gray's Inn was otherwise forbidden territory. The lawyers didn't take kindly to a bunch of half-trained common boys with bows and arrows shooting willy-nilly on their lawns. We frequently got a sly shot or two at a tree or even a window. The older members were never quite sure what to make of us. I'll put some more hot water on the tea." . . . *almost hit her when she gets like that. Annie warned me she was moody. The sword of a jedak is never drawn in anger. It's him I'm sorry for . . . and stared across the endless plain* . . . Rising he glanced out into the street and saw an attractive woman with gleaming black hair and brilliant blue eyes, in a grey two-piece suit and navy high heels, walking rapidly along the opposite pavement as if in agitated flight. Her gloved fingers gripped the hand of a small cheerful boy no more than six who skipped beside her and was clearly her child. His blond curls somewhat out of place in Endymion Road, he wore a grey flannel windcheater, grey shorts, grey socks to his knees and brown Oxfords. It seemed to Mr Kiss that the pair must be on a formal outing for they were otherwise too well dressed for Brixton.

Never know these days that last one was too close to be us they tell us they're going to stop but they never do. Harry ought to be here. Those bright little pearls like children in Tooting when I was a girl those steps were a staircase to wonderland, Uncle Leon used to say. Oh why won't it stop I don't want it to hurt I didn't do anything wrong why is it always me gets it all I don't all I did was look after my child there's a war on someone's going to come along anyway. Even Marge thinks that.

Almost solicitously Josef Kiss, kettle in hand, watched them until they reached the end of the street and disappeared.

the bellowing challenge of a bull mangani echoes through the forest

Norma Mummery and her son David are taking the short cut to the tram-stop at Brixton Hill. Marjorie Kitson, whom David knew as Aunty Marge, had offended Norma obscurely, making her leave early, and now she allows few of her familiar responses to her child. Always happy on an outing, and enjoying the sensation of his mother's black glove on his skin, David marvels over Aunty Marge's poodle, Roger, and how the dog was able to beg and roll over. For two hours they had played in the garden while Aunty Marge and mummy talked about shortages and women who could get extra meat or fruit, the usual topics. David cannot remember a time when his mother meeting her friends had not at least touched on these subjects.

As Mrs Mummery and her child turn the corner into the main road, where half the trees are in full leaf and half are blackened victims of incendiary bombs, where piles of rubble lie between forlorn, boarded-up villas built in anticipation of a rising Brixton aristocracy and most of them almost immediately turned into lodging-houses, a scarlet and brass tram begins to start up, its rail sparking on the overhead line; a vivid emissary from some brighter age. David relishes the rare sight of these sparks. All drama over, the tram begins her stately journey down the hill and David gives his attention to the street again, immediately fascinated by a disembarked passenger wearing a sailor suit, the hat high on his curls, hefting a large kitbag onto his shoulder and grinning amiably at a giggling woman who reaches out to touch him. The sailor's skin is the dark brown David's mother identifies as "chocolate" when she looks at material or paint. Even the man's hands are dark, reminding David of Marzipan the Magician in *The Rainbow*, though Marzipan's lips are bigger. David is astonished to find there really is a person of that colour. He thought he had only dreamed of him, this same man. It was like seeing Roy Rogers in the street or one of the Bruin Boys come to life. His mother is also curious but whispers, "Stop staring. It's rude." Whistling, just like any other homebound Tar, the sailor passes them by. "Where's that man from, mummy?" David thinks of a magic land. "From America or South Africa or somewhere," she says. And David is satisfied.

"Why was that lady laughing?"

"She was making a fool of herself, I suppose. Touching him for luck. That's what you do with a black man."

"Because he's magic, like Marzipan?"

The conversation improves her mood and she relaxes. "Oh, maybe, Davey. I don't know. Anyway, I think it's rude. People are people." She looks momentarily into the middle distance. "Not that he seemed to mind." With a sigh she settles to wait at the tram stop.

My son is my life.

Mombazhi Faysha, known as Basher to his shipmates, rolls down Electric Avenue, back to his digs, chanting to himself within himself as is now his habit. Here come the sailorman. Here come the African sailorman with his bag on his back and his big fag hanging out of his mouth. Here he come. Come down the road. Coming home to a home which want him. Coming away from a home that don't want him at all. Coming home to the lady calls him Captain. Hello Captain. Hello darling. Here come your own little bushman baby African little sailorman cheeky sweetheart and what he got in his bag for us this time?

Here come the sailorman back from the War, all the way from Cape Town, all around the world, all with his different stuff in his bag. Here come the sailorman. Here come the African sailorman to tell you about Shanghai and Sydney and Calcutta and anywhere else you want to know. Been everywhere. Been on the convoys and on the old bad steamers what run between Borneo and Rangoon. Been on the North Sea convoys taking food to the Russkies. Been in the sea thought to die in the sea to drowned in the sea to be all swallowed up. Not me. Been drunk on docks from Liverpool to Lagos. Not this year. This year the African sailorman save up his pay. Stayed on board, paving his way.

Here come the African sailorman with a medal on his chest and a dignity no damn colour bar going to lose him.

Here he comes, with a dignity no curse, no unconscious insult, no white fool will ever diminish. Here he comes, sauntering up Electric Avenue, tipping his hat to the turned heads, greeting the people who know him with a jaunty "Hi, there!" and "Good to see you, missis!" Able Seaman First Class Faysha, come through the World War and all the dangers of the Seven Seas to put down his kitbag, to set it at the feet of his lady love and tell her his plans. For he is going to settle down ashore. He means to get himself a job with prospects. He means to marry Alice Moss and make an honest woman of her.

He reaches the little green front gate. There are climbing roses in bloom along the wall beside the house's door. From inside a dog begins to bark. He gets out his latchkey and strolls slowly up the path, taking his time, step by step. He touches the key to the lock. Already he can hear her running down the hall to greet him, her own darling bit of beauty.

My beauty my gentle beauty my sweet my faith's salvation my own little wonder my brave and tender love. Thank God. Oh, thank you God!

Brixton bears her scars as gladly as her sons once sported razor-wounds; she's full of dusty plane trees, rosebay willowherb, hollyhocks and poppies, butterfly bushes everywhere, no longer quite the entity she was. The bombs fragmented her identity as they have broken up so much of London. She is missing many of her houses, missing whole streets almost, because she bore the brunt of the first flying-bombs. Misdirected to the uncrucial south, the enemy thought they had got the range on London's factories. As she was the closest witness of the Battle of Britain, with the planes going up from Biggin Hill and Croydon and half-a-dozen other airfields, so South London, selected to confuse the enemy, to draw him away from the city's heart, takes the V-bombs. She throws up her dust, her ashes and her black smoke still stinking where dirty children play, grimy with the detritus of a thousand air-raids.

When the news came that Hitler was beaten South London began to stir again; then came the rockets. The rockets almost finished her. The rockets threatened to drive her mad. So many fiery swords hanging overhead, falling without warning, falling without logic, without motive. Falling as the Nazis in their death-throes killed at random, killed for revenge, killed because killing had become their habit, their only fulfilment. Killed as they had always killed.

Nobody cared much for Brixton. Brixton was an unimportant target. Brixton could be dispensed with. All Brixton ever spawned was subhuman, violent and greedy. All Brixton ever sheltered was failure and the excluded. Had the Wehrmacht and the Panzers moved upon the city, Brixton would have been sacrificed. She had been expendable almost since her conception; a place of brickyards, a railway suburb, never respectable even in her early years.

Violet was her flower and that's what we called her though her name was Nelly. Not even christened Eleanor. Not christened at all, for by then her parents were between faiths you might say, not completely lost to the Jews, not yet claiming C of E. Only half-absorbed. It would be left to Nelly and her sisters to change their names as they changed their pasts and bury those alien ancestors for good, trivialising all that had gone before, devaluing their own lives as they devalued the lives of their forebears . . . I write this down because I am dying, because I have been sent to die, as I deserve, alone, for I too have denied those ghosts their rightful voice. I was afraid. I could not face such evil. I could not survive such fear. I prayed, as so many of us prayed, not for enlightenment, not for knowledge, but for ignorance.

Beryl Male is not sure it is a good idea to be seen driving through Brixton but she reassures herself of anonymity here. She has learned of a recent death of an old lady on the Tulse Hill side, who has some good pieces, a couple of worthwhile paintings, perhaps, and some promising bric-à-brac. Beryl needs it for her shop in Kensington Church Street. The larger premises need filling as quickly as possible and a house clearance, if cheap enough, will do the trick.

Her figure kept trim only by savage self-discipline, her costume carefully chosen so that while she does not appear wealthy she does look decently upper-class, she sports a new perm, her mousy hair tinged towards brunette, and drives with some pride a new Wolseley which she has waited for since 1939, her polished court shoe just a little uncertain on the accelerator for she has never controlled a car this powerful ("the same as the police use" said the salesman). Her sharp features are more attractive when softened by fat. She has light brown eyes, pale pink skin, has shaved her eyebrows as thoroughly as she shaves the rest of her body, and smells of some severe cologne which she calls her shark repellent and always wears into unknown territory. She pulls her new car up beside the tram stop and addresses a young woman and her child. The woman looks reasonably smart and well-educated. Beryl's mouth forms a condescending grin. "I'm so sorry to bother you. I'm trying to find Tulse Hill."

"You need to go back that way." Awed by the new car the woman points roughly east. "Look for Brixton Water Lane, back there on the right, then turn right again and that's Tulse Hill itself. You'll see Brockwell Park on your left. There's a big ack-ack gun. I think it's still there. As a matter of fact that's where we've just come from." And she laughs at this coincidence.

"Thank you so much," says Beryl absently. She winds up her window.

Norma and David Mummery watch her turn in the road, almost in the path of another tram which, apparently affronted, clangs and rattles.

"Hoity toity," says Norma Mummery. Her glove tightens on David's hand.

"What's that over there, mummy?" David points to a massive Gothic pile, Victorian stone and green wrought iron, but the tram is coming and blocks the view as she hurries him aboard. "Thornton Heath Pond only." The ancient conductor seems to suspect a plan to go further.

"We'll get off at the ABC and walk down." Mrs Mummery fishes in her handbag. "One and a half, please, to the ABC Norbury." She hands the conductor a threepenny bit as David climbs the stairs. He likes the trams much better than buses for there is more adventure to them. A tram's stairs are outside, unprotected from rain or wind, and a boy can stand with his back to the curved metal, pretending to be aboard some more romantic vessel. David also likes the polished wooden seats whose backs move to let the passenger face either direction. He likes being able to see the way he's come. He ascends swiftly, followed by his reluctantly indulgent mother, and sits down in time to take another look at the iron gates and the castle beyond. His mother smiles. "That's the prison. It's where you'll wind up if you go on the way you're going."

"I haven't done anything wrong!" David is tickled by his mother's joke.

"Not today you haven't." She hugs his shoulders as he looks back at the prison with considerable interest. After reading, in terror and bafflement, *Great Expectations*, he has a clear idea what convicts are and wonders casually if his father could be found amongst them. Although he is fairly certain Vic Mummery is not in the War he can get nobody to tell him where his father actually is. Streatham Astoria, his favourite cinema, now lies ahead and he carefully inspects the posters to see what films are showing. "Oh!" His mother brightens. "George Raft. Perhaps we'll go later on in the week." David's own happiness increases.

nice piece of skirt get up her I bet all the Americans

Knocking briskly on the polished oak of the large Queen Anne villa, Beryl Kiss was satisfied to note the house was detached with a good-sized garden, its own garage and slightly neglected; the home of someone of reasonable means and a solid middle-class pedigree. It was to houses like these that Imperial Civil Servants had retired. She could almost smell the furniture, could guess how much colonial bamboo she would find, what sort of pictures would be on the Morris wallpaper. Lately she had developed an interest in English paintings, including the early PreRaphaelites, and good quality 18th-century furniture. An elderly woman opened up the door and drew it back. "Oh?" Beryl had expected a daughter, someone younger. "Miss Boyle-Unsworth?"

"You're Miss Kiss. Come to take a look at my sister's things?"

"Of course. Yes I have."

The woman was shy. Stooped with arthritis she had been much taller once, perhaps almost six feet. Her skin healthy and flushed, she wore her dark grey hair tied back in a somewhat eccentric pigtail. Green eyes, a wide nose, thin lips, turquoise and tortoise-shell earrings, bracelets, torque, a kind of chatelaine holding a cameo, a belt low on her waist. Beryl Kiss catalogued her. The whole effect was old-fashioned bohemian as if she had worn the same clothes in Chelsea or Bloomsbury from the turn of the century. "My sister was a widow. Her husband died before the War. He was a doctor in Singapore, you know. Ran a hospital there. I shouldn't think you'll be interested in most of this stuff. All a bit out of date. Not really antique. But you were recommended by Mr Victor and so I thought I'd give you first crack so to speak."

The gloomy hall was full of the anticipated dark bamboo and oak so polished and grimed it was almost impossible to identify. There were several pictures to which she would give more attention later.

"Very kind," said Beryl Kiss. "Mr Victor's your solicitor?"

"My nephew's solicitor. My sister's solicitor, that was. My own solicitor is in Rye. Where I live." Miss Boyle-Unsworth spoke rapidly, with an unusual lisp. She might almost have been German, or even Jewish, Beryl thought. She followed her through into the front sitting-room which had the familiar chairs, matching sofa, various small tables, pot plants, photographs. But as she trained her eye Beryl noticed that the photograph frames were the best examples of Liberty Cymric silver. There was a good deal of Cymric in the room; vases, mirrors, clocks, all solidly resellable but chiefly indicating a good chance of finding something really valuable. In almost unconscious response to this Beryl nodded, displaying restrained disappointment. "Ah, well. Let's look at the other rooms, shall we? I feel a little awkward, you know. Mr Victor's an old friend . . ."

"It was good of you to come."

"I'll be as quick as I can. I'm sure – "

"No, no. I've all the time in the world. I'm stopping overnight at my London club. So I'm in no hurry."

"Where are you staying?"

"The New Cavendish."

"You'll know Lady Kenwick. And Mrs Berengori, perhaps?"

"Not intimately. I use the club infrequently these days." Miss Boyle-Unsworth gave out a faint, uncomfortable smile.

"Lady Betterton?"

"We're fairly well acquainted, yes." The smile showed relief.

By this mixture of social display, flattery and mild intimidation, Beryl established both her status and control. "You must let me give you a lift. I'm going that way after this."

"I've no wish to remain here any longer than necessary. I'm obliged to you. It's hard to get a bus here. And a long walk to the station."

"Let's have a quick look at the other rooms, shall we?"

By the end of her tour Beryl Kiss had noted a small Holman Hunt, two good quality Palmers, a variety of medium-rank PreRaphael-ites and English water-colourists, a Sargent, a Whistler and what was almost certainly a Manet, the signature obscured by its heavy frame. She had also seen two pieces of Sheraton, a Wedgwood dining-service, a fair amount of Minton and some fine Meissen figurines.

As she let her into the car, she gave Miss Boyle-Unsworth the impression of someone making difficult calculations and, just before starting the engine, murmured, "If seven hundred and fifty would be acceptable . . ."

With a gesture of embarrassment Miss Boyle-Unsworth accepted gladly. "It seems very generous. Are you sure? I'd really like to see the back of it. In the circumstances the sorting was, well . . ."

"I presume a cheque will be all right? I'll write it out when I drop you off." Beryl put the car into gear.

"I'm sure there's no hurry. But since nothing's insured it would probably be best." To Beryl's considerable satisfaction Miss Boyle-Unsworth was blushing.

"If," said Beryl sympathetically, "you're prepared to leave the keys with me I could see to everything. I have some very trustworthy people."

"That would be a great weight off my mind." Miss Boyle-Unsworth settled with somewhat less discomfort into her seat.

"These things can be very difficult." Beryl moved smoothly towards the crossroads, under a railway bridge stained by fire. "My own parents were killed last year. My brother and I had to go through their things."

"Not a bomb, I suppose." Grateful for common ground.

"Yes, but they were in a train."

"How awful."

Beryl changed gear, trying in this action not to reveal a sense of triumph.

fish and chips rock salmon everyone knows it's sharks that landmine hit the convent and the greengrocers went up at the same time if he don't come home ready for it tonight he'll come home tomorrow and find the milkman in his bed no luck with the vinegar it'll be a while till we're back to normal that shtoonk he shits in his gatkes and everybody loves him what a bonditt what a bonditt, the schlub, and his father the best baker in Brixton slonce juz gaslo

Crossing by the traffic lights by Brixton Town Hall, Dandy Banaji waved at Beryl Kiss's car but she was busy talking to an older woman beside her. Dandy watched the Wolseley's decisive path towards the invisible river then walked up to the bus-stop outside the Bon Marché Department Store where he would have a better selection of buses to take him back to his borrowed apartment in a block just off Smith Square, Westminster, where every other resident seemed to be a politician living there only part of the time, so weekends were singularly peaceful. He would be sorry to leave. He stood looking across the road at a damaged house, wondering how many people had been killed when the V2 hit it. With V-Bombs you never had a chance to get to the shelter. The V1s had been bad enough, but you could hear them before they started to descend. The V2s were completely silent; you could be sitting in your front room listening to the wireless and the first sign of a V2 would be the whine as it came down out of nowhere. How much longer could Londoners, whose morale had deteriorated so badly at the end, sustain the rocket attacks? There was still a public ban on such discussion but it remained a talking-point at the Department, though they had nothing to do with London's civilian affairs.

He boarded a 109 which would take him to Westminster. He sat downstairs on the bench seat. They got to Stockwell and the leafier reaches of Kennington and he felt obscurely that he had left the most dangerous section of the war zone. Having no telephone of his own, Josef had asked Dandy when he got home to call a Mrs Kiss in Harrow to say he was delayed in Southend and would come up in the morning. Presuming the woman to be a relative, Dandy was surprised by his friend's secrecy, for he felt they were intimates even though Josef had only begun inviting him home to Brixton in the last few months. Was the woman Josef's mother, his sister-in-law, his wife? You could never know what the English were hiding. He took out his notebook and recorded these observations, since as soon as the Japanese were defeated and things got back to normal in India he planned some articles about English life and manners for one of the papers out there. His writing became hard to control as the bus vibrated. If the Indian papers were not interested he would approach a New York journal. *The Nation* had published some of his work before the War, though its editors blew hot and cold and one couldn't rely on their integrity. Replacing the cap on his fountain pen, he noticed how the sleeve of his light sports jacket had frayed. It was the only decent summer jacket he had and as soon as he could afford it he would take it to the Invisible Menders in Piccadilly for leather cuffs and elbows to be put on. As the bus crossed Westminster Bridge Dandy returned pen and notebook to his pocket, preparing to disembark.

I thought those bastards had had enough with the Blitz but there's always a few. I call it treachery. I call it what it is. Yes, I've known the bleaker bits

217

of London. I've lived and worked in parts of Fulham, Somers Town and Notting Dale. Compared to them Brixton's a suburban paradise. I know what being a copper's all about. Notting Hill has the real what I call thieves' kitchens with criminals drinking together in the basements then going upstairs to their lodgings. Without leaving the premises they can find a fence or get a prostitute. It's what my sergeant used to call the whole colourful spectrum of vice . . . Taxi drivers'll refuse to take you into Notting Dale. There's hundreds of stories about the ruling families, used to be all-out battles with the police, they barricaded us in our own station once, we used to patrol in threes down there. No, give me old Brixton any day, even with the gangs back. You know where you are with those lads. Notting Dale's got real villains. The East End's overrated on that score, believe me. I'll take another half. Are you sure that bloke didn't recognise us?

Savouring every action, Josef Kiss washes his dishes, stacking them neatly in his little wooden cabinet; he makes a paper cap and with a khaki elastic band secures the top of the condensed-milk can; he goes to sit in his comfortable chair. When as a lad he left home to go on the stage this was the first room he ever took, inheriting it from a comic juggler who retired to the Kent coast. The room is arranged like all his rooms, though he keeps fewer treasures here save for a small wind-up gramophone. Instead of posters featuring himself he displays some group photographs, chiefly from his childhood, though one was taken at the nearby Springfield Mental Hospital. Dandy Banaji is the only other guest Josef Kiss has ever admitted since he brought a girl from the chorus at the Grand Theatre soon after he took the flat and before he was married. He has never used his flats to deceive his wife in anything but matters of privacy. Had he not gone mad and given up his true calling he might at least have let her know about this one, but when his decision to retire from mind-reading was received so poorly he grew to distrust her. Their intimacy ceased. The house in Harrow is in her name and almost paid for. Whatever happens to him, that and a considerable amount of life insurance makes her future fairly certain. She always received his lies without question and he cannot know if she really suspects nothing or does not care how he spends his time as long as she is also allowed her privacy. He wishes it were not too late to discuss such things but now the lie has hardened and become a matter of habit.

They have achieved a miserable *status quo* which neither presently wishes to threaten. So they go on. He still loves his Gloria and perhaps she loves him, but she wanted so much for him to become a star and she cannot cope with his mysterious resistance to his destiny; she had dreamed of supporting him in his climb to fame and fortune, of commiserating in his noble failure, but nothing had prepared her either for his unnatural lack of ambition, or to know ambition for herself alone. Sensing her frustration and helpless to satisfy her, he sympathises but cannot change.

"Gloria, my dear." He glances through the shielding nets to the street outside where a yellow-and-white mongrel sniffs at rusty metal dustbins placed to one side of a gateless path. Even the sunlight cannot relieve the squalor, the suggestion that here all the city's hopeless souls must finish their lives. In the socialists' Utopia will such misery actually be stamped out? Will a Wellsian marble city rise from the ruins? Josef Kiss hopes desperately that it will not, for he is in love with London as she is. To change her radically is to threaten his own identity: to threaten the identities of her remaining millions.

He imagines Endymion Road as a thoroughfare in which gentlemen and women in chitons and sandals come and go, like an idealised scene from Periclean Athens, and is so amused that he laughs aloud. "Oh, why not? Why bloody not? Good luck to you, Mr Attlee." He shakes and the room shakes with him, the little Chinese vases, a present from Patricia Grant, the actress who courted him for an entire season at Scunthorpe in 1942, rattling together and threatening to fall from the mantel onto the blue and orange tiles of the grate in front of his gasfire. He controls himself long enough to rise and adjust the vases. Sometimes when he feels miserable about his situation with Gloria he consoles himself with the knowledge that the Belle of Scunthorpe was once his for the asking. He had enjoyed her company and taking her to dinner or making little trips to the country, but always on the understanding he was already spoken for. Even the sight of the RAF uniform in the alley behind the house in Harrow had not changed this for him, though he understood that sooner or later affairs must come to a head. He was determined to put that moment off for as long as he could.

polyphony but even the most progressive halls are reluctant perhaps

219

because people want to be reassured by tradition in wartime; yet that hardly explains the amount of progressive literature and poetry, even painting, emerging now

Clearing his throat, he wonders suddenly what they are all waiting for, why there is a mood of expectation throughout the city. Has everyone become so familiar with dramatic events they now demand them on a regular basis? Is war a drug? Is everyone hooked? If England were to sink into an exhausted stupor what would the politicians find to bring people back to life? Another war? The socialists could scarcely build their brave new world in a couple of years. Josef Kiss hopes civil strife will not follow, for he believes people can be like dogs once their adrenalin is running and if separated from fights with enemies will frequently turn and attack friends.

His drift takes him into dangerous waters. Politics reminds him of his sister and he grows alert with a sudden suspicion she is nearby, possibly looking for him, having used her influence with her friends in high places to flush him out. All Londoners have heard rumours of secret ministries possessing lists of every bolt-hole, every soul's habitat, Muscovian in complexity. At the window again he cranes to look the length of Endymion Road, but even the dog has gone. Only a ragged blackbird, its missing tailfeathers showing it to be the survivor of some cat's over-sophisticated game, sits in the tree outside the window and pipes an anxious call. But Josef Kiss knows the blackbird for an alarmist who has cried "Cat!" ever since his escape. The other birds have ceased to listen. Opening the secret drawer in his writing-table, he removes one of his store of strong prewar peppermints with which he these days consoles himself. He sucks, he considers the odds, he relaxes.

He is back in his chair, his features serene. The nets fall in folds at the window resembling so many fine bars, slender rods positioned in the casement behind which are a roof, some foliage, a distant yew, the blue sky. By moving his head upward a little he could see a bombed ruin, one of the large houses which made such an orderly thing of Brixton Hill. But Brixton Hill has almost lost any recognisable form. Only the tram-rails are consistent, crossing with telephone lines and electricity ducts, with sewers and gaspipes to form a great cat's cradle binding Brixton like steel wires in concrete, perhaps the reason why the suburb has not completely collapsed beneath the flying bombs.

Dozing, he sees the gathered mists of an ancient Surrey hillside before it was London. Gentle, early-morning summer mists, daisies and dandelions cover the grass; a sandy track follows the path of what is now Brixton Hill, and out of the mists roll the bright shapes of covered wagons, elaborately painted and carved with ancient illumination, traditional figures; gypsy caravans drawn by shaggy ponies as sturdy and enduring as their owners. They are followed by other more ordinary carts, carrying goods towards London Bridge to provision all those who crowd together on the other side. There are unkempt drovers' dogs, like Old English Sheepdogs, and bullocks, mules, big carters' horses, all going to trade with the city before returning to the countryside again. A few of their number they'll leave behind. He tries to distinguish faces but by concentrating too hard he loses the rest of the picture so he relaxes again, watching as the procession moves perpetually towards him.

This pleasant and unremarkable vision comes to him frequently. It is as if the rest of the nation is perpetually in motion on the city's periphery, as if London is the hub around which all else revolves, the ordering, civilising, progressive force which influences first the Home Counties, then the entire nation, ultimately the Empire and through the Empire the Globe itself: a city more powerful than all cities before it, perhaps more powerful than all cities will ever be, for New York cannot equal it, nor Washington, nor any city Josef Kiss can imagine. London is the last capital of the great city-based civilisations and henceforth the new empires shall be built in the name of ideals and crusades, in the name of holy abstractions. The golden age of cities has achieved its absolute fulfilment. London has surely reached her maximum expansion and must now begin to shrink until, as Athens or Rome, her memory shall be greater and more enduring than her stones.

The mist gradually envelops the gypsies, the drovers, the herds. Josef Kiss tries to peer through it but by now realises he is actually sleeping. Soon his dreams will be completely out of his control.

Late Blooms 1940

CHLOE SCARAMANGA came back from attending to the new Sicilian Flower Birds; she was enthusiastic. "They're settling in beautifully. Who told us they were bad tempered?"

Seated in sunlight which slanted through a low window from the west, Beth Scaramanga had been sorting out some old embroidery. The round wicker basket which had belonged to their mother was full of rich pieces, many representing other exotic breeds, for as well as boarding cats and dogs and growing roses, the sisters bred chickens; they were famous in the poultry fancy for their success and until 1939, at Earls Court, had regularly won major prizes. There had not been a show this year because of the War. Breeders were apparently afraid of losing their best birds. The Scaramangas had been contemptuous of this caution and tended to take a lofty view of "our country cousins" who had so little, in their view, to fear. Bank Cottage, lying in the shadow of North Kensington's gas holders but hidden by high yew hedges, with its own mooring on the canal, its view of the cemetery's trees, shrubbery and flowers, was much as it had been when built by Bishop Greville for his head shepherd in the middle of the 17th century. Its stone and timber and thatch had been dutifully maintained by Scaramangas since the family inherited it two hundred years earlier, and was a perfect example of its kind. The town had grown up around it then become part of the city so that the sisters might still consider themselves true Londoners. They had been born and raised in the Royal Borough and if they died penniless tomorrow Kensington would have to give them a proper funeral. While the family home remained in Edwardes Square the cottage had been let to a variety of bargees and artists, but when their father had died shortly after their mother they discovered his debts to be considerably greater than any assets, so they sold the house then refurbished and redecorated Bank Cottage, whose land was theirs by ancient deed and which could not be claimed by Crown or Council, turning their hobbies into a living. They were as successful as they wished to be and, though the only ways of coming and going were by the towpath or by boat since the Gas, Light and Coke Company would allow them no legal right of way to Ladbroke Grove, they were as content as they had ever been in Edwardes Square. Neither had much cared for Kensington society but had put up with it for their mother's sake. In Bank Cottage they had successfully weathered a Depression and fully expected to weather a War.

Chloe Scaramanga entered the kitchen to put away her gloves and basket. "I think I'll make a cup of tea. Like one?" She wore a blue French blouse and an old beige skirt. Her pretty skin was reddened by exposure to the weather.

"Really you should let me. I've done nothing."

"I'm up and about. What are you planning to do with all those bits? Cushions?"

"Nope." Beth was decisive. "The vicar's getting 'em next jumble sale. To help the war effort."

"They'll be snapped up. The workmanship's so superior. But it seems a shame."

"They passed the time when we had more on our hands. But they are pretty. Remember Jack?" She held the piece up.

Jack, their Cochin cock, a golden buff with huge feathery feet, had been their third prizewinner.

"What a character." Chloe crossed to the Welsh dresser and took down the Nurenburg tea caddy. "He never changed. Right from a chick. That Mrs Cocker's opened. Did you see?"

"And smelled. We've been even luckier this year." Beth plucked loose thread off her flowery summer dress.

Chloe brought in the big wooden tray with the teapot covered by a red knitted cosy, two cups, the sugar in an old French porcelain bowl, two yellow-and-black plates, a Staffordshire milk jug shaped like a cow and a Christmas biscuit tin on which Harlequin and

Columbine danced. Beth moved her basket for Chloe to put down the tray and pull her own chair closer, then both looked through the open window at their roses and relished the air. "You can't believe the War's still on." Chloe poured a little milk into each cup. Both brothers had been killed in 1918 and Chloe's fiancé had been shot near the Roumanian border in 1921 during the Russian fighting. When they referred to the War at all it was usually to dismiss it as "that nonsense" and even should the Germans conquer London they did not expect to be greatly disturbed. Nine years of living in relative isolation at Bank Cottage had given them a sense of invulnerability. Hard to find even from the towpath, the cottage possessed a single tall wrought-iron gate which led directly to the steps of their mooring. Occasionally passersby were surprised to see the Scaramanga skiff shoot out into the canal and head towards Little Venice. The few bargees who still worked the canal were affectionately protective and the Gas Company employees, taking only a dismissive interest in two loonies who raised chickens they refused to slaughter, understood the Scaramanga sisters to be under the protection of the bargees who brought down the coke and whose anger they feared. Unaware of this, the Scaramangas thought the men polite and decent and only occasionally did Beth complain to the Company if she felt men working on the tall holders were threatening their privacy.

Picking up her cup, Beth Scaramanga realised that the early September weather reminded her of something she did not much want to think about.

"When is the jumble sale?" In the light from the window which softened her somewhat angular features and emphasised the beauty of her lips, Chloe looked so much like their father. Inheriting her heart-shaped face and curly brown hair from their mother, Beth otherwise resembled her sister. Chloe's lovely hair was strawberry blonde, from the Hackwood side, and she had the golden "faery" eyes which Pope had described after meeting Caroline Hackwood when a guest at the Hollands'. Proud of her sister's eyes Beth had hung the portrait of Florence Hackwood in their little spare bedroom so that guests might note the similarities and liked to show off her sister's looks whenever she could. She knew she was pretty but she lacked Chloe's originality and at 36 was not as striking as Chloe at 39. Remembering their conquests, she smiled;

224

there had been so many that they had become the object of scandal. Some of the scandal had been undeserved but she had enjoyed her reputation, for it gave her a certain kind of freedom and she wondered what might have happened if she had stayed on in Paris when Jay had gone off to Italy with her sailor. She could not imagine she would be any happier than she was. And she would have had to come home eventually, with France throwing in the towel as she had done. Beth was not surprised by their surrender; the French had always been Huns with fancier manners and better taste, quite as rude and almost as arrogant, making the Germans better allies than enemies. She still loved Paris but had never been completely won over to the idea of the entente cordiale.

Her sister was suddenly laughing. "Bethy! You're miles away!"

"I suppose I was thinking how lucky we are to have so much of our own food. Eggs every day if we want and a good price for those we don't want. Though I'm still not completely sure of Mr O'Keefe."

"If we're breaking the law someone will make us stop sooner or later. We're doing our bit, Bethy. The vicar's always ringing up for something."

Beth winked at Chloe. "Aye, aye!" Both held the opinion that Mr Goozey was smitten, but they were not entirely sure which of them he wanted. Given the amount of work he had, his excuses for calling grew feebler by the day. He was limp and handsome and his wife, they had heard, was now living in America with her lover, though he called himself a widower. His two sons were at school and his daughter was looked after by his housekeeper. The Scaramangas had visited him several times at his Dalgarno Road vicarage to watch him blush deep red the whole time they were there. Since they got so little sport nowadays they made the most of him.

Chloe was certain Beth was the vicar's choice, but Beth was not convinced. As Beth returned to her reverie Chloe slowly slipped into her own, wondering at the intermittent nature of what she called her sex-drive for there were no other signs of menopause. After settling at Bank Cottage she had continued entertaining her lovers there but Beth had gone to visit hers or had taken them down to Brighton. The men had come to bore her in conversation as well as in bed, and it became unbearable to give them the

225

responses they always seemed to need. Gradually the men grew resentful and stopped telephoning and while she had not wanted them to do anything else she missed the pleasure she had expected to enjoy into her sixties. She had discussed this with Beth who had always been more selective and anyway preferred women. "I've less choice, really." Beth had told her. "But I suppose I'm in much the same state, too. Funny, isn't it?"

Chloe had read that in wartime women's libidos became affected. They lost all biological urges or else acted like rabbits, perhaps wanting to produce replacements for the killed. She had a poor opinion of most psychological sexual theories. She was sure there had to be social causes for the phenomenon.

Both sisters swayed a little in their chairs as if drugged by the scent filling the room, which had filled it all summer and every summer. Outside one of their cocks began a noisy display. Beth knew it was their Laced Barnvelder, a slightly aggressive Dutch bird. If he continued his nonsense, she decided, he was not long for this world. Earlier, Chloe had decided he sounded rather like Mr Churchill and that was now his name. She always hated killing but they had reduced numbers in the coops drastically, cutting space allowed for chickens to make room for dogs and cats since, with the evacuations, more people were boarding their animals. They had three Springer spaniels, two Pomeranians, an Alsatian, a bull terrier and a greyhound, as well as the usual half-dozen Pekes which, like the Persians in the cattery, enjoyed being together. The Scaramangas specialised in Persians and Pekes. The animals were not a great deal of trouble, and several took the space they could charge for a single Dane. They also had a couple of Siamese and various English domestics, including a very fine Red with eyes as fiery as his fur who spent much of his time in the house because he was Beth's favourite and his owners had decided to sit out the War in Australia. She called the cat Riley and whenever they received a cheque for his upkeep she thought it was like being paid to maintain one's own pet. She would be sorry when the War ended. Liking dogs best, Chloe found only the present batch of Poms appealing. It was hard to get decent food for the animals, some of whom were decidedly disgruntled by their new diets. She reached for her *Woman's Weekly*.

Very suddenly Mr Churchill stopped crowing and it seemed the entire world had been stilled at the same second. They heard nothing from the gasworks, nothing from the canal, no traffic in Ladbroke Grove, no trains from the lines on the other side of the gasholders. The slight breeze rustling the yew branches was gone. There were always such moments but this continued, and for an answer Chloe looked to Beth whose eyes were fixed on a nearby yellow and pink Madame Ravary where a bee close to the heart of the flower had paused as if in expectation. Time itself might have stopped, save that Chloe, experimenting, saw her fingers move and knew that if she wished she could easily get up, while the lapping of water from the canal meant that too was unaffected. Or was Time moving backward?

Chloe made herself concentrate on the familiar creosoted beams of the ceiling, the whitewashed plaster, the pewter and copper decorating their walls, the big old-fashioned hearth with its black fire irons, its brass toasting machine, the trivet on which they boiled their winter kettles, each of the windows looking onto a little neat lawn surrounded by crowded flower-beds, the whole enclosed by their great impenetrable hedge. She reminded herself of their security. She still regretted replacing their leaded windows with clear glass, for all it allowed more light. She now began to experience a kind of claustrophobia as the silence wore on. As if for the last time she took stock of their bookcases, each shelf protected by pleated linen curtains so spines could not fade, their cabinets of china and silver gathered during travels or inherited from obscure relatives, their bijouterie, the family pictures in big pewter frames above the fireplace, the good-quality Turkish rugs on the slate slabs, brought years ago from the Lake District, which were always so cold.

And the moment grew longer still, like the period before a Singapore typhoon or a storm in July. But this was September with no hint of thunder.

Then the silence broke at last. Chloe heard a distant plane climbing, its engine labouring as it sought altitude beyonds its capacity; when the sound died away she heard metal striking metal over in the train yards.

She looked at the clock. It was four-thirty. The silence returned, as if the city kept trying to resume normality and, failing, tried again, and failed; as if she were a beast alerted but uncertain of the source of her danger.

Could this silence, Chloe wondered, have anything to do with an air-raid? Had the authorities ordered London mute so special listening posts could more easily catch engine noises and count how many planes were coming over, where they were headed, when they would come? There was one huge detector horn pointing at the sky on nearby Wormwood Scrubs, another in Hyde Park. But nobody really expected an attack any more.

The single aeroplane, perhaps a Gladiator, came back, doubtless heading for the Farnham aerodrome. It was flying low now, seemingly in a hurry.

As if emerging from a daze the bee began gathering pollen from the rose while the breeze returned to make the yew branches shiver and, realising she had been holding her breath, Chloe expelled air from her lungs with a great sigh, smiling. Beth turned, shaking her head. "Angels passing over."

"All this nonsense makes you behave in such an odd way sometimes." Chloe reached towards the teapot and plucked off the cosey. "I hate superstition and that's what it is."

But Beth was still nervous; Chloe noted the way she kept her hands on the arms of her chair, letting her sister pour more tea without actually offering her cup. Now the scent of the roses had grown almost unbearable, as if the late summer heat made the most of everything it touched and Chloe's dreaminess continued, though the sensation of dread had passed, for the Saturday traffic could be heard again, far away on the canal bridge, while noisy bluebottles, bees and wasps, bustled about in the humid air. Even the sight of a fat horsefly drifting in through the open window was welcome to her. The fly buzzed almost enquiringly, perhaps wondering if its life would be spared should it enter. Chloe made a kind of helpless gesture. Why not?

Beth showed distaste. She hated flies. She almost had a thing about them. Without an equal distaste for fly-paper there would be dead bluebottles and wasps everywhere.

"I'm sorry. I suppose I'm still feeling a bit funny." As she rose to get the Flit-gun Chloe felt she had somehow betrayed the fly, luring it to its death with a false assurance, and when attracted by the garden's sweetness, the animal dung and the chicken meal, it flew out again Chloe subsided in enormous relief.

228

"It's so close all of a sudden." Beth pulled at the front of her dress. "As if there really were a storm brewing."

"There isn't a cloud anywhere." Chloe made to look.

From the kennels at the back Tommy, the youngest Springer, began a rapid barking. The dogs responded, some with low, disturbed howls, some with high-pitched yaps, agitating the chickens and the cats so that soon the entire menagerie had joined in. "Oh, God, the racket! This is the last straw!" Chloe put down her cup. "It has to be a rat."

Following her into the kitchen Beth said, "I'll get the cricket bat." They used the bat to club the rats they trapped. Chloe unbolted the yard door to find all the dogs in their outside run, crashing about, yelping and shrieking, flinging their bodies against the stout green bars the sisters had bought at Lord Burnford's estate sale which were altogether more elegant than ordinary wire; such attention to detail attracted the best clients. In the middle of the chaos, cocking his head from side to side, the liver-and-white spaniel who had started it off sat growling to himself as if utterly astonished by this turn of events. "Tommy, you little Turk!" Beth banged at the railings with her bat. "What have you seen? Stop it now, the lot of you! Oh, those bloody Poms, Chlo! I can't stand it when they yap. It goes right through me."

It seemed to Chloe that her sister's methods merely added to the general discord, but it was too late to try calming the dogs now. Leaving Beth to attack the railings she walked round the whitewashed walls, past the new buttress which looked as if it had been there forever, to see about the cats. She paused beside her favourite Mrs Darlingtons; these white roses had the sweetest scent of all. Wherever space was not used for vegetables or animals there were flowers. This summer there had been an astonishing variety, with old-fashioned hollyhocks, snapdragons, cornflowers, honey-suckle, peonies, nasturtiums and dozens of others. While the dogs yowled and grew still more frenetic and Beth's bat rang on metal, Chloe watched two big peacock butterflies, attracted by her buddleia bush, weaving and diving in a delicate air-battle. The sisters had found some chrysali in the toolshed in spring and watched over them until they became caterpillars, then butterflies, so she regarded them as she regarded her chickens, almost as offspring. Three or four meadow-browns wandered about in the

229

heavy garden air, but their time was almost over. She could tell. She went to calm the cats, to find the Persians mildly put out, offering the odd enquiring miaow, but with their unrelenting growls and moans the Siamese were as loud as some dogs, striding around in aristocratic dismay, tails fuzzed, as if responding to a territorial challenge. When she spoke softly to the loudest, a great muscular chocolate-point, it paused immediately to listen. "Now, now, Choo. What have you seen?" Coming up to the rails the cat stroked its powerful head against them. She reached through to scratch him behind his ears and he began to purr. "That's better isn't it?" The best Siamese were always rational.

For a second time there came a sudden descent into silence. Smiling triumphantly Beth rounded the corner, her cricket bat over her shoulder, and Chloe heard a drone in the early evening sky, very muted, like a distant bee. Beth heard it too and lowered her bat. Looking up, the sisters stood side by side, seeking the source. "Over there," Beth said at last, pointing with the bat to the south-east. She shielded her eyes and became admiring. "Good heavens! What a terrific flypast! There must be at least a hundred machines. Where could they be going?"

The vista was obscured by the gas-holders but the swarming bombers were thick as locusts, a real morale-booster. Squadron upon squadron filled the air, presumably heading for Germany. There was no end to them as they flew in stately procession. Soon the roar of their engines drowned the world and their wings blocked out the sun.

It was Beth who first became uncertain. "Hear that?" The noise had grown unfamiliar, the roar of the planes supplemented by a kind of staccato coughing, like an old man clearing his throat. Slowly she let the bat drop, her face bloodless. "Oh, Christ, oh, Chlo!"

"It's the Germans, isn't it?" Chloe's arm embraced her sister's bare shoulders. "It's a raid."

"But so *many* of them. Oh, Christ, Chlo!"

Now the ground vibrated rhythmically even though the bombs fell miles away to the East, on the docks and factories of Woolwich, Whitechapel, West Ham, Bermondsey, Bow, Limehouse, Poplar, Stepney and Canning Town.

They heard an awful whistling, like human voices in agony.

"We should have let them put that Anderson in." Chloe was almost inaudible. They had refused a shelter because it would take up too much valuable garden space. Nobody had warned them to expect anything like this.

They heard the anti-aircraft batteries banging uselessly, hitting nothing, and the Germans came wave upon wave, in unimaginable numbers. The bombers maintained their formations as tightly as any Roman phalanx and the sound of their engines was a constant oscillating drone. Already the black smoke boiled up from the docks and the shrieking sky had turned a terrible pinkish yellow, the colour of a rose.

"Those are incendiaries. The whole city's on fire. Nobody could live in that." Chloe spoke as if to convince herself of an unacceptable truth.

"Why don't they stop them?" Beth's tears would not stop. "Where's the damned RAF?"

Overhead the black formations wheeled with horrible precision while the Scaramangas stared up just as if they were at Farnborough watching a display, not considering they might be more secure inside the house, for the bombers had surely dropped every bomb they carried. North Kensington was spared.

The sisters remained fixed in their embrace, unable to take their eyes from the east and the monstrous fires. "They'll lay waste the whole of London." Beth's lips seemed cracked from the heat. "And make everything rubble. Then they'll invade. Won't they, Chlo?"

Because she could think of nothing comforting to say, Chloe remained silent. The sky had grown dark as twilight yet still the bombers came, invisible in the smoke before emerging, their cargoes released, to climb beyond range of the ack-ack guns firing from Regent's Park, Hyde Park and Wormwood Scrubs.

"They've killed everyone." Beth lowered her eyes at last. "It'll be worse than Spain. They'll wipe us out, won't they Chlo? Unless we give in."

Chloe shrugged. "We'd better have a cup of tea. It's getting chilly."

As they went inside the telephone began to ring. "It'll be the vicar." Beth grinned. "Doing a collection for the victims."

Chloe picked up the black receiver. "No, no," she murmured. "Oh, no. They're not after us, are they? It's the docks and factories they're going for, of course. They probably exaggerated. The East End. Really? Yes of course. No, we're fine. Haven't so much as heard a whisper of a bomb. Yes, he's very well. No. I will. Thanks for phoning. Yes, of course." Replacing the telephone in its cradle she said almost casually, "That was Mrs Short. You know, Torquay with her little boy. Puffy's owner."

"It was nice of her to phone." In the kitchen Beth was not surprised to find the water still on. "What happens if they hit the gasworks, Chlo? We'd be goners, wouldn't we?"

"There's not much chance of it, Bethy. Do you want to be evacuated?"

"Now. Yes."

The drone of the planes, the explosions and the guns had grown familiar. Were the Germans planning some kind of round-the-clock affair; would the bombers go away just long enough to take on more bombs and fuel, returning to bomb again?

Chloe hesitated before she switched on the wireless.

A man's voice, calm as oatmeal, reported the raid. The RAF was beating back the German bombers. People should not panic but make their way to the nearest shelters. For a while Chloe listened until it became clear they would hear no real information. As Beth came in with the tea Chloe turned off the set.

"I put some water on the old," said Beth. "It was strong enough. Do you mind?"

Chloe shook her head. Her body felt enormously heavy.

"Should we try to get to a shelter, do you think?" Beth arranged cups. "Where's the nearest? They sent round a sheet, didn't they? A long time ago. The gas-masks are in the bottom of the sideboard, I think. Still in their boxes." Beth let out a high-pitched laugh. Chloe refused to be irritated. Giggling had always been her sister's response to anxiety.

"Mr Goozey was talking about the crypt, wasn't he?" Chloe wondered if she should phone the vicarage.

"I bet he did, ha, ha." Beth's hand trembled on the milk-jug.

"This might just be one of a kind. Like a warning. Like in France. There can only be a finite number of bombs. And they're not only fighting London." Chloe refused an impulse to close the curtains.

"They want to wipe us out." Beth always expressed her worst fears, though she was at least as courageous as Chloe. "Couldn't

232

you see that? First the East End, then the West End, then the suburbs. What's the odds the King and Queen have already made a run for Canada?"

"They're going for munitions plants and stuff. It would be a waste to do anything else."

"They mean to break our spirit, same as Spain and Poland. John said it's that sort of warfare. Aimed at civilians."

"John doesn't know everything. He spent most of his time in a Spanish camp."

"He knows more than we do, Chlo." She did not want reassurance.

The ground was still vibrating as Beth poured their tea and Chloe decided she would at least close the windows. The garden scents were completely swamped by the acid-smelling smoke. She remembered she had been airing the bedrooms. "I'll just nip upstairs and shut those, too." She had become aware of an odd sensation in her stomach and groin, almost pleasant, and had an unnatural feeling of elation. Perhaps she had expected the raid and was relieved the worst was at last upon them. Reaching her bedroom, she looked across the city at the wall of flame, certain that the entire East End must be ablaze, like a second Great Fire. There could not be enough water or people to extinguish it. When Chamberlain had declared War last year many of their friends had volunteered for auxiliary fire work only to look for something more worthwhile to do in the absence of serious bombing; being a fire warden had come to be synonymous with not doing your bit properly. Now, of course, they were needed and not available. But she wondered if any human agency could cope with such fires. And what if it spread this far? They had always considered themselves lucky to have water so handy, particularly since the roof was thatched. Would it do them any good? She decided that if the fire came too close they would load what they could into their boat and head for Oxford, even if it meant throwing themselves on the mercy of their obnoxiously stuck-up Boars Hill cousins. The animals, she supposed, would have to fend for themselves. She drew the last window shut with a bang.

"Are you all right up there?" Beth sounded shaky, faint.

"I'm fine, dear. Just mooning. I'll be down in a sec."

Chloe expelled the breath she had been holding, closed the door of the spare bedroom and set the latch carefully in its place, as if to add protection against the bombs. In the early stages of a crisis Beth always made a fuss but then became cool as ice, whereas Chloe was inclined to start calm and grow gradually despairing. She paused on the landing to look down into the garden. All the insects, all the butterflies and birds were gone, as in a fairy tale where the world changed from summer to winter in an instant. But the flowers were still there in the gloom and she could see part of the cattery. The thoroughly terrified animals were completely silent, staring upward as the black planes flew low overhead, their monumental drone occasionally broken by other engine notes. Perhaps the RAF fighters were arriving at last. Again she wondered how there could possibly be enough of them.

As she returned downstairs she decided to relay her guess as news. "The RAF's turned up," she told her sister. "In time to save our bacon."

"Is it the Spitfires?" Beth thought Spitfires beautiful.

"Don't go outside just yet." Smoothing her skirt Chloe sat down. "The shrapnel and so on."

Beth said vaguely, "It probably looks worse than it is."

Chloe had seen a vision of Hell. She recalled newsreels of Spain and the fighting in Europe, then realised she had again been holding her breath. This time she let the air out gradually.

"Are you tired?" Beth wanted to know.

"Aren't you? Shall we bring a mattress downstairs? To be on the safe side. Would you feel better?"

"Much." Beth placed her warm cup against her breastbone. "This is the real war at last, eh, Chlo?"

"Real enough for me."

"It was like the end of the world."

Chloe nodded. She heard machine-gun fire quite close, the whine of a fighter's engine, a coughing note from a larger plane. Without wishing to alarm Beth, she strained to interpret the sounds. At first the embattled planes seemed immediately overhead, then the noise grew fainter, returning to the same steady, unerring drone. There was sweat on her forehead and palms, on her lip. She looked about for her handkerchief before rising to go into the kitchen. As she washed her hands she heard an altogether different noise, easily identified: a distant whistling, growing rapidly louder. She hardly had time to rush at Beth and fling her to the flagstones behind the sofa as the bomb struck with a great thump. No glass shattered; she heard no eruption of noise and earth, just a faint, awful yelping from the garden.

"Stay there a moment, Beth." Hardly believing they were still alive, Chloe crawled to the window. The bomb had seemed so close and had probably been dropped as an afterthought, or by accident, from a retreating plane. Still convinced of her imminent death she peered over the window-ledge trying to see the dogs while the yelping grew worse and the other dogs now joined in frantically, but she could see only that some of her roses had been pushed down, as if by rain or a heavy wind, and that bits of twigs and leaves were scattered on the grass verge. She stood up.

"Beth, dear, will you stay here?" Carefully she walked towards the kitchen as if more rapid movements might draw deadly attention. "Stay here, dear, for my sake. I'm going to look outside."

"Chlo. Just phone the police."

"There's no point if we don't know what it is."

Through the kitchen window Chloe could now see the kennel. Something had dropped through the mesh and timber roof and partially buried itself in the ground. It was dull, metallic, roughly circular and there were stencilled numbers on it. Stubby fins at the top still pointed up through the ruined dog-run's roof. The bomb had killed Tommy outright. She could see half his head, with one eye still open, under the nose. Perhaps Tommy's body had stopped the bomb going off. The other injured dog was Puffy. The little Pom still yelped, his back leg crushed and trapped. The rest of the dogs cowered in corners, eyes rolling, tongues lolling, like crazed wild creatures, utterly unlike the pets she had fed a few hours earlier.

She walked carefully back to the sitting-room. "We'll get those mattresses. Yours and mine and the one from the spare bedroom. And we'll put them against this far wall. I think it's all we can do."

"Is it a bit of plane, Chlo? A parachutist?" Beth was rising to her feet, imitating the slowness of her sister's movements.

"It's an unexploded bomb. I've no idea what the drill is, so we'll phone the police as soon as the mattresses are down. They'll send someone. We'll probably have to leave the cottage while they do whatever they usually do."

"But who is it making the noise?"

"Mrs Short's Puffy. His leg's caught so we'll have to put him to sleep somehow. If he moves about much more he might just set the bomb off. Don't they have all sorts of extra triggers and things?" For a moment she thought she could hear it ticking, but it was the marble clock over the fireplace. "It's just as well Mrs Short didn't phone later."

"Call the police now." Beth was much cooler. "First. Or shall I?"

Carefully Chloe went to the telephone and picked it up, dialling 999. Almost inevitably the number was engaged.

By the time she got through to the vicar there were tears in her eyes, though her voice still sounded calm to her. "I wonder if you'd mind sending a message to the police station. I know it sounds silly, but there's an unexploded bomb in our garden. Yes. Right through the poor dogs' kennel. Killed one, injured another. Yes, we should put it down, I think. Shall I wait to hear from you? I'll phone the vet in the meantime. He'd be risking his life. I don't think he should . . . Yes, I quite agree. Thank you. Perhaps we shall. It's very kind of you." She replaced the receiver, drew breath and dialled again. "Oh, good evening Mrs Lundy. This is Miss Scaramanga at Bank Cottage. I know. Isn't it awful? You can? Yes. No, I haven't heard either. Of course, I shall. Yes. Would it be possible to have a word with Mr Lundy? Oh, I see. Yes. I'm so sorry. I hope everything . . . If he could ring me when he gets in."

Crossing to the sofa she almost fell into it. "He's over there somewhere."

"Over where, Chlo?"

"A function in the City. He'd gone on the bus. She doesn't know what's happened to him. She's trying to keep the line clear in the hope he'll phone."

Their telephone rang. Waving her sister back to her seat Beth jumped to answer it. "That's very kind of you, Mr Goozey. Yes, I can imagine. We'll come to you, then, shall we?"

"We must try to do something about the animals." Chloe felt unnaturally cold. "Does he want us to go to the crypt? You do it, Beth. I'd better stay here, though."

Beth was still talking to the vicar. "There's just a couple of things we have to do first. Yes, I'm sure they said that. I can understand absolutely the sense of it. Don't worry. We won't take any silly chances."

Side by side on the sofa again, the sisters knew they would not leave Bank Cottage. A little later they went upstairs to bring down the mattresses. As best they could they barricaded themselves against a blast. When the vicar phoned again they told him they would come as soon as possible. After a while Puffy stopped yelping. They hoped he had died. Taking electric torches, they carried the dogs into the house two at a time, careful not to alarm them in case they disturbed the bomb. When the sisters had finished they turned their beams onto the sinister case and saw it was actually impossible to leave by their gate since a metal fin blocked it. To escape Bank Cottage they would have to crawl through the thick hedge. Almost comforted by this knowledge, they went into the cattery to collect all the cats and put them in the spare bedroom. The dogs remained downstairs with them. Some had blood on their fur which they began to lick. Chloe wondered if she should wash the dogs. Beth shook her head.

The phone rang again. Beth answered it. "I'm awfully sorry, Mr Goozey, but we're stuck here." She began to giggle. "We can't actually open our gate because of the bomb. Perhaps we'll cut through the hedge tomorrow, or they'll send a man from the gasworks. Oh, really? Well, if you really could get someone over now that would probably be an enormous help." She looked enquiringly at Chloe, who shrugged.

"Mr Kiss? We'll listen out for him."

PART FOUR
FAST DAYS

The last burned church, St Stephen, Coleman Street, is memorable for its connection with the Great Plague of 1665. This hideous calamity, which fortunately preceded the Great Fire (what would have happened had the Plague broken out after the fire, among the wailing refugees, sleeping on carts in Bunhill Fields?), is something which is happily unlikely to occur again. As an experience of horror, it beat the Great Fire hollow: it also, in my opinion, beat the bombings of 1940. To have lived through the Great Plague seems to me as remarkable a feat (though not as questionable a one) as that of an ancestor of my own who lived through the Black Hole of Calcutta. By being the biggest of London epidemics of the Plague, the 1665 outbreak has come to seem the only one. A glance at the records, or the letters of any earlier period and any earlier reign, however, show what a constant menace the Plague was felt to be; it gave an insecurity to daily life, to which the Germans have now introduced us. The really curious fact about the Great Plague is that once it had subsided there was no similar outbreak again in England. The cessation was glibly attributed to the Great Fire: but in every other city in England the Plague ceased at about the same time.

      – James Pope-Hennessy, *History Under Fire*, 1941

Early Departures 1940

JOSEF KISS, accepting a map and an electric lantern from the hands of the vicar, set off on foot into the blackness, at his back the red flames of Bermondsey; ahead an unexploded bomb. He knew nothing of war or fires or planes but had a little rudimentary first aid training from the St John's Ambulance Brigade, a tin ARP hat and an armband to show he was an Air Raid Warden. He called himself an Air Raid Privateer, an *espontaneo*, since the authorities had refused his sacrifice, rejecting him from the Home Guard, even from the Volunteer Fire Service. He had acquired the armband and the helmet for himself, adding the official-looking trousers, Wellington boots and donkey jacket. Having decided in their bureaucratic response to the evidence of his medical record to permit him no active function in the War, the authorities had forced him to become a freelance roving Warden, ready to assist whoever needed him. Tonight was to be his first real trial. If there were actually an unexploded bomb at Bank Cottage (which was not marked on his map: only the gasworks was shown beside the towpath) and he conducted himself well he would consider promoting himself. If he did badly he would probably dismiss himself.

A happy coincidence had led him to this trial. Leaving an audition at the Kilburn State on the other side of the canal, he had seen the planes and remembered the tin hat and armband in his satchel. He needed transport to take him East again, towards the fires, but nothing was going there. London seemed completely unprepared for the raid. He had tried to phone, to present himself for duty to the

243

appropriate authority, but nobody knew what was going on. It was as though the government had already decided London could not survive concentrated bombing. All their arrangements were for swift burial of the dead, setting up psychiatric units for shell-shock victims, trucks and buses to take units of the Home Guard to defend the outskirts against an expected land invasion. People actually needed information, fire-hoses, ambulances and transport to the scene of the bombings, but these had not been planned for.

That Mr Kiss had been taken by surprise was not unnatural: that those in charge were equally bewildered was perhaps more alarming than the raid itself, which must surely be the worst in history. On the other hand he was rather glad he was not attached to any official group which might already be halfway to Sussex by now on a wild-goose chase. When he had arrived at Dalgarno Road, searching for a fire-fighting team or a first-aid post, he had found only the church and an anxious clergyman ushering people down into the crypt. He had presented himself to the vicar who had asked him to wait before inviting him back to the rectory to offer him a cup of tea. While Mr Kiss tried to discover the whereabouts of the nearest ARP station the telephone rang and he learned of the unexploded bomb at Bank Cottage. Mr Kiss desperately wanted to go into the main disaster area to save those who still lived, to help extinguish the fires of Whitechapel and Stepney, but when the vicar could find no volunteer for Bank Cottage and learned the women were now trapped there Mr Kiss offered to try to cut them out and perhaps get an idea of their danger. In his bag even now he carried the vicar's personal hedge-trimmers and an old-fashioned ear-trumpet left over from a jumble-sale. His lantern had come from the front of the vicar's bike. Mr Kiss had a whistle on a lanyard. This, like most of his kit, was borrowed from the props room of The Lyric, Hammersmith, and whenever he saw a group of people he blew it loudly. "Unexploded bomb!" he explained as he passed. "Could go up at any minute. Bomb-bombadi-bomb-bomb!" He closed his mind to their casual insults.

Following his map and the vicar's instructions, he descended the concrete steps at the side of the road-bridge to find himself on a dusty towpath smelling of rot, damp and wild plants. The planes still roared over, but in fewer numbers, and he could clearly hear the London anti-aircraft emplacements sending up a steady stream of tracer fire while searchlights sought their targets. The air began to stink and his eyes were stung by smoke. It was impossible to imagine what it must be like in the thick of that terrible destruction. He checked his compass, although he had a fair idea of his bearings, and struck off at a roughly westerly direction. To him the darkness seemed desolate; foul-smelling water lapped near his feet and red chaos filled the ruined world behind, so he reassured himself from time to time by blowing his whistle. "Bomb! Bomb! Unexploded Bomb!" Hoping the sound would also reassure the waiting women, whom he imagined clinging to one another as they sat beside the phone, praying for it to ring, while outside the monstrous infernal machine ticked remorselessly on.

We get smug, Mrs C, when we're chosen over someone else – especially if it's a wife or husband. We never seem to realise that the advice we give out to our lovers, together with the homilies, is as stale as the situation itself. What petty treacheries are gilded as words of wisdom by our inflated egos! What wretched deeds, what ruthless greed, do we disguise as love! It's fair to say that the greater the betrayal, the fuller the sentiments we have to invest in our ignoble actions. And think of that pity, that ghastly pity, we feel for those who are suffering from our acts! How coldly we dismiss them. Are we all the same? Or do some of us at least accept that what we do has no moral justification? I thought it was finished, down to the bone, but he got the marrow out. Mrs O'Dare had twelve different blokes. One for every month, I said. Apostles, more like, he said. Quelim na foske, oh my god you're better than I

Mr Kiss began to hurry, his mock-ARP helmet bouncing on his head. Though he knew he was not entirely in his right mind and if he were caught would immediately be locked up, he was genuinely concerned for the Scaramangas. Again and again he blew the whistle while behind him the whole sky boiled and threw up gigantic sparks, funnels of red flame, unstable dirty orange mountains, yellow, white and black smoke. He paused, transfixed, watching and listening. The city was actually shrieking. He had never imagined a single air-raid could be so fierce, and part of him now felt glad of the errand of mercy taking him away from the blaze's heart. His impulse to head towards the danger had subsided, not only because it was impossible to believe any creature could have survived but also because massive images had begun to form in the vast fire: crazed horsemen rode foaming horses over cliffs of smoke; naked giants writhed in the valleys, their eyes glaring with pain and fear; from the darkness of caves hideously distorted figures shambled as if in pursuit, and all the beasts of the apocalypse leered, gibbered and slavered as they took shape from the chaos giving them birth; while the black, crimson-eyed angels of the Pit, their swords burning with mercury and molten brass, rose in mocking challenge to survey the dying city. He groaned, less sure of reality than he had ever been, for this air-raid was itself unimaginable. He turned his back on the fires and began slowly to pick his way along the towpath again. Then all at once a wave of anguished voices hit him and he gasped as if winded, yet resolutely kept his momentum and direction, his lantern revealing patches of grass, the occasional pile of dung and, when the light touched water, a dark oily spectrum.

The voices came again, fiercer and more urgent than before, striking him with such force he almost fell. Each voice was an individual, each one in such terrible confusion, such ghastly physical pain, such psychic agony, that he found he too was shouting with them; his voice joining the millions to form a single monumental howl. The noise was like a bomb-blast, hot and ravening, threatening to tear the clothes off his body. His whistle fell from his lips, bounced on his chest; he might have been kicked in the groin as he doubled up, the breath pouring out of him. He desperately tried to recover himself. "Oh, God!" He was attacked by all the demons of Hell, by every tormented soul pleading for release. Breaking into a run he stumbled and fell face down on the towpath. "No! Leave me alone! I'll stop! I'll take the damned drops! Please!" He gripped at the ground.

There were words, faces, more fantastical forms and now a wind came howling up the canal, making the water spray and swirl, drenching him. A motorboat went by, faster than any boat should go, its engine high and nervous; if it struck anything its occupants would almost certainly be killed. The voices subsided. They became distant whispers. Mr Kiss got to his hands and knees, patting around until he found his lantern. The battery was still working but it had become loose. He adjusted the screw at the top then used the light to find his map and helmet. Angry with himself he wiped sweat away from his face, dusting off his clothes and glaring at the nearby wall. He could make out gigantic, faded black letters on the brick: GLCC. This meant that he had reached the gasworks and according to the vicar need only go another hundred yards or so before he came to Bank Cottage. He began to sing, to drown the whispering in his head:

> Sweet London, she's the town for me,
>   Her women are so gay-o,
> And the sweetest that you'll ever meet
>   Are the ones who'll steal your pay-o.

> Oh, Maggie, Peg and Bess and Nell,
>   They're welcome to my money,
> Because I'd rather rot in Hell,
>   Than miss their tender cunny.

And, thinking he detected the laughter of Lucifer himself in the sky above, he swung his lantern, first on the wall, then on the water, in jaunty time with his baritone, almost daring the Devil to strike him down. The towpath had narrowed and the water was filthy with debris disturbed by the fleeing speedboat. Pausing by a mesh fence topped by barbed wire to protect hills of coal and coke, he saw beyond it the towering tubular shapes of the great gas-holders; like Romanesque citadels they loomed up into the darkness. He fancied they might shelter the sleeping gods of London who would burst out at any minute to take vengeance on their attackers. They were about two-thirds full and, knowing nothing of the nature of gas, he wondered if they would explode or merely catch fire if an incendiary hit them. It seemed to him folly to leave them expanded but he supposed there was no easy way of ridding them of gas. When the fence ended and the brick wall began again he felt safer, and a few feet further on he came to the dense hedge which looked more solid than any of the gasworks' defences and knew he had found Bank Cottage. He stopped, settled his tin hat on his head, and considered his next action.

Eventually Mr Kiss put his whistle to his lips again and blew three short blasts, calling into the hedge: "Hello, inside! Hello, inside!" There was no reply. Unclear as to where the cottage exactly lay behind the hedge, he walked on, following the leafy barricade until he stopped short at a couple of hand-rails set in the ground ahead of him. The lantern showed he had come to the mooring mentioned by the vicar. Now he must turn left. From the East came a sudden massive roar, like some fabulous monster released into the world, and he began instinctively to throw up his arm to protect his eyes. A burst of bright fire revealed a path scarcely a foot wide ending in a line of bricks which dropped away into the little basin where he could just see the shape of a small skiff. Metal rungs led down to a landing-stage about fifty by thirty inches. He turned carefully and found the heavy wrought-iron gate with its massive mortise lock and barbed wire woven into the top. Flashing his unsteady lantern through the bars he immediately saw one entire fin of the bomb, a section of another. By twisting his neck to the right he could see what he thought of as the main fuselage disappearing into some sort of shed. Even if the gate were unlocked he would not be able to move it more than a couple of inches before the iron came in contact with the steel, and he remembered vaguely that German bombs were supposed to be magnetic: one of those long government memos had warned people not to touch an unexploded bomb with metal. He felt disproportionately gratified that his ear-trumpet was ivory and horn.

> "She was beautiful as a butterfly
> And as proud as a queen,
> Was pretty little Polly Perkins
> of Paddington Green . . .

"Hello! Hello, inside! Hello, the cottage!" He had now forgotten the owners' name. "Sisters? Ladies? Hello! This is Warden Kiss. Sent by the vicar!" He waved the lantern's beam at the windows which were blocked by something other than blackout material. "Are you all right in there, my dears?"

A muffled response.

Mr Kiss cupped his hands to his mouth. "Can you speak louder, madam?"

Her voice was completely drowned by a formation of Heinkels flying unusually low, their silhouettes occasionally picked out by the searchlights and the hissing tracer fire. Mr Kiss wondered if they were about to strike and if so what the chances were of their selecting the gasholders as a target. Then the German planes had banked and were gone, back into the smoke drifting from the East.

"Is it about the bomb?" A woman's distant shout.

"That's right, madam. I can't get the gate open."

"Don't open the gate!"

"I can't. It's locked. I understand. I'm going to try to make a hole in the hedge. If you hear anything, it'll be me!"

That of course was the year I got pregnant. Can I ever forget it? That pain. More intense than any pleasure, before or since. A dreadful thing to remember. And the mess. I've never been able to skin a hare since. Even the chickens sometimes remind me. What's she saying?

Mr Kiss pushed his helmet back on his head and removed the vicar's hedge-trimmers from the bag. The yew-boughs were extraordinarily thick at all points, and woven together, for the hedge had clearly been there for at least two hundred years. Would it be possible, he wondered, to burrow under it? He guessed the roots were as deep as the boughs high. He could feel the women inside controlling their panic, trying to comfort themselves, losing themselves in a past which seemed a bewildering welter of relationships; lives lived, he though, enviably to the full. They must know as well as he how difficult it would be to get through to them. Experimentally he threw his mass against the foliage; as if irritated by the disturbance it rustled but scarcely moved. Within the house came the sound of excited dogs. He heard chickens. A whole menagerie. Then a woman cried out again.

"Nothing to fear, madam!" Taking off his helmet, he scratched his head; his hair was greasy from the smoke, as if he had gone too close to an abattoir. What he needed was either a sharp axe or a long ladder. "Hang on inside!"

bits and pieces who the hell will inherit No good asking I wish

Josef Kiss edged his way around to the towpath again and kept his eyes on the ground, not looking at the fires and the shapes in them as he headed back to the gasworks and the mesh fence. He played the light over the wire and the piles of coke behind it, then taking the hedge-clippers he began working on the fence, surprised how easily the strands parted under the blades. Soon he had a large hole into which he could work his body and squeezing through stood at last, only superficially scratched, in the foothills of the nearest coke pile. Overhead more planes went past, but they were too high to identify. There came a series of rapid explosions from the general direction of Bow, as if a gigantic jumping-jack was going off. The voices began to shriek again in the distance. Thankful for a certain amount of practice, he forced them to subside. Crunching through the coke he came at length to a gate secured by a piece of twisted wire which he found more difficult to cut, but eventually it parted and he pushed the gate wide.

As he entered this yard a light appeared suddenly ahead of him as a hut door swung open. He heard excited Cockney. "Who the blazes is it? Len! Phone the coppers. It's looters!"

"Oh, bugger," said Josef Kiss.

Why has he gone away, Chlo?

"Presumably to get some sort of reinforcements." Chloe licked her lower lip. "The vicar said he's a Special Officer. He knows what he's doing. If he thought we were in real danger he would have done something."

"Well, I hope he didn't shift it. I thought I could hear the awful thing whirring again. Are they clockwork?"

"I wish I knew." Chloe sipped her cold tea and prayed for the telephone to come back on. It had gone off immediately after she last spoke to Mr Goozey.

She had stopped listening to the wireless because the news was so vague. The reassurances were clearly unrealistic. Now that it was on again it kept playing the quieter movements from Holst's *Planets* and the contrast between this and what she had observed outside was to her sinister, yet as her faith in the authorities weakened her sense of humour grew stronger. "We need a few rousing bits of timpani from *Mars*," she said to Beth. "Make the whole thing seem like a proper show."

"We'll have all the timpani we want soon if that bloody thing goes off. I bet they've sent one chap in a gas mask. Just like when the stove leaks and you get a chap to look at the trouble, another to make notes about it, another to work out what's wrong with the pipes, another to bring the parts, another to size them up, another to fit them. Our first chap just came to look at the trouble. In four or five weeks someone will come to make notes. It'll be two months before we have a man to deal with the bomb itself." Beth grinned as she stroked a spaniel.

"Well, at least we've plenty of eggs." Chloe found herself shaking with laughter.

Beth joined in until they were in tears. "Oh, my sainted aunt!" gasped Beth. "Oh, Chlo! Oh, Chlo!"

They staggered into the kitchen to take stock of their provisions. They drank another glass of sherry each, then carefully put the stopper in, as they had done last time. They began their inventory.

They had a whole loaf of brown bread. There were two rashers of bacon in the meat-safe and over half-a-pound of margarine. They had seven packets of Brooke Bond tea, a pound of Assam and a pound of Darjeeling, almost a pound of ground Colombian coffee, a huge stack of tins which had been brought to them by their rich Oxford cousins before they left to weather out the War in the Cotswolds. From Harrods and Fortnums, most of the tinned stuff was unsuitable for casual eating.

"We're well off for artichoke hearts and asparagus spears." Writing the numbers down on her spiral notepad, Chloe set them to giggling again but they controlled themselves long enough to make an inventory of the tinned hams by brand, weight and shape of can. Then they decided to cross-reference the pâté-de-foie-gras by ounces.

"We can do a whole category by weight." Beth gave her sister a strange, shared look of crazed irony. "We go from, say, four ounces up. So we find every tin that's four ounces or under and put those on their own list. Then we do five ounces and so on. What on earth is this?" Reaching into a dark shelf at the back of the pantry she encircled something with her hands. "Not another bloody bomb?"

"That's the Stilton were were supposed to eat last Christmas." Chloe made a face. "It'll be all right this, won't it?"

"Perhaps we should eat as much as we can now. After all, those about to die stuff themselves silly . . ."

Chloe smiled awkwardly. "That's not the right spirit, Beth. We agreed. Some of these tins don't have weights or anything on them. Shall we put them under height, perhaps? Or what about diameter?"

The electricity went off. Almost at the same time there came a heavy thump on the roof. "Oh, God!" Beth put down a tin of salmon pâté. "It can't be."

They became aware of a voice overhead bellowing either in pain, command or reassurance.

"It sounds like the same chap." Chloe led Beth to the table where she had placed the torches and found one almost immediately, switching it on. She played the beam on the other torch for Beth to pick up. Meanwhile the noise from above had turned into a series of random thumps and shouts.

"He's on the roof!" Beth's laughter was less manic. "He's brought the electric cable down! My sainted aunt! He'll be electrocuted!"

"And set the thatch on fire."

From above Warden Kiss's voice came clearly now: "Hello, inside! Are you all right?"

"He's parachuted in! Well, he's resourceful at any rate." Beth called up in his general direction. "Be careful, warden, you'll kill yourself. That's our power line!"

They heard more voices from further away and as they went upstairs they heard him scrabbling outside. They went into their spare bedroom, which was now awash with cats. The Persians looked up in mild enquiry while the Siamese stalked and lifted noisy, enquiring faces. "Keep them away, Beth," said Chloe, opening the window. "There you are, warden!"

Against the glare of the burning city they made out a pair of legs in Wellington boots, a shower of thatch, a torso and finally a head and shoulders. The arms were stretched high above the rest of the man's plump body. He was younger than they had expected and oddly good-looking. Marked in white paint with the initials ARP, his tin helmet was askew. "Good evening, ladies." He began to pant. "Help has arrived!"

Because Chloe was better at keeping a straight face, Beth withdrew to calm the cats. "It's very good of you to come so quickly." Chloe was grave. "Do you know you've brought down our electricity cable?"

"Was that what it was? Oh, bugger – excuse me. Oh, bugger! We used a ladder, you see, to get over the hedge. Len and Fred lost control of it. I came forward rather rapidly and landed on the roof. Luckily the ladder's wooden or there might have been nothing left of me, eh? I'm terribly sorry. Ah!"

"What's up, warden?"

"I'm not sure if my arms will hold out much longer." He glanced down. "What's that directly below?"

"A Grand Duc Adolphe de Luxembourg." Chloe squinted. "A

bit bushy at present. Not too thorny, really. I think we've seen the last of any serious growth this year so I suppose if you were going to fall on something . . ."

"Eh?" Warden Kiss groaned.

Beth had taken pity on him. "Here, let's see if we can get you in this way. I'd hate the roses to suffer." And she stretched past Chloe to seize the waist of his trousers. Chloe imitated her. "There. Now let go with one hand and get the sill if you can. That's fine. Quickly. Oh, yes, a leg. Very good. You're surprisingly agile. I'm sorry, I didn't mean to be personal . . ."

Warden Kiss got his massive knee onto the ledge and shifted his hand to the window-frame. "A lot of people find that odd, given I'm a bit on the portly side. It's hard to upset me. I suppose I'm just very healthy. But I've ruined my jacket." At some stage of tonight's adventure he had torn it. "Will your roof be all right, ladies?"

They helped him in and soon he was standing in the spare bedroom, rather surprised by the numbers of cats. Beth let her torch-beam rest for a moment on the portrait of Florence Hackwood. Mr Kiss noticed the resemblance immediately. "Is that you, all dressed up?" he asked Chloe.

"Just an ancestor." Chloe became embarrassed. "Well, the one thing we have left is a lot of gas. And tea. Would you like a cup?"

"I was thinking I should be evacuating you." Mr Kiss was diplomatic. "It's very kind, however. I've had nothing since I left the vicar's. It seems ages. You'd given me up, eh?" A great gust escaped him as if he had absorbed half the explosions of the night.

Beth glanced away. "Oh, no. But where did you find a ladder?"

"I requisitioned it." He was proud as a schoolboy and took her question as a statement of approval. "There are two night-watchmen on duty next door. Elderly and not too handy, but they had the ladder and it was my only chance of reaching you. I really am terribly sorry about the electricity."

"We were just hanging around anyway." Beth imitated her older sister's expression. "We haven't had any excitement for at least an hour."

Seemingly oblivious of her sarcasm, yet not insensitive to her situation, Josef Kiss recovered himself. "You'll have to go out more or less the way I came in. Then I'll take a look at the bomb. One of the gas chaps cycled off to get his boss. I suppose it isn't in their interest to have a great big bomb ticking away next door. The threat of losing money should bring them round in a hurry!"

"We'll wait for them, shall we?" Chloe shooed the more curious cats back into their corners. "Poo! Crispin!"

Beth was closing the window and said apologetically, "His revenge. You know what they're like." As they descended the stairs she explained the situation to Warden Kiss. "It was all we could think to do. But they're fussy beasts and hate us for it."

At the sink Josef Kiss lifted his lantern so that Chloe could fill the kettle. "I've no cats of my own. Only children."

"We board these for other people." Chloe hesitated then lit the gas. "How many children do you have, warden?"

"Two and another coming. To Harrow. I sent my wife to stay with her relatives in Wales but she found the culture too different. She was charged the price of a crust for the boy who's teething so she said she'd rather die free in her own home than pay to live with the Welsh."

"Poor thing." Chloe considered taking a Dundee out of its tin. "Such a lot of people have come back thinking the worst was over. I feel – oh, dear – all those children in the East End!"

Beth helped Josef Kiss off with his coat. "I can mend that. We've an oil-lamp. Electricity's always been a luxury for us. This old place is completely self-sufficient if we need it to be. We're always prepared. Not for unexploded bombs, of course."

Chloe thought Beth's laughter abnormally high-pitched and self-conscious and put the kettle on the gas with a significant clang. "See if you can sort out the biscuits, dear."

"There's that madeira cake."

"I'm not sure this demands madeira, Beth."

Realising she was in her sister's poor graces, Beth stood for a moment fingering the tear in Mr Kiss's coat.

"I'll be able to do that." He reached for it. "I'm a dab hand with a needle."

"You were in the navy? Wounded?"

"In the theatre. One learns to take care of oneself."

"You were wounded?" Chloe looked up from the stove. "Poor man. We had expected an octogenarian, you see."

Beth let the coat slide onto the back of a kitchen chair.

Chloe made a gesture. "Why don't you squeeze round a mattress and go and sit down, warden. They'll absorb the main force of the explosion, I suppose. The walls are over two feet thick. Rubble-filled. Stone. They knew how to build."

Knowing he was always better off when he had something to do, and the activity with the ladder having temporarily deadened his reception, Josef Kiss made a great effort to collect himself as the little voices came again. From habit he drove them away with his own words. "My dear Miss – my dear lady, there's little time to waste. I have a listening instrument in my bag. If you'll permit me to go into your garden . . ."

The oil-lamp came on. It was supported by an art-nouveau lady in a flowing gown who held the bowl of green crystal from which emerged the lamp itself, and a slender funnel covered by a translucent shade of milky blue. "She's a beauty." Mr Kiss beamed. "French, is she?"

"Belgian." Chloe motioned. "The garden?"

"I dropped my bag there. It contains my bomb stuff."

"Well, if you like. While the kettle's boiling. Should we do anything?"

"Nothing. That's the front door, is it?"

"We never moved it. We use the kitchen door mainly. On the other side."

He went to push up the old-fashioned latch. "You're astonishingly rural here." He was complimentary.

"Yes." Beth grinned again.

While Mr Kiss looked outside for his bag Beth and Chloe, as they had done since girlhood when fearing to be caught laughing, struck one another violently on the legs and shoulders. "You're making a fool of yourself," whispered Chloe amiably. "You don't even like men."

"I was only being hospitable."

"The oaf's brought down our power. Now he's going to blow us to kingdom come. There's such a thing as overdoing hospitality in these circumstances, Beth." But Chloe could not remain serious.

Helplessly Beth banged on her sister's arm. "He'll think we're hysterical."

"Aren't we? He's pretty funny, though. So fruity. A thespian of the old school." Chloe stopped as Mr Kiss put his helmeted head

255

into the room, smiling as if he had heard every word and wanted to put them at their ease.

"Found it. I'll have a listen. Then I'll make my report."

A loud, horrible noise burst from Chloe's nose and she made an equally disagreeable sound as she drew a fresh breath. Clutching at Beth, she sat down hard on the sofa.

"Are you unwell, dear lady?"

"She's just a bit – it's the tension." Beth knew she was turning red. "She. Hee-hee. It's all right. Hee-hee. Oh, God!"

"If you're sure." He had his khaki bag in his hand. He closed the door. Chloe caught his eye for a second and was certain she detected a knowing look. She began to feel they might be underestimating Mr Kiss and shivered. "I think I'll make the preliminary inspection, anyway," he told her. "And have my tea later, if that's all right."

She felt obscurely ashamed of herself and raised a hand as he left, almost in salute.

Mr Kiss made his way around the outside of the house. Back in their coops the fancy fowl had settled down for the night. They uttered a few small comfortable sounds as he reached a little gravel path and followed it until he saw the dog-run, the ruined roof and the dead animal beneath the bomb's nose. Then the beam of his lamp caught movement; it was reflecting Puffy's pain-filled eyes. The little creature began to pant, whimpering very softly. There was a delicacy about it, a fragility to its suffering, that made Mr Kiss take the beam away and begin to murmur to the animal. Puffy's leg was still caught under the bomb. He squatted down in the darkness. The bomb was warm to the touch and actually seemed alive; he moved his hand to find the dog's head, petting it. Before he had considered the action he had taken the garden shears from his bag and begun carefully to dig at the ground under the trapped leg. He worked slowly, fixing his lantern in the crook of his own leg to keep the light steady, pausing whenever he thought he might touch the bomb and praying the thing would keep from shifting, supported as it was by earth and the shattered, bloody corpse of the spaniel.

He could feel the intensity of the Pom's pain growing worse as pressure came off nerves, but the dog lay obediently still, licking his hand as Mr Kiss rested before taking hold of its leg in his palm and with his free hand slowly drawing the little creature away from the casing. The leg was virtually pulped but he did not know enough to tell if the dog would have to be destroyed. From his bag he removed the ear-trumpet and his empty sandwich-tin, gently wrapping the Pom up in the canvas. Puffy made no loud sounds but sustained the same small regular whimpering.

Mr Kiss shook his head, sighing as he stood with the dog in his arms, looking at the bomb in the lamplight. The thing was making an increased and significant murmuring and must soon explode.

Walking slowly back to the house he pushed open the front door with his foot.

dying in such a silly situation not at all the saviour I imagined

"Oh, he's alive!" Beth ran to take the dog. "Poor Puffy."

Chloe said respectfully. "That was brave of you, Mr Kiss, and very kind."

"Kind?" He sat down. "Look here Miss Scaramanga, you will have to leave. We'll put that ladder over the hedge and you can climb into the yard. Fred will help you."

"It's really that serious?"

"I think so. Have you a toolbox?"

"Nothing sophisticated."

"Could you get it? Then we'll go upstairs and try to lean the ladder across from your spare bedroom."

"You sit here and have your tea. I hope it's hot enough. You were out there for ages. I'll call to Fred, shall I?"

"If you wouldn't mind."

Beth handed him the cup. "Have lots of sugar. You need it."

"I'm not normally a sugar man." He let her put three lumps in and when he took the cup from her it rattled violently. "Bit tired."

Beth went to the foot of the stairs between the kitchen and the sitting room and raised her voice. "Can you hear me Chlo?"

"Loud and clear. You stay with Puffy and the warden."

"Have you done this lots?" Beth offered chocolate wholemeals on a blue and white plate. "Disexploded? What's the word?"

"Disarm or neutralise." He sounded casually cool even to himself. "I've had my share of unexploded devices, you know. But frankly there's nothing worse than a flat night in Cleethorpes, as the comedians say."

"Where?"

"Cleethorpes." He finished his tea. "Take an overnight bag, but hurry. I'd guess it's a matter of quarter-of-an-hour one way or the other."

"I'll take Puffy. At least if he can't be saved the vet will put him out of his misery. Good luck, Mr Kiss."

He nodded. He was pouring with sweat. He grinned at her from under his false colours. "Old Bertha'll be harmless as a baby soon."

funny how it's never what you expect or imagined I wonder if he knows

When Beth had taken the dog upstairs Mr Kiss grasped the oil lamp by the lady's slender waist and carried her with him for company as much as for her light. One of the dogs tried to follow him out and he ordered it gently back. "There's no telling what mischief you'd cause."

Settling himself beside his bomb again, Josef Kiss was scarcely aware any longer that he was playing a part. He was convinced that he had a sense of the bomb's mechanism, could, as it were, read its primitive mind. He scratched his head, then carefully laid his hands on the casing, wondering if it were possible to will the bomb into passivity. When he detected a movement behind him, a beam of light, he looked up.

"The tools you wanted." Puzzled, Chloe stared at him. "You are all right, are you? I thought they usually sent a team."

"We're undermanned, at present, as you can imagine." He took his hands from the metal as she placed the toolbox beside him. It was wooden, painted green. He gave it what he hoped seemed an expert eye. "You'd better go. Have you sorted out the ladder?"

"It's fine. Is there anything else you need?" Her voice had that oddly intimate note of camaraderie which the War had specifically developed in people. He enjoyed it. It relaxed him.

"Perhaps you'd better warn people against using the towpath. There's other houses, I gather, in the vicinity. Len and Fred should go, too."

"Well, good luck, Mr Kiss." The hand she reached down to him was warm. They had become friends in those moments. She went back into the house and he peered hard at the bomb's nose, thinking he could tell where it unscrewed. He knew that you unscrewed the cone first, then you severed certain wires. He paused, waiting for the sisters to get over the hedge and on their way to the vicarage.

"Next comes the Queen, so pretty indeed,
How nicely she sits on the velocipede,

258

With high heels and buckles she treads with ease,
She's getting quite young is our Queen,
That Alderman Salomon out of the lane,
He holds up so stately poor Vickey's train,
Prince of Wales and Prince Tick will come
   if they can,
  Just to open the Viaduct and Bridge.
Horses and donkeys will caper like fleas,
No more sore shoulders and broken knees,
The animal Society may take their ease,
  Goodbye to the once Holborn Hill.''

He sang as usual to hold the unwelcome voices and thoughts at bay. At least here he could not see as much of the sky and its population. He raised the beautiful lamp and played warm light upon the nose cone. There was a notch clearly designed to take an instrument. He put down the lamp and opened the toolbox, removing a screwdriver. Fixing it into the cone for leverage he tried to turn it. From within the casing came a vicious hiss, the kind a disturbed viper might make. To Mr Kiss the sound was evil, but he ignored its warning and pushed again.

The cone grated and turned, further mangling the dead dog's body beneath it, for Tommy's corpse was still proving helpful, offering just enough room between nose and ground for Mr Kiss to work. Bit by bit he continued to loosen the nose, screwing it deeper into the dog's body until it was clear he could not continue. Getting to his feet, the bomb still grumbling behind him, he went back to the cottage to find some clothes line, two chairs, a set of straps. Everything he wanted was in one of the kitchen cupboards. The light from the lamp filled the kitchen and he looked around him for a second admiring the crowded neatness, the comfort of the place. He became determined that it should not be destroyed.

Outside he was sure he could smell cordite mixed with the stink of urine, faeces and Tommy's bloody flesh. With the rope, straps and chairs he rigged a harness from which he could suspend the main mass of the bomb to stop it dropping through what remained of the roof. Hauling on the clothesline he gradually raised the bomb a little higher. Though still attached to the casing the nose was now unscrewed some six inches. As it swung up the bomb hissed again, a far more violent warning, and something within it began to click rapidly, like a telephone being dialled. Suppressing an urgent need to vomit, Mr Kiss picked up the ear-trumpet and placed it carefully against the casing. He could hear machinery whirring and grinding like the innards of a clock about to strike. While he had no idea what was actually happening he knew he must act as quickly as possible.

Again he attempted to achieve some kind of rapport with the thing's crude brain, but if the bomb were sentient at all it was not in that section. First he whistled a few bars and then he began to sing again:

> "I wish I was in the land of cotton,
>   folks down there are not forgotten,
> Look away, look away, look away Dixieland . . ."

The bomb shuddered and he thought it must surely explode, but it merely growled and grew hotter to the touch, as if offering him a final warning.

He returned to the nose and slowly unscrewed it completely, lowering it onto the cushion he had placed over Tommy's body. Now with the aid of the electric lamp he could see wires and coils. He was almost certain he could see a thin plume of smoke issuing like ectoplasm from the centre. The entire contents of the machine was a mystery to him except he knew the thing went off on impact, which meant the explosive itself was in the main casing. There was a terrible constriction in his chest, as if his heart were being squeezed by a demonic fist. Wires led from the cone into the body of the bomb. He ignored these and instead picked up the vicar's shears, still trying to sense how the bomb was constituted. The clockwork noise started again, faster, and he advanced towards it, shears extended. The bomb began to growl loudly. He would have been unsurprised if it had turned towards him, glaring and snarling. It had a distinct Nazi character. But he refused to be intimidated. With a gasp, almost a sob, he rammed the shears into the works and snipped. He snipped twice more, trusting to whatever instincts he had, to whatever luck was still with him, then snipped again as the bile rose in his mouth and he felt he would drown in it. For a fourth time he snipped, severing every possible wire and the bomb seemed to shriek. It grumbled, whimpered and grew silent.

Mr Kiss let the shears fall onto the dead dog and when he at last allowed himself to vomit it was into the cone, almost an act of vitiation, but also over the dog, so there would be only one mess to clear up. Even in these circumstances Mr Kiss retained the habits of a man who lived alone. He knew for a certainty that he was still mad as a hatter. Though he had risked his own life and might well have saved theirs, what he had done had been insane. The oil lamp was beginning to burn low. Lifting it, he went to the gate and tried to pull it back, but while it was no longer blocked by the bomb it was still locked. The harmless bomb turned slowly in its makeshift rigging, hanging like a drawn murderer.

When he had rattled the gate uselessly for a moment he returned to the house, carefully searching cupboards and drawers until he discovered a likely key on a ring. By now the dogs were barking, jumping and leaping at him as if to acknowledge their salvation.

"I'm Kiss the Idiot," he informed them affectionately. "I'm Kiss the Fool. Kiss the Unexploded Bomb. You were my only witnesses, and even you didn't see me wrestle with it. Your friend is avenged. When people learn how hopeless and unnecessary governments are, then perhaps they'll start fighting this war in earnest with some chance of winning. But who'll find out first, us or the Germans?" He guffawed. He grew sober. "Well, that's a bloody easy one. Might as well be optimistic, lads." Weeping with pleasure he hugged them, sniffed their fur and did not go immediately to unlock the gate but kept the dogs with him in the house while he sat for a while on the sofa and enjoyed the cottage's atmosphere, for it was a better, more sophisticated retreat than any of his. Although he now felt extremely tired it would be unfair to go to sleep. People would be wanting to know what had happened. He went upstairs to the bathroom. The immersion heater was no longer working but there was warm water. Wondering how long it would be before the electricity cable was repaired, he washed as thoroughly as he could and looked with curiosity at his round, bright face framed with a halo of light hair in the mirror. "By God, J.K., you stymied the bugger!" And he threw back his head, shouting with joy, marvelling at his good fortune.

"Come lads and lasses, be up in a jiffy,
The Queen is about to visit the City,
That her visits are scarce we think it a pity,
She will open the Viaduct and Bridge.

With the Lord Mayor Elect like a porpoise,
Big round as an elephant in his old corpus,
To see this great sight nothing with stop us,
Gog and Magog shall dance with the Queen."

Feeling considerably elated he cleaned off his jacket and put it
back on, resettled his helmet on his head, returned downstairs,
placed the toolbox carefully on the kitchen table, put his own things
back in his bag and looked around to make sure everything was
shipshape, then he closed the door on his eager new friends and
walked to the entrance to find that the key fitted. Locking the gate
behind him, he strolled onto the narrow path beside the canal,
smelling its rich mixture of scents. The sky was still on fire but the
shapes and the voices were held at bay by his singing.

"All the good clothes that is got upon tally,
They'll put on this day as they look on the valley,
Dusty Bob, Tom, and Jem, and African Sally,
    These bye-gones will visit the Queen.
All the old horses will jump for joy,
'Twas up Holborn Hill that did them annoy,
I remember truck dragging when I was a boy,
    Good luck to the Viaduct and Bridge."

Near Ladbroke Grove steps a couple of dim shapes moved ahead
of him and he turned his beam to see that a tape had been drawn
across the towpath. Behind it stood Beth Scaramanga in her
summer dress with a Chinese silk dressing-gown over it, a
somewhat doddering Special Constable with grey hair and shining
cheeks and a young, excited lad in a cheesecutter cap at least two
sizes too large. The distant flames made virtual silhouettes of them
and their voices were punctuated by the frequent explosions, the
fearful confusion of an East End which surely must be fatally
wounded.

Beth Scaramanga called behind her. "It's okay. Is it okay,
warden? Are you back?"

"The bomb's safe now." Josef Kiss grinned appreciation at his
gall. "You can sleep in your own beds tonight."

Smoking a cigarette, Len the sour nightwatchman climbed
awkwardly down the steps as the boy climbed up. "I never
expected to see you again, old man. The company's got a lot to

thank you for. Bloody boss wouldn't come near the place. He got
the Specials to cordon everything off. You fixed the bomb, then?"

"Snicker-snee." He knew a pang of conscience as he let Len shake
his hand.

*ghastly for them yet there's something horribly exciting my liver's still
sitting there unless the bloody rats got it I wish it wouldn't go on so funny I
think I'm a gonner she couldn't get the smell of wood-shavings out of her
nose look what they're doing to the East End is it because of the Jews do you
think?*

"Fred's gone with Chloe to have Puffy seen to at the vets."
Taking a packet of Gold Flake from her handbag, Beth offered him
a cigarette. When he refused she said automatically, "Mind if I do?"
before striking a match. "So the house is all right?" Her eyes were
large in the flame's glare.

"As rain, Miss Scaramanga." Raising his steel helmet he handed
her the gate keys. "The dogs probably need a bit of attention. And
someone will have to deal with the mess. It's pretty awful. The dog
that was hit and so on." He was too embarrassed to mention his
own contribution.

"Won't you stay with us for a cup of tea? Or perhaps the night, if
the cats haven't completely ruined the spare room. You must be
beat."

"I'd better get over to Harrow I think. The wife and kids might
be worried you know, though she wouldn't expect me to be there."
He pointed eastwards.

"Of course, our phone stopped working. Can I do anything?"

"Give my regards to your sister. It was a delight to meet two such
civilised and beautiful women."

"Haven't you a number we can reach you at? An office? A
station?"

"Just think of me as a ship passing in the night. Some
unanticipated Zorro." In truth he would have liked to rest in their
company, enjoy their admiration, at the cottage, particularly since
Gloria became nervous when he was in this condition. She was not
at all entertained by him and would not want him in Harrow. After
he found a working phone-box to ring her up and say he was all
right, he was not sure what he would do.

"No, really. We must thank you in some way,"

"You're a bloody brave lad." The Special Constable's voice was high, cracked, Edwardian. "Don't you let no one tell you otherwise. This is like Arthur's last fight. At the old Paddington Baths."

Framed against lurid smoke above them on the bridge's steps Chloe paused. "Mr Kiss? Are you all right?"

"He's done it, Chlo. The bomb's out of action."

"You'll stay and have a drink, Mr Kiss?"

extraordinary day but not altogether a disaster she wore that gown that was nearly a crinoline you couldn't get away with it unless you were gone with the wind, as it were, and I can't blame anyone, you had a jar full, looked like rubies I saw them in the sunlight that time and a jungle green as a picture it was like being in a picture but just that little burn was bad enough oh there'll never be one who'll ever come up to what you imagine or hope for it's so stupid to hope just a child crying, and a young woman is the man dead help us help us I'm broken

"His wife and kiddies will be worrying about him." Beth had adopted a slightly proprietorial tone.

"Perhaps you could stop in tomorrow? Do you have our number?"

"LAD 9375," said Beth. "Please write it down."

He took his book from the donkey-jacket's pocket and with a stub of pencil noted the number. "I would very much like to call on you again. If I could get in touch with Gloria – I am rather tired. A long day. Not what I was expecting. Would be delighted to accept."

"You're more used to all this than we are!" Beth helped the Special Constable roll up the length of tape.

Josef Kiss felt the truth about to emerge and suppressed it. "Well, if you'll keep a look out for my return, I'll be back. I will be back." Removing the ear-trumpet and shears from his bag he put these and the electric lantern into the Special Constable's hands. "Would you be good enough to return these to the vicar?" He bowed hugely to the lovely sisters who had adopted the stance of Celtic heroines made still more splendid by war.

makes you sleepy after a while the smoke tore all the clothes off that old woman stark naked in the street just like those pictures she had from her cousin in Germany what are they trying to do to us? What did we do to them? Why do they hate us? Do all men hate all women just because we gave birth to them, hate life, hate anything that lives tear it and soil it and rob it of dignity identity anything of its own how can it be our fault burn it and smash it even the organ grinder's monkey little charred body not two minutes from here will they ever reach me the trick is not to think about it but it's quiet as the grave quieter than I've ever known it night or day but so bloody hot even when we try to do what they want

Josef Kiss ran up the steps and looked through the shifting darkness for a phone-box. He decided to head towards Notting Hill. He could still feel the warmth of the two women at his back, almost equal to the heat from the agitated sky. He knew that he was splendidly, selflessly and probably platonically in love. He glimpsed a demonic black horse rearing over the roofs of Cambridge Gardens and forced his attention on the road ahead where, by Ladbroke Grove Underground Station, he knew he would find a phone.

> "The banners and flags will go in rotation,
> Emblems of things of every nation,
> The workmen of England and emigration,
>   And old Besley fighting for Mayor.
> Lawrence is down as flat as a flounder,
> On his belly stands the trumpet type founder,
> The Aldermen in rotation playing at rounder,
>   When they open the Viaduct and Bridge."

must stop this going back to I was happy why can't I accept the present constant where I hoped why can't I give up the past the tropics never leave my mind almost a punishment

> "The cabman will dance in every passage,
> Cow Cross is done up, you won't get a sassage,
> You can travel the Viaduct like a telegraph message,
>   Now they've opened the Viaduct and Bridge."

hurts

When he reached the shadows of the railway bridge he stopped singing and leaned against the wall while the brightly dressed old lady in the box used the phone. He would not see the Scaramangas again for another eight weeks.

Premature Burials 1946

"I'VE LEFT my moorings for a bit, old man." Josef Kiss lets a splendid hand fall on Dandy Banaji's shoulder. "I'm offering you a choice: Drift with me and risk a wreck on the reefs of authority or strike out now for the shore." In the cold rubble, his feet and the bottoms of his trousers obscured by mud, he stands looking towards the river. Before the Blitz, Southwark's biggest warehouse had been here, full of books and toys. He brandishes a piece of charred tin. "A kiddy-car!"

"Where would you drift?" Dandy Banaji is amused and concerned. "I suppose you can't say."

"Keep your options open and come anyway." The summer rain has brought a fresh smell to the ruins, of poppies, dandelions, daisies, of small shrubs and grasses, some periwinkle, a little London Pride. For a moment a small brown butterfly flies around Banaji's head then descends on a clump of rosebay willowherb. "Join me for a bit and take some jolly memories back to Bombay."

Dandy has no wish to disappoint his friend, suspecting that his own imminent departure is at least partly why Josef Kiss has deliberately stopped taking the opiates which usually keep him in control of himself. "What if you're wrecked," he speaks with careful good humour, "and sink to the bottom? Do I come too?"

"That couldn't happen for days. They'll salvage me well before then." Mr Kiss is the picture of delighted self-mockery. "Please come."

At the best of times Dandy can rarely resist Josef Kiss's charm and today an obscure sense of guilt conquers any good judgement he has left. "Very well. But only if you decide a direction."

"West. Always west on these occasions. We go to Tower Bridge, Dandy dear, and take the boat upriver, perhaps to Hampton Court. I'd like to enjoy some spreads of flowers, not these rogue patches." Clambering up a huge slab of broken brickwork resembling the stranded bridge of an antique galley, he peers intently at the sparkling water full of untidy flotsam, broken furniture and old iron, the diluvium of War. "The sun's out again. It'll be wonderful. We'll buy sandwiches for lunch or eat our ration books if forced. Wait!" Exaggeratedly comic he claps his hand to his forehead. "I know what you're thinking! Is it concern, sir? For a relative? No? A friend? I thought so, sir? A friend. A lady – no, no – a gent. You think he's going bonkers do you sir? Off his rocker, sir? Am I right? Well, only time will tell, sir.

> "Let us drink and be merry, dance, joke and rejoice
> With claret and sherry, theorbo and voice;
> The changeable world to our joy is unjust,
> All treasure's uncertain, then down with your dust:
> In frolics dispose your pounds, shillings and pence,
> For we shall be nothing a hundred years hence!"

And with this he sweeps Dandy along with him, his brightly striped blazer giving him the appearance of a gracefully animated pavilion. "We'll put the ruins behind us and look only on pleasant prewar things unsoiled by death's dusty stink. We'll escape out of this city of sweat, of mists and yellow succulents; out of crime and grime and signs of the times. This is better than your Mrs Duxbury's eh? On a Saturday? Better than Mr Duxbury's allotment or Mr Rodrigues's Meccano set? Better even than the Streatham Locarno or the Empire, Leicester Square? Better dear Dandy than an evening of Sinhalese Ballet at the Cultural Centre? Almost as good as India's independence, eh? And what an independence it'll be! Everything Mr Gandhi's dreamed of or had nightmares about. And you're going to see it first-hand. I envy you, old chap."

"Come with me." He has said this more than once.

"Ha! I'm at present psychically bound to London and its environs, my would-be Hythloday. And I'm a married man with a number of

responsibilities. To my children in particular. My responsibilities
to my wife are these days limited. But that's another sauce
altogether and we shan't taste it today. Ha, ha, ha! Come along,
Dandy boy. Come along!"

Leaving the wasteland behind they find themselves on Bank
Side strolling under Link Street's iron viaduct and passing the
unlikely flamboyance of the Cathedral, striking towards London
Bridge. There is a hushed quality about the air as if the
corrugated-iron fences and untrustworthy brick walls, the
temporary scaffolding and asbestos sheets, the leaning ruins now
constituting so much of Southwark's landscape are actually
absorbing sound, but once they set foot on London Bridge,
heading for Steam Packet Wharf and Billingsgate, the smell of
dead fish almost a tangible wave, the world grows less grey and
the rays of sun which failed to warm Southwark begin to take
effect. In the market with its Victorian fancy ironwork and 18th-
century classicism, Dandy as usual displays open fascination for
the porters' peculiar basket hats stacked one on top of the other,
the bustling camaraderie, formal obscenities and the unexpected
good humour of the place, then they are past Custom House
Quay's austere Arcadian building, as packed as the market
galleries and smelling almost as strongly of fish, out onto more
bombsites and temporary metal stairs leading up rubble slopes to
Tower Hill's neatly cut lawns, a sharp comparison to the
surrounding tumble of damaged and gutted buildings, and the
White Tower's pale glittering granite, its royal flag at full mast.
Back on the cannon-defended embankment, ready for any Dutchy
who tries to sail up the Thames, by Traitor's Gate, Josef Kiss
remarks how he would relish seeing the heads of Mussolini, Hitler
and Hirohito grinning on the ancient spikes, forced to stare
forever across the water at their lunatic destruction. When the War
was still at its height he had arrived at Downing Street bearing the
Polish cavalry sword presented to him by Count Obtulowitcz in
1941, offering to do the job himself. This gesture cost him a
month in Orchard View, a private hospital near Canterbury
officially taken over for people the Blitz had driven mad, where,
having no record of his prewar lunacy, they treated him with
rather more sympathy than he had come to expect. At the little
green wooden ticket office he lifts a marvellous boater to the

smiling old woman in the window and munificently purchases two tickets. "Change at Westminster, Captain Sanders, love."

Returning with Dandy Banaji to the little tunnel taking them to Tower Pier they see the steamer's funnel giving out blobs of dense smoke as it prepares to leave and Josef Kiss rolls rapidly ahead roaring for it to wait, while perhaps for the first and last time in his life, the startled boatman does as he is told.

if the fair comes back this year we'll go he was killed you know on a chairoplane and funny enough he never trusted the buggers as much of a dynamiter as this he dropped a jumping-jack or two into a pillar box it's the jewboys still up to their tricks they'll buy up all these sites believe me

Under its aft awning the boat holds a miscellaneous collection of passengers while an entire mixed party of schoolchildren occupies the forward parts. Shuddering, Josef Kiss moves as far away from them as he can. "The smell you know," he whispers, "reaches maximum when they get to ten or eleven and doesn't completely fade until they're almost twenty. I have difficulty with it, even around my own kids, whom I love." A large woman with a picnic basket makes space for them in the stern. Josef Kiss touches fingers to boater. "Much obliged to you, madam."

"Don't mind if I do." Mysteriously amused, she wears a dress printed with enormous California poppies, her handbag of some gaudy fabric, her high-heeled sandals having rubbed her heels bright red reveal that she has painted her legs with special dye in place of stockings, giving Dandy Banaji a sudden vision of her naked, piebald and enormous, and to disguise his embarrassment he laughs along with her whereupon she offers him a cigarette which he refuses. "Oh, go on, treat yourself."

"I'm afraid I don't."

"All the more for the rest of us." She lights a Weights. "You over here with the uh . . .?"

"May I present, madam, Colonel A. J. Dadderji, Commanding Officer of His Majesty's Royal Bombay Horse, three times winner of the Victoria Cross, twice winner of the Oaks, but being incognito he doesn't wish to be recognised." Josef Kiss announces this with ponderous gravity.

"Go on!" Her own not unintelligent eye catches Dandy's. "Your friend's taking the mick."

But it is too late for Dandy who is by now happily infected. "I'm just a simple maharajah, actually."

"Yeah? With elephants and emeralds and stuff?"

"Only a couple of hundred elephants and a few dozen emeralds. It's a small state, really, Banajistan."

"Good enough for me." Placing the picnic basket on the other side of them she takes his arm. "I'm Mavis Essayan and that's almost as funny a name as yours isn't it? You're very light-skinned. I thought you was a gyppo at first or an Eye-tai. My young man was supposed to meet me here and take us to Kew for a picnic but I don't mind sharing with you. And your mate, of course."

"You've made a conquest, your highness." Josef smiles as if considering himself some courtly cupid. "We'd love to help you eat your lunch, madam. And Kew's our destination too."

Dandy says nothing of Hampton Court, for plainly the adventure has begun and there will be random changes to accommodate whatever Fate determines. He rather likes the fat woman and Josef Kiss's present mood inspires him to suppress his normal reserve, so he does not discourage her. The river grows clearer of rubbish as they sail west and the boat's wake no longer has a grey tinge like scum in a thrice-used bath. They are heading into more salubrious waters. "Well, that's all right then." With an air of satisfaction she addresses Josef Kiss. "You know we don't go all the way to Kew?"

"I do, Miss San. We change at Westminster Pier, below the Shot Tower and across from Queen Boadicea."

"It's Essayan. A lot of people make that mistake. And you?"

"Forgive me. I am Kiss. Josef Kiss."

"And what were you in, Jo?"

"Bomb Disposal," says Dandy. "And Civilian Rescue. A hero. Almost a saint."

"Oo, I wouldn't like that." Mavis wriggles her shoulders. The boat passes between a burned-out dock and the remains of an office block where cranes and bulldozers work to clear the site. "I never saw the Blitz, thank god. I was in Norfolk with my sister. We were Land Army which was hard work but a good life compared with some and we had a lot of laughs. Were you over here during the War, Mr . . . Colonel, your highness?"

To his friend's admiring astonishment Dandy Banaji embarks on a fantastical account of a war career spanning several continents, rivalling Hollywood, and culminating with his single-handed dropping of the Atomic Bomb on Hiroshima when the American Air Force failed to liaise. By the time they board the second steamer Mavis is in fits. "Well this really is a bit of fun. Frankly I wasn't much looking forward to today. The bloke who never turned up's a friend of my brother-in-law's and talks nothing but electricity."

puritanical mixed race Scot purse-lipped pursuit of narrow-minded prejudice posing as principle fanatical reactionary broke Ben's heart he was so kind and practical Ben said they should always have the right to choose my solicitor's a Jew and my barrister's a bloody Indian on top of that my solicitor's also a woman so if we wish Mr Wheatstraw we can give in now it'll otherwise be a total triumph for them Will this mean a major upheaval hardly what I'd have called nice should never have done that but it was putting her out of her misery really and all for three fucking pound

As they head past Vauxhall and Chelsea signs of the War grow fewer, though the enemy habitually picked out river targets like warehouses and power-stations. Josef Kiss has no desire to remember those days and far prefers his invented present.

"Good old Battersea." Mavis affectionately addresses the great deco chimneys. For many Londoners the survival of Battersea Power Station remains a more potent symbol than St Paul's miraculous emergence from the flames of the Blitz. "Have you ever seen inside? Ben took me. It's like a film, a castle. Modern but nice. You know, like a really high-class West End picture palace." Much of the surrounding destruction has recently been levelled and grass grows over it, smooth as a cricket pitch.

"This is the start of the Battersea to Hammersmith swimming race." Josef Kiss grows silky with nostalgia. "Anyone can go in for it. There were hundreds before the War, kids mostly. But now it's older people still do it. Rival residents of Battersea and Fulham. Parents throw their children in to make them swim. That water was never clean. It's all power stations, of course, past Hammersmith, though the trees around Putney and Barnes and that stretch of Hurlingham and Bishops Park make it seem countrified and healthy. It did nobody much harm and the water was almost always warm. In 1920 my Uncle Edmond, the hatter, the dandy, who knew royalty and rode his own horse at Newmarket, a great

Gentleman Amateur in everything but name, swam this course sixteen times before he was pulled out. They thought he was dead. They think all our family's dead now. My sister certainly wishes us dead but then she's in politics. An Alderwoman and a Prospective Member of Parliament, she sold her soul early on. Got a good price, too."

Buffalo Bill and Texas Jack scan the lonely river for signs of Broken Knife and his Blackfeet I'm largely a cigar man now and that's silly with a war on the lost treasure of Troy's supposed to be in Kensal Rise. It was taken from Berlin by two Nazi SS officers in 1944. The gold brick business was never better hot and put it up those thighs

When a small swarthy man in a dull sports jacket motions with his hand from the other side of the bench his wife hisses at him to shut up, but he has been grumbling for some while. She darts a blue-eyed apology, exceptionally pretty. "You're talking rot!" he says. "I've lived in Fulham all my life. We get the Boat Race, Putney to Mortlake. There's no swimming race. I ought to know, chum. I work for the local paper."

"Ever ready to bow to the gentlemen of the press." Josef Kiss frowns. "However . . ."

"You're making a fool of yourself, Dickie." Tugging at his jacket his wife explains apologetically. "He's a printer. Thinks he knows everything."

"I read the blasted thing from cover to cover, don't I? Every blasted week! There's no such thing. You shouldn't be allowed to say there was. Posing as a river guide!"

"I am Kiss, my dear sir." Seizing a metal support he rises on his side of the boat, dignified in the face of petty attack. "You've no doubt heard of the Kiss and Banstead Expedition of 1928? Banstead was killed of course by natives upriver. But I went on to chart this entire stretch, my dear Dickie! You'll not remember, either, I suppose, Dickie, the Viking fleet sailing as far as the Palace of Fulham to sack the Bishop's treasury? Where were you during the raids, Dickie? No, sir. Don't sit back, sir. Stand up, sir, and be counted. You have accused me of perjury!"

"You're loony." Blinking, Dickie looks to his wife. "He's bats."

"Call the captain!" Although there is still a self-mocking sparkle in Mr Kiss's eye it is clear to Dandy that his friend is in danger of losing control. "I'll have this settled. Captain!"

"Just say you're sorry." Dickie's wife continues to pull at him. "Just apologise."

Dickie weighs this up. "Well, I apologise, though I still say you're lying."

"Extremely civil of you." Josef Kiss turns to smile benignly on his entire audience, most of which has moved discreetly to other parts of the boat. He raises his straw hat. "I too am sorry, for suggesting you were a coward."

"He's much obliged," says Dickie's wife. "Now for god's sake shut up, Dickie. You're always doing this. You think you know it all. Then you make a fool of yourself and me."

"Never you, dear lady." As he resumes his seat Josef Kiss wags a gallant finger. Smiling at him she returns to her *Reveille*, the scandals of the stars.

"Oh, look. Swans!" Mavis Essayan takes a tighter hold on Dandy Banaji. "We'll be at Kew before you know it. Do you like Kew, Mr K?"

"Do I like Kew, lovely Mavis? I adore it. The heat! The fecund stench!" He rolls his eyes like some beatific Jolson. "Mavis, you can't know what Kew means to me. I was married there."

"I didn't think they had a church. A registry office was it?"

"It was in the eyes of the Lord." He blushes at his recollection of rapture.

she cannot be she cannot ever be as sweet and vulnerable and intelligent as me the boy's in work at last got him in the canteen and he had his trousers down before I could blink bloody hell fire it was better than I'd dreamed and never again just my luck took the bus up there but they'd all gone don't know what to get the little bugger for his birthday squirt it on his face boys little sods little bitches little fuckarse beggars fuck a dozen before breakfast

> "Come all pretty ladies and listen to me,
> I'll sing thee a ballad of sweet chastity."

When Dickie and his wife disembark at Putney Bridge the printer glares over his shoulder as he stands on the pier waiting to go through the gate, but Josef Kiss is oblivious, looking past tall plane trees to Victorian flats scarcely touched by the War and Putney High Street which is much as it was in happier years before Austerity removed goods from its windows and forced imaginative use of cardboard models. Since Swinburne lived here Putney has borne the air of a self-contained village, though it is bordered by Wandsworth, Wimbledon and Barnes. For a second Josef Kiss considers following an impulse to jump ship and visit Old Barnes Cemetery in the middle of the Common, a cemetery unfenced save by wild brambles and one of his favourites, another small patch of arcadia in the city, but Kew holds even more attractions, if only bitter-sweet ones, memories of prewar lust.

only me and him still on the stake still alive crying out while they laughed I thought I was dead and ran nobody ever found the baby I'll go back as soon as I can wigs can they tell go out to Egypt first chance I get

Now they share the vessel with seven silent nuns, evidently members of a strict sect, three young army cadets smoking ostentatiously and continuously, several middle-aged ladies in the ornate hats associated with formal shopping expeditions, who not being together are almost as silent as the nuns, and a pale, gloomy individual of about thirty, wearing dark worsted in spite of the warmth, sitting by himself at the front of the boat as it pulls again out into the river.

"You're an odd pair to be going about together." Mavis transfers her hold to Dandy's unresisting hand. "How did you meet up?"

"It was in the Blitz," says Dandy. "He was at the Windmill. I became his fan."

"What were you doing there? Is Kiss your stage name? You a comic?"

"I suspect so, Miss Essayan. I've done most things in the theatrical way."

As they move towards the great Gothic warmth of Hammersmith Bridge, its sandstone pinnacles and turrets freshly touched by rain and tinged pink by the sun, the quality of the water becomes magical, a little misty, flanked by thick mysterious willows, and they steam past ducks, a swan, some optimistic fishermen enjoying their Saturday afternoon, waving people in pubs to right and left, shouting children who run along the banks. "Not much further now," Mr Kiss reassures them, "before we're round the bend."

"I always forget how much it twists and turns." Mavis peers over the rail to look at the wake, now a cheerful brown and cream. "You always think it goes straight. Then it catches you by surprise."

"Can you really go all the way to Oxford by boat?" Abstractedly Dandy stares below the surface.

"And beyond if you want. But not on a big steamer. We could get to Henley or Kingston. Before the War a company ran the river regularly but I'd guess all its boats went to Dunkirk with Mr Miniver. They had motor cruisers, steamers, punts, skiffs, launches. Very busy, the river before the War."

"I suppose there are more regulations now." Dandy looked up. "And fewer people. It's a shame."

"It'll all be back just the same one day." Mavis is in no doubt. "Mr Attlee's promised. Just the same, only better."

"That's the spirit." Josef Kiss hears only confirmation of her desires. "Wider and deeper. We'll have the *Cutty Sark* doing Greenwich to Oxford in half-an-hour. Cram on more sail! Avast there!"

In mild astonishment the nuns look back before returning to their contemplations, while, with a somewhat artificial somnambulistic air, some of the passengers move slowly to the other side of the boat. Removing his hat, Mr Kiss stares thoughtfully in their general direction. "I smell mutiny, Colonel Dadderji. Stand by to break out the muskets. Of course it was sheer folly to have brought a woman with us."

An elderly boatman, his face a map of broken veins, testament to several thousand pints, peering from his little wooden cabin places a patient rag down on the brass engine casing and fixes his wheel with a piece of wire. "What's up squire?"

"The crew, sir. We can't drive them much longer without risking trouble." Josef Kiss's stance apes conventional melodrama.

"Well, that's no problem then, is it?" The boatman responds with weary sarcasm. "We'll put them ashore at Kew. Same place you get off, guv'nor. He ought to have a keeper," he adds warningly to Dandy and swings the little steamer with some force through a pleasant stretch of water with a wide stone bridge ahead, a long ornamental wall to port and a path lined with tall shady chestnuts. "Here we are, ladies and gents. All change! Women, children and loonies first." The quay comes in sight.

I am the ship all those years and meanwhile we die of thirst what the fuck does the bridge care they'll bring in Turks and god knows what before they'll give a fair day's pay to an Irishman smell the room from a mile away nobody ever guessed he had a drink, let alone three bottles a day neat as a pin to the public at large

275

"Look!" Mr Kiss is delighted. "A Wood white. You don't see those in London any more." He is first to the gangplank, in pursuit of the butterfly which darts to the bridge's shadows.

"Has your friend always been barmy?" Mavis curtseys, joining in the general spirit as Dandy takes the picnic basket and hands her ashore.

"Always," Josef Kiss tells her amiably, rejoining them. "We'll go up that little bit of road and through the turnstile there." Pulling change from his baggy white flannels he makes for the walls and the somewhat baroque gates of the Royal Botanical Gardens. "Three please!" He puts three brown coppers on the dark worn brass of the kiosk where an old man wearing a greasy peaked cap, deep in gloom as if discomfited by the sun, counts them through the shrieking turnstile. Breathing the heady air of the Gardens they regard an apparent infinity of trees, lawns and flowerbeds.

"Oh, bluebells! Just look!" Mavis Essayan gasps. "Like a picture."

In the distance beyond the monkey-puzzle trees stand two buildings of iron and glass looking like smaller versions of the Crystal Palace before it burned down. Dandy points. "What are those, Mr Kiss? They're marvellously Victorian."

"Ferneries and as I recall Succulents. They are shrimps in comparison to the Palm House or indeed the Temperate House. We go over there first." He gestures with his boater which he has removed to wipe sweat from the band. "The Filmy Fern House in fact. Are you game, Miss Essayan? It will be hot in there."

"And muggy. I know. Just a quick look round's always enough for me."

As Josef Kiss leads them along the pathway, Dandy and Mavis trail to admire roses, peonies and the fragrant blooming trees.

When he stands beside the doorway to the filmy Ferns Dandy is reminded suddenly of India. The glass and green-painted iron, the black lettering on white notice boards, are a style somehow typifying the more acceptable aspects of the Raj, yet he knows a moment of disapproval.

Josef Kiss pushes at the sign marked ENTRANCE PLEASE KEEP CLOSED and stands poised on the brink. "Opium! How wonderfully fecund! Doesn't it make you reel?"

Shoulder to shoulder on the grillwork they close the door behind them. "It's like the prehistoric past." Dandy stretches to sniff a frond. "A primaeval past. One would not be surprised to see some beast – some great lizard – blundering towards us."

"Coo," says Mavis. "I hope not." She adds as an afterthought: "I wouldn't mind meeting Victor Mature, though. In a loincloth."

Peering through a spray of delicate giants, Mr Kiss presses the flat of his hand hard into the damp mould and brings it to his nose growling with pleasure, then prowls slowly along the walkway as if stalking game before, like Cro-Magnon, pausing to test the air and growl again. As fascinated by his behaviour as they are by the plants, Dandy and Mavis hesitate at his back until, with the air of a native guide sensing dangerous country, Josef Kiss leads them out into the dry sunshine of the park where it now feels cool. "It does you good to start with the filmy ferns. Our roots as it were, encouraging a sense of history. Not *Two Million Years BC,* dear Mavis. More like two billion. Time! Oh, Time! They have survived – indeed are now nurtured by us – when every other species has perished, and are the basis of our life. They provide our oxygen. They know the secrets of the dinosaurs and Neanderthal. It's all written in there somewhere. But we'll never crack the code. We have lost the knack. We no longer identify ourselves with such things."

"Was he in Codes, then?" Mavis asks Dandy as they hurry behind the striding Kiss.

to the Sunday pictures would look a treat in his window box don't half make you randy George why couldn't you wait you saw all those gates going by all those fences you must have known I couldn't say anything to you and you never thought to ask did you in a world of your own half those soldiers go whoring down the As You Like It not after whores I mean but doing it those bloody stinking Knightsbridge stables with our quarters right over them I hated horses I hated riding them feeding them mucking them out I never did a more stupid thing in my life than joining the fucking Horse Guards god that sort of smell will make you sick for days shove it in he said the horse won't mind

> "A scarlet coat and a smart cockade,
> Are passports to the fair;
> For Venus' self was kind, 'tis said,
> To Mars the god of war."

"Bombs, as I said. And entertainment. He could have done anything. It's as if he's –"

"Touched?"

"In the old sense, yes."

"But harmless."

"To us. Oh, yes."

There is clear water ahead like blue steel under the sun. "Broad Walk," calls out Josef Kiss. "Turkey Oak on your left. Weeping Beach coming up. Weeping Beach is where they planned to strand me, but I kept my wits, my compass and my map. And here we are. It's happening, Dandy. The sounds are getting louder and they're beginning to rhyme again. I know what's being thought. I can see the ladies, though happily I'm still invisible to them."

"All different kinds of special trees." Mavis wiped her red forehead. "We'll sit down in the shade and have our picnic soon. I suppose you like cheese and tomato."

"And cucumber." Dandy speaks with wistful hope.

"Do you know, I thought of making ham and cucumber because my mum had a tin she offered to swap for my sugar but I changed my mind at the last minute. I didn't really want to waste the ham on Derek."

"Just as well. I'm a vegetarian."

"Personally I always trim the fat off. Phew! I'd forgotten what a hike it is here."

They have reached the pond with its fountains and water-lilies, its willows, its little brown ducks and black coots. A few children hang about on the stone stairs throwing pieces of bread to the birds. Behind them, like a country seat imagined in the previous century by H. G. Wells, imposing in its curves and planes, almost faceted, shines the massive Palm House, its interior foliage offering profound adventure.

Josef Kiss comes to a mighty stop, like some predevonian loco, at the foot of one of the fabulous beasts flanking the high greenhouse. Carved from granite they are on a similar scale to the building. "The Queen's Beasts," explains Mavis Essayan to her new friend. "They're the animals supposed to guard England, aren't they? Unicorns and things. And dragons I suppose."

"I think it's a griffin." Dandy frowns up. "Though I'm not too good on English fable. I think they have a rather stand–offish air."

Two groups of children in clashing uniforms file by in opposite directions.

"They do look a bit snooty now you mention it."

claimed Hitler was living on the same landing in the house in Oxford Gardens I'm old and scruffy and I shuffle up and down Chiswick High Street when I used to swan along Bond Street a king of jazz ek kali bhutni si deraoni suret tell me it's trayf please god I know my toches from my torah thinks that's the only way to drive a taxi then after that they all went to live in Finchley

"Up before the beak. Evicted from the bin. A night in the lockup." Josef Kiss lowers his head, a friendly bull feinting in play. "On the road to Portsmouth. Never got any further than Tooting. Wormy, wormy, wormy, though my turds are wormy, will your arms still spurn me? Could your eyes still turn me? Sholom! Sholom! Don't think I can't hear what you're saying. I've got my ears, you bastards. You lying bastards." Josef Kiss turns his face on them, ablaze. "Oh, Dandy! They're coming through again. All at once. No, it's fine. I don't need help. Let them come. I'm used to it. *Old Jenny, creeping Jenny. Ah, Jenny, weeping Jenny. Sweet old Jenny girl.* Can't you just smell all those hundreds of hybrid teas? There are the white roads rising out of nowhere, leading over low hills, going nowhere, leaving the city. I went to Eton, he went to Slough. All good chaps here. That's me in my hey-day. They said I brought a much-needed dignity to the music hall. Is there no heart in you any more? What is this turnabout, this Blitzkrieg, all of a sudden? You said you loved me. A week ago we were talking of a holiday. How long have you been planning this? You raised no warnings, issued no ultimata. This is complete treachery. Traitor! Traitor! Traitor! You're crazy – you've no idea what profound respect – what I feel – Lorna, I love you like you're an idea come to life. Tumble fumble trundle bundle humble. It's still the same old story. How many doors do you pass and get the identical house whine. Dinners for sinners, schleppers for lepers. Social services are here to stay. He's turning into the spit of his loudmouth dad." He smiles at his companions, whom he has now silenced. "That's a taste of what's going on in here. Or rather what's coming into here." He taps his shaded head. "Little currents of electricity in the air carrying the voices of all our times. People like me are individually tuned, no two the same. Look here," he bends to stroke a large red rose, to cup it and smell it, "that rose has a name. All roses have names. This is Le Comte G. de Rochemur. A fine swaggering name for such a grand rose, eh? With such a big scent. Smell the Comte. You'll love him."

Striding quickly away, he passes into the Palm House.

"Are you perfectly sure he'll be okay?' Mavis takes a smell, steps back from Dandy and adjusts her dress. "Is he often like this?"

"To tell the truth, I've never seen him this far gone. Yet as you said yourself, he clearly isn't dangerous."

"It's not exactly what I was looking forward to. I wanted to sit quietly and enjoy the park, eat our picnic. You do what you want but I'll be there under that tree." And she moves off with a rolling petulant gait. All Dandy can do is follow his friend into the Palm House.

Inside it is hotter than any jungle and Dandy is almost physically struck by a powerful smell of damp earth and rotting vegetation; so many different scents. The perforated cast-iron walkways are littered with fallen stamens and fleshy pods, with massive leaves and unidentifiable parts resembling human organs. There are dull pinks and livid reds, sullen yellows, peculiar greens. He cannot see Josef Kiss through the foliage.

"Josef! Josef Kiss?"

The voice he hears has a strange echo. "So you're now saying a Roman, no matter if he was born of British parents, is still a Roman, never a Briton? Because you'll say he is the power, the colonial boss. But a Briton living five years in Rome can he be a Roman? Because he is a subject. How can this be explained?"

Dandy looks for the source but sees no one at all, hears only a bump as a door shuts. At this moment he is alone, save for the disembodied Kiss. The voice is muffled now, coming from somewhere close to the humid centre, amongst the plants them-selves where visitors are forbidden. "Ecstasy, ecstasy, don't run against it, don't challenge it, don't even confront it! Oh, god, that was what it was like in the fire. Ecstasy. Can't, won't fight it. Don't fight the fire. Oh, god, this is more than Heaven; it must be what Hell offers then takes away. I didn't try to warn anyone. I never complained. I tried to live with it. Is that you, Dandy, old boy?"

"Josef. Do you need me for anything? Where are you?"

"The Turkish brothers come here every week but on alternate

Wednesdays and Thursdays because of Petros, who is a Greek, you see. Some vast percentage of the original population of Cyprus now lives in England but they sometimes have trouble getting on. The irony is that it was the British first divided them. When the voices start, Dandy, you get this messianic need to tell everyone. They're scared of that. Don't worry them and they'll leave you alone. Am I scaring you, Dandy, my dear?"

"I must admit I'm a little troubled. Worried you'll get into a jam."

"Then help me out as best you can. This is self-indulgence on my part. I've already said you don't have to stay."

"I'll do what I can." Dandy makes a helpless motion. "Shall I join you in there too, old man?"

From the densest clump comes an agitation, the sounds of pods falling, as if Mr Kiss is involved in some unguessable act of transmutation. "Best not, I think. I used to have this sense of urgency. A need to communicate my experiences. But since they aren't interested and I'm not frightened any longer, I've stopped doing that. There are plenty anyway who think I'm probably sane. The poor souls without imagination are genuine victims, actually barmy. I find it hard to understand that people can be so badly harmed. For my own part I'm merely twisted and transformed. There's no real damage done at all! This is where we courted, Dandy, my wife and I. Gloria curled about me as tightly as any vine. Can you imagine making love in all this earth and vegetation? Don't you envy us? It was our best time. We were never caught, though sometimes a keeper received a hint. Well, there were footprints and broken branches sometimes, which we didn't hurt deliberately. It was in the heat of our passion, Dandy. Can you guess how hot that must have been? To make this House seem cool? Oh, it was wonderful. Our first child was conceived here. Which is why we called him Silvester. I'll leave it to you to guess why son number two is called Leicester! All I do is rhyme away. Can't stop no matter what I say. Amongst Rhode Island Reds I'm a hero. Single-handed I conquered their fear-o. With a crow and a cluck they recall my good luck, for they know I'm not Nero but Pierrot!" There comes a burst of laughter then an almost sexual convulsion from the central clump of palms and at last Dandy spots his friend, shinning relentlessly upwards, like some Papuan coconut-hunter, a

281

massive ape, a pink orang, his boater on the back of his head, his striped blazer covered in leafy mud, his trousers slowly reducing to tatters.

"We're denizens of a decadent place, Dandy. A world of ignorance. Those steady missiles. It was all that stuff on the other side of the Viaduct that horrified me in the end. I'd visited Mrs Mackleworth down there only a day or two earlier. Oh, the miserable smell of her rooms. Of her and her foul little dog! How beautiful she was! It's a sin. It makes you feel sick. I wondered if somehow I had willed the incendiary onto her. Did many people feel that sort of guilt during the War? A fanciful enough notion, an egocentric notion, since Hitler and his planes were after all the active agents. The Temple, Dandy! Don't you mourn it? I saw red. Really red. Bright like a light in my eyes. They were just kids doing the killing. Our kids and theirs. That awful calm face in the rubble. The poor GI who never wanted to be here in the first place. Just bone and gristle and blood all on one side. Is there much point to carrying on? A shadow like a negative against the night. Oh, this is not exactly what I had come to expect. It really is a rotten shame. Bad show, not playing the game."

Dandy watches his friend, unsure if the words are Mr Kiss's own or if he is quoting what he believes he hears. Perhaps it is a mixture. Josef Kiss is close to the top of the palm now, reaching for whatever fruit grows below the branching fronds. "This could be the very gourd I'm out of."

"Mr Kiss, I have a feeling you'll get into worse trouble if you don't come down. Josef, old friend!"

"Remember the White Zombie of Norbury, SW, Dandy? That was me. They never caught me. What a bloody tragedy, those poor little babies. Is Mrs Saleem still alive? The last time I was up a tree for any length of time, Dandy, was in Hyde Park. I was chased there by a gang of boys. They had razors. They wouldn't let me come down. I was rescued eventually by two ladies and an alsatian dog. People aren't so bad. I was looked after very kindly. When the fight was over, when the arrests had been made and the drunken crowd outside the pub dispersed, all that was left was a persistent bitch barking and barking. Barking at her own dim memory of violence. Does that mean much to you, Dan – ah!"

"Oh, Josef! Mr Kiss come down. You'll kill yourself."

But Josef Kiss rights his graceful mass, swinging back against the bole and clasping with beaming triumph a single fruit. He glances at the glittering roof as if hoping for infinity. "We're so set, Dandy, in our cultural arrogance we can't realise how we continue to ring increasingly barren changes on a few themes and techniques, while elsewhere good new voices are being raised. And we can't hear them. We've become too conservative, Dandy. Who's to take over? Did I foresee this or is it a forgotten memory and therefore an illusion? Bloody sunsets over Barnes or maybe Hammersmith. Those bricks were baked for such sunsets. A tricky city. Who can guess she has so many aspects and who can determine which if any are accidental? There are more bricks – harder, grey ones – which look at their best in summer rain. Some improve in winter fog. Did people choose these effects, Dandy? What genius, if they did! What genius, anyway, if they didn't. The Germans were rotters to bomb it all. Do you know what it's like? I suppose you must. Taking hold of all that pain and hammering at it till it assumes a manageable shape. It should be a woman's world this next one. Oops!" He pauses carefully. "I think I've caught a testicle on the tree. I'll have to go up an inch or two."

"And then come down, old man. Mavis has the picnic ready. There are cheese and tomato sandwiches. And lemonade, I think. You could do with a break." Dandy jumps, hearing the squeak of a door.

"London's undramatic variety means that no metaphor is ever very accurate. You can't impose upon it the way you can with Paris, New York or Rome, a single image. Is that fair? It's my home lair. The same's doubtless true of anywhere." He frowns and his voice grows more sonorous. "We've little choice where we begin the 70 year dash and are hardly better at arranging where we'll end it. I'll stick to what I know. I've known too much anyway. I was recalling the government official who came to look at the craters. All topper and teeth, we said. We were covered in dust and other people's blood not to mention their shit. We'd worked for twenty-four hours. 'You chaps look all in,' he said. 'Better take a break.' We'd been leaning on this bit of wall listening to the baby crying somewhere down in a cellar underneath the rubble. He hadn't heard a thing." He sniffs the fruit, a curious ape. "They told me I was loopy. They put it down to the horrors of War. I was lucky my records went up in 1941. It gave me a fresh start and made me a hero instead of a victim. Which helps a great deal – ugh!" He has bitten into his trophy. "This isn't a fig or a banana or even a damnable paw-paw. What right has it? Suppose this were a desert island? It's terrible to be on your own and hearing voices. Worse if you haven't even got a decent fruit to gnaw. Behaving oddly, am I?" With knowing intelligence he stares down at Dandy and winks.

"My good chap!"

"They tried me with a seance, my ladies I mean. We all linked hands and I got in touch with the spirits. Believe me, it's no fun on the other side. I thought at first it was neighbours knocking or builders. It went on and on. Then I realised they had no neighbours. One more shadow comes swiftly into focus then swiftly fades." He becomes obscurely concerned. "Dandy?" He's staring up into the glaze. "Don't let my wife know about this, Dandy, old boy. I gave you her number, didn't I? If it comes to trouble notify my sister, Beryl Male, WHITEHALL 8762. Beryl's my official next of kin. Not Gloria." The intimacy leaves his voice as he drifts onto a more general subject. "Seeking an antidote at the old chemist's Gothic house amongst asymmetrical retorts and test tubes I thought I might have a chance but he was a charlatan, the same as the other. The Thames was red as that rose we looked at, red all over. A vast melted ruby. Then night fell. I just needed a job. It seemed easy. The Celts, he said, have magic." He moves his body a little further up the tree, to a curve, high above the other great flat leaves and fronds, staring into them as another might look for shapes in a fire. "All bloody oppressed people have bloody magic, I said. Or religion. Or both. It's in our nature. That was the medium, you know. She got twitchier than usual and eventually went mad. Locked up permanently. Every so often I see her again, wherever she is and wherever they put me . . ."

He balances his heel against a boll and turns carefully to lean with his back to the tree, apparently comfortable as he continues to inspect his prize, picking at it with his nails. "Gloria. Gloria. This is the scene of our sweetest times. You cannot guess the number and complexity of the roles I assumed in those few years, Dandy. Little Mike, the escape artist, stayed out of it. He was killed by a V2. 'It's a baboon colony, Mr K,' he used to say, 'and I don't have to join. I don't necessarily get any of the benefits but I do get to choose who I mix with.' He mixed with half the down-and-outs in the Balham Salvationist Hall in the end. They couldn't tell which had been people and which was the next day's menu. My God, Dandy, you should be up here with me. Everything rises. The stink makes you drunk. We thought of calling the boy Pan, but it wouldn't have done him much good at school. Pan Kiss is not a fair name. It's not even very melodious. There's black sand running through my glass. Black ram crawling up my arse. Pack rats ruling us from Mars. I think I've got ants, Dandy. Or termites. Maybe merely aphids. Oh, bugger. Get me a spray!

> "When I drain the rosy bowl,
> Joy exhilarates my soul;
> To the Nine I raise my song,
> Ever fair and ever young . . ."

"Come down, old man. We'll have our lunch."

Pale, Josef Kiss grasps the tree behind his back with both hands and carefully lifts a leg to shake it. Something falls from the ruined trouser to the thick mulch below. Dandy is too late to see what it is: either it is inanimate and buried or it has scuttled quickly away. He is suddenly startled by a fresh presence.

A small angry voice speaks at his rear. "I'd think you'd better get down off that tree at once. I've already notified the Head Supervisor and he'll be ringing the police. They take a dim view of the likes of you in Kew."

"Thus making two of you who do. You think perhaps I'll rue discovering this clue to jumping the human queue. Is it 'Ha Ha' now, but soon 'Boo-hoo'?" Tossing his fruit disdainfully, Josef Kiss hits the keeper on the hat. "Do you, sir, intend to have me dragged away?"

"As soon as you're down," says the small fat man grimly, all pompous offence. "You can't make a fool of me doing that. You only harm yourself."

Josef Kiss is contrite. "I understand your position. You're horrified at what you perceive to be desecration. Whereas of course I see it as celebration. It's the same problem with Stonehenge, I believe. This is my favourite spot on Earth. I love nowhere better. I have not only fine memories of a fine time, but memories of a fine woman, a fine fuck, a fine conception."

"That really is enough! Have you any idea what it took to grow that tree? And protect it. All through the War I looked after it. And you're doing I don't know what damage."

"It will be a healthy tree still, possibly healthier for its experience of real life, a bit of decent company."

"Please don't be angry with him." Dandy Banaji hates his own placatory tone. "He's a war hero. Shell shock, you know."

"I've seen shell shock, sir." The keeper remains firm. "And it never took that form. This chap's an exhibitionist. I wouldn't be at all surprised to see the Press pouring along Broad Walk any minute."

"If I wanted cheap publicity," says Mr Kiss with dignity from above, "I would have climbed to the top of the pagoda. I can see it from here. It looks lovely. Another reminder of my salad days with Gloria. This is a pilgrimage, sir. Like some people make to Jerusalem. And evidently just as objectionable to the majority. How will you get me down? Wait for me to be eaten to bits by your trained termites?"

name of Nutbrown worked at Buckingham Palace he said it was a perfect play Sicilian willowherb in the ruins James Parr and the amoeba aesthetics om sani rana om sani rana sed efris nogod called it The Fallen Phoenix said I was the image of him

"Gather ye rosebuds while ye may
Old time is still a-flying;
And this same flow'r that smiles today,
Tomorrow will be dying . . ."

"That's definitely not shell shock."

"He really doesn't mean any harm." Dandy is desperate.

"Let the authorities decide that. I was in the ARP, a full-time warden as well as doing my job."

"Little Hitler," says Josef and folds his arms.

"Please Josef, get down. You need to take your tablets old man." Without malice, Josef Kiss ignores his friend.

Eating an apple Mavis wanders in, her picnic basket under her arm. "Blimey!"

Taking paper from his pocket Dandy writes out a name and number. "Could you please find a phone box and tell this lady her brother has got himself in a jam?" He gives her two pennies. "I'll look after your basket. Please, miss."

She glances at the number. "Well, I suppose." Impressed by his urgency she leaves but takes her basket while Dandy, staring in silence at his friend, observes that he has closed his eyes and appears to be sleeping.

"I don't care if he breaks his bloody neck." The keeper offers this in an intimate undertone as if by ceasing to plead for Mr Kiss, Dandy has become a confidant. "And he will. One slip. He can't really be asleep."

It seems to Dandy that Josef Kiss is listening to distant music, for his expression has gradually taken on a seraphic cast. Dandy and the keeper fall silent, looking up as sun strikes through the dusty glass to strike full upon Mr Kiss's massive frame. His position on the tree seems an impossible act of levitation. After a while the keeper speaks. "He's got to drop soon." Then the door of the Palm House opens, allowing a drift of cooler air and two policemen to enter, followed by a man in an expensive lounge suit; he is grey-headed and sallow with thin, bright red lips, deep-set brown eyes. The policemen have the pallor of men who have worked for a long time on night shift.

"What's the trouble here, Varty," says the man in the suit.

Varty points at Josef Kiss above.

"Good God! How did he get up there? Why doesn't he fall? Has he fainted? Is he dead?"

"He's sleeping, I think." Dandy Banaji finds it impossible to keep a note of pride from his voice.

"This is his friend, sir," says Varty to the Head Supervisor while the two policemen glare resentfully at the tree and its occupant; as conservative as most of their kind, they had hoped for a rest in Kew and have no training to cope with this situation. "Who does he think he is?" asks the shortest. "King Bloody Kong?"

"Mickey the Monkey more like." His companion looks carefully at Dandy. "Is he violent, sir?"

"No. He was injured in the War. A hero. Shell shock." Dandy can only repeat excuses already offered, hardly able to believe them himself. The real explanations are almost unvoiceable. The audience of five falls into silence again. Mr Varty checks his watch.

"Not a bet, then," says the Head Supervisor after a while. Dandy shakes his head.

"Wake up. You'll kill yourself you soppy date!" cries Mr Varty.

"More a banana, really," says the taller policeman.

"Off his rotten coconut!" His companion sniggers.

Dandy is shocked. "Please, gentlemen! He's in trouble. He's in pain. He's in torment. Can't you tell?"

"He looks rather happy to me." Slightly ashamed, the Head Supervisor taps at his leg. "Has he escaped from somewhere?"

Dandy sighs and shakes his head. "We came for a picnic. I hoped the flowers and trees would have a calming effect. But I hadn't understood his special affection for these palms. He was here before the War."

"Not up that tree he wasn't." Mr Varty's initial outrage has subsided. Now he stares with neutral curiosity at Mr Kiss. "Though I think I've seen him here before. With a lady." He frowns. "He must be fixed to it. An invisible wire?"

"Shouldn't we get a net or a blanket?" One of the policemen is bright red and running with sweat. He loosens his tunic. "From the Fire Brigade?"

"I'll go and ring them." The Head Supervisor seems glad of an excuse to return to his office. "Keep an eye on things, Varty."

Dandy Banaji wonders if he is witnessing something like a miracle, yet knows this could be nothing more than a show put on by his friend to attract attention. He enjoyed, after all, his life on stage. Is he merely extending his area of performance?

A further half hour passes while the four people on the grid observe the large man on the palm. Mavis Essayan comes in for a while to report having made the phone call, watches, tries to chat, then wanders out again. Mr Varty puts up the CLOSED notice and locks the door behind her. For a while a small crowd of people congregates outside as if waiting for the place to re-open. Then it disperses. At length a sharp-featured woman in authoritative black and white raps on the glass to be admitted. Her hair is so tightly permed it might be glued to her head. Admitted by Mr Varty she strides with touchy hauteur towards the tree. "Good afternoon, Mr Banaji, how are you?"

"Not too bad, thank you, Mrs Male. Yourself?"

"Well. Busy." She flicks a distasteful glance up at her brother. "Not in the best of moods, needless to say. Do the Press know about this?"

"I don't think so."

"We can handle it," she informs the policemen, "with as much discretion as possible. You know who I am?"

The tall policeman is vague. "Yes, ma'am, I think."

"I am Mrs Male of Westminster City Council. My husband is Doctor Male of the New Jerusalem. That gentleman is my brother. He was injured in the Blitz."

"Poor devil," says the short policeman, who is by now sweating worse than his companion, "I had a feeling it was something like that."

Dandy Banaji shrugs. "He was more or less fine most of today," he tells her, "then we found some bombsite he recognised and he decided to take a trip on the river. I think he was trying to calm down."

"But he decided to make a exhibition of himself instead. Did you tell that woman to phone, Mr Banaji, or was it Josef?"

"He doesn't want to alarm his wife."

"She deserves to be alarmed. She's done nothing for him. Has she a reputation to consider? Josef! Josef! Wake up!"

Without opening his eyes, Josef Kiss begins in a sing-song to talk again:

"The stolen pythons were about ten feet long and eventually discovered in the old Abbey grounds by two Bulgarian wives but the thieves were never caught anyway Trent altered his employment policy after that, selecting, where he was able, Jews for every new position so when Hopwood returned he almost immediately remarked on it. 'It's what you asked for,' said Trent. 'Almost your last words before you left.' Hopwood was bewildered. 'I never said anything of the sort. All I asked you to do was liven things up. Get some juice into the firm.' Trent was no longer mystified. 'Juice? That's where I misheard you.' I can detect you, Beryl. Your mind is like a worm in my heart. I know what you want me to do. The meathooks in the thumbs again. The ribbons of bloody flesh. What a monster you are. I know you, you see. They don't. Your talents were lost here during the War."

And he opens his marvellous face so that it seems to shine brighter than the sun, surrounded by a golden halo; the face of a demigod, a messenger from Olympus; an angel.

"Josef! The police are here!"

"Perhaps I should have got Gloria to come, after all. I'd forgotten

289

the intensity of your fury. Ah!" He slips an inch or so downward and recovers, holding his back tightly against the tree. "Go outside, Beryl. You'll meet a very interesting man. His name is Mr Alemada. He's an amateur ornithologist. 'I'd be a pro if I had the right bits of paper. But I've been on the BBC ten times and given a cheque for every appearance, including *In Town Tonight*, so I suppose that makes me at least a semi-pro. What I'd love to own one day would be a field recorder. The sort the BBC have now. A Grundig or one like that, but they're a bit beyond my means at present. Here's a bower bird. Isn't he a beauty. You can buy records these days, of course – ' He's fading. He's on his way out. Catch him, Beryl. Ask him, Beryl, at Victoria Gate. 'It wouldn't be the same as doing your own. I had the loan of a record-making machine but it didn't pick up too well, even just in the garden . . .' Oh, hurry, Beryl. Hurry and ask. He's almost gone. Why won't you believe me!"

"I shan't be tricked again." She is surprisingly oblivious of her audience. To Dandy this exchange has the air of an ongoing argument begun in childhood. "There's no Mr Alemada. And if there were he'd be in league with you. Like those boys you made me go after."

"That wasn't my fault. 'Show us your pants. Show us your bottom. No, I won't. No, I won't.' I came and saved you, Beryl. But you always said it was my fault. I never could discover the reason for your anger against me."

"You sent me there."

"I didn't."

"Come down, Josef. Bernard will give you some medicine. He's expecting you at the New Jerusalem. He's sending an ambulance."

"Stop that! Can't you improve your mind, Beryl?

> "My mind to me a kingdom is,
> Such perfect joys therein I find;
> That it excells all other bliss,
> The world affords or grows by kind:
> Though much I want that most would have,
> Yet still my mind forbids to crave."

Led by the Head Supervisor, through the door of the Palm House, their helmets flashing like gold, run in full kit three members of the London Fire Brigade carrying a ladder and a collapsible net. They are followed by Mavis Essayan. "I'm with the party," she says. "I'm allowed in."

"You'd better let us know what we should do." One of the firemen pushes off his chinstrap and removes his helmet to reveal a rosy skin topped by blond curls. "Coming down, are you, old chap? Blimey! It's Jo Kiss. Hello, Jo."

Mr Kiss is clearly pleased to see the fireman. "Good afternoon, Don. Everything okay with you? The missus?"

"Not too bad at all, Jo. So you're the loony, are you? I'm sorry to hear it." He turns his back on Mr Kiss to address all the uniformed men, including Mr Varty, who has rejoined them. "That's Jo Kiss. He's famous in my section. I've known him since the first couple of weeks of the Blitz. He saved more lives than the rest of us put together. He was with us in Holborn, too, when we were sent over there. He had a knack of finding people who were still alive, didn't matter how deep or how long they'd been buried. He was like a bloody dog, only better. He got hundreds to safety. What a shame. Poor Jo." He returns his attention to his old comrade. "Would you come down for me, Jo? If I got the ladder there?"

"I wouldn't like to put you out, Don." With careful slowness Josef Kiss scratches his head. He seems to maintain his position by will alone.

"He's got to be arrested." The Head Supervisor has an air of frustration and disappointment. "I want that clear. People can't be allowed to do this whenever they like. We're a Royal Park, you know."

"These men are my colleagues, sir." Josef Kiss speaks in stern and level tones. The sun glows upon his golden flesh, his noble rags. "They will vouch for me. I had good reasons to climb this tree. It is my wedding anniversary."

"Oh, good God, force him down!" says Mrs Male viciously.

"You want him charged, then, madam." The short policeman has assumed the patient voice of one who disapproves of superiors' actions. His sympathies are with the firemen, men of action like himself.

"There'll be an ambulance along in a minute. Just get him into that."

"These men will tell you who I am!" Josef Kiss speaks with

ponderous gravity, clearly relishing the situation. "I am Kiss the Saviour, friend of the cat, the dog and the chicken!" Giant pods now fall from surrounding palms, cracking open as they strike the iron grids at the onlookers' feet. A strange smell fills the lush greenhouse as once it might have filled the world at the dawn of creation, as if some new and glorious thing were about to be born.

of those lovely leafy courts behind Gamages Mr Fitzmary's aunt had one and then they went to Jersey where I heard they collaborated Paternoster Row used to stink of printer's ink and fogs wasn't in it Dr Fadgit's real interest was in modern dance he said give me a cup of coffee very quickly if I drink it suddenly I shoot up as it were but don't warn me or it won't work kept on at the Deptford pumping station long past his prime but he got a lot of support from the Church

> "On Richmond Hill there lives a lass,
> More bright than May Day morn;
> Whose charms all other maids surpass,
> A rose without a thorn."

"Brigade H.Q. is on the Albert Embankment," says Don to one of the policemen. "The river firefloat, it is. *Massey Shaw.*"

the coal officer come round and the next thing is the Flying Squad is interested in talking to me giving him a quick bunk up in the cupboard under the stairs when who should come straight through saying he wants to read the meter

Through the Palm House's other end, which the officials have forgotten to block, there enters a pretty dark-haired woman with her small son who carries a book and is dressed in white shirt and shorts, white socks and plimsolls. On the front of his shirt is a green stain from where he has been lying on the grass.

"Sorry madam. We have an emergency on. Madam, we're temporarily closed. You must go." Mr Varty waves her out.

Becoming confused Mrs Mummery takes a grip on her son and turns him round. Offended, helpless against so many, she leaves.

breast feasting they had a car and a fridge just looking at the menu he says cheek I said cheeks look good to me he said what's that smell then we watched the tanks go by and all I had to show was the subscription to Mickey Mouse Weekly *that Errol got mind you he was interviewed twice*

From his tree Josef Kiss watches the Mummerys, Mavis Essayan and several others, whom he recognises from their thoughts, move

slowly towards Victoria Gate and the river from where they will
return to their homes, then his bottom scrapes another painful inch
or two down the tree and he yelps. It is in the nature of a palm to be
able to hold him in this way, but it is becoming increasingly painful;
moreover the agitation below makes further meditation impossible. Now his temptation is to open his arms and fly down into
their net, but this might badly damage the trees and he has no wish
to do real harm. The palms are after all the most tangible memory
of his greatest happiness. He gives thought to his problems.

> "When you first came to town,
> They called you the Roving Jewel,
> Now you've been here six months,
> They call you Katy Cruel.
>> Oh, would I be where I am not,
>> Then I could have what I have not,
>> If I had I would not.
> Diddle–iddle–day.
>> O, dee–di–do–di–do day!

"You'd better try to get your ladder over here, Don," says Mr
Kiss at last. "I'll come down now. It's impossible to find anywhere
to be alone."

*the queue at Australia House last Tuesday did you see it my tits were
burned but there's no mark on them now and he'll never try it again ach,
man you won't get me back to that bloody mess my shit went pure white*

"I had a spell like that once." Another fireman shakes his head
before taking hold of the canvas-bound ladder. "Same reasons
really. The Blitz. I was in hospital for months. I got to believing I'd
invented the sun and could put it out whenever I liked. But not the
sea. That was like an enemy. Funny really, because water's your
greatest friend in this job." As he talks he helps unfold the ladder
and move it so that the top comes just below Josef Kiss's
downpointed toes in their muddy pumps.

u gory blekitnawy na zachod rozany

"No poles!" cries Mr Kiss bewilderingly. As he gradually lowers
himself towards the ladder he looks out through the glass again and
sees, driving slowly up a tranquil Broad Walk, the familiar white
and red private ambulance. He pauses in his descent, almost afraid.

"Here I am, old chap."

"Will you come in the ambulance with me. Just as far as the hospital?"

"Naturally, old chap. Whatever you want."

"Don't let them refuse you. There always has to be an anticlimax when you're fundamentally sane. You might as well witness it. Only the truly mad make spectacular endings." He beams happily down on his glaring sister and begins another song.

"I take it you'll be paying for the damage, madam?" The Head Supervisor's miniature smile only barely threatens her.

Abstract Relations 1950

MARY GASALEE shifts very slightly in her sleep. While Sister Kitty Dodd detects the movement, she is used to it so settles comfortably in her wicker armchair leafing through a *Woman's Weekly* thinking about her holidays, her true love. Sister Katy Dodd believes Mary Gasalee to be a miracle of innocence saved from the sins of the world, immaculate and blessed. *Thank God she's happy in there at least some of the time it's when she cries out it's the worst and nobody ever hears her but me and Susan and Susan's thick as a post and never knows what to do about anything.* Rather like the guardian of some well-established shrine, Sister Kitty Dodd has a benign proprietorial interest in Mrs Gasalee, for the nurse was here when Mary was admitted to Bethlehem Special Wing and has been here ever since. When doctors bring their guests to have a look at Mary Gasalee they defer to Sister Kitty; they turn to her for answers. Mary hasn't aged a day since she was brought in, yet almost every function is alive and healthy. Even her brain reveals considerable activity, as if she is hibernating. Hers is the rarest form of narcolepsy. There have been other cases, of whom Alfred Gordon Blount at the Maudsley is the most famous. Sister Kitty knows one must simply wait for them to wake up; measuring reflexes, heartbeats, breathing and so on does not tell very much except the obvious facts of her being alive. She feels pain. She feels the normal range of sensations. She is fed. She is cleaned. They wait.

Daddy said he thought he'd mix something new with WEETABIX – more than a breakfast food Oh, the excitement of Weetabix cookery – even for amateurs! It goes with everything. It's wheat, malt, salt and sugar. It's all goodness. It's all ready. It's all right! POPULAR PACK 9d. Now carry breathing comfort in your handbag!

Watching his vapour trail circling towards the cemetery Mary runs between the gates down the broad path dividing graves and under the rose bowers of the Garden of Peace where the plane has crashed. Through the flames surrounding the cockpit's Perspex she sees with relief that he has bailed out and, looking for his parachute, notes something black swinging in the clear sky; she watches him land on the Chapel's far side and, glad he is safe, turns to leave the cemetery at the main road entrance where almost every house is flattened; there is not one shop she recognises but the trams are running again and she is lucky to reach the corner as a 79 to Smithfield draws up at the stop. She jumps aboard as if pursued. Recognising her the conductor gives her a friendly smile and shoving his cap on the back of his head begins to whistle. She is delighted to see him again for it is her old friend Ronald Colman full of cheery resourcefulness and gay good manners. – All the way, Mary? He jingles his coin pouch.

– Yes, please.

– I bet we're off to visit grandad.

The tram's machinery grumbles and snaps, the brasswork shudders, the curved scarlet metal sways and jolts, squealing on temporary lines through North East London's smouldering streets, the blasted rubble still giving off familiar greasy smoke. – Your young man get down okay? Against regulations Ronald Colman sits on the seat opposite and cheekily lights a cigarette.

– Seemed like it, says Mary. How's Claudette?

– Never been better. She's in the WRACs now, doing her bit like all of us. Thank goodness the winter's over. You don't expect snow in May, do you? The way it makes the concrete burn. You've got to laugh.

ancient symbol of the chemist's craft, still glows brilliant and mysterious in many a chemist's shop window. It tells all passers-by that there is within

When the tram arrives at the Smithfield terminus Mary is glad to find the meat market still in one piece, its rococo painted iron and stained-glass panels an unlikely background for the rushing porters, their aprons crusted with blood, who seem frantically busy as usual even though there is hardly anything to buy or sell. When she can she comes here during periods of inactivity at the end of a day's trading or during certain quiet afternoons. You could buy a cheap cut of steak here for a penny before the War, and a really good cut would cost you far less than in any butcher's. The bookstalls had stood outside in the street before the incendiary bombs had found them; using incendiaries on libraries and newsagents for the same reasons they burned literature at home, the Germans had charred and pulped the books, filling Farringdon Road with little heaps of blackened muck, like corpses, an occasional half-burned cover visible in the pile. She makes her way towards the stained red, gold and blue of that great sturdy bridge across her home valley; Holborn Viaduct withstands the raids side by side with St Paul's and carries buses east to west or from Oxford Circus to the City over acres of destruction, for the Germans have wiped out every building between here and Charterhouse Street. There are temporary wooden walkways across the ruins where little boys and girls play games of hide-and-seek and old men turn over pieces of brick and timber in the hope of finding a treasure or a lost document. On the other side of Farringdon Road the bombs have touched but not entirely destroyed Saffron Hill and Bleeding Heart Yard, their houses looking as invulnerable as the houses now perished. She remembers the pavements lifting, rising and falling like ocean waves, the awful heat, the wind that sought to suck your clothes off, to tear your eyes from your head, and she looks about her for her yellow doll.

When a husband starts like that you know he's got something up his sleeve.

– Time has passed in the Land of Dreams, says Beryl Orde the impressionist, one of Mary's prewar wireless favourites. Beryl can make you think she is Greta Garbo, Gracie Fields, Jessie Matthews, Wee Georgie Wood, anybody, and, while she is pretending to be Maurice Chevalier now, Mary would know her anywhere. Whirling round Mary greets a Beryl whose long face is droll as ever.

– How do, our Mary? She has in real life a Liverpool accent. Haven't seen you up at Broadcasting House recently. You been ill, love?

– I've been back at the cemetery looking for my doll and my

young man. His plane came down today, but he was safe, so here I am!

– Your doll's all right, too love. I saw her a couple of days ago. A few air raids won't hurt her. But we'll put out an SOS on the programme if you like.

– Wouldn't that be going too far? Mary laughs. I haven't heard you for ages, Beryl. When all this is over I'm looking forward to listening in again.

– I was sorry to hear about your grandma. Still, it must have been quick.

– No, I don't think so. Mary is suddenly resentful of Beryl but doesn't want to show it for fear of making her go away. Have you had your hair done? It's more curly. She fingers a red lock. She enjoys the moral support celebrities can give.

– Well, love, she's in a better place now.

–Oh, yes. And so am I. Trying to laugh, Mary sighs and sits down on an old steel safe lying at an angle in the rubble; she stares miserably towards the Thames where mist still lies on the water.

– Oh, yes. Recalling a time when the river's banks were lined with women tied to stakes all burning like horrible candles under a hot summer sun, their fat making sickening yellow smoke, perhaps a defeated army, martyred in some failed rebellion. Mary cannot remember either their cause or their circumstance.

– Hey! Beryl Orde pulls a face. Who's this?

Mary forces out the memory. – Gracie Fields. Give us a song, Gracie!

– Turn father's face to the wall, mother, never more mention his name, for he brought disgrace on the fam-i-lee . . . She takes Mary's hand and together they skip along the makeshift bouncing boardwalks while in the ruins on every side men work to salvage usable materials, their heads covered in sacking, their faces grey with dust. Soon they are climbing swaying wooden steps up to the Viaduct itself. It gives Mary a sensation of adventure to approach the familiar bridge from such an unfamiliar angle. – Well, she says, this isn't any better than it was, really. The Germans haven't won, have they?

– We've beaten them. Or rather Russia has. It doesn't make any sense but Mr H and all them Narzies never did make sense. They only got as far as Dorking. Dorking would be enough to put anyone off. In their printed cotton short-sleeved frocks they lean on the blackened crimson balustrade near the City's coat of arms and beside a rather haughty black iron Greek lady representing Commerce. They stare casually out to south and east, enjoying the views of St Paul's and Blackfriars. Sharing the same cigarette, three elderly men in Home Guard uniforms pass them on the other side and board a moving bus as it goes slowly by, but in the main High Holborn and the Viaduct are deserted. — Did everyone get evacuated from round here, Beryl?

— Mostly dead, I'm afraid. The comedienne puts out a sympathetic hand.

— It's peaceful at any rate. Like an early closing day. Refusing to cry, Mary looks again towards the river, surprised no more mist is rising. A few black stakes are left but all the bodies are gone. What had they resisted? Warfare itself? There are a couple of odd-looking boats on the water.

— They've been dragging that, says Beryl. All the rubble. Farringdon Road was flooded. Jerry hit the storm drains and sewers. It was like every lost and old river had come back. It wasn't nearly so bad where we were, but they bombed St Anne's, Soho. The ugliest spire in London and now only the spire's left of it! Beryl giggles and turns into George Robey, the Prime Minister of Mirth: — But, I say, but the King and Queen were *marvellous*, weren't they? Rolling up their sleeves and shifting piles of bricks, singing songs and making everyone cups of tea!

Mary is surprised. — I thought they went to Canada.

— They were meant to. Of course in the early days they weren't at all popular.

— I was there. We booed them. Rich bastards. What do they know, people said.

— They're still better off than the rest of us. Beryl adopts a Scottish accent Mary can't identify.

— They were snooty at first, says Mary. All sympathy and no tea as my gran said, but I suppose they just become what the times need, what people need them to be. That's how they manage to stay on. Did they turn Buckingham Palace over to the homeless?

— Not quite, darling. Beryl as Gertie Lawrence winks at her friend. They only had to make a teeny bit of extra effort. They didn't want to go too far, after all.

299

– They still seem like frauds to me. Mary grows gloomy.

– I think values are a bit different in the Land of Dreams. Beryl wants to change the subject. She is basically a conventional person and this disloyal talk makes her uncomfortable. Did I ever mention how I once got lost on the roof of Mount Pleasant Post Office. They told me about a short cut through a door, over a flat roof and then in another door. It was before my career got properly started and I was working as a messenger. Anyway, I found the door out but couldn't for the life of me find the other door in. I peered through skylights where people were working at desks, rapped on windows trying to ask the way. Nobody noticed me. It started to rain. It was all offices up there, not sorting rooms or anything. You'd be surprised what you get to see. Little things, mostly. But I saw two women at it. Two women, mind, kissing and cuddling. What d'you think?

Mary does her best to understand what is supposed to be remarkable but her imagination defeats her. – I used to live just behind Mount Pleasant. You know Phoenix Lane?

Clearly upset, Beryl looks at her watch.

Mary wishes she knew how to win Beryl's approval back. She hasn't a clue. – On the roof? The skylight? Gosh!

– Here's my bus. Beryl is abstracted. I've a broadcast in half-an-hour. Goodbyee, don't cryee, wipe the tear, baby dear, from your eyee! Look after yourself, love. She jumps on a Number 25 crawling across the Viaduct towards the West End and waves from the stairs as she climbs to the upper deck.

Mary watches her settle herself in the back seat and light a cigarette. – I'm sorry. Mary shrugs. I'm not fit for the world I suppose. Her grandmother said that as she smiled and patted her face as if in approval. Mary strolls slowly along the bridge's unyielding iron towards Holborn station whose girders gleam like wholesome bones against a pale blue sky. Outside the broken brickwork and collapsed stone facings of the main entrance Mary's father, wearing his Khaki, his Sam Browne and his puttees, with his Lee Enfield at ease, stands guard. Adjusting his cap above his green-gold eyes he grins and blows her a sneaky kiss. – Wotcher, love. If an officer comes along just keep walking. I'll say you were asking me the way. How's your mum?

– I heard she went to Canada with the Royal Family.

300

– That'd be typical. Still, she has her good points.

– Then I heard the Royal Family came back. Maybe Mum was with them.

– Why don't you ask, love? They're inside now. Let me know if you hear anything. He winks at her and grins again.

Mary enters the airy main hall, its battered iron rafters full of exotic birds. For a moment a small kestrel perches on her shoulder, then takes purposefully off in the direction of a pigeon. The concrete concourse is deserted apart from some porters near the various platform gates and the King and Queen who sit at a card table by the ticket office drinking cups of tea. When she approaches, they look up. King George is thin, what Mary's gran would call weedy, hardly any size at all, more like a schoolboy, and his wife is a plump little doll beside him. Mary feels huge and clumsy. – Excuse me if I don't curtsey. I was brought up not to.

– That's refreshing anyway, says Queen Elizabeth. Your dad's all right on his own is he?

– He said to ask if Mum came back from Canada with you.

Glancing across the table at her husband the Queen seems distressed and King George folds his hands together in front of him.

– Y-y-your m-m-m-mum's n-n-n-not here.

Mary had forgotten his stammer. – Don't bother trying to tell me. You look all in.

– He's been helping get bodies out. Queen Elizabeth dabs at her mouth with a dainty doily. Poor thing. He was never very fit. I blame his brother for all of this. What was your mother's name, dear?

– She was a Nellie Felgate. It was my Grandma Felgate told me she was in Canada.

King George takes out a pack of cards and begins a game of patience. – It calms him down. Queen Elizabeth brushes at beads of sweat on her forehead. We don't know any Felgates, sweetheart. Do we, Davie?

– N-n-not since we got b-back from C-Canada.

Significantly his wife glares at him. – We haven't been to Canada since before the War.

– This was before the War, says Mary. Perhaps even fifteen years ago. I mean, I'm not very old.

– Well, you can see dear she isn't with us. The Queen becomes

301

abrupt. She never married your father, you know. He was a professional soldier. Here today and gone tomorrow. She should have known better. You were luckier than most having Mrs Felgate to look after you. And your grandad. They don't come any sweeter.

– That's a lie, says Mary. Well, it's not a lie, but what you're saying must have a lie in it, because you'd never say that about my grandad if you knew him. He said you were festering sores on society's backside and you should be kicked out and all your property redistributed.

– We are the spirit of this country, my girl. Queen Elizabeth folds furious arms across her little round stomach. You should be ashamed of yourself.

– He said you were a stupid extravagance. If we needed a ceremonial Royal Family to hold the Empire together we could still get one far cheaper than yours.

– The Felgates were as common as muck. The Queen snorts. And so were the gloody Gasalees. They were pirates. All kinds of scum. You should be ashamed of yourself. But we're used to this. Don't think we haven't read *The Daily Herald* and the *News Chronicle*. But live and let live, I say. You could be had up for treason, you could. Your head could be put on one of them spikes down at Traitor's Gate.

Mary as always grows defiant when threatened. – My grandad said you're a bunch of Huns at heart and you'd show your true colours sooner or later. He said you didn't have a pot to piss in when you arrived in this country and now you own half of it. And your lot goes on about Jews!

– N-nobody said we was p-p-perfect. King George VI looks up from his cards. C-calm d-down, k-k-k-kiddy. There's a wa-wa-war on. W-we all have to s-stick together. I've had a h-hard d-d-day and s-so's your m-mum.

– Steady on! The Queen grows alarmed. Who said I was her bloody mum?

– S-s-slip of the tongue, s-sorry l-love. King George turns a couple of cards.

Mary is like a terrier and can't leave them alone. – My grandad said you should be shoved out of London and made to live in some village. He said that's where you belong. If you don't like it here, he said, you should leave. Go up to wherever it is in Scotland and stay there. But that's when he was feeling kind-hearted. Usually he had the lamp-posts already picked out for you. By size.

– Your grandad's dead, girly. In a swirl of powder-blue chiffon Queen Elizabeth sits down. And so's the rest of your bloody family. You'd better watch your step. You're all alone now.

Disgusted by this low blow, Mary attacks again. – He said you hadn't changed, not underneath. I suppose he was right. What did you do with his pension?

– N-n-never t-touched it. Still at his Patience, King George loosens his tie. L-look I'm going to c-c-call the p-p-police if you g-go on l-like th-th-this, m-m-m-my g-girl. We-we d-don't have to p-put up with y-your r-r-rubbish. We're d-doing our b-bit. Everyone s-says s-so.

– Not in the East End they don't.

– Salt of the earth, the East End! The Queen has regained control of her temper. It's the foreign agitators down there, fifth columnists and the like, who stir the ordinary people up and make them discontented. We go down there and show we care and it soon stops. We even take the kids with us. They're in uniform now you know. What more do you want?

– I wouldn't mind some money back. Mary knows it is her grandfather making her so furious. He would have loved this chance and she owes it to him to take it. If she stops to think, they don't seem too bad as people. Fairly ordinary, really, if you forget their funny voices.

– Nobody cut off your pension, that's all I know. Mary decides to leave it there and turns her back on the King and Queen as they start to tell each other how common she is. Returning to the outside of the station she finds her father has gone. Because of her bad behaviour he might have been removed from duty. – Dad? Or deserted.

When a mob of policemen come running at her, just as they ran at crowds in Cable Street before the War, she turns to head along Holborn until she reaches Hatton Garden and wonders what they have done to Gamage's. On a false trail the police disappear down the steps into Farringdon Road gleaming with water, for the tide is rising. She feels exhilarated as if she's done something worthwhile and brave like Patrick and is happier than she has been for ages.

– Say what you like in the Land of Dreams! Whistling jauntily she heads for Tottenham Court Road, convinced that if she goes into Shaftesbury Avenue, along St James's and down the Mall, she'll find Buckingham Palace and a heap of grey rubble in the road. Why else would the King and Queen have to be sitting at a card table on Holborn Viaduct Station drinking tea and playing Patience like any other homeless couple? She feels a little guilty and wonders if she was too hard on them but her first loyalty remains to her dead grandfather and that loyalty has been more than satisfied today.

Britain can be fun!

Turning another page of *Woman's Weekly* Sister Kitty Dodd relaxes in a sudden sense of well-being which she's convinced comes from her patient. *That's the message we'll be sending the world next year with the Festival of Britain and the jumper illustrated opposite should be fun to wear, since it incorporates the symbol of the Festival Lady on a lightweight, summer knit.*

Sister Kitty Dodd picks up the free booklet she's received telling her about the Festival's wonderful events and sights. She has already decided what she wants to see but will send the brochure to her brother in Cork at his request, since he and his wife will be over for the Festival and intend to make the most of it.

> "No pipe did hum, no battle drum
>   did sound its dread tattoo,
> And Britannia's sons with their great guns,
>   sailed in on the foggy dew . . ."

Finding herself in Soho Square again, Mary sits on her usual bench to take her ease in the soft warmth the sun people have left behind them. On her left is Hermione Gingold and on her right June Havoc. – This is the life, eh, my dears? Hermione Gingold offers them one of her belly-laughs.

June Havoc's pale yellow uniform looks rather like something fanciful from a musical comedy and gives her skin a sallow cast. Would she take offence if she were told? – I saw that doll of yours, Mary. Do you know the one I mean? The Royal Family were trying to find it for their little girl.

– They don't have a little girl any more. They've joined the WRENs. But if you see the doll I'd be glad if you could keep an eye on her. Mary is particularly fond of June, whom she sees as being rather vulnerable.

– This was in Canada. She'll be back here soon, I'm sure. Do you know how much it costs to get there now? Over twenty pounds. June opens a compact and frowns at what she sees. That's without meals. What ho! She snaps the compact shut. Here come the chaps.

Heaving round the corner from Falconberg Street, arm in arm, in perfect step, their fresh pink lips pursed to whistle Barnacle Bill, come three sailors of identical height.

> "Johnny Todd he took a notion,
> For to sail the ocean wide,
> And he left his fair maid waiting,
> Waiting on the Liverpool side . . ."

– You look as if you could do with a bit of fun! Hermione winks lecherously at them. Avast there, my jolly jacks. Fresh ashore are we?

– Fresh ashore, ladies! They speak as they whistle and sing, in unison. And on the town!

– Looking for company? June pulls her uniform straight and pats at her back hair.

– Good afternoon, says Mary . . . boys. She lacks the confidence of the two stars and is close to losing her composure. She wants to giggle.

– Steady the buffs, murmurs Hermione.

– I'm a respectable married woman.

– Oh, no, dear. Not any more. You're a pretty young widow. Remember?

– Patrick died?

– Long, long ago.

– I saw his plane. It doesn't seem very long.

– It often doesn't, in the Land of Dreams.

Alert as a wren, Sister Kitty Dodd detects a slight change in her charge's breathing and checks instruments, tubes, wires feeding, measuring and evacuating Mary Gasalee and, discovering nothing strange, relaxes again with her magazine. *Now that she'd dispensed with her little turn, Chris was in the mood for love. She wanted nothing less than to lie in Jean-Louis' arms and let him pet and adore her. And yet there was not a hope in the world! Every now and then she caught his eyes over*

305

some bare shoulder, pleasingly on hers. But, as a result of her moment of
limelight, she was in demand.

Linked arm-in-arm the three women and the three sailors stride
off through the Square, heading cheerfully in the general direction
of Piccadilly Circus. – All the nice girls love a sailor, all the nice girls
love a tar . . . Borne along by the others, Mary realises her legs are
weak and has no idea what she is doing or what it will lead to;
nonetheless she is enjoying the high spirits and the company of the
sailors, who slightly resemble a hot-water bottle she was given one
Christmas and hardly offer danger. Mary joins with everyone in the
whistling. – Ship ahoy! Ship ahoy! By doing what they do and
keeping reasonable harmony she feels her cares dissipating. She is
still proud of how she has conducted herself and is sure her
grandfather would also be proud of her, and her grandma, though
she would never say so. The colours are pale and bright, pastels of
infinite variety, and she has never seen London cleaner. Even the
ruins seems scrubbed, as fresh as the skins of the sailormen. – Well,
you know what sailors are! She thinks about going to the Windmill
where she and Pat had such a good time when he came home on
leave. There's nothing like a sing-song to lift you out of the blues,
Pat said, the night before he flew away and their house fell down. –
Free and easy, bright and breezy . . .

June Havoc marches with boyish gaiety alongside her particular
Jack. – Where are you from, sailor.

His lips are a red bow, his eyes round and Mediterranean blue.
His is scarcely a man, without a trace of hair on his face, and has
curls so fair they are almost white. – I used to be in the Horse Guards
but I couldn't stand it. Polishing the bloody helmets and breast-
plates all night, blancoing up the trousers and the belts, not to
mention the horrible posh queens trying to chat you up. It's a real
sleazy life being a fancy soldier.

– My Pat's friend told us that. Mary nods and hands out
chewing-gum from her little velvet handbag. Everyone takes a
piece without breaking step. They are going down Shaftesbury
Avenue now, the shops full of cakes and coloured cellophane as if
the sun people are expected.

– Take my tip, says his friend squeezing Mary's hand under his
arm, and get into chemicals. Or electrics. After the War that'll be
what's booming. Use your loaf. I'm tired of being shoved around

like someone's hot-water bottle. When I was a kid I lived just near here.

– So did I! Mary welcomes this normal conversation. Where was that, then?

– Just off Leather Lane. Near Hatton Garden. Know it? He lifts almost invisible eyebrows.

– I thought I'd seen you before.

– We used to go up and down Hatton Garden looking in the gutters for diamonds, hoping some old bugger had dropped one. It's the largest diamond market in the world, you know. Bigger than Amsterdam now, of course.

Hermione, more or less in the middle, is slightly in the lead. She always decides what they're going to do. – We'll go and see a musical, she tells them. Something good with Fred Astaire. Round the corner in Leicester Square. He's lovely to watch, like he's dancing on air.

– Makes all the people stop and stare! June laughs in her wonderful, half-defiant way.

– My dad ran a stall in Leather Lane. Mary's sailor is more interested in carrying on the ordinary chat. He specialised in old hardware. Pliers for sixpence, ninepence a pair. He worked and slaved to pay his share. With an honesty that's getting rare. Where did you say you lived round there?

Mary feels that she's somehow failing to fit in again. – Calthorpe Street. She is hesitant. In the Peabody's first, then we had our own house. With a cloth on the table and carpet on the stair! She feels a return of earlier triumph and the sailor's tone becomes more respectful.

– My dad was helping run a pig club up Percy Square. You might have seen him. Always a smart dresser, a camel hair coat. People used to think he was a bandleader.

Eros is back in the Circus, gleaming all gold and silver on a dais the colour of emerald glass and Mary gasps with pleasure. Hermione's sailor turns to her. – Ron used to play with Harry Roy, didn't you Ron? Used to play the old trombone. Still does. You should hear him. He's in our ship's band. You're going back to Harry Roy after the War, aren't you Ron?

– If he'll have me, says Mary's sailor and begins to whistle again.

I saw you last night and got that old feeling,
When you came in sight I got that old feeling.
The moment when you danced by, I felt a thrill,
And when you caught my eye, my heart stood still . . .

– Built on the ruins of Bedlam, Liverpool Street was named for a Lord.

The faces grow indistinct as they turn off Shaftesbury Avenue into the warm streets where the sun people shop. Their voices remain clear and various, but slowly her companions cease to act as mediums and go on their way towards the Circus leaving her surrounded by a great busy crowd, but Mary is perfectly happy, for the sun people protect her. She catches the conversation from all around her and sinks into a couch under an awning on the boulevard. – I let my legs swell up again. I'm getting careless. That's right Brentford eyot. We met on the towpath. Yes, that was lovely. Yes. *Mr Blacker emigrated from Borneo in 1948 you should hear him going on about anarchist plots and gambling and stuff it's an eye-opener well they took all his rubber still if you need anyone to make you a kayak he's your man coffee will be his ruin he took that girl with him and showed her what to do what did she learn well, she's not telling soft memory playing in harmony tranquil springs did you feel cold all of a sudden there was a light coming out and we realised the mountain was below he shot his son apparently and was going to kill himself I was under the doctor for three years let's welcome Walter de la Mare flying his own Douglas DC3 coming home from visiting relatives in Australia a lucky escape that's the third time she's tried it and next time I'm going to let her do it*

The sun people come and go about their business in the little Soho shops and cafés, buying tickets for the pictures and theatres, sitting in the bars and chatting to one another. – *What did our boys bring home from the Continent? Nothing to what the Americans found nothing to what they found in the East all I ask is a bloodless death*

Mary Gasalee takes a sip of her pink cocktail. It's like being a little girl again, she thinks with contentment. This'll do me for the moment.

blazing a new trail I suppose and eating humble pie it was kill or be killed she's filling in for her mum what am I to worship now I asked we landed on water look she not only has my heart she has my pen there was this clatter of falling sticks that's how I knew Mrs Gasalee

308

"Mrs Gasalee?" Sister Kitty Dodd sometimes talks to her patient. "Are you okay, dear. Mary? Are you all right?" She goes to the window and opens it, breathing in the not unpleasant smell of rotting vegetables and lilac. "All the loonies are on the lawn today."

but the flowers smell wonderful at least. Cowslips, barbarees and hart's horn henbane she had to buy a lot of it in Chinatown it's where they sell it now Limehouse nowhere else and there's not much of Limehouse left not that she knew of I could only see her in the firelight moving in the room what has this to do with the sun she had this familiar she said a cat called Gog older than London she said how am I to survive her whole shop and studio was bombed out the smell of burning stuff all her potions and chemicals was terrible like petrol the smoke only worse I thought honestly they'd see things in it you know like in those films but I suppose it was unfair really she did a lot more harm than good in our neighbourhood and then they brought her here

A debutante can get away with wearing her white frilly debutante frock and look like Merle Oberon in the gown she wore at one of those fabulous Venetian balls. But any girl with a white fluffy ballet-length dress can garland it with paper roses, make a wreath for her hair and achieve the same effect. Sister Kitty Dodd shakes her head. She herself will have to find a costume for the weekend after next when the hospital holds its annual fund-raising gala. – *Personally, I love the Charles II period with its satins and laces, ribbons and frills and rich materials, or there are many ideas from the Knights of the Round Table or the Beau Brummell films or the Oscar Wilde plays, with their bustles and great hats and elaborate ball-gowns.*

– Oh, God in Heaven, I'm being eaten to death.

Mary Gasalee looks up from her drink to see her old friend Merle, in a magnificent magnolia gown, hurrying along Old Compton Street as if on her way to greet her beau. She smiles with relief when she recognises Mary. – Mary, dear! I thought you'd left these parts. I'm to stay in control. But who will instruct me? What has it to do with the sun? Am I to win anything? There was firelight moving in the room. Whose head is it? Did you ever meet that little scoundrel Freddy Bartholomew? He's cooking something up I'll swear! Why can't I see? Oh Mary, come and have a cup of chocolate at Radice's. You'd die for it. Did you ever marry again?

Mary rises and hugs Merle. She smells of the most delicious perfume. – Weren't you on your way to a party?

– I've just come from one in Venice. They buzzed the bridges night and day. There were just too many connections. Then they landed on the water. Look!

Merle's gesture was so uncharacteristically dramatic Mary knows a moment of fear, but it is only the brown and cream entrance to the Polish patisserie. She laughs in relief. – What has this to do with the sun?

– Ask that in California, dear. With her pale blue fan she brushes crumbs from one of the white iron chairs and expertly seats herself. These people spend half their waking hours on the trot. They cross and recross London at least a dozen times a month. As if they're gathering information for something or someone. I get to wondering if there's not a pattern in it. The way the old beggars' guilds and street tribes used to work, you know. Doctor Male's arrived. She looks up as the scarlet-faced lady they all call Mrs Dumpling comes to take their order.

– Two cafés-au-lait, please, Mrs D. Is that all right for you, Mary, dear? What do you think of him?

– I haven't met him yet. Mary wishes she was wearing something other than the cheap print frock her granny cut down for her.

– Well, you won't dear will you? Not here dear. How many of those clinics are there in London? The kind he wants to set up? Admittedly, it will take the heat off us. Was her skin always on the dark side or do you think it got like that in the fire. Fires turn you red, though, don't they, dear? Then black. So I suppose you could go brown at the half-way stage. At a certain split-second. Like a gypsy really. Mary, on the other hand, has such soft pale skin. So unspoiled. It's perfect skin. Mary, dear?

Mary is surprised to discover herself dozing off. It has been a long time since she was in her own bed. – You said something about dressing up. A ball?

– *If you want to be amusing and witty in your costume, what about the 1920s? You may be sure to get a laugh by wearing the type of dress of twenty-five or thirty years ago. The earlier twenties period has been overlooked and is just asking to be caricatured. Have you, perhaps, some idea of those "chocolate-box" hair styles all loops and dips and the headband worn low on the forehead and sprouting antler-like ornaments and the low-waisted swathed frocks and the apricot-coloured stockings and fussy shoes? I myself have only just realised that clothes of this period may well be found*

310

stored away in the attics of middle-aged aunts and cousins because they have now become almost "period'.

– I haven't any aunts, I don't think, says Mary. I might have cousins but they're not much older than me. I wouldn't know where to look for them.

– We could think about transferring certain people to out-patients on condition these clinics were regularly attended, you know. Worth thinking about. How long have you been with us now?

"Nearly twenty years, sir." Sister Kitty Dodd sets aside her *Woman's Weekly*.

– Good night baby, good night, the milkman's on his way . . .

Mary and Merle have stopped for a cup of hot chocolate in Fleet Street. Horse-drawn vans and motor vehicles of every kind pass to and fro as if there had never been a petrol shortage. They notice a couple across the road. Escorting an ebullient Janet Gaynor, the rather sour-faced Nils Asther stops outside a huge stone wall which Mary thinks must be the Fleet Prison. – Those gates really frighten me every time I go past them. I was behind them once, same as you. That's so much worse, what goes on there.

Mary makes to wave to Janet but Merle plainly doesn't want to be seen by either of them. Mary drops her hand.

– That man's a swine, says Merle. He deserves to be locked up. I can't tell you what he did to his wife.

– He does look a bit of a lounge-lizard.

– Worse.

Merle is unusually critical. Behind them at the next table Mary overhears two sun women in murmured conversation. – *Then you go in. Don't think anything sentimental. Don't think he looks funny. He's not actually deformed you know but put on some fresh make-up he likes you to look your best it sort of cheers him up but just remember there's no need to suffer he's not unhappy he'll get normal again don't worry they say it's like restoration work* Mary tries to turn her head to see the women better but Merle stops her. – Don't leave me, Mary dear. I need you.

Flattered, Mary leans towards her friend. – Did I tell you how lovely your dress is? You should have been with us earlier. We had some real fun. With these sailors. Oh, Merle! What is it?

Merle lowers her eyes but it is clear she is close to tears. – I worked in a circus before I came here. Still did until they closed it down. Bertram Mills' is all that's left, at Olympia. There's no

Winter Circus in London now, only in Paris, in the Boulevard du Temple. Do you know it?

– I've never been to Paris, Merle.

– There's no difference, really. I don't think there's any difference between this century and any other, actually. I mean, are there more of us these days? She looks up to make sure Nils Asther and Janet Gaynor have gone. She is almost whispering.

– You know, people who need the tablets. Forgive the euphemism, dear, but we're not allowed to say "mad" are we? What do you think? Shall we ever get out of here?

– There isn't a future at the moment, Mary tells her kindly. Not for me at any rate. I'm sort of sticking to the present. If you take it a day at a time you can avoid the responsibility. I'm too weak for anything else.

– You're too hard on yourself. Or too soft. I'm still a pretty good painter. It's a question of confidence, I suppose. Children always bear pain so much better than adults, don't they? Is it because they don't know any better? Oh, Mary, I hardly know my arse from my elbow, as your grandad used to say. There are very few people here who haven't at some time found an alias useful. Eh? Merle sighs. Like your dad.

Mary feels urgent sympathy for Merle, but has no idea how to help her. She finishes her chocolate and leans back in the chair to watch the busy traffic. – I had this old First World War photo as a little kid. I thought it might be my dad: a really young fellow with an almost girlish face. But he had sergeant's stripes. I got a magnifying glass and looked at his cap-badge but it didn't mean a lot to me. He was probably educated because he had lovely writing. I thought he was a toff. He went to Canada I think and probably my mum after him but my grandma never heard and of course they weren't married. The badge on his cap looked like some sort of animal lying down, maybe a deer. It was signed Yrs Sincerely Edward S. Evans but I suppose that doesn't mean much to you. It was a comfort to me.

– Well, he might have died. Merle looks concerned. I wish I could do more to help but my flames are now hidden like yours they feed off my blood *that's why I'm so pale the flames need so much yet there's a consolation I suppose after all how many other women have not survived these fires in Dresden in Tokyo in Madrid they found her in Richmond*

312

Park she said she'd followed Robin Hood to the Greenwood we never found Robin Hood but did come across a deer shot by a two-foot arrow fletched in the colours of the Royal Toxophilites identified as 14th-century but there's lots of people know about that sort of thing these days I'm told they never caught Mr Hood whoever he was he's had at least three bucks

– That's illegal, isn't it? Mary takes hold of Merle's hand. Her friend's eyes have taken on the hot, flat appearance of a sun woman's. The pupils have virtually disappeared. The shooting of the King's Royal Deer. Well, you were in it. You should know.

– Illegal as hell. Merle shrugs and pulls herself together. She strokes the folds of her magnolia dress. Aren't you thinking of Olivia de Havilland? But what are they going to do about it in the blackout? Do you really plan to stay here forever, dear? I don't mind, but I was wondering. Her voice has grown softer, with a slight Irish accent. He asked me to come back to him a free woman. We should never have parted. Was it my fault I said that I couldn't read minds? But he needed fantasy more than me, poor thing.

I think I'd have died I wouldn't have known what to say I was crying all the time all the way on the plane but he was so weak he needed so much he was like the rest and saw me as the strong woman the mother is that fair

In her sleep Mary Gasalee frowns. Sister Kitty Dodd adjusts the light sheet covering her to the shoulders. Having enjoyed a discussion so self-important and irrelevant that Sister Kitty Dodd is as always left feeling almost in a state of shock, the doctors have left. "You could do with getting out of here. I don't like their drift, my darling, and that's the truth. Anyway, my new boy's a real charmer. You'd love him."

I've played my part all right I've held on to it whatever it is I didn't say a word that's where the kestrel lady lives she must have twenty hawks in that house all raised from eggs they said something about tracing the source of the heat all those poor buggers out in Asia I don't know how they do it they set fire to themselves a handy little brewery and a pub next door to it on this old spot that ivy alone has got to be four hundred years old once I commanded thousands and my decisions made a difference to our history all I'm asking is a private room they steal things from you in this ward not just the inmates either the nurses are the worst am I unduly sensitive that notices different qualities in engine smoke and car fumes that likes to watch sunsets crawl through smog I belonged to a secret charitable group that's all the London Owls is that you Peter looks like trouble on the escalators

313

Mary Gasalee rubs at her eyes. She hates being inside and now they seem to be in a room together.

— Don't do that, dear, you'll make them all red. Merle hands her a delicate handkerchief.

Now at last she was in Jean-Louis' arms — dancing. He danced wonderfully, lifting her off her feet. He was whispering sweet things into her ear, but Chris knew now they were fairy-tales. And this, she was thinking, this Summer in Paris, is just one leaf out of the story-book of my life. It is a short, gay, beautiful little page. But the pages must be turned over and it won't last, only as a memory. Sister Kitty Dodd reads on with some resentment. This is not at all what she wants or expects from the story.

— I'm sorry, says Mary. I suppose I'm likely to start making a fool of myself again. I seem to do the same things over and over. Sometimes I go out not wearing any pants. I really offend people badly. I say things I don't intend to say. I always wind up in the same places when I'm trying to get somewhere else. Did you ever know such a silly person?

Merle takes back her handkerchief. — You won't find that doll here, my dear. Not to keep for yourself. You'll have to go outside one day. Nothing's ever resolved in the Land of Dreams.

— They're resolved too much and too often elsewhere. Mary is sharp, frightened. You know that, Merle. You're a woman of two worlds. Besides, you must give me time.

"How long?"

"It's been nearly ten years now, sir, but I think we're seeing some improvement." Sister Kitty Dodd stands up in honour of the great grey Specialist who has let the others go on ahead of him. "But I'm not sure about the electric shocks, sir. It could do more harm than good. She sort of retreats, sir."

"I think you know what you're talking about, Sister. Thank you."

Rather flattered to be taken seriously, for normally she feels nothing but resentment of the stupid doctors who come and go through her patient's room, Sister Kitty Dodd sits down, reaching to stroke Mary's lovely face. "I'll not let them get you, Mary. Not while I'm here."

— I can't be expected to do everything in a few days. Mary knows Merle is disapproving, even though she remains sympathetic.

314

– Will they give you more time, Mary? Merle's voice drops to an urgent whisper. You have all the patience in the world. You're the most patient of patient women. You're an example to everyone. But sometimes patience can destroy you. Better to fight, like your armoured women. The sun people will look after you wherever you go. Think what you'll miss, too. Katharine says the same. She told you that last week when you went out to Whaddon to look for your Patrick again.

Mary fears she is about to weep, then realises there are no more tears. – Patrick's dead, she says. He died instead of St Paul's. I hoped he'd get to see those sparrowhawks you mentioned. The ones that are nesting in the Prudential now. I had a postcard but I suppose that got burned, did it? "Chumming up with a nice bunch. Weather couldn't be better." Of course, I saw him after that. He made us go downstairs and then there was the raid. We were going to try to get into the Trocadero while he was on leave. He had quite a bit of money. But it's different about the doll. It can be repaired. I suppose you're right, though. I might never find her here. I'm not ready to give up. I stick things out once I've decided on them. I always have.

– So you'll pull through, dear. Shall we have another cup? Merle looks up in surprise. The traffic has disappeared and along the broad road swing June Havoc and Hermione Gingold linking arms with three sailors in brilliant blue uniforms.

– Oh, we do like to be beside the seaside. We do like to be beside the sea . . .

Mary waves to them but has lost her urge to join them.

– I've clicked this time, Mary! cries June, blowing her a kiss.

Merle looks after them fondly, her expression full of its old angelic sweetness. – We all deserve a little freedom.

Sister Kitty Dodd picks up her needles and her wool and stares closely at her charge. It is as if subtle invisible currents move on Mary's skin, suggesting expression. At the same time baffled and encouraged by this mystery, Sister Kitty Dodd returns to *Woman's Weekly*. – *Work for 2-in on these last 22 sts. Cast off.*

"That's where I went wrong."

With some contentment she continues with her knitting convinced that everything is now working out for the best.

Alternating Couplings 1956

FOR DAYS Mrs Gasalee had been visiting the greenhouse at the far end of the walled garden wondering when Josef Kiss's natural impulses would lead him to her. She had waited so long she was beginning to doubt he was after all a twin soul. He found her there at last, amongst the potted African violets and fuchsias, the dark greens, scarlets and cerises, sitting in the wet heat and reading *The Amazing Marriage*.

"They have been experimenting with me." He inspected a pale gold pod, a whiteish blossom; the orchid had been trained to climb a trellis stretching to the streaked glass of the roof. "I was curious so I let them. They drugged me. They put me behind screens of different materials. They showed me infantile pictures, mostly in silhouette, and they asked me to say what they were looking at while I was blindfolded. And so on. Are you familiar with the lunatic fringe of the psychological profession?"

"I'm not sure." She wore her cream rayon dress with the green cuffs and neck. "For a long time after I woke up I was very dozy. The way you are in the mornings after a really thorough night's sleep. That's where my memory is vague. Everything else is fairly clear."

He sniffed the flower. "It's a familiar smell but I can't place it. How fragile!"

"Icing." She closed her book. "Ice cream. It's Mexican, I think. *Vanilla planifolia*."

"Clear? You mean, before you fell into your sleep?"

316

"And during. It's what vanilla extract comes from. I dreamed a lot. I had a wonderful time. But of course I knew I was dreaming."

"You deliberately stayed asleep?"

Drawing a long breath of the sweet exotic air she stood up from the folding wooden chair, her incandescent hair rising like spume about her head and shoulders. "I had no particular desire to wake up."

He put a tentative finger to a leaf. "You're fond of tropical plants. Or were you hiding here?"

Her green eyes were frank, silvery with desire. "I thought you'd come here." She spoke with soft significance.

"You read my mind." He smiled. Forty at least, he had clear radiant skin, very pink, and in this antique light his own eyes were the sharpest blue she had seen; from these she knew he must be gentle without weakness, realistic without cynicism, and her love for him informed her blood, suddenly making her shiver as she watched him cup the orchid to study it, approaching the flower with a peculiar egalitarianism, as if he would be neither surprised nor upset if the plant decided to take the same intimate interest in himself. "Yes, vanilla, of course. I'm glad you want to be friends. I was hoping that was it. Bethlehem isn't the best place to meet people. Most of them are ordinarily mad, if you follow me, and consequently not very good company."

"You're not mad?" Amused she shifted her foot on the floor's wooden slats.

"Not ordinarily. I suspect I might have been once. I experienced something very like it for a while, shortly after VJ Day, perhaps inspired by the Atomic Bomb. I hope not. I don't recall thinking very highly of myself at the time. I felt almost sorry for the people of Hiroshima but we'd had our fair share of bombs and it didn't seem an exaggerated reaction, not then. In retrospect perhaps we shouldn't have done it. Well, it was at the Round Pond in Kensington Gardens one autumn morning around dawn. I was walking there, trying to decide whether to head North towards Hampstead or South towards Battersea, when I ran slap into a demon. He was about eight or nine feet tall, bright green, fanged, with glaring red eyes and an evil grin. I seem to remember he also had a forked tail, like a dragon you know."

"You were dreaming?" She plucked at the cotton against her spine.

317

"Not at all. I was wide awake. He felt very solid." He lifted his eyes from the pod he had been inspecting. "I was horrified."

"I should have been." She pushed damp hair from her forehead.

"You misunderstand me. I was horrified by the crudeness of my imagination. 'Good morning, Mr Kiss,' he said, this demon, 'and is there anything I can be doing for you on such a lovely day?' He had a strong Celtic accent, not exactly Irish but with those same old-fashioned speech forms and rhythms. Perhaps from one of the more remote parts of America. I didn't want anyone to see me talking to something that was visible only to me, and a dreadfully banal hallucination at that, so I held my tongue. 'Come now, Mr Kiss, there must be a secret desire you'll be harbouring, eh?' he went on. I pushed past him, feeling my knuckles graze his scales." Josef Kiss transferred his attention to a fuchsia's flower, like drops of blood streaked by milk. "I continued on my way. He followed, hissing and mumbling and promising me the world. 'Is all madness so banal?' I remember thinking. I felt his fiery breath on the back of my neck. I suspected he would carry me down to Hell willy-nilly. I kept walking, paying no attention to him. Eventually, somewhere near the Albert Memorial, I gave him the slip."

"Did he pester you much after that?" She noted the wrinkles in his linen jacket; they seemed to form a map, perhaps of the city. His cotton trousers were equally crumpled but in a different kind of pattern; she wondered if you could read a person's life in their clothes, just as you could in their palm.

"I never saw him again." There was sweat glittering on his chest, in the open collar of his Hawaiian shirt. "The encounter made me pull myself together, I can tell you, and curb my imagination. I've met too many people impressed by their meetings with the devil and sightings of flying saucers and angelic visitations. I'll have none of it. There's nothing more boring and anti-social. Madness is a dreadful state and I pity anyone who suffers from it. For my own part I'm an hysteric with certain crude telepathic gifts which I have no interest in promoting. Neither do I want someone else to believe in this gift. If they did, my entire life might be devoted to the kind of fantastic idiocy I've suffered these last few days. I'm as sane as you are, Mary Gasalee."

"It's good of you to say so. But what are you doing here, if you're sane?" She made a clumsy coquettish joke of it, lifting her shoulder and brushing back her moist hair, surprised by her own apparent flippancy, then met his eyes with hers, drawing the deepest of many breaths. "Am I being cruel?"

"It's a reasonable question." He did not alter his own gaze. "I'm here partly because I hate taking drugs to keep myself calm. I resent the strictures imposed by those who demand I be less irritating. So I stop. Sometimes I merely need a rest in a bin like Bethlehem which, incidentally, was never my favourite but unfortunately I was arrested nearby and tried at the local magistrates court so I came to be consigned to this hospital where my dreadful brother-in-law is Chief Consultant. But I'm grateful now, Mary Gasalee." Her hand was ready as he reached to hold it in both of his.

"And I'm glad." She almost sang the words. "Oh, I am."

"Smell the mulch in here." He beamed. "It's almost as heady as Kew's. Forgive me."

"What?" She was surprised.

"No. I was speaking of an earlier incident." He resisted her thoughts; he was not sure he could bear them. Meanwhile she experienced a frisson which she had thought specific to The Land of Dreams.

"A woman." She too rejected this hovering mystery. "You're married? Gloria?" She intended to tug free, but had no resolution.

"Gloria lacks time for me. I don't blame her." He spoke rapidly, attempting to deal with and dismiss the problem at the same moment. "But I'm not unfaithful to her. This will be the first time, dear Mary, I've confessed attraction and as it were taken action." He stopped, gasping. He was closer to her. *If he had eight wives*, she thought, *they would not have my right to him*. "We scarcely see each other. We hardly live in the same house. This is not to smooth any guilt, Mary, in me or you, but to tell the truth of it." *I would open the truth of my mind but you would run away, you would die, both of us possess too much of this power perhaps it would be I who ran away.* "In spite of pale blue warrior's serge sneaking into sunset alleys I refused the excuse. I had no wish to engage another's emotions, for this was my private battle, or to perform a simple vengeful act of counterdeceit. There was one small infidelity in Scotland, but that was for soup. Personally I can't afford such deceptions. I am professionally committed to deceiving the world. It would be certain folly to deceive my friends."

"I'm not deceived. I never could be, I think." As she reached to kiss his cheek she felt sick with lust. The close air of the greenhouse, almost like water, was dragged into her lungs and held there. She shivered and let it go, a single gust, and he was embracing her; her shoe was falling away from her foot as her right leg curled about his and she sought a balance on the creaking catwalk between the earthy trays, anxious not to overturn a bloom, to break a pot and alert the House, to do harm in the exercise of her own passion. Although it had become familiar over the days, she gasped at the sweet richness of the scents, and the cerises, purples, reds and whites, all fuchsias, over his shoulder became still more vivid as she embraced a body at once hard and soft like the organ she felt swelling against her stomach, her thigh. He was vibrant. He held her. She let herself be lifted up then securely lowered until they both lay under the sweating racks, visible only to another occupant, and there was muddy damp on her back, on her bottom, but his hands already grasped her legs and his lips held her mouth as she took ownership of him in her arms, this monster of delight, this fiery, unfoolish Falstaff, whose trousers she now inexpertly helped unbutton. He was scarcely less practised. She had never anticipated such an encounter; had neither hoped for nor feared it. Her fancies had been conventional, her heroes shared with her contemporaries, their courtships conducted in French châteaux, in rose-bowers or ballrooms.

This, she thought, *is the closest I'll ever come to a rose-bower and God knows how I'll explain the mud.* She thought she heard him chuckle in response. *My new dress!* Sister Kitty Dodd had gone out for it only four days earlier not knowing it was her seduction gown, her bridal weeds, her party frock, specifically designed to achieve this moment beneath the flowering rarities, the hothouse succulents *I knew he would find this irresistible he loves jungles he identifies them with sex he can't resist me here oh Jo the elastic cuts like cheesewire give me a chance hold yourself sir hold on a second! stay! good they'll be comfortable there just pray to heaven nobody sees my knickers waving on my foot where are my shoes ah* "Ouch!" *it's been so long take your damned time Jo for Christ's sake what a grunt what sweat what pouring rivers running over him and off me and the damned water everywhere can you catch stuff in this mud only vanilla pods and greenfly and fuck and fuck and cuckoospit and whatever else the poor plants suffer from not me I'm not suffering god*

*almighty I'm not bloody suffering there's a little kink in his cock I don't
remember that on Patrick this one's for you my dear this first one's for you
and then you'll have to go away for good back to heaven Pat it's over for you
my dear this stuff's for the living God God God fuck him god almighty this
will do nicely this will do for a long time but I must get out of here into the
real world where we shan't have to worry who's going to find us oh I know
he won't marry me but it's too late for that anyway I'm the mother of a girl
Josef Kiss by Christ Josef Kiss you're on fire yourself and so am I this whole
damn place will steam up the plants will drown oh all those smells those
tastes and feelings this could kill you easy this could be killing me now we
are you my darling Mary Mary no tenderer flesh no warmth so good no
darling honest sweet cunt full of such giving such life this could be the end of
a dream and I'll be dead in a minute who the hell cares this is the miracle this
is the true bloody miracle goodbye Patrick Gloria farewell have this one on
us I'll see you in heaven soon enough if this isn't heaven already. "Ow!"
that's a stone let me shift you bastard darling there oh he moves when I move
he moves with me and I with him and there was nothing like this in all those
months of wedded bliss with poor dead Patrick who never had a chance to
grow into a man who died a boy I've wasted too much time I had no idea of
what the waking world could offer and she is everything everything she is
all I ever desired and I hold you Josef you are mine informed made a god by
my demand created*

And then comes red oblivion and flashes of something better than
fire, better than the golden needles which stroked her dreams,
better than life or death or any pleasure she had ever guessed at.
What's this? Shuddering and holding him and trembling and she
knows she's groaning, but he's groaning too and she can't tell
which voice is which and she doesn't know what's going to happen
next what's due for delivery it's like a baby but without the pain and
then she gives herself up to something she's never resisted before
because it was never there to resist and which she would not have
resisted because it is more glorious than anything more profound
than love though perhaps the foundation for a love she now guesses
at and understands what makes the women in the books so helpless.
They're not fools after all. She wishes she could tell them she is
sorry, then he's at something, pushing her so hard she shouts he's
hurting her on a board and he slows down then he stops then he
pulls himself back and out and she's looking at the silver streaming
from his red and purple penis, from his glowing pink-gold skin, his

silky brazen body, soft as down, burning like the sun but never for a second threatening to consume *Mary Mary Mary. Mary!*

"Blimey." Mary Gasalee was limply paralysed. "Blimey! Are you okay. Gosh, look at the mess! Oh, gosh!"

He was shaking as he laughed. All his muscles and fat and beautiful veins, his skin and his hair, were dancing under the slender rays slipping through from above, in the heated murk, in the amniotic mud, for she and he were born together, born within the mulch intended for the orchids and the fuchsias; a well-augured beginning, perhaps.

"Let's do it again in a minute. What d'you say, Mary?"

But she shook her head. This must be decently sustained and not lead to mere habits and appetites, for she knew in herself that would only produce a swift death. Death was part of it already, for humans were only human, but she would put off the moment for as long as she could. Besides, she had plans in mind, schemes for her introduction into the world, a new Mary, a Mary who could never have existed before she went to sleep and who might never have come to fulfilment were it not for Josef Kiss, yet she owed him no loyalty save for the pleasure she took in the sight of him, the pleasure his massive, subtle body could give.

"We'll not do it again until tomorrow." She was grave, a little girl making rules. "For we're prisoners here and they will bring it to a stop if they find out, Josef. And what's to be explained already? Mud all over a new dress. Pants covered. Trousers soaked. Shirt and jacket filthy. Hair caked. Where did we have our accident? It can't happen in summer, in a dry garden. We need a hose quick. We should separate and give them the slip somehow. We'll meet up again when the coast is clear. We'd best be going to ground till then."

With an air of contentment Josef Kiss picked mud from his knees. "You're talking like my demon."

"Perhaps that's me. Perhaps I'm who you met but didn't know it. When I was dreaming and you were imagining things. Could we have met? Was that how we managed it?"

"Oh, Mary. Do you have a lust for symmetry? That's dangerous in these days, the urge towards ontology." He winked respectfully. "You're a force to fear, I think."

She was unimpressed. "I suppose that's why you talk to devils and I only talk to film-stars. We need a hose, Josef." And she caught his eye and they were both lost again, with him on his back blowing like an ecstatic whale and she riding him, some Amazonian spirit, astride that massively rippling bulk.

to rise forever in this golden light could Nirvana offer as much his square jaw clean cut strong hands lace at throat and wrists now all eyes are on the field as the KLM Silver Gull banks for a landing flown by the one and only J.H.Squire the man who introduced jazz to England and today is our most popular broadcaster

By the time Josef Kiss and Mary Gasalee went their individual ways, re-soaked as if by accident, sufficiently free of compost and foliage, he to General Psychiatric (Men) and she to the Special Wing (Women) it was teatime. Only Doreen Templeton remained in the Recreation Room and was so involved with her writing (since admission two days ago she had sent off some thirty letters to various politicians) she did not notice Mary's appearance. Reaching her little room undetected Mary hoped no one would see significance in the damp footprints she had left along the marble corridor. She knew she could get away with few assignations in the greenhouse and that anywhere else in the grounds was equally likely to be detected. Sister Kitty Dodd was always full of the lengths some patients would go to "do it" and how frequently and easily they were apprehended "at it". Moreover Mary had not as yet completed her master plan. Josef Kiss was no disappointment; indeed the experience was far better in reality than in her imaginings and she knew that she loved him; but before anyone suspected what she was up to, before she found herself attached to Mr Kiss, she was determined to introduce young David Mummery to the pleasures of the flesh: an ambition further encouraged by her new-found messianism, a wish to share her joyous knowledge with at least one more individual, and David Mummery was the only other inmate who stirred her. If Mummery could be taken tonight or the next morning, she could by tomorrow evening be back in the greenhouse with the gorgeous Josef Kiss, ready to let Fate decide when the inevitable detection would occur.

By the time Sister Kitty Dodd found her she was stripped and in the bath. "Oh, Mary, dear, you heard already." The mildness and the innocence of the nurse's tone told Mary her secret was still safe.

"Heard what, sister?" She moved a sponge to cover a bruise.

"Your daughter's here at last with your cousin. Her exams are over and they told her in Scotland. She's seen you before of course but you haven't seen her, not for a good few years anyway. It's Helen, down from Scotland, and I must say your cousin seems a nice man. I've met him before. Do you remember him?"

Remaining still and mute, Mary huddled as much of her body as possible below the waterline. "Dear, dear, dear."

"Do you remember him?" Sister Kitty cast about the bare bathroom for something to occupy her hands. She pushed at a piece of broken linoleum with her foot. "Mr Meldrum?"

"Yes." Mary's lips went under. For a second they grinned.

"Oh, Mary. You're frightened, dear. But it's all right. They're nice nice people and care so much about you. Helen's overjoyed and a bit nervous same as you but full of it all, dear. Oh, Mary she's waited such a long time, fifteen years. She's a young woman almost."

Feeling obscurely that she had deserted her daughter, Mary wondered if Helen hated her. Or did she resent Helen? Doctor Male had told her Gordon Meldrum and Helen were coming that afternoon but so intent had she been on courting Josef Kiss she had let it slip her memory, and now her guilt was worse because nobody guessed the truth.

"Oh, Mary, I'm an idiot not to realise you'd be nervous. Will you wear the new dress?"

"It's ruined." Mary lifted her head a fraction, brushing soap from her eyes. "Spoiled at least."

"Come now." Sister Kitty believed herself teased.

"One of the gardening men thought I was going to hurt him and he panicked. He had a hosepipe. He pushed me and I fell in the dirt." She did not blink.

Sister Kitty Dodd was outraged. "They shouldn't let these people out in the grounds. Who was he?"

"I don't know. It was my fault, really." Sure Sister Kitty would see her blushing Mary sank back down under the water.

"Well, there's your smart brown." Indistinct to Mary's ear, the nurse was determinedly cheerful.

Mary came up again, a shifty naïad. "Yes, I'll wear that."

"Helen isn't going to care what you're dressed like, she'll be so glad to see you." Picking up the big white bath sheet, Sister Kitty spread it before her. "Out you come, my little madonna!"

spent spent spent

Progressing some twenty minutes later in brown and beige towards the mottled marble of the front hall, Mary Gasalee was recomposed chiefly because she recalled the pleasure of her recent escapade and partly because she was no longer afraid of being found out. Sister Kitty Dodd stood solicitously ahead of her, beside the door of Doctor Male's office where such meetings were usually conducted. Mary might have returned to the Land of Dreams, her sense of detachment was so great. Sister Kitty Dodd's voice was unclear and meaningless, then momentarily it was as if the polished oak of the office door opened directly onto a yellow beach where bright surf rolled (she had still to visit the coast) and then vanished to reveal three beached sea-beasts, fabulous and sinister.

" . . . picayune," whispered Doctor Male. "Oh, here you are!" He was like an etiolated plant, more vine than man, and his hands were reaching tendrils as they touched her to turn her towards her family. "Here you are!"

The girl's white face was framed by pale red flame and the man beside her was merely a dark shadow, for both stood with their backs to a great stained-glass mock-Celtic window through which the afternoon sun blazed.

"This is Helen." Doctor Male's voice was a soft rustle. "And this is Gordon Meldrum, whom you doubtless remember."

"No." Her daughter's hair was almost strawberry blonde, lighter than her own. She wore a short-sleeved blue dress, a little gold chain, a gold bracelet. Mary was not surprised by the resemblance Helen bore to Merle Oberon. She had her grand-mother's looks.

"We never really met." Gordon Meldrum had a deep, re-assuring voice and a pleasant, hesitant manner, though Mary was slightly repulsed by the strong smell of pipe-tobacco in his barathea jacket and white flannels. When he moved slightly to one side she saw his grey wide-set eyes at last, his thinning sandy hair, his narrow lips smiling. "Good afternoon, Mary. I'm so pleased you're better." He made no attempt to embrace her.

"Hello," lunging forward Helen spoke with girlishly false

enthusiasm, "mother! Gosh, you look super. I'm really glad you're better." She paused.

Mary smiled in appreciation of her daughter's generosity. They had no experience in common and Helen had grown used to her mother being little more than a corpse. "I used to dream about you, Helen." She gestured. "That is, I dreamed about my baby. What I thought of as my baby. I thought in my dreams that you might be dead." She sighed and moved an apologetic hand. "I'm not expressing myself too well but I'm very glad you're not dead. Which seems a bit negative." She found it hard even to move her hand now.

"You look smashing." This time Helen's enthusiasm was more than conscientious. "So young."

"That's right, you look like sisters." At his unknowing re-discovery of this brush-salesman's compliment, Doctor Male seemed to expand with gratification. "Exactly like sisters. A couple of years between you."

"But that's not normal, is it?" Mary Gasalee was grateful for his banalities, which helped her form a bond with both her daughter and her evidently amused cousin.

"This is a very unusual situation." Doctor Male spread his hands and it was as if some carnivorous rain-forest plant had detected a food source. "I'm sure nobody will mind if I leave for a while. Sister?"

A sentimental smile fixed on her mouth, Sister Kitty Dodd was reluctant to follow Doctor Male out. She was almost hypnotised by her own pleasure at their reunion. "Call if you need anything. I'll bring you some coffee later."

Mary sat down in the window seat across from the great stained pane and waved at the geometric greenery, the garden visible on both sides of the gravel drive. "Lovely. Especially the roses. Did you come by train?"

"By bus." Gordon Meldrum was grateful for this familiar intercourse. "From West Brompton. The 30 goes all the way. It's handy. We've used it before, of course, when we visited. While you were asleep. Helen's known the route better than any, I'd say, since she was quite small."

"You live near the graveyard." Mary was not clear about what she had dreamed and what Sister Kitty had told her. There was also a letter which she had mislaid soon after she woke up.

"Brompton. It's Earls Court, really. Nothing very salubrious. All the posh people like Mrs Pankhurst are dead and in the cemetery! We're probably the only people living in Philbeach Gardens who aren't Australian or Polish. But it's lively enough and convenient, and Helen doesn't have far to go to school." He moved to peer down at the rose bushes, symmetrically distanced, red and white.

"In King Street, isn't it? Hammersmith?" Mary shifted to allow him more room and to move away from his smell. "Sister Kitty Dodd says it's one of the best schools in London and hard to get into." With some relief Mary felt normality returning as her recollection of lust faded.

"Fairly," said Helen. "I was lucky." She came a few steps closer.

Still not completely adjusted to the brightness in the room, Mary thought she saw tears in her daughter's eyes and wanted to reassure her. "I'm not mad, dear, or anything. I'm not ill. I've just been in a sort of shock. You must have heard the general opinion. I was stunned when the house fell in on us. I held you so tightly. We were lucky. Your father's forethought, of course. But it's long ago and I'm not sad, though I'm sorry not to have been with you while you were growing up, but I couldn't have given you anything like what Gordon and Ruth have so it's worked out very well, really."

"Look here, Mary, we benefited, too." Gordon's voice was gruff with controlled emotion. "And Helen's thought everything over. We've talked about it, of course, and need to discuss it with you now. We need to know what you want and how you feel."

"I feel very good. Very free, I suppose." Unable to bring a conventional reply to mind, Mary shrugged. "Very good. Ready to be free, anyway. I feel like making up for lost time."

"Well, you would." As if to assure himself that his pipe was still there, Gordon patted at his pocket. "I'm sorry, Mary, this is actually harder than I thought. I was thinking about you and Helen. I wish Ruth could have come, but she has this stupid therapy stuff. She'll be along as soon as she's a bit better." He was trying to avoid displaying his considerable fear for his wife.

"Is she on the mend?" At that moment Mary would rather have discussed Ruth.

"Oh, yes. Oh, yes." Another reassuring pat to the pocket.

"She's lost a lot of weight." Helen's tone showed she felt this reference to her foster-mother was almost a minor betrayal.

"I'm so sorry." Mary now felt a need to console and calm her daughter. "She doesn't deserve it. I've heard how marvellous she always was with you. Please give her my love and tell her I hope to visit her soon if she can't make it here. I'm anxious to get away. Doctor Male said there's a sort of half-way house I can go to, with my own room. When I'm used to the outside world I can apply for a flat."

"You could live with us." Gordon spoke with hasty affirmation. "I mean you're welcome to stay as long as you like. We all think it would be a good idea if you moved in. It seems the best thing and would cause fewest disruptions."

Mary's answering grin was frank and grateful. "You're a saint, Gordon, really. But I won't do that to you. You know it wouldn't merely be an inconvenience, it would be an emotional nightmare."

At first he seemed wounded by her candour, and clearly had not expected it. "Well, we could give it a shot. Ruth needs a hand, and will until she's better, so it wouldn't be a case of taking in a poor relation, Mary. We need you, I think."

"It would be a good way of trying to get ordinary." With ungraceful force Helen bent forward and took her mother's hand. "I love Ruth and Gordon. I think of them as my parents, but I never thought of you as anyone other than my mother."

"Helen's always called us Ruth and Gordon." Gordon had grown fiery red. "I mean, it's not as if she didn't know where and who her real mother was. There was never a mystery. So you've been 'mother' or 'mum' and we've been 'Ruth' and 'Gordon'."

"I've got three parents now." This romantic last from Helen seemed either rehearsed or borrowed. "I'm better off than almost anyone." Mary noticed how her daughter's bare arms had caught the sun.

"Well, perhaps I can find a little flat round the corner. We'll see." Mary was not ready for what they offered; the familiar love and good-heartedness her daughter took for granted but which was scarcely real to her. She thought she would prefer to be on her own, with only limited social intercourse, until she felt up to more. On the other hand if it might be her duty to stay with the Meldrums; if Ruth were desperately unwell, she might have to defer her plans at least for a while. She owed as much to Ruth. But she found herself resenting this possibility. "Life was certainly simpler in the Land of Dreams."

"I beg your pardon?" Gordon began to stand up. Helen tightened her hold on her mother's hand.

"I dreamed a lot while I was asleep." Mary gave in to an urge to explain. "Sometimes it was like a continuing story and I came to know people quite well, just as in this world. Not real people, I suppose." She lowered her eyes. "They were almost all famous filmstars." And when she giggled this set Helen to smiling.

"Filmstars, mum?"

"The Royal Family, too, and the odd prime minister. And my father, who ran off actually not too long after I was born. I think he was a tinker."

"Who did you know best, mum?"

"Merle Oberon and Katharine Hepburn. Do you still have them?"

"I love them! Who else?" Helen's interest was absolute.

"June Havoc. Ginger Rogers, whom I didn't much like. She was narrow-minded when you got to know her. Janet Gaynor. And Ronald Colman did an awful lot of different jobs. I suppose he couldn't settle. He drove a tram and was a postman. And a milkman. That must have been from *The Thirty-Nine Steps.*"

"Wasn't that Robert Donat?" Gordon was civil, tentative.

"Possibly." She acknowledged his politeness. "I got them mixed up sometimes. I found out from the magazines they have here. And films on television that are old as far as everyone else is concerned but mostly not very old for me. See how much I have to enjoy?" She was making a small plea for her liberty.

"You're certainly looking on the bright side, Mary." Gordon still seemed put out by her failure to respond positively to his generosity.

"I knew you would, mum." Helen now sat closer, her body relaxed, and Mary smelled her sweet scent, enjoying her warmth, her girlish plumpness and the domesticity they offered her suddenly had a greater attraction, though part of her mind remained engaged on her seduction of Josef Kiss and her planned seduction of David Mummery. She knew her family considered her some sort of lost soul, a baffled innocent, but since waking she had

329

gained experience amongst all kinds of people, many of whom were at the extremes of emotion, and she had also had some excellent guides in the Land of Dreams. Gordon Meldrum was offering her peace and quiet and she had enjoyed that for fifteen years; now she desired adventure. If it was possible she would have toured the world. She had been particularly impressed by the television and radio documentaries and was a keen follower of Armand and Michaela Denis. She decided to change the subject. "You were doing exams weren't you, and then you were in Scotland?"

"That's when I heard you'd woken up. They hadn't wanted me to get over-excited."

"They never do." Mary scratched the back of her neck. "Round here they try to calm you down if you start laughing at Norman Wisdom too loudly. Do you like Norman Wisdom?"

"Well, yes, a bit." Helen was embarrassed.

"Not your cup of tea. I don't think he'd be mine if I were outside. Gordon, did they tell you a date?" Mary turned her head.

"They seem to think you could leave at any time now. They have to arrange accommodation. That's one of the things I wanted to talk about. Like you, they think this halfway house is the best bet first." He extended his hands. "Then you can come and stay with us."

"It would be lovely to have you with us." Helen became enthusiastic again. "I could show you all my things. I've kept stuff from when I was a little kid. I've a dog called Muffin. He's pigheaded but I love him." She began to list her possessions, her joys and hobbies.

While understanding how her daughter could not know why she looked forward to a life of partial solitude and considerable experiment, Mary felt that Gordon's failure to perceive her needs was further proof of their validity. She remained grateful to the Meldrums for their love and goodness; her daughter had enjoyed a better life with them, and many more advantages than she could have provided.

Gordon Meldrum, studying her with a kind of embarrassed concentration, sensed her thoughts, and as soon as he could he said to her, "Everyone's much better off than before the War, Mary, because of full employment and higher wages. Really, we aren't particularly wealthy, you know. Everyone has a fridge, a washing-machine, a television set. Loads of people have cars. And better housing. We took advantage of everything being blown apart and started from scratch. In a few years time the problem will be what to do with all our holidays and cash! Ordinary kids are going to university. It's the classless society now. Labour or Conservative, it doesn't make a lot of difference. We're enjoying the benefits of austerity. Of the rationing and so on."

Mary tried to think of some way to acknowledge his decency. "I seem to have slept through the worst of it all. I've read the magazines and I've listened to the news. They complain about people growing greedy, but they don't seem any worse than before the War. My memory's probably clearer than most, not cluttered up. I can't wait to see it all. You'll be able to show me some of it, won't you darling." This last word to her daughter had only a slightly forced ring, but brought a pause and halted the progress of their relaxation. "I'm a bit tired." Gazing down into the garden Mary thought she saw Josef Kiss and David Mummery walking together beside the rose beds, but they were almost at once hidden behind the bushes. "I'm socially a little inept. I was virtually a child when I was knocked out."

"It's amazing how sophisticated you seem." Gordon was glad of a chance to offer this honest observation. "It's almost as though you were doing one of those 'Learn in Your Sleep' courses where they plug you into a gramophone and you do a foreign language or something. I'm amazed."

"I've been catching up. I've been reading a lot, you know." She squeezed Helen's hand. It was hot.

Knocking loudly on the door, Sister Kitty Dodd called eagerly: "Is it all right?"

"I still love E.Nesbit, though I suppose I shouldn't," Helen offered by way of an intimate revelation. "But I read more modern writers, too. I'd like to know what you enjoy best."

Raising an eyebrow at the others who nodded forcefully Mary called, "Come in!"

There was a single sharp squeak from the tea-trolley as Sister Kitty Dodd wheeled it through the door and brought it to a ceremonial halt before Mary and Helen Gasalee. "Who's to be mother?"

It was Gordon Meldrum who lifted the pot at last as Sister Kitty backed for the door telling them she would leave them at it. He poured three cups three-quarters full. "Do we all take milk?"

Mary reached for the jug. "I'll do that at least." When their hands collided across the sugar-bowl they laughed together.

"I hope you'll give it serious consideration, coming to live with us. And you can stay for a weekend, I gather, when they put you in the temporary hostel. Ruth's longing to see you." Gordon was a relentless St Bernard.

"Of course." Mary was surprised how readily her mind expanded to accept a wider range of possibilities. She could enjoy her adventures and become familiar with the commonplace at the same time, but the hospital's plans, her relations' plans, Josef Kiss's plans, even her daughter's plans must not influence her. She would continue on her own course. As if to affirm this she placed reminiscent fingers to the bruise steadily coming to prominence on her calf. There were others, hidden on her bottom and her outer thigh and she bore them with the uncomplicated delight of a child sporting cuts, grazes, or operation scars. Presently they were the only tangible signs of fulfilled ambition.

Almost in silence they drank their tea, ate several Oliver biscuits and some Garibaldis. Helen was encouraged to finish the plate. "I can call you mum when I'm talking about you because I always have, but it's hard calling you mum to your face."

"You can call me Mary if you like. The same as Gordon and Ruth."

Helen shook her head. "It would seem like letting you down. I've always loved you. They say you saved my life. But you know that."

"No." Mary became confused. "I didn't. I thought I'd lost you somewhere."

"No. I was in your arms."

"I thought I'd lost you."

"No." Gordon nodded emphasis. "She was in your arms when they found you. It was a miracle you were alive. You hung on to Helen through the whole thing. You were burned as you know on your back, you still have the scar, but you wouldn't let Helen go. You wouldn't let them take her until you reached the hospital. You held her all the way." He was crying.

332

Mary frowned, not sure if this was anything more than another sentimental half-truth. The War had produced so many. "It was just after Christmas."

"December 30th. I talked to an Air Raid Warden." Gordon held up the pot by way of enquiry but no one wanted more.

"You shouldn't feel upset." Mary was nonplussed. "Things aren't always what they seem in the Land of Dreams." She yawned.

While her relatives collected themselves and prepared to leave, Mary, with a delicious resumption of lust, wondered if she still had time to hunt down Mummery.

Successive Movements 1964

I BELIEVE that 1964 was my most significant adult year, Mummery had written on hospital stationery. In my mind it stands as the chief watershed between 1954 and 1977, though I am hard put to say exactly why. I met the Black Captain again. My books began to be published with regularity. I discovered the subterraneans. I saw my first love again; the older woman to whom I had given my virginity in a bed of pink Livingstone Daisies whose petals only open in bright sunshine.

It was a hot day in 1956. My mother had gone to a Bournemouth nursing-home and I was staying on my own at a guest-house where my seductress was a resident. Her pursuit of pleasure was at that time completely unselfconscious, and doubtless the swaggering, foulmouthed youths who threatened me in the High Street would have called her a nymphomaniac. She eventually succeeded in presenting a more conventional image to the world, but when I first knew her she was like a miraculously successful Frankensteinian experiment. Rousseau would have marvelled at this living example of all his dreams, this *Erdgeiste*. She was resuming her life after a long period of inactivity. Bedridden for years, she suddenly recovered, and I met her just as she awoke determined to take from the world all it could offer. I'm still not sure how she found me the alcohol.

It is embarrassing to admit to a nervous breakdown as a schoolboy but my mother's health was poor and I was regularly victimised by our local Teddy-boys. We lived in a private house on the fringe of a big council estate and my accent, developed at my public school and amongst my immediate family, made me their natural prey. I was mocked, pursued and challenged to violent and impossible contests. My best friend Ben French, living on the estate and going to the same school as the Teds, was almost as vulnerable, chiefly because of his association with me. Their leader, Ginger Burton, threw knives at him in the playground; one pierced his arm, another his hand. Our arrow tips replaced by dart heads to give extra penetration, we took our bows to the allotments and laid for Ginger, but he never came by on his own; he moved at the centre of a great pack. I thought of him as our local Ivan the Terrible. Discovering assassination to be out of the question it never occurred to us to ask help from our parents or to go to the police. We relied on our own resources and they were insufficient.

Facing the gang when I walked home from the bus-stop after school or when I went out in the evening, together with my anxiety around my exams, caused me enormous stress and consequently brought about my mother's collapse. As she moaned in her darkened room I grew obsessed with the Suez situation, which I saw in terms of Hopalong Cassidy books. 10 Downing Street was the Bar-20 ranch in danger of attack while Tex, Skinny, Buck, Red, Johnny, Pete, Lanky and the boys were out chasing rustlers. Since only Hoppy and his wife Mary were left to defend the Bar-20 against bandit or Indian attacks, it was my clear duty to offer what help I could, so wearing a check shirt, a wide-brimmed khaki hat, an old waistcoat, a pair of chaps made from a hearthrug and two air-pistols in matching holsters, I turned up one morning on Hoppy's doorstep. A few minutes later I sat in his living-room and, while my Aunt Iris wrung her hands on the sofa and two friendly PCs calling me "lad" said everything would be all right, I continued to assure them that the ranch would be defended to my last shot. When my uncle came from his conference with Mr Eden he knew immediately what I was talking about. "Well, pardner." My Uncle Jim put his hands on pin-striped hips. "I reckon th' old Bar-20 could use a few more hands like you. And if'n it was up to me, I'd hire you on like a shot. But I guess yo're plumb needed over at yore own spread just now. Yo're sure the best man t' go. An' don't worry about us. Th' boys'll be back in th' bunkhouse afore you can say 'stampede'. Hoppy tol' me straight – I want Th' Kid t' go an' keep an eye open for trouble over on th' Southwest Range."

It was at this stage I realised my Uncle Jim was not my Uncle Jim at all but an evil twin. As the police took me to a waiting car the pseudo-Uncle Jim came with me to the door. He said he was sorry he could not come home with me since he was needed by the PM. "I mean Hoppy," he said. Here was confirmation of the deception, since my Uncle Jim, not Anthony Eden, was Hopalong Cassidy. This impersonator was trying to pass off Dude Eden as foreman of the Bar-20! I laughed in his face and less than a day later sneaked back to find out why the real Hoppy was being held prisoner on his own ranch, but this time a plain clothes thug wrenched my arm behind me and was about to do worse when my Uncle turned up. I remember Detective Sergeant Culpepper listening in astonishment to a distinguished civil servant begging me in the language of the prairie to ride home and take care of my sick ma.

In Norbury for several days I defended our house, patrolling from window to window as my mother's small melodramatic voice called to me. "Davey, what are you doing?" I assured her that everything was fine, since I saw no point in alarming her. Satisfied at last that the danger was over, I took the 109 from the High Street back to the Bar-20. I now reasoned that my Uncle Hoppy had deceived not me but traitors in his own camp; he had given me a secret warning.

They found me with one leg over the spikes on the garden wall, the metal barb impaling the fleshy part of my inner thigh, making it impossible to go forward or back. A reporter on a routine job took my photograph so by that evening the story was in all the London papers.

Only the *Standard* had the picture of a boy in home-made chaps, his Boy Scout hat moulded like a Montana-style stetson, hanging by his leg and hands from the Downing Street spikes, but every one carried versions of my attempt to rescue Uncle Hoppy from the outlaws. I was "The Whitehall Kid", "Young Roy Rogers" or "Tex Mummery", and I was said to be a circus rider, a US cattle-baron's Etonian son and Anthony Eden's nephew. That evening I left hospital with twenty stitches in my leg and learned I was to stay with my Aunt Charlotte. My Aunt Daisy was tending my mother. I was told I had caused a great deal of trouble. Soon after this my mother and I were sent off for separate rest-cures, I met my first lover, and I was taken up by Josef Kiss from whom I received my initial knowledge of London and her legends.

Pubs were the nodes from which radiated Mr Kiss's lines of travel; lines so strictly maintained that after a while I could predict almost exactly where in certain circumstances he would be at any given time of day. I became his protégé. I would leave home early in the morning to seek him out. Even when I occasionally failed to find him I enjoyed exploring the city. I loved to see him in Holborn emerging from elaborate pub doorways, from nondescript Mayfair drinking-clubs, from mysterious Soho alleys. Once I witnessed his mountainous body running ponderously down leafy Haverstock Hill towards the tube station as he held his black felt hat, his stick and his gloves in his hand, his ulster flapping in the wind, all flamboyant, self-confident, knowing vulgarity. "I've just come from my psychiatrist, Bolton. Oh, god, I feel so cheerful!" This to a scrawny baffled bookseller arranging the sixpenny tray outside his shop. "It won't last, of course. But isn't it a lovely day?" Unaware of me he vanished through the gate of Belsize Park Station, replacing his hat as he went, pulling on his gloves, stick under his arm, ticket out of his waistcoat. I had to run to catch him.

I knew very little about him in those days. They said he was a man of the theatre, an old performer from the golden years of Variety. "I think," said Bolton the bookseller to me later, "he had a magic act, but I imagine him more as an old Shakespearian ham, like Donald Wolfit." I had seen Wolfit several times on television.

"He sounds nice, darling." Mrs Bolton, a curly-haired shadow, came from their back room to where I stood, my hand on the threepenny bargains. "Is Kiss a Jewish name?"

"He comes in about once a month, browses, but hardly ever buys, passes the time of day. He likes cheap silly fiction."

"Perhaps he's down on his luck." Mrs Bolton dusted a Dickens or two.

"Those clothes aren't tat and they're not old. They must be specially tailored for him. He arrives in a taxi often as not, to see a private doctor round here. A head-shrinker."

"Somehow he doesn't look the type."

"That's what he says, anyway." The bookseller had not desired

337

a conversation on the subject. He had merely wanted to be heard while he told an anecdote and expressed an opinion.

For me all this was a betrayal of Mr Kiss, and consequently I never went back to the bookshop. Instead I would wait in the stationer's opposite until my friend came flying down the hill, talking to anyone he even faintly recognised, almost never noticing me until the last moment. Eventually, having heard many similar opinions of Mr Kiss, I took them in my stride, and began to feel superior to the people who offered them.

When I was seventeen Mr Kiss let me go into his pubs. He had dozens of acquaintances, most of them far more eccentric than he. To a boy who had left school so early he provided a marvellous education. I never really returned to school after my breakdown but went to a special tutor for a while, then to evening classes, then to my first job as messenger for a shipping office in the City. My employers, two grotesque characters whose faces were permanently flushed with drink, told me the office was expanding.

Actually they increasingly employed staff and tried to fit us all into a single large room above a coffee warehouse in Pepys Street. By August 1956 there were twenty-two people in the room, only two windows admitting air, and London was experiencing a heatwave. I escaped frequently since my main job was to take Bills of Lading back and forth from various consulates and dockside offices, giving me plenty of time to read while waiting for the documents to be certified, or using public transport. At this time I began, with no clear idea of publication, to write my articles about London. Sometimes when I came across a previously undiscovered corner of the city I would forget my job altogether and arrive back at the office very late or after it had closed. In the summer heat I grew dozy but inevitably in the crowded madness of that modern sweatshop rows broke out. The final dispute had little to do with my lateness or my vagueness; it involved a friendly remark I made to a secretary in imitation of the general lewdness around. After I left I was told she was the manager's mistress and I had unknowingly struck a nerve. She took mild offence but he took considerable umbrage, giving me my cards and ten days' pay and telling me to clear out on the spot, which I cheerfully did, and by the following week was working for a Management Consultants in Victoria whose atmosphere was a complete contrast to the crazed misery of

338

my first job. Josef Kiss was of considerable comfort during those teenage years and gave good advice whenever I asked it. Soon I was selling small pieces, usually of five hundred or a thousand words, to many periodicals including *John O' London's, Everybody's, Lilliput, London Mystery Magazine, The Evening News, Reveille, Illustrated, John Bull* and various juvenile periodicals. In those days, although we yearned for the pre-war Golden Age of magazines and newspapers, there were plenty of publications left, and soon after my nineteenth birthday I became a full-time freelance, thanks to Mr Kiss's encouragement, his suggestions, his submissions on my behalf to editors he met in various Fleet Street pubs.

He told me he had spent his early years in Egypt, where his father was a serving soldier, had not returned to London until he was six and consequently was called "Gyppo" at school. "Eventually I impressed them by reading their palms, looking at their tea-leaves and so on. From being considered an outcast, almost a foreigner, I gained a certain amount of respect in the Theobald's Road area."

He had stories about his travels abroad, his experiences in the film and theatre worlds, the characters he had known. He was familiar with Europe's great cities, both before and after the War, and several parts of North Africa, especially Marrakesh. There was an idiosyncratic quality to his reminiscences and sometimes I would go home and record them, his Boswell. "I was living in those days," he informed me for instance in May 1964, "at the Grand Hotel Lafayette in Bucharest. The heyday of course of the Gypsy Nation as we affectionately called it, though Carol wasn't the first king they'd ever had. In Victory Square, I think. I forget what it's called in Roumanian. Very fine. The Grand Hotel Lafayette. I'm not sure it was the best or most famous hotel in Roumania – that was probably the Athénée Palace, though perhaps I'm remembering a film I was in with Peter Lorre just after the War. We used some library footage of Bucharest . *The Mask of Dimitrios*. The book was better. Lorre regularly stayed with friends of mine in St Mary's Mansions, Paddington, a very odd group of buildings. Secluded in the middle of idiotic urban ugliness near the Church Yard and Paddington Green, made famous by Polly Perkins, of course, it has horrors of every type around it. Motorways, grey blocks of flats, hooligans. You should think of living there. I would. It's convenient and very cheap. Get a flat at the back, overlooking the graves. The Lafayette was considerably better than the place we called L'Hôtel du Porc. It was near the park, naturally, but run by pigs. No, that was probably Hungary. You're not familiar with that exceptionally romantic period of Balkan history. The relaxing thing for me was that away from London I received very few voices." His discursive style was confusing until you realised he always returned to the point. He only occasionally spoke of his "voices" and was plagued far worse than I with a sense that sometimes he heard the whole of London in his head.

During the sixties we walked a lot at night, enjoying the darkness when a good deal of danger seemed to have disappeared from the city. In June 1964, on one such walk, through two little rows of Georgian cottages off Praed Street, we heard a sound so loud, so penetrating and chilling, that neither of us wished to believe it had been human. The sound issued through the city's early-morning gloom from an upper room in Sale Place and we knew it could only be the expression of some terrible sexual apotheosis; the culmi-nation of desire achieved after decades of waiting, as if the creature crying out had prepared itself, like a particular species of insect, for this one terrible moment, the shuddering memory of which would satisfy it for the rest of its life, just as until now the anticipation had sustained it. The experience was dreadful for me, but worse for Mr Kiss who gasped and pressed the heels of his hand to his forehead, weeping and groaning and trying to speak, begging for the noise to go away, long after it had ceased to echo through the Paddington alleys. Clearly there was more inside his head that only he could hear. Later, as we rested in the lobby of one of the district's cheap hotels, where his friend was porter and the rooms could be had for a lower rate if you took them for a whole night, Mr Kiss said, "Never let anyone persuade you, Mummery, that there is no such thing as pure evil. Those who merely believe in good and who easily dismiss the existence of evil are nothing but sentimentalists conspiring with the wicked, though they do not know it. Certainly there is divine goodness, but equally, as Zoroastrians would tell us, there is unmitigated wickedness. Embrace the one by all means, but by so doing you must fight relentlessly against the other. You may take this as a statement of truth. *I have read their minds.*" He was soaked with clammy sweat and still shaking. His friend, the seedy old janitor, fetched him a glass of whisky which he drank in a single swallow. "Tomorrow," he said "I'll get some stronger tablets from that swine Male. Phew!" On impulse next day he made one of his rare voluntary excursions from London, leaving on the early train for Oxford as if he still sought to escape the horrible sound we had heard in Sale Place. I saw him off at the station. As he promised, he was back by that afternoon, but shortly afterwards he signed himself into one of his private mental hospitals and I was only permitted two visits in that entire month.

These hospitals were generally no more than hiding-places for embarrassing relatives of the rich, and I always found him in a nostalgic reminiscent mood, frequently talking about London before the War, which suited me because it was extra fuel for my little books. After the Sale Place incident, he spoke chiefly of his father, who had been killed in a train accident. He mourned, he said, the passing of the Age of Steam. "The steam you could see eveywhere! From trains and ships both. On cold mornings the men's breath mixed with it. You saw fog forming before your eyes. My father said it would do him in because he had developed bronchitis after he got back from the Middle East. But he loved it, the sight of steam, I mean. He used to smoke those full-strength Capstans, too. Well, we know better now, but he didn't realise what was causing it. 'You got to laugh ain't you?' he'd say. 'Better than crying, anyway, isn't it?' He was in hospital but he signed himself out. This was during the War, too. He didn't feel safe. His brother had died in the same ward and it was obviously bad luck. I remembered going to see my uncle there. My father said he was the nicest geezer he'd ever known though it was his own brother. He was sweet-natured and so was his wife, an unusual combination. He was a real character, did all the cooking and when he sang 'My Old Dutch' he meant every word, it was better than listening to Albert Chevalier. We lived with them when we came back from Egypt. She's still alive, the only one left, in an Old Folk's Home over near Epping Forest. My cousins keep in touch with her. I see them occasionally but they don't think much of me. They admire my sister."

Josef Kiss's sister Beryl Male is the present Minister of Arts, a job requiring someone who hates and depises everything but the crudest forms of opera, and is the only woman on the government whom Mrs Thatcher even slightly likes, though it's certain she will not get any significant cabinet post until the Tories tire of their leader and elect another man. My Uncle Jim remained a kind of unofficial amanuensis to a number of disenchanted Tory radicals until he died, so he continued to have some idea of what went on within the Party. To his regret he never met Josef Kiss but knew Mrs Male fairly well, believing her typical of a politician willing to embrace corruption even before they gain any sort of real power, "as if by becoming corrupt they will, by a process of sympathetic magic, consequently become powerful." My Uncle Jim had known such types all his life, but only in recent years had they begun to rise to positions of prominence. "Ours is probably a genuine example of society undergoing a period of decadence," he said shortly before his death. "Decadent government in a decadent country. The Civil Service is no longer effective, having ceased to attract the right people, and there's no dynamic elsewhere. They show a genuine desire to achieve sterility. All this ludicrous emphasis on zero-inflation while they're lining their own pockets as fast as they can. It's reactionary conservatism of the narrowest kind, and it's deeply hypocritical. We have a disenfranchised intellectual class; a dis-enfranchised working class; a disenfranchised urban population and while the government doesn't trust the Civil Service, the Civil Service despises the government. I rather wish I'd died a few years ago when there was still some hope under Macmillan." I heard Macmillan, by then Lord Stockton, in the House of Lords once. He was ninety or so and evidently frail, but it could have been my Uncle Jim speaking. Macmillan shared with my uncle a strong dislike of his later successors. The two men remained good friends; better finally than my uncle and Churchill. All relationships with Churchill deteriorated, especially as he became senile until in the end the Party fielded a corpse as its leader. My uncle felt his chief should have retired with better grace. "He desired power for so long that when he got it he could not give it up. If he had looked after himself better he might have lasted with a bit more dignity. But he was always self-indulgent." My uncle only spoke of these things as he himself approached death. He felt the Royal Family had been tainted by the same new cynicism he observed in British politics. "They've borrowed the sort of publicity machine Wilson loved so much." When he witnessed Prince Charles standing on an apple crate in order to appear taller than Lady Diana Spencer, he decided our end as a decent nation had come. He died a few months after their marriage, lamenting the folly of kings and making increasing references to the fate of the French. His one joke on the subject was that by the end of the century Charles the Third might well have become as devout and as discreet a Catholic as Charles the First. "A clear sign of the imminent Dark Age, David. Pray for a Cromwell!"

Josef Kiss also feared a looming Age of Darkness, but his auguries were less political. He felt we had not learned the lesson of the Nazi War, that evil was too readily ignored both by people wishing to make quick venal gains or by those who simply hated to face its existence. "They concentrate on the killing of whales while whole nations of their fellow creatures perish." This bleak and rarely expressed aspect of my friend's character greatly discomforted me. I had my own periods of deep depression, though my mania was now used to fuel my best moments of inspiration, and I could not bear the weight of this monstrous vision. To counter it I recalled the miracle of my own existence the suggestion of divine providence. What I call the Legend of the Black Captain speaks for itself.

In 1964, when the excitement of the Beatles and the New Liberality was first being felt, I met the Black Captain for the first time since the War. I had begun to doubt his existence. He wasn't of course a Captain. He had been an ordinary Able Seaman at the time. But he existed. I've written the full story in my book. We met entirely by coincidence in a doctor's waiting-room. Sitting across from him that morning, I was sure I recognised him and overcame my embarrassment enough to ask him if he had been in the Streatham area during the V2 attacks of March 1945. He admitted he had been on leave then. He lived in Brixton, he said. "Did they call you The Captain?" I asked. When he laughed I knew I was at last speaking to the man who had saved my life. I tried to tell him about my latest research but he seemed baffled.

In 1964 I was working on a peculiar book about the city's "lost" tube lines whose maps exist only in Masonic libraries. There are many tunnels under London, some containing complete lengths of line, some with platforms, ticket offices and all the paraphernalia of an ordinary London Transport stop. There are, too, older tunnels, begun for a variety of reasons, some of which run under the river, some of which form passages between buildings. I became so fascinated by this knowledge I completely forgot to control myself while I worked night and day on my book which was becoming much more than mere journalism. I discovered evidence that London was interlaced with connecting tunnels, home of a forgotten troglodytic race that had gone underground at the time of the Great Fire, whose ranks had been added to periodically by thieves, vagabonds and escaped prisoners, receiving many fresh recruits during the Blitz when so many of us sought the safety of the tubes. Others had hinted of a London under London in a variety of texts from as far back as Chaucer. Eventually I grew determined to look for this race myself.

My first expedition into the huge vaults of the Fleet sewers was relatively painless. Taking a frogman's breathing equipment, fisherman's waders, powerful lamps, ropes and a supply of food and drink, I had no difficulty in finding a manhole through which I could enter the underworld. My main concern was how to avoid the teams of "flushers", the sewermen patrolling the area; but side-tunnels, forgotten and disused passages of all kinds, provided cover and gave substance to my theories. The complexity of the warren was astonishing and the beauty was often breathtaking; a world as various, as wonderful and as mysterious as anything on the surface, yet more peaceful, comforting in its strange isolation. It had considerable wildlife. One night, moving steadily upstream through slightly phosphorescent foam and mist, I heard the grunting and squealing of feeding pigs. They moved away at my approach and as fast as I waded they kept ahead of me. I glimpsed only the shadow of a large boar. I knew the legend about a fierce pig colony breeding there since the Fleet was first roofed, but these were shy animals. Perhaps they provided fresh meat for their world's human inhabitants.

Night after night I descended, frequently hiding in tube stations until they closed and then exploring disused branch lines. I came upon the frozen ghosts of Metropolitan platforms; their news-stands and benches waited for passengers who would never arrive. I found two skeletons, both of children, but from the clothing it was clear they had only fairly recently preceded me. For all the sparseness of evidence I refused to give up my search for the Secret

Nation. These people were as adept as Amazonian jungle dwellers at misleading explorers.

As I tried to contact them by leaving notes and gifts, my offerings became increasingly elaborate: radios, hampers of food, books, all kinds of battery-operated gadgets. Then one marvellous night my faith was at last confirmed! The gifts were accepted! Thereafter whenever I returned, whether to sewer, tunnel or station, they would be gone, and soon I left them in regular places, addressing pages of notes to the natives, pleading with them to show themselves to me. In September 1964, I was rewarded. I watched in awe as shadowy, black-clad figures appeared from the tunnel depths. Some seemed a little simian; all were below average height. They stood looking at me, their eyes glittering, but whenever I moved towards them they would immediately vanish.

"What can I bring you?" I asked. "What do you need from up there?"

I was answered eventually by guttural, muffled voices. The subterraneans seemed chiefly interested in the ephemera of over-ground society: pin-up magazines, records, comics. Like other primitive tribes lacking previous contact with our civilisation they were fascinated by our most trivial artefacts.

To provide my new friends I began to sell my own possessions. Soon my flat in Colville Terrace was virtually bare, but my book was growing. I worked all day, sleeping only fitfully, and visited the tribespeople at night. I would ask them simple questions about how long they had lived underground and who led them, but they answered cryptically or contradictorily until I came to realise they understood me no better than I understood them.

When I begged to be taken to their realm to meet them on their own ground, they always refused with emphatic grunting and head-shaking.

My obsession grew until eventually I decided I would have to follow them secretly, so one night, in a section of the old World's End line abandoned due to seepage from the river, I met the shadowy natives with the usual gifts of a transistor radio, fresh batteries and copies of *Playboy* and *The Beano*. I wore rubber-soled boots and had dressed entirely in black. Parts of the line were waterlogged but other sections were fairly dry, and as the subter-raneans slipped back into the deeper reaches I was able to follow.

Thinking me gone, they made no attempt to move silently and I heard their garbled beast-like voices as they shuffled ahead of me up the tunnel, giggling and squeaking.

At last they slipped into a storm drain and I was forced to crouch low, then entered a wider sewer which I guessed was somewhere under Fulham Broadway. Their voices echoed and were further distorted but I caught an occasional word such as "home" and "late" and assumed we must be nearing their camp, but then to my absolute astonishment I saw them ascending an iron ladder towards one of the manholes I myself had sometimes used! As I made forays into their world, so they made forays into mine! What an obvious and simple explanation for so many London legends and folktales of cobbolds and gnomes creeping at night from the sewers to steal food and carry off children! In the city these creatures had replaced the Gypsies in popular folklore. Before following them into the upper world I let them go ahead, then carefully inched up the ladder into the cool drizzle of a May night, but sadly, by the time I had been narrowly missed by a special bus, I looked across towards Fulham Town Hall and saw only a couple of schoolboys sheltering from the rain. When they noticed me they yelled something and ran away.

I returned frequently to the World's End, but I must have frightened off the tunnel-dwellers for they never revealed themselves to me again. Soon after this episode my doctor suggested I take a holiday. I spent it exploring the rather less complicated mines and fogous of North Cornwall. As I calmed down I saw things in better perspective, realising I had almost destroyed myself in pursuit of an obsession and encroached on freemasons' privacy. My little book *Looking Backward: The Truth Behind the Fiction* sold fairly well in Watkins' and other specialist shops.

I'm sure these interests developed out of the pleasures of the Blitz when we were allowed to make homes for ourselves in the Underground. People were very cheerful and friendly to me; and there was a marvellous feeling of safety there, even more than in the old Anderson shelter where I had originally slept. It was a treat to use the Underground during the Blitz itself but it was only later, when the doodlebug raids began, that we slept down there regularly.

The doodlebug threat virtually over, and the War evidently

coming to an end, I was sent by my mother round the corner into Manor Road to buy a long tin loaf at the baker's and to get her ten Player's cigarettes at the tobacconist's next door. If there was any change I could have a stick of licorice wood which though almost inedible was not rationed. I remember very little after I reached the shops. I think I heard a whistling sound before suddenly a vast sheet of fire appeared in front of my eyes and I was blinded, lifted as if by a crane and swung upwards where it seemed I was momentarily suspended until I fell at length back to the ground.

I tried to shout but I couldn't find anything to breathe. The noise seemed to force my skull open and I crouched holding my arms and knees to offer as small a target as possible. When eventually the roaring stopped I stood up. I was covered with a grey-pink dust from the pulverised bricks and there was broken glass down the back of my collar, glass in my hair. My arms were wet with blood and my sleeves were gone. I still held the shopping bag, though it was full of plaster, and the money was in my hand so I began to walk towards the bakery to complete my errand. Only gradually did it dawn on me that the baker's had vanished, together with most of its neighbours. I stopped. At my feet was a baby's leg in a little knitted blue bootee; the pram containing other parts of the same baby was twisted up several yards away, clasped by the hand of a faceless woman whose whole upper body was nothing but bloody pulp. Nearby a child, a girl of about my own age, was screaming but no sound came from her mouth. I saw four or five other corpses, most of them blown to bits like the baby. Walking through the rubble to where the baker's had been I discovered more lumps of bone and flesh, most of it nameless meat, but no loaves. My mother's friend Janet was never identified. Past the back alleys of the shops, the houses beyond had their windows blown out, their roofs broken. There was still a storm of dust coming up from the crater and I could hear people screaming from within the piles of rubble. I heard a familiar voice shouting. In her pinafore, her hair in a turban, my mother came running up Manor Road shouting "David! David! David!" I told her I was all right but hadn't been able to get the bread or the cigarettes. She kept me near her for a couple of weeks. Then one Saturday the next V1 hit my school in Robin Hood Lane, and while no children were hurt I was allowed to stay at home for the rest of the War and have ever since remained grateful to the Germans.

More clearly than the V1s I remember the V2s whose only warning was that dreadful scream as they came on you from nowhere. In wartime one tends to look back on earlier periods of terror as if they were relatively untroubled and by the time the War ended people spoke of the Blitz as if it had been a Golden Age. Inmates of Auschwitz presumably recalled Sachsenwald as others might yearn nostalgically for a childhood holiday.

I can still feel the pavement lifting under my feet, the weird wind pulling the clothes from my body, the sudden silence as I went deaf, then the roaring as hearing returned, the flash of light, the awful heat and the dust covering me from top to toe. Few survived as I survived. I remember how bitterly people complained of the posh Westminster, Knightsbridge and Mayfair residents who were able to direct the bombs over working-and middle-class areas of the city. My Uncle Jim told me we were sending back false information to the Germans making them think they had struck critical targets when they had actually been devastating unstrategic suburbs. He was not surprised when after the War the Labour Party received such a massive vote from people convinced they had been betrayed by their own government. Churchill, the British Bulldog hero of posters and newspaper features, was by no means universally loved. Only in the 1950s, with the Empire shrinking and the British beginning to grow less confident, was he knighted and turned into the demigod we now remember. My mother felt he had actually prolonged the War, though she would never tell me why. "Ask your Uncle Jim," she would say. My Uncle Jim of course said nothing.

In 1964 my Uncle Jim visited me at the Cornish rest home. He was staying nearby with old friends who lived in an elaborate castle raised on an offshore crag and invited me to dinner there. I refused in case I embarrassed him, for I still remembered the earlier episode at Downing Street, but he laughed when I mentioned this. "Truthfully, David, I enjoyed every moment of it, except when you hurt your leg. You brought a note of domestic farce to something which until then had been merely a foreign tragedy. Eden enjoyed the story no end, you know. You took some of the heat off him. He told me there would always be a peg for you to hang your guns and hat at the Crazy D. It didn't seem politic at the time to tell you this. 'Nuff t' say, y' played a better hand than y' knew an' me an' th' boys was plumb grateful to you, pardner!" This praise meant much to me and could not have been better received had it come from the foreman of the Bar-20 himself.

Alive by a miracle, by the agency of the Black Captain, I would gladly have given up a dozen of my own extra years to my Uncle Jim. I wish he could have lived longer to enjoy his retirement. He was an old-fashioned egalitarian Tory, courteous and humane and open to all new ideas which might increase people's liberty. He showed as much understanding and sympathy for black power as he did for the woman's movement and seemed to accept the principles with as much enthusiasm as any left-wing radical. I loved him more than I loved anyone else, even Josef Kiss, whom in some ways he resembled.

In 1964 I met the woman who would eventually reintroduce me to my first love. Eleanor Colman came to that same Cornish rest home shortly before I left, and later back in London she recognised me. She dressed eccentrically in the most vivid shades of lilac blue, turquoise and lavender, like an overdone Sargent, and though there was no telling exactly how old she was, she did draw a pension. In fact she was getting her pension when she saw me behind her in the Westbourne Grove post office. We went across the road for a cup of tea and a bacon sandwich. Everyone knew her in the café.

"I'm as old as the hills and older than the Tower of London," she told me when I asked her age. We shared an interest in the city's mythology. She went so far as to claim to have known the actual founder of London. "Brutus the Trojan, dear. He's still alive and doing very nicely for himself in the antiques business. Appropriate, really." After I had met her in the same café for a few times I asked if we could visit his shop. She was amused by this. "He doesn't sell 'em dear. He makes 'em. You know, with the old bit of chain and the hammer and the blunt chisel." He worked nearby, in a Portobello Road mews occupied by totters until it was taken over by poets and painters. Eventually Nonny introduced me to Mr Trojan. He was even older than she was, and so wizened it was impossible to tell what he had looked like as a youth. His piercing green eyes staring out of his brown skin like fresh buds on an ancient tree, he showed me at Mrs Colman's request how a piece of furniture was artificially "distressed" to give it the right appearance of age. "You can antique anything up." He was quietly proud. "Even buildings. They do it all the time in California." For a Trojan, he had a fine old-fashioned Cockney accent, the Edwardian kind sounding almost upper-class to my modern ear. "Cockney's the original language of London," he said. "It might even be the original language of the whole world, like Romany. Your silly rhyming slang was mainly thought up for American tourists in the 1920s. They had as much rhyming slang over there, though they've forgotten it. But Cockney's the real old cant. Comes from India, like my dad."

"He was in the Indian army?"

"He was born there, same as me. It's us you got to thank for all this." And he waved his hammer in the general direction of the West End. "You're not related are you to Vic Mummery, the speedway star?"

"There's someone else I want you to meet," says old Non.

Again I lie in the cool and comforting arms of my original seductress, though I am no longer so greedy to explore her sexuality. The maturity she has achieved cannot affect her relish for the world. Forty years old, she has the skin and figure of a girl, the assurance of a goddess; her wisdom and kindness are timeless. Kissing and fondling me, she speaks of her life in the world while outside her window the relentlessly harsh traffic of Shepherd's Bush Road gradually fades. Now the years' accumulation of misery and failed dreams, of banished illusions, is washed from me in gentle heat and I become the child I was when she first took me into her. I smell the Livingstone Daisies, the rich roses, the new-cut grass, the maple trees spreading over us. Afterwards I will walk bemused through ornamental gardens, geometric gardens, cottage and rock gardens, watching the sun fall towards a high wall's spikes, the same that speared me when I tried to save Hoppy and was sent here to be introduced to the most exquisite pleasure. I will walk through air still and hot as the split-second after a bomb has dropped, before it begins to tear at you, before it seizes your eyes and tongue and wrenches at your limbs. There are some moments like that and one comes to lust after them. But they are elusive, almost never found in the tranquil security of an ordinary bed. Usually they must be sought in the eye of the cyclone, in the moment before death, in danger and terror, because that is the only way most of us know how to create such moments, but in her wisdom she can do it here, amongst her own domestic things, because she like me has experienced a miracle; like mine, her life was unexpectedly resumed.

I think my lady sings to me for I have the impression of a delicate tune. I sigh and my blood begins to catch fire. It is not, she says, a damaging fire but a fire which heals and replenishes, promising eternal delight. There is a fire which destroys, she tells me: an evil fire created by warlike, depraved and wicked men. Our fire, which struck down at us amongst the flowers, is the creation of the opposite force. Our fire heats a crucible in which female and male principles unite and become impervious, strong perhaps immortal, though the flesh dies.

My lady kisses me. Soft, searing fire on me. It makes me gasp and she laughs. She touches me wherever she desires. I cry out. Her fingers are healing knives which exorcise the past. In my distress she has sought for and found me and I am no longer tired. She brings me another future; she provides another life.

Variable Currents 1970

LIMPLY STONED in the rear upholstery of the Rolls, David Mummery tried to explain to Mary Gasalee and Josef Kiss from beneath the flopping brown brim of his felt hat how the Swinging Sixties' chief appeal was that they allowed grown people to dress up as Cowboys and Indians. "Though it's not Hoppy's style of course."

"Well, you've got the boots, the belt and the jacket." Humorously Mary fingered his buckskin fringes. "And the beads are pretty."

"An outfit only a cissified 'breed might wear to a rodeo." He was serious. "Try signing on at the Bar-20 looking like this and you'd soon find out what the other punchers thought of you." His mood changing, he fell giggling back into beige padded leather.

They were on their way to the Kensington Summer Festival. For different reasons Mr Kiss and Mrs Gasalee had originally been reluctant to accompany Mummery until he insisted on picking them up in the car belonging to his friends Mark Butler and Piers Swineburn, who had partly guaranteed the expenses of the Festival being held in Holland Park which might include appearances from John Lennon and Mick Jagger. For his part in the Festival, the biggest event of its kind to be held in London, Piers Swineburn, Lord Wheldrake, had received his usual publicity. *The News of The World* had nicknamed him "Lord Pot" after he admitted on TV that he smoked marijuana, but his friends called him Worzel. He had cheerfully loaned David his car and driver. Jack the Jock, dressed as if to attend an Apache rain-dance, steered the Rolls out of Ladbroke

Grove. Sitting amongst all the young passengers in their elaborately pretty clothes, Mary remarked on how they reminded her of Fairies, each one a Titania or an Oberon. She and Josef Kiss, like two rather ordinary mallards in a flock of birds of paradise, even enjoyed a puff or two on the joints passed from hand to hand until a broad and benign smile came to Josef Kiss's magnificent lips as they drove slowly beneath the tall green trees of Holland Park Avenue. "I believe I might have discovered an excellent substitute for the ghastly drugs they prescribe me. What are those golden builders doing near mournful ever-weeping Paddington? Standing above the mighty run where Satan the first victory won, where Albion slept beneath the fatal tree. Is it run? Have I served thee well, David?"

"Better than I deserve, Mr Kiss." David was content.

Turning to the young blonde in blue 1920s silk who had boarded at Colville Terrace and introduced herself as Lucy Diamonds Josef Kiss beamed. "I have been his guide through this perilous city for years. I am familiar with every crack in every paving-stone from here to Hornsey, to Harrow, to Hounslow, Hammersmith, Hayes, Ham (East and West), Harold Hill – London's encircled by more aitches than ditches. Houndsditch is both. You know, Lucy, Londoners follow tracks as well-worn as any Lapland reindeer's. Take the lines of retirement. East Enders retire to the south-east coast. South Londoners go to Worthing and Hove. Actonians usually go further west, to Bournemouth, say. Even on their way to their dying grounds they refuse to cross unfamiliar sections of their city."

"That's amazing!" Lucy widened her panda eyes in profound curiosity. "Like ley lines. Is it to do with flying saucers?"

"Being followed by them, you mean?" Mary glanced up.

"That's a thought." In the front seat with tall redheaded Annie swathed in batik on his lap, Mark handed back one of the joints the two of them were rolling almost non-stop. "What is?" Jack's hairy hands were light on the wheel. He was huge, Scottish, a kind of solicitous nanny to his young charges, and had been head roadie for Led Zeppelin and The Yardbirds.

"A thought."

"Being followed by a flying saucer." Mark tried to look in the rearview mirror and almost fell on Jack who amiably pushed him upright.

"More likely a pig." Jack chuckled and watched the road.

"A pig!" Laughing loudly at this notion Mary looked back but saw only Cortinas and Escorts, the occasional Rover. She was fond of pigs.

"The Shire Counties," Annie's accent was Belgravian in its extremity, "are absolutely totally grotty, you know. Don't you think? A sort of squashy dough of privilege surrounding the Big Pie that's London. Right?"

"Or the Big Stew," Lucy offered brightly.

"Or the Big Sausage!" David cackled.

"The Big Toad!" Mark watched Jack blinking to turn left.

"Toad?" David was lost.

"Of Toad Hole. That's where I live."

"Far out!" Josef Kiss uttered an enormously gratified sigh.

The car, a stately and luxurious tumbril of musical-comedy vagabonds, drove through baroque iron gates that once led to Holland House but now approached its ruin, a victim of the War's incendiaries, where on the remains of a stone veranda the first of the day's rock groups was setting up. Already the park's lawns were filling with glorious youth, a few miserably hot policemen and a number of curious locals standing in little knots to stare as much at the audience as at the roadies and musicians. "Testing. One, two, three. Testing. One two, three. Hi, David!" From the platform Worzel Swineburn, Mark's fellow Old Etonian, with a Zapata moustache and Geronimo hair, waved before passing his hand upwards to indicate the perfection of the sky. "Beautiful!"

Helped by Lucy and her curly-haired friend Beth, Josef Kiss emerged unsteadily from the car and adjusted his panama. "Isn't it odd no matter how society changes it continues to be organised by young Americans and old Etonians who clearly know a secret they never reveal? I suspect they learn that the trick of maintaining power is to be as flexible as possible. Before the War they would be sitting down with Kikuyu elders or Pathan khans to enthuse over roasted snakemeat or boiled sheep's eyes, or becoming leaders of the Socialist movement. There are worse ways of achieving the same ends and they are frequently fairly graceful, at least."

Mother will you hear me out. By God, Mother, will you hear me out!

354

Startled, Josef Kiss glances a question at the frowning Mary Gasalee who shakes her head and for a moment they look around for the voices' source but discover no obvious origin. "Perhaps hashish is not after all the answer," he murmurs as she joins him together with Lucy and Beth. "It doesn't dampen anything." *Full of vermin if I had my way I'd put them all up against a wall and shoot them.* Mr Kiss raises an enquiring eyebrow to a glaring policeman. Producing passes the party is allowed through the temporary barriers into tents where bands and their crews prepare. The place smells strongly of patchouli, other aromatic oils, hemp, alcohol and grease. On skimpy sleeveless vests the men sport the faded names and logos of chic rock-and-roll groups, *Love, The Grateful Dead, Fleetwood Mac.* Some have tattoos. Seated on bikes they have wheeled into the marquee, Hell's Angels sweat in denims and leathers, drinking beer from six-packs and scowling at young girls in long tapestry skirts and linen blouses, bandannas and beaded necklaces, who work behind trestle tables serving orange juice and wholefood. *Bloke muck they smear it everywhere and so proud of themselves for it poker kill only way the bastards.*

"Flowing and waving out of the Phoenix and the Sun, out of the Abbey and Hambro Life: on they come! There they are, lad. There they are! Flaring and roaring, the great flags flapping. What do they offer but peace of mind? Yet human nature has not been changed by Insurance. Not a whit." Carelessly Josef Kiss takes another long pull on the pipe he has been offered while refusing Lucy's proffered sugar-cube. She shrugs and pops it into her own mouth. "This is interesting," he continues, looming over the grinning young man who attempts to tune a guitar with help of a small amplifier under his foot. "You think me wiser than I am, I see. Your name is Jamie, am I right? And you dropped out this summer? You were at Sussex University doing English before that? Yes? Thank you, sir. Thank you very much, sir . . ."

Mary looks to David Mummery, who merely shrugs, for he knows it is cool to be neither concerned nor disconcerted.

"Freedom!" Amplified on stage, a musician raises his healthy young fist, giving Josef Kiss something of a turn. "That's all very well."

how can he still be alive after that and they say it's no more than a disappointment I hurt that I hurt that in me I hurt no them I hurt them

"David says you do a mind-reading act, sir." Mark Butler's black skin is given extra vibrancy by the ivory he wears at throat and wrists, his accent is so thoroughly of the ruling class, his stance so deferential, that Josef Kiss, flummoxed, can only smile in silence like some beardless Mr Natural. "We were wondering if you had time to do your act today, sir. We've a little fair, over behind those trees: helter-skelters and so on, mimes, clowns, monocyclists, jugglers, or if you'd care to do half-an-hour this evening while a group's setting up? I mean, we're not trying to –"

"My dear boy." Josef Kiss raises a benevolent hand. "You've a generous spirit. I am not myself today and caution is in abeyance, yet neither am I crazed. This experience is delightfully new to me and if most of the people here are a little naïve, a little arrogant, they are also in the main well-mannered. No doubt if good will were all that were needed to improve the world we should see perfection in a matter of weeks. Yet you'll note that your class remains in control. It can't help itself and therefore this movement, wonderful as it is to enjoy on a summer's day, has as much chance of ringing in the millennium as your Church of England."

"If you've any tips, sir, I'd like to hear what they are. In the meantime, what do you think about my idea?" Mark shifts his weight.

"I'll read their minds for them. Why not? I've read a lot worse. But I warn you, my act was never very popular. Some minds here would be best left unexposed. People adopt all kinds of disguises." With deep approval he draws again on the pipe.

"David says you're the best the business has ever known, sir, so I'm sure we'll all enjoy it. Will Mr Banaji help you?"

"If he can make it away from this afternoon's copy."

Emily Croak felt my prick pinched my boots and is up the stick

Used to ignored warnings, Josef Kiss lifts his panama, moving with amiable dignity from the tent, through the metal barriers, down towards the sound of calliope music. Catching up from behind, Lucy Diamonds tugs his arm with her little hand like a child and fills him with pleasure. He misses his own teenagers who now run a street theatre group in Amsterdam, the hippy mecca, the symbol of an achievable millennium. "I thought I'd stay with you." Lucy requires his security. "I'm really interested in London and the flying saucers and everything."

356

Sensing the child's nervousness, Josef Kiss is nonetheless flattered by her curiosity. "I'm on my way to the fair. Do you like fairs?"

"Some of them. Some of the things." She sounds cautious but begins to skip almost with excitement.

"How old are you?" Having already guessed he wonders what she will reply. "Where did you live before you came to London? I hope you don't mind these questions, Lucy? I need to know a little about my merry-go-round partners."

"I'm seventeen." This is probably untrue. "I was born in Berkhamsted and came to London this spring. I live in Notting Hill and that's where I met David. There's a whole lot of us in Powys Square, it's a Housing Trust place. It's good. David lives round the corner in Colville Terrace. We go to Finch's. Do you know it?"

"I know the gents there very well. The crunching syringes underfoot!" He makes a joke of it, believing it inappropriate to lecture her, to warn her, to discuss the future, though his paternal impulse is to take care of her for he believes young women are the bohemian fallacy's worst victims since so many exploitive young men exist. "And I hate the service. I prefer Hennekey's, further up the hill."

"Me, too." Lucy hugs his arm. "But most of us go to Finch's."

Amongst the youthful crowds many lie on woven blankets, needlework quilts and Afghan rugs, sleeping under the sun, as bright and as proud as the peacocks who remain the park's permanent residents. "This, like Kew, was once a private botanical garden." Mr Kiss pauses beside a bougainvillea. "Lord Holland was a great patron of the arts. His was a decent family, all in all. It's unfair they suffered perhaps the worst damage of the War to an old family seat. The fire here was terrible. A tiny fragment of the house, a few bits of wall and the Orangery were saved. The Library went up. Addison was a guest here, of course. Addison Road was named after him."

"A poet?"

"A man of letters, a satirist, political journalist, a person of some substance. Few today possess some of his qualities, let alone all. Anger is presently given very unsophisticated expression, maybe because the writer is not really in danger now. Look at poor Locke, forced to live in Holland or lose his head! With more to risk, Addison wrote with greater point and ferocity. I can't remember if

357

he lodged in a gatehouse here. There were two. The Troy Court bomb got them. This whole area was a trampled mess after the War, Lucy. You wouldn't recognise it. Only the hardiest trees and shrubs weren't blown apart or crushed under debris. Yet here it is again, London's loveliest park with its wild trees and completely unexpected aspects."

"It seems very nice. I love the birds. And the flowers." She speaks as if to the park's creator.

"You've known better, no doubt, in Berkhamsted?"

"Oh, no!"

the Nazis taught us that people who love Art can be absolutely bestial there's only Vardy left now and she's married to a Pyrtle shot every round at the pub's burglar alarm and it still rang the entire weekend not much of a house really but it's hundreds of years old they were playing chess on it I got a phone call in California saying my grandma had died she never liked me much oil and keep it up his arse I said we'll soon get it ready

At last they reach the main lawn and the fairground with its striped canvas tents, coconut shies, chairoplanes, whips, dodgems and a whole variety of other rides and stalls, its crowds and noise. The profits of the fair will go to charity, which is why Piers Swineburn and his friends got permission to use the park.

hairy quim show her what for little bitch won't say no to James Bond playboy millionaire stud fuck sharp legs

"Wotcher, Jo!" Scratching at his earlobe Mr Kiss turns, conscious of a growing feeling of disgust. "Who's the little lady by your side, then?"

John Fox, the bantamweight hood, incongruous in his Carnaby Street loose-fitting suit, his wide-brimmed hat, his longish hair, still has, for all its moustache of sorts, the face of a thug. His paisley cuffs hold wideboy cufflinks, little roulette wheels, and beside him stands his sister Reeny in her usual shapeless purple but with a white leather bolero, a headband around her bright red hair. In mirror shades, seemingly embarrassed to be found in their company, Kieron Meakin wears a frilly Tom Jones shirt, green loon pants, cowboy boots, a butcherboy cap and a neat beard. "Long time no see." He glances into the middle distance.

"You've a knack for picking 'em Jo-Jo." Reeny Fox cast a lewd eye over the child.

As Josef Kiss looks gravely upon the trio Lucy is surprised to hear issuing from his chest something like a very distant growl; then he clears his throat. "Lucy, these are the Foxes. As unconscious of their doom as the rest of us, no doubt. And this is Kieron Meakin, known to all as Dorian Gray."

Kieron throws back his handsome head and laughs with self-conscious heartiness. "I'm not that bad, Josef."

"Doubtless worse, judging by your company." A bullish, angry snort.

"Still the same snotty bastard you always were." John Fox shrugs his minute but evil shoulders. "Just saying hello. We're here for the music, you know. They say the Stones are playing free later. When's that?"

"Tomorrow, I told you!" Reeny waves an *Evening Standard*. "It's only hippies today. Sunday's the big day, eh, Jo-Jo?" She is as ever oblivious of disapproval. "I wouldn't have thought this psychedelic was your cup of tea, squire." She leers again at Lucy. "Are you all right, love?" Meant to communicate maternal sympathy, her voice is out of practice, for it is several years since she enjoyed any real success as a procuress.

"Oh, come on, Reen!" John is aware as anyone of her lost touch. "Let's have a go on the rifle range. Take care, Josef."

Remaining in place, Mr Kiss fixes Kieron with a steady stare. "Well?"

"I've given it up." Kieron blushes. "Really I have. I don't do nothing like that. I'm straight." He lacks some of his old swagger.

"No longer the jolly highwayman?"

"Leave it out, Jo, please. That's well over."

"How are you earning a living? Where's Patsy?"

At this Kieron relaxes, grinning. "I'm part of the alternative society now. I'm dealing acid and speed. Patsy's still in Chelmsford."

"What is it a tab?" Lucy speaks up and Josef Kiss draws a deep breath, expels it, takes charge of himself and begins to move on, not listening to their exchange but depressed to hear Lucy's laughter; then he allows himself a look back and sees her following him, running as best she can in her long brocade skirt. "He's got a nerve, Mr K!"

"He's a wicked lad." In his relief he almost sings the words.

"Worse in some ways than the Foxes. And much trickier than his brother."

"What's bad about them?" She draws alongside again.

The fairground has absorbed them. They stand near the bright red and yellow railings of the bumper cars listening to the jolly distorted "Sergeant Pepper", the thumps, the screams, the high-pitched laughter, the crackle of the poles on the overhead power like so many miniature electric trams. "Almost everything." With an effort Josef Kiss speaks lightly. "John and Reeny are Bow Foxes. John's brothers are big-time villains. He has neither their nerve nor their blind ferocity, and sticks to the more romantic fringes of crime: smuggling, gun-running, a spot of white-slaving, selling chorus girls to Arabia. Reeny used to provide younger girls to brothels, but now she only does a bit of drug-pushing and whatever else comes up that doesn't take her far from home. She's the laziest of the Foxes. The last time I saw Kieron was in court with his brother Patsy swearing to me he'd have nothing more to do with them."

turtles and all these really incredible sort of intersecting rainbows like a lot of layers in the same cake sort of

"He seemed quite nice." They join the queue for the next spin of the cars. An older black woman turns to smile an apology for her boisterous little girl.

"His charm once worked well for him. He was pretty. But when the charm doesn't do what he wants, he threatens. There are a lot like him. His brother Patsy is merely violent. Or was when he went inside."

"You wouldn't think those people would want to come here if they're not interested in peace and love. You probably think that's silly."

"Fifty percent of the people here," with thoughtful courtesy Josef Kiss helps Lucy into her glorious red and silver car, "are in some way exploiting the others. I believe that's always true. But time will prove me right or wrong." With a vicious twist of the wheel he moves the car out of the general mass in a long, skilful curve bringing him up behind his first victim, a white and green No.666 piloted by two young men with dark curls and ostrich-feather hats who from the rear resemble Edwardian ladies out on a spree, and when the cars collide with a monstrous bump their hats

360

almost fall from their heads as Josef Kiss speeds away thumbing his nose in challenge at his stunned targets. "My prowess in the dodgem ring is legendary," he boasts to the startled girl. "My friend Dandy Banaji and I are probably the world's two greatest dodgers. We are rewarded with free rides at certain funfairs the length and breadth of the country, but have two favourite rinks, the best on three continents. One's in Kew, the other's on the end of Brighton Pier. We have spent whole weeks at both. The flash boys who hop on and off and display their abilities so proudly bow to Dandy and me as their masters!" While he talks he performs complicated manoeuvres, never once being bumped unless it suits him, always achieving his goal. Lucy becomes thrilled and impressed. "I bet you're an ace in a real car, Mr Kiss."

"I've never driven one, Lucy. Would you trust yourself to someone who handled a real car like this?" Seeing David Mummery and Mary Gasalee standing on the sidelines behind the wooden barrier watching him, he exchanges a wave.

heads know and music that's Marrakesh but never sold my arse

"That's his favourite fun." With some relish Mary Gasalee breathes in the burning oil and cheap perfume, the sweet candyfloss and peppermint rock, the sweat of the crowd, the grease of hamburgers and hot dogs, reflecting that the dreamlike quality of a good fair makes her nostalgic for the world she lost. She loves the tanned and dirty faces of gypsies running the stalls, the frank sexuality of the boys and girls enjoying the rides, the incoherent noise of rifle shots, squealing girls and machinery, engines thumping, calliopes gasping, crackling tannoys, distorted music, yelling roustabouts, groaning metal and wood, the crash, the clatter, the range of excited voices as people are hurled through the air, dropped, swept up, spun violently this way and that, whistling and shrieking in voluntary helplessness, trusting their limbs and lives to miscellaneous collections of rods, pistons, chains and wires, to scurrying lads in dirty jeans and torn shirts who leap and dance amongst the whirling cars, the violently coloured wooden animals, their faces as old as Pan, their bodies as hard as Sparta. Mary Gasalee laughs with all her force and David Mummery actually gasps to see her come to life again.

"Dave! Davie!" A huge woman with peroxide hair, wearing a turquoise blouse, black skirt, fishnet stockings and high-heeled shoes, a short Union Jack apron displaying the slogan "England Needs It" and a healthy pink forearm covered in multicoloured plastic Hoop-la rings. shouts at him from the stall behind them. "Dave Mummery! It's Marie Lee!"

Looking in surprise from Mary Gasalee to Marie Lee as if he had up to that moment considered them a single person, David begins to smile. "Haven't you got a greengrocer's shop in Tooting, Marie?"

"I'm helping me Uncle Harry. Come and introduce your friend. Hello, love, don't worry about me. We're old pals. Childhood sweethearts." And she laughs to show she is joking, though David seems to recollect a more profound memory.

"You were together in Mitcham," Mary says. "In the Rocky. You helped look after him."

"Have we got something in common? That's right, love. He was my mum's favourite." Marie lifts her voice to a penetrating squeal. "Bob! Look who's here!"

Her brother turns from where he leans against the central pillar of a quiescent chairoplane. His features have hardened and are lined with dust, but his black eyes gleam as they have since birth while his slicked black hair keeps the same birdlike sheen. He wears a leather jerkin over a plaid shirt, his jeans torn, his white cowboy boots scuffed and oil-stained. A thin cigarette in his lips, Bob recognises Mummery at once, directing towards him the same disdain he showed twenty years ago and amusing Marie. "Still the civil bastard you always was, Bob. What you been up to, Davey? How long you going to be here? Are you with one of them bands? Or are you still doing the writing? I saw your mum, did she tell you, five or six years back. She said you was getting into the papers and stuff. So I looked out for you, but must have missed the ones doing you. Are you rich and famous yet? I've got three kids, two girls and a little tartar of a boy. My husband's running the shop but I stick to the stall. I can't stand being cooped up. This your lady friend?"

"Sort of." Mary shakes the warm red hand. "You don't do this regularly?"

"No. I'm a proper didicoy. Half the fair people live in houses now. The real gypsies are a dying breed."

"Your mum all right? And your dad?" Mummery moves closer

to the Hoop-la stall with its pegged and numbered boards, allowing a group of amiably staggering Hell's Angels to pass.

"Dad's had a bit of trouble with his heart and his eyes and doesn't do the horses anymore but mum's fine, still selling heather and pegs up Ken High Street most days in the summer. It's always been a good pitch. She goes up on the Northern Line. Is your mum okay these days?"

"She's having a rest in Bournemouth. Some family trouble put her under a bit of a strain."

"She was always highly strung." Marie held her tongue.

city loving me loving me city pretty women with their cozy bums fall all over me kiss me make me laugh so nice to me love me love them all pretty pretty women

Taking lazy pleasure from her friend's happiness Mary feels that all she needs is Katharine Hepburn to emerge from behind a sideshow to make her own day perfect. She yawns as if to eat the fairground's thick, hot air.

Rising blood. Who pollutes who stares I saw red really red bright like a light in my head I was the favoured guest of Saladin Lord of Arabia this little cunt'll do me me buy'm some Ten Commandments, some Lucky Mojo Oil, some Auntie Sally Good Luck Oil and I get some Adam and Eve Root and Devil Backbone and then we see who go to Kingston first who make bad headmess soul-sticksman got me now who make blokemuck that London town she stinking with it say it in Italian say it to the Lion here she come no other feeling like her here's the headmess Christ Almighty it hurt me so damn bad pork all leaving Babylon snow geese rising out of Whipsnade Zoo turning into pink flamingos time going consume me time is my nation fire in the head fire in the mind I won't pay it no attention time coming soon who gone sentry you want to know what gone wrong in my soul what got sick in me what harden my heart what harden my artery what harden up me mind get to me brain get to me head making me zombie man looking forward to a night of the living dead selling red silk scarves down the lane baby says give me is there much point in carrying on? Oh, this is really not exactly what I'd come to expect it really is a rotten shame. Bad show not playing the game. She the guide little knickers those eyes got to be right eating ribs in remission pay out me money roots my roots are in pigshit man they're in the stinking muck of Notting Dale when it was swineries, tanneries and a racetrack well it still a fucking racetrack now why feel like doing the derby the fiery bridge it's just a bloody rainbow what's it worth personally put a swordstick through his ribs they can't charge me that and get away with it I can't think why they ever looked him up. Bloody women!

Bloody, bloody, bloody women.

In distress at this unexpected but familiar experience Mary Gasalee, seeking the source of terror, sees John Fox in the crowd arguing with his sister. They have not seen her. Furiously John Fox gives Reeny a handful of coins and Mary wonders why he is in disguise until she sees Kieron and shudders, looking to escape, but then all three have gone blindly by. *Dresden dancers and Coventry queens. Oh, fuck! oh, man!* She is by no means alone in the Land of Dreams. With some relief she smiles. *This is not a well-spun web Mr Kiss. What do you say Mr Kiss? What do you say?*

Are you trying to ape, emulate or parody my style, David? And posing at that as a damned spider. What do you want from me?

Only that you recognise me as the white zombie of Holland Park as you once haunted Norbury. The Red Race has come to the end of its time. Is the Temple still burned down again? The end of the Metropolitan Line why they let the fucking Turks in anyway they favour them that's why well, there's a lot more of us. Open? Did it get has it ever been rebuilt going round and round round and round searching every station seeking out my nation don't find me destination the new generation it isn't just a fashion not just a rhythm not just a pattern more me education and poetic imagination

Why it come through better with a bit of rhyme and metre

"Or do we add that?" Two heads turn enquiringly towards Mary and realising she spoke she shakes her smiling head. "Sorry, I was thinking aloud."

Racist flames I poor cow but nice got no tits that woman is risking too much I don't know how she can keep sane I foresee the demise of the tin can he's been carrying that rubbish bag off and on my bus for the past two weeks and the smell's getting too bloody much for me

things are looking good and black to go down St Saviour's Pimlico and see if I left it there she'll never believe me stripping everything off I wish in these empty nights I could be back in Kerry why did I ever take up such bleak work

It's like the old herb garden in Bishops Park it hasn't changed since Tudor times it's full of lovely plants and huge ancient branches there are patterns everywhere in those leaves I've never seen so many faces this is

*like everything's crystal like stained glass happy enough to sit here with my
tapes playing the voices of dead or absent friends*

   *Tiger tiger burning bright in the forests of the night good times following
the War Doctor O'Rourke would died of heart attack in the hall while
visiting a patient I wonder if she's a nurse she said keep your house cold and
you'll never be short of company thinks I'm gay well let him maybe I am*

   *Mrs M can't run no more death he catch up quick now she no hide she no
get out and she up against it you can't help feeling sorry down she go and
what a fuss it all is now what a noise she making all tears and shouts then
suddenly she quiet suddenly she calm right down like a lamb about to be
slaughtered pouty and passive and though she'll never look death in the face
at least she's stopped fighting him.*

   But this is no more than a holiday. Scrapehead seed.

   "Hey! All right!" A great shout from the denimed Angels; young
black dudes in their big chequered coats and Jimi Hendrix feathered
hats start to clap as through the fairground trot the little Shetland
ponies drawing carts driven by pearly princes and princesses in
miniature pearly suits all sewn with thousands of tiny buttons while
behind them march their bowing Cockney parents and grandparents showing off home districts as aggressively as Angels
displaying their Colours. PEARLY KING OF PIMLICO. PEARLY QUEEN OF
DALSTON. Their proud, knowing, friendly faces look no different
from the gypsies, the travellers, the first settlers who returned to
London after the desolation, drifting in from all the compass points,
bringing their carts to market, some to settle, some to stay on the
outskirts and grow lavender; some to put down roots in Kent and
plant orchards; horse people from India to found the New Troy,
powerful kings and queens, arrogant creators of cities and
dynasties wherever they paused; always travelling on again,
perhaps to the other planets, to the stars; unremarked carriers of
civilisation, showing few signs of it in themselves, but spreading it
like a virus across the universe. Tamers of monsters and fighters of
gods, they force Gog and Magog to kneel. Burned and humbled,
these giants are made to serve the strangers they despise. To a
blaring silver band London's founders march, their cunning
silver-white armour resembling ordinary suits, yet each flashing
plate of it has been taken from creatures of sea-rocks, sandy beds
and shallow salt pools, from the island's estuaries reaching all the
way upriver to London, the sweetest pearl, the largest of all pearls, a

conquering and rapacious pearl, mother of pirates, protectress of bandits, queen of merchants and goddess of soldiers, a miraculous warrior-whore who once threw pearls like a noose around the world but now wonders if the white which flakes her skin is wealth or merely leprosy.

The bells are jingling for the yellow robes of dancing turnip-heads, the wide, wet mouths of angrily non-violent skipping mind-blown palefaces chanting against the coming of Chaos and Old Night, as if a self-comforting moan will do the trick and all Hell repelled by two untuned cymbals whose very meeting is a taste of the eternal cacophony, but here's an easy crowd, drunk and drugged and dopey with the heavy sunshine, the sweet pollen and the ashy heat of glowing caterwauling fun. What comes out of India? Can it be everything? David Mummery is shoved by hard arms and shoulders. "Sorry mate." And Marie's brothers all go by in twisting, finger-snapping parody of the Hare Krishnans, their belts decorated with the moon and the stars of old harness whose particular use they have almost forgotten, the ancient signs which some of their blood still revere, all good Catholics, dancing after the very fanaticism which drove their people here, mocking that which their ancestors most feared, for in flight they became stronger than Israel, laying down a net across the world which only the fractured atom can shred, a spread of roots so fine they can hardly be seen, a web of lanes, like the secret paths which Hereward followed or Robin took through English oaks so thickly grown no ordinary people could make their way yet through which the elven men could skip and dart, these nutbrown forest devils in their Lincoln Green; free travelling folk never driven from houses for they did not know houses until they chose to found them, to split their wattle, to fire their bricks, to chip the stone and cut their thatch. Onto the merry-go-round they go, up on the gay steeds, the lifting red-grinning bright-eyed hard-maned horses; straddling their timber saddles as they begin the old-time waltz, up and down and round and round.

Here's Mary Gasalee, her thick hair flowing like windblown flame, her lips apart in fine delight, her skirts hitched up to her thighs; and here's Josef Kiss, roaring upon a charger which has galloped this course for a hundred years, his hat brim pushed back by the speed of his progress, his white clothes flapping on the very

366

point of transformation as if he might at any time turn into a monstrous fowl, to carry love to every one of us and protect us from evil, and here's David Mummery the cowboy in the prefaded jeans, Buffalo Bill jacket and Clint Eastwood sombrero, only his neckerchief in tune with his earliest dreams to ride a range where Tex Ewalt quoting Shakespeare or discussing the nature of reality and the theories of Kant would teach him to shoot and Hopalong Cassidy would reveal to him the secrets of punching cows while a woman as proud and as straight as any great queen, able to ride and shoot better than most men, would bring out the hero in him. And Lucy Diamonds, feeling the beginnings of the tab's glorification, gulps and giggles and wonders why the beast she mounts is moving his mouth and flexing his legs. Will he ride away with her and if so where? And Leon Applefield in harlequin leather coat cut high at the waist and full in the lapel, a leather butcherboy on his handsome head, with white jeans and two-tone patent-leather shoes, swings aboard a prancing mare to disarm a Scottish lass who can't believe her luck. And Kieron jumps on and so does John Fox who, glancing in disgust at his sister's sugar-coated face, takes a fastidious lick at his own pink cotton candy. And we're all aboard for the Summer Festival, the happiest carousel ride in the history of the town, to beat any Hampstead August or Mitcham Easter or Scrubs, Wandsworth or Putney, or all the heaths and commons left for the travelling shows to set their escapements whirling, to stop Time or make it pass quicker, whatever is required. The waltz grows louder and faster and the air's cool on the faces of riders clinging tight, some with barely checked dismay and others with grins of terrified pleasure, for none expected a merry-go-round to deliver so much speed. They're galloping to high heaven as the world spins round them showing them for a fragment of a second a familiar face, an attractive stranger, some mysterious shape.

"Faster, faster, faster!" Josef Kiss yells like a man who's bartered his soul and is running from the devil. "Faster, my bold, bad steed!" And he leans from his own mount to put a kindly arm around Lucy and deliver a mischievous, a good-hearted kiss upon her cheek, throwing all the anxious fear the acid has alerted back into the crowd so she smiles again wondering at so much beauty and is no longer in danger of falling, for she has a tender guardian who lusts for her to know not his organ but the future. And amongst the scattering of myriad jewelled stars within layer upon layer of reality, in the multiversal vision permitted her merely from exchanging a few shillings for a chemical-soaked sugarloaf Lucy sees the comfortable faces of the crowd embalmed in the entire spectrum of light, clad in unconsuming, life-bringing flame, in colours like unknown but infinitely precious metals, yet there is ordinary dirt in their fingernails, their cheeks have ordinary smears; only their make-up pours and writhes from their flesh, revealing commonplace skin and bone, unchanged people in their variety, with their everyday expressions still, with their small frustrations and great abiding passions; she thinks she could read their minds but would be too afraid.

"Yi-hi-hi-ki-yay!" David Mummery folds one leg over his saddle and wishes he had some rolling tobacco or even a chaw while Mary Gasalee simply delights in the roar that drowns all words, in the music which changes all emotion, in the steady, wave-like movement of her steed carrying her nowhere and away from nothing.

Over at the house, up beyond the trees, the first band of the afternoon begins its lazy rock, lifting its fingers to the crowd, its fists, its confirmation of a heaven on earth. *Lou has seen the deserts of my burned-out brain, she has held me and she's loved me as I cried in pain and she's led me back to sanity and made me whole again, because you love me, don't you Lou. Lou with your long hair, Lou with your long hair, Lou with your long hair hanging down.*

A cheer is raised and now we know the Festival has really begun. More and more people arrive on the grass before the makeshift stage. Life has never been so sweet. John with Yoko wanders about behind the stacks and Mick and Pete and Eric drop in to share the vibes. In their feathers and silks and Indian cottons, in afghans and bell-bottoms and flowers they call themselves the children of the sun. On the tarmac path leading down to the youth hostel Kieron Meakin has hopped off just in time. His beautiful face slowly relaxing into lines giving him the look of a depraved baby, he nods his plumed head to the music while John and Reeny Fox, more awkward because they refused his drugs, tap their feet and follow him, snapping their fingers like obsolete variety performers determined to prove they have lost none of their youthful pep. And anxious to make the most of his remaining looks and charm Kieron turns his back on them, smiling like the god of light himself upon a girl's soft face and a curtain of pure blonde hair.

The band looks ready to play until the end of the world, until the end of time, and its song does not so much finish as fade into introspective guitar breaks and self-involved cross-rhythms with the occasional angry burst from an unconvinced and impatient bass. Already these musicians are of a later generation, their poses no longer spontaneous but studied, remembered from mirrors and the music press, borrowed from old men of thirty who still give blessings on this wonderful high summer. Backstage are almost as many journalists as musicians and crew-members, almost as many photographers as tall, unreadable princesses who in fairy finery have come to fuck a star. Meanwhile the calliope plays the same old waltzes, racing and undulating bearing its elated cargo in a full circle every thirty seconds and David Mummery, escaped from himself at last in his days of dope and hope, throws round his head to shout his pleasure at Josef who holds the hand of his acid child, at Mary who like some Boadicea upon her humiliators, some haughty Elizabeth, some ebullient Nell Gwynn, both stern and joyful, rides her mount with almost the relish she rode her early lovers, never muffling her laughter or her shrieks, with perfect, natural poise. Mummery believes he sees all his friends in the crowd and is looking for his mother when into his field of vision, whirling down the helter-skelter, cackling like a crazed jackdaw, her purple scarves and lavender blouse, her lilac and cornflower skirts and petticoats flapping like frantic signals, her face the epitome of glee, speeds Old Non, utterly alive and thoroughly kicking, and disappears from his sight until the merry-go-round starts to slow. Mary offers her money to the skipping gypsy boy. "I'm staying on!"

They all stay on except Lucy whom Mr Kiss directs to the safe-keeping of Beth and Annie who lie on the grass listening to her revelations, then groaning wood, well-greased machinery and a breathy calliope signal the start of a further circulation.

"Wait boy, wait! I knew this was where you lot'd be! Keep your brakes on." Old Non has found her friends. "I'll get up next to you shall I, Mr Kiss?"

Josef Kiss lifts his hat. "Honoured, Mrs C. You've chosen Nellie." He indicates the scrollwork lettering on her horse's neck as with dignified grace Nonny arranges her tiny body upon the saddle. "This ride had better be good. I'm used to the best."

The merry-go-round begins to turn.

The waltz is picking up, growing less sedate with every gyration. Sitting on the ground Lucy watches them, her eyes like new-born stars, clapping her hands in time, encouraging her friends to join in. David waves to the Black Captain and his wife who stand by a coconut shy. Over on the fringes of the fairground the shrubs and borders are blooming, their scent for a moment cutting through all the others, then he smells grass and oil but rejects the threatening memory of pain and suddenly alert Mary Gasalee leans from her seat to put her hand to his head and kiss him so that he beams. Never before has he enjoyed so much good company or felt so happy with his lot. He starts to whistle to the tune, which becomes "The Emperor Waltz". Overhead the gold of the sun merges with the blue of the sky and the platform tilts and rolls like a long-haul clipper feeling her first thrust into open sea. Taking the reins in her hand Mary stands up in her stirrups, exaggerating the movements of her mount as if it were really alive and she's riding it into infinity.

"Are you happy, Mr Kiss?" Old Nonny shouts at the top of her lungs.

"Never happier, Non. That continuing echo. It doesn't really fade, yet there's a hint or perhaps merely an expectation of decay, which gives me at least some hope of eventual release!"

"Do what, love?"

"I'm happy, Non! Here's both excitement and equilibrium in one. What more could I want? Where else would I find it?"

"It's the waltzes I like. I can't get enough of them. It's all rhumba and jive on the wireless now, isn't it?"

Marie Lee stands beside her Uncle Harry in the Hoop-la stall. "Here you are, love. Six rings for a bob. Six for a shilling, darling. It's all for charity. Very good, sir. Very good. Take what you fancy. Anything off the top shelf. Danny's really speeding that bugger up ain't he? Is he trying to kill them?"

"Safe as houses." Uncle Harry Lee is admiring and winks. "He's doing it because they're your mates." His weathered features crack like a nut to reveal white teeth. "They're enjoying themselves. They stayed on for a second go. Don't the music make you want to dance? Our merry-go-round's taken worse punishment in her day.

Remember the War? The old dear's having the best time of all. I'd swear I've seen her before. Is she a gypsy?"

"Oh, Christ!" David Mummery addresses a loving world. "Don't let it ever stop."

The music drowns all other sound and every misery. David watches the punched paper music sheets drop in folds, one by one, into the box which holds them at the centre of the ride; he waves to Marie's brother, recognising the gnomish face at last as, draining a Carlsberg, Danny steps from his ornamental control cabin, a cone of stillness in the eye of the cyclone, to cast an incurious eye over his cheerful passengers.

"Wine, Women and Song". "Tales of the Vienna Woods". "The Blue Danube". "Morning Leaves". "The Skater's Waltz". "The Cuckoo Waltz". "The London Waltz". "The Artist's Life". The calliope was invented for such tunes. "The Gypsy Baron". gives way again to "The Emperor" and Time does not so much stand still as reach and then repeat its apotheosis. If they could they would all gladly live this instant forever.

PART FIVE
THE ANGERED SPIRIT

This is the book of a city which will not be destroyed, the London of ages past and ages yet to come. It is a record of London as it was before the Blitzkrieg and the V weapons scattered death and ruin and fire about its streets. Much has been written of the London of those bitter times, and the whole world has paid tribute to it. When Mr Churchill told his countrymen that their lot for many a day would be blood and tears, toil and sweat, he spoke with a heartfelt awareness of the awful shape of things to come. He had nothing else to offer, but his countrymen were to find new hope and renewed vigour in the cup of bitterness.

At Dunkirk the soul of a nation was reborn and before long London was to prove to the world that once more England was true to herself. The capital unfurled the banner of courage and became the emblem of the nation's endurance. London bore the full brunt of the Hun's barbarity, and the long nights and days, the terrible nights and days punctuated with horror upon horror, were a challenge answered with a matchless fortitude.

"London can take it," became the common man's cry of defiance to a frustrated foe. "He also serves who only stands and waits," and the Londoner who stood waiting during those holocausts by day and night served his country as bravely as any knight in armour.

375

That Londoner was Mr Standfast, Mr Greatheart, and Mr Valiant in one, a shining figure whose only armour was his good humour. The Londoner, proud Cockney, became a warrior, and London became a battlefield. The little houses that were Home to thousands of Londoners vanished hideously. The streets they loved became unrecognisable. The churches in which they had worshipped, where they had been christened and married and had laid their loved ones, were wrecked. The inns where they had met and talked and laughed together were grim disfigured skeletons. The bricks and mortar which had been their London became ugly heaps of rubble. The Londoner's little world tumbled about him. Gone were the old familiar places.

Arthur Mee's LONDON, *Heart of the Empire, Wonder of the World, 1948.*

The World's End 1985

THEY STROLLED through streets, Josef Kiss and Dandy Banaji, so upwardly mobile there was scarcely a house without the scaffolding, the knocked-through downstairs, the dormer window which indicated the new optimism, the optimism of appreciating capital, replacing the old optimism of ideals which had ceased to be in vogue by the late 70s. Mr Kiss looked about him in resigned astonishment. "I remember when World's End really deserved the name, don't you, Dandy? A church surrounded by rusty corrugated iron, a miserable chip shop, a fly-specked newsagent and a run-down-pub. You could wind up here of a winter evening and the most entertainment was feeling the cold grease forming on your skin while you watched old newspapers blow across the overflow from a blocked drain."

"I lived across there in sleazy Langston Street." Dandy pointed with the umbrella caution had made him bring into this early September day. "Now there's art galleries, Penguin Books, wine shops. And look at those warm red blocks and the bit of greenery. Council flats! I'd be proud to live here now. Christine Keeler does. But I suppose I couldn't afford it. Where are all these wealthy people coming from, old man? That's the mystery."

Mr Kiss was decidedly unmystified and flared his nostrils, a disgusted boar. "From the damned Home Counties, always London's bane, her worst enemies, her potentially deadly parasites. They're driving out most Londoners and taking over our houses, street by street. My sister's Party encourages them in their

377

destructive investments because it helps develop a brutish and disenfranchised unemployed class. Complaining all the time, these half-educated drones are filling up Fulham and Finchley with their stripped pine and snotty little ill-trained babies, taking over our resources, creating ghettos as they go. London will soon cease to be cosmopolitan. Those pale-faced parkers are all the bloody same, Dandy! They should be kept in reservations, limited to South Ken and to Chelsea, not encouraged to move into Clapham and Battersea and God knows where else. You hear them moaning about the people who were born there as if those were the interlopers! It's classic imperialism." He looked appreciatively up at the red towers of World's End as they progressed towards Eel Brook Common. "Think of South Africa, Dandy. Think of Texas. Do you know what these immigrants call black people? Tea-cosies. I know people born in Bow who've had to move as far as Stevenage to find a house they could afford. And who's getting the houses in Bethnal Green, my boy?"

Knowing better than to interrupt his friend in one of his editorials, Dandy merely raised a politely questioning eyebrow.

"Bloody brokers, Dandy, from Haywards Heath and Beacons-field who now have the gall to blame the disruptions they cause on black people! Soft-palmed whites, Dandy, are the real cause of London's trouble. They should be pushed out, or at least made to qualify for residency through paternal origin. Or have to live in Tower Hamlets for three years on probation.

"Keep the bastards in Guildford and Thame dear boy. They stink and they hate cities. They don't belong here. They're trying to turn London into some appalling Dorking. We should set up barriers to check everyone who comes in."

Not entirely sure he was following all this, Dandy Banaji cocked his head on one side as they rounded the dogleg of King's Road and strode on towards the exemplary stronghold of improvement grants, terracotta restorations, BMWs and double-parked Volvo estate cars that was Parsons Green. "Who –?"

"Those scoundrels from the Thatcher belt, Dandy! Thatching this and Thatching that. It's rural blight, old lad. Arcadian spread. It's hideous! They've no right to throw their weight about in London. Give 'em Westminster as a free zone, but draw the line

378

there. The City saw this coming, you know. We were warned about it a hundred years ago!"

Still not really wanting to halt his friend's drift Dandy spoke mildly. "It all sounds a bit like a scenario for an Ealing comedy. *Passport to Pimlico* or *The Napoleon of Notting Hill . . .*"

"I'm not suggesting autonomy, Dandy. I'm merely saying that people who actually live here and were born here should get priority. It's not just the Sloanes and Yuppies. It's stockbrokers, estate agents, investment counsellors . . ." His imaginings nauseated him for a second. "TV producers. There should be a quota."

"Like Indians."

"If you accept that logic you should accept this. The Margaret Thatchers have moved, Dandy, to a private estate in *Dulwich* but they were born in some dreadful part of Kent or Surrey. Repatriate them to begin with. Their new security-guarded estates have been built on the torn-down homes of ordinary Londoners. They have displaced no doubt some decent artisan who opted for voluntary retirement and went unenthusiastically off to Shoreham-by-Sea. The only citadels still unstormed are the ancient council estates, the strongholds of a beleaguered working class, and these they plan to starve out by an active policy which turns them into dangerous slums. Then in the name of slum clearance they'll be able to drive these last defenders out to Harlow or Milton Keynes. What slimy foes we face, these days. With my own sister as one of the leaders!"

They crossed brave, irredeemably bleak Wandsworth Bridge Road to stand on the corner facing Eel Brook Common which, with the coming of the new money, had begun to take on the sheen of a used-car salesman considering the possibilities of retiring to Marbella.

"I knew this part only vaguely," Josef Kiss drew back a cream sleeve, scratched his wrist, then tugged a silver Albert from his waistcoat to consult the old watch it held, "as Beyond World's End. Now they move here, these awful nesters, and set about fencing, as Mummery might put it, our range. Not a mile that way," his stick swung roughly south, "there's a bridge across the water to Putney. We should have held the rotters there. I've no objection to them staying in Barnes. Look at them. Running to fat, to high blood pressure, to delusions of gradeur. Twickenhamites! *Yah*, they cry

379

and *Bye-ee*. Is this the world we wanted, Dandy old scout? The women all pregnant in Laura Ashley pinafores and Mothercare frocks, with shopping bags from 'Notions' or 'Wild Idea' and Habitat smocks. Look at them, Dandy, and tell me I am wrong. And wherever they go the bland standardising merchants follow. W.H.Smith and Marks and Spencer, Wimpey and Rymans, just as their predecessors took the wake of the waggons into the West. Safeway and MacDonald's and the Abbey National, Boots and Our Price, until every street once holding idiosyncratic haberdashers and chaotic hardware stores, little picture-framers and bookbinders and cafés and junk shops, where sometimes you found nothing you wanted and sometimes things you didn't know existed, are all gone, gone, gone! The rates go up and the rents go up and the prices go up until the indigenous population is forced to trek to our city's outskirts, to massive industrial estates by buses which take an age just to get food at those monstrous Asdas because they can no longer even afford to buy groceries in their own territory. Dandy, am I wrong?"

"Well, old boy, I suppose there are benefits." Dandy looked with dismay at the public toilets which were closed down and boarded up, their mock-Tudor windows filled with three-ply. He had been planning to relieve himself there.

"They're coming in from Middlesex, from Surrey, Kent and Essex, from Hertfordshire and Beds. They're swimming in from the Shires to steal the benefits of our life and our work. From Berks and Bucks, they come, timid, prejudiced and mean. We're surrounded by them." Josef Kiss looked with loathing upon a bald young man in a bulky blue sweater and boating trousers escorting an angular young woman with lustreless mousy hair, Clark's shoes and an apologetic summer dress. "Bloodsucking sods!" The couple broke into a rapid walk. He looked upon this rout with the satisfaction of someone who has won only a minor victory in a losing war. "And there isn't even a decent bus or tube comes here. I suppose they all drive." He went to look at the schedule fixed to the 22 stop. "This won't get us to Scrubs Lane in time for tea." He glared along golden New King's Road, past the big plane trees and the boutiques. "Wine bars!"

"I think we'll either have to walk over to Fulham Broadway and get the 28 or take the tube." Dandy wiped his forehead, feeling overdressed in his tweed sports jacket and flannels. "Or I'll stand us a taxi, if you like."

"It would cost over a fiver, dear lad. No, no. The bus will do us." He turned, taking purposeful strides towards Harwood Road's as yet ungentrified grime.

trying different drums well you can't have them clapping four four to the bloody tabla I said and he said he was a Huguenot journalist what's your paper I asked him Dutch treats in old Soho put an urban freeway straight through that was the Italian news from Mr Parrot anyway down at the creche when he came out of it he was as good as blind played Pantalone and did it very well considering it was called Ancient Lights *or the* Rival Mediums *and they were talking of George Robey but they can't cut that deep and not do damage can they my aunty knew she was a lesbian all along but never was prejudiced we weren't in those days you leave me alone and I'll leave you alone was how it went and of course there was always a gloss on it but what's the difference now really football for the family's a bloody joke Godfrey's rather putting it on we feel no city lacks some pleasing sight up a bang bang up a bang bang up a bang bang taking hold of that pain a hammering at it till it assumes a manageable shape barking in Essex barking Babylon all the pork gone soon no more pork no more Babylon up a bang bang up a bang bang up a bang bang the old catholics are the worst who the bloodclot now*

As she descended the steps to the towpath Mary Gasalee noticed how the old cast-iron fences had been painted a cheerful light blue while the studs and struts were gold and red, reminding her of Holborn Viaduct and the colours in fashion when she first came back from the Land of Dreams. The towpath too was well-tended and looked a treat in spite of the inevitable graffiti. Children were no worse than they had been she thought when all they could use was chalk or bulky tins of paint but now they possessed the indelible marker and the spray-can. The wall and corrugated fence around the abandoned gasworks had its fair share of slogans, only a few of them lewd, most of them mysterious. Yet the grass verges were tidy and the canal cleaner than at any time in its long history.

When Josef Kiss had first taken her to Bank Cottage, Mrs Gasalee had arrived with her shoes caked in yellow mud and more than once on the way had been afraid she would fall into the filthy water and be poisoned. Now men and boys fished there and occasionally an elaborately painted barge went by like a scene from *The Water Gypsies*. She smelled the roses almost before the impenetrable yew hedge came in sight and the clucking of hens, barking dogs and mixture of scents reminded her as always of a country farm. Arriving at the little cut she was glad to see the boat still moored in its place but evidently unused for some time, while the freshly painted railings reminded her again of stories heard from Josef and the Scaramanga sisters, almost epic in their telling. Filled suddenly by a delicious sense of occasion, she pulled the string to set the bell ringing on its spring and dogs began their usual riot until round the corner like some benevolent witch bent by her scoliosis but beaming came Beth Scaramanga, her eyes as clear as bluebells, her age worn like a wonderful tapestry. "Mary, little Mary. The roses knew you were coming. They've been lifting up and looking for you all day. Come in, dear. You're early, but it doesn't matter."

Mary basked in the comfort of this gentle and welcoming eccentricity. "You're looking spendid, Miss Beth."

"And as old as the hills, eh? While you never change. You must be fifty by now, Mary."

Mary found no intended flattery. "I'm sixty-three, silly."

"It really is a miracle." Leading Mary down the crazy-paving beside the wrought-iron railings of the kennel, the rich splendour of roses and fresh-cut lawn, of cornflowers, fuchsias, hollyhocks, lupins and snapdragons, the conventional magnificence of the English country garden, Beth arrived at the front door they used now in preference to the kitchen's where a couple of sacks of chicken feed had been placed and where sat the unkennelled cats, a companionable chocolate-point Siamese and two somnolent blue Persians.

"You make me feel years younger, anyway." Mary wanted to hug Beth. "Coming here takes all my cares away."

"Nice of you to say so, dear, though we too have our dramas. Chlo, love, it's Mary."

If undoubtedly her hair was tinted to a shadow of its old glory Chloe had kept much of her stature and retained her queenly presence. Putting down the knife with which she had been cutting sandwiches, she wiped her hands and advanced to embrace Mary. "My dear! I see you're still living with Peter Pan in Never-Never Land!"

Mary laughed. "It's the Land of Dreams as well you know. And a long time ago. But you could pass for Katharine Hepburn, Miss Chlo."

"We were planning to go to Italy this year again, but Beth talked me out of it at the last minute saying she didn't want to be machine-gunned at the airport. We never go by plane, anyway. I said there was more chance of being shot at Harrods. Have you been anywhere, Mary?"

"Only to Scotland, my daughter's, where it rained. Isn't this an awful year? Today's the best so far."

"Oh, I don't know." Beth frowned.

"You're senile, dear. I'll take your things, Mary." And Mrs Gasalee was put in one of the large floral armchairs with her plate and bone china cup ready for her tea.

demolition expert a scorcher when the most dramatic news was from the tennis courts and cricket fields barmy about women and Jesus hated them loved him decided to cycle to Windsor but only got as far as Hampton Court at that gay night club quite a good time following the War but Dr O'Rourke got taken on the common that time done for buggery they said but it was what he was buggering was the point they said he had a parrot tangled up in the chuppah noch say what you like he was a pisher and you talk to me about mama-loshen dropped her in the canal the little minx and teach the lot of them a lesson ws ki bat per mat jao yeh ciz ws ke kam aegi call himself expert of what me say dema a mi spar-dem and that's good enough know what I mean su carne es del color de un calavera blanqueada open-heart surgery he said you'd better check there's one in there first I said einen frohlichen Tag im Bett do you have any broken biscuits no way that sod'll come back in here I don't care how many sixpacks of Extra Strong he's got in his boot baby was you mouth sewed up Miss Freezer and Mr Sebidey you are a very bad habit et vous?

As David Mummery was escorted round the house he paused to look at the fancy chickens, which fascinated him, to greet a couple of dogs. "I thought it was forty-four years." Beth Scaramanga tried to ignore his shaking hand. "But Chlo told me it was forty-five." They were celebrating the anniversary of Josef Kiss's heroic defusing of the unexploded bomb. "Did Ben French get in touch? He phoned to say he couldn't come. He's cut up about something. But the Captain's on his way and Mrs Captain. All our veterans! Are you cold, dear?" He wore a scarf and an overcoat.

"Not much," he said and followed her into the living-room, where he stooped to greet the woman he had loved for his whole adult life. He kissed her on the cheek.

"David." Mary was a little alarmed by his peculiar flush, but said nothing. They paused very briefly in private communion before Beth Scaramanga cried "There's someone else!" just as the bell rang.

"How's Clare?" Mary said.

"Fine. She's working today."

"Look at all those butterflies outside. It's as if they don't go anywhere except here. Have you seen so many in London?"

The newcomers were Mombazhi and Alice Faysha. Guided in by his wife the tiny African displayed his usual beaming embarrassment. Talking about the traffic and the difficulties of parking around Ladbroke Grove, he lifted his hand in a genial, rather vague, salute and entered the shadows of the house. Alice went to hug both Mary and David. "We haven't seen you since I don't know when. We hardly ever get out now, what with our own cats. We're thinking of moving, you know. Brixton's not what it was."

Glad to see them, David shook the Black Captain's delicate hand with all his old enthusiasm. "I'm going to the gate so Beth doesn't have to run back and forth. I'll see you in a minute." David had spoken so Beth could hear his intention and she was grateful, opening the front door wide for him as he passed into the garden and paused to sniff the soft crimson of a Mrs Anita Porteous, admiring the big chocolate-point which slammed its head against his leg to regard him with huge enquiring blue eyes, and he winked at a big silly Cocker who put her face on one side as she sat down, her tail disturbing the dust. He observed that the green paint was new, that the stones were freshly whitewashed and the timbers whitewashed, all doubtless in preparation for this reunion. The thatch too was only three or four years old. His eyes did not always focus properly at present but today everything seemed very clear. He wondered where one found a thatcher in London. He could not imagine this house ever changing or belonging to anyone but the Scaramangas.

Voices came from behind the hedge, the angry music of Mr Kiss in one of his tirades against change, the amiable flute of Dandy Banaji who loved London less critically, perhaps because he had chosen the city as his own. They came round to the gate and in some surprise paused on the other side, the huge whiteclad eccentric with his gloves, cane and panama, the neat, conservative, almost dowdy Indian whose head did not quite reach Josef Kiss's shoulder. David smiled and unlocked the gate.

"You've caught the sun, Mummery. Life treating you well?" The great hand fell upon him with a friendly thump.

"Good afternoon, David." Dandy touched the younger man's sleeve. "Mr Kiss has been ranting against middle-class settlers all the way from Clapham. He blames his sister for every evil."

"You have a point there, dear boy. Well, I'm hungry." With pachydermic purpose he proceeded down the path while behind him Dandy stopped every few steps to admire the roses then ran to catch up reminding David of Dumbo and his friend Timothy Mouse. As they disappeared he heard the phone ringing in the house and a few moments later Chloe called, "Come in David, there's nobody else due. We can start."

the most marvellous caves met him in the French pub years ago could hardly speak a word international demand for London property has reached unprecedented levels in all price ranges dyed her cats pale green, lilac and pink so much for middle-class sensibility the bring and buy Byrds, Beatles, Monkees the singing sixties

"It was Helen." Mary settled herself back on the Liberty's couch. "She'll be along later. Her train was delayed outside Crewe."

"His ambition, his life's work, seems to be to translate the works of T.S. Eliot into prose," remarked Dandy Banaji of Collier, the fashionable wordsmith, and giggled.

"I thought Eliot had already done that," Chloe said, passing.

"I know for a fact," Beth Scaramanga murmured confidentially to Alice Faysha, "that a baby was born in St Mary's that had two faces. One on the front of its head, like normal, the other on the back. But they hush these things up, don't they? Like tails and hair."

London's spine the district of Notting Hill is almost entirely the product of the present generation eight years wasted suspected poltergeists forward I the dunseye jane do chazzer all leave Jerusalem onun bugün yüzmesi lâzum shokran merci all pork going to fry up soon no more pork

Chloe gave David a cup of tea. "Not much voodoo round these parts." She spoke over her shoulder to the Black Captain. "It's hard to get the right supplies. But you wouldn't know anything about that."

"We have some rights," Beth insisted to Josef Kiss. "There's a disenfranchised middle-class which has nothing but cars and pride, which gives the country its working lives and is repaid with some status, a small pension, a little place on the coast. My father came over that bridge five mornings a week. Three weeks summer holidays. We weren't rich. Not really. We'd just always had the houses."

"I was referring to geography, not class, dear Beth. These new immigrants are all of a type. Things have seemed worse, I suppose. Bleak wishes. Cold, small dreams. The power failures. The three-day week. The collapsing pound. The light on only along one side of the street. The oil crisis. But they still seem only poor excuses. I have remained sceptical of government explanations since the Blitz."

"Oh, I remember!" Beth brought him down to the arm of her chair where he balanced with a kind of monumental grace. "You said you'd be back in a few hours and we didn't see you for weeks. The look of you! The things you'd seen!" She spoke for the benefit of Alice Faysha.

"It was the first I fully understood how detached governments become from ordinary people." Mr Kiss made almost a ritual response. "I never went home. I worked in the East End all that time. The carnage was disgusting. Expecting London to collapse, the authorities made no real provision for defence. The ordinary people pulled the city through. They forced the tube stations to give them shelter. Against official disapproval they set up street groups, volunteers, amateur firefighters. It wasn't Churchill or the King of bloody England who kept up our morale. It was men and women whose homes and families were bombed to bits discovering their own resources. But it was hard work. Frequently we had only our bare hands to dig away bricks and concrete and all kinds of filth, trying to find anyone who might still be alive."

"But you could find them, Josef." Chloe smiled. It had been years since they had discussed the reasons for this celebration. "The Great Dante could find 'em. Give us the Great Dante, Jo, for old time's sake."

Mr Kiss was glad to get to his feet, close his eyes and place the tips of his fingers on his forehead. "Tell me sir am I right? Is your left collarbone broken sir and giving you a fair bit of pain? Is a girder resting on your right leg just below the knee? Stop me if I'm wrong madam. Are you somewhere just above the door of this collapsing cellar? Thank you madam. Thank you very much sir." Only David Mummery, moved to tears, did not applaud. "It was the one time my skill ever did anyone any good," said Mr Kiss. "It was as if I'd been specially bred for the Blitz. I could sniff out the injured and ignore the dead. I've not been of much use since."

"You didn't tell us any of this, then." Chloe refilled his cup from the pot she was carrying round. "Though you were horribly angry. We were astonished by the change since you had seemed so jolly and level-headed when you defused our bomb. We were afraid you'd been blown up somewhere else."

"The bombs never seemed to stop pounding out of the sky, one batch after another." Mr Kiss sipped his tea then replaced his cup in its saucer. "Shrapnel flying everywhere, whole districts undulating like heavy seas, tarmac and paving-stones bursting upwards as if to release the hordes of Hell; walls falling in, heat forcing you to the ground, wind dragging flesh from bone, joints from sockets. When it died down you returned to getting what water you could onto the fires and when the fires died down you carried on digging. I hated the Germans but I hated our leaders far more. I wasn't alone in that. People weren't allowed to report how we felt. We were depicted as valiant, chirpy Cockneys, taking our hats off to His Majesty. They didn't say how they were too scared to let any aristocrat go into the East End for fear they'd be torn to pieces, how Churchill's life was in danger from the salt of the earth. They were all the same to us. They hardly got bombed at all and any concern they displayed was a fraud."

Beth shook her head in amused disagreement. "Josef! Not everyone hated Mr Churchill. He was the man we needed, you know."

"They needed us much more, Beth, as cannon fodder. They only started fighting properly when their own districts got bombed. If you had ever tried to drag the mangled, bloody mess, that looked like the muck a butcher discards, from its mother's arms so that she could be carried off to have her legs amputated, you'd have some idea what I meant. It wasn't their wealth or empty sentiment or

387

their deep shelters we hated, it was their disgusting failure of imagination." Mr Kiss paused to finish his tea, took control of himself, apologised.

shall I go for money or friendship this ain't a deal where you're allowed to keep both unnatural lovemaking sad holiday at the Kenilworth my viking

Surprised by his friend's open display of anger David Mummery looked over at the Black Captain, his own saviour, wondering how Mombazhi Faysha would respond, but the African sailorman was oblivious to Mr Kiss's outburst. "Jellied eels in chile vinegar. You can guess what that was like first time!" He raised his eyebrows for Beth Scaramanga's amusement. "And of course the Holborn Empire's gone, along with Mudie's, that used to be on the corner of Museum Street."

"Blasted to bits with all its books," confirmed Josef Kiss, amiable again. "I went there one day to exchange my Sabatini for a Tennyson Jesse and there it was, nothing but a massive crater. Mudie's gas lit up my Holborn winter evenings. Do you remember those round lamps? Even at long distance the Nazis had a knack for burning books. They got the publishing warehouses over in Southwark during the Blitz."

Now he carefully lightens his tone, feeling too much adrenalin building up in him. According to his theory adrenalin had a way of mastering all tranquillisers, enough to put him over the edge.

they murder us with all their complacent follies they are creatures without reason. They are hateful creatures who have only a will to power, a wish to sustain that power at any cost they never hesitate they can merely be checked

David Mummery remembers the first morning he went with Josef Kiss to the Clinic and was surprised by its ordinariness. "The Bedlam Outpatients," Mr Kiss had said. "I pick up my tablets once a week and I keep in touch with all my spies. As doubtless you guessed, very few here are mad, though the tablets can sometimes be of use. We let them patronise us and call us by our first names, the way policemen do when they wish to diminish us. They used to call everyone 'sir' when I was your age. Is that a sign of the times? Are we more democratic? I think not. What a powerful, terrible weapon is liberality in the hands of the English." He taught me, thinks Mummery, a means of surviving, more or less within the system, and passed on the same trick to Mary. The Black Captain came by it himself. Friendships grew outside the Clinic, for patients had much in common. Sometimes even marriages and children result. David met his Clare there though she had told him she would never be Mary Gasalee.

"She played the cello," Alice tells Mary, "at the old Vienna Café. Really lovely classical performer she was. Killed by the Zeppelin raid on Bloomsbury in March 1917. Of course that was nothing like the Blitz. Only a taste of it really. But it killed her, just the same. Just the same as if she'd been in Hiroshima for that matter. Lovely player, my grandad said."

I saw dark grey sand like graphite running through his hour glass. Time is a mad spider. There was fireweed rich upon the rubble, following the lines from Oxford and to Oxford it went all the way home to the slopes of Vesuvius. The Willow Herb burns pink against the dark blue of the coming night

"I was sent regularly," Mummery tells Chloe Scaramanga, "to the Port of London Authority. The street I always walked down was called Seething Lane. I imagined the ground at the time could start to bubble and heave, changing shape, becoming completely unstable, just like in the War. Yet it was such a solid little thoroughfare."

And they never mentioned the looting the predatory armies prowling the city's streets invading parks gardens and houses. There were murders accomplished under cover of the general slaughter. Were we better or worse than our enemies? But the newsreels showed us all doing our bit, fighting on, taking it, defiant and brave in the face of monsters, only some of the monsters we made ourselves. Why did they think it necessary to deceive us when we had proven ourselves so thoroughly? Why couldn't they respect us. What were they afraid of? That the meek might, after all, inherit the Earth?

"Didn't they remind you of burning swords? I believed we were the victims of Heaven itself." Chloe Scaramanga hands round the salmon and cucumber sandwiches. "As if we were being punished. The German planes you could understand but those V-Bombs came from nowhere, like unjust Fate. David, you must tell us how Mr Faysha saved your life. It's only when he's here he'll ever speak of it," she told Alice proudly.

The Yours Truly 1980

CARRYING HER white wine over the lime-green carpet to the ornamental iron table, Mary Gasalee refused her threatening panic until she was sitting down, her back to the engraved glass of The Yours Truly, named for Jack the Ripper, and surreptitiously removing a pill from its case slipped it to her mouth, washing it down with the Graves, though she was supposed not to, and swallowed just in time for here came Judith, still aglow with lust and defiance, on the arm of her handsome beau the clothes designer Leon Applefield, star of screen and Sunday supplement, a great catch and some years her junior, in from the racket of Whitechapel High Street, he in a white linen overcoat and fedora, she in baggy black and red, looking her exotic best. "Mary!"

Judith had left Geoffrey Worrell in 1979, the day she found out about his secretary's pregnancy. Since by then Judith was illustrating half the magazines in Fleet Street, especially *London Town*, there had been no serious problems over the divorce. She had met Leon when Lewis Griffin, now a Tory MP, had sent her down to Applefield's to draw his new dress lines, and they had hardly been apart since. They spent several months in California, the rest of the time in London. Leon's daughter Bianca loved Judith. They owned a massive domestic revival house, once the home of Tillot-Kent the English impressionist, next door to where Josef Kiss rented a room, overlooking East Heath and beyond it Parliament Hill, Highgate Cemetery and Upper Holloway. Judith's hair was streaked to match her clothes while her fashionable make-up made her ageless.

She wore net gloves, daglo stockings and what might have been "Mitsouki", which reminded Mary of Lady Olivia Brooke.

"Another white wine?" Leon was always politely suspicious of Mary. She nodded and smiled, enjoying her friend's pleasure and merely thinking Leon a bit self-involved but less of a bore than Geoffrey. Sitting down on the bench, Judith pulled a red plush chair in closer for Leon. "Remember when we came here looking for your past?"

"And found some of it!" *Only it had been from the Land of Dreams.*

"I'm not sure we're going to be able to do much," said Judith. "Is he here, yet?"

"This meeting was his idea. I said we'd support him any way we could."

"Oh, yes." Judith nodded rapidly. "Of course. He's not here yet, poopsie." Leon Applefield set down the glasses.

"Wine bars in the East End." He removed his coat and folded it expertly, with unconscious care, putting it on the stool beside him. "We came down through Bethnal Green. I couldn't believe it! What's happened to the costers and the Cockneys? I thought Ben was supposed to be here."

"He's on his way." Judith laid a calming hand on Leon, who returned her an appreciative smile and made his shoulders drop, trying to relax. He sipped his Côtes du Rhône. "Still basically an old pub, though, isn't it? I haven't been in this bit of London for years. It's like a theme park!"

Mary was not sure what a theme park was. "Have you seen Katherine Dock and round there? It could be a set from *Oliver*."

"Disneyland," Leon agreed. "Or rather Dickensland. I know. Hello, hello. Here's the man himself." And he rose to greet the tall blond in lumberjack shirt and tight Levi's, cowboy boots and brass-buckled belt, who with his deep blue eyes, square jaw and firm lips resembled a caricature of the All-American hero. Mary thought he should have been wearing a pilot's uniform. He had lived in America and been a Radio Officer for Pan Am among other jobs before settling again in England and becoming a poet. "Hi, Leon." He hugged the elegant designer. Mary regarded them with delighted amusement. They were both beautiful but the combination of styles made her think she had wandered into a comic-strip story, particularly after the man-to-man embrace.

Ben French kissed Mary warmly and Judith more carefully, as if afraid her make-up would come off on his lips.

"I'm buying." Leon went towards the bar. "What is it?"

"Double brandy if you don't mind." He winked at the women as if he were getting away with something. "I need it at the moment. I've just come from the lawyer's office. They're going to try to send me down, apparently." He made an effort to brighten himself up. "Well, as long as it's only a few months I said I don't mind. Where else would you find so much ass?" But he was frightened.

"Well, then, perhaps we won't bother with the petition." Judith lit an elongated cigarette.

"I'll happily reliquish the pleasure." Again Ben winked and reached a demanding hand for one of her menthols.

"It's a bit late for all this." Judith cleared her throat. "I'm giving these up." She put her own cigarette out. "We only heard yesterday, when Mary rang. And she'd only heard Sunday. I suppose you're worried about disease. Why did they arrest you?"

"Because I was there. They've arrested me before. Three big trials in the early seventies. Everyone turned up, then. That was the magazine I was doing. Poetry and short stories they claimed were obscene. I got off. But these days nobody much cares what happens and the police are busting everyone they couldn't get charges to stick on ten years ago. They haven't forgotten! It's not only me. There's comics people, distributors, importers. They're seizing drug books, gay sex manuals, anything they disapprove of. Well, my little shop was chock-a-block, wasn't it? *Dykes on Bikes, Marijuana Papers, Cocaine Casebook, The Lesbian Reader, Gay News,* you name it. They seized the lot and the case goes up to the Old Bailey any day."

"Well, we're all behind you here. I've been phoning people I know." Leon got out a slim leather-covered notebook. "George Melly, John Mortimer, Jonathan Miller, David Bowie. I've still to contact Paul McCartney. They've all promised to do what they can."

"But they think it's my own bloody fault, eh?" Ben guzzled the drink.

"Some do," Leon agreed. "And the papers don't seem very interested, I must say. I was surprised."

"You probably told them I was a poet, Leon, and that was

enough to finish me off." Ben always pretended to aggression. He smiled.

"It's true they don't like that, most of them." Mary had been surprised. "I started calling you a journalist and they perked up a bit."

His smile widening, Ben reached to hug her, sipping the remains of his brandy. "I'm really grateful, believe me. The rats are all scampering out of the old bilges now. And my straight publisher, the bastard, told me he's going to hold off publication of my new poems until after the trial. The only chance I ever had to sell a few!" He laughed, sniffing suddenly as something acted in his nose to make his eyes water. "Oops!" and he dashed for the bathroom. Leon exchanged glances with Judith but Mary failed to understand their significance.

"I wrote to Dandy's friend, Mrs Male," said Judith. "She's in the government. I haven't heard yet."

"I can guess what it'll be though." Mary did not like to mention that Beryl Male was Mr Kiss's sister. "She's been talking a lot about the moral majority lately and she's pretty solidly in the Mrs Whitehouse camp."

"Well, she goes on a lot about liberty for the individual." Leon shrugged. "She was my MP in East Kensington. I voted for her as a matter of fact." And he uttered a silly, self-mocking laugh.

"Walked ten miles in a pair of borrowed boots to do it, did you?" Ben French came back and looked at his empty glass. "What are you, then? Uncle Tom's role model?"

Leon became angry. Then Ben reached to pat his face. "I can't help it. I have this knack of knowing where people are at their weakest."

"You've got a bloody death-wish," said Leon, calming down.

boycott won't do it the toy and fancy weeds god's call ruffians all of them fucker fucker fucker did it down the dump fucker fucker fucker did it down the bog fucker fucker fucker did it down the alley

Josef Kiss, Dandy Banaji and David Mummery entered together in time to break what was left of the tension. Leon rose to buy more drinks. "Sorry I'm late." Dandy was pale with a fury he had not yet made coherent. "Somebody put dog muck through my letterbox this morning. At least, I think it was dog muck. I've lived in that house for – well, you know how long it is, Judith."

"Twenty-five years, at least. Are you talking about Wimbledon?"

"And two Sikh newsagents had their windows smashed. A Bengali got a Molotov cocktail through his front door. Luckily it didn't do much damage. Isn't it wonderful?" He was close to tears. "Hi, Ben."

"Sit here." Ben French shifted his huge body to accommodate Dandy while Mary moved the other way for Josef Kiss. David Mummery brought over a fresh chair and removed some folded sheets of paper from his jacket. "These are copies of the letters I've done and lists of people I've contacted. About you, Ben."

"Helen's written to the papers in case her name might do a bit of good." Mary shrugged. "But they think she's crazy because of her feminist articles. They only seem to take her fiction seriously."

"Have we brought all of this on ourselves?" Josef Kiss took hold of the straight glass of bitter Leon handed him. "My sister's of that opinion. I telephoned her, Ben, for the first time in some while, and was surprised that she was pretty well up on your case. Then she said it was clear it was your own fault since you challenged the authorities. I thought you were merely selling books to customers. Your mistake, Dandy, was to believe the self-approving lies of a powerful class in decline. We are now proving ourselves as thoroughly greedy and rapacious as any other baboon colony." And he subsided while he drank down his pint.

"Well, I can't believe it." Leon was honestly baffled. "I mean it's hardly part of my experience. Especially in California."

"You've joined the upper classes, laddy." Josef Kiss meant no harm. "Your letterbox is safe at least until the government needs rich 'aliens' as scapegoats." He cleared his throat. "I hope it won't come to that. It seems ironic so few of us stood so bravely against Hitler for so long to earn the liberty to express our prejudices and hatred so freely."

"I know what racial prejudice is." Leon felt somehow slighted. "But I really thought things were getting better."

"For you." David Mummery disliked the designer, whom he knew through Lewis Griffin. Tommy Mee was a partner in a couple of Leon's subsidiaries. "The further away from common reality you go, the better things look. Money does that, Leon. The middle classes, no matter where they started from, really hate to

394

hear bad news. They'll discount it or discredit it in any way they can. Being middle-class is accepting this conspiracy of lies. It's like getting the Queen's Speech every day on telly or in *The Times*. When she talks about people from all walks of life she means from the public services, the farms or the forces. That's all they want to know. If the SS came round to drag you away tomorrow, Leon, there's not many would even admit they'd seen it . . ."

"We're not here to discuss Leon's potential discomfort but Ben's immediate danger." Mary broke in not unsympathetically and David calmed down, as he always did for her. "Have you heard from your uncle?"

"He's ill." David was apologetic. "His wife won't admit it. She's a Christian Scientist. I spoke to him on the phone but he was in so much pain he hardly recognised me. I'll go down to see him tomorrow. You understand, don't you Ben, that I won't ask anything of him if it will make him worse."

"I'm overwhelmed as it is. Give the old buffer my best, if he still knows who I am." Ben spread his hands, offering them his bravest grin. "This is the greatest company I've had since 1968. It's like old times."

"Not quite." Josef Kiss was wry. "In 1968 you had a fair chance of winning."

I think I would like to be married to him now, Mary Gasalee decides. *But the chances have never been less good, I suppose.*

"Punk pessimism." Judith is baiting Mr Kiss, not knowing his liking for the new dandyism, which he believes to be the best since the Regency.

"Aha." His own pint emptied Josef Kiss stands to offer a fresh round. "If only I could begin my life with their advantages. Conscious theatricality has always seemed preferable to pious imitation. More wine for all?" He appraised their glasses and ambled away.

They discussed the strategy of Ben's plea; they argued with his solicitor's ideas, his counsel's proposed defence.

"Here's to you, Ben." Josef Kiss put down the tray and lifted his beer in salute. "We survive. We are all veterans of the psychic wars, I think."

How many other women have not survived those fires? In Dresden, in Tokyo, in Vietnam. There's no precedent. We were lucky. Tomorrow we

395

could be unlucky. But Mary smiles with the rest to give Ben courage. She has was awake all night and much of the previous night since Fiona Patterson Hall turned up almost naked on her step and weeping. A former friend of Helen's, Fiona was liked by Mary for her argumentative disposition, her sense of justice and her generosity. Coming home from the Hammersmith Palais Fiona had been raped near Charing Cross Hospital and had come to Mary because she remembered she lived nearby, but she had not wanted Mary to call the police until Mary had chosen to take responsibility. When a decent policewoman had done her best to get a description and a doctor had been called Fiona was still frightened and was now at Mary's flat in Queens Club Gardens, full of Valium in Mary's bed. The policewoman told Mary the chances of catching the man who had worn Rasta locks ("which means almost nothing these days, it's a fashion") were not good. "I don't think he was even from round here." Fiona was further confused because she worked for a civil rights group and had not wanted the police to know the man was black. "They're all beasts, dear, never mind the colour," the policewoman had volunteered. "Men with no other power take it out on women, kids or dogs. They're used to getting whatever they want. This job's terrible for that. What you learn, I mean. I hate them all sometimes, and I'm married to a lovely bloke."

"It can't just be financial," says Leon. "You're not going to tell us you believe in original sin. I thought I left that behind in the Baptists."

"Oh, I believe in it," Mary speaks to escape her inner thoughts, "and I'm not a bit religious, though I sneak into a church occasionally, when they're empty. It's a good way of marshalling your thoughts. But I do believe in original sin, yes."

"And that's the view of the most innocent woman on the face of the earth!" Gratefully Dandy finds himself laughing. He looks at the carpet, wondering why a particular pathway from the bar to the fireplace is so threadbare.

"I've never had some people's opportunities." But Mary doesn't believe everyone to be wicked. "Some people are really and truly bad, Dandy. Horrible minds."

"I'd turn them into pet food," offers Mr Kiss comfortably. "That's this year's slogan for me – 'Can a hooligan and save a kangaroo.' After that we'll work on getting rid of the flies." He is already slightly drunk. "Back to business. Would any of us be useful as character witnesses, Ben?"

dumpy-di-do, dumpy-dumpy-di-do; dumpy-di-do, dumpy-dumpy-di-do
come me mouf darlin come me bottom

"I've got Davie's list of names and I'll give it to the lawyer tomorrow." Drawling, Ben scratches his head, anxious to avoid further talk of his coming trial. "Does anyone want to hear my new poem?"

Mary agrees with Josef and David that Ben is one of the worst poets she has heard, yet it seems unkind at this moment to refuse him his audience and he is already unfolding a thick wad of paper from his shirt pocket. Both sides of the sheets are filled with his small, rounded writing. Even before the poem begins she longs to escape into the Land of Dreams. *Oh, Katharine I could use some common sense. All my women friends have gone bats at the moment.* Just before she left to come here she had been asked by Fiona to talk about her long coma. Mary has only told Helen a little of her dreams. "Why would you want to know about that? It's a fairly common condition, you know. In the ambulance after they got us out they thought I'd been hurt and they hadn't realised it. I was burned on my back. I've still got the scar. But they thought it must be internal, because I fainted almost as soon as I got Helen onto the bed. They did all the tests while I was asleep. I suspected for some time they had changed my face, too. It was fifteen years before I woke up and they said I hadn't aged a day. I thought they were being nice to me but people still think Helen and I are sisters. It's as if I was allowed to have back the lost years. Yet they were surprised, they said, at how sophisticated I was. Well, I'd had some pretty sophisticated company, in the Land of Dreams. They thought I hadn't aged because I'd had no experience. I'd had loads of experience. What do you want to know, love?" Fiona was already sleepy: "Why you woke up, I suppose."

"Things
  in miniature
don't interest me
much.
There's
    a
dullness about

the microcosm.''

Begins Ben French in deadly imitation of the late Pound's tones. They are stuck. Their decent sympathy has brought them to this.

God knows, thinks Josef Kiss, *if there's one thing I'm prepared to thank my sister for it's her refusal to spend our taxes supporting this sweet lad's ego. On the other hand it would be wonderful if day after day their committees had to sit in dusty marble halls listening to the declamations of every experimental novelist and concrete poet applying for Arts Council grants. Each committee should be chaired by my sister and they should have to hear at least three chapters or a small volume of verse.* Imagining his sister's wonderful discomfort, he begins to smile broadly. She would soon beg for a Home Office Under-Secretaryship where all she had to worry about was jockeying crime statistics and showing support for the boys in blue. And the panel members should be made to display paintings, sculpture and tapestries by artists to whom they gave grants, living with them in their own homes for as long as they had their jobs. And performers should perform at their own dinner-parties. And they should personally be hosts to visiting opera stars, which might easily be the worst ordeal of all. He begins speculating cheerfully on the exquisite punishments available within this kind of privatisation process where the individual patron was revived, and when the system might be shown to work with a degree of success. *Instead of the State (namely ourselves) being the patron the panellists are given sufficient funds to support some creative person in their home.* His expression of appreciation for Ben French's awful rhetoric grows fuller as he imagines Sir Nigel Spence having to supply bed and breakfast to Eduardo Paolozzi. Would Art continue to seem such an attractive career? His delight increases when he thinks of his sister becoming landlady to some lunatic construct-maker or an *avant-garde* timpanist so by the time Ben French's meaningful drone reaches a welcome conclusion, Josef Kiss is able to applaud with genuine enthusiasm while Dandy Banaji, looking panicky and betrayed, rises to buy his round, praying closing time comes before Ben determines to entertain his captives further.

"Frankly," he murmurs to his ex-wife's boyfriend as they stand side by side at the unmodernised urinal, "I think he deserves to hang."

"You should try the meat-hook technique." Leon buttons his

fashionable fly. "I learned long ago, as an interacting parent, that you can keep an appearance of interest if you imagine the object of your hatred, the one who is boring you, I mean, hanging by their thumbs from meat-hooks. I first used the technique on a teacher of mine, the sweetest old boy who ever lived, but the most boring bastard in the world. I hated to hurt his feelings, so I hung him up on his meat-hook. Everyone should choose their own method, of course. I'm not saying mine would suit you."

"It'll do until I think of something better." Dandy speaks with deep feeling.

Dr Fadgit's real interest was in modern dance he said he was always forgetting the time he took them both up to Bethnal Green the West End is awakening he said flying squad was interested in taking one had to find five hundred by the next day how else am I going to do that but thieving some more I said how you get it is up to you they said and you tell me coppers aren't bent

Watching Dandy and Leon coming slowly from the Gents Judith does not immediately assume they are discussing her, but when she sees Leon smile a little condescendingly she wonders if he is boasting since Dandy's reaction is one of mild approval and she rises in her seat then resettles herself, unable to rationalise her impulse. She wants Mary as an ally but her old friend is leaning towards Josef Kiss. Judith wonders how old Mr Kiss must be, guessing a good sixty-five but a plump man is always harder to date. Momentarily Judith's grip on her own dream falters and she feels close to terror, then everything falls back into place. Leon settles beside her squeezing her wrist. *Oh, God. This one's got to last.*

"What a miserable grey place London's becoming." Ben French enjoys his fourth double brandy. "When I came back in the mid-sixties things were happening, you know. There was colour everywhere and the people were all good-looking and got excited about what they were doing. Now I might as well be in Wyoming. If they'd let me stay in Wyoming, of course." And he bellows with an infant's zest.

old flame sold me his points or so I thought poppy up the little john down the bloody drain a huge pile of coupons the idea is to put up London's first real scryscraper if that bugger knows about birds then I'm a baboon's aunty karuna khien chan mai kao chai try an orang utan then

"I can remember everything. The Zeppelins, the Blitz, the V-

399

Bombs the lot. I went through them all. I've still got a bit of Zeppelin in my leg and a sliver of shrapnel in my cabinet at home."

Looking across the bar into the other side of the pub Mary sees Old Nonny talking to the publican and remembers who first brought her to The Yours Truly. Her impulse is to wave but she knows Nonny will be flummoxed by so many people and start to show off. Mary remembers Old Nonny taking her to visit the travellers under the motorway at Shepherd's Bush, the camps in Southall and Brixton and the Old Kent Road. "I've a fair bit of gypsy in me," Nonny told her. "I'm on the dark side." Mary had told Nonny how her dad was supposed to be from old Romany stock.

"But then there's all the Africans we've had in London." Non is saying. "Since the seventeenth century there's been thousands living here. All absorbed. I don't know what people mean nowadays. There's a bit of every continent in the world in the average Londoner. That's why this city's a combination of all other cities, too."

Mary watches Nonny leave through the engraved glass door. No gypsy had known her father. Sitting in their elaborate vans, offering her cups of tea and fanciful lies they didn't expect her to believe, they had denied all knowledge of him. They had been suspicious of her or taken her for an easy mark, asking for money, claiming the Ptolemies and the Kings of India as their ancestors and speaking in that same mock-powerless whine affected by alienated peoples everywhere. Never had Mary felt such hard little bodies as those children, like tiny horses pushing against her. Twice they had stolen her handbag and returned it at Non's insistence but wherever she heard of a colony she would conscientiously visit it, though the only gypsies who had ever seriously tried to help her were David's friends, the Lees of Mitcham, who introduced her to travelling gypsies in Kent who in turn took her up to the Appleby Horse Fair in the Cumbrian hills where she searched amongst the vast gathering of traders for one person who might remember her father before he went to Canada. Back in London the bookie Prince Monolulu, wearing a fanciful mixture of African and Arabian clothes, who covered all the major horse races, claimed to know her dad. "He's a very rich man today who raises horses in Ireland. He made his pile in Canada though. I'll find his address." But when she went back to Epsom the next week he had made a mistake. "He worked on the docks for a bit," her grandmother had said, "when the ships were big and plentiful. He joined the army and eventually went to Canada." Nobody had known him at the docks and the army refused to help so she remained disappointed, wishing she had taken time to know him better in the Land of Dreams.

Ascending like an expanding balloon in all her finery, Judith pats Ben on the shoulder. "Good luck. You know where we are. And we'll stay in touch." Leon guiltily unfolds his linen coat and slips it on, removing his expensive hat from the peg.

"Ciao!" Dandy is unable to resist this tiny sarcasm.

"I'll come and see you." Judith assures Mary. "Soon." And a kiss is blown.

"Oh, damn all these bastards." David Mummery sits hunched over his empty wineglass. "What are we going to do about it? I sometimes wish I could get hold of a machine-gun."

"And what would you shoot, Davie?" Ben French rolls back on the bench, almost as drunk as his friend.

"Who cares? Does it matter? The stags in Richmond Park!"

"They'd hate that," says Mary Gasalee.

The Merry Monarch 1977

IF, MUMMERY wrote, I was never able to repay the Black Captain in full, at least I was able to help him at the 1977 Notting Hill Carnival when he was in some danger. I remember waking up on the first morning of the holiday and looking out of my window to see that the police had barricaded both ends of the road. There were youthful uncomfortable coppers everywhere. My friend Ben French had been on his way to see me. I could make out his Ford van at the barrier where an inspector in a Hunnish sort of peaked cap and carrying some sort of swagger-stick was waving him away. I pulled on a pair of trousers and ran downstairs to the street. "That's my car, officer!" I shouted on the spur of the moment. "He's bringing it back to me."

Looking like a Surbiton bank clerk drafted into the SS, the inspector addressed me in a kind of conspiratorial drawl. "I'm awfully sorry, sir. We're not too sure what's happening." He looked anxiously and suspiciously up and down Colville Terrace. "We've been told to expect trouble but we don't know where it's going to come from." It seemed he saw me as a potential ally and I knew then that for him black people were the enemy. I was never so close to so many nervous policemen. After Ben was let through and had parked I said to him, "There's going to be a riot today. I don't feel like staying around."

"Flakey fuzz," he said. "Always bad news." He was back again from the USA where he had run some kind of communications company. He had trained as a radio officer in the RAF and then gone to work for Pan Am but he was also a poet and now ran his own bookshop in Brighton. I only saw him about once every two or three years. At that time he had a deceptively conservative appearance, with very short hair and leisure clothes which were about five years out of fashion. This was because people had frowned at long hair in Wyoming. His face was tanned and he was a great deal fitter than I. It was good to see him apparently so well.

We sat and drank coffee in the window of my kitchen, looking down on the policemen who milled about in honest confusion. There seemed nothing vicious about them but they had been brought in from outlying suburbs and, having no experience of crowds, thought they were going to be slaughtered at any minute by Zulu assegais. In fact the only serious trouble at the Notting Hill Carnival was usually started by jumpy policemen like these, while the local station was notoriously racist so that it suited them to make the most of existing prejudices, particularly when the Kensington and Chelsea Council had been trying to stop the Carnival ever since it had grown into a major West Indian Mardi Gras, attracting people from all over London and from other cities, its parades growing bigger and bigger, the costumes increasingly elaborate; the liveliest and happiest event the city had known since the End-of-the-War street parties. Drafting in hundreds of police reinforcements the local authorities had circulated "ratepayers", a euphemism for respectable white residents, warning that while they had tried to stop the Carnival they had failed and so a riot would not be their fault. It was clear they hoped any trouble would give them the excuse to ban further Carnivals. I had no wish to be beaten up as a result of their political manipulations. Ben agreed to drive us to Hever where as boys we had ridden our bikes, have lunch in a local pub and grow sentimental about old times. It was a perfect day and the sun shone on the American's fantasy that was Hever Castle, a dream of Olde Englande. Like Windsor no real mediaeval castle had ever looked so lovely. It was a splendid, easy day for us, as good as any we had known as lads.

That evening when we got back to town the area seemed fairly quiet. People were wandering about in Ladbroke Grove, sidestreets still had police barriers and Portobello Road was crowded with drinkers who had overflowed from the pubs, but everyone seemed in good humour and I decided I had grown overly suspicious of potential trouble. When Ben had driven home I rang my friend Mary Gasalee to see if she still wanted to come to the Carnival, arranged to meet her mid-morning the next day and went cheerfully to bed, lulled by the distant, pleasant rhythms of reggae and soul.

Around two that morning I was awakened by an increasingly loud buzzing as if an enormous wasp colony had begun to swarm; then came the sound of police sirens, of helicopters passing low overhead, of loud reports. It was as if a full-scale war had broken out in the Notting Hill streets. When I got up and went to look cautiously through the window at Colville Square I saw groups of people being herded about by police armed with riot shields, truncheons and special visored helmets, yet still I took this for an isolated incident until it dawned on me that the buzz had grown to a roar and from not very far away came the crash of breaking glass, of metal smashing against metal, of voices raised in outrage and anger. Then I saw a young black man, his face covered in blood, run past my window with about ten policemen in pursuit. It seemed after all that the authorities were supplying the initiative for the trouble and I was witnessing my first police riot.

That night I was too frightened to leave my flat, but lay awake listening to the sounds of violence. In the morning I walked through the debris to the newsagents in Elgin Crescent where several of the shops were being boarded up by their proprietors, though only one seemed to have been damaged. A mixture of whites, blacks and Indians, chiefly proprietors of the shops, stood about discussing the night's events. The paper I bought had front-page pictures of "rioters" clashing with police, suggesting as usual that the police had been defending themselves against an insensate enemy. I learned bottles had been thrown and a couple of cars turned over but there were no details of how it had started. The surrounding streets were virtually deserted, almost hushed, but there was broken glass everywhere as well as a more general litter always left after a Mardi Gras. A couple of shopkeepers were laughing about the reports of widespread looting, saying anyone was welcome to their stock. I had read that Kensington councillors were warning there must now be a bloodbath while police were claiming they had successfully controlled the mob which had injured several officers.

I walked up an empty Portobello road to Talbot Road and from there to All Saints Road. These days the area does have a tense ghetto atmosphere, but ten years ago there was no line of young black dudes whistling at women and offering dope for sale, making machismo displays and threatening violence to any white. I still had friends I could visit at The Mangrove Café, a sort of unofficial and long-established HQ for the Carnival organisers, one of the few restaurants in the area serving good soul food and where people of any colour could meet. A couple of men I knew slightly told me they were baffled by the night's events when police had suddenly begun to search people for drugs, arrest them on suspicion of being pickpockets or carrying weapons and busting in with truncheons to almost every ordinary celebration.

Inevitably there had been angry protests, exchanges of shoves and blows: "Then the coppers went off their nuts, man," my friend Floyd told me. "They just started hitting everyone. It didn't matter who. Women, kids, you went to ask them what they think they doing and they just hit out at you. It was crazy, right?"

If the unofficial black leaders had not stopped young lads from retaliating things would have grown much worse. I went home urgently and tried to phone Mary but she was already on her way. By the time she arrived a parade had begun and, apart from groups of French and Italian boys evidently there in hope of excitement, everyone else seemed anxious to forget the previous night.

"Just let's enjoy ourselves." Mary was less nervous than I was. She was delighted by the sight of all the floats with their reggae and steel bands and their floral fantasies, the bizarre tableaux, the children's renderings of Heaven and their favourite TV shows all mounted on slow-moving trucks and surrounded by people of every race on earth. We joined a great prancing procession, jogging behind a group of Bird Dancers, sporting the feathers of lyre birds and bower birds and birds of paradise, their huge plumed masks nodding in time to the rhythms of the bands, their great feathery feet reminding me of the Scaramangas' exotic chickens; while behind us came "Zulus" with lion-manes and ostrich headdresses and zebra-striped shields, "Ashanti" dancers with brightly painted wooden masks and decorated rattle-sticks, Rastas and Baptists and Panthers, all taking part in a festival of unification, the time of release and comradeship and purification which everyone looked

405

forward to, black and white, and which brought exotic colour and life to the depressed slums of North Kensington; a great clattering of drums, the steady booming of the basses which made even the most repressed foot want to begin tapping.

Only the police, pale and wary, pacing along the pavements on both sides of the parade, failed to be captured by the spirit of the Carnival. Earlier, police had enjoyed themselves here but there had been far fewer of them. In some places there were today more police than civilians and as we turned up leafy Cambridge Gardens, heading towards Portobello Green, I noticed police with shields and helmets in the shadows under the arches of the motorway and again saw dandified men in sharp coats and panamas, in butcherboy caps and stylish harlequin leather, cooling out their people. I knew how much the police owed to these dandies, who kept far better law and order than any half-panicked paleface looking with nervous hatred from under his helmet.

As we neared the underpass in Portobello Road, where all the fashionable shops are now, I saw a phalanx of armoured police break into a trot pursuing three young French men and some of us dropped out of the parade to call to the police, asking what they had done. When the police paused, the French lads picked up stones and began throwing them and at that moment two black lads came running from another sidestreet, half-a-dozen more riot police at their heels. Here and there scuffles broke out until from their parked buses hundreds more police poured in on us, completely disrupting the parade, smashing into Carnival floats, knocking over little children and women as more and more people began to panic and run while those who attempted to remonstrate with the police were arbitrarily clubbed. Taking Mary's hand, I kept to the side of the wall under the arch and up into Tavistock Road which was still relatively quiet, from there into All Saints Road and The Mangrove whose cool, brightly painted interior seemed a genuine sanctuary. By the time the police did arrive, filling All Saints Road and coming to a stop outside, The Mangrove was full of people considering it a point of honour not to respond to the uniformed men and making a great display of carelessly laughing, joking and drinking our coffee. About a third of us were white, most were couples, and we felt united like the defenders of the Alamo or, as my friend Jon Trux decided, like soldiers at Rourke's Drift awaiting the Zulu attack.

The police were already goading and challenging us, but we carried on as if nothing were happening. At one point Jon Trux and a friend wandered out to ask an inspector where they were from and why they were there. From Weybridge, the inspector said; they had been warned The Mangrove was the nerve-centre of the troublemakers. As far as he knew we were planning civil chaos while we ate our curried goat, our flying fish and yams. When Jon Trux attempted to explain how the police were the ones in a volatile state the inspector, looking from his cowboy boots to his almost waist-length hair, repeated firmly that he was here to make sure we didn't start trouble and advised Jon and the other whites to leave while they could. When this was relayed to us it caused more amusement. "I don't think they'll actually attack," advised Elton Grahame of the *Gleaner*, "but a couple of *Sun* and *Daily Mail* photographers up on the corner of Macgregor Road would really appreciate it if we went for the coppers."

Since the sounds of violence had resumed on all sides of us it seemed safest to stay in The Mangrove with my friends. Mary seemed to be enjoying herself and getting on well with everyone, even though the police line outside was clearly primed for trouble, and some of us started a game of cards. A little later, however, there began one of the most astonishing rituals I have ever witnessed in my experience of many demonstrations and riots in London and Paris since the fifties, for as the people inside The Mangrove dined and talked with considerable style and urbanity the ranks outside continued to build up until through our windows we saw nothing but visored helmets, shields and sticks. Then with apparent spontaneity the police began to beat rhythmically on their shields with their riot clubs, for all the world as if they prepared for battle, apparently trying to challenge us to break ranks and attack them. It was Elton made the joke about our thin red line as we sat smoking an unostentatious joint at his table and waved casually at the police. "The natives are damned restless, what?" he said.

Mary remained amused and surprised, though unfamiliar with Notting Hill's recent history of racist police campaigns against The Mangrove and black activists, but it was soon obvious to her that the police wanted to force into a fight people characterised by the press as anarchist thugs. The monotonous beating of the clubs on the shields all but drowned out the other sounds of desultory violence, of yells, police whistles and sirens. Someone turned up the restaurant's PA so we soon had Bob Marley and Big Youth competing with the police, again reminding me of old John Ford films where C. Aubrey Smith would wind the gramophone and put on a dance record to combat the sound of native drums. It occurred to me that the banging of the shields was to exactly the same rhythm as the ritual clapping of chanting football crowds. Every so often they would fall silent to hold a conference with a senior officer while the unwholesome shapes of reporters and press photographers slunk back and forth like jackals on the edge of expected slaughter; then the sound would begin again. At dusk, when we escorted Mary back towards Colville Terrace and my flat, they had not stopped. We watched the rest of the events on TV which gave the impression that half London was erupting and the entire black population had risen in arms intending to slaughter all policemen. Imperialism doesn't die, I thought; it doesn't even change its approach very much. The police had gone berserk, like soldiers at Amritsar. Even seasoned Metropolitan officers would eventually agree on that.

I took Mary to Notting Hill Gate so she could get a bus home to Hammersmith and as we walked up the posh residential section of Portobello Road we saw hundreds of people still heading down the hill, most of them drunken white continental youths presumably hoping to take part in any fighting still available. One group ran after a pair of constables until they saw a whole mob of police emerge from a nearby mews.

To reassure Mary I would not get into trouble I told her of my instinct for avoiding really bad violence even though I had been beaten up by the police here and abroad several times merely for accidentally wandering into their path. But as I strolled home, keeping to the more salubrious side of Ladbroke Grove with its big houses and crowded flowery gardens, I heard pounding boots behind me; a fresh detachment of riot police had been released from a bus parked in Arundel Gardens and was running down into Ladbroke Grove towards the intersection at Elgin Crescent where the buses turn. The remains of a parade, two floats with torn coverings and ripped bunting, had stalled and a bus was stuck behind them. A few West Indians were standing around the floats and explaining what was happening but when they saw the column of visored men pouring down the hill several of them simply broke and ran and others got hastily back into the trucks. I recognised one of the people still on a float, there with his lovely buxom wife Alice who had been very kind to me during one of my bad depressions. The man I'd always called the Black Captain was looking vaguely around as if wondering if he should try to get away. His wife had nicknamed him the Captain because he had been a sailor when they married. The Black Captain was in fact so small he was often mistaken for a child, though he was at least fifty-five. I think I understood the danger more clearly than he did and found that I too was running towards the floats, with the idea of asking them back to Colville Terrace, a few minutes away, but the police reached the flatbed trucks first and struck them with massive force, instantly surrounding them. I saw them drag a driver from his cab, saw the Captain put his arm round his wife and try to push through the circle of police but I think this action spurred them to further terror, for it was not the first time I had observed police become murderous upon realising a black man had a white woman friend. By no means a brave person, I am proud of whatever instinct made me force my way through the heavy serge uniforms shouting "Press" at the top of my lungs and waving my expired NUJ card. Whether the press card or my authoritative middle-class tone, to which the police are conditioned to respond, worked I don't know but I managed to gain the float at the moment a mob of visored men hauled themselves up over the edge and fell upon my friend to Alice's outraged screams. Pulling myself onto the truck I cried: "Stop that. You men! I say, stop that at once."

They heard me. They paused. They looked from me to their inspector. "What's going on, chaps?" He had seen my press card. "Was the lady being attacked?"

"This gentleman is Sir Mombazhi Faysha, the Bardonese Ambassador," I said, "and the lady happens to be his wife."

The inspector directed a look of fury at his brightly polished shoes. "I'm very sorry, sir. You understand my men are under considerable pressure. Fall back, chaps, while we sort this out." And he offered the Black Captain a reluctant salute. I helped Mombazhi Faysha and Alice down. Everyone else had drifted off and the floats were empty. They appeared to have released the driver of the float but now the bus driver began to blow his horn and half his passengers were in the street shouting angrily at the police, in no doubt about the cause of the obstruction. Mombazhi was holding his cut head. "You bastards!" Alice was still uncontrollably angry. "You bastards. You terrible bastards. My husband defended this country in the War. He saved people in the Blitz. You are wicked, horrible men!"

"It was an honest mistake, madam." The inspector barely disguised his hatred for her. She looked at them all, trying to read the numbers deliberately hidden under capes.

"You cowards!" said Alice.

"They never change." One of the women from the bus sniffed with hearty contempt. "I'll sing you a song and it won't take long. All coppers are bastards."

Unused to such responses in the Home Counties, the inspector began to look visibly shocked. He and his men had automatically assumed they were there to defend grateful white residents. "You ought to go back where you bloody came from," added the woman. "Didn't they teach you nothing at Hendon College, dear?"

I helped Mombazhi and Alice up Elgin Crescent and we stopped at The Merry Monarch for a drink before going indoors. The pub was packed with black youngsters talking fiercely at the top of their voices about their plans for the pigs, but it was the quiet men in corners, or leaning on the bars, who would make the decisions. They had the air of men like Hopalong Cassidy, Tex Ewalt, Red Connors or Johnny Nelson who said little, sized up a situation and took only what action was necessary when it would be most effective. They would be able to control the swaggering youths, but I doubted there was anyone of similar calibre on the police side.

"My God," Mombazhi tried to control his trembling hand and lift his Guinness, "that was truly frightening. I didn't know what was happening. Then they were all over us."

"They're vermin." Alice remained cold and angry. "Even worse than in my day when most of them left women alone but now they feel they can do and say anything their filthy minds come up with!"

During the demonstrations of the sixties and seventies women were always more at risk from policemen who grabbed their breasts and genitals at any opportunity and used the foulest descriptions of what they would like to do to them. In court in the

City of London one day after a demonstration outside the Old Bailey in which friends had been involved, I heard one young woman tell magistrates what the police had said and done to her and consequently got roundly ticked off by the female magistrate who said that she hoped the girl didn't use that kind of language at home and offered an extra reprimand, a harsher sentence, merely for telling the court the truth. The same jolly bobby who appeals to everyone's sense of fair play and community spirit can, when that technique fails, resort swiftly to brute force.

"That was as bad as what happened in Germany before the War." Alice paid attention to her husband's wounds. "It's what you see in those newsreels. What was the point of fighting them?"

"We didn't," I said. "We just defended ourselves when they attacked us."

"That's not fair." Mombazhi was recovering. "You're too young to remember. We did something when Poland was invaded. We weren't as bad as you youngsters like to make out and there was a good spirit during the war, too, no colour bar, hardly anywhere. The Americans noticed that. Alice and I couldn't have got married in America, not easily."

"Now we're running behind the times," I said. "The class system is the most enduring aspect of our culture and will strangle us in the end, sustaining itself when the whole bloody country is in ruins."

"Well." Mombazhi looked on the bright side. "Even ruins don't last forever."

I remembered the Streatham V2.

Lying on my back in what had been someone's garden I watched the rubble falling around me, striking the ground and sending up clods of earth, dust and more debris while walls kept collapsing. I could not move. I was in a sort of shallow grave, my face pressed against clumps of pale foxgloves, pink and golden. I can smell them now, as I write. I watched the massive tidal waves of white and grey smoke smothering us all as we lay on a beach at the edge of the world and then felt the planet being blown apart around me until I was on the only surviving fragment, drifting in space. The smoke and dust were very hot and hurt my nostrils and lungs, they clogged my throat so that it was almost impossible to breathe. I was trapped under something not very heavy but I couldn't get my legs free. I think it was part of a body. The smoke rolled closer and gradually the rubble came to rest. There was an odd silence now, but the smoke was denser than ever. I saw this shape drifting in it and at first from the way it moved thought it must be some kind of signal balloon for it bobbed almost at random on the air currents, but it was elongated, the shape of a boy. For a second I had the idea it was my own ghost breaking free of my body and trying to find a way of reaching Heaven but then the shadow dropped and rose again and it was a human figure which had picked up a much larger man very easily in one hand, then stooped again and in the other hand now held the limp body of a woman; then it floated up a foot or two above the ground and drifted back into the smoke.

Like everyone I was used to the idea of being killed, so I suppose I took this vision for a hint of a world to come. Then the figure, empty-handed again, drifted back and I saw him hovering over me, smiling encouragement and reaching out his tiny hands. He was familiar to me. I called him Marzipan the Magician and had seen him briefly once before, only a mile or two from where I now lay. Although hatless he was dressed in a sailor's uniform and was black as a stoker with the most benign expression I've ever seen on a human face. I think I was crying and supposed myself to be hallucinating since I was an imaginative child and had already seen ghosts.

Drifting down until he was a few inches above the ground the black sailor touched me, asking if I was hurt, and I said that I didn't think I was.

"There's an unexploded incendiary or two just behind you." His accent was exotic, warm and extraordinarily reassuring to me. "We're not sure when they're likely to go off. Can you feel your feet and fingers?"

I told him they hurt a bit but I thought they were all right and watched him roll something off my legs, felt his hands as gently they inspected my limbs, my ribs, my head. I grew sleepy, perhaps because of the smoke, then he lifted me up and actually flew with me. He had enormous strength, for I wasn't much lighter than him. A bushman from one of the South African tribes, he was here on leave visiting a friend in Brixton and had been out shopping with her when the two V-Bombs had dropped. She had mild concussion. He had remained behind to help the living get out of the wreckage and had already saved my mother but she remembers little about it saying I must have imagined him flying. "Because of Peter Pan at Christmas."

I remember a phrase, however, which I thought at the time was Romany: *Ek ardmi upa si gill gia!*

Many years later, when I met him again, I asked the Black Captain if he knew what it meant. I did not tell him the circumstances in which I had heard it. He was very amused by it. "It's what they call low Hindustani. They use it in ports and on ships all around the Indian coasts. You have to know a bit when you're working those particular routes. It means 'a man has fallen from aloft'."

I have never told him where I heard the phrase and I suppose I shall never know who spoke it. He had a way of blocking my questions on the subject.

I am however absolutely certain the Black Captain flew. I know that if he had not been able to fly he could not have found me before the other bombs went off several minutes later. He has never denied what he did but he also refuses to confirm it.

"If it did occur then it was a miracle," he told me once, "and miracles tend to be over very quickly, sometimes before anyone realises what has happened."

With his usual kindness, the Black Captain laughed at my confusion.

The Axe and Block 1969

STROLLING with tranquil relish through Brick Lane's crowded market stalls, Mr Kiss remarked how Sikhs and Bengalis had taken over traditional Jewish trades. Bakers and butchers, pawnbrokers and tailors called Goldstein, Grodzinski, Litvak or Pashofski, were now called Das, Patel, Khan or Singh, but the business had the same element of exoticism to liven up the drab, decrepit Whitechapel streets where Cockney mock-auctioneers, watch-sellers, Crown and Anchor operators, china salesmen, jellied-eel vendors, religious cranks, haggling octogenarians and sharp-eyed children filled every available space; little cafés blossomed in gaps between houses and bagels sold next to kebabs or pie and mash while someone fried latkes opposite a Chinese take-away. Ignoring stalls piled with bolts of cloth, ladies dresses, suits, cheap toys, mysterious confectionery, school books, gramophone records, hideously gilded oriental ornaments, Josef Kiss paused beside a mass of cheap Italianate bijouterie, waiting until David Mummery and Dandy Banaji caught up with him. "This proves my point. Bad taste is universal while good taste is almost always specific. This stuff is enjoyed across every continent of the globe. It's discovered in Los Angeles and Chicago, Paris and Hamburg, Tel Aviv and Baghdad, Bombay and Peking, Sydney and Tokyo. The sunburst clock, for instance. Wherever you go you'll always find it. But Arab good taste, my friends, is unique. Witness their talent for architecture. As is English, French or American." He picked up a jingling gold-painted photograph tree. "This would sell as well up the Amazon, in Papua, on the Gold Coast, in Uxbridge, St Denise, Oxnard or Skokie." He added a lamp shaped like a rearing horse, an ugly cat. "The triumph of the tabloid, the soap opera and the blockbuster, indeed the dictator and the demagogue, are all explained! How much?" he enquired of the Sikh proprietor, who frowned at him suspiciously. "Fifteen pounds the lot, it's all legit." The Sikh rearranged the photograph tree next to a silvered teapot. "That's less than they cost me, mate." And was relieved rather than offended when Mr Kiss, as if in confirmation of his pronouncements, returned his collection to the stall and continued on.

hum pati uss ko dia that yachna so show me what is schlock und zu verkündigen das angenehme Jahr des Herrn him obeahman the oldhead tickle me fancy I'll give him tickle me fancy

"A character witness! Ha!" said Mr Kiss.

"Kieron?" Mummery brought his attention back to his friend. Crowds as dense as this one made him sweat with discomfort.

"The jolly highwayman and his brother, yes. For some while I'd wondered how he got his expensive clothing and cars." Mr Kiss stood in a doorway waiting for Dandy Banaji to push through the mass of people and reach them. "Clearly he wasn't involved in ordinary thieving yet Mary said Kieron boasted of his romantic adventures on Hampstead Heath. She thought he was selling cars. Eventually they were caught. But it took years. Some off-duty policemen laid a trap for them at Jack Straw's Castle, I think, or the Spaniard's Inn. Patsy's still in hospital. There's lots of casual encounters on the Heath at night as you know. Kieron, the pretty one, lured them out, then Patsy beat them up and robbed them, frequently with Kieron's help."

"I can't believe Kieron would be so vicious." David waved to Dandy.

"He said he hated homosexuals because they always chatted him up but I remember that night some years ago in Berwick Street when you called out to him and he winked and told us to keep quiet. A moment later we saw him arm-in-arm with an old businessman. Apparently he was doing the same thing then, though with more risk. Since Wolfenden a lot of homosexual men lost their caution. Kieron reckoned he and Patsy pulled in a couple of hundred pounds a day on average."

Having enjoyed Kieron's company and relied on him as a willing link with the underworld, Mummery was depressed. There was no denying his crime was distasteful. Dandy joined them as Mr Kiss was finishing. "So it was stand and refuse to deliver." The Indian wore a black seaman's sweater and jeans and seemed uncomfortable in this unnaturally casual clothing. He did not feel much sympathy for Kieron's victims. David felt overdressed in his white suit with its flared and cuffed trousers while Mr Kiss, as usual, wore his linen and panama with casual pleasure. The styles of the sixties had not caused him to alter his appearance, but now he no longer appeared eccentric. He led them from Brick Lane and into Whitechapel High Street which seemed almost deserted in comparison. "He starts at the Old Bailey on Monday. Mary was almost a mother to him for ages and she went to see him. Apparently he's denied nothing because he hates, he says, queers and that justifies his actions. I've known burglars who excused their crimes as long as they were committed against people they despised – stockbrokers, Jews, heiresses, darkies. He said he was a victim of the War when he was on the King's Cross Meat Rack supporting, he said, his family by selling his bottom to horrible old men for a few bob."

"The Meat Rack couldn't have existed when he was a boy." Mummery said. "He's my age. It's recent. It's gone on around those Soho amusement arcades since Wolfenden."

"True," said Mr Kiss, pausing again, to stare with horror at the rebuilt skyscrapers confronting him. "Hardworking women have been driven off the streets but little boys are everywhere displayed. What have you heard about his interest with that property development business. Do John and Reeny still want to get hold of Bank Cottage?"

"The gasworks is closing down." Mummery pulled a map from his pocket. "I'm not sure when, though. It was in the local paper."

"So now the land's a choice area for redevelopment." Through sunshine made magical with oil and fumes, Dandy headed East with his friends in tow, noting how the rebuilt, unfeatured monuments of Whitechapel were given at least a shred of sightliness by the haze. "This fits in with the schemes to privatise the Westway bays and make the place a fashionable shopping-arcade. Can South Kensington speculation work in North Kensington?"

"They'll not take Bank Cottage!" Josef Kiss directed them to the traffic lights and the pedestrian crossing. "Nor drive out the

Scaramangas! They've had letters from the council alleging complaints about their fowls; alleging rats and other vermin, alleging unsanitary goings-on of every sort, and we all know this is untrue. The accuser's letterhead revealed everything. The John Fox Partnership indeed! That little sniveller's probably the entire partnership. And as for the disputed deeds, they have rights going back before Magna Carta. They'll need more than a couple of Housing Trusts demanding land for the overcrowded slums, since the gasworks and the railway between them can settle that entire problem. The Foxes have undoubtedly overstepped the mark at last!"

"The Scaramangas feel the council may be able to evict them." Dandy paused again, baffled by the newly arranged streets, broad and featureless, and consulted Mummery's map.

"Not while there's breath in my body." Mr Kiss was firm.

"How will you stop them?" Mummery was curious.

"I have some ideas. If everything else fails I shall have to mesmerise them. When Mary brought Kieron to our last reunion I warned her it was a mistake, but then she was besotted with him. I could see his fingers counting the potential profits. Without doubt he told the Foxes of Bank Cottage."

Heading for the Tower, they crossed through sluggish Sunday traffic to enter Leman Street. Mummery nodded towards a derelict warehouse. "That was one of my early publishers. Mary worked there. My first job was over that way, closer to the Mint, off Seething Lane. These rebuilt streets are even more depressing now. The Co-op's pretty much all that's left." He waved at the marble and stone headquarters whose motto, "Labor and Wait", took them back to more optimistic times. A door or two from this, with fresh paint and clean repointing, new window-frames and brass that was almost incongruous, as if Time itself had begun to lose shape and allow a little of everything into the same period, was a Georgian house, complete with window-boxes. Mummery offered it a disapproving eye. "Leman Street was all theatres years ago. It's fallen on hard times since it attracted its Italian population. Perhaps the old Commedia dell'Arte plays are performed in secret courts and upstairs rooms once you go through Half Moon Passage." They wandered past an ugly police station of the kind featured in depressing English thrillers of the forties, to East

Smithfield, skirting St Katharine's Dock where Josef Kiss refused he said to lay eyes on the site of any restaurant to be called The Charles Dickens and entered Wapping High Street, which current- ly consisted of half-demolished warehouses and corrugated-iron fences. They stood in a small group at the locked gates of Wapping Old Stairs where once the immigrants came in their thousands, many thinking they had reached America. "And now, of course," said Mr Kiss, "the Americans are reaching them. Such are the virtues of patience."

When reluctantly Mr Kiss allowed Dandy Banaji to talk them into entering the premises of a large Victorian pub near Tower Bridge, he was relieved to find the interior largely unaltered though he insisted that the name, The Axe and Block, was new. "Doubt- less attracting bloodthirsty tourists who come to gawp at those awful instruments of death our ancestors spent so much of their ingenuity upon."

The pub's huge cast-iron roof supports were decorated in Stuart style with cherubs, elementals, plants and animals all in delicate plaster. A jukebox exuded the bass part at least of the latest Beatles song and because it was Sunday the place was crowded with local men and women standing at bars with pints and ports and lemons, rums and Ribenas, lagers and limes, or leaning against the great arches of the main room, playing slot-machines, pinballs, darts and bar billiards as the smell of beef pervaded everything while plates of roast potatoes and cabbage, Yorkshire pudding and horseradish sauce were hurried to waiting tables. Without asking their prefer- ences Josef Kiss ordered three pints in straight glasses, bringing them in his big hands to where they stood at the window looking into a Thames which in the peculiar light shone like polished lead."Not a ship in sight," complained Mr Kiss, "save those forever anchored. Sundays or weekdays, ships were always on the move here. Cargoes from the world, passenger ships, too. What on earth are we to do with all these unused docks and warehouses?"

"Make them into airship posts," offered Mummery with predictable alacrity. "There's an article in *The Illustrated London News* about how they'll provide cheaper and faster cargoes. It makes sense. We've the technology to build much better ships than, say, the *Graf Zeppelin*."

"Which would blow us all to kingdom come!" Dandy Banaji

pursed his lips above his glass. "I remember the R101 being expected in India and never getting further than France. Everyone was killed."

lae orid she' hilw' giddain min fadlak hayeza hayesaen fucking megilla

Too often bored by Mummery's obsession, Josef Kiss changed the subject. "We planned to discuss the defence of Bank Cottage."

"What do the solicitors say?" Dandy looked up at barren skies.

"There's nothing anyone can ever do except appeal against a compulsory purchase order. This means the Foxes have at least one friend on the Council. The Scaramangas are disputing a claim that their smallholding harbours vermin endangering surrounding residents. There are no vermin to speak of at Bank Cottage, and precious few surrounding residents. Counsel's also examining the wording of the original Royal Grant of the land. The sisters meanwhile are at their wits' end and convinced they're to be thrown out. Anything we can do will help. I had wondered about paying a visit to John and Reeny."

His glass empty, Dandy gave his attention to the bar. "No time like the present. They're only up the road, after all, and Reeny always holds her At Homes on a Sunday afternoon."

butter cross gone down Dalston and then he said the bus was no good where the fuck does it go down the bloody drain I said boozed out of his brain of course and no way could he get it up which was a small mercy at least

Feeling his nerve failing, Mummery drank more than the others. By closing time they had wandered up to Tower Hill, found a taxi letting off a tourist near the White Tower and ordered it towards Gunmaker's Lane in Bow where Reeny, her husband and her brother shared a decrepit 18th-century merchant's house whose back fell sheer to the Grand Union Canal. As the taxi drew up in the gloomy street Josef Kiss instructed his friends to let him do the greater part of the talking and they agreed, Dandy speculating briefly if the Foxes merely wanted Bank Cottage for their own retirement since they already lived near a canal, then opened the rotten oak gate which had once been dark green to advance along the broken paving stones and a flight of steps whose railings were missing or falling out, up to the peeled wood of the front door where John had fixed a cheap white bellpush which Mr Kiss pressed with his umbrella. It was not long before Reeny Fox, clad in a kind of Hawaiian muu-muu made of purple and green deckchair fabric, greeted them glass in hand without surprise. "Long time no see. There's some lovely girls here today. You'll get on like ninepence." They followed her through passages of mouldy, shrinking wall-paper on which various posters and magazine pictures had been pinned. Faces even more ravaged than Reeny's peered at them from every shadow. "Darlings! This is Jo-jo, Davey and Dandy. Wonderful old pals of mine. We've done everything together, haven't we, boys?" Lifting a scarred chin towards Mr Kiss she blew a mixture of tobacco and gin fumes into his face.

"John here?" Mummery remained terrified.

"He'll be glad to see you, lovey. And Kieron, of course. Is that why you're here?"

"Kieron's out?" Dandy was surprised.

"Bloody murderous bail. John and me got stuck for it. We owe him a favour. Isn't it awful what they're doing to him? And all for a couple of bloody brownhatters. Makes you wonder."

Heavily painted women looking as if they had arrived shortly after the fall of Berlin waved and patted mouldering velvet sofas or Indian cushions. With lessening panic Mummery gave in to his sense of familiarity, feeling he had been invited to spend the afternoon in one of the lesser circles of Hell, and even accepted from Reeny a glass of punch tasting like methylated spirits. "It's what Georgie brought," she indicated a man lying prone and pale green under the feet of two ladies playing Happy Families. "He's a chemist or something in a hospital. It's pure, he said. So drink up."

"Well," Mummery was almost amused, "nothing's changed in ten years. The last time I was here she'd managed to get an entire detachment of the Royal Canadian Mounted Police in, plus half the chorus from the Windmill or whatever it's called now. She's still something of a catalyst. I'd thought this was long over."

They made their way through room after room filled with people in various states of drug euphoria or inebriation while Reeny put her fingers to her lips and beckoned them to follow her up another flight of steps whose carpets were actually worm-eaten. Largely untouched since the 19th century, the house was lit chiefly by gas globes with a few electric lamps strung on wires. Reaching a landing Reeny tapped in code, opened the door and brought in her three friends. "Guess who? Old home week, eh? They must have heard you was here, Kier."

Looking up briefly from a mirror on which had been drawn out a thick line of cocaine or sulphate, Kieron put the empty shell of a Biro to his nose and inhaled noisily. "Well, well, well. I'm touched." He offered them some of his drugs which John Fox pointedly folded up in a piece of paper, but they declined. "I'd hoped you'd all be witnesses."

Glancing distastefully at Dandy Banaji, whom he disliked, John Fox murmured about a nosey little wog until Kieron's eye, suddenly sharp, silenced him and he sniffed, his nose pouring with liquid, putting the palm of his hand under it in an effort to stop the flood until Dandy passed him a Kleenex. "Is it just about Kieron?" Plainly the Scaramanga sisters were on John Fox's mind.

"We're a bit skint, actually." Mr Kiss was apparently frank. "We heard you were interested in that old cottage near the Scrubs."

"Well, the Council is." John was shifty. "And Horace thought . . ."

"We wondered how much it was worth to you to hear about the catacombs." In an obscure gesture of passivity Mr Kiss removed his panama.

"Do what?" John Fox gathered his brain together.

"The cemetery catacombs run right under the canal. They've been there for centuries. You've not heard about them? If you wanted to get in to Bank Cottage to have a look, and had the bottle for it, you could go through the old tunnels and come up right inside the hedge. I found it during the war. I could take you myself."

"What do you get out of it, Jo-jo?" John moved the paper packet round and round in his fingers. There was a hint of triumph in his horrible stance.

"We'd expect a couple of grand. What's the land going to be worth when it's cleared? A hundred thousand? A million?"

"More than that!" Reeny spoke to her brother's furious regret. "They want to build a leisure complex and supermarket there but while there's just one residential building it's impossible. Some fucking law, eh? It's got to be knocked down before they stick a sodding preservation order on it, see? We offered the old dears a good price ages ago, through our company. But they weren't interested. Now a mate of ours is going to get them out anyway. The beauty of a site like that is that you never have to build on it. It appreciates more and more. You just borrow against it!" She was glad to show off her new financial know-how.

"Well, then, my info's worth two grand to you." Mr Kiss spoke with something close to a leer.

"You'll get it when you show us the way through those tunnels," John Fox reassured him. "We could send a team in and flatten the place in hours and nobody the wiser. It's perfect. When can we have a butcher's." He added, awkwardly, as if to show his sincerity, "Mate?"

"Tonight all right? What about you, Kieron? Anyone else coming?"

"I'll think about it." Obscurely, Mummery had lost heart on the subject of catacombs.

"I'll come. It'll make good copy, whatever else!" Dandy beamed.

"You'll keep good and mum, Mr Bumblebee." John Fox glared at him. "Why tonight, Jo-jo?"

"While they're at church. I saved their lives, dear boy, and they couldn't even see their way to lending me a couple of ponies. Well, one has to raise the readies where one can."

"If we could get in there we could frighten the knickers off the old slags." John Fox spoke with breathy relish. "Okay, Jo-jo, you're on. And I won't go back on my word. Coming, Kier?"

"There's the trial tomorrow. I've got to be there exactly on time or they do me for contempt. You going to be a witness, Jo?" His air of carelessness betrayed his terror.

"Oh, yes, I'll be happy to," said Mr Kiss in a gust and turned his head as his face began to grow red.

"I think you went too far, Kieron." Mummery wanted to express his disappointment. "It was scummy, doing those gays like that."

Kieron's handsome features became defiant. "It wasn't like they've made it out, Davey. Those bastards are all really geeky, clammy sods, honest. They'd make your stomach turn over if you ever saw them." He took the packet from John Fox's fingers and poured himself more powder.

suck cunts suck cocks shove it where they want it all the same fuck dirty slag whore fucking shit suck get the bitch tied up get the big nail hurt me hurt you little girl fuck dirty mouth all bloody stink dead now pulp fuck shit filth piggy

It was growing dark by the time Josef Kiss, unsupported by Mummery, led John and Reeny through the gates of Kensal Green Cemetery beneath sweet-smelling trees massive in the shadowy sunset. Electing to stay with the car, Dandy Banaji held back, watching the two dwarfish figures following the much larger one along paths through tombstones and monuments until they were lost among the gravestones on the far side of the chapel. He was still not at all sure what Josef Kiss intended to do but they had been made to wait outside two tube stations while Mr Kiss went to relieve himself, and this Dandy knew to be unusual. Mummery had been let off near his home just before Ladbroke Grove bridge.

After a while, Dandy reluctantly got back into the car, rummaging around in the filthy interior until he found a magazine. Once Reeny had run massage parlours in Earls Court and Bayswater and her magazines tended to reflect her old calling. Astonished, Dandy took in pictures of people encased by rubber suits and gasmasks, nipples pulled out on long pieces of string, hanging by wrists from crudely-made crucifixes and gallows, spreadeagled against walls. Leaving the car door open so that the light stayed on he turned the pages this way and that and did his best to work out what was actually happening. Josef Kiss had said that he had first met Reeny in a brothel but had never really described the circumstances. Once an enthusiast for these places, at a certain stage Mr Kiss had suddenly stopped talking about them. Dandy believed this change had come during the time his friend had lived with Mrs Gasalee.

Two hours went by while Dandy indulged an innocent but increasingly baffled curiosity with more magazines which he mined from the car's floor, stratum upon stratum of elaborately ritualised despair, while he wondered how difficult it was to negotiate the catacombs or indeed if Josef Kiss had taken the awful pair to Bank Cottage at all, for Dandy knew the sisters rarely went to church and that his friend would never betray the sisters, that he was clearly bent on scotching the Foxes' ambitions by means of one of his usual convoluted plans.

By midnight Dandy lay dozing with a copy of *Seminal Sentiments: The Romance of Rubber* over his face when a warm finger touched his wrist, startling him so that he inhaled the faint smell of mould from the paper and was coughing when he pulled himself upright. "Josef!" He peered at his misty friend who carried the somewhat sickly stink of the farmyard about him while his clothing was damp, his trousers soaked almost to the knee. "Where are the others?"

"John and Reeny are still engaged, dear boy, but I have the car keys so I think I'll drive us home." He had a mighty air of satisfaction.

"You don't drive." Dandy felt dreadful. He picked stuff from his eyes. "You haven't done something to them . . .?"

"I drive after a fashion and I'm in a mood to do so tonight. I feel celebratory." He eased into the seat and savoured the wheel.

"You've marooned them down there?" Dandy sucked in his lower lip and peeled a piece of paper from it with his teeth.

"They have had a vision of their own future, that's all. They have witnessed what they will find a little further along their chosen road. They'll be rescued eventually, dear boy, no doubt by some honest flushers. My studies of underground London, learned from Mummery and my father-in-law, never proved of much practical use, except during the war, when I was anyway a mere tyro." Mr Kiss's large hand enfolded the gearstick.

"But where are they, Mr Kiss?" Dandy's voice rose to a squeak.

"They've doubtless made it as far as White City station by now. Not the present one, of course, but the abandoned one. Or they might be passing down Counter's Creek and be reaching the area where the motorway is under construction somewhere in the vicinity of the old Portobello tube station, also abandoned. From there it's questionable which direction they choose but they might get all the way past Olympia to Chelsea where there's an outlet to the Thames."

"How on earth will this escapade stop them forcing the Scaramangas from Bank Cottage?" Dandy nervously scanned Mr Kiss's face for signs of his old lunacy.

Josef Kiss started the car inexpertly and it jumped forward. "Tomorrow, Dandy, we'll get a preservation order on Bank Cottage. You will enlist the help of my sister. She'll do it for you. And once that's fixed Bank Cottage will cease to be of interest to the developers. Meanwhile, for a day or two, the Foxes will enjoy an experience few Londoners can match. Almost mythic, really," he murmured as Dandy watched him steer out into Harrow Road, grateful there was little traffic about. "How impressed they'll be when they discover the truth of those old legends." And he began to laugh with the rich, windy roar Dandy loved, then broke into one of his songs:

> Jerusalem fell from Lambeth's Vale
> Down thro' Poplar & Old Bow,
>   Thro' Malden & across the Sea,
> In War & howling, death & woe.
>   Spectre of Albion! warlike Fiend!
> In clouds of blood & ruin roll'd,
>   I here reclaim thee as my own,
> My Self-hood! Satan! arm'd in gold.
>   Rolling, we're rolling in the ruins.
>   Rolling, we're rolling in the ruins . . .

Days later Dandy met Mr Kiss at Essex Street where the old steps led down through the Water Gate and found his friend even jauntier than before. From this regular meeting-place they could walk up into the maze of Covent Garden or down to the embankment and cross the Thames at Hungerford Bridge. At first the buildings had been in bombed ruins and now almost all that remained of the original street was the old Water Gate which, before the building of the embankment, had led directly down to the river. There was a hazy cast in the sky for the day was extremely hot, and Mr Kiss seemed to exude a faint, triumphal glow. "We'll have some thunder before evening, Dandy." From his pocket he dragged a photo-copied letter, handing it across as they descended the steps towards the shrubbery. It was from the Scaramangas' solicitors informing them that their cottage was now listed Grade I, that the Kensington and Chelsea Council had passed their premises as healthy, that their Royal Grant was valid and that the cottage was indisputably theirs in perpetuity to remain in their hands or those of their assigns forever.

Dandy congratulated Mr Kiss. "They must be over the moon! Did you mesmerise the Foxes?"

"Perhaps a touch, dear boy, but Mummery got hold of some gypsy friends from over near Wormwood Scrubs and they were only too pleased to join in the fun. Mary helped, too. Between us we haunted them for some time. They were very pleased to be led out eventually and still see me as their saviour, since they believe I became lost, too. The whole idea of Bank Cottage is now terrifying to them and I doubt if they'll ever take the Tube again."

"So you remain the Scaramangas' hero." Dandy was affectionate.

Mr Kiss continued to glow. "A delightful feeling, dear boy, and well-earned. The Foxes will return to what they know best. The only bad news is that the jury found Kieron Not Guilty at the Old Bailey. The witnesses were almost all his victims and were made to seem disgusting and unreliable. Can you feel the tide turning against us, Dandy, my dear?"

"Oh, come now, old chap, this is no time for pessimism!"

Strolling West towards Charing Cross Mr Kiss tilted his panama against the sun. "Another two or three years, Dandy, should find the passing of our particular Golden Age."

The Pilgrim's Gate 1965

FROM THE far corner of the carriage as the Tube clattered through darkness between Victoria and Sloane Square, Mary Gasalee surreptitiously watched two old men balancing a board between them to play a game of chess probably begun on the Circle Line when it had started up that morning, passing King's Cross and High Street Kensington at least thirty times. Their matted white beards stained with tobacco, their shiny tweed overcoats and dark trousers crusted with dirt, their old brogues scuffed thin, they were virtually identical; occasionally they passed a wine bottle though they were not apparently drunk. Once she had used this line for comfort, reading or watching other passengers, trying to find a means of blocking her voices, refusing to become emotionally involved with so many desperate, suicidal, bewildered, vicious, violently frustrated, unwholesome or wounded minds, some of which planned in extraordinary detail the prosecution of unspeakably terrible crimes. Now welcome drugs helped shroud her brain but she missed the ectasy she had also felt.

She looked up at the station map over the old men's heads and, seeing there were still five stops before Notting Hill Gate, checked her watch. She was in good time to meet her daughter at the little Italian restaurant they both liked. It was getting on for six. At exactly five-thirty she had left the Palace Hotel, Victoria Street, where she was popular and had every chance of becoming manageress. Earlier, Helen had phoned her at work to suggest they meet; she had some wonderful news. Mary wondered if she might be ready to announce her engagement since for some months Mary had sensed an unusually passionate love affair going on, though Helen had not even offered her the boy's name. She reached her station and got up hearing one of the old men speak with quiet satisfaction: "Check, you stupid old bugger." His friend tittered knowingly in reply. She had enjoyed their companionship. For as long as she could remember she had seen old men like these on the Circle Line, ever since she had been released from Bethlehem Special to stay at the St John's Wood halfway house which she had left as quickly as possible because they had frowned on her friendship with Josef Kiss. At first she had tried to see both Mr Kiss and David Mummery, but Mummery's mother returning from the rest home had worried when he was out all night and gradually Mary had realised her mistake in continuing such a confusing affair. Josef Kiss on the other hand offered consistent understanding and had been willing to help her and Helen try to piece together what had happened before and after she had been rescued from the flaming house. This had become her obsession for a while though Helen's interest had decreased as her books were published. Mary had all four of Helen's books on her shelf at home and frequently borrowed them from the library to make sure they got plenty of stamps on them.

Moving with the rush-hour crowd she reached the slow, groaning escalator and stood looking blankly at advertisements for underwear and cigarettes passing on her left. Reaching the top she crossed with the crowd to the barrier where the ticket-collector waited, and waved to Helen who, very fashionably dressed today, stood on the other side, her hair cut in a short page-boy; she wore high boots, lemon-yellow stockings, a red mini-dress and carried a PVC satchel-bag. Relieved that her daughter had discarded her previous dowdy black and was taking an interest in her appearance, Mary kissed her. "How are you, dear?"

"I've got some smashing news, mum. We'll have our usual tea first, okay?" In its frame of auburn hair Helen's pale oval face shone with excitement as they moved along the tunnel and took the stairs to Notting Hill Gate's South Side to pass the Coronet Cinema with its somewhat dowdy dome and enter Maria's, where they were enthusiastically recognised by the plump, black-haired middle-aged proprietress. "Mary! Helen! Aren't we looking the dog's dinners! Going to a show tonight?"

"Something like that, Maria." Slipping into one of the nearest booths Helen picked up a menu, knowing exactly what she was going to have, and Mary smoothed the cloth, the lace doilies, straightened the cruet and the place-mats, looking across the busy street at Woolworth's where people seemed to be buying nothing but potted plants, coming out with aspidistras, mother-of-thousands and Busy Lizzy, as pleased as if they had looted some unguarded nursery. Rather surprised at the variety of flowers and shrubs everyone carried, Mary sat back on her bench, glad to see the pretty young people in their bright clothes, and reflecting that almost overnight London had become as beautiful as any place she had ever been in the Land of Dreams.

Although it was late, Maria brought their usual pot of tea, their scones, butter and strawberry jam, while Helen talked about her research job at the BBC's Schools Service, full of the opportunities of the new Channel 2. "You'll have to get yourself a colour TV at this rate, mum."

"Oh, the old one's good enough for my cowboy programmes and the documentaries. *Don't try to understand 'em, just rope, throw and brand 'em.* I wonder if any cowboy ever sat down and tried to understand a cow? That Eric what's-his-name's my heartthrob, and Rowdy Yates I guess."

Helen shook her head in mock disapproval. "Not what someone from the educational side wants to hear, mum. We say there are too many cowboy programmes."

"I like the old films. *Pat and Mike. Bringing Up Baby. The Petrified Forest.* They're all a bit old-fashioned, I suppose." Finishing her last scone she decisively licked jam from her fingers. "Okay, my dear, what's the big news?"

"Well," Helen paused, "you know I've been writing books for a publisher who more or less just supplies private libraries?"

"Mills and Boon. Yours are by far the best."

"That's what this agent I got said. His name's Mr Archibald. He asked me to write a couple of chapters of my new one, plus a plot outline. I was a bit unsure, but Delia, the girl I share a flat with, said I should risk it. So I did. And what do you think?"

"Mr Archibald sold it for you?" Mary enjoyed the game.

429

"Exactly. And do you know who to?" Helen almost sang. "To Collins! They do all the successful historical novels and thrillers. Agatha Christie, Ross MacDonald, Hammond Innes. You name 'em! And do you know how much for, mum?"

"Five hundred pounds!" Mary picked the largest figure imaginable.

"Two thousand, mum! Isn't that incredible? Now we can move into a nice flat and do almost anything we want."

"We?" Now, thought Mary, for the real revelation.

"Delia and I. We've been thinking of getting a flat in Linden Gardens or Orme Court, across from the park."

"That would be wonderful, dear. Why don't I ever see Delia?"

"Oh, you will mum. She's dying to meet you. She's a nurse, you know, and works odd hours. She's the warmest-hearted person you've ever met. Anyway, what do you think of your little girl now? Miss Moneybags. Mr Archibald says with Collins behind it the book will sell forever and might even be a best-seller or a film. I'll make hundreds more."

Cunningham or even Nikoleieff maybe that Cage piece the movie's good

Drawing deep comfort from her daughter's pleasure, Mary drinks another cup of tea. Everything has worked out for the best, she thinks. She has a mental vision of coming upon a row of red-bound Macmillan Classics, their titles stamped in gold each bearing the name of Helen Gasalee. She has not told Helen how she had each Mills and Boon book redone in scarlet cloth.

"There's more," says Helen, "and it's just as good. I told you we were doing a series of programmes on the Blitz, how people coped and all that. I had to talk to people about the War. Human interest stuff. It gives a better idea of what things were really like. One of our other people came up with this old chap living in a caravan down near Euston Station who'd heard we were looking for people with good stories. We have to screen the public, of course, because some will say anything just to be on TV or get the money, but everything he said checked out. He worked in the National Fire Service during the War, over in the Tottenham area. He remembers both of us, mum."

Mary feels she will be sick, then her legs begin to tremble, then tears come. She is unready for this. She opens her handbag and begins to look for money. "Would it be possible to thank him?"

"I've arranged everything. In about five minutes a car's going to draw up outside and we're taking it to Euston. He's very anxious to see you. He keeps saying it was a miracle."

"A miracle we were saved at all." Mary looks out at the traffic, fearing something she cannot identify. "Maybe he knew your father and gran and grandad. What's he doing in a caravan?"

"There's a sort of temporary site in an old railway yard. He was on the road for years. A bit of a gypsy, apparently."

"I always had an idea I had gypsies somewhere," says Mary, wanting breath. "Oh, look at those roses!"

pointed out where I went wrong burning concrete vision of harps and Mr Fitzmary falling phoenix in the perfect play Sicilian widow little lamb correo para mi shaygets shlong oysgemitchet

The hired Rover took them up behind Euston Station into a dense medina of tiny alleys and narrow roads which had once been mews for the demolished houses of the gentry and were now occupied by the rag-and-bone men who stabled their horses and stored their wares there, by small mechanics' businesses, by sculptors, brass-founders and second-hand merchants. The district had a depressed and hopeless air, even in the heat of the powerful evening sun, and from everywhere Mary heard the ringing of hammers, the smashing of glass and sawing of timber, smelled horse-dung, wood-shavings, hot metal and burning rubber as they passed through a nest of streets below the railway arches to a patch where the sheds and brick stables surrounded a large bare concrete quadrangle, a single standpipe sticking from its middle. About this pipe were gathered dirty children dressed in ageless rags; they could have belonged to any previous century or any yet to come, and stared with dull, suspicious eyes as the Rover parked at the far end of the concrete square near where seven or eight caravans had been grouped together, most of them metal-bodied with chrome decoration and chipped silver paint, and a couple of the traditional horse-drawn kind, all intricate yellow, red, blue and green painted scrollwork reminiscent of North African or Afghan truck-decoration. There were no horses in sight but instead across from the caravans piles of broken cars had carefully been picked over for their reusable parts; the rest of the metal was folded for easy stacking, to be sold for scrap. Leaving the nervous driver in the Rover, Helen and Mary walked slowly past the staring children towards the caravans. As they approached, other faces appeared at windows and doors; faces as dirty as the children's, their eyes hiding any curiosity. Emerging from an old painted van a man spoke softly in what seemed to Mary a West Country accent. "And what can we do for you, young ladies?"

Mary became a little nervous of his insinuating tone, his cocked head, his dark, handsome eyes, his dirty skin adorned with gold. He smelled of oil and mud, like a newly-sited fairground, and there was tobacco on him, too, for he smoked cigars when he had the chance, though presently he merely held a thin roll-up in his stained fingers. "We're visiting Jocko Baines." Helen's returning stare was unfriendly, even challenging. She disliked the man. "He's expecting us."

"Jocko! Jocky!" Replacing his cigarette in his lips, he sat on his step appraising them. "Nice figures. You sisters, then, girls?"

"Thanks so much for your help." Helen waved to the face that came to the window of the largest chrome caravan. She led her mother forward through a thin litter of sweet-papers, newsprint and miscellaneous cans. It had been some time since Mary had been close to such poverty and she was surprised the local council had not done more about it. Stinking of burnt oil and metal, a train went by overhead, its clatter violently aggressive, giving off a film of filth which slowly settled on washing hung out to dry. A dog barked.

Wiping soap from his face, Jocko Baines opened the halfdoor of his van admitting them to an interior both cool and clean in which everything was neatly positioned, even the little jug of rosebay willowherb, poppies, cornflowers and daisies, wild flowers evidently gathered from the railway embankment. A small television on a shelf above a built-in couch displayed *Coronation Steet*, its sound turned down. Every wall bore framed pictures, chiefly on religious themes: Christ turning the water into wine, feeding the Five Thousand, raising Lazarus from the dead; or mottoes: *Bless This House, Home Sweet Home, What Mean These Stones?* all rather dampstained as if bought in a job lot from a junk dealer, and the place smelled of fried food, sweet Old Holborn tobacco, mothballs. Cadaverous Jocko Baines, as well-scrubbed as his van, had short military-style greying brown hair, grey-lined skin, greenish eyes and wore a collarless blue and white shirt, dark blue braces, a pair of grey flannel trousers, old-fashioned clog-shoes with laces. He was

432

too small for any of his clothes and his voice contained a faint Northern brogue under the London accent.

"I know *you*, miss," he told Helen, "but it's a long time since I've seen this one." He winked at Mary. "Care for a cuppa, love?"

They accepted his hospitality, and filling the kettle from a large jug he lit his Calor gas ring, whistling snatches from popular Italian operas, parts of arias, sometimes less than half a bar. "You still living in London the pair of you? Still together?"

"I live in Bayswater." Helen seated herself on white leatherette. "Remember? And my mum lives in Hammersmith just off Shepherd's Bush Road."

"I was based in Shepherd's Bush before they moved us here. I wasn't always a traveller, of course. I used to be a docker. I lived in Limehouse before the War when it really was Chinatown. They're very polite and clean, Chinese people, in the main, though I never got on with them close. I was in the anarchists then. Cable Street and so on. We fought the fascists off all right and we fought their mates when they came over. Now it's all happening again, but it probably won't be so bad. There's a bunch of Arnold Leese's old outfit still over there not far from where I used to live, off Holland Park Avenue in Portland Road. Did you ever meet him or Mrs Leese? He's the one called Mosley a kosher fascist. I'm not Jewish myself, though a lot of people think I am. My dad and mum were settled gypsies. I went back on the road again for years until I got too old for it, but they never refused me my pension. I loved the docks. Did you know the docks when they was a going concern, love?"

Hating to break his flow, Mary shakes her head; she looks for personal pictures but finds none.

"How much do you remember of what happened to you?" He stretches suddenly towards the kettle as it begins to boil.

Unhesitatingly and to her own surprise, as if she is back in the Land of Dreams, Mary answers him almost by rote. "I watched the black staircase falling away all around me. I held tight to Helen feeling the sting of the fire on my own skin. I think it was burning, at least in patches, but there was no really bad pain. I couldn't believe I was hurt. I wondered about Patrick. I lost my footing and fell forward. Fifteen years later I woke up."

With an air of satisfaction, Jocko Baines pours water into a brown pot. "Well, love, it did you no harm in the long run. We called you our Little Angel. You kept us going through the rest of the Blitz. The rest of the War, really. I think London's getting too old. I think she's hallucinating, do you know what I mean? She's sort of senile, remembering only bits of her recent past but a lot about her childhood. She's a couple of thousand years old, after all."

She can't be, I did see it, she can't be though. Or didn't I see it, after all? She's not after me. She's not testing me.

Jocko Baines takes cups from their hooks, wondering if the women realise how much they are disturbing him. "I talked about what happened a lot, we all did, but most of the lads in the NFS got killed a year later in that big Blitz we had over by Holborn Viaduct." He put the cups onto saucers. "I miss the ships, mind. I'm not against change. I just miss the ships. I'm not even a Cockney, but it's the same for me as it is for them: I worked most of my life in the docks, since 1928. I got laid off in the forties when they gave my job to a younger man, just demobbed. But never say die. I spent all I had on a caravan and a little pony and set off round the country doing whatever odd jobs I could. Became a regular travelling tinker, like my dad. I had a knack for mending stuff. Then I came back to London and this."

Through the window Mary watches dirty children playing with old rubber tyres from the nearby dump, rolling them back and forth across the concrete while their mothers seem prematurely aged by a lifetime of hanging out washing which never gets clean. "You'd think they'd do something."

"They want us to go away. We steal chickens, don't we, and start fights. That's what they think. Or they believe we'll put the evil eye on them." Chuckling, Jocko Baines precisely fills three cups with tea. "Milk and sugar?"

"You were in the Fire Service the whole War were you, Mr Baines?" Helen accepts the thin china cup and saucer.

"Our dock was one of the first to be hit so I got called up into temporary fire-fighting. It was horrible to be in that yet I miss it sometimes. I did it off and on throughout. I thought of the Blitz as a person. The Blitz was like a mother to me. I never had so much attention. I'm not saying she was kind, though she brought out a lot of kindness in people. She wasn't strict and she wasn't fair and she laid about her at random or let you alone when you were expecting the worst. When she went for someone else it was always a relief but you missed her when she wasn't there. I'm not the only one that misses her. The doodlebugs were completely different. They had no personalities, just sudden unexpected death. We hated them." He sits down under his TV. The picture warps as he moves below it, getting settled. "There was us and the regular Fire Brigade blokes with a big engine and ladders and water and everything, but they couldn't control that one. Yours. It had almost the whole row. You get to understand these things and we were certain there couldn't be a soul that hadn't been burned to death. Me and Charlie McDevitt went in all the same, using axes we borrowed from the regulars. We'd seen something moving, you know. They told us it was pointless but we thought it was worth it, anyway, so we got these old blankets and soaked them with hose-water and we went in. Your house had completely collapsed and was blazing like a torch but there was a sort of tunnel where the flames hadn't caught. We went through that, calling out, asking if anyone was there. You did things like that. Bloody silly, you'd be told, but you'd be surprised how you sometimes heard a voice calling back to you. I think everything had fallen through in yours. All the way from the top to the bottom of the house. What we'd seen moving was burning timbers and bits of wall. We thought they were being flung around, the way it was sometimes, almost like poltergeists were in there. You know, troubled spirits. It was something to do with the heat and the way the bombs acted on the air, but it was always spooky. Sometimes a house would go crazy like that, flinging itself all over the place, like it was in pain." His mouth has grown dry. He sips his tea.

"But you found us!" Mary laughs. "It wasn't an illusion in our case." She is now feeling unnaturally elated.

Frowning, Jocko Baines collects the teacups and puts them in the sink. "Not exactly, love. That was the strangest thing of all." He reaches for his jacket hanging on a hook behind the door. "Do you feel like a quick one? The local's all right. They know me. They don't mind gypsies."

Wondering what else he can possibly have to say but glad to spend time with the man who saved her life and, more importantly, Helen's, Mary agrees. Locking his caravan door, Jocko murmurs about thieving kids. "Never used to. Now it's better safe than sorry. This isn't the best site I've ever lived on. I'm thinking of getting a car and hooking up the old van, driving back out. London's not my home, you know, though I've lived here most of my life. I came down with my dad from Huddersfield. We walked. People were kind to us. We lived off turnips and potatoes in the fields and anything we were given. We did odd jobs. My dad got a job in Mitcham, over in the toy factory there, and kept it until the whole bloody place was taken over by the Meccano people." He leads the way off the mephitic site and round the corner to a small grim pub whose cracked walls have been pebble-dashed and whose old wooden windows have been replaced with aluminium frames as if it has barely survived a recent bomb attack. They follow Jocko into the single murky bar. He makes them sit down on the cracked red plastic of benches through which horsehair pokes. Over the dartboard Mary makes out a picture of a mediaeval traveller from Chaucer's day and sees that the pub is called The Pilgrim's Gate.

swollen up I told him you're getting careless silly pig but it was a proper little motorbike and really changed his life for him he was a Master Baker too and did part-time at the City of London Theatre near Liverpool Street do you know it was built on the ruins of Bedlam you should see what they dug up

At their request Jocko brings them two halves of lager and a pint of mild for himself, then sits down in the chair opposite staring from woman to woman, his pleasant weathered features suddenly full of delight. "You really don't know how – well, it's a real treat to see you both. Best thing that happened in the ruddy War."

"You were going to tell us how you saved us, Mr Baines." Helen is smiling, enjoying his pleasure.

Jocko takes a deep interest in his drink. "Would it seem sort of bad manners, Mrs, if I asked you if you had a scar of any kind on your back? Kind of boot-shaped?"

"I've got a burned place where they couldn't do anything with plastic surgery." Mary again feels short of breath. "As if someone stepped on me. Really, Mr Baines, if you're going to apologise – "

"It wasn't my boot, love. Oh, no." Emphatically he shakes his head. "I've got cancer, you know, in my bones. I'm having treatment. Found out a couple of weeks ago. I was wondering if this wasn't a sign. I want to touch you both for luck, if you've no objections."

With mixed feelings Mary stretches out her arm and with a little hesitation her daughter imitates her, whereupon respectfully Jocko Baines touches first one and then the other before sinking back in his seat, his unhealthy skin enlivened by a blush. "You never know do you? There's more than one miracle been heard of in the world. My wife died of it, too. In the lymph. Carried all through her in six months. She was a big, healthy woman. Fonder of life than I was, really. It's always the way, isn't it? What was I going to say?"

"How you and Charlie McDevitt pulled us from the fire." Briefly Helen puts the tips of her fingers on her own bare arm.

"I wouldn't have said that. We were in the fire all right. It got hotter than hell. You know what fires are like better than I do. We couldn't stand it. Our clothes were beginning to smoulder and that's a very bad sign. If the smoke hadn't been blown away – almost sucked away by something out there – we'd have been gonners. So we get out of the house, with timbers coming down still, with a wall crashing not a foot from Charlie's heels. It's a near thing. They keep playing water on the fire as a matter of course. We know bloody well nothing can live in it." His voice takes on a distant chanting rhythm.

"But I thought it was you who saved our lives." Mary has a sense of anticlimax. "You mean you only know who it really was?"

"Well, I reckon I do now. Good heavens, love, we couldn't get near the place after that first time. Nobody could. And yet we still thought we could see a person moving in there like at the core of the fire. We'd seen that happen once or twice you know. It's corpses sometimes being shifted about by the heat. They seem to be dancing. A lot of people noticed that during the Blitz. No, me and Charlie didn't save you, love, though we had a good try at it!" Laughing he shakes his head again, draining his glass. "But you know that really, don't you? You're pulling my leg, eh?"

Helen rises up to fetch more drinks. Jocko is grateful. "That's what I call a nice modern young lady," he tells Mary approvingly. "You got to be proud of her."

"I am. Someone must have saved us, Mr Baines. Are you sure you don't know who it was?"

"Not unless it was God Almighty, Himself, of which there is a strong possibility." He lifts his ailing shoulders.

Returning, Helen distributes the beer. Over in the corner of the pub an old man strikes piano keys in a bizarre, almost random, way, his left hand simply marching up and down the black notes in a single fixed shape, his right playing some dimly recognisable tune while Jocko Baines grows more enthusiastic. "You're a legend all over North London. I've spoken to a lot of travellers who've heard the story in one version or another, but I'm the only one still alive who saw it for certain. I saw you do it, love, with my own eyes. Charlie McDevitt and me saw you. So did the regular blokes. We couldn't believe it. We were convinced you were dead, even while we watched it happening. You just came walking out of that house. There was hardly a brick or a stick of it left that wasn't roaring flame. You just came walking out of it, your baby in your arms. A slight little thing, you were, hardly any different then than now. A girl yourself. But your dress was hardly touched, except for that one place where it was on fire. Like the shape of a boot. It was as if the fire couldn't harm you. It was just like that story in the Bible about Shadrach, Meshach and Abednego, only for the little bit of flame on your back like a fluttering wing, the colour of a rose. You walked out of the lot, love. Don't you remember? Picking your way along a path with your dainty little feet as if you were strolling through a field of daisies. And by the time you got to us even that bit of flame was out, your dress smouldering, you know, as if someone had left the iron on it a bit too long and the flesh underneath bubbling up."

Scratching his jaw, Jocko Baines regards the two stunned women as if puzzled by their strange silence. He becomes embarrassed again. "It wasn't the only miracle of the Blitz." He begins obscurely to try to reassure them. "Don't get me wrong. I'm not making any claims. There were a lot of weird things happened in the War. And a lot of horrible things, too, like the coppers we caught looting over near Seven Sisters who got drowned in the canal and I could tell you the blokes that did it. But what happened to you was the only thing I ever saw I'd call a miracle, and that's why I remember it so clear. It were a vision of innocence. I said to Charlie it was like a child and *her* child had been taken into the bowels of Hell and then allowed back to Earth. 'Walking unscathed out of the mouth of Hell' was in fact exactly how Charlie put it and he'd confirm it if he was here now. Blimey, you've both gone pale as ghosts. Don't you remember any of this?"

"I don't believe . . ." begins Mary.

"I'm not sure I understand." Helen puts her hand on her mother's arm. "Are you saying mum walked out of the centre of a fire so hot it had driven you back? I'm sorry, Mr Baines. I gathered you were on the team which found us buried."

"She had you in her arms, miss. Tight and sort of covered against her breast. Both of you should have been dead. You were never buried. That's all I'm saying: What I saw." Almost offended by her questioning Jocko shrugs. "I suppose it was just a fluke, but we thought it was a miracle."

"And then what happened?" Anxious not to upset the dying man, Mary leans forward, almost spilling her lager. "I fainted, did I?"

"You didn't faint until the ambulance turned up, love, and they took the baby off you. Then you just sank down, like, in a heap. They put you in with her, but you were still talking like. We got your name and everything. And your age. And look at you now. That's something else you can't easily explain, can you?"

Glancing about her, as if for escape, Mary wonders if she is back in the Land of Dreams. A certain quality of light in the pub sometimes accompanies the sun people when they are merely trying to mix and enjoy themselves with mortals. *Don't come a lot prettier, like angels . . . Thought she had to be a snotty bitch, told his fortune in the laundry while it rained, if I live this one down I'm lucky, one more second and I'd've been all right. The spit of Lord Derby there's a gate but it's locked now knickers off or I'll* "And it couldn't have been anyone else?" Mary restores her normal grip on herself.

"You've the same mark, you said." Jocko Baines turns his gaze on her, suddenly sympathetic, perhaps understanding. She looks in panic to Helen, who has closed her eyes for a moment.

And all the town's great organs give voice in myriad ways. Mr Balhar's definitely one of them and the same goes for the Spaniard's my guess it's not hard work in fact it's bloody easy she's going to faint.

"Mum!" She holds a pound note out. "Could you get her a double brandy, Mr Baines?" Helen steadies Mary with her other hand. "Mum!"

I hate this world, says Mary. *I love Josef and Helen, they're worth living for, but I feel so guilty. How could I do such a thing? Millions of other women died in those yelling fires, died of fright even before the smoke took them. None of us should have died. And that's the outrage.*

439

The Old Bran's Head 1959

SCARLET AS the plush on Reeny Fox's worn-out ottoman, David Mummery shaped his fingers to the chord of F and did his best not to stare at the Guardsman who having removed his own trousers was now unhooking Little Daphne's brassiere; elsewhere most other guests had reached various stages of undress but still safe in his plaid shirt, and baggy green corduroys David kept to his corner, his banjo on his knee. Reeny had offered him ten bob and free booze to entertain at her party before he realised its nature or its location. The house off Warwick Avenue, Earls Court, was one of John and Reeny's "earners" and David was already friendly with some of the whores who knew him from Soho and enjoyed treating him as a kind of mascot. "Come on Davey, lad, let's have another of them filthy songs of yours!" Skinny Brenda exuding California Poppies chucked him under the chin. "He knows dozens. You wouldn't think so to look at him, would you?" She addressed her elderly estate agent who was almost as red-faced as David, though for different reasons. Opening the door John Fox looked in, winking at David and giving him the thumbs up sign before returning to run the gambling in the basement. Clearing his throat with another glass of gin David began a fresh ballad.

> *"There is a pretty piece of work,*
> *It is up in high life,*
> *Upon my word an amorous lord,*
> *Seduced another man's wife,*

> *She was a lady of title,*
> *She was charming, young and fair,*
> *With her daddy and her mammy once*
> *She lived in Belgrave Square . . ."*

He had never understood why men and women so throughly familiar with the lewdest behaviour found such relatively coy songs uproariously funny, yet predictably they had already begun to laugh. The appreciation of the whorehouse, he decided, probably had more to do with the power of words than the actual nature of the songs, for people were impressed by the most obvious double-entendres. As he sang on, the approval of his audience, now thoroughly beyond the undressing stage, helping him to relax, Mummery wondered how he would ever describe such a scene as this. He felt like a Babylonian minstrel and wished Patsy Meakin and the others had agreed to come instead of accepting a gig at The Two I's and already discussing how much to demand for a recording contract. There came a huge wave of laughter as he reached the chorus. Some of the whores even tried to join in.

When the phone on the sideboard next to him began to ring Reeny, naked but for some peculiar pieces of wood and equipment which looked as if it belonged in the kitchen, wobbled over to take the call. "No, dear. I'm really sorry, lovey. Nobody to be spared tonight. And Moira can't travel any more, as you know. I wish I could help, darling. You could come over if you're really lonely. Okay. See you soon, dear."

She left the phone off the hook, returning to embrace her enormous businessman so that they merged into a single formless mass.

> *"Your Molly has never been false, she declares,*
> *Since last time we parted at Wapping Old Stairs,*
> *When I swore that I still would continue the same,*
> *And gave you the 'bacco box mark'd with my name."*

Naked on a bed in Acton, resenting gathering his courage for nothing, Josef Kiss puts back his own telephone. "Well, ladies, we are to spend the night without company, it seems." The young women positioned on various pieces of furniture, on bookshelves and tables, merely continue to smile. *Mr Kiss, can you eat fire?* They offer him sweet roses, they wear the feathers of exotic fowl.

441

"In Fulham town, as people say,
A couple courted, night and day;
So firm and constant were their loves,
They bill'd and coo'd like turtle doves.
So merrily passed their time away,
They did so often toy and play:
The happiest couple that ever met,
Were Red-prick'd Jemmy and Randy Bet . . ."

Mr Kiss, Mr Kiss, can you eat fire? These beauties have often reminded him of sirens but not of the sea. They are particularly fond of Essex Street late at night, the steps of the Water Gate, the little alleys behind Fleet Street, the Thames Embankment near the Temple. *Mr Kiss, Mr Kiss, can you read fire?* And of course his eyes go to his little coal fire for there's no gas in this Acton bedsit and fuel has to be bought by the bag. All in their early twenties, they wear silk lingerie and most have long red hair. They seem genuinely anxious for his opinion but he cannot think why they should want it. How could he possibly return the pleasure any one of them could bring him? They delight in flattering him. *Mr Kiss, read our minds. You know what's in them already, don't you, Mr Kiss?* Perhaps they do not offer him pleasure, perhaps they really do value his opinion. Always he has believed his knowledge would be a guarantee of company, when he needs it, until his death. Not always happy to be alone, especially when he returns to Acton, which is a far larger room than any of his others, Mr Kiss has tried to make the place seem smaller by filling it with draperies and clutter and books, but instead has succeeded in creating a far more sinister environment of crevices and mysterious crannies, folds and shadows. When his sirens appear here he can never be sure if they are unaccompanied. Do they have masters? He imagines demons, like that he once met at the Round Pond, for whom these women act as lures. He does his best not to acknowledge them. Only outside does he feel safe in their presence. Then he will cheerfully go to seek them, at Essex Street the Temple, beside the Thames.

Mr Kiss, will you kiss my fire? Will you taste my flames, Mr Kiss, for I am sweeter than anyone, sweeter than your true love. Read my lips, taste my mind, eat my fire. I will set you to burning, Mr Kiss.

442

"In London Town, not long ago,
A laundress lived as you must know,
Who had a daughter young and fair,
Whose beauty made the male sex queer.
Now Betty was a clever maid,
And help'd her mother at her trade,
'Til one day with grief I tell thee quick,
Her mother lost the copper stick,
It was such a rummy copper stick,
A long, a strong, good copper stick,
An instrument to do the trick,
But alas! she lost the copper stick."

Sing with us in our flames, Mr Kiss. Can you smell our lavender? Our roses? Stroke our feathers, Mr Kiss, will you eat our fire?

His ladies are worse than the miscellaneous voices, few of which refer directly to him or wish to tempt him, yet all these flame-haired women want him. They open their legs to reveal their private parts, they hold their breasts in their hands, they suggestively lick their red lips. Only a real whore can ever take his mind completely off them, but Reeny's unhelpful tonight. He pushes past one of his women to get to his wardrobe, selects a suit of near-yellow gabardine, a straw hat the colour of butter, a lace-trimmed shirt, and at length he marches from the room in full thespian splendour, leaving his sirens behind him, taking to the primly desperate streets of mock-Jacobean Acton.

"All round about did Betty look,
In every corner, every nook,
But vain her search fate was unkind,
The copper stick she could not find.
Up stairs ran Bet to escape the rout,
And from her window she peep'd out;
When underneath the little miss,
A youth came up and began to piss."

sings Josef Kiss in a rare antisocial mood to sleeping West London.

"He show'd a member long and thick,
A regular one to do the trick,
And Betty who saw it cried out quick,
'By jingo that's my mother's copper stick!' "

443

It is not even, he rationalises, closing time, when staggering songsters evicted from their pubs fling their voices like imprecations to unseen gods into Acton's second-rate night. From here he will walk via Shepherd's Bush, Notting Hill Gate, Hyde Park, Green Park, the Embankment, Essex Street, to Fleet Street and a hidden court, a pleasanter retreat. Acton is his penance, his testing-place; he has a room there because it lies to the West and he knew little of the far Western suburbs before he came. He considered White City and Ealing but the one had been too miserable, the other too bland for his purposes and Chiswick was altogether out of the question, for with Hogarth and Norman Shaw it possessed a little character. Acton, it can be said with fairness, has none.

> "Just like a shot down stairs she flew,
> And the street door wide open threw,
> And catching hold of the man quite cool,
> Pull'd him into the hall by his lanky tool.
> Says she mother has lost, oh dear,
> A copper stick, I do declare,
> But as we're going to wash tomorrow,
> This here for a copper stick I'll borrow.
> It is so very long and thick,
> Just the sort to do the trick,
> May every woman – when in the nick,
> Always find such a jolly copper stick."

"Goodnight ladies." He raises a grave straw to a couple of young women in ballerina skirts, lightweight mackintoshes and thinly-rolled umbrellas who lift their nose and ignore him as thoroughly as he ignores his temptresses. Down The Vale he strolls, into Uxbridge Road, that sluggish, half-dead, miserable thoroughfare of pawnshops and second-hand clothing, of limp fried fish, tired-out prostitutes, ugly newsagents and chemists whose main trade appears to be in condoms and cures for piles, past Wood Lane's tall-tiered BBC which overlooks all this wretchedness with a kind of high-minded myopia, and crosses the littered scrub of Shepherd's Bush Green where half the condoms bought that night have already been used and discarded, to reach eventually Holland Park Avenue, its huge houses reminding him of grand 19th-century balls, of

444

every possible elegance, of mysterious embassies, of scandal and terror and discreet detections, of enormously powerful tycoons who are superficially benign but actually plan to rule the world, perhaps the only avenue of its magnitude in London where the houses actually display their backs, seated on elevated embankments, obscured by tall trees, by walls and hedges: perhaps, like the BBC, disliking to look northward where Notting Dale begins, her slums more violently independent and thoroughly wicked than any Acton can create, where policemen patrol in threes or sometimes refuse to venture and taxi-drivers never go, which has created a population to match anything from the East End or Brixton yet a race distinct from all others, though even this is endangered by city planners who since the War make Standardisation one of their holy words.

Into Notting Hill Gate itself he strides where the wind always howls through new white towers, housing professional people of the better type who, like cultivated Danes set between Saxons and sea-raiders, occupy the border; those towers raised on the ruins of 18th-century grog-shops and haberdasheries somehow manage to channel air and send a typhoon with enormous force along Notting Hill's high street when elsewhere all is calm. Architectural magazines the world over now refer generally to this phenomenon as a Notting Hill wind trap. Safely beyond it, his hand no longer on his head, Josef Kiss unbuttons his pale jacket to the night and breathes a less boisterous breeze. It is nothing for him to slip through the Kensington Gardens railings and take the Broad Walk past the Fairy Tree, crossing, with the moonlight upon him and huge oaks and chestnuts faintly hissing, to the placid reflections of the Round Pond, to pause where he first met his demon as if challenging the creature to materialise, but when neither it nor the tempresses appear he moves, on, full of the secure tranquillity which comes when one is alone in a large yet enclosed space. He yawns, lifts his head up and begins a further song:

> "My bride, my bride! My luscious frisky bride,
> No other one I'll kiss beside!
> With belly plump – and round and fair,
> And your little spot all clad with hair!
> You make me queer – when I feast my eyes,

On your private charms – and your ivory thighs!
I'm on my bride! I'm on my bride!
Till from her floods the lecherous tide,
And her eyes with lust and passion glow,
For the treat I'm giving her down below!
If her belly should swell – when oft I fill,
What matter! What matter! My bride I'll ride still!"

This brings him to the Serpentine and the statue of Peter Pan. "Peter, goodnight. I share your sentiments, if not your future. Oh, I think I do. But that's the yearning in me, not the reason." Across the water ducks cackle like demented witches and he imagines a hundred magical crones turning the water white with their brooms before shooting upward in rehearsal for All-Hallows Eve through the exotic trees into a sky so beautifully black that it can scarcely be real with its half-moon shining, a couple of pearly blue clouds, sharp, unhidden stars hardly twinkling the air is so clear, to wheel and dive in joyful display and he will lie beneath a rhododendron, secret witness to their Sabbat. He takes the path under the road, looking to where the daytime bathers swim.

"I love, oh, how I love to ride,
My hot, my wheedling, coaxing bride,
While every throb and every heave
Does near of senses her bereave.
And she takes the staff of life in hand,
Til she makes each pulse and fibre stand!
I love her Cunt! I love her Cunt!
And on it I will ever be,
In spite of every randy whore,
I'll kiss my luscious bride the more!
And when the devil shall for me glide,
He'll find me lock'd in the arms of my randy bride!"

Only at this point does he think of Mummery, to whom he taught a great many of these old music-hall and tavern songs, and realises it must be his protégé he heard at Reeny Fox's. "Well, there are worse places for a youth. He's a good-hearted boy and the girls will treat him kind, I'm sure. But he'll have to watch Reeny and John, and even Horace. Or let me watch 'em for him."

By the time he reaches Park Lane and slips once more over the railings to stand looking towards Marble Arch and the late-night taxis and limousines or a rare bus, every window lit, negotiating the street like a sinking liner through a reef, he realises he has forgotten to bring the tablets which cushion his brain against the world's thoughts, and took nothing while he sweated it out in Acton, whereupon he decides to avoid another park and go by Oxford Street instead, the faster route. It seems to him the air grows close and he mops himself with navy blue silk refusing panic by whistling some ancient interlude half-remembered from a Restoration play in which he acted some bumbler, some tongue-tied countryman to be made sport of by a couple of London bloods. By the time he reaches Bond Street where sight of a couple of policemen temporarily silences him and some straggling youths see him as an opportunity for fun, then change their minds, the air grows almost too thick to breathe yet he forces out a couple of verses of "The Gypsy Lover" before he thinks to consider his heart, wondering if the slight numbness in his left side, his occasional difficulty with enunciation, might suggest the mildest of strokes. To be on the safe side he controls his breathing and his heart-rate, walking slowly across an Oxford Circus lit by window displays whose frigid mannequins seemed perfectly cool displaying the New Look but wear the current styles rather awkwardly, and turns into Soho Street keeping his pace as even as possible until reaching Soho Square, where he sits down on the first bench, he sees with surprise that his sirens are emerging from the gardener's shed in the middle of the square and wonders briefly if they have come for his soul. Do they represent Death? "Good evening, ladies." Here it is safe to address them directly.

Can you eat fire, Mr Kiss? Have you ever eaten fire?

"Oh, in a manner of speaking, ladies. Not professionally, however." He looks up, noticing the absence of the moon, the heavy clouds. Sweat is clammy on his forehead. He looks towards Greek Street's lights and has it in mind to pay a visit to a lady friend in St Anne's Court but then hearing growling from behind him turns prepared for any sight, any monster, then realises immediately he heard thunder. A storm is closing in. He laughs at himself, watching lightning fork over the ruined tower of the church, and decides to move on. If he has to shelter from the rain he would

447

rather do so in some more familiar place. "Good night, dear ladies."

Walking back through Sutton Row, past Foyles and into Charing Cross Road, he crosses to High Holborn on his way to the Viaduct. It is still difficult for him to see all the new building and he remembers when he hunted without sleep, night and day, amongst the ruins, listening for the whispers of life, for a brain that had not died. The thunder roars overhead now, like a wave of bombers coming in for the kill. The lightning reminds him of ack-ack guns, tracers, searchlights. He pauses. There is still no rain. As he starts across Chancery Lane he glimpses a figure lying face down in the road, two broken plastic carrier-bags of shopping spilling their contents, and at first he thinks it is a drunk, then sees a woman of about twenty-five, thick-set with long brown hair, blood gouting from her nose. She wears a cheap cotton dress, almost a sack.

When Mr Kiss goes to help her up she climbs nervously to her feet and reluctantly lets him lead her over to the side of the road. He sits her down on the steps of an office building and goes back to retrieve her shopping, chiefly potatoes, onions and carrots, doing his best to get everything into the burst bags and somehow tie them up for her. Lightning reveals her bleeding palms and knees. He tries to turn her further into the lamplight. She has fallen badly.

"She's okay, is she?" The voice comes from further down Chancery Lane where car lights glow, presumably the driver who hit her.

"She probably needs to go to hospital," calls Mr Kiss.

A door slams and a beefy man in a string vest and grey flannels tramps reluctantly back. "It wasn't my fault, mate, honest. She'll tell you. She walked into our rope."

Trying to clean her wounds, which seem chiefly superficial but some of which might need stitches, Josef Kiss looks at her enquiringly and she nods. A drop of rain falls through the air and lands on the pavement mingling with her blood. She begins to cry. "The rope," she says.

"I was towing this geezer who'd broken down." The beefy man points back. "We'd stopped at the light when she crossed between us not seeing the rope. And it tripped her, of course, when we tightened up. I stopped as soon as I saw what happened. You're okay, aren't you, love?" Every question contained the desired answer.

"What's your name?" Josef Kiss asks her gently.

"Eve." Her face is sweet, rather dull. She nods willingly at the men.

Two women emerge from the stairs of Chancery Lane Tube and pause, watching, before deciding to approach. They are both in their thirties, with worn, cheerful faces which their elaborate make-up cannot disguise; they wear pastel rayon dresses and several petticoats as if they have been out for the evening. "It is Eve, I thought so," says one. "What happened, love?"

"She's just tripped, that's all." The man in the vest looks as if for confirmation towards a doorway, where Mr Kiss notices for the first time a figure hanging back in the shadows, his hands in his pockets, perhaps drunk.

"Did you see this?" Josef Kiss stands up while the women attend their friend. The man remains in the shadows, unwilling to involve himself. "Didn't you try to help her?"

The man in the shadows lifts a hand to his head and adjusts his cap. "She just tripped, like he said. Her own fault. Silly cow wasn't looking where she was going." Carelessly he slouches into the lamplight as if resentful of his being called as a witness, and he sniffs. "She's not bad hurt." He wears a greasy donkey-jacket, a dirty green shirt and black moleskin trousers, his hair wet with sweat, moulded over apish features. "It was her own fault." He glares at the other women, at Eve. "Pull yourself together, silly cow."

Pushing up the sleeves of their light frocks, placing their coats over the nearby railings, the women help Eve sit up straight. One of them tears her handkerchief to stop the worst of the bleeding on Eve's right hand. "We'll get you back, love. You can stop at my place until we see what's to be done."

"She can go home. She's okay."

The woman ignores the man. "He been knocking you about, has he, Eve?"

Only now does Josef Kiss realise there is more than a casual connection between the man and the woman and he looks up to question the driver but the lights of the two cars are already disappearing down Chancery Lane. "Hi!" shouts Mr Kiss and drops his arm, disgusted.

While Eve explains to her friends what happened to her the apish man stands at a distance like a half-wild dog watching them. Eve looks bewilderedly from him to Mr Kiss, almost as if she fears the two might be in league. "Can you move your fingers?" calls the man. "She's okay. It's a lot of fuss about nothing. If you can move your fingers you're all right." He looks up towards the tube station then back towards the Viaduct.

Mr Kiss feels his anger grow and tries to suppress it, for he fears it. It could lead to his own arrest. "Is he with you?" he asks Eve.

"Supposed to be." Eve begins to weep uncontrollably as the initial shock wears off. She tries to rise then sits down again heavily on the concrete. More rain falls around her, more blood flows from her face and hands.

"What a bastard. It's all right, lovey." One of the women looks to reassure Mr Kiss. "We only live over the road. We can take care of her now."

Mr Kiss thinks he remembers seeing the woman near the flats bordering his own in Brooke's Market. But he will not move on. He looks over at the man who has returned to the doorway. "Is that her husband?"

"Her old man." The other woman seems to be making a distinction. She tears at a petticoat now and binds this around Eve's fingers. "It's all right love. Never was any good, Billy Fairling."

Billy Fairling, as if alerted to danger by this identification, lunges across Chancery Lane and passes them by, perhaps, thinks Mr Kiss, to get help after all.

fuck all them berks no push me cows all bloody always bloody bloody make you fucking sick all blood mess dirty sick fuck cow all bloody bloody sick cow

Billy Fairling is sloping off and has almost reached the corner stones of Furnival Street, opposite Brooke Street and the red Prudential. "Hi! Mr Fairling. Your wife might have to go to hospital. Aren't you going to help her?"

"Busy," says Billy Fairling crossing Furnival Street into half-lit gloom. He moves towards Fetter Lane and the mighty Viaduct while the rain comes down in heavier drops, the thunder groans.

"We'll see to her," says one of the women, perhaps in alarm.

"Honestly, it's just across the road." She folds back her sequined skirt to get a hand under Eve. "Come on, love."

"Then where's he going?" Josef Kiss growls like a disturbed Labrador. "Why isn't he helping?"

"Oh, about now he always hangs around near *The Sporting Life*," says the other woman. She speaks with some relish as if to fan the flames of Mr Kiss's evident disapproval. "He thinks if he gets one early he'll have a better chance on tomorrow's horses. So he'll be off to Farringdon Street."

Baffled by their apparent lack of anger or resentment, Mr Kiss stands looking after the disappearing Fairling. Almost as stunned as Eve, not quite believing that the cars have simply driven off when one might have taken her to hospital, he finds it inconceivable that the injured woman's husband has simply abandoned her, yet all of them seem to take it for granted. The other woman begins to pick up the shopping-bags and makes a kind of sack out of her coat while her friend helps Eve hobble across the road at the traffic lights. They seem embarrassed by his presence, as if he observes some delicate intimacy. "Awfully nice of you," says the woman with the shopping in artificial tones, her attitude deeply suspicious as he continues to stand there; perhaps she suspects any man's motives in this kind of situation. Josef Kiss feels obscurely ashamed for himself, for his sex.

Mr Kiss? Can you read fire? She sits on top of the cast-iron Dragon marking the old gate of the City. Naked she pretends to ride it, winking cheerfully at him.

The rain is heavy now and the thunder is directly overhead. With an explosive crack lightning strikes the Prudential's conductor and Josef Kiss begins to run. It is rare for him to move at any pace other than a stately walk, but his shame and his temper have got the better of him.

Mr Kiss, Mr Kiss? Her voice grows faint and is absorbed by the reverberating thunder, a bellowing baffled beast.

Fairling is ahead of him on the Viaduct and will take the stairway down to Farringdon Road if he intends to make his way to the offices of *The Sporting Life*. The rain is now so dense Josef Kiss can hardly see, but he dives into the arch above the stone steps and by the time he reaches the middle landing Fairling has stopped beneath the dim gas globe looking back in surprise, his face made even more brutish by the shadows. "Something wrong mate?" He is mild.

"Eve is badly hurt. You should go back to help her. I understand she's your wife."

"In a manner of speaking. Anyway, friend, it's none of your business." His tone remains tactful. "Her mates are there and there's nothing seriously wrong with her. It was her own fault, the silly moo. She's always tripping over things. Ruined her bloody shopping."

"What was she doing with the shopping at this time of night?" In the face of such insensitivity Mr Kiss's question is lame.

"None of your fucking business." Billy Fairling shrugs, adding, "She'd left it in the pub, hadn't she?"

"You were supposed to bring it home?" Mr Kiss feels he has the whole miserable scenario. "And she came to fetch it."

"I told you it was none of your fucking business. Now fuck off, mate. It's my wife, so stop interfering where you're not wanted." Fairling's tone is placatory and clearly he does not like the look on Mr Kiss's face. He licks his lips, unwilling to turn until he is sure he will not be attacked from behind. "She just fell over. If she was badly hurt that'd be different, wouldn't it? But she's not."

"How the hell do you know? If you had an ounce of sympathy . . ." Mr Kiss pauses, aware of his own lack of realism in making an appeal.

"I fucking saw what happened. Those blokes were right. I told them it wasn't their fault before you ever turned up. So bugger off, mister, will you? Be a good chap and stay out of other people's affairs, eh?" There is aggression in the whine, a suggestion of Birmingham.

Taking Mr Kiss's silence to mean that he has won his point, Billy Fairling makes to continue his journey down the steps.

"Stop," says Mr Kiss suddenly, with urgency. "Go back, Fairling. See what you can do for her. It's the only decent thing." He is yearning for the man to see the justice of this.

"What?" Fairling is genuinely amused. His unhealthy features twist in mimicry of Mr Kiss. "The only decent thing, is it? Oo-er, what d'you think I am, mister? Douglas fucking Fairbanks Junior?"

The thunder echoes through the arches of the Viaduct just as some years ago Mr Kiss listened to the sound of falling bombs here, and rain descends in such massive sheets it almost drowns the noise while lightning makes the street outside momentarily blue. Billy Fairling looks warily at Mr Kiss, regretting his direct display of aggression. "Look here, I didn't mean to get you upset, mister. Maybe I'll go back when I've finished an errand. All right?"

No expert at hitting other people, Josef Kiss's next action is not premeditated and his bunched fist lands by chance in Billy Fairling's right eye. Fairling staggers and catches himself on the railing. "Here now, stop it! I'll call the rozzers. I told you I'd see to it!" He shrieks with alarm. "I'm an ex-soldier!"

Mr Kiss finds his left fist striking Fairling's nose and feels bone give way. His right fist flies out again and now Fairling loses his grip, staggering down the remaining steps and into the lamplight under the Viaduct where he stands befuddled, bleeding almost as badly as his wife. "You gone mad? I've got a bad leg!"

Inarticulate, Mr Kiss growls again, his voice echoing the thunder. When Fairling tries to run towards Ludgate Circus Mr Kiss follows him, catches him, strikes him on the back then on the ear. "Pick on your own fucking class!" wails Billy Fairling mysteriously. Mr Kiss kicks at his leg and Fairling slips on wet stones, going down and either pretending to be knocked out or actually losing consciousness. His pale suit soaked through with his own sweat and the pouring rain Mr Kiss stands over him, fists still bunched, snorting and panting like a battle-crazed bulldog. "You bastard! you swine!" For perhaps the first time in his adult life he is at a loss for words. "You bloody, bloody, bloody rotter!"

He is crying when Old Nonny, her finery protected by a yellow cycling cape, starts to pull at his sleeve. "Mr Kiss. That'll do him. No more, Mr Kiss. Leave it out. Let him be. Mr Kiss!" She speaks as if to her Lulu.

The thunder grows louder and the crash of the rain seems far away. Old Nonny's voice is high and authoritative as the wind.

Panting, gasping, Josef Kiss wonders why London women's voices grow shriller as they get older. Non's is often like a bird's call. He remembers she lives somewhere over in the streets beyond Smithfield which survived the bombing and whose foundations went back well before the Fire.

"Oi!" She grows fiercer. "Mr Kiss. You know what they'll say if they find you!"

He decides that when they next release him from whatever mental hospital they choose for him he will go to Holland and visit his family, for he is curious to see how the policeman is doing now he has turned into a writer. "She got the success she deserves, I suppose."

Billy Fairling stirs on the ground. A tooth is broken, a lip swollen. "You're a fucking loony."

"Absolutely right." Josef Kiss becomes almost genial, though his anger remains. "I'm the Fleet Street Monster. Want some more?" He watches Billy Fairling get up. He watches him walk rapidly away into the raining darkness of the deserted streets.

"Come on, Mr Kiss." Old Nonny takes him by a hand quite as bruised as Eve's now. "There's no point in losing your freedom until you feel like it, is there?"

"That man's a conscienceless animal." Unanticipated, a terrible sob escapes from his chest.

"Most of them are, love. Come on. I know where we can still get a drink." Old Non tugs at him. "Mr Kiss, dear."

The thunder does not pass and seems permanently positioned over Holborn Viaduct. He looks up at the bridge's elegant outline, a symbol of his own hopes. The rain falls steadily and horizontally through the yellow shafts of light. There is no wind. He turns at her guidance. Every so often lightning shows him the City, St Paul's, the Old Bailey and half-a-dozen churches, for the rubble of the war is everywhere around, unbuilt upon, its purpose undetermined. Mr Kiss continues to cry, his monstrous hand gripping Nonny's tiny one.

"It can't be any bloody surprise to you." Old Nonny pulls him through the dark over the muddy bricks and broken concrete where the mauve fireweed has been beaten down by rain. "You must have seen more than your fair share of dirty deeds, Mr Kiss."

The smell of the rain on the ruins helps him collect himself and he pauses for a moment in the cooling night trying to get his bearings with each flash of lightning. He draws breath. "I suppose so, my dear. But they pain my sense of justice, you know." Unusually, he is in new territory yet has covered this area a thousand times in peace and war.

"There's precious little justice in this old city, Mr Kiss. Except for what we make ourselves."

454

The thunder seems to shake the whole of London and he imagines buildings quivering, threatening to fall. Old Nonny cackles. "Come on, darling, almost there." She nods at a faint gas lamp shaded to attract minimum attention. Again Josef Kiss is puzzled not to remember this particular alley, though it resembles many he knew before the War. Under the lamp rain runs like a river down the ancient paint of a sign displaying a crude head with a grinning, bloody mouth, staring eyes, a crown of branches wound into its wild hair: The Old Bran's Head. "Mummery's written about this place." He was relieved that the world was still real. "London's first pub."

"Mr Mummery don't know everything."

Old Non pushes open the narrow door and hinges creak. There comes a tremendous explosion. As more thunder and lightning gathers around the Viaduct it seems the whole City has gone up. The two veterans look back, marvelling. "Now that's what I *call* a bit of a cock's egg," says Non, beginning to whistle. "They remember you in here. You saved their little sons in 1941."

Mr Kiss's anger has left him full of self-hatred. He stands waterlogged in the doorway of The Old Bran's Head displaying only his humiliation.

Nonny tugs at him, her ancient eyes disguising sympathy. "You did your best, Mr Kiss. You always have. But the world's not going to improve by an effort of will, is it? You should be grateful you get your own way most of the time. Some of us are used to never getting it. Some of us just know we'll never change the rules."

Mr Kiss takes a grip on himself. "We can keep trying, though, Nonny, my dear.

> "They hang'd his body on Tyburn's Tree,
> 'Twas in the jolly month of June;
> But they hang'd his cock at Execution Dock,
> And as he danc'd he sang this tune:
>> Hey diddle, my love,
>> Hey doddle-o-lay
> The jaunty cock crows at the break of the day!"

And he strides with his old step up to the stained oak of the bar, demanding of the bewildered publican two pots of his finest porter.

455

PART SIX
DEPARTURE OF THE
CITIZENS

Serene and unafraid of solitude,
I worked the short days out, – and watched the sun
On lurid morns or monstrous afternoons . . .
Push out through fog with his dilated disk,
And startle the slant roofs and chimney-pots
With splashes of fierce colour. Or I saw
Fog only, the great tawny weltering fog
Involve the passive city, strangle it
Alive, and draw it off into the void,
Spires, bridges, streets, and squares, as if a sponge
Had wiped out London, – or as noon and night
Had clapped together and utterly struck out
The intermediate time, undoing themselves
In the act. Your city poets see such things . . .

But sit in London at the day's decline,
And view the city perish in the mist
Like Pharaoh's armaments in the deep Red Sea,
The chariots, horsemen, footmen, all the host,
Sucked down and choked to silence – then, surprised
By a sudden sense of vision and of tune,
You feel as conquerors though you did not fight. . . .

Elizabeth Barrett Browning
from *Aurora Leigh* (1856)

Josef Kiss

WITH MRS GASALEE for the first time beside him in his Fleet Street bed, Mr Kiss revealed that his mental powers were limited to London: "I could never properly read minds in the provinces. Perhaps I would have been more popular there."

Relishing the significance both of his hospitality and this admission Mary turned her eyes to the small leaded windows made a precious white by the snowy air outside and pressed her soft skin to his soft skin for warmth. "Yes, it's much the same for me. It would have been more comfortable to have moved away. And you didn't consider that?" He smelled faintly of roses.

"Not seriously." It was Sunday so Johnson's Court and its surrounding streets were almost completely silent save for starlings and some sparrows; three pigeons settled on the sill before flapping off again, their plumage magnified and distorted by the glass so that they might have been ravens.

Since Mummery's drowning that autumn they had found themselves spending more time together, as if Mummery alive had divided them while in death he joined them, a victim of tardive dyskinesia, that most dramatic side-effect of psychiatric drugs whose frequently sudden symptoms resembled senile dementia with an increasing inability to control shaking limbs, so that Mummery, believing himself possessed by something like Parkinson's, had thought to exercise the disease from his system. Had he stopped taking the pills it might have been possible to have sweated the symptoms away but the doctors had insisted he continue with the drugs and one afternoon, struggling with his shuddering limbs, he had slipped from the towpath on his way to visit the Scaramanga sisters and their adopted child. One inquest witness told of Mummery's declaring he was swimming and needed no help, but his increasingly spastic movements had alarmed a local hairdresser who jumped to rescue him. By then he had sunk; a police frogman eventually found him tangled in barbed wire thrown there when the gasworks was demolished.

"Would it suit you to get married after Christmas?" Mary Gasalee took hold of her bit of blanket and wrapped it under her bottom. "I celebrate my birthday around the thirtieth of December." Her friendly kiss on his pink shoulder made him smile.

"A winter wedding would be wonderful. Would you want to live in Palgrave Mansions?"

"Well, I have my cats there. Siamese like company but would travel I'm sure."

"Let's keep all our places, then. It's never bad to have options. Unless you'd considered going out somewhere. To Mitcham or Epping or, I don't know, Uckfield?"

To his clear relief she shook her head. "The reception. Where?"

"Only Bank Cottage. If the Scaramangas and their pinch-faced protégé agree." He turned his huge head so that his blue eyes looked directly into hers. "Did they really find that changeling in their chicken-house?"

"Burrowed up from below like a fox, having heard of secret passages to a magic kingdom underground."

"Some land of dreams? You noticed him in Putney and Kilburn and maybe offered him a clue. Can he read minds?"

"He says not. He's sane. He's wholesome. He's happy now, a great help to your old ladies, is already preparing fresh roses for next year's shows, has improved the addition to the cattery and can't benefit from much further school. He reads as greedily as we ever did. The mother's a traveller who drinks and wants nothing to do with him while his father was killed a few years back in a knife fight at The Kensington Palace Hotel. Remember when the gypsies were banned from the place for months and had to use The Elgin across the road? Chloe thinks he's psychic but for his sake won't labour that. He seemed in such fierce pain when I first saw him, too. Now he's cured, they think." Abandoning her struggle for

462

warmth, she rolled to the edge and stood up, her slight, rosy body glowing in the pale light.

swinging sweet as the park in May a song and a flame in every mouth

They began to dress. Looking up from the wash-basin where he had been spraying his armpit with deodorant, Josef Kiss moved his head slowly, turning his body after it, lastly his eyes. "Ha! My ladies. Where can they be?"

"Those ghosts? Those women?"

"Regular as clockwork. You've driven them out, Mary, my sirens of the fiery see whose bishop was a Duke of Hell, tra la!" He drew on the fresh corduroy shirt she had bought him in Burlington Arcade. "With promises of lust tormenting me. I knew each of them well." Almost a song, at least a litany. "For years they haunted my retreats: my temptresses of burning streets, those slaves of demons, whores whose wares were heat and ecstasy, who lured me from the shores of sanity and sought my consignment to cold eternity. Cold blood forever, sweet Mary! With this fore-knowledge and enormous will did I resist them and was royally rewarded, for then you came to me. *Mr Kiss, Mr Kiss, can you eat fire?* Their lips writhed back, sensuous to the teeth. Their eyes flared, flickered, rolled. Oh, how they ogled me, Mary, dear. Like yours their hair was delicate fire upon silky skin. Molten. But they were coals which, once you held them, flared to searing life then died. *Oh, Mr Kiss, Mr Kiss, can you feel pain?* Ha! I'm no penitent who needs such pay or seeks out guilt like mother's milk. I'm Kiss the Mind Reader, greatest in his day, tra la!" He buttoned up the fine navy trousers she had made him buy in Jermyn Street. "The supernatural has no imagination. Its world by and large is one of dull banality. They say that's Hell, Mary. Well, there'll be no Hell for us while we live and breathe, eh?"

"I hope not. Where shall we honeymoon?" She had been listening only to his voice, not his words.

"Well, Kew springs to mind." He studied the trousers.

"I'm no Gloria. Are you confusing us?'

"There isn't another botanical garden in London worthy of the name!"

"I'm too old, and so are you, to make love in a public nursery, particularly in winter. But we could fill one of your places with potted plants. What about Hampstead? There's central heating there."

463

"The paper would peel. It's Morris. The plaster would crumble."

"Not if the pots were under glass."

He caught her drift and gathered her to him in the great folds of cotton she was wrapped in. "A little Hampstead hothouse and thoroughly secret. Could we bear it? I'm seventy-four!" This notion so tickled him he could not stop from shaking. He wept and he roared. "Oho, I'm seventy-four!"

She joined in. There was no stopping herself now. Here she was, a child bride at sixty-two. Could they live forever? She doubted she had ever left the Land of Dreams. Instead of entering the real world could she have actually brought the real world into her own? If so they had infinity if they wanted it, until it bored them. She fell upon him as she had fallen from the first and laid him out upon his bed, that recent virgin bed, and kissed every sweet happy part of him again and again for they had all the time they could ever want.

"I'm seventy-four!" He came within her tender belly. "By God, these are rewards for a saint!"

"There's never been a jollier saint, Josef Kiss!" She climbed off him. "Which reminds me, we have to marry in my church."

"You're a Christian? What?"

"St Andrew's, where I've prayed for you, Josef Kiss, and prayed for the souls of the dead, where I shall pray for our marriage and make it last forever. You'll trust me in this?"

"Of course."

"I suppose the cats won't be allowed to attend. It's a good thing they like you."

"Animals usually find me sympathetic."

"They feel sorry for you. They're rarely moved that way. How long can we stay off the treatment?"

"As long as we like. There's another promise to you. Since my sister's Minister Of Health the Clinic won't be long for Putney or anywhere else. She's already told her Parliamentary peers that she'll close them all down. Downing Street's certainly earned its name since Mummery was a boy." Mary had let him read their drowned friend's bequest to her, his memoirs.

"And how will the other loonies fair, Josef? The Black Captain and poor Mr Hargreaves and Old Nonny and all?"

464

"They're there for the company and comfort, same as us. We'll carry on meeting."

"Without Mrs Templeton?"

"Doreen is merely neurotic with a will, poor creature, to possess the least actually harmful disease she can find. Similarly Gloria's mother was able to give herself heart attacks more or less on cue, though her timing grew a little off. The Scaramangas might agree to Bank Cottage as a venue."

"Or we could offer Palgrave. The cats would enjoy the extra people . . . We'd never have to endure those doctors again."

"They'd have to find real jobs. There's plenty overseas."

In topcoats and hats at last they locked the Fleet Street door behind them and moved through air so silvery it might have been the remains of some old-fashioned fog, on their way to The Edgar Wallace where Dandy Banaji awaited them for their lunchtime Sunday drink. He wanted to tell them how he had gone into business.

There was still frost on Fleet Street's paving flags and the granite, the marble from grander days, the tile and Portland stone all sparkled, rimed as if touched by Ymyr in an ancient lay, and Josef Kiss reflected how northern myths had moulded this place making soft news hard and forging a bludgeon, creating cynics of boozy berserkers living as their spiritual ancestors had done by rape and robbery, by violence and dogged heartlessness, pouring daily ashore after a hard pull up some bitter river; but Sunday mornings were by and large free from the press. Mr Kiss had longed for the predicted exodus to Wapping or even Southwark though these creatures religiously celebrated habit, mocked all change and feared it, naturally.

He felt the pressmen's present battles had as much immediate concern as battles between King John and his barons, seeing little difference in the wretched tycoons and the majority of their minions save that the minions craved the power the tycoons merely abused. Living brutally and because of brutality, any news-paperman left with a trace of wit or humanity seemed at least a messiah. The stink of blood, long-spilled or fresh, became choking as you walked towards the Law Courts, past the Wig and Pen and all manner of ports, cheeses, flagons and roasts, so many bastions of dying creeds and misspent faiths, fortresses of misshapen, misused and bruised ideals, of dreams gone wrong and lies given the shape and polish of universal truths, of wicked men forever planning war against a world they hated. "Tra, la la!"

In a panelled corner of The Edgar Wallace, on a stool, Dandy Banaji awaited them, his motley scarf wound so many times around his throat his head seemed like a wizened cherry on a melted sundae.

"Meet," said Mr Kiss with all his fondness for the well-worn phrase, "the future Mrs Kiss."

"Congratulations." Dandy hugged them both. "And not before time. I'll get your Campari Soda, Mrs Gasalee, and Mr Kiss, you'll have your usual pint?"

"He's not surprised." Mary loosened her coat, speaking for Dandy.

"Are you?" He paused, money in hand. "Josef's the essence of predictability."

"I expected some exclamation. But I agree, Josef's a slave to his habits!" She touched her fiancé's sleeve.

"I'm sworn to change!"

She took the Campari from Dandy, plucking out the slice of lemon to nibble.

"I've asked George Mummery to join us." Dandy returned to his resting place. "You know what I've been up to lately?"

"Tourists." Mr Kiss made a pious face.

"I do a literary walk most weekends. I speak a little Japanese. Most of them don't have any idea what I'm talking about or who I'm talking about even when there's a translator with them but they love the fish-and-chip shop at lunchtime and so does the proprietress. It's now worth her while opening Sundays. She's English, but the rest of her family's Chinese. I began with that Jack the Ripper tour and found there's half a dozen of them, same as Sherlock Holmes. An American lady runs a T. S. Eliot. I'm surprised she has any business. I include T. S. Eliot but he'd never bring in a whole tour alone, not even Barrett Brownings can pull that kind of interest. Only the Dickenses and Shakespeares pay as singles. After that it's twelve poisoners on five famous sex-crimes, that sort of thing. '

"Wotcher, Dando!" A bucolic barrel-shaped man in a Harris Tweed suit waved a small meerschaum. "Drink up, I'll get these. Your mates?"

There were introductions. Irritated by Mummery's cousin, Mr Kiss thought the man should have been at a racetrack taking bets but George Mummery was so friendly and at ease with himself it was unfair to think ill of him. *Snobbery on my part coloured by Mummery's contemptuous descriptions of his father's side of the family*

When Dandy had introduced George Mummery as the inventor of the Royal Scandals tour they retired to sit about a table. "I'm always open to suggestions," George Mummery told them genially, "and if they turn out lucrative I'm well-known for paying a percentage. It doesn't do to rip people off in this game. You can't have enemies. It's already cut-throat. If I could have copyrighted Royal Scandals I'd be a richer man today but, you see, it's the same as the street selling I used to do. I had a lovely line in nodding puppies up and down Oxford Street when eight bloody Turks moved in. There were more nodding dogs between Bond Street and Tottenham Court Road than in an A3 traffic jam on a Bank Holiday Monday. The bottom dropped out and there wasn't a damn' thing I could do. I had a billposting business but the heavy mobs duffed me up twice and you can't go to the law because half of it's illegal anyway. So that was out. This touring's better, though you've got God knows how many Australians and Americans coming into it. Students. Housewives. That's the trouble. No Turks yet, but give 'em time." He laughed at this obscurely before sinking his pint.

"You're in business now with Dandy, are you Mr Mummery?" Mary Gasalee was anxious to move the conversation on. She wanted to get back to her cats. She wanted to make love to Mr Kiss in her own flat.

"Let Dandy tell you about it while I get them in again. Can you tell we're after capital?"

At his friends' surprise Dandy grew embarrassed, offering an explanation. "The paper had a staff shakeup. In India the politicians change and everyone's people change. I lost my job. It's to do with the tourist trade, too. George heard the café on the corner opposite The Old King Lud was coming on the market so we plan to reopen it as The New Ludgate Chop House, done up, you know, in the sort of Victorian style tourists prefer, like those new hotels along Piccadilly which look as if they've been there for a hundred years. Anyway, it's a chop house. The Natwest's interested but we could do with some extra capital."

"A real old-fashioned chop house, know what I mean?" George Mummery returned with his hands full of unspilled glasses. "There's not a proper chop house left in London, right?"

"I loved them." Mary Gasalee smiled for confirmation at Mr Kiss. "I ate at one almost every day when I had my job near Aldgate."

"There'll be original marble tables in all booths, cast-iron stands and wooden chairs, enamelled dishes on gas burners, gas lamps and a blackboard menu." George paused to spread his hands indicating an imagined sign. "All You Can Eat For 1/3d: Bread and Butter 1d Extra."

"You'd go bust," said Josef Kiss with simple conviction.

"Oh, no you wouldn't." Mummery was equally convinced. "Because you have to belong to a club. For two hundred quid a year you're issued with old coinage to pay for so many meals. Dees for pees, see. Like getting chips in a gambling club. Non-members can only enter as guests and can change a cheque or cash or credit cards at a pound to an old penny in the shop next door – Mrs Evans Sweet & Tobacco Shop. Disneyland's shown the way, it's the combination of a thoroughly maintained atmosphere, attention to detail, obvious exclusiveness, totally protected fantasy. Believe me it'll be bigger business than any Irish Pub or Olde Englishe Grubbe concept this side of the Atlantic. They won't be able to copy me this time. I'll make the Chop House one of a kind. A real club, that's the secret. The tourists have to join or come as guests of members. They'll be desperate to get in, the way they queue in the rain at The Hard Rock. The food's absolutely basic chops, steaks, sausages, peas, fried potatoes, the sort of stuff any caff in London's doing for a pound fifty – and I'll get fifteen quid a plate for it. That mark-up'll buy me my house in Highgate. It'll buy us all houses in Highgate." He sniffed as if to emphasise the perfection of his dream. "What do you say?"

Jolly highwaymen rogues of the open road Sixteen-string Jack, Claude Duval, Dick Turpin and Jack Sheppard, take a tankard with the Jew they mean to rob

"In what way," Mr Kiss and his bride-to-be went back into the chill to walk silently up the Strand towards Charing Cross, "can I make it clear to Dandy how terrible I consider the scheme? Or must I lie to an old friend, out of work and desperate? For almost his whole life London has been his living. Why shouldn't he benefit from this trend? Holborn Viaduct and Ludgate Hill, not to mention Blackfriars and Fleet Street, have until now largely escaped becoming mere themes but is there any point in further resistance? Mightn't it be better to join the final fantasy? It would amount to capitulation. To Beryl and all she stands for. No. I'll not conspire in this."

"You think it's deceptive?" Mary Gasalee was not greatly worried. She believed civilisation to be a process of self-mythologising.

"Worse." Josef Kiss paused beside the Church where once he had found consolation, Wren's St Clement's Danes, erected over the graves of Harold Harefoot and his Viking colony. "It's self-deception. It's a gigantic charade. It'll be the end of us. A farce."

Mary took his arm to move him on towards the tube's warmer air, the patient promise of her home. "Better than a tragedy," she said.

469

Mrs Gasalee

SEATED IN the chair recently vacated by Katharine Hepburn who had been visiting Mary for old time's sake, Judith Applefield reflected on an irony. "I've been a bride lots of times, but never a bridesmaid. Who proposed?"

"He did, but I'd made up my mind for ages. I really love him a lot Judith." Having taken down the heavy curtains she had used for years, Mary had replaced them with pastel blinds. Her flat smelled of paint and polish and even the furniture had a reborn look. "Helen's delighted. She thinks Josef's wonderful. A reincarnation, she says, of a proper London wit. Well I think he's more than that but she's very romantic, Helen. It's her job. Will you do it?"

"As long as I don't have to get myself up in organdie or come as something hideously Fergie-esque."

"You haven't the figure for it. Just watch the hair-dye and the orange blush. This is a church and I know the vicar. He'd be embarrassed but manful. I don't want to put him out."

"Trust me," Judith hiccuped. "Who's best man?"

"Dandy, of course, though there's a slight strain there at the moment. He's potty about some business scheme we won't put any money into."

"Leon thought it was worth risking a bit on the Chop House."

"It's principle with Josef, and Dandy knows that really, but if Leon's up for a share others are bound to be."

"Tommy Mee was before his heart attack. He was chairman of Big Ben Beef Bars and the Professor Moriarty's Thieves' Kitchens.

And David's cousin Lewis, the MP, is in. Tommy was talking about exclusive franchises in key capitals – New York, Tokyo, Hong Kong, Los Angeles. And Tommy could smell money in a wino's fist. Josef's worth a bit, surely, now. Make him come in."

"We're not Tommy's class. But good luck, anyway."

"All right. I'm off to the Commonwealth Institute to do my bit on a stall." Judith laughed at herself. "I don't really change do I? It'd be the WI if I'd stayed with Geoffrey." And when she left she was whistling "Jerusalem".

Followed by her Siamese Gabby and Charlie, Mary returned to her old-fashioned kitchen to check the stove. Opening the main door with a black iron rod she looked inside. The fire glowed like rubies and she contemplated the familiar world she saw in there. For years she had been tempted to consider the stove a gateway into the Land of Dreams. Had it been rude of her not to invite Katharine Hepburn to the wedding? Enjoying the intense heat, the cats began to purr and she picked one up in each arm to sit down in her old wicker chair, leaving the stove door open for it had grown bitterly cold outside. It was unusual to have snow before Christmas. She wondered if the Thames would freeze as it had done once for her. She remembered the huge silver fox cloak worn by Merle when she had crossed the ice trapping her scarlet and gold boat while a fire burning on the far bank sent up black smoke; all the waterways had been frozen and the roads blocked by snow. No trains or buses could run and even the sewers were made impassable by great icicles. That had been in 1947. Her dates were from old newspapers wherever she found them, giving her some idea of the sequence of her life before she woke to see Sister Kitty Dodd smiling down at her. "Awake at last, my angel. I bet you feel like a little bit of breakfast." She had been sorry to leave Sister Kitty Dodd and would have stayed in touch if the nurse had not in 1956 taken an assisted passage to Australia and, married, was now living in Queensland.

Merle Oberon had said it was the worst winter in living memory. From below Waterloo Bridge they had walked up a completely frozen Kingsway like the giant ice sculptures of the Japanese. Their breath the colour of May they turned into High Holborn and saw a sleigh drawn by reindeer pass, its driver hidden beneath a canopy. When the reindeer reached the gigantic bomb crater just across from the Prudential's redbrick castle and the Tudor parade of Staple Inn which had survived the Great Fire and the Blitz Mary was afraid they would fall in but Merle squeezed her hand pointing at the reindeer which lifted themselves and the sleigh high over the crater and landed beautifully on Holborn Viaduct before vanishing into the gathering fog of Cannon Street.

Mary and Merle had gone shopping in Gamages which was decorated for Christmas as it was when she worked there before she met Patrick. In the toy department full of imitation holly and mistletoe where a Santa Claus gave away presents, she had demanded a yellow doll. She had not been entirely happy during the interview perhaps because Santa had refused her. She could hardly believe the richly coloured lights were merely electric.

Jumping into her lap Gabby, her largest cat, began to pat at her face with his paw making her laugh and stroke his head; she supected he was jealous of her memories. She was a little sad that Katharine was returning to America for good but although she saw her friend rarely now she would be sorry not to have her advice; at the same time she was now less certain and less concerned where the Land of Dreams ended and where reality began. She thought it would be marvellous to introduce Josef to some of the delights though not the horrors she had known. They could go to Soho Square and meet the sun people who did not burn but offered you their warmth. She would like him to see that magnificent squadron of fighting women led by Joan of Arc and Boadicea riding across the Viaduct on their way to Oxford Street and Tyburn Field to their great battle against the Grey Host led by Death Himself. She had seen the grey figures like monks fleeing the Vikings running for the safety of the mist, but it was some time before she learned what had happened.

The year she had been able to go as far as Tyburn had probably been 1950, judging by the fashions in the shops, and then it was paved; there were fountains in it, all signs of the conflict gone, but soldiers guarded a memorial at the centre and one of the soldiers was her father. Not recognising him at first she had been intrigued by the man in black shirt and trousers, a white sombrero and black high-heeled boots who was talking to him. Her father had eventually introduced this Western dandy as Hopalong Cassidy but when she mentioned this to David Mummery he explained how all

472

she had met was a film actor posing as the famous cowboy. At any rate she had not been greatly impressed by the man. "Hoppy sneered at pearl-handled sixguns and fancy frippery," David told her. "It was wrong to deceive your father like that."

How much of David's life, she wondered, was happy. He had almost always been melancholy. His mother was still alive in a retirement home near Brighton, and when Josef Kiss had gone to tell her the news she had seemed sorrier for herself, or at least her loss, than for her son. Josef's impression was of a deeply unhappy and frustrated woman who had passed on her low expectations and disappointments to David, who had been wary of joy. At first whenever David had begun to relax with Mary he had almost unconsciously jerked himself back to alertness until eventually she found ways of calming him. But even his calm never lasted for long, though he had been worse she recalled as a boy. Only when reading or writing did his tension ever fully disappear and latterly as the tremors increased all over his body and his speech and thoughts grew slurred, even these escapes eluded him. Witnessing this deterioration had been a desperately painful experience, particularly once Josef Kiss had discovered the cause, and they had tried to get him to end his own drug dependence but he had been warned officially that if he stopped taking his pills he would be put into the hospital again and this frightened him horribly for he had witnessed the fate of helpless senile patients in institutions and he feared the loss of dignity or becoming the victim of some sadistic nurse. Mary now felt she should have made him stay with her while she weaned him from the drugs, though by then he was on some sort of Probation and had to report every week to the Clinic, whereas she and Josef were still volunteers. At the Clinic they injected him with the special shot with its timed release so it was then actually impossible to give up drugs. She would no longer be sorry to see the end of the Clinic and prayed something worse would not replace it.

Four or five years ago she had learned how Doctor Male, now soon to be her brother-in-law, had argued for surgery on her own brain and for all she knew had convinced his wife of the remedy's financial benefits to the Health Service. Even without money pressures such cures went in and out of fashion. When she and Josef tried to warn everyone of the causes of David's death, few had listened; indeed the doctors had insisted they themselves were showing signs of dementia and threatened them with new even more terrible medication. Consequently they had taken nothing for weeks and felt no worse for it, especially since they were so frequently together and could give each other support. Picking the cat from her chest where with long legs stretched it clung by its claws to her shoulders she moved to the dresser where the new compact disc player Helen had given her was set up. She touched a button. A favourite record was already in the machine and she returned slowly to her chair and the old, warm room filled with the *Enigma's* opening bars.

Held, like Ben French's, at the Kensal Green Cemetery, David's funeral had been particularly miserable because so many of the mourners had been wondering if his fate might soon become their own. She thought that a funeral service for an AIDS sufferer must have a similar atmosphere, and perhaps people had felt much the same when loved ones died during the Great Plague. This reminded her how she had recently learned that the Great Fire of London was not responsible for the end of the Plague but that the Plague had simply burned itself out at the same time in every great city of Europe, its disappearance as mysterious as the cause of the Fire. At the beginning of the Blitz she remembered some people saying how it was a good thing that the bombs were landing mainly in crowded slums of the East End which could be rebuilt after the War with wonderful new houses containing every modern amenity in green and airy surroundings. Wren's vision had been no better translated, but even he had not suffered the concrete high-rises of Tower Hamlets, Haringey, Fulham and Kilburn, warrens even more depressing than those they replaced. In the slum streets where she had been raised it had been possible to enjoy a certain sense of freedom in the sky above you and the earth beneath you and you could always see the landlord coming, but she felt sorry for the tower block dwellers, with feet overhead and heads below their feet, forced to submit almost every domestic function for a committee's approval. Built on clay, London's natural development was not vertical; Londoners had not been prepared for that way of life and it would be years before they became used to it; then perhaps conditions would improve.

Meanwhile there was too much misery in the hives; she was

familiar with the great groan, a thousand complaints combined, the dull pain of the hopeless and sick of heart told to anticipate a better world but everywhere observing the evidence of decline while the democratic future they had been promised had become nothing but two sharply divided classes of Londoners; between them a defensive ditch of misunderstanding and distrust, of lawless violence and violent authority. There were hardly any gradations in a city become almost feudal again. She was one of the few lower middle-class people left in the Gardens, for most of the others had been bought out or evicted long-since, their places filled up with young women wearing headscarves and tweed skirts who cried shrill slogans to one another heedless of the hour and were sometimes accompanied by brash, ill-mannered young men whose unhandsome gloss was not improved by a covering of expensive cloth, who addressed everyone including themselves in a form of banter and hectoring rudeness which she supposed had always passed among them for wit.

At present May saw few changes that were pleasant and had some sympathy with Josef's notion of a people following the Roman way with uncanny directness to make a whore of their mother, pimps and procuresses of themselves; people who were what John and Reeny Fox had aspired to become yet because of their class had in the end failed. Reeny was in Holloway serving two years for conspiracy while her brother was said to be in Dublin working as a barman under an assumed name. Nobody knew what had happened to Horace.

Tommy Mee is selling a birthright that isn't even his to sell, David had written in his memoirs, those miscellaneous notes, part reminiscence, part diary, part essays, which filled seventeen quarto leather-backed notebooks in which he had also pasted old theatre tickets, programmes, restaurant menus, wine labels, a whole collection of small mementoes as if his moments of pleasure were so few he had done everything possible to preserve them. David had continued to write that it was not very important if the government sold oil and gas reserves or offered car companies to American buyers but what really disturbed people was the package selling of things constituting their fundamental sense of identity. *What a poor substitute nationalism is for that. It's a brutalising process, similar to what happened to slaves taken from their own countries who become dumb and dazed because they have no future. Then the slave-owners point to them saying 'Look, they're little better than cattle. They have no initiative. They have no ambition. They are barely articulate. What good are they?'* It was not a problem, she reflected, one experienced in the Land of Dreams.

Madame Pearl spiritualist Tarot card reader palm and psychic reader healer and advisor superior falling phoenix voices in the city Jane up the Cally call it amoeba aesthetics

Josef had said it would take a miracle to make things better now. As Charlie, the other Siamese, moves from his place below the stove and jumps into her lap to join his friend, Mary remembers Old Nonny standing beside Josef in the pub, her gaudy little figure so dwarfed by Josef's bulk she might have been a beautiful shrub blooming in some monumental shadow. Silent as Josef bemoaned change, Nonny had winked at her then, when Josef paused to take a bite at his pie, had said, "You just love this city more, that's all. Depending on your point of view it'll get better and it'll get worse again. A city London's size is everything to everyone. I've seen it all before, every dream and every nightmare. It's bound to get better."

"So you do believe in miracles, Nonny?"

She had chosen to respond innocently to his irony. "Oh, I believe in *small* miracles, you know."

As usual Mary had enjoyed the exchange, for Old Non could always defuse Josef when at his most depressed he became too pompous. She realised with satisfaction that of late he had hardly been pompous at all. On these occasions Old Nonny liked to give Mary demonstrations on the handling of men. "If I'd had a daughter you'd have been the one."

Mary was surprised by this. "I thought you'd raised a load of kids, Non."

"Raised, dear? No. Whether I *had* them or not's between me and London Stone, as they say, but I've got the instincts of a bird, love. Kick 'em out of the nest as soon as they can fly. People are best left looking after themselves, though that's not to say I'm against mucking in. A helping hand's better than a wagging finger. You had the right idea love when you nodded off until your kid was able to fend for herself."

Mary Gasalee is not sure she agrees with Old Nonny but Old Nonny frequently fails to agree with herself and always tells Mary not to listen to her. "I'm barmy as a fruitcake. I'm certified, I am, potty as they come. A four-goose bozo, as the Yanks used to say during the War. Not the full shilling. The lights are on but there's nobody home. I've been going senile for years. Anyone will tell you I haven't got both oars in the water. Look at it how you like, Old Non's round the twist, dear, but she's not complaining. Think of the interesting people you meet in the bin." She smiled with genuine affection upon Mary. "As long as you don't take yourself too seriously, dear, it pays to be dotty."

To the irritable complaints of her cats Mary rises to stir the fire as the last movement of the Elgar begins, reaches for the enamel scuttle and throws on a little more coke. For a moment the flickering red flame turns blue and copper-coloured and she remembers Patrick leading her and the baby downstairs to the Morrison, where there hadn't been room for him to sleep with them comfortably. "Anyway," his grin had assured her, "I've got a charmed life, me." He had told her already how he had several times escaped death while overseas and when the bombs began to fall she had not really believed the wave was coming in her direction and even as she heard the rhythm of the Junkers' engines the regular booming of distant explosions like the beating of gigantic hearts she had still thought the sound came from the graveyard behind the house and imagined the ground opening up, with massive bodies erupting, swords in hand, to do battle with invading planes; then the whine directly overhead told her the truth and the bomb had come; she had heard it burst through the roof, seen plaster crash from the ceiling above the confines of the table, felt a tremendous bang and her breath was gone. Clutching at Helen she noticed how they were covered in dust. The house undulated around her like the cakewalk at the fair when the gypsy boy had made her skirt blow up around her face. There was another crash, probably a second bomb, and the walls began to fall inwards as a fire blossomed pink, yellow and red like a vast rose so that she thought it was just gas at first, with no fierce flames, but then it was roaring all around the Morrison and she began trying to crawl from the shelter as debris drummed on its steel roof and one side of it fell in. Her memory is mixed up. Shortly afterwards Olivia de Haviland dressed like a bird of paradise in her exotically feathered cowled cloak had arrived; though it might have been Merle Oberon, for Mary confused the

477

two sisters. She had forgotten her child when she entered the Land of Dreams but she knew Olivia de Haviland or Merle Oberon had saved both her and Helen. She was now sure they were not the real actresses but people who took their familiar forms and could live in fire like the sun dwellers who sometimes shopped in Soho. With all her old tranquillity she smiles at the stove's flames which seem now to be dancing for her entertainment.

A little later the doorbell rings and singing softly to herself she hurries to greet her lover.

David Mummery

I SHALL always, David Mummery had written, love three people: My Uncle Jim, my friend Josef Kiss, and Mary Gasalee. My feelings towards my mother remain ambivalent while I have no strong feelings for my father. Ben French was always a good friend and I retain affection for Lewis Griffin who helped so frequently in my career and while my girlfriends have not been what I would call lovers they have all been kind. Some time ago I came to realise how impossible it was for someone like me to live any way but alone, a fact to which I'm now reconciled and am not particularly sad about because I suppose I mistrust affection in most people and care only for those whose interest in me seems distant or neutral. Frankly, I had hoped to find more clues to all this at the Clinic but was disappointed. I frequently wonder how things might have been if I had never signed on for mental treatment or indeed if I had not taken it into my head to lend the Bar-20 boys a hand during Suez.

My Uncle Jim told me he was against sending me to a mental hospital but there was some pressure on him after the newspaper stories and there were few choices since my mother was having her own breakdown elsewhere. It was impossible for him to look after me and my aunts had responsibilities to their own children though I stayed with them for brief periods. My favourite cousin died of polio when I was young and I never liked my other cousins much. I think I probably loved her too for she appears frequently in my dreams and my feelings towards her are always warm. Her final years were spent in an iron lung and soon after she died I would have vivid romantic dreams, complicated adventures in which I rescued her from the green Martians of Barsoom, from Viking raiders, Apaches and Corsairs. Perhaps losing her made me reluctant to commit myself to any woman though there was one I dearly wished to commit myself to, perhaps because she never showed any strong romantic interest in me or because she was my first love and one always feels the first might have been the truest.

Even when I became unbalanced my Uncle Jim never condescended to me but seemed to appreciate my fantasies just as he had understood about Hopalong Cassidy and the defence of Downing Street. I drew from him my abiding interest in the mythology and legends of London for he loved to tell me about Gog and Magog, Boadicea, Brutus the city's legendary founder, and all her other heroes and demigods. On walks he would speak of the layered ruins like geological strata beneath our feet since unlike most old cities London bore few obvious signs of her antiquity; Tudor London was all but burned to the ground and Hitler bombed what remained, while all her old rivers are turned into sewers and entire temples, churches, citadels lie below her modern concrete. Traditionally Boadicea is buried under Platform Ten at King's Cross Station, Bran's magical head lies beneath the Celtic burial mounds of Parliament Hill, Gog and Magog, the giants who ruled Lud's Town before 1200 BC when the Trojans conquered, still sleep near Guildhall and King Lud, who was once a god, might be found frozen within the foundations of St Paul's. My Uncle Jim was first to point out how London is so full of ghosts. There are almost as many as the living, a spirit citizenry which includes Nell Gwynn carrying a perpetual scent of gardenias haunting Dean Street while the Tower alone houses hundreds: Anne Boleyn and Lady Jane Grey and Walter Raleigh. Less exalted creatures like poor Annie Chapman, the Ripper's victim, continue to walk the meaner streets nearby. Lord Holland, killed for supporting the divine right of kings, stalks what remains of Holland House; Dan Leno haunts the Theatre Royal and Buckstone's appearance at the Haymarket certifies a long and successful run; Dick Turpin rides from The Spaniard's Inn across Hampstead Heath, ghostly coaches roll willy-nilly from Brixton to Barnet, in Ladbroke Grove a Number Seven bus rounds the corner from Cambridge Gardens and passengers foolish enough to board it are lost forever. Nearby, in

Blenheim Crescent, a Rolls Royce Silver Ghost is sometimes seen, full of nuns from the long-demolished Convent of the Poor Claires. Underground you might meet at least a dozen phantom tube trains, hordes of Blitz victims, many of whom were blown up, drowned or crushed in the carnage of the Balham Tube Disaster. The ghosts of the Blitz proliferate; at The King's Arms, Peckham Rye, they fill an entire pub every night, celebrating their convivial final moments and at Tyburn, where most of the great rogues swung, there's a festive crew of highwaymen, dynamiters, freebooters, privateers, seditionists, horse-thieves, traitors, burglars, sheep stealers, rapists and murderers jostling around the site of the old gallows where now stands Marble Arch, useless even for ceremony. London never had a knack for producing impressive monuments of the kind in Washington or Paris, perhaps because the builders always had a tendency to skimp on materials.

When he retired my Uncle Jim chose to live away from London but Rhodesia disappointed him; he said it was like a hotter Surrey with fewer theatres. He had been born, raised and had worked all his life in London, mostly in Whitehall and Downing Street. You developed a habit of expectation in London, he said, and to live near the city was a bit like an ex-alcoholic buying a house next to a pub. He chose to break his ties but I think he regretted it. I suspect the decision had not been his real desire, for Aunt Iris had wanted sunshine because of her disease and he had made up his mind on that basis but she had not much cared for Rhodesia either and came back complaining that the place was full of black people, her feeling about Africa in general which she expressed frequently, I suspect, because she chose deliberately to hurt my uncle whose old-fashioned ideal of the British Empire might have been as unrealistic as hers but was at least founded on the notion of a Commonwealth of equals, intermarrying, mingling their cultures, building a world free from racial and religious prejudice, while my aunt, raised in some singular and narrow form of Christianity, had a rather larger investment in the *status quo*.

My Uncle Jim was disappointed I went into politics only on the radical fringes and even then not very enthusiastically, but pleased I chose to become a journalist and writer, though he would sometimes ask, rather as a mother might demand grandchildren, when there was going to be a novel. I would tell him I was working on one but knew I had little leaning towards fiction, being too fascinated by the semi-fiction of Londoners' beliefs, by actual miracles such as my own and others close to me. This experience of miracles formed the chief bond between us all. The Black Captain moved from Brixton saying the young people spoke a language he could scarcely recognise, a patois which had actually developed in London, a secret language no one in authority, no parent, could fully interpret, adding with some disapproval that there was not much African left in it. He had been insulted by these children too often, he said, and while he did not blame them for their anger he hated their lack of feeling. "Why should they call me Babylon Pork who has always cared for all people?" He saw the same lack of imagination, the same ritualistic hatred, in black and white. He moved to Southall, where the people were mainly from the Indian sub-continent and were more reasonable, but when I visited him there shortly after he and Alice had moved in they had an unhappy, uprooted air which I felt they could not easily lose. "Mind you," said Alice, "I think we'd feel better if we thought all the trouble we'd had as a mixed couple in the early days had been worth a bit more. Are we any further forward? Yet I do regret we didn't have kids."

That last time I visited The Horse and Groom in Mitcham I felt uncomfortable. There are parts of London or places on the fringes of London where you only see white faces and that is usually where the intolerance runs highest. I can still see those Surbiton policemen in their riot helmets banging their clubs on their shields and trying to lure us out of The Mangrove. "Most of them have only themselves to blame," said my Uncle Oliver, the Sentimental Commie, "they went and voted Tory too long." The Sentimental Commie also blames women for allowing themselves to be turned into second-class citizens and thinks rape victims frequently lead on their attackers. He claims none of them would be in trouble if they understood the value of Marxism; the last Neanderthal Man blaming the world's ills on the passing of the bone knife. When old Mrs Templeton tells him to shut up and, weeping, leaves the pub, my Uncle Oliver says she's upset because Doreen's in trouble again. Doreen has been in Banstead for the last three weeks because she wheeled away another baby saying it was evidently badly treated by its mother and she was saving it from battering. I've no plans to return to Mitcham again. There's a housing estate where the old gypsy stables used to be. Ma Lee died. She had always said she wanted an old-fashioned gypsy death and funeral in the open under the sky but her relatives had her cremated at Streatham Cemetery in a ceremony lasting a few minutes. I was not invited and as the last cars were leaving I put a bunch of wild flowers on the marble outside the chapel. An elaborate wreath from Marie and her husband had been made of her favourite roses in the shape of the word MUM and someone else had left a huge bunch of lavender. Gypsies were born outside and died outside, Ma Lee had said, but only rarely these days was someone burned in their own van. "It was wasteful. I never agreed with it. Besides, I'm a good Catholic." In the end neither her beliefs nor her faith had been respected.

Sentimentality, my Uncle Jim would say, was never a substitute for principle. "Sentiment is what the majority of English people thrive on, though it's dreadful to see it taking over the party leaderships." At best he hoped a society like ours was a kind of interim period between the giving up of useless old habits and the development of vital ones. "But we haven't even invented the vocabulary yet, let alone taken the action." He believed he had most in common with Bertrand Russell and Harold Macmillan. "I too should have been happy to step from the eighteenth century directly into the twentieth given the chance." Which was why his hope was invested in America. "Still suffering from the follies and ambitions of the nineteenth century, Europe also possesses an unhealthy nostalgia for the period. America is not quite so badly contaminated by their malaise."

My Uncle Jim died before Reagan's foreign adventures shook the faith of his fellow idealists, and he too was given a funeral which acted as a denial of almost everything he stood for. I remember the discomfort of his mourners at the Service my Aunt Iris demanded he be given by two Christian Scientists who used the occasion to promote their particular faith and suggest my uncle's death was somehow his own fault because he had Given In. My Uncle Jim had liked to quote an American who believed one of the cultural distinctions between her people and the British was that Americans honestly believed death to be optional. I don't know how much he wished to prolong his life but his wife never offered him the chance. On my way home in the ostentatious car, which for obscure reasons I had hired in order to honour my Uncle Jim, I sang "Bury Me Not On The Lone Prairie", "Ghost Riders in the Sky", "Your Cheatin' Heart", "It Wasn't God Who Made Honky Tonk Angels", "Lovesick Blues" and other snatches of his favourite Hank Williams, Willie Nelson and Waylon Jennings songs I could remember. These three had been his great enthusiasms, along with Elgar, Holst and Percy Grainger. I remembered visiting him with my mother and her sister one afternoon and hearing over the last bars of "Country Gardens" almost bestial noises coming from another room then my uncle's name being called over and over again. "Winston's not himself today." He had taken the arm off the record. His chief's senility he found difficult to admit, but it was obvious even to us. In Churchill's final years as premier a great many people were unwilling to accept their hero's decline because they had a vested interest in his image, but my uncle simply grieved for him.

I was glad my friend Ben French came to the funeral for he had always enjoyed our visits to Downing Street. My Aunt Iris had attempted to dissuade people from attending but Ben had been impressed by the famous faces, mostly from the worlds of politics and journalism. "I'd no idea your uncle was so well liked." Lord Home stepped backwards onto Ben's foot and turning shook his hand asking him how he was. "Fine," said Ben, "and your good self? You knew Sir James personally, did you?" They chatted for some time, neither having any idea who the other was. Home was the only ex-prime minister to attend, but with the exception of Mrs Thatcher all the others still living sent wonderful messages. It was perhaps the oddest and unhappiest occasion I've ever witnessed, as if in punishment for some dreadful sin my Uncle Jim had not been permitted a proper burial. Although his friends and colleagues made the best of it they clearly thought the choice of place and service to be inappropriate, given that everyone knew my Uncle Jim to be a thorough-going Anglican. I suppose the obituaries, the valedictions, partly consoled me for his wife's vengeful send-off. When she died, in equal pain and bravely, neither my mother nor I went to her funeral but thought we would let the Christian Scientists preach to the converted. My one triumph is the blue plaque dedicated to him on the wall of the house where he was born in Church Road, Mitcham, and should anyone ever care to search for it they will a find a piece of discreet graffiti in a shaded corner of Westminster Abbey, for so many years his local church. It reads *Happy Trails, pardner.*

Ben French and I took my mother to a nearby pub for a drink after the funeral. My mother had always been as fond of Ben as she had of me. With undisguised distaste she asked after his mother and seemed relieved to hear she had died of a heart attack. As always when she met an old friend of mine she recalled my boyhood and youth, asking after people whose names I had forgotten and whose faces I could not for a moment bring back. It was Ben however who told her of Patsy Meakin's arrest for drug-smuggling in Malaysia, where he is still under sentence of death.

My mother named girlfriends, slight acquaintances, relatives of Ben's. In some ways Ben was fonder of her than I had ever been. He answered patiently, willing to listen to memories which had taken on the nature of legends and whose words I no longer heard. With considerable pleasure, forgetful of her grief (Jim had been her favourite brother and she his favourite sister) she talked about our escapades as boys and her own wildness as a girl. Ben, who lived in Brighton, offered to drive her home and I went back to my flat in Colville Terrace to lay out my collection of toy soldiers while listening to Ives's *Holiday Symphony* and Copeland's *Billy the Kid.* My Aunt Iris had already thrown away all my uncle's record collection when she had his cat put down so I had nothing specific I could play. I put on The New Riders of the Purple Sage and The Pure Prairie League and took from the shelf where I kept my small collection of such books a copy of *Tex of the Bar-20* and read for my own pleasure and the spirit of my Uncle Jim a scene where Tex teaches Miss Saunders the art of pistol shooting while the two discuss the nature of reality in relation to the writings of Kant and Spencer, little knowing that in a short while Tex will have to resort to his twin sixguns in order to defend himself against Bud Haines, the hired killer, in Williams's Hotel, Windsor, Kansas. Then, for my own consolation, I removed one of my copies of *The Magnet* from its plastic envelope and read about Billy Bunter's adventures in Brazil. There was a time when this sort of activity was better for me than medication, but sensational fiction like drugs quite frequently lose their power with prolonged use. It was through desperation rather than aspiration that in recent years I resorted increasingly to Henry James and Marcel Proust. I am no longer sure what quantities of the various benzodiazapenes I carry in my system, for they have a tendency to build up, but I'm sure they're no better for me than the German Romantics. When I once attempted to convince my doctor to prescribe Tieck on a National Health form all he did was recommend a higher doser of Largactyl. I have discarded all my junk and now keep my rooms spare and as neat as possible. It is best when one lives alone to maintain everything exactly in its place. Mary Gasalee says my flat is very "Hi-Tech" but that is because it's tidy. I have cultivated a liking for steel shelving and plain varnished woods without decoration while she's attracted to an earlier aesthetic which she probably equates with social stability. I'm no longer sure what people with her taste want since I have become determinedly of the 20th century, albeit the first half. We move through Time at different rates it seems, only disturbed when another's chronological sensibility conflicts with our own. Choices as subtle and complicated as this are only available in a city like London; they are not found in smaller towns where the units, being less varied, are consequently less flexible. Past and future both comprise London's present and this is one of the city's chief attractions. Theories of Time are mostly simplistic like Dunne's, attempting to give it a circular or linear form, but I believe Time to be like a faceted jewel with an infinity of planes and layers impossible either to map or to contain; this image is my own antidote for Death.

The Celebrants

THE ROADS south curve into shapes redrawing pictures hard to expel from his mind; like legs, like stockings, like women's thighs on the newsagent's top shelf, too high to snatch at, too frightening to demand. The car continues her alarming journey. Surely it can't be taking him away. The lady in the newsagent is kind to him but were he to ask for one of those magazines she might tell Auntie Chloe. What would Auntie Chloe do? Would she send him back? He could never hope for her approval again unless he could make her understand how afraid he is of the magazines. He is scared of what the women seem to be offering. What price is being asked? Something or someone is being betrayed.

The motorway curves to the West running beside rooftops and high-rises, the crowded caravans of his relations. *Please, please, please let me get there. Please, please, please don't let the car break down.* He has not enjoyed this afternoon with Granny who made him feel sick, not because of her age, her wandering mind or even her unfamiliar smell; it was the filth of her kitchen, the dirt and the dog hair all over her little van: visiting Granny has made him learn how to repress his gagging. He can still smell the urine, the sour stink of old cat turds, the boiled food.

In his khaki cardigan, his aftershave, his fresh shirt, Uncle Mikey steers the car off the white road down into the maze beneath, turning left into Edgware Road then taking another left until they go west once more. "Enjoy seeing old Nick again, did you son?" The boy has no love for old Nick but always pretends to a strong interest in the labrador. Glad of any attention diverted towards it the dog will sit panting and grinning in its own armchair, sometimes beginning to get an erection.

Uncle Mikey had taken him to see Granny because everyone at Bank Cottage was going to the church but he is allowed home for the party. Although his mother's rapidly changing moods, from smothering hugs and kisses turning so often to shrieking battering rage, had not prepared him for their consistency he had accepted the Scaramangas' affection without suspicion. He has always tried to make his own order in the chaos at home and now they help him in this, encouraging him so his work at school improves and he has more friends. He will never do anything to risk losing what they give and he loves animals and flowers so enjoys being of use to the sisters, feeding dogs and cats and chickens, learning about roses. He never suspected such a sanctuary could exist in London.

Driving up Harrow Road Uncle Mikey stops at the canal bridge; it is almost twilight and an evening mist hangs over the frosty water. "Gran was pleased with her Christmas present, anyway." Uncle Mikey seems at a loss. "You got a knack for knowing what she likes. I never did. I won't come in, because of the parking. You be all right?"

"Thanks." He climbs from the Uno. "See you, then." He makes an awkward gesture.

"Be good, lad. God bless." Uncle Mikey puts the car into gear.

The boy walks down concrete steps to a towpath which earlier was muddy underfoot but now crunches, hardened by the cold. There is a smell of old leaves, mould, smoke, the weeds in the canal. Still warm from the car, bundled in his anorak and scarf, the thick gloves knitted for him by Aunt Beth that Christmas, he takes his time walking home, relishing the still silence of the canal, the winter solitude, but when he draws close to the yew hedge he sees smoke rising and for a second fears the cottage is on fire for the unfamiliar thatch always worries him, but it is only the chimney; the fire must be going full blast. Now he hears music and all kinds of human voices, dogs and chickens and cats clearly disturbed by the routine's alteration. The silly chickens always make him smile. He turns along the little path above the reach and the golden varnished rowing boat which next spring he will be allowed to take out and, pushing open the big metal gate, walks past the dogs who make a huge fuss as they recognise him so he stops to pat them, to talk, while behind him all the uncurtained windows are bright with yellow light and he can see people everywhere within, upstairs, in the kitchen. As he turns to open the back door he almost expects to see people in the cat-run but there are only the usual complacent Persians and discontented Siamese. As he enters the house Mary Gasalee sees him; she seems flushed and her skin glows almost as warmly as her eyes when she hugs him in welcome. "Afternoon, Mrs G." He has always been fascinated by her and never expected to know her.

"It's Kiss now." She looks across to where her huge husband smiles down, a cross between a Buddha and a Regency buck, upon Dandy Banaji. "Are you going to have a glass of champagne with us to celebrate?"

"He hates the stuff. Have some apple-juice." Aunt Chloe helps him off with his coat. "How was your Gran? And old Nick? It's in the fridge. Don't mind us. We're all a bit tiddly, dear."

On his contented way to the kitchen he pauses between Joe Houghton and Leon Applefield who are arguing about Hockney. "What can you know?" says Joe belligerently. "What the hell can you know about painting?" And when Leon Applefield begins to laugh Mr Houghton laughs too. The atmosphere of happiness is impossible to break. Seated at the piano, with a turquoise scarf on one wrist, a lilac scarf on the other, aquamarine chiffon around her throat, Old Nonny plays anything anyone asks but mainly Cockney music-hall favourites. He recognises "Knocked 'Em In The Old Kent Road" and "Wot a Marf!" because Mr Kiss sings them for Aunt Chloe and Aunt Beth when he comes for tea. Although the cottage is small the carpet is rolled back and the furniture pushed against the walls so Judith Applefield can dance with Mr Faysha while Mrs Faysha is in the arms of a tanned man with very blond hair who was at Mr Mummery's funeral. His name is Joss and he lives in California. Standing in the kitchen with his glass of apple juice the boy takes pleasure in their enjoyment but is barely able to understand what goes on for his mother's gaiety had usually been with one other person and had an odd unspontaneous quality as if she tried without success to introduce some feeling into her body.

saved from the blitz nobody can tell when they talk of walking into the bowels of hell my auntie said he had a speedway brain but I was a child when they died on a train my father was jolly my mother was mad my granny was good but my

Upstairs Helen Gasalee and her friend Delia Thickett, a delicate pretty woman with smiling lips, thick black hair, round glasses and permanently sardonic eyes, hold their champagne flutes in both hands and talk to Josef Kiss's ancient agent Bernard Bickerton who discusses the BBC budgets and how damaging they are for the smaller performer; he insists on referring to Mr Kiss as "your father-in-law" and asking Helen when her next play is going to appear on TV. She wears dark blue velvet and pearls borrowed from Delia, while Delia sports a fashionable scarlet two-piece and Bernard Bickerton believes her to be a well-known actress though it is clear he cannot place her. "Well, those two are set up for life. It's hard to say where Josef would be today if it weren't for the Fish Finger."

"What a refreshingly odd collection of people." Delia is quietly enjoying the day. "Where are they all from?"

"Mostly mum's Clinic. You know, it was axed by Auntie Beryl, but they're all going to meet here every month instead of every week. The chap over there is Greek and the other two are Turks, brothers. Mum says this is the first time they've spoken. That one's a postman, I think and there's a painter downstairs who teaches at the Slade or maybe St Martin's and is gay but gets upset if it's mentioned. His boyfriend was beaten up by Kieron and Patsy Meakin, those jailed friends of mum's, and he's been a bit weird ever since. Mum hates to mention the incident, which is typical!" Helen smiles. "She got so used to her own company in the fifteen years she slept she never feels much need to talk now." She wishes Gordon Meldrum had been strong enough to come up from Devon.

"Well, she's lively enough this evening." Delia turns her back on Bernard Bickerton who has not paused in his monologue.

Outside snow falls into the darkness and the evening mist forms shapes above the canal; it is like a fairy kingdom. From the window Delia Thickett can just see over the hedge and across to the dark trees and shrubs of Kensal Rise. She is delighted by her first visit to Bank Cottage particularly since Christmas, which they had decided to spend in a smart London hotel, had been disappointing. Wearing paper hats and blowing streamers they had eaten Christmas lunch at the Café Royal surrounded by other couples equally unable to relax, desperately calling "Happy Christmas" across the tables. Only the waiters who, Delia suspects, had been drinking longer than the guests seemed to have a good time. But with the light and decorations of the tree all still up this party is complete compensation and they have sworn never to plan a sophisticated Christmas again. As if sensing their feelings Old Nonny downstairs begins to play "The First Noel" and everyone around the piano joins in. "I'm nipping down for another mince pie," says Delia to Bernard who nods amiably in reply and continues. "And poor old Donald Wolfit, of course. God know how many livers have gone the same course." He waved a wizened hand too pale for his bright blue blazer.

"Cancer, old cock," says Arthur Partridge the dusty baker. "Give me the Blitz any day of the week."

Ally, now living in a hostel, but still afraid her husband might pursue her, smiles at him with nervous desire. "Was it bad, then? Or do you mean you've got it?"

"I'm talking about where it comes from," Mr Partridge explains. "I'm talking about sewage. I'm a fool to be this close to the water, really." Thanks to Ally's habitual passivity he expands and becomes self-confident and for her part she enjoys a peculiar sense of power, of security. Only occasionally does she glance into the night.

sweet pork all leave Jerusalem all that troubled Babylon no way the children cry no more sorrow no more pain all the people come home again

Seeing Delia stepping carefully down the narrow stairs in her high heels and scarlet petticoats, Mary pauses, smiling. "You two all right?"

"It's the best time we've had in ages." Delia kisses her surrogate mother. "We went up to watch the snow over the canal. Then I came down again for some more champagne."

Going over to the living-room table Mary lifts an opened bottle. "Do you mind pink? I like it best but it's supposed to be vulgar. What chorus-girls drink."

"Pink'll do fine." Sensing a figure behind her, Delia sees Josef Kiss steering through the crowd, a liner through tugs, and when he opens his mouth she half expects him to utter a sonorous boom like an old-fashioned steam whistle. "I haven't said congratulations, yet."

Even his chuckle has something of a maritime note and he nods his magnificent head in acknowledgement, engulfing her hand; he might have been blessing her. On impulse Delia stands on tiptoe to kiss his cheek. "Thank you!" He is flattered. "Any second we're off on our honeymoon. We're just saying goodbye."

"Where are you going? Is it a secret?"

"In a manner of speaking, my dear. North, you might say, to our own particular tropic." An intimate wink to his wife.

Delia think they look ageless as trees. Are they reborn every spring? "Well," she says good-humouredly, "I hope it's all you dreamed for."

"Oh, yes, it will be." Mary is ebullient. "I'll just find Helen then I'll get my coat."

"I could do with being somewhere hot myself." Delia steps over to inspect the Christmas fir's glinting red, gold and green decorations which are old, richly detailed, no doubt Scaramanga heirlooms, probably German, and then she glances beyond the guests to the brighter light of the kitchen and sees the child, with a tall glass in his hand, smiling not at her nor at anyone else but simply displaying his pleasure, and she realises that this must be for him a perfect Christmas. Making her way through the dancers in the middle of the floor, past the piano where Old Nonny now gives an energetic rendering of "Boiled Beef and Carrots", Delia thinks she will have a word with the boy.

Upstairs Mary and Josef Kiss put on their coats talking to Bernard Bickerton who, standing between them and Helen, bemoans the good old days of Independent Television until Mary, her new multicoloured raglan unbuttoned, moves decisively past him to embrace her daughter. "We'll be up, dear, after the honeymoon."

humming bird no sweeter nose butterfly no lovelier rose all flame and quiet desire making this please the phoenix pyre and let old London live again

Later Mary and Josef Kiss step into mist, into pearly night, where the snow no longer falls and the air overhead is so clear the stars are bright as newly minted sovereigns. Settled on hedges, roofs and towpath, snow softens the lines of the cemetery's trees, sharpening the shapes of marble angels and granite tombs, and everything is perfectly tranquil, timeless, still. Relishing this easy magic, they

492

make their way slowly along the canal which begins to freeze while their friends' voices grow distant; they hear the piano play an unfamiliar waltz then the dogs stop barking.

Mummery dumb Mummery numb Mummery doomed in the noonday sun Mummery deaf Mummery cleft Mummery lost for the cost of a gun Mummery bound Mummery found Mummery downed by the drowning town

When they have walked arm-in-arm up the steps to Ladbroke Grove on their way to find a bus or a taxi to take them to their tropical Hampstead honeymoon they hear nothing more of their wedding party; a silver curtain hangs upon the canal bridge and everything beyond it is invisible.

"Perhaps we'll have more luck going the other way." Josef turns to look back at Notting Dale's gaudy bustle.

"No." She leads him forward. "That's not the road to the Land of Dreams."

Enjoying her lighthearted irony, Josef Kiss lets her guide him through a mist which disperses as they reach the other side and he feels they have actually crossed to a new world as fantastic, as complex and as eccentric as the one they leave. Here, though, it is still early. Harrow Road lies deep in snow, the streets deserted. Amber light from lamps and windows throws silhouettes across the whiteness, trees, kiosks, steeples: A shadow city waiting to take on any shape or character they wish. In one another's arms they stand at the crossroads, content to await whatever transport comes their way.

Sighing with considerable pleasure Mary removes a glove to see the new wedding ring, gold bound with silver, which Josef's Clerkenwell uncle made specially for her. Josef's own is identical. "Have you ever known a night like this?"

"There are a few in every year," he looks contentedly about him, "when the entire city seems at peace with itself. But this is something better." And he raises his voice in celebration of their union:

> "From Paddington to Camberwell
> Their Joy resounded o'er the Town;
> From Hammersmith to Highgate's Hill
> The jolly Bells chim'd round & round;

Voicing the News from Mayfair to Bow,
When Madcap Mary wed Gentleman Joe!"

An hour or so later Old Nonny, out for a breather, crosses the bridge and sees them still embracing, their lifted faces full of sublime concentration, oblivious of all around them as if listening to some invisible choir. Feeling that she has blundered upon a profoundly private moment Nonny slips back into the mist and returning to the towpath leans on an old wall, lighting a cigarette. She has come into the air coatless. "If I stand here too long I'll turn into a lolly." Addressing the water she has less than half the cigarette before throwing it away, its tip glowing for a while upon the surface of the snow and sending up a tiny frond of smoke, then she turns, making her way quickly back to the warmth of Bank Cottage, deciding after all to accept the Scaramanga sisters' invitation to spend the night.

There are shadows on the path, breath pouring so white she half-expects to see writing in it; people in heavy overcoats and furs: Helen Gasalee, Delia Thickett, Leon and Judith Applefield full of good spirits, singing snatches of carols and hymns. "Nonny! You disappeared!" Leon Applefield puts his arms around her little body and picks her up. "We wanted you to give us another tune!"

"There'll be plenty more chances." She cackles with pleasure.

"Not if you walk about in this dressed like it's spring." Delia is typically solicitous.

"Don't worry love it'll take an H–bomb to kill me!" Returned to earth Old Non blows her a kiss. "See you at the anniversary!"

Rounding the hedge she passes through the gate ready to play again whatever is asked of her.

"Thank goodness!" At the door Beth Scaramanga carries little Lulu the Pom in her arms. "We thought we'd lost you."

Barking Lulu wriggles until Nonny takes her from Beth, laughing as the dog enthusiastically tries to lick her face. "Careful, you'll have all me make-up off. What a horrible thought. Some-times," she explains to Chloe, "I get a bit claustrophobic and need to be on my own. The smoke's not very good for me, these days. I will sleep over if the offer's still on."

Like the others Beth admires Nonny's independence but is concerned about the old woman's health. She is relieved by Nonny's decision. "You could stay longer." She is joking. She knows Nonny's nomadic tendencies. "Wouldn't it be odd for a lad to be raised by three old crones like us?"

"The best thing that could happen to him."

Back in the sitting-room Nonny seats herself at the piano and lively as always gives them "One of the Ruins The Cromwell Knocked About A Bit" and "Love's Calendar".

"There's a cottage in a meadow to the south of Kensal Field,
And when the beeches and the chestnuts their lovely harvest yield,
The golden glow of autumn in her beauty doth reveal,
An old yeoman and his mistress, his daughter and his son,
At their gate beside the merry brook which to London Town doth
    run,
And with smiling tranquil faces they sing this old sentimental song
Of heartbreaks heal'd, of battles won and of sorrows overcome."

In the morning Nonny and Lulu slip downstairs to the kitchen to find only the boy up eating his cornflakes and reading *Little Dorrit* which he closes politely. "Say cheerio to your aunties for me, dear. I've got to stretch me legs. Look after yourself. I'll see you soon." Then softly as any ghost she opens the door and is gone.

It is several years since Nonny had any home she thinks of as permanent, though she keeps her Smithfield room. She prefers to wander the city's old paths, many of them obliterated by fire and bombs, crossed by new roads, broken by tunnels or viaducts, yet as familiar to her as secret marsh trails existing here before London was built where the Thames was shallow and easily forded on swampland cut by myriad streams now all diverted, sewers. More complicated than any electronic circuit, no longer always visible, the paths Non follows grew out of singular tensions, eccentric decisions, whimsical habit, old forgotten purposes, so that she appears to move at random when actually she travels ancient and well-used arteries, though most would not recognise her signposts since she steers by association, by an instinct as profound as any jungle hunter's, and will say her skill is nothing more than common sense.

Brilliant and exotic as a fabulous bird she migrates from pub to pub as Josef Kiss once did, paying with her stories for her suppers and her drinks. She knows something about every district, every street, almost every house in London and can tell the old tales of

Brutus, Boadicea and Dick Turpin with the same vivid relish as she recounts the newer legends of the Blitz. She knows which ghosts haunt cellars beneath modern concrete and glass, whose skeletons are buried where. She tells of uncanny presentiments, impossible escapes and unexpected bravery; she speaks of David Mummery, rescued by the Black Captain; of Josef Kiss who reads minds and by this means saved a thousand lives, and of Mary Gasalee walking unscathed from the inferno with her baby in her arms. Such stories are common amongst all ordinary Londoners though few are ever noted by the Press. By means of our myths and legends we maintain a sense of what we are worth and who we are. Without them we should undoubtedly go mad.